ANDRE GONZALEZ

Arielle Lucila Series: Books 1-3

For Natasha.

"Greed makes man blind and foolish, and makes him an easy prey for death."

—Rumi

Contents

II   Secrets in the Vault

III   Dirty Money

GET EXCLUSIVE BONUS STORIES!

Connecting with readers is the best part of this job. Releasing a book into the world is a truly frightening moment every time it happens! Hearing your feedback, whether good or bad, goes a long way in shaping future projects and helping me grow as a writer. I also like to take readers behind the scenes on occasion and share what is happening in my wild world of writing. If you're interested, please consider joining my mailing list. If you do, I'll send you four FREE novellas as a thank you!

You can get your content **for free,** by signing up at **https://andregonzale z.net/join-newsletter/**

I

Angel Assassin

Arielle Lucila Series, Book 1

Chapter 1

Arielle Lucila jammed her pistol inside the man's gaping mouth. Her arm didn't so much as tremble. Like anyone, the twists and turns of life had shaped her sense of purpose in the world. Pain and tragedy had chipped away at her like a patient sculptor hacking off chunks of marble to create a timeless masterpiece. She was exactly where she was supposed to be.

The man lay flat on his back, his dark skin glistening as sweat covered every inch of his face. It had been a treacherous two-hour manhunt for the Mexican drug lord known as El Guapo. His bloodshot eyes dripped with desperation, begging for mercy.

Arielle had come into this mission on her own, confident she could bring him down along with the rest of his cartel, and securing the perimeter around his mansion in Culiacán, Sinaloa.

She had arrived the night before, scouting the area from a distance with night-vision goggles to familiarize herself with the landscape surrounding the private mansion. An iron fence with spiked tips secured the property, and she had found only one exit along the rear, where El Guapo could slip out in case of an emergency.

Weeks of studying the area with satellite maps left her confident she only needed one other Angel on the mission to watch that rear exit. She never knew who manned that post, nor did it matter. Twenty-one cartel members populated the property, and she killed every single one of them on her own, sniping a cool dozen from a perch in a tree one hundred yards away before moving closer to the mansion. The rest retreated inside.

Arielle always loved that part of the job, seeing several grown men scatter like terrified ants. Maneuvering toward and through the mansion was plenty more difficult thanks to the cameras planted throughout the property, but she had learned the layout like her own home, and was ready for the trapdoors and hiding spots where El Guapo's goons hid to ambush her.

The Road Runners, the secret organization she had joined many years ago, had unlimited resources and had no problem paying off the architect who had created El Guapo's famous mansion for the original blueprints and designs. This mission, like every other before it, proved rather straightforward thanks to the advantage they always had. It almost wasn't fair, until you considered these gifts were used to kill people like El Guapo, with forty known murders under his belt, and hundreds more by the hands of his cartel.

Arielle wasn't driven by hatred, but rather a respect and appreciation for life. Those who used others' lives for their own gain had no reason to exist in her world, and she'd see that none of them could shatter the lives of innocent families again. She knew the pain too well, its scars having hardened her soul in the years since she lost her own family.

She brushed aside those thoughts before they distracted from the task at hand. Not that El Guapo posed a threat—Arielle had shot him once in each leg and crushed his arms with a crowbar. She enjoyed this part of her work, making those who caused so much suffering live through their own moment of personal hell before she turned off their lights.

"I'll admit, this is a beautiful home," Arielle said, forcing the gun deeper into the drug lord's mouth, causing him to gag uncontrollably. "It will need a good cleaning after the mess your people made today, but I think we can turn this into something useful for society, don't you think? Maybe an orphanage, or senior home. I don't know, a rehab center for drug addicts seems appropriate to me."

El Guapo's eyes bulged out of his sockets, begging her to stop, but she saw the look of acceptance and defeat in them. It was a look she knew too well, one that made her heart skip a beat each time she witnessed it. She never saw regret or remorse, but rather, shock. How could someone so powerful and connected end up in such a predicament? Maybe their lives flashed through their minds, or perhaps they calculated how they ended up looking death straight in the eye. She didn't care either way.

Arielle felt the man pushing his tongue against the pistol, trying to force it out of his mouth. "Fighting until the last moment," she observed. "Admirable, but not enough. Do you actually think you're going to walk out of here? Look around—I did this all by myself."

She paused and looked away, inviting El Guapo to do the same. His head dropped to one side, eyes scanning his office where four bodies formed a trail of death from the door to behind his desk.

He grunted, fighting to speak, and Arielle shook her head. "I used to let people like you say some final words, but I've found it to be a waste of time. Let me guess, you want to call me a crazy bitch?" She grinned and pressed the pistol deeper, cutting off the grunts as El Guapo's face reddened, his lips turning a shade of purple while his body convulsed. "You're choking. And unless you can give me one good reason to shoot you instead, I think I'll wait this one out."

The gagging stopped as he fell silent. The only sounds were his hands rapping on the hardwood floor while his entire body tensed. He was only seconds away now. Arielle knew, again, by the distant look in his eyes. They stared in her direction, but focused behind her. *Through* her.

It only took another minute until the convulsions softened and the drug lord lay motionless. His balled fists relaxed, fingers opening into a slight curl. A cloudy haze took over his eyes, prompting Arielle to reach forward to brush his eyelids shut. She kept the pistol in his mouth, not wanting to take any chances—she had made that mistake only once before.

Arielle remained on top of him for the next ninety seconds for good measure, listening for any sounds throughout the house.

Silence.

She had done it. Killed an entire cartel on her own, and the only injury she had to show was a small graze from a bullet that had caught her on the calf.

Two-day recovery, she thought, mind already wondering about the next mission.

She removed the pistol from El Guapo's mouth and stood over his body, still keeping it cocked and aimed at his face. "You sick man. All those children, police officers, and judges you killed. All the people you took advantage of to do your dirty work. You'll get yours wherever you end up."

Arielle lowered the pistol to his chest and fired three rounds, the corpse not so much as flinching as it absorbed each hit. She had once shot a dead drug lord in the face and couldn't stomach the way it looked.

Before she called headquarters to confirm the job was complete, she wanted to browse El Guapo's office. The most powerful man in Mexico surely had something worthwhile for her to keep as a memento. She started at his desk and rummaged through the drawers, finding bundles of cash, forged documents, and plenty of guns and ammunition. She expected as much, but froze after finding a framed picture buried under a mountain of fake passports.

The portrait was slightly grainy, suggesting it had been taken several years prior, and showed a young boy with his parents. Arielle held the portrait next to El Guapo's face and concluded that he was indeed the young child in the photograph.

"Maybe we weren't that different after all," Arielle said. "How many times were you alone in this office and pulled out this picture to have a cry? I do it about once a week still. The pain never fades, does it?"

She stuffed the portrait back into the drawer before any compassion could drip into her mind for the man who had murdered hundreds. Keeping her targets as dehumanized as possible was crucial to her job's success. And her mental health.

Now she wanted to get out as quickly as possible and closed the drawers before crossing the office toward the exit. That's when she looked out the window and froze once more, catching her reflection with those of the dead bodies on the floor behind her.

Dammit, she thought, sensing the trip down memory lane. Her face tingled as she fought the urge to cry. That quick glimpse of her reflection was all it took. It was the same reflection she had seen the day her family was killed.

That fateful day was only five years in the past, the pain nowhere near vanishing. She had joined her parents and brother for a day of Christmas shopping at the mall, having spent some time at home after graduating from the CIA. After the holidays, she was supposed to start her new life as an agent.

That never came to fruition after a gunman opened fire in the mall, killing dozens and wounding several more. The Lucila family had been caught in the wrong place at the absolutely wrong time. The gunman had barreled out of a clothing store, having used a dressing room to slip into tactical gear and load multiple magazines for his AR-15, and opened fire in every direction. The Lucila family had been across the aisle, waiting in line for a pretzel.

Arielle had stood in front of the line, and that was perhaps the only reason she survived. Her mother and father caught multiple rounds to their backs and collapsed to the ground instantly. Arielle's brother, Antonio, recognized what was unfolding and shoved Arielle from behind, sending her crashing into the pretzel stand counter. Blood had splattered across the walls and floor, Arielle slipping in it as she struggled to get back on her feet.

Antonio saw the shooter turn his attention in their direction, and he lunged toward Arielle, absorbing the bullets meant for her, in the most heroic action she had ever seen in her life—even to this day. She had been close to her brother, growing up only two years apart. As for their personalities, Antonio couldn't have been any more different from Arielle, the CIA agent. He preferred quiet nights in, and long weekends in the mountains where he'd take a handful of easels and paint the landscapes of the Rockies. She didn't even consider him brave; he being the older brother who ran out of the room if a spider was present, leaving his little sister to squash it.

Knowing him at his most intimate level only made Arielle wonder what had taken over his instincts to jump in front of a bullet. She might never know, but she swore to never waste another moment of her life. Doing so would be a dishonor to Antonio.

The gunman had fled the area and continued his rampage in a different part of the mall, and that was when Arielle had pulled herself onto her hands and knees, and saw her reflection in the clothing store's window, blood splattered across her visage, dead bodies on the floor all around her.

She hadn't realized in the heat of the moment, but that image would remain burned in her mind for the rest of her life. Only twenty-seven years old, she had a long road ahead of processing this tragedy over her remaining days. She could close her eyes and mentally go back to that moment, her jaw hanging, lungs filling with the unbearable stench of gunpowder, death clinging to her skin like leeches. Aside from the imagery, she could also recall the emotion she had felt that day, the instant numbness that filled her entire body once she finally stood and saw the three people she had loved her entire life lying dead on the floor. Perhaps it was survivor's guilt, but she had no problem picturing herself lying next to them, drifting off to whatever afterlife might await.

And now, as she stood in front of the window in El Guapo's office, it all came flooding back.

Chapter 2

Later that evening, Arielle arrived back in Denver, headquarters of the Road Runners under the leadership of Commander Martin Briar. The mission to kill El Guapo had been a rare one that didn't require any time travel to complete. Only the advance team had traveled back in time to scout their target and craft a plan for Arielle.

The Road Runners owned a fleet of private jets, and Arielle always had one at her disposal, a perk of being the top-rated Angel Runner. She had left Sinaloa within an hour after killing El Guapo, and now drove to the downtown Denver office to meet with the commander.

The Road Runners, a top-secret time-travel organization, had origins that dated back a handful of decades after they had branched off from a group called the New Age Revolution, who had been in the time travel business for centuries. The two groups had split in a schism over the differences of how they thought they should use their unique abilities.

The Revolution used time travel to manipulate governments and societies all around the world, implementing their own people to call the shots and create a world best suited for their selfish desires, leaving everyone else to fend for themselves.

The Road Runners wanted to do good, using knowledge from the past and future to enhance lives in the present. They were a curious bunch, always investigating historical events, trying to stop future tragedies. But the Revolution, a group who vastly outnumbered them under the leadership of a lunatic, Chris Speidel, had always tampered with their goals.

After years of bloody war, Commander Briar was the one to finally get the job done and claim victory for the Road Runners only one year ago. The Revolution had since fizzled away, some members joining the Road Runners after a rigorous initiation process to confirm their loyalty. The Road Runners remained the lone organization within the time travel world, enjoying a peaceful transition under Commander Briar's leadership.

The Angel Runners—Angels, for short—were a subset of the organization that focused solely on missions, typically in the past, to prevent devastating crimes and tragedies from happening. They kept a live ranking of all Angels based on missions completed among other factors, and Arielle had risen to the top spot after five years with the organization. Being the top Angel afforded several perks, like access to private vehicles and jets, and scheduling flexibility.

And of course, one-on-one meetings with the commander. Arielle reflected on their past as she walked up the steps to their downtown office building, a street-level unit in the Ballpark District that appeared as a marketing agency. The main level, though employed by time travelers, *did* serve as a marketing agency for businesses in the Denver area. They operated at a slight loss, but it didn't matter, as the Road Runners had access to virtually unlimited funds.

Below the marketing offices, through a back door in the manager's office that led to the basement, was where the serious business took place. Arielle entered the building and strolled to the back room, nodding and smiling to her colleagues who ran the marketing front as she passed.

The stairwell had always been a strange sort of purgatory between the worlds, engulfed in sheer silence thanks to its concrete walls. She reached the bottom and pulled open the door, stepping into the Road Runners' bustling headquarters. Large monitors lined the walls, dozens of Road Runners sitting behind their desks in the office's bullpen. Some spoke on phones, others clattered away on their keyboards, and someone was always glaring at the monitors.

The monitors displayed live maps of different areas of the continent, small blips moving around that showed Road Runners' current locations.

The Road Runners in the office preferred to assist from behind the scenes. There was no shortage of needs for the organization, and people were always willing to jump into whatever role to help the team. Winning the war had brought a fresh sense of unity and purpose for nearly every member. Now that they no longer had obstacles to making the world a better place—plus no longer fearing for their lives—the Road Runners had jumped into their new era with vigor and motivation.

Arielle scanned the office that stretched fifty yards to the back wall, looking for familiar faces, but finding none that weren't already tied up with work. Her stomach growled, and she debated going all the way to that back wall where their kitchen housed plenty of food, but she stopped by the commander's office first.

The door was closed, so she gave a sturdy knock on the frosted glass window.

"Come in!" a man called from the other side, and she pushed it open.

Commander Briar sat behind his desk, scribbling on a stack of papers before looking up. A grin took over his face. "Arielle! Always a treat. Congratulations on your most recent mission. Did you really kill twenty-one cartel members by yourself?"

Arielle smiled. "I did."

The commander rounded his desk and gave Arielle a quick hug before leaning against the wall and crossing his arms. He shook his head. "I see these reports about your missions, and I swear, they sound made up. How on Earth does one person kill twenty-one of the most dangerous men in Mexico?"

"Twenty-two, once you count El Guapo."

Commander Briar chuckled. He was a middle-aged man showing more gray hair each time Arielle stopped in. Early wrinkles appeared around his eyes and mouth, and Arielle assumed the conclusion of their war had aged the man at least a decade—he had a much more youthful appearance beforehand. "Yes, of course, can't forget about him. I actually spoke with Darius—remember, he was hiding around the mansion's rear just in case—and he said it was an absolute treat to watch you take all of those thugs down. I guess he was perched up in a tree and watched the entire show through his binoculars. Left quite the impression on him."

Arielle nodded, upset that she was just now finding out Darius had been her backup. The two had a long past in the Road Runners, starting together in the same training class and rising through the ranks together. It would have been nice to see her old friend, and maybe even grab dinner with him. "Well, I'm glad he could help out."

"Have you thought more about the offer I made to you before this mission?" Commander Briar asked.

Arielle knew the question was coming and still wasn't sure how she felt about the proposition. "I don't know, Commander. I've never had an issue going into these missions on my own. I've done how many now? Like 400 or something—I've lost count. I just don't see why we have to change things all the sudden."

She knew he would consider her opinion, but the commander ultimately made the final decisions. He had suggested Arielle work directly with a small team on future missions. Teams that prepared for a mission already assisted her, but Commander Briar's proposal was to send this team into the field with her, getting their feet on the ground for more comprehensive research.

"It's not your experience I'm worried about—you're clearly at the top of your game. We are in a time of peace, and with that, my primary focus is minimizing risk. You made it through this mission, just as you always have, but at some point you're going to meet your match. Your missions are dangerous, and involve some of the most violent human beings to walk the planet. I just don't want anything bad to happen to you."

"What would this team honestly bring to the table that I can't already do myself?"

"It's not about ability—it's about lightening your workload. Lapses in judgment stem from a lack of concentration. Our thought process behind this is to allow you more time to worry about what you're actually going to do on your missions, then execute it. Imagine arriving at your next destination and all the preliminary work is done. Or say you get there and find something isn't right. Instead of having to make adjustments on the fly, you can delegate that work to your team."

Arielle nodded. "And who would be on this team? I hope it would be permanent, and not a constant rotation like it has been."

"It would absolutely be a permanent team. We want you to develop chemistry and cohesiveness. We want them to anticipate your needs before they arise. That can only happen by dedicating their time to nothing else. We have a couple of names in mind: Felix Francisco and Selena Nicole. Are you familiar with them?"

"Yes. I've worked on some missions with Felix—he seemed to know his stuff. And Selena is that actress, right?"

"That she is. We stole her from Hollywood right before she attracted major attention. We took a peek into her future. Had we left her alone, she had an incredible career ahead, like on Meryl Streep's level. We paid a ton of money to get her to leave Hollywood and join the Road Runners, but she'll be worth every penny. She can act any role, and under pressure."

"Okay, I don't see the harm in trying it for the next mission. Have you found anything for me yet?"

"How many days are you looking to take off?"

Angels could take as much time off as they needed in between missions. Most opted for seven to ten days. Arielle usually took three.

"Two days—I get bored too fast."

Commander Briar chuckled and shook his head. "Of course. I'll have to get back to you in the morning to see what we have—I haven't looked yet myself. Been busy."

"Oh? Are things finally in motion with the laboratory?"

"They are. Construction began a week ago, and they estimate a month for completion. It's brought a lot of work and moving parts—I have to hire a whole new team to run the lab."

"Exciting. Congratulations, Commander. I know this has been one of your biggest goals."

After the war had ended and Chris Speidel was split into multiple parts and buried around the world, the Road Runners recovered perhaps the grandest secret that belonged to their foes: The Book of Time.

Its writings dated back centuries and outlined the origins of all aspects of time, including time travel. Initially, to join the world of time travelers, one would need to get a special Juice from the Keeper of Time, which had been Chris Speidel. The Road Runners had worked hard in trying to reverse-engineer the liquid to create their own, but they could never quite get it correct. The Book of Time contained the recipe, and Commander Briar moved forward by creating a laboratory to mass produce the Juice, ensuring they could always recruit new members to their organization, and provide unlimited Juice for their existing members. Not only did they have the recipe, but they discovered Chris had been creating a limited version of the liquid. One intended to hinder certain aspects of time travel.

"Thank you. We've come a long way since that night in the woods. Sometimes I think back and can't believe everything that's happened."

"I know—it's been quite the ride. At least we have the future to look forward to. I want to hear more about what you've found in the Book of Time. Maybe before my next assignment? It's been such a game changer not having to fall asleep and worry about my body being left behind in the present. This new method is much more efficient. And safe."

"Of course. There is some good stuff in that book. Time portals all around the world that we never knew of. We're trying to figure out how to best use them."

A steel safe sat on the bookshelf behind Commander Briar's desk, and Arielle nodded toward it. "You still let him keep you company?"

The commander grinned. "I know it might be a little morbid to keep the head of our greatest enemy in such plain sight. But did we not earn this? I enjoy having the reminder of how bad things can get. Helps me keep perspective."

Arielle thought back to the night in the woods when Commander Briar had successfully murdered Chris Speidel. She had driven him to the mission and was the first to meet him at the scene after time had been frozen for two hours. It had been the highlight of her career, getting to be part of the most important mission in the organization's history. After that, her career skyrocketed.

"I suppose that's true. I should go now. I'll be back in two days, if that works for you?"

"Definitely, enjoy your time off."

"Thank you, Commander. Give the lieutenant my best."

Arielle let herself out of the office and escaped the headquarters before anyone stopped her. She had become quite the celebrity within the Road Runners—a common occurrence for any Angel who cracked the top three in their ranking system.

Chapter 3

The next morning, Felix Francisco entered the Road Runners' head-quarters at eight o'clock sharp for a meeting with the commander and another colleague about a new role. He ran fingers through his sandy hair, assuring it was properly slicked to the side. Felix rarely worried about his appearance, but made it a point to spruce himself up when visiting HQ. He still felt lanky, despite recent efforts to bulk up at the gym. And he always struggled with self-consciousness, thinking his skin was too pale and his hair too light. He knew this insecurity stemmed from his Hispanic heritage, and being teased by other kids throughout his childhood for not being "brown" enough. Those ghosts of playground bullies past still haunted him today.

Felix dealt with all things technology for the Angel Runners when preparing for their missions. After a scout had deemed which areas and times of day were safest at the mission's location, Felix worked on setting up surveillance and bugging any phone lines and homes for the subjects in question. His tasks were some of the first steps to ensure a smooth mission, and if done correctly, could lead to their targets walking straight into a trap. He made the Angels look good while getting little of the credit, and that was fine in his eyes. Felix didn't need the spotlight and preferred to excel behind the scenes.

Since his work contributed to the Angel Runners, he had a spot on their sacred rankings, but would never break the top 100 Angels, since he never worked in the field and captured the bad guys himself. He was, however, the highest-ranking Angel in his role. He had counterparts all around the continent, and most would call Felix for advice. He didn't mind, and was happy to share his knowledge.

He stood outside of Commander Briar's office, informed that he was finishing a call before their meeting. He stood on one side of the doorway, while a woman stood opposite, scrolling and tapping away on her cell phone.

She looked familiar, but he couldn't pin down her name. With Felix standing six feet tall, he figured to have at least six inches over the young, athletic woman. She looked up for a moment and batted her brown eyes at him, brushing back her long, wavy brown hair with a slender finger. Felix guessed she lived near a beach, judging by her dark, sun-kissed skin.

He looked around the office for any familiar faces, but didn't find anyone he recognized. He used to work in the Denver office regularly, but had shifted to working from home one year ago after buying a new house and transforming the basement into a state-of-the-art office.

The organization didn't mind. Felix could get more work done if he felt the urge in the middle of the night—something that occurred more often than not. He had been both blessed and cursed with an overly active mind, earning a Firestone Medal from Stanford University, while also fighting insomnia most of his life.

The office door swung open and Commander Briar strolled out, his signature wide grin lighting up the room. "Felix, so good to see you!" He turned to the woman. "Selena, welcome. Are you both ready?"

Felix had no idea the meeting participants included the famous Selena Nicole. She was a rising star within the organization, earning a reputation as one of their best field scouts. She was also known as a loose cannon, enjoying lively celebrations after missions. For someone like Felix, driven by data and logic, Selena was too much of a wild card.

"Good morning, Commander," Selena said. "Can't say I'm much of a morning person, but happy to be here." She grinned at Felix before they both followed the commander into his office.

"Please take a seat, you two," Commander Briar said as he closed the door and shuffled around to sit behind his desk. "Can I get anyone a drink? Or even some breakfast?"

"I'm okay," Felix said.

"Do you have mimosas?" Selena asked, brushing her light brown hair behind her ears as she crossed her legs to get comfortable.

The request caught Commander Briar off guard, but he smiled and nodded. "One mimosa coming up." He typed a quick message on his computer before leaning back in his seat. "Have you two met before?"

Selena shook her head. "Not that I recall."

"Felix meet Selena. Selena meet Felix." The two looked at each other and exchanged awkward nods. "You may not know this, but you two are actually some of our first members recruited for your skills. Before, we only recruited relatives of existing Road Runners, or people who had their lives ruined by tragedy, as has been the norm for years. Commander Strike believed we had the potential to strengthen the organization by recruiting top talent. Felix, you were top of your class at Stanford. Selena, you were very much ahead of your time at Juilliard. We took gambles, not knowing how it would play out pulling regular citizens off the street to join our group. But you two have performed so well. I'm expanding our recruiting efforts to bring in more members like you."

"Why thank you, Commander," Selena said with a wide smile. "Are we getting some sort of award? I'm not entirely sure why this meeting was called."

The door knocked and opened. Commander Briar's assistant, Rolando, entered with a mimosa and placed it on the desk before leaving without a word.

"No award," the commander said, gesturing for Selena to take her drink. "I wanted to talk to you both about an opportunity. The Angel Runners have been running so smoothly since we've restarted them after the war, but we feel we can do even more. Having the Angels broken into set teams is the best way to improve our efficiency. As is, we have so many moving parts: different area scouts, different advance teams. And while everyone is fantastic at their job, no one does it all the same way.

If we had a dedicated team working with a specific field agent on each mission, the consistency will yield even better results."

"So you want *us* to work on the same team?" Selena asked, nodding to Felix.

"Exactly."

"And what if we don't have the chemistry you hope for? Are we able to move to different teams until we find the best fit?"

"We will evaluate those scenarios on a case-by-case basis. We're going to align our teams based on talent and trust that all Road Runners can work together. You two are the best at what you do, and that's why you'll be together as a new advance team for Arielle Lucila."

"Arielle Lucila?!" Selena jumped from her seat and gasped.

"That is correct. You two have earned it. What do you think, Felix?"

"I'd be honored," Felix said, beaming in a rare show of emotion. "I've done a few missions for her in the past, and all ran smoothly."

Felix rarely fawned over celebrities, but Arielle Lucila was one person he couldn't help but admire. She seemed to have superhuman abilities, having the same technological knowledge as him, combined with a plethora of other skills. He had worked with her on missions before, but had done little directly with the top Angel, instead focusing on the preliminary work. This new opportunity would change his life now that he'd have a front-row seat to watch the organization's phenom carry out her missions.

"I want to be up front with you both," Commander Briar said. "I know the chance to work with Arielle is a high honor, but understand she is a person of great intensity. She is prompt, strict, and monitors every detail. I've had more than my fair share of complaints from other advance teams about how demanding she can be. It can take a toll on your mental health if you're not prepared. But I think you can handle it. Who knows—she may even lighten up once she has her own dedicated team for each mission."

"I'm not concerned about it," Felix said.

"It takes a lot to upset me," Selena added.

"That settles it then," Commander Briar said. "I'm still working on finding the next mission for Arielle, and expect to meet with her tomorrow to discuss it. I'd like for you both to come to that meeting and get to know her a little better. Does that work?"

"Yes, sir," Felix said, overcome with glee. "Should I not worry about the mission they assigned me last night?"

"Toss it. We'll shuffle things around tomorrow. For today, enjoy the time off—it's supposed to be a sunny day. Maybe you two can take some time to get to know each other better."

Felix looked at Selena as she took a sip from her mimosa. "Sounds good," she said. "You like breweries or rooftop bars better?" she asked Felix.

"There's actually a Rockies game this afternoon. Do you like baseball?"

"I hate baseball. Gotta be the stupidest sport. But Coors Field has both a brewery *and* a rooftop bar, so I think we can make that work."

Felix grew antsy thinking about spending the afternoon with Selena. She was already planning the rest of her day drinking before even finishing the mimosa. He wondered if she was an alcoholic, or just a young adult enjoying her life. Her reputation spoke for itself, and he couldn't argue that he was now working with one of the best, no matter how off-the-walls her methods were.

"Sounds like you two have it settled," Commander Briar said. "If you wouldn't mind, I have a ton of work this morning. Glad we could get together for a moment. So good to see you both."

He stood up and extended his arm across the desk, shaking Felix's hand while Selena chugged the rest of her drink to free up her hands. "Thank you for this opportunity, Commander," Selena said. "We won't let you down."

Chapter 4

Five hours later, Selena and Felix enjoyed a drink together at the Coors Field rooftop bar. Felix had babbled for the last thirty minutes about baseball stats and standings, and why the team needed new ownership if they ever wanted to win a World Series.

Selena quickly grew bored with the conversation and dreaded if this is what the rest of her career with the Road Runners would consist of. She needed to change the subject to avoid the urge to jump off the rooftop deck. Felix was a nice guy, but had a glaring lack of social skills. She knew the type, having worked with plenty of his counterparts on other missions. The tech team came off introverted, rarely accepting invites to celebrate successful missions with Selena.

"Tell me about yourself, Felix. How old are you? Do you have a girlfriend? How did you end up with the Road Runners?"

His passion for discussing baseball immediately waned now that he had to talk about himself. The gentle grin that had remained while he rambled about home runs and batting averages turned into a slight frown.

"Uh, okay," he said. "I'm twenty-four and single. Had a serious girlfriend in college, but we broke it off before graduation."

"Oh no, I'm sorry to hear that."

"It's okay. She went off to Europe. She invited me, but I wasn't interested in living out of a backpack for three months. I guess we realized then how we didn't quite agree on what life should be like after college."

"I suppose those things happen."

"I don't know. It kind of came out of nowhere. So that's my love life, or lack thereof." Felix giggled, taking another sip from his rum and Coke. "Anyway, as far as me joining the Road Runners, they approached me at Stanford. It was literally the day after graduation. I had been applying to all kinds of jobs and had interviews lined up all summer. They used their marketing firm in Denver as a front to get me to interview."

Selena nodded, her story not much different.

"From the beginning," Felix continued. "I thought it was all a prank. I had applied for a software engineering job with them, and after speaking on the phone and learning the salary, it felt like a scam. I researched the company and found they had been around for a while, so not some start-up in over their heads. Then they sent me my flight tickets and hotel reservations. I still had my doubts, but it was a free trip for a broke college graduate."

"Did they take you back in time at your interview?"

Felix nodded. "I'm very focused on facts, so they needed to persuade me. I was about to walk out of that building, then they showed me the basement, gave me a sip of Juice, and took me back to when I was in elementary school. Just a kid playing at recess with his friends. But it was me."

"And have you been doing the same work since joining?"

"Pretty much. I've bounced around to work on different projects and have expanded to some other fields, but technology is always at the core. Research and preparation, too. I find the currency for the year we're traveling to and make sure we have enough to last the mission. I bug the phones and hack into computers, but also get all the weapons and wardrobe ready for the missions."

"Wardrobe?" Selena asked, expecting that to be the last thing Felix would handle.

He chuckled. "Yeah. My mom is a fashion designer in San Fran, so they figured that somehow qualified me to handle the wardrobe for missions."

Selena looked Felix up and down, wondering how the technology genius dressed in faded jeans and a Star Wars t-shirt was qualified to handle fashion for some of the world's greatest assassins.

"I know, I know," Felix said. "Why don't I dress nicer? I just want to be comfortable. Honestly, the wardrobe part of my job is just research. How did people dress in the particular era and locations? Does that change based on their class or job? That's all I do . . . but I have an eye for it. Guess that *was* passed down from my mom."

"And she still does fashion design?"

"Sure does. My parents didn't have it easy. They came here from Colombia after they got married. Worked together for a cleaning company that served businesses all around San Fran. One of the stores was a clothing boutique. It took my mom over a year to work up the courage to just tell the owner that she loved the clothes and had always had an interest in fashion. After that, the owner started giving my mom scrap materials, then eventually full materials to let her create new things. It all sort of grew from there. Now my mom is the top designer in NorCal, and my dad helps her run the shop."

"Such a beautiful story," Selena said. "I love hearing things like that." She placed a hand over her heart.

"What about you? What led you to becoming such a legendary actress? How old are you? Like twelve?"

Selena didn't expect a joke from Felix, and her jaw dropped in surprise. "Very funny," she said, slapping Felix on the arm. "I'm only a year younger than you. My childhood was . . . interesting. Parents divorced when I was eight. I had grown up in Florida, but after the divorce, my dad moved back to France and my mom moved to New York."

"You're French?"

"French and Spanish. I'm fluent, too. I spent the summers in France with my dad, and the school year in New York with my mom. I watched a ton of movies on those seven hour flights. I could never sleep on planes—still can't. But that's when I fell in love with the work of Julia Roberts and Hillary Swank. From that point I knew the only thing I wanted to do was act. Here I was, an eight-year-old girl not even aware of what a pain in the ass it was to fly across the world to see my parents. But I didn't notice—I was too busy practicing accents and pretending to be someone

I wasn't. Looking back, I think that's how I dealt with the pain. If I didn't have to be myself, then it was like my parents were never divorced. I just lived in my own world, even more when I stayed with my mom—she worked two jobs and I rarely saw her."

"I'm sorry, that sounds so hectic. I can't imagine."

Selena shrugged. "It's like anything, I suppose. You get used to it, and it becomes your normal. It wasn't until I was older that I realized my mom was working that extra job to save money for college. By then, I had acted in high school theater and kept inching toward a career in acting. I ended up going to Juilliard, earned my Master's, and moved to Hollywood. And that is where the Road Runners found me. Made me an offer I couldn't turn down." Selena paused and shook her head. "I still wonder if it was worth giving up my dream of winning an Oscar. But that's the thing about Hollywood—your background and education don't guarantee a thing. I could have spent the next twenty years chasing something that might have never happened. That made it hard to pass up the money the Road Runners offered. I mean, my God, I've already made more than Meryl Streep in the past three years. I'll have to settle for thanking my mom by putting her in a mansion."

"Can't argue with that."

"I know. It just feels like I sold out for money. The worst part is the fire still rages within me. I want to win an Oscar—I don't think that desire will ever leave me."

"And maybe you will one day. You're already climbing the ranks. The Angels at the top get to do whatever they want. Maybe you'll make a connection in Hollywood *because* you're a Road Runner. Don't give up on your dreams."

"Oh? And what are *your* dreams?"

Felix tossed his hands in the air. "To become a billionaire." He laughed. "I know that sounds silly, but I see these guys who create websites or apps and become billionaires. And I'm so much smarter than them. And I want to do it the hard way, not by cheating with my time travel abilities. Obviously, I could have a billion dollars tomorrow if I really wanted, but it's the journey I want—the challenge."

"A billionaire? Wow, that's definitely ambitious. And do you know what you would do with all that money?"

Felix shrugged. "Donate it. I don't need it. I'd probably start some scholarship programs and open better schools in low-income areas. My parents did everything they could to make sure I had the best education—sounds like they had a lot in common with your mom. The hardest part about all of this has been keeping my life a secret. We're a close family and know everything about each other, but I know my parents just won't understand the Road Runners or time travel. So I tell them I work as a software engineer for Google. When they ask about work, I just speak technical jargon until they lose interest."

Selena laughed. "Well played. I've just told my parents that I'm struggling in Hollywood. They think I'm waiting tables at night and doing auditions all day. I guess at some point I'll have to change my story to explain why I drive a Lamborghini. But until then, I'll let the good times fly. Another round?"

Felix examined his cup as if he had forgotten about it. "Okay, sure."

Selena grinned, oblivious to the baseball game happening in the background, and slapped her hand on Felix's shoulder. "I'm glad to be on your team," she said. "It should be interesting to see what Arielle thinks about working with us, but I get the sense that neither of us really gives a shit."

Felix laughed. "I'm just here to do my job."

"I'll be right back with our drinks," Selena said, turning away and pushing through the crowd toward the bar. She already felt better about Felix after having cracked his hard exterior. Her father had once told her that if you wanted to know a person's true self, give them a couple of drinks. She'd yet to see that plan fail, and with it, looked forward to working with her new teammate.

Chapter 5

Commander Briar called for a meeting in his office the next morning, inviting the new super-team to gather in the same room for the first time. Arielle arrived first, eager to learn what her next mission would be, curious how things would work with a permanent team in place. For all of her career with the Road Runners, she never had to worry about developing chemistry with those working on missions with her. She rarely had to mingle with the advance team and never had to consider others when diving headfirst into a mission.

"Excited?" Commander Briar asked from behind his desk, his eyes drawn to the computer screen in front of him.

"I don't know why I feel a little nervous," Arielle replied from the wall she was leaning against.

"I know why. Ever since you lost your family, you've done a good job of closing yourself off to others. This new structure is forcing people into your circle, and I apologize for that. But understand that we are doing this in the best interest of our members and the entire organization. Our top talent was too widespread, either physically or logistically. This is more about refining our ways."

"No need to apologize, Commander. I understand, and I know I'll be fine. It's just a big change."

"I'm sure there will be kinks to work out in the beginning, but in the long run, I think we'll all look back and won't believe it took us so long to do things this way."

A knock came from the door.

"Come on in!" Commander Briar shouted, and the door swung open to reveal Selena and Felix. "Have a seat, you two." The commander waited for them to take their places, Felix dropping a briefcase on the floor. "I can't believe this is finally happening. Arielle, meet your new team, Felix and Selena."

Arielle stepped forward and shook their hands. "Good to see you, Felix. Selena, I've heard so much about your work—looking forward to teaming up with you."

"Likewise," Selena replied with a soft smile.

"Alright," Commander Briar said. "Before we jump into the details of your first mission together, does anyone have questions?"

"Not a question, Commander," Arielle said. "But I want to say something to the team. I want you to know that I have been riding solo for a long time. I've gotten used to doing things a certain way, but please don't think I'm closed-minded. I'm always open to feedback and new ideas. Don't be intimidated by my status as top Angel—if you think we can do something a better way, then just say it. This goes for our work and for me as a person. I'm not interested in drama or tension, and just want a solid relationship where we can all work in harmony."

Felix and Selena didn't reply, but only gave quick nods, and Arielle immediately worried that she had come off as too aggressive.

Commander Briar recognized the awkwardness in the room. "I think what Arielle is trying to say is just talk to her. Open communication is key. I've had plenty of discussions with all three of you, and it's clear this whole thing is going to have a learning curve. You're going to figure out how to work together, but it takes time. You might each have to make sacrifices based on the way you've done things before, but as long as you arrive at solutions as a team, I don't foresee any problems."

Arielle leaned back on the wall, feeling like the first day of school when she had to make new friends. How was anyone supposed to know, upon first impressions, if they were making the right choice? Could personal friendships blossom in forced professional relationships? It had certainly happened in the past, but so had shoddy relationships and rivalries. If they were going to all work together for the foreseeable future, then Arielle wanted personal relationships. True chemistry came from a deeper understanding of one another. What made these people tick? What did they like, or hate?

"Understood," Felix said.

"I'm not intimidated by anything," Selena said. "So you don't have to worry about me. I'll call you out if needed."

"Well then," Commander Briar said. "Let's talk about the mission, shall we?" He closed his laptop screen and reached into his desk drawer to retrieve a file, dropping it on top of the desk. He flipped it open and splayed out three different pictures of a chubby middle-age man with pale skin, a receding hairline, and stubble peppered across his jaw. "This is Mason Gregory. In 1988, this man was found shot to death in his car in the middle of nowhere. He left no paper trail, but the murder makes us believe he was killed for a reason. That's where we come in. Our primary focus is to save his life. His family fell into a tailspin afterward. Kids grew up to be drug addicts, wife suffered from lifelong depression. The murder really rippled through Mason's community."

"Sorry, Commander, you haven't mentioned where this is," Arielle said.

"Apologies. This is somewhat local. Pueblo, Colorado."

"So this is it?" Selena asked. "Just stopping a murder for this random guy? Was he even important?"

"Sorry to burst your bubble, Ms. Nicole, but not every mission is going to be high-profile. Mason worked for a credit card processing company in Pueblo to take care of his wife and two kids. A family man, from what we've gathered. A *regular* man."

"So, why does this warrant our attention?" Selena asked. "Even if missions aren't high profile, I've at least always worked on ones that have a widespread impact."

"I don't appreciate you undermining the work we are doing. The range of impact for a particular mission should make no difference to you. And this murder affected the entire town. Back then, they were a much more tight-knit community. Mrs. Gregory and the police department had made some false accusations that caused others around town to attack innocent people over rumors they heard. They never found the actual killer. That information is *not* our priority, but naturally something you'll figure out if you successfully stop this murder from happening. Think of this mission as a practice run for you as a new team. We aren't going to just thrust you into something magnificent on your first go-round. Learn how each of you works. Learn your strengths and weaknesses, both individually and as a team. If you don't like it, Ms. Nicole, then we can put you on the next flight to Hollywood to figure out your life from there."

Commander Briar leaned back and crossed his arms, his lips pursed tightly. Selena said nothing and allowed the room to hang in awkward silence before Arielle spoke up.

"When do we start?" she asked.

Commander Briar broke his stare-down with Selena and looked at his top agent. "Whenever you'd like. That's probably up to Felix to decide how much time he needs to get weapons and other matters in place."

"I have fast access to weapons in pretty much any year," Felix said. "I have a guy in the Springs—not too far from Pueblo. We can stop on the way and load up."

"We're driving together?" Selena asked, disgust buried beneath her appalled tone.

"Why wouldn't we?" Felix asked. "We're working as a team now. It's up to Arielle how far back we should start."

"I like doing two weeks prior to the murder," Arielle replied. "In my experience, that is plenty of time to figure out what is going on and stop it."

Felix pulled out a notepad from his briefcase and started writing.

"If we can have the file, Commander, we can grab a conference room and start planning out the mission," Arielle said.

"Eager as always," the commander said. "But not so fast. I want to make sure you three are all aware of your specific roles. Felix, you will get the weapons, clothing, and handle any bugging of necessary properties.

Selena, you will immerse yourself in Pueblo for those two weeks and learn everything you can about Mason through his wife, Lindsay. And Arielle, you handle the items on the down-low—scout suspects, follow leads, whatever it takes. Are we clear?"

"Understood, sir," Arielle said.

Commander Briar shifted his glare to Selena, who only responded with a nod.

"Perfect," the commander said, closing the file and sliding it across the desk. "The mission is all yours."

Chapter 6

Arielle marched down the hallway with her new teammates by her side, all heads in the office's bullpen following them, as they had never seen such a group of high-profile Angel Runners together at once.

The main conference room was still occupied by the Council, a group of seven Road Runners who served as a sort of Supreme Court for the organization. The Revolution had destroyed their original offices in New York toward the end of the war, and their new location in eastern Washington State was still under construction. Arielle chose the conference room next door to the Council, a smaller space with a lone table, six surrounding chairs, and a 70-inch flat-screen TV hanging on the wall.

They entered, and she closed the door, giving them complete privacy within the frosted glass windows that served as walls. She dropped the file on the table and leaned back into a seat across from Felix. Selena had taken her place at the end of the oval table.

"Before we jump into the mission details," Arielle started. "I think we should talk about how we like to do our work. Let's get an understanding of each other's styles."

"What's there to understand?" Selena asked. "We're all the best at what we do. Let's do our thing and kill bad guys."

"It's not that straightforward," Arielle replied, stuffing her hand into her pocket to pull out a pack of gum, quickly popping two pieces into her mouth. She liked to chew gum when she wasn't in a peaceful state of mind, and Selena seemed set on pushing her buttons at every opportunity.

"Felix, you do all the prep work. Are the two weeks enough time for you, honestly?"

"They are. When missions get dumped on my calendar, I typically work with one week before they set the agent to jump in. Two weeks is perfect."

"And you, Selena?"

"I can make it work."

"Okay," Arielle said. "Let's plan for an arrival two weeks before the murder. After we're done, we can evaluate and see what we liked and didn't like, and make adjustments from there. We don't have to set anything in stone. Obviously, for these smaller missions, two weeks should suffice, but at some point we're going to get a big one, and that can require anywhere from six months to a year."

"You've spent a year on a mission?!" Felix asked, shaking his head. "I can't even comprehend working on one mission for that long. What was it?"

"Two snipers in D.C. killed ten people over three weeks. In 2002, I believe."

"And you needed a whole *year*?"

"Well, keep in mind, the bigger the event, the more resistance I get from the past. I have to literally tiptoe around the event and the suspects before making a move. It's never as simple as finding the suspect and shooting them dead. The past doesn't allow that. See, we don't just fight the bad guys, we are fighting the past trying to preserve itself."

"The past is the hardest puzzle to crack," Felix said, staring blankly at the wall.

"The point is—this is a long, dangerous process. That's why it's important to not tinker with anything in the past. We all need to gather the materials and information we need, and I have to figure out how to best use it without the past trying to throw at us every roadblock it can."

"You know," Selena said. "We can help. Well, I can't speak for Felix, but I am comfortable helping you. My role required I go through the same field training as you."

"Good to know," Arielle said. "Hopefully it doesn't come to that, but

I'll keep it in mind."

"And I'm just fine staying behind the scenes," Felix said.

"Let's talk about Mason Gregory then," Arielle said, opening the file to a picture of the heavyset man standing in front of a grill loaded with burgers and hot dogs while he smiled over his shoulder with a spatula in hand.

"What a horrendous name," Selena said, more to herself, scrunching her face as if she had just tasted something sour.

Arielle glanced up, but paid her no attention. "Mr. Gregory had two kids with his wife. Amanda, aged six. David, aged three. He lived in Pueblo and worked at CreditConnect, a credit card processing firm. This job was also in Pueblo, so we believe he spent nearly all of his time in town. However, authorities found him dead in eastern Pueblo, nowhere near his house or office. Police reports contained interviews with the wife, and she had no idea why her husband would have been in that area."

"An affair?" Felix asked.

"The wife says not likely, but isn't that the point? We'll investigate an affair, but I also want us to keep our eyes open for drugs. Whether that was him using or involved in some sort of dealing ring."

"I don't know," Selena said. "Seems there can be all kinds of possibilities. Sounds just far enough for privacy, but not far enough to arouse any suspicions at home. He could make it home in a hurry if needed."

"Could he have been living a double life?" Felix asked. "I know that seems absurd to us today, but think back before social media and cell phones—it would have been much easier to get away with that sort of thing."

Arielle shrugged. "These are all excellent suggestions, and hopefully we'll be able to figure it out after a couple of days of tailing this guy. I'm thinking we find a place to stay together. Probably a hotel with adjoining rooms, or even a house, if we can find something that works—the Road Runners have no problems with buying properties in the past and flipping them in the future."

"You tell me," Felix said. "I've handled plenty of real estate transactions for the Road Runners."

Arielle rubbed her chin as she thought. "Let's plan for it. We can stay in a hotel while you and Selena pretend to be a couple looking for a new home."

"I don't really think that's necessary," Felix said. "I can get a home on my own, no problem. And within a day."

"Well, you're quite the Eighties man," Selena said. "Can do it all yourself."

Felix chuckled. "It's not like that. I'm just saying, we have unlimited resources. It's not like I need a co-signer or something to buy a house. If you want to buy the house, go for it."

"Unfortunately, Selena makes a valid point," Arielle said. "It's the Eighties, and if a woman tries to buy a house on her own, it will draw suspicion. Keep in mind, this won't even be two decades after women were *allowed* to get a mortgage without a male co-signer. Even though it's legal in 1988, there was still discrimination."

"So we're just going to roleplay and pretend to be some strange family who lives together?" Selena asked, crossing her arms.

"Exactly."

Selena rolled her eyes as she looked to the ceiling, remaining silent. It had quickly become apparent that Selena kept people on their toes, and left many wondering what exactly was happening inside her head. Arielle supposed that was simply the nature of a talented actress.

"I think we should do a house," Arielle said. "Hotels don't make it easy to mingle with the locals, and we're too many for an apartment. Felix, think you can have a house purchased within three days?"

Felix snorted. "With a duffel bag of cash, I can have a house in three hours."

"That won't be necessary. I still want you to take your time and find something that works for what we need. We need to be within a fifteen-minute drive of our target's home and work. We shouldn't face any major streets or highways. And we need as few neighbors as possible, preferably none if we can swing it."

Felix nodded as he jotted this information down. "I'll see what I can find. May take me longer than a couple of hours—they didn't exactly have Zillow back then, so I need to drive around or speak with a local realtor, if that's okay?"

"I'm fine if you work with a realtor who isn't popular. Well-known realtors know everyone in town—we can't have that. Find someone new and inexperienced—you just need them to find out what houses are available for sale. And come up with a backstory for why you are buying. Something that keeps suspicions low."

Felix parted his lips, but remained silent as all color flushed from his face.

"Is something wrong?" Arielle asked.

"I-I just don't know how to do all that. I normally tell them I moved to town for a new job, and that's it. Never had to worry about so many rules, let alone a backstory."

"I'll help you," Selena said. "That's literally the first part of my job—creating a massive backstory for who I am and why I'm in town."

"Perfect," Arielle said. "Do you two want to work on that now? I need to head home to pack some things before we start this mission."

"We can do that," Felix said. "And I'll head into the past this afternoon to start the home search. Let's tentatively plan for two days from now to start the mission."

"Friday it is. I'll text you both my phone number—if anything comes up or you have questions, just let me know."

"Thanks, Arielle," Felix said, watching her pack the papers back into the file and sliding it across the table to him.

"You hold on to that file. We'll review it more once we're in 1988 Pueblo, but I think we're at a good starting point for now. Talk to you guys soon."

Chapter 7

Arielle stormed out of the headquarters with her head down to avoid conversation with anyone who might want to strike up a chat with the organization's top agent. She had kept her composure in the conference room, something she had no problem doing, but deep inside, her stomach churned. And once she stepped outside, her arms immediately trembled.

The meeting felt forced, unnatural. Too much talent had been gathered in the same room, and Selena had an ego that Arielle simply couldn't dismiss. They were bound to clash.

She debated calling Commander Briar to express her concerns, but already knew his response. They hadn't even started the mission yet, hadn't given it a fair shot working together as a super team. He wouldn't budge on this new experiment for the Angels, and she was stuck figuring out how to best make it work.

"It's just part of the job," she muttered under her breath as she started down the sidewalk toward Sixteenth Street Mall to grab lunch. She had gained so much freedom and flexibility in her role that she often forgot she was indeed working a job, no matter how unconventional it may be. She still had to report to someone and take orders without question. It was more like the military than a corporate job.

"Just one mission," she whispered to herself as she tore down the sidewalk, still fighting to get her arms under control. Few things bothered Arielle as much as unnecessary change. Everything had been working up to this point in her career as an Angel, so why the sudden decision to throw a wrench into their system? Her new team had no natural chemistry, and while it could develop over time, she had a hard time imagining it. It reminded her of the times in middle school when a teacher would assign groups for a project, and everyone came together and pushed through as quickly as possible. All to return to their usual bubbles and not having to mingle with others.

Arielle had already walked two of the four blocks between the office and the mall, increasing her pace with each step while the whirlwind of thoughts and doubts swirled in her mind like a hurricane.

A shriek echoed down the alley on her left, freezing her mid-step as she snapped out of her trance and spun around. At the far end of the alley, about fifty yards away, a woman ran from a man wearing raggedy clothes. The woman tripped and fell, the man promptly lunging toward her, flailing for the woman's purse slung around her shoulder.

Without a second thought, Arielle broke into a sprint toward the mugging, the brick exterior of the surrounding buildings passing by her vision in a blurry reddish-brown. "Hey!" she screamed, closing the distance in a hurry. "Get off her!"

Once Arielle was within fifteen feet, the man moved into a crouched position and looked over his shoulder, his eyes immediately widening as Arielle leapt into the air, rearing one foot back and thrusting it crisply into the man's forehead.

His head jerked sideways as the strength in his body vanished, leaving him to tip over and collapse beside the woman.

"Oh, my God!" the woman cried, scrambling to her feet. "I was running late from lunch and thought I'd take a shortcut through the alley. This guy jumped out from behind a dumpster and started chasing me." She looked down at the man, bobbing his head from side to side, while he mumbled incoherently. "Guess that's the last time I'll be taking shortcuts. Who are you?"

"My name is Arielle, and I've taken plenty of self-defense classes. I suggest you do the same. The world seems to get a little more dangerous each day."

"You can say that again. I could hardly see you because he was over me.

Did you come flying out of the sky? One minute, I thought I was about to die, the next he's on the ground and you're standing behind him."

Arielle studied the woman. Middle-aged, clearly dressed for work in a button-up blouse, knee-length skirt, and high heels. "Did you say die?" she asked, scanning the man for a weapon, spotting a switchblade clutched in his hand. "I don't think so."

Arielle stepped toward the man and kicked the knife out of his hand, followed by a stomp on his face that sent a stream of blood from his nose.

The woman gawked at Arielle, jaw hanging open as she stared back at the man on the ground. She clutched her purse a little tighter, clearly intimidated by Arielle. "Do we need to call an ambulance for him?"

Arielle let out a faint giggle, quickly realizing that didn't help ease the woman's worries. "No, he'll be fine. Hopefully, he learned his lesson and won't try to mug women in the middle of the afternoon!" She directed this last sentence toward the man, shouting it to ensure he heard her within his daze.

The man moaned as he continued to rock his head, eyes barely open while he rubbed his face with one hand and his shoulder with the other.

"See. He's alive," Arielle said. "Nothing to see here. You can get back to work now. Sorry this asshole tried to ruin your day."

The woman turned and took one step away before stopping and spinning back around to face her heroine. "I don't know who you are—or if you're even real—but thank you."

Arielle couldn't help but let a laugh slip out. "You think I'm part of your imagination?"

"No. I see you standing right in front of me. Maybe you're a guardian angel or something. You look way too sweet to kill grown men with your bare hands."

"Well, I can assure you I'm a just a regular person. Happy I could help."

The woman gave a tight-lipped grin before returning to work. Arielle remained standing over the moaning man.

"Are you homeless?" Arielle asked him, her shadow covering his face as he opened his eyes and allowed them a moment to focus. She already knew the answer, judging by the man's tattered pants and scattered holes across his shoes. His eyes had welled with tears that he promptly blinked away.

"Yes," he said. "I'm sorry."

Arielle offered her hand to the man. He stared at it for at least twenty seconds, looking from it to her face, trying to gauge his next move. He eventually gave in and grabbed it, Arielle pulling him up to his feet.

"You don't need to apologize to me, but you should have to that poor woman. You may have just changed her life forever. Now she'll always walk around looking over her shoulder, paranoid that she's going to be attacked. For the rest of her life. Can you believe that? *You* did that." She jabbed a stern finger into the man's chest, a move that caused him to flinch.

"I'm sorry, lady. I just wanted to take my girlfriend out for a nice date night. Dinner and a movie."

"And you felt this was the best way to go about it? Robbing an innocent woman on her way to work? What were you going to do with that knife?"

He shook his head, avoiding eye contact with Arielle as he gazed at the ground, licking his dried and cracked lips. "I've never hurt no one. Just use it to scare people."

She studied the man, sensing genuine guilt and regret for what had just unfolded. She had spent enough time in downtown Denver to understand there were a wide range of causes behind the growing homeless population. For many, it was a choice. Those who chose this lifestyle rarely caused a stir. The man in front of her, however, radiated desperation and shame.

"Look at me," Arielle demanded. The man lifted his head until their eyes met. Behind the fear and struggle, she saw a broken man. Everyone faced some demons in their life, and some people let those demons get the best of them. "You've already proven today you can change a life. You have that capability. Put that same energy into yourself, and I know you'll be able to turn your life around. It's never too late."

The man's eyes welled again, prompting Arielle to shake her head.

"Stop crying. I'm sure you've had plenty of time to feel bad for yourself."

The man sniffled and watched cautiously as Arielle reached into her pocket. She pulled out a small wallet and opened it up, flipping through a thin wad of cash.

Arielle whipped out a bill and held it in front of the man's face, showing a clear look at Benjamin Franklin. "Go have your date night. Take your girlfriend to see a movie, then go to dinner somewhere you can sit down. I want you two to talk about the next steps you're going to take to get your life back. I know you weren't always in this position, but you can get back. Fight for your life while you're still on Earth. Are we clear?"

"Yes, ma'am," he said, studying the hundred-dollar bill before Arielle forced it into his hands. "Thank you."

"I never want to see you again. Good luck."

The man gulped before he spun around and ran off, limping every other step until he disappeared from the alley and returned to the bustle of downtown Denver. Arielle watched him the whole way, arms crossed and head shaking, thinking about an ex-boyfriend from years long gone.

Chapter 8

"You're telling me you've never wanted to pretend to be someone else?" Selena asked Felix. They had remained in the same conference room to hash out details for the upcoming mission.

"I guess not. Don't see why I would pretend to be something I'm not."

"But you've gone on these missions before. And you just tell them you want to buy a house? Don't they ask you questions?"

"Sure, and I tell them the truth. I'm in town for an indefinite amount of time. I'm from Denver and need a place to live. Not interested in paying rent. And that's always been enough."

Selena shook her head in amazement at how long Felix Francisco had survived taking dangerous trips into the past. Amazed at how any human on the planet could simply go about life and everyday interactions as the happy-go-lucky guy he seemed to be.

Since acting had been flowing through her veins at a young age, perhaps Selena couldn't relate to others who lacked the same passion. She, too, knew herself and was comfortable in her own skin, but she had an obsession with acting. Trying to figure out the best way to portray a character and bring them to life required patience and precision. Most of all, it gave her a rush each time. She was always herself around family and friends, but meeting new people always presented an opportunity to test out her skills.

"You've never even gone to a bar, met a girl, and told her a little white lie to get her interested?" Selena asked.

Felix shrugged. "I rarely go to bars. And why would I want to start off a relationship with a lie?"

Selena clenched her fists. "Acting isn't lying. It's an *art*. No different from a painter, writer, or musician trying to capture a moment in life."

"I get that, but if you go around pretending to be someone else, how is anyone supposed to get close if they don't know who you really are?"

Felix always spoke in such a calm tone, regardless of the topic. It drove Selena mad how he could sit there so nonchalantly, while her emotions boiled within.

"Whatever. Let's talk about your backstory."

"Fine with me."

Selena scoffed. "The purpose of creating a backstory is to make you seem three-dimensional. You've probably been going around on your trips like a pretty generic person."

"Isn't that what I want, though? To be forgettable so they never think about me again?"

"It depends who you're dealing with. Another aspect of acting is to feed off your surroundings, and that includes the people you encounter. People remember others who are just like them. In your line of work, yes, it is important to be forgotten, and that will be easier to achieve if you understand your backstory. Say you played sports growing up. If you find yourself in a conversation with someone in the past and that comes up, avoid discussing it to make yourself more forgettable. Compared to meeting someone who was focused on theater in high school, there's no harm in you mentioning that you played sports."

Felix nodded. "Okay. Makes sense. So what should I use in my backstory?"

"Since you can likely get away with being the same 'character' each time you make a trip into the past, you're honestly fine using your personal history as your backstory. That way you don't have to keep track of details that aren't true of yourself. Your biggest focus should be on knowing when to chime in with something, and when not to."

"So I just have to be myself? And this is all you did to become the best scout in the organization?"

Selena offered a crooked grin. "It's a lot more complex for me, mind you. I interact with a variety of people on each mission. I need to fit in with groups of people who are nothing like me. I need to be accepted by them if I want any chance of learning valuable information they would otherwise keep secret from strangers. I've portrayed bartenders, churchgoers, strippers, book club members, engineers. Hell, anything you can think of from all sorts of eras in time. I have hundreds of backstories that I've used, all while juggling how to best use my character to get what we need from locals."

"Can't lie—I'm impressed. Never realized how much thought went into what you do. All my work can get so technical, I guess I never imagined that anyone else had to think so much to make these missions work."

"My work may not require the level of technical education like yours, but there is plenty that goes into it. More than meets the eye. I suppose it's like anything else. Those who have mastered their craft can make it seem easy to do. In reality, it's just years of practice to reach that point."

Felix nodded. "I've learned a lot already from this conversation. Excited to put it to use."

"Oh, good! When do you think you'll head to 1988?"

"Later today. Need to tend to a couple of matters for the mission before jumping back. Probably need to circle back with Arielle one more time."

"Ahh, yes. Queen Arielle. What do you think of her?"

Felix let out a nearly inaudible laugh. "I've worked with her before. This isn't something new for me."

"Then humor me. Tell me what it's like."

"You don't like her. You make it obvious."

"I like her just fine. I'm just not a person who automatically bows down and gives respect to someone based on their title. Respect should always be earned, especially by people with as much power as Arielle Lucila."

"And you're not going to tell her this?"

"I don't have to tell her anything. A true leader exposes their character to you, not the other way around. So we'll get to see soon if she's the real deal or not. I suspect she is, but I want the proof."

"Well, I've worked with her, and I can vouch she *is* the real deal. She has a rare combination of confidence and humility. Strength and intelligence. It's kind of intimidating to be around someone who can change the direction of your life."

"Felix, darling, there is no need to ever be intimidated by another human being. Regardless of the person they might seem on the surface, they are regular people like you and I. Everyone has skills, flaws, passions, and fears. Even Arielle. I'm sure within the next month we'll all get to learn those about each other. And that's the beauty of life, isn't it? Celebrating one another despite our flaws and differences."

She caught Felix with a distant gaze as he calculated a response. Selena had spent plenty of time around other brainiacs, and while she admired their self-control during conversation, she rarely lost an argument. They were too busy thinking, talking themselves out of each response until they found the perfect one.

"Look," she said. "I've followed Arielle's career. She's incredible. She sets the bar for the rest of us. Professionally, she's everything we strive to be. But with these new permanent teams, our relationships are going to become more than professional. It's about to get very personal, so I hope you're ready to open up. I know that's a traumatic thought for you, but I'm just warning—it's coming."

"I would never. Work is work and life is life. The two never have to intertwine."

"You keep thinking that. But it's going to be weeks of *living* together. At some point, the conversation around the mission is going to run out and we'll start talking about life. How we got here. Where we want to go. Our childhoods and hometowns. It's natural for people who spend a lot of time together to discuss these things. You already started telling me about yourself at that awful baseball game. I know your type."

Felix snorted. "You know nothing about me."

"There are only a few personalities in the world, Felix. Let me guess. You're a closed box who never tells anyone about your feelings. You can probably count your friends on one hand. And there's nothing wrong with that, because your friends are likely high-quality—always there when you need them. Your family and friends are the only ones who know the real you. Only they don't. Because the way you think of yourself is so much bigger than anything they could imagine. You're not just good at your job—you're the best. Yet, you don't have to proclaim it—you just show up and work every day. Your actions speak on your behalf. You want someone to share your life with beyond the holidays and random nights out with friends. You want someone there all the time to share your incredible success with."

Selena paused and stared at Felix, his jaw hanging open. "I . . . uh."

"You don't have to say anything. I know I'm right. See, part of acting is understanding the personalities of the world. Not just how to portray them, but how to interact with them. That's something I've understood from a very young age and a reason I had the success I did as an actress. I started studying the psychology of personalities in middle school and analyzed everyone I met—still do."

"People aren't that simple. Humans are more complex than that."

"They are, but also, they aren't. There are only so many combinations of personalities that exist. And humans will often have a bit of each within them, pulling out different ones in unique situations. But we always return to our home base. We can't run from ourselves."

Felix scratched his head. "What you say makes sense, but you can't reduce me to something you read in a book."

"I'm not reducing you to anything. I just understand what makes you tick. I know your buttons, if you will. There is more to you than everything I just mentioned. But I also know once you trust me and Arielle, you're going to open up and tell us everything about yourself. That could take months or years, but it will happen. You know it, and I know it."

Felix pursed his lips and nodded. "Okay. I don't want to talk about this anymore. I need to get ready for this mission and buy this house. But I'm sure you knew I was going to say that."

Selena giggled. "I'm not a psychic, but thanks for the flattery. I'm sorry if it disturbed you, but now you know a little about me."

"Sure do. I know I'm not gonna say a damn thing around you that isn't work-related. You and Arielle can do as you please, but I still plan on keeping my life to myself."

"Okay then," Selena said, crossing the room to the door and opening it. "I'll just get out of your way, Mr. Francisco, and let you do your work. See you when the mission starts."

Selena stepped out and slammed the door shut behind her, knowing that simple act would cause Felix's mind to stir in a frenzy.

Chapter 9

A knock on the door startled Felix after his mind wandered for the last five minutes. Selena had left in a rage, and he couldn't figure out what exactly he had done to spark it.

"Come in," he said, hoping it was Selena returning to apologize. Instead, he saw Commander Briar and immediately jumped out of his chair, circling the table to meet him at the door. "Is everything okay, Commander?"

Their leader rose a calming hand. "Nothing to worry about. May we come in?"

Felix craned his neck for a look and saw a short man hiding behind the commander. He was young, college-aged, with spiked black hair.

A new recruit, Felix thought.

"I saw Selena leave, and figured you were getting ready to start the mission," Commander Briar said. "Was hoping to catch you before you jump back in time. This is Eddie Alvarado. We just recruited him from Nicaragua, and he's spending the next month shadowing our team here at headquarters."

"Nice to meet you, Eddie," Felix said, extending a hand. "My family is originally from Colombia, so we're not too far from you."

"Beautiful," Eddie replied, his accent strong but clear. "My family used to vacation in Santa Marta every summer when I was a kid. We took a cruise from Nicaragua across the Caribbean. One of my fondest memories from childhood."

"Oh, how cool!"

"Sounds look you two will hit it off just fine," Commander Briar interjected. "Felix, I've brought Eddie to spend just the initial part of this mission with you. I want him to see how the setup process works upon our arrival into a new era."

Felix felt his palms become slick with sweat. "Wait, so he's going to be by my side while I buy the house?"

"Yes, is that a problem?"

"No, sir. Just making sure I'm clear on the instruction."

Everything was changing since the war had ended. Commander Briar's top priority was to increase recruitment efforts, and that meant more training. Now Felix had to adjust his plans to factor in having someone by his side.

Another backstory.

"Perfect," the commander said. "Once you buy the house, send Eddie back here and he will shadow elsewhere."

"Understood."

"I'll leave you to it," Commander Briar said, patting Felix on the shoulder before leaving the conference room.

"Let's head out," Felix said, starting down the hall. "We have to drive to Pueblo."

Eddie stayed by Felix's side as they stepped outside and walked down the block to Felix's car.

"Whoa," Eddie said, stopping as Felix unlocked the car. "This is what you drive?"

Eddie whistled as he squatted to admire an all-black 2020 Mustang Shelby GT500.

"Was my dream car for the longest time," Felix said. "She's my baby. But it's not what we're driving today. We're traveling to 1988 and need to blend in. Can't exactly roll down the street in this thing." Felix reached in and pulled out his backpack, slinging it over his shoulder before locking the car again. "We're taking that one." Felix nodded to a silver car parked two spaces in front of the Mustang. "A 1985 Acura Integra."

Eddie threw his head back and laughed. "Well, that's a bummer, but it makes sense."

They got into the Acura and Felix fired it up, giving a minute for the engine to warm up. "So what kind of role are you looking for with the Road Runners?" They pulled onto Blake Street.

"I was actually a driver and a realtor in Nicaragua before getting recruited. Commander Briar wants me to handle real estate for select parts of Central America and the Caribbean. I volunteered my driving services, but he said there isn't much of a need for that."

"Interesting," Felix said. "Sounds like we're becoming a lot more business-focused. Did he mention what sort of real estate?"

Eddie shrugged. "I'm not sure. I've gone through the basic training and orientation, and now he wants me to shadow multiple teams across the continent to see if my skills might plug into other areas as well. He was adamant about me joining you on this part of your mission, since you'll be buying a house."

Felix pulled the car onto the freeway and floored the accelerator as they started their trip to Pueblo. "That's funny, because I don't consider myself an expert on real estate by any means."

"Well, how many transactions have you done?"

"Somewhere around twenty."

"And you never work with a realtor?"

"Only the selling agent."

"Mr. Francisco, my friend, you're an expert, even if you don't know it. No one makes that many real estate transactions without knowing what they're doing."

"I've never thought of it that way. I'm not exactly negotiating—we have unlimited funds, so I just pay whatever the asking value is."

Eddie nodded. "The commander mentioned that. He's wanting to do more with our real estate. Says there's a lot of unused property. So I think he's more interested in selling."

After the war, the organization outlined plans to generate more funds aside from playing the stock market in the past. Having a team of in-house realtors would make that easier. The organization was growing, and that meant more exorbitant signing bonuses for people to leave their regular lives behind and dedicate to a life of secrecy.

"Do you have your Juice?" Felix asked.

Eddie stuck his hand into his pocket and pulled out a bottle no bigger than the miniature shooters you could buy at the liquor store. A light purple liquid swirled around inside.

"That tiny bottle is all they give you?" Felix asked with a chuckle.

Eddie grinned. "Oh, no. I have my big one at home. They required us to travel with the smaller one and leave the big one behind. Something about an incident where a lady dumped her Juice and vanished into the future."

"Wow. I didn't realize there was a new rule about that. Must only apply to new bottles of Juice, because I haven't heard of that."

"So you know the story behind it?"

"It's a long one. We'll have to chat about it another time."

"I haven't time traveled in quite a while. All of our training was physical and educational—nothing with time travel itself."

Felix furrowed his brow. "You haven't taken a sip on your own? You don't need permission to time travel, only to do missions."

"I understand. But I haven't done it since the day I got my Juice."

Felix thought back to his days of training. Depending on the type of work a recruit wanted, the training program could take anywhere from four months to two years. Even if Eddie was on the lower end of that scale, it seemed absurd for someone new to the world of time travel to have no interest in visiting different eras. "Why not?" he asked, not sure what else to say.

Eddie shook his head. "It's odd. Going through the transition, or whatever it is. Arriving in a new world—an *old* world—and breathing in the air. For the life of me, I can't wrap my head around it. Part of me thinks I've died. And there are too many rules—I'm scared to mess anything up. The last time I went back to 1954, I saw my grandmother as a teenager. She spoke to me, and we talked for ten minutes. The experience was . . . life-changing. But it scared me. I can't process it."

"Look, Eddie, I think any Road Runner you meet has gone through similar thoughts. It all seems like something out of a cheap film, but it's real. You need to be careful if you go into the past and interact with your family. The simplest thing can lead to you not existing. Say that conversation you had with your grandmother prevented her from crossing paths with your grandfather. Just like that, you could stop existing. That's why you'll hear most people don't even take the risk. And if they do, they keep a safe distance to avoid interaction."

"What happens if you prevent your own existence?"

"You die. See, the past is sensitive. Your life exists in the past and has branched into several possibilities for your future. The time we're in right now, we call it Original Time—some refer to it as Real Time. If you die in the past, you die in your Original Time. That's why it's important to prepare for these missions to ensure maximum safety. One slip on these missions can end it all for you."

Eddie nodded. "And that's what scares me. I'm comfortable in my Original Time. I know this world and the safe places—and dangerous places. Staying in the present is low-risk. Once I venture into the past, I'm basically a tourist in a foreign country."

"Then travel to a safe time. We know history—pick an event and check it out. Be a spectator. You don't have to speak to anyone or do anything. Just check out the world and come right back."

"I've thought about that, but it seems like a waste of Juice."

Felix shook his head. "You can't waste Juice. When you run out, they just get you a fresh bottle. We have the Book of Time, thanks to winning the war, and can now produce all the Juice we want. In fact, I'm surprised that wasn't the first team Commander Briar started with. He had mentioned dedicating a new location to strictly produce Juice."

"Maybe he needs the real estate first," Eddie said with a crooked grin.

"Very good." Eddie was growing on Felix. He rarely enjoyed meeting new people, and especially dreaded being forced to mingle with a stranger. But Eddie had a natural calm about him, a welcoming aura. "Do you have questions on the basics before we hop back in time?"

Eddie squirmed in his seat and fiddled with his fingers. "Honestly, Mr. Francisco, I need a refresher on *everything*. There are so many rules—I don't know how you all keep track of them so easily. You make sure every piece of the plan is in place before the other team members get there—weapons, passports, finances... there's so much to learn. I suppose it doesn't help that I haven't time traveled in so long."

"First off, just call me Felix. Please. As for the rules, it's best to learn them as you go. There are rules you may never encounter based on the type of work you do. The two biggest to keep in mind, however, are to never encounter your past—or future—self. And never stay beyond the point of your Original Time."

"So if I were to travel back to yesterday, I'd need to return before the day ends?"

"Exactly."

"Okay. And what happens if you don't?"

"Look, time travel is all fun and games as long as you respect the rules of time. We're dealing with multiple dimensions here. If you stay past your Original Time, you'll remain trapped forever. And that means there will be two of you existing in the same world at the same time. Remember, only ten minutes pass in our Original Time, regardless of how long you spend in the past or future. That means there is no reason you should ever allow it to become a close call. If you have business to tend to from the prior day, make multiple trips back and forth. It's just not worth it to get stuck. We've studied the Book of Time and this rule is confirmed—there's no way around it."

"And if I encounter myself?"

Felix twirled a finger beside his head. "You'll lose your mind. A mental implosion is the best way to describe it. There have been a wide range of reports to what exactly happens. Some people turn violent and go postal. Others completely separate from reality and their life free falls out of control. Again, you're dealing with multiple dimensions, and the rules of time just can't allow one's past self to encounter their present self. Sadly, most of these time travelers who fall victim end up on the streets, walking in circles all day, talking to themselves about nonsense. The encounter completely damages their mental circuit board, if you will."

Eddie shuddered at the thought. "Say no more—I'm convinced. Last question before we jump back, what exactly are we able to change in the past?"

"You can *try* to change whatever you want. The bigger the event, or the more people an event had affected, will cause the past to resist your changes. History likes to preserve itself, especially the major moments. If I go back in time and change the color of the car I bought, not much is going to happen. But if I go back and try to change, say, a presidential election, my very life will be at risk. The past has no limits on what it will do to stay the same. That's why our missions are so thoroughly researched—we have to be ready for anything."

"And buying a house in the past is pretty straightforward?"

"Usually. As long as the house doesn't have some sort of historical significance, it's not considered a major event in world history."

Eddie nodded. "Okay, I think I'm ready."

Chapter 10

Arielle finally returned home after the excitement downtown. She had given up on lunch, losing her appetite after pounding the homeless man within an inch of his life. She had always tried to avoid the homeless population when strolling through downtown, not out of fear or elitism, but to avoid the emotions that accompanied witnessing someone living on the streets.

The drive home was a blank spot in her memory, her thoughts too consumed with her ex-boyfriend, Kevin Fletcher. Some moments in life were impossible to close the door on, and the chapter with Kevin had proven the most difficult for Arielle.

She parked her car in the garage of her tri-level home in the suburb of Thornton, Colorado. Arielle lived in a gated community with neighbors ranging from surgeons to attorneys to business executives. It was a quiet, upscale neighborhood, with plenty of luxury vehicles parked in the driveways, her BMW not out of place.

She slipped inside and kicked off her shoes, racing down the hallway toward her living room, where she dove onto the couch, trying to shake the ghost of Kevin.

He was still alive, as far as she knew, having lived on the streets for the past two years after getting kicked out of rehab for an opioid addiction. Their relationship had been strong and full of love before Kevin suffered a torn ACL while playing a club soccer game on campus.

As Arielle had learned, the addiction was not something that happened overnight. Everything had been fine through Kevin's surgery and recovery in physical therapy, which spanned eight months after the operation. He took two pain pills in the morning with breakfast, and two in the evening with his dinner, to allow for total comfort while fighting his way back to full strength. Kevin had been an athlete, playing multiple club sports, so no one expected a struggle in his recovery.

What Arielle didn't know—nor did anyone—was the increasing tolerance Kevin developed against the drugs. This led to him taking more than prescribed, and it started out innocently enough. Arielle had been by his side throughout most of the recovery, tending to him in his off-campus apartment after long days of classes. He'd complain of increasing pain and would pop an extra pill with dinner, sometimes before bed. She should have seen the signs, but by the time Kevin started taking ten pills each day, it was too late.

Arielle often beat herself up, still to this day, for not putting a stop to it. It had been the only regret in her young life, and she wondered at least once a week what her life would look like today had she put her foot down.

A tear streamed down her face, prompting her to jump off the couch and run up the stairs to her bedroom, barreling toward her closet as she swung the doors open and dropped to her knees, rummaging through a pile of shoes until finding an old tattered box against the back wall.

The box wasn't much bigger than a typical shoe box, and she pulled off the lid to find the remaining memories of her past relationship. She sifted through the photos of her and Kevin on various vacations they had taken during their four years together. Some showed them posing in front of major landmarks. The photo on top had the happy couple grinning in front of the Eiffel Tower.

Under the portraits were a couple of handwritten notes Kevin had penned during their college years, slipping them under her dorm room door in the middle of the night so she could wake up to a romantic greeting. He had written about a dozen notes like this, but only two had survived long enough to make it into the box.

She kept all the jewelry he had gifted her—necklaces, earrings, bracelets. He had always talked about finding the most special engagement ring when the time came.

The emotions had become too strong, so Arielle pulled out her cell phone and scrolled through her list of contacts, partly dreading, partly wanting to make a call she had done roughly once every three months. She found Riann Fletcher and tapped the name to dial while she stood to pace the room, waiting for an answer.

It rang four times. "Hello?" a tired voice answered, prompting Arielle to check the time, forgetting California was an hour behind. She often lost track of the date and time during her life as a time traveler.

"Hi, Riann. It's Arielle. . . how are you doing?"

"Arielle!" the voice immediately brightened up. "I'm doing okay. Always great to hear your voice. How are you?"

Even though she knew this phone call would stir up more emotions, Arielle felt instant relief at hearing Riann's optimism shine through the phone.

"I've been alright, drowning myself in work. Having an off day, though. Passed by a homeless man, and it's made me think about *him*."

"Of course," Riann said, her voice softening. "Happens to me often, too."

"Have you heard from him lately?"

Kevin would randomly reach out to his mother, speaking with her two or three times a year for a few minutes. Sometimes from jail, other times from a stranger's cell phone. But only during the rare times he sobered up enough to think of calling.

"Heard from him a couple of months ago, actually. We talked for three minutes. He was at a park. Sounded okay, but I could tell he was still so far from himself. Still in San Francisco. Said the only other place he'd go live is San Diego, but that he was fine with things the way they are for now. I guess he made a friend with someone who runs one of the shelters and they guarantee him a bed at least three days a week."

The pain never stopped upon hearing the love of her life suffering in the world. Kevin went to school for marketing, and even dragged himself to the finish line of graduation. That summer, with internships and interviews lined up with seemingly every tech company in Silicon Valley, was when everything spiraled out of control.

"Well, that's good," Arielle said, glad to hear Kevin was still alive.

"I suppose. You know, they say the worst pain a parent can feel is having to bury their child. But let me tell you, I think this is much worse. My son is such a danger to himself and others that I can't even let him into my house. And because of that, I have to fall asleep every night knowing he's sleeping on a park bench where anything could happen. He could die at any moment, and I might never find out. Each time I hang up the phone, I accept it may be the last time. I just don't know."

Riann's voice wavered, causing Arielle to break into fresh tears.

"I miss him," Arielle said, sniffling. "I miss what we had together. How he loved me and made me feel like the most important person in the world. We had our whole life planned out together."

Riann sighed. "If only we could go back in time and change it all."

Riann had no idea about the secret world of time travel. Arielle hadn't told anyone, not even her grandmother, who still lived in New Mexico. Kevin's injury happened shortly before Arielle had lost her entire family, and only a few weeks before the Road Runners had initially approached her.

She could have jumped back in time right after the injury happened and prevented it. In that moment, the change would have been minuscule, the past likely offering no fight since no one's life had been severely altered yet. But they didn't know what would come down the road, and once it did, it was too late. Arielle could count the number of mistakes she had made as a Road Runner on one hand, and trying to prevent Kevin's injury had been the biggest. She experienced firsthand what happened when you tried to change the past without a plan, and that made her never overlook another detail again.

"That would be nice," Arielle said, her leg bouncing out of control. "I guess all we can do now is hope for the best. There's always a chance he cleans himself up and gets back on his feet. It wouldn't be the first time something like that has happened."

"You're so positive, dear. I used to be, but it's hard for me to keep the hope. My son is gone, my husband is dead. I guess I'm supposed to be alone in this world, and that's okay."

Arielle had no response. Riann had been alone ever since Kevin wound up on the streets. She couldn't make recurring visits to her once future mother-in-law, especially as she climbed the ranks within the Angels. The thought had crossed her mind on plenty of occasions of recruiting Riann to the Road Runners, but she brushed it away. Even with a beneficial background as a nurse, Riann would certainly spend all of her time trying to tinker with her past. Trying to bring back her husband and son would certainly kill her.

"I should get going, Riann. Thank you for talking with me—I needed to vent to someone who understands how I'm feeling. I'll call again soon."

"Of course, sweetie. Don't work too hard, and I'll look forward to our next chat. As always, you have a place to stay if you're in the area."

They hung up. Arielle stuffed the box of painful memories back into her closet, and collapsed onto her bed.

Chapter 11

Felix and Eddie sat in the parking lot of an abandoned gas station in Pueblo.

"I still don't understand," Eddie said. "We're about to go back in time to buy a house. It doesn't reset when we return to today?"

"Nothing ever resets," Felix explained. "We can go back in time and change things, and they will remain. Even when we jump back forward to our present day, the past will have caught up by the time we arrive. For example, say we went back in time and stopped Lincoln's assassination. That change will remain, and the history books will reflect it by the time we're back. It's perhaps one of the most fascinating parts of our work—changing things and coming back to learn how it affected the world we live in today. Commander Briar actually has an interesting story of when he went back to 1996 and stopped the Columbine shootings from happening."

"Columbine shootings?"

"My point exactly. How old are you, twenty-one?"

"I will be, later this year."

"I didn't know about it, either. I was a baby when the shooting would have happened in my Original Time. But the commander had gone back and stopped it, so it never occurred. Now people like you and I grew up never learning about it. Instead, we know the story of when Columbine caught fire and burned to the ground."

"I was wondering if you were referring to that Columbine," Eddie said, shaking his head. "Didn't like 200 people die in that fire?"

"Precisely. See, the past still corrected its course. It seems as if that school was destined for tragedy. Commander Briar stopped one from happening, but the past still made sure it took its victims. Now, we haven't found this to be a universal occurrence. In fact, it is the exception to the rule. But it is something we urge our members to keep in mind when they tamper with the past—there will always be consequences when you return."

Eddie stared out the windshield, studying a crow that had landed atop one of the old gas pumps. "What about us? We know the past, but Road Runners are changing it every day, right? How are we supposed to keep track of everything that has changed?"

"You don't. Our knowledge of events is fluid, so when something changes in the past, our memories will reflect those changes. Road Runners never watch the news because there is no point—it's *going* to change, most likely, at some point. Honestly, though, the missions we work on nowadays aren't well-known enough. Say we stop this murder in Pueblo from happening. It's only going to change the lives of those close to it. The victim's family, the suspect and their family, and perhaps a few members of the area. But beyond that, no one outside of Pueblo has even heard of Mason Gregory. It's not often we take on a major mission, like say, the Lincoln assassination, but when we do, everyone in the organization is notified and ready for what might happen."

"What has happened?"

Felix shook his head. "Afraid we don't have time to go into all that right now. We have to get back to 1988 and buy this house."

"Okay, my bad, sorry for all the questions."

Felix cracked a small grin. "Check your vocabulary. People didn't say 'my bad' in 1988—keep that in mind. I avoid slang unless I'm comfortable with a particular era. Otherwise, I'll speak as neutrally as I can."

"Understood."

"You ready to go?"

Eddie nodded, holding his gaze to the crow. Felix wondered what he was thinking about, remembering how anxious he used to get in his early time travel days. Every trip, no matter how well planned, had always felt like crash-landing in a foreign country. And in many ways, that's exactly what it was. Many new members treated time travel more like a vacation. Few understood the elevated levels of risk they were stepping into. Time travel and the past had rules accompanying them, and there had been plenty of stories of new Road Runners who never came back from their first trip.

"Let's do it," Felix said, reaching over to open the glove compartment and pull out his flask of Juice, spinning the cap off. "We're going to February 11, 1988. Be sure to touch part of the car with your hand to make sure we go together."

Eddie remained silent as he pulled out his small bottle and twisted the cap off. Felix noticed the liquid shaking within the man's trembling fingers.

"Hey," Felix said, placing a hand on Eddie's shoulder. "Nothing to be nervous about. Quick, easy trip."

"Thanks," Eddie said, his voice distant and occupied.

"Cheers," Felix said, raising his flask and taking a quick swig. Eddie followed suit, and they both replaced their caps and leaned back in their seats. "Give it a minute and we'll be on our way. Slight rumble, but that's just us passing through."

They sat in the car, both men staring forward while they remained undisturbed in the abandoned gas station. Within a minute, they felt the rumble, and the world turned black.

* * *

Seconds later, they arrived in 1988.

Eddie shot forward, rubbing his head and eyes. "I don't remember it being so fast."

"You were probably just nervous last time. That can make the simplest of tasks feel like forever. But see, quick and painless. Now we're here—let's get to work."

"Were you able to research who we should speak with?"

"I tried," Felix said, opening his car door and sticking a leg out. "But I couldn't find anything. No databases of realtors from 1988 were available, so we'll have to do it the way people used to, and find a phone book."

Eddie scanned the area, finding the gas station active and with customers strolling in and out of the store's front door. "This is the same place we just left?"

"Yes," Felix said in a hurry, stepping all the way out of the car. "Let's go."

Eddie followed, Felix already near the entrance after hustling across the parking lot.

"You always end up in the exact place you left," Felix said over his shoulder. "The landscape will obviously change depending on what year you go to. Go back another two hundred years and this area is probably swarming with Native Americans."

Felix opened the gas station's door, poked his head inside, and closed it back shut. "This way," he said, strolling down the sidewalk and rounding the building's corner. On the backside were bathroom doors, but more importantly, two payphones, each with two thick cords dangling from the bottom, metal cases connected to the other end.

"Wow," Eddie said. "I don't think I've ever seen an active payphone before. I've seen some that were old and out of service—just chunks of metal—but never one I could pick up and make a call."

"It is fascinating to look back and see how far we've advanced. Just think, this giant phone book was essentially Google." Felix raised the steel box and dropped it on the base of the payphone's booth. "Almost five inches thick."

He flipped open the Yellow Pages and searched for the section starting with the letter R, slowing when he reached it, running a finger up and down the pages until finding the section labeled with "Realtors".

The two splayed open pages contained nothing but lists of realtors and their phone numbers.

"Goodness," Eddie said. "How do we pick? That guy has twenty years of experience." He pointed to a paid advertisement of a grinning man with slicked back hair, calling for all home buyers and sellers to call him for their real estate needs.

"Nope. Twenty years of working in this area means he's connected and knows everyone. We don't need our realtor telling everyone in town about us. Look at this one." His finger slid down the page and stopped on the name of Joseph Graham. "This is our kind of guy. Says he has three years' experience. That means he knows the area well enough, isn't entirely new to remember us as early clients in his career, and just maybe we can push him around to get us a better deal on his commission."

Felix picked up the phone, dropped coins into the slot, and dialed the number.

"Thank you for calling the office of Joe Graham. How can I help you?" a woman answered.

"Hello, I was hoping to schedule a time to meet with Mr. Graham today. Looking to buy a property in Pueblo and would love some guidance."

"Let me check. Mr. Graham is out at a showing right now, but it looks like he has an opening this afternoon. Three o'clock, if that works for you."

Instinctively, Felix pulled out his cell phone to find it showing a time of 00:00, and hurriedly stuffed it back into his pocket. "I'm sorry, ma'am, what time is it right now?"

"12:30, sir."

"Okay, perfect. I'll be there at three."

They hung up and Felix copied down the address from the phone book before closing it and returning it to its proper place.

"Forget your cell phone doesn't work?" Eddie asked.

Felix nodded. "Gotta remember the little details. It can get confusing because some technologies exist in different eras. The thing is, the technology itself has to exist in the year you're visiting. There *are* cell phones in 1988, but they're not too common yet, and the technology is vastly different for my phone from 2022. You'll notice we rely on two-way radios during any missions after 1940. It's an old technology that has remained consistent throughout time—therefore, it's highly reliable for us."

"So we have some time to kill before we meet with this realtor?" Eddie asked.

"Yep. It's twelve-thirty right now. I see you have a watch—that's another important thing to bring on any trip, so you don't look like a fool pulling out a device from the future like I just did."

Eddie checked his watch and promptly adjusted the time. "I never leave the house without a watch, so I guess I'm good there."

"Let's drive around and find somewhere for lunch. We can eat and get to know each other more. I'm sure you have more questions about our . . . business."

Chapter 12

After two hours at a local diner where they munched on burgers and fries, Felix and Eddie returned to their car and headed for the realty office of Joseph Graham. They had asked their server for directions, and were delighted to find the office a quick seven-minute drive away.

They pulled into the parking lot of a two-level building surrounded by nothing but open fields. An entire business park would develop in the coming years, but for now, the solo building housed realtors, insurance agents, and accountants. It had a brick exterior with blackout windows, and couldn't look any more vanilla if it tried.

Felix found a spot in the front row, and the two men made their way inside. They entered a lobby with a front desk impeding their path to the elevators, an older gentleman nodding off in his chair behind the desk.

Hank, according to the name tag clipped to his shirt, startled back to consciousness upon seeing them enter. "Good afternoon. How can I help you?" Hank had dark skin with contrasting white hair and a goatee.

"Hello," Felix said. "We have an appointment with Joseph Graham."

Hank cracked a grin. "Joey is a good man. Suite 206—take the elevators up if you like."

"Thank you."

Felix strolled around the desk, Eddie following two steps behind. They rode the elevator up one level and found themselves in a new hallway, filled with a dozen doors and plenty of silence.

"Do you ever wonder if we encounter other time travelers?" Eddie whispered.

"We certainly do. Even with only one percent of the world's population having access to the ability, that means there are a little over three million time travelers in the United States alone. It's highly likely you have crossed paths with a fellow time traveler."

They moved down the hallway, Felix grumbling once he realized their destination waited at the furthest end, a frosted glass door with bold lettering that read: *Joseph Graham Realty.*

"Just follow my lead," Felix muttered.

He opened the door and stepped into the office, a young red-headed woman greeting them with a wide smile from behind a reception desk.

"Good afternoon, you two. Are you Mr. Francisco?" she asked, pushing a pair of horn-rimmed glasses up the bridge of her nose.

"Yes, ma'am," Felix said, approaching the desk.

"Perfect. Mr. Graham had a last-minute cancellation and is ready for you a few minutes early. Please, follow me."

She stood, and the two men gazed at the curves outlining her slender figure before following her down a short hall where an office awaited with its door open.

"Mr. Graham, your three o'clock is here."

A man not much older than Felix, stood from behind a massive desk that nearly took the entire office space. He wore a metallic suit, had a gaudy gold watch on his wrist, and smelled of cheap cologne.

"Mr. Graham," Felix said, extending a hand to shake. "My name is Felix, and this is my associate, Eddie."

"Pleasure," the realtor replied. "Just call me Joe. Now, how can I help you gentlemen today?"

Joe sat back down on his throne and gestured for Felix and Eddie to do the same.

"Well, Joe," Felix said. "We have cash and are looking to buy a house in the area. Hoping we might get something this week, if possible."

Joe leaned back, his hands clasped in front of his mouth as he stuck out his index finger to his lips. "You one of those rich gay couples moving here from Denver?"

Felix laughed, while Eddie remained silent and confused.

"No, definitely not us. Is that a thing?"

"Goodness, yes. The gay community has been making its way down here to Pueblo. Can't blame them—it's one of the few areas outside the big city with a more accepting community. Though, if you ask me, I don't think folks down here are as much accepting as they are disinterested. Most just mind their own business and don't worry about what others are doing."

This statement was fantastic news for Felix, and precisely what they needed to set up shop for a mission. "Interesting," he said. "I'm curious. How long have you been doing real estate?"

"I've been doing it in Pueblo for the last year, but started in Denver a couple of years ago."

"What brought you down this way?"

Joe shrugged. "Less competition. The Denver market can be absolute cutthroat. You get into some of those up-and-coming neighborhoods, forget about it. The suburbs are still growing, but Pueblo is exploding. It's a gold mine down here for real estate—both residential and commercial."

Felix nodded, as if accepting this explanation. While it wasn't his field of concentration, he had picked up plenty of skills in negotiation for times just like this. He had every intent on securing a property and only paying four percent commission to Joseph Graham. "Well, that sounds great. Me and Eddie are business partners, and we're looking to expand our operations here in Pueblo."

Joe shot forward. "So, you're looking for a house *and* an office?"

Felix had to fight from bursting into laughter. Joe's conclusion left him looking like a dog desperate for its owner to throw a ball in a game of fetch. "Just a house. We conduct our business right from home."

"Oh," Joe said, deflating and leaning back into his comfortable position. "Well, I don't see why we can't find a suitable home for you. What kind of space do you need?"

"Preferably two levels, plus a basement."

Joe leaned forward again, though not as aggressively. "For just you two?"

Felix hadn't encountered such a nosy realtor in his previous housing transactions, and wondered if Joe might not be the best choice after all. Was he the guy to show up at random to check on his clients?

"We'll both have some family stopping by from time to time. Would like to have guest rooms for them."

Joe nodded. "And what kind of budget are we looking at?"

"You tell me. We have the cash."

Joe's eyes lit up like a child unwrapping the first present on Christmas morning. "What you're looking for is definitely on the higher end for Pueblo. Probably somewhere around two hundred thousand."

"And your commission?"

Joe looked up, calculating how much money he could massage out of Felix's wallet. "Eight percent."

Felix immediately scoffed, all part of his act. "Mr. Graham, don't insult me. Maybe I should have clarified. We're expanding our business. We're looking for a realtor to handle repeat business. I suggest you don't swing for the fences on this one purchase and think of the big picture."

Joe nodded and leaned forward, planting his elbows on the desk. "My apologies—I really wasn't under that impression."

"And you thought high-balling me was wise, anyway? I know the average commission is between six and seven percent."

Joe shook his head. "I'm sorry. Don't hold that against me. I'll do six percent."

"Three."

Now it was Joe's turn to scoff, and he leaned back as he tossed his hands in the air. "Three percent? Have you lost your mind? The absolute lowest I'd consider is five."

"Very well," Felix said, standing from his seat.

Eddie looked up at him, confusion smacked on his face until he remembered he needed to follow whatever Felix did. Felix was already halfway to the door when Eddie rose, and Joe shouted, "Wait! Don't leave."

Felix paused with his hand outstretched toward the doorknob for added dramatics.

"Four percent," Joe said, nearly muttering it under his breath. "And I can't go any lower."

Felix pivoted around and returned to his seat. "Deal."

The men shook hands.

Joe reached into a desk drawer and pulled out a binder. "Let's look at some properties."

For the next hour, they flipped through dozens of pages of properties from around the Pueblo area. Joe had access to everything currently on the market, along with some expected to be listed soon. Felix and Eddie consulted on each property until whittling a list down to their top three. Joe assured them if they truly had cash to spend, they could expect no competition for any property they desired.

Within minutes of choosing their favorites, all three men were on the road, Felix and Eddie following behind Joe's Toyota hatchback as they set out to tour the three homes. Fortunately, during their two hours together that evening, Joe didn't once ask what kind of business his new clients were running.

Felix found this suspicious, wondering why the nosy man omitted this simple question after prodding about nearly everything else. Perhaps he felt intimidated after Felix turned the tables on him in his office.

Regardless, Felix was glad it was one less lie he'd have to tell and keep track of. By the end of the night, Eddie had returned home to 2022, satisfied with learning enough of the real estate process Felix had taken him through. Felix called Joe to let him know which house to place an offer on the next morning.

It was the exact house he had sought. Three floors with bathrooms on each level, a fully finished basement, and a quick ten-minute drive from Mason Gregory's home. Since the house was in an upscale, spread-out neighborhood, the nearest neighbor was an entire quarter mile away. They'd enjoy complete privacy while working on their mission to solve—and hopefully, prevent—the murder that would soon turn the community upside down.

Chapter 13

The next morning, Felix had traveled back to 2022 to call Arielle and let her know the address and details of the new house he secured for their mission.

She had been awake since six o'clock, reviewing the electronic mission files and getting in the right mind frame to start within the next couple of days. When Felix had called at eight, Arielle was deep into Mason's work history, mapping out all the areas he had worked since his first job scooping ice cream at the local parlor as a sixteen-year-old boy. The Angels had members dedicated to doing this tedious work, but Arielle always wanted to absorb as much information as she could about her subject. Some argued it was unnecessary, while others said that was what made her the best. She simply viewed it as another weapon in her never ending arsenal. Anyone could master firearms, sword fighting, or hand-to-hand combat, but for Arielle Lucila, knowledge trumped everything.

She took the new address and added a sticker on its location in their travel atlas. Felix planned to meet them back in 1988 once Arielle and Selena arrived in Pueblo. Right when Felix hung up, she dialed Selena.

"Hello?" Selena answered, voice groggy.

"Are you still sleeping?" Arielle asked, trying to soften her voice to not sound like a scolding mother.

"Yeah . . . what time is it?" Selena mumbled in response.

"Eight."

"Ugh! I just fell asleep four hours ago. Why are you calling so early?"

"Are you hungover?"

"Hungover? No. I might still be a little drunk."

"Jesus Christ, Selena, we are about to start a mission. You can't be doing this stuff."

"'This stuff'? Get off your high horse. We all have our ways of blowing off steam. No need to crucify me for being twenty-three. Maybe you should try it sometime. Let me guess, you spent last night working. You were probably up as late as I was."

"I did some work, yes. But I also got eight hours of sleep, especially on the eve of a new mission."

"You're such a grandma."

Arielle paused and pursed her lips. No one within the Road Runners organization had ever spoken her to like that before. "We're arguing about nothing. As long as you're ready to work, it doesn't matter what you do in your free time."

"Thank you, that's all I ask. So why are you calling me so early?"

"Felix found a house for us. Great location, tons of privacy. We should all be able to move in over the next few days, but I thought you might want a head start to scout the area."

"So leaving today? I can make that work in the afternoon. Have a couple of matters to tie up here first."

Like sobering up, Arielle thought, but didn't cave to the temptation of shooting back cheap insults. "Okay, great. Today is Thursday, so if all goes well, I should be there either tomorrow night or first thing on Saturday morning."

"And we have our own rooms in this house, I take it?"

"Yes, it's huge—lots of space for all three of us."

"Good. Okay, anything else?"

Arielle sensed the shortness in Selena's voice and fought away more snarky comments. "No, that was all. Have a good morning, and I'll see you soon."

Arielle returned to her home office to gather her notes and files, stuffing them back into the bulky binder that housed all information for the mission. She had done enough research for the day and needed to clear her head. She found herself in the awkward phase before the start of a mission where all preliminary work was complete, and most of what remained would have to wait until she arrived in the new city and year.

She left her office and moved down the hallway to her bedroom, passing the portraits of her family on the wall, avoiding eye contact with them, as she needed to maintain her intense level of focus.

Once in her bedroom, she rummaged a stick of gum from her nightstand drawer and popped it into her mouth while turning on the TV. Arielle rarely had time to watch TV, so she didn't bother keeping up with new shows. They came and went while she worked, rising in popularity around the world while she couldn't pick one out of a lineup.

Instead, she used her 70-inch television to play music, finding her favorite channel that played pop and hip-hop music from the early 2010s. fun.'s "We Are Young" came on, mentally taking her back to her senior year of high school when it had first released and exploded up the charts.

Her college days were typically the memories she reminisced, perhaps because high school seemed like another lifetime. Always a popular student since day one in high school, they had voted Arielle the most likely to become famous. And while no one in regular society had ever heard of her, she had indeed become a living legend among the Road Runners, all before her twenty-seventh birthday.

Arielle crossed her bedroom and stood at the window, looking out to the vast landscape that stretched miles into the distance, the Rocky Mountains glowing under the early morning sun. She wondered where her life had gone. Deep down, part of her wanted to quit the Road Runners and run off with her accumulated fortune. She could live anywhere in the world, and spend her days drawing pictures, binge watching TV, and cooking world-class meals for dinner. She supposed these desires stemmed from her old life when she used to find joy in doing such therapeutic activities. Even in CIA training, she had time to watch a couple of episodes at night before falling asleep. She used to read a book each week, and now couldn't remember the last time she had even seen a set of bound pages.

The most frustrating part was considering how much time she spent on private jets, providing plenty of time to enjoy leisurely activities. But all she could ever do was sleep. Even with a consistent routine of eight hours each night, her time awake was so involved and active, by the time she reclined in the luxury of the Road Runners' private jets, a nap was all she wanted.

Her life had gone under constant transformation since surviving the mall shooting, yet she only realized it when she had down time between missions to reflect. And it never hit her all at once, but in bits and pieces. Sometimes she would realize how losing her family left her alone. Other times revolved around losing her soulmate.

Today, however, she couldn't help but dwell on how she had become a Road Runner. It was something she rarely considered, but now, staring down yet another mission from her massive empty house, she wondered if it was all worth it.

Her father had always preached the importance of not letting a job consume one's entire life. And he backed it up, always home in time for dinner, and never missing his children's extracurricular activities. *Family isn't everything—it is the only thing.* She thought of the words he used to say at least once a week.

The phrase rang true, but Arielle found it impossible to keep living up to it when she had no family nearby. She never felt guilty about essentially marrying her job after she lost everyone of importance. It had been a gradual process as she found herself back at the CIA, her evenings left to either sulk and mourn, or hit the books and learn everything she could. She always chose the latter and never looked back.

When the Road Runners reached out to her, days after she had returned to the CIA, she dismissed the encounter as nonsense, perhaps a scammer trying to get a cut of her family's life insurance. But once she returned and had some time to clear her head, she thought back to meeting the man who offered no name and had spewed a bunch of random facts about her life that no one had any way of knowing. It felt sleazy at first, but after further consideration, seemed more legitimate considering what the man had known.

She had called him back on the phone number listed on the plain business card he left for her. They spoke for an hour, the man identifying himself as Brendan Costner, a recruiter for the Road Runners. He explained the work his organization focused on trying to make the world a better place, and didn't explain the bit about time travel until the very end, once Arielle had expressed an interest in joining.

She thought back to the precise moment, one that she supposed would have been laughed off under normal circumstances. But she had grown so vulnerable during that time of mourning, and slept on the matter. The next day, after hours of research into the science from those who believed time travel was at least a possibility, she called Brendan back and agreed to meet with him in person.

Within a week, she met him at the Denver office and enjoyed her first taste of time travel. She had traveled back to the year 2000, and stopped by her fifth birthday party at a park, keeping a safe distance with Brendan by her side, explaining the rules and restrictions that came with the territory.

Seeing her family, much younger, and herself, was all the proof she needed. Of course, her initial thought was that she had been killed and had fallen into a strange purgatory. But when they returned to the present time, and all was the same, she ran out of ways to explain it away.

Life had knocked her down, but just as quickly yanked her back up, flinging her into a whole new world. Her only regret was not getting to say farewell to her previous life.

Chapter 14

By the evening, Arielle had grown antsy after packing her bags for the mission. She went down her checklist five different times to ensure not a single item had been missed, zipping her suitcase closed and sitting on the foot of the bed as she racked her mind for any last tasks to handle before jumping back. Only ten minutes would pass in 2022 while she spent a couple of weeks in 1988, but she didn't want to return home to a long to-do list.

After enough stalling, she retrieved her bottle of Juice from her nightstand drawer, took a sip, and lay on the bed while focusing on the date of June 24, 1988. The night of the murder of Mason Gregory.

Arielle preferred to jump into the past before traveling to the location. A two-hour drive was more than reasonable, and once she experienced the rumbling of the world, shifting through the dimensions of time, she arrived in 1988, in the middle of a dirt lot, her suitcase by her side as she had kept contact with it through the time travel.

Jumping through time always left her head cloudy, but the sensation typically wore off within five minutes. Arielle lived at the top of a hill, having done thorough research to find the prime location for her chaotic lifestyle. She had few neighbors in the immediate vicinity. No matter when she had to travel to the past, she could guarantee the location would either be her house or the dirt lot.

From there, she had a one-mile walk to a Hertz car rental location that had opened in 1978. If she traveled to a time before that, it was only an extra half-mile to the nearest gas station that had a payphone to call a taxi to either take her to the airport or a different car rental agency in downtown Denver.

She didn't mind the walk, even though she had to lug a 50-pound suitcase through the dirt—and sometimes mud. It gave her just enough additional time to mentally prepare. Because once she arrived at either the airport or a car rental agency, all other matters in her life took a backseat to the mission.

Arielle climbed to her feet, slightly off balance, as she hadn't completely shaken the fog from her brain, and drew in a deep breath of the crisp 1988 summer air. The Denver metro area had yet to see its boom in population, so she always enjoyed traveling back to the days of less pollution and crowds. Being near the foothills of the Rocky Mountains also put her back in touch with mother nature, grounding her, and reminding her how insignificant a speck she was in the universe.

"Here we are," she whispered to herself, grabbing her suitcase and starting her trip down the hill. She had to take careful steps. One false move could send her tumbling to the bottom. Rocks and dirt decorated the ground, the occasional weed tickling her ankles.

It only took five minutes for her to reach the bottom, at which point she turned and looked back to the top of the hill, her mind filling in the blanks of where her house would one day stand on this magnificent landscape. As much as she dwelled on her past life, she never let a moment pass without feeling some gratitude for the lifestyle she currently enjoyed, no matter how lonely it was.

From the bottom of the hill, the nearest road waited another quarter mile away, where she would find flat ground and the sidewalk leading to the strip mall that hosted the Hertz rental agency. Arielle hurried to it, thankful no rain had fallen to turn the ground muddy. Her calves and thighs burned, and she cursed herself for having skipped her workout routine the past two days.

Arielle took great pride in her twelve percent body fat, adhering to a strict diet and exercise routine. The only time she strayed was in between missions, often eating a pint of ice cream and enjoying a glass of wine. Sometimes on the missions, she had no choice but to eat junk food, depending on when and where she traveled to. She required her temporary residences to have full kitchens so she could cook a healthy meal in the evenings.

Her stomach growled, and she wondered if she was actually hungry or if the past was already trying to slow her down. She expected as much resistance from the past, but also couldn't recall what time she had eaten last.

The most important rule of time travel, and perhaps the most difficult aspect to understand and adapt to, was the past refusing to be changed. No mission was as simple as barging into a room and shooting a future murderer years before they had the chance to commit heinous crimes. No matter how dark it might be, the past was only interested in preserving itself.

Arielle remembered how they explained the past in her early days of training with the Road Runners. Her instructor, the third-ranked Angel Runner at the time, likened the past to the Pando, a tree colony comprising over 40,000 individual aspen trees, yet still considered a singular living organism.

The thousands of trees all intertwined within the same root system. If a person were to go underground and cut just one root, it could lead to the death of hundreds, or possibly thousands, of trees. Tampering with the past was to be treated with the same caution.

While stopping an isolated murder seemed the right thing to do, on the surface, the Road Runners always had to consider the consequences of such an action. A dedicated team always studied the ripple effect—or butterfly effect—but they only had access to so much information. The rest of the work had to be carried out by the Angels in the field once they gained a true understanding of all the moving parts within the mission.

On top of uncovering where all these potential roots led, another factor that weighed on the team's mind was how wide of a reach the particular event had in the past. The wider the reach, the more they could expect the past to protect itself.

It was the main reason their missions focused on fixing more small-town tragedies, instead of things like trying to prevent Hitler's rise to power. The bigger the event, and the more lives affected, only opened doors to chaos if they tried to tamper with it.

The past understood what lay within one's heart and soul. It understood when Arielle had traveled back to significant moments in American history—the Battle of Gettysburg and the moon landing—to gather more information. Not to change anything.

"The past is our ultimate ruler," Arielle muttered under her breath as she reached the sidewalk and increased her pace, grateful for the flat concrete. Respecting the past was the only way to understand all the nuances of time travel. The past held no prejudices, and would stop anyone trying to alter it using any means necessary.

The Angels had learned after enough failures what sort of things to expect. Arielle already expected events like flat tires, gas running out, random explosions, and outsiders to serve as roadblocks in her mission to save the life of Mason Gregory. Every mission had thousands of little details to consider, and Arielle looked over nearly all of them, despite having dozens of fellow Road Runners with jobs dedicated to doing just that.

A sign hung over the side of the road showing the names of all the businesses within the strip mall. It wasn't quite the evening yet, so its lights hadn't been turned on, instead catching an orange glow from the sun starting its descent behind the mountains.

Arielle's stomach fluttered—she always got a small amount of jitters before starting a new mission. This one had a few more than usual, now that she had a dedicated team working with her. She didn't have total control over every aspect of the mission, as she had become accustomed to. Felix and Selena were already at their shared home, hopefully hours into research and planning. As of right now, Arielle was the missing puzzle piece to the mission.

She stepped into the Hertz office, eager to begin.

Chapter 15

The drive to Pueblo took the two hours as planned, but Arielle faced a delay at the Hertz office. When she arrived, she found no one from the staff for fifteen minutes. They had apparently taken a break to swing by the neighboring ice cream shop.

A man and woman eventually returned and apologized profusely, citing it as their slowest time of day when customers never came in. After filling out all the paperwork, Arielle didn't hit the road until a few minutes before six o'clock, and she had to speed to make up for lost time, since the murder took place between nine-thirty and ten.

The first part of any mission was a brief observation of the tragedy to ensure it actually happened. Unlike detectives looking for a missing body, the Road Runners had the advantage of going back in time to confirm the incident was a murder and not a case of someone running away or being kidnapped.

Since Mason Gregory's body had been discovered hours after the murder, this initial observation was more to confirm they had the correct time and location. From there, Arielle and her team would work backwards to find the best opportunities to prevent the crime from happening.

Arielle arrived in Pueblo just after eight o'clock. Everything had been marked out on her map, which she studied under the bright lights of a gas station where she had parked to figure out the next several hours. The site of the murder had a circle drawn around it, and less than a block away was another circle where she would park, the location confirmed to be in the shadows where the murderer would never see her.

Her stomach growled, and she couldn't put off eating any longer, especially since she wanted to be at the site no later than nine o'clock. It was a Friday night, and the restaurants she had passed looked jam-packed with the weekend crowds and families. She wouldn't have time to sit down and order, dread settling over her now that she'd have no choice but to eat fast food.

"First day of the mission and already stuck eating a burger," she said, shaking her head as she studied the map. Arielle pulled out of the gas station and turned back onto North Main Street, where the bars and restaurants lined both sides of the road. She passed a Wendy's and Taco Bell before seeing the bright yellow sign of a Subway, and immediately swerved over a lane to turn into the sandwich shop's parking lot.

She always chose the sandwich chain when possible—there weren't many other options for non-greasy fast food when traveling into the past, and she counted her blessings every time she found one, since they still hadn't become as widespread as many of their greasy competitors.

Arielle ran in and took five minutes getting her sandwich, deciding to drive to the murder scene and eat from there. She returned to Main Street, driving away from the center of town, toward the outskirts.

She got onto Highway 50 and headed east, into the darkness of the night. It took five minutes until she escaped the neighborhoods and businesses of Pueblo; the landscape turning into open fields as far as she could see. After ten more minutes, she exited the highway after passing a group of industrial warehouses. She turned onto a frontage road that connected all the warehouses and turned off her headlights once she found the one with a tattered sign that read *Big Z Home Office.*

The lot had two parking lots, one on the north and south sides of the building. The murder would occur in the north lot, which was already abandoned, two dim lights casting a weak glow over the empty parking spaces. Arielle's hiding spot was between the two lots where a row of roughly twenty trucks stood with trailers backed up to the warehouse. She parked next to the first trailer, engulfed in darkness, as this area had no lighting. A small courtyard, only thirty yards long, separated Arielle from the northern parking lot. She had a clear view of the lot, and with her binoculars, shouldn't have any problems witnessing the murder, even in the night.

They had informed her the warehouse closed at eight o'clock, and that appeared true, as she had yet to see a single person walk from the building. It was already 8:45 once she killed her engine and unwrapped her sandwich to eat. She rolled down her window to keep an ear out for anyone passing by, but had already fallen lost in her dinner.

Shortly after nine, a pair of headlights appeared from the south, startling Arielle into crumbling up her empty wrapper and tossing it aside on the passenger seat. She reached under her seat where she had stashed her pistol and pulled it out, just in case.

The car moved at a snail's pace as it crawled along the road in front of her. Her stomach tightened once she had a clear visual of the vehicle, a 1982 Honda Civic.

It's him, she thought, already knowing what Mason Gregory drove. The show seemed to start early, and she was glad to have arrived on time. The car continued past Arielle and finally turned into the north lot, parking right under the lone lamp.

She could only see the silhouette of the car, and immediately doubted her position was good enough.

The car's door swung open, and out stepped a heavyset man she knew was Mason. His silhouette stood in front of the car before taking a seat on the hood. His arms fumbled in his pockets for a moment before she saw the flicker of a lighter. Mason remained in the dark, sitting on his hood, a lone orange ember from the tip of his cigarette standing out strong through Arielle's binoculars.

Doesn't have the look of a man who thinks he might die within the hour.

She mentally ran through a checklist of possibilities that she always considered when investigating a murder. Did the victim seem startled in the moments leading up to it? In this case, no, Mason seemed completely fine, from what she could tell. Someone afraid wouldn't have stepped outside of the car. This suggested he was meeting someone he knew, and that always helped narrow the pool of potential suspects. The location opened the door to many more questions. Why would a family man like Mason be out? Granted, it wasn't *too* late, especially for a Friday. The deserted warehouse suggested a potential drug deal, perhaps an off chance he was indulging in a romantic affair—though something nefarious was seeming more and more likely.

Arielle braced to witness a crime of passion, perhaps an escalation of events that left Mason dead in his car. The file mentioned that they had found him dead with a bullet wound to the head, slumped forward over his steering wheel. He was a large man, so it wasn't likely the suspect took the time to lug him back into the vehicle—someone definitely shot him while behind the wheel.

She watched Mason through the binoculars, the soon-to-be dead man still minding his business, puffing a cigarette without a care in the world. A motor roared from the opposite end of the property, prompting Arielle to spin around and drop her binoculars. She found the new set of headlights and followed them as they crept toward the north lot.

"Jackpot," Arielle said, recognizing the vehicle as an older muscle car. Even though it was too dark to make out the exact make and model, just knowing it was older would drastically help narrow down the suspect in this affair.

She regained her focus and watched as the car pulled up and stopped right in front of Mason's car; the headlights turning off to leave them in darkness. A man stepped out of the vehicle and circled around, shaking hands with Mason and leaning on the hood to face him. The two chatted, heads nodding, and it appeared nothing more than a couple of friends catching up.

They carried on like this for twenty minutes, Arielle growing somewhat bored as she watched the entire muted conversation through the binoculars. At one point, Mason accepted another cigarette from his acquaintance, the two appearing to laugh multiple times. For a moment, she wondered if she had possibly stumbled across the wrong suspicious meeting in the middle of the night, and doubted the second man who had arrived was the actual killer.

That was, until their conversation ended and Mason returned to his car. The other man paced back toward his vehicle, but hesitated as he walked in a circle in front of his door before returning to Mason's car.

Mason rolled down his window, and the two exchanged more words for another minute. The man reached behind his shirt and whipped out a pistol from his waistband, promptly stuffing it through the open window and blasting a slug into Mason's head. Arielle couldn't make out the gory details, but there was no mistaking the flash and bang that accompanied the lone shot.

The man stuffed his gun back into his waistband and hurried to his car, hopping behind the wheel and speeding away, sending smoke into the air from his screeching tires. Arielle followed the vehicle through the binoculars and noticed it was missing a license plate. She instantly knew she was dealing with a professional criminal, possibly even a hit man. The body of the car could have been a Camaro, but she still couldn't get a clear enough look. It didn't help that a lot of the older muscle cars had fairly similar body types.

"Shit," she muttered, shaking her head. Arielle had hoped for a simple mission, but should have known better. The Road Runners didn't give the top Angel simple missions—those were for newbies still cutting their teeth on this new life. For Arielle, her missions would forever be complex and take at least multiple weeks to resolve.

She turned her attention back to Mason, able to see his silhouette slouched over the steering wheel, not a single movement coming from his vehicle. That was how the warehouse morning crew would arrive to find him, and how he would remain for the rest of the day while the police and a team of detectives investigated.

And that's where Arielle, and her team, had to step in and fill the gaps.

Chapter 16

After witnessing the horrific scene, Arielle took a swig of her Juice to jump back to June 10, 1988, the same day her teammates had arrived in the past.

Arielle reached her home for the next two weeks at 10:15 and already had hundreds of thoughts running through her mind on the way over. There were always unanswered questions in any murder case. But she braced for even more than usual on this mission, since all the information they had on Mason Gregory didn't portray a man who should have even been in the empty parking after hours.

She lugged her suitcase up the walkway, unable to see the yard in the night, as the light on the front porch only illuminated the three steps that led up to the entryway. All the lights on the main level were on, and she saw the movement of shadows through the windows as she reached to open the oak door.

It opened before she could touch the doorknob, Felix greeting her with a wide grin. "Welcome home!" he said, stepping aside and opening the door all the way.

Arielle stepped in and scanned the area. To her left was a living room, fully furnished with a light gold sofa and two love seats, all centered around a wooden coffee table. An obnoxious chandelier hung from above, lighting up the room that only had a fireplace to look at. She saw the adjoining kitchen where all the blondewood cabinets complemented the matching kitchen table. Flowery wallpaper decorated the top perimeter of the room.

"My goodness, we really are in 1988," Arielle commented. "I've seen old pictures of my grandma's house, and this place looks a lot like it."

Felix chuckled. "And to think this house used to belong to a home decorator. This is just how the times were."

"The place came with all of this?"

Felix nodded. "I guess the last owner had a sudden family emergency and had to move to Georgia. Only the closets are empty. Even the basement is full of stuff they left behind. I figured we might as well hire someone to come clear it out, since we'll be holding on to this property to resell down the road."

"Fine with me. Where's Selena?"

"In the other living room, watching TV."

Arielle continued through the kitchen, into the dining room where a long table with eight seats sat in the middle, fake plants standing tall in each corner. A tall china cabinet stood against the wall, displaying vintage plates, mugs, and teakettles.

From here, she saw Selena sitting on a couch with a glass of wine in hand, watching videos on the old MTV channel—one that used to base its existence on music.

"Hey, Selena."

"Evening, Arielle," Selena replied, standing up and crossing the room to give Arielle a quick hug. "How did it go tonight? Did you see the murder happen?"

"She just got here," Felix interjected. "Give her a second to settle in."

"It's fine," Arielle said. "I need to talk about it."

No matter how much death she witnessed in her line of work, murder never lost its shock factor. And it always disturbed her old memories of the day in the mall.

Selena returned to the couch and turned off the television, patting at the open space beside her. Arielle obliged and sat, Felix getting cozy in a love seat to their side.

"I'm not sure what we're dealing with," Arielle said. "I think a professional killed him."

"Well, shit, that complicates things."

Arielle nodded. "It's nothing we haven't dealt with before. We've handled the mob, the cartels, plenty of hitmen. Sure, it makes things a *bit* more complicated, but we'll be okay."

Felix nodded, the wheels clearly turning in his mind.

"So, how do you propose we spend the day tomorrow?" Selena asked.

"We need to learn Mason's routine. Let's tail him for three days. Figure out what time he leaves the house in the morning. When he comes back home. And what he does in between. He's definitely involved in something that I don't suppose his wife knows about. Once we figure that out, we'll be able to track down the killer. Also, the killer was driving an old American muscle car. I couldn't make out any details, but it was a dark color, and could be a Camaro. Just keep an eye out for any vehicles in that range while you're out and about. I'll tail Mason—Selena, will you be trying to get close to his wife?"

She took a sip of wine and nodded. "That's my plan. I'll be waiting for her to go *anywhere*, at which point I'll follow her and accidentally bump into her. She'll have no choice but to become my friend. I'll find out as much as I can."

"Do you ever do things like get invited over for dinner?" Felix asked.

"Quite often. It's not a guarantee like I want it to be—maybe fifty percent of the time someone is comfortable enough to invite me over. Not bad, considering I'm dealing with people I've just met. Would you invite a stranger over to your house after meeting them a few days earlier?"

Felix laughed. "I invite no one over. For any reason."

"Challenge accepted," Selena said with a smirk. "Arielle, I'm going to get us a dinner invite to Felix's house in 2022 by the time this mission ends."

"I'm sure you will," Arielle said. "And what do you have planned for tomorrow, Felix?"

"A visit to the weapons warehouse in Colorado Springs. Any special requests for either of you?"

"I'll take a tommy gun," Selena said with a chuckle.

"Very funny. Seriously, what do you need?"

"Just a small Glock to keep in my purse," Selena said. "I rarely need anything else."

"I'll make the same request for each mission," Arielle said. "A nine millimeter, an AR-15, a lightweight butterfly knife, throwing knives, and some liquid poisons."

"Damn, girl," Selena said, taking another swig of wine. "You're crazy! What are you going to do with poison?"

"You never know. You think you can get all that for me?"

Felix had opened a notepad to jot down his weapons list, and nodded as he slapped it shut. "Shouldn't be a problem. And if either of you think of anything else, just let me know. I won't be leaving until nine o'clock tomorrow morning. I'll also stop to get clothing, just in case you need to blend in more around town."

"Thank you, Felix," Arielle said. "Your attention to detail is always appreciated."

Selena tipped her wine glass all the way back to finish the remains. "Anyone want to play some cards?"

"It's almost eleven—we need to get to bed."

"Ah, that's right," Selena said. "The queen needs her beauty rest. Felix?"

"It's been a long day," he replied. "Count me in tomorrow night—I'm running on fumes right now."

"Wow," Selena said. "Okay. You two enjoy your sleep. I'll be up for another couple of hours if you change your mind."

"Good night," Arielle said, returning to the foyer to grab her suitcase and haul it up the stairs. She would be asleep within fifteen minutes of settling into the master suite, replaying the image of Mason Gregory getting shot in the head.

Chapter 17

The next morning found Felix at the kitchen table, a pot of coffee brewing, its irresistible aromas filling the house. He was ready for the day, and just wanted to enjoy a cup on their back patio, an elevated space with breathtaking views of the Rocky Mountains to the west.

Selena came downstairs, a robe tied around her body, her hair rolled up into a messy bun. "Good morning," she said. "You make enough for me to have a cup?"

"I made enough for all of us," Felix said, standing from the table and going to the counter where the pot was just about ready. He rummaged through the cupboards and pulled out three mugs, aligning them next to the coffee machine.

"You're my savior."

"You stay up late like you said?"

"Of course. I'm a night owl. The only time I'm in bed before midnight is when I catch a cold. Even still, I'll stretch it until eleven. There's just something about unwinding from the day that gives me a new boost of energy—no matter how busy I was during the day."

"Well, today should be a busy one. Was Arielle awake up there yet?"

"Her door was closed, but it sounded like she was moving around. She's probably been up since four o'clock, plotting the day."

"We all have our methods. I suppose there is a reason she has been the top Angel for so long."

"If that's what it takes, then I guess it'll never be me."

"That's what you don't get, Selena." Felix's tone shifted. "*We* don't have to reach that high. We're Angels, sure, but we're role players. I know you don't follow sports that much, but every successful team has role players to support the superstar. They know they'll never be the star of the team, but they are the best at their specialties. Combine all of that around a superstar like Arielle, who also has leadership qualities, and there is no stopping that kind of team. *We* can be a super team. Even if Arielle gets all the credit and recognition, we'll know that we're the ones who made it possible. And as long as we accept that as our role, all the other fluff and rankings won't matter anymore."

Selena joined Felix at the counter as he poured coffee into the mugs. "That makes sense. We are highly regarded in our own ways."

"Exactly. You're the best at what you do. And I'm the best at what I do. Just because we don't have as wide a range of abilities as Arielle doesn't make us any less. People come to us for advice and direction."

"I'm honored to be working with you two," Arielle said, her voice startling them as they spun around to find her standing in the kitchen's entryway. "Felix, I'm impressed. Never heard you open up like that. You're quite the team player."

Felix's face flushed with embarrassment. "I . . . sorry, Arielle."

"No. There is nothing to apologize for. We need more of that. We *are* a team and will only succeed if everyone is carrying their weight. I'm sorry if I've ever seemed too solo. It's not you guys—I've just always had a certain way I like to do things. This is a change for me—for all of us. I have faith that we'll have this all figured out by the end of the mission. And if I ever stray, just reel me back in. I can't stress it enough to you two—always tell me what's on your mind."

"Coffee?" Felix asked, nodding to the steaming pot sitting on the counter.

"I'd love some."

For the next twenty minutes, they all sat on the patio chairs outside, enjoying their morning brew and mountain view. Arielle ran through her plans for the day and asked for the same of Felix and Selena.

Felix hadn't grown any less intimidated since Arielle's arrival, still ready to jump at any request she had, but their morning meeting started softening his perspective toward the top-ranked Angel. He saw her more as a human than the superhero others around the organization often portrayed.

Arielle slurped her coffee and smacked her lips after each sip. Felix always caught these sorts of details with everyone he met, and was relieved Arielle had such subtle nuances.

"I need to get going," Felix said, standing from his seat and soaking in one more view of the mountains. "I can arrange dinner plans for this evening if we think we'll all be back in time."

"You're a chef, too?" Selena asked.

"Well, yes, I am an excellent cook, but I rarely cook during missions—not enough time to grocery shop and all that. I can make us reservations somewhere, or find takeout to eat here."

"It's impossible for me to know where the day will take me," Arielle said. "When will you be able to set up surveillance on the Gregory property?"

"I scouted the area—well, I drove by it when I first got here. Looks like entry should be easy enough. As far as bugging the inside and tapping the phone line, that's more up to Selena finding out the safest time for me to enter the home when it's empty. I need at least thirty minutes of guaranteed alone time in that house."

"If you can have it set up today, I can plan to join you for dinner. If not, I'll have to stay near the property. I need to know all of his movements."

"I should be able to do that. That's part of what I'm picking up at the weapons warehouse—they store all of our spy gear, too."

"Sounds like you're on top of it," Arielle said. "My apologies—again, I'm not used to having a fully functioning team like this."

"I'm all for double-checking things to make sure nothing is missed. But I really need to leave now—don't want to be late."

Arielle waved her hands to hurry Felix back inside the house, and he left with a quick nod to both women on the patio. He patted his pockets while crossing the house toward the front door, confirming he had his wallet and keys.

Satisfied with everything, Felix stepped outside and ran down the steps to his car.

* * *

Felix arrived at an abandoned office building in Colorado Springs and killed the engine. The Road Runners loved using commercial buildings for their own, whether abandoned or active. For the active ones, they operated similar to the mafia, using the main level of an office as a business front for the public, while operating their secret existence in the depths of the basement.

This location in Colorado Springs was an abandoned one, an older building falling apart. The windows had webbed cracks, chunks of the wooden exterior hanging on for dear life. Even the "For Lease" sign hung crooked. The colors and wording faded after years of the sun beating on it. This part of town had been abandoned after being run down by crime. It was the only part of Colorado Springs where few people dared visit—making it a perfect hideout for the Road Runners.

Felix only had to pass through the rough neighborhood, and doing so in the early morning proved non-threatening. Once he arrived, he couldn't see another soul in sight. The front of the building faced open plains, tall yellow grass ruffling in the morning breeze.

He stepped out of the car, the ground crunching beneath his shoes as he checked around the area once more to ensure he was alone. Felix climbed up the three steps and pulled open the door, the hinges screaming loud enough to draw attention. He hurried inside and closed the door shut behind him.

"Hello?" he called out down a long hallway, his voice bouncing and echoing back. "Anyone in here?"

Felix didn't expect a response, knowing the weapons warehouse was underground, but he made a habit out of declaring his presence whenever entering one of these buildings. On a prior mission, a homeless man who had been hiding out in a similar building had startled Felix when he burst into the place without a care in the world. The man had pulled a knife, and Felix had to react with the combat skills he hadn't used since his early days of training. His line of work rarely put him in danger, and that's why he took a more proactive approach now.

No one responded, so he continued down the hallway, its wallpaper a faded yellow tint after years of suffering water leaks that likely went unrepaired. Heavy wooden doors lined the hall, portals into the former office spaces that once were. In his early days on the job, Felix liked to explore what lay behind the doors. He had an itch to catch a glimpse of the life that once was, but after going through so many and rarely finding anything of interest, he now pressed through toward his destination, a man on a mission.

He reached the end of the hall, where the stairwell waited under an exit sign. The stairwell fit in with the rest of the place, but as he descended, the surroundings started to morph. The walls had fresh paint, even though they were black, and a functioning light fixture hung above the door at the bottom landing, also painted black.

"Like I'm entering a house of death," Felix muttered under his breath before knocking. It made a hollow thud that echoed all the way back up the stairs. He braced himself for the fellow Road Runner he was about to meet, since the people in this position were hit-or-miss in terms of their social skills and general awkwardness.

The door swung open, the first one in the building that did so without a loud creak. A man appeared in the doorway, nearly filling its entirety. Felix found himself eye level with the man's bulging chest and had to raise his head to meet the eyes of the behemoth. He had a bald head and a thick, black beard connecting one ear to the other.

"Felix?" the man asked, his voice slightly softer than a grumble.

"Yes, sir," Felix replied, unsure why he felt nervous all of a sudden. "And you are Lou, is that correct?"

The man nodded, revealing his teeth through the jungle of his beard as he cracked a friendly grin. "The one and only Lou Garrison at your service." He stuck out a meaty hand to Felix, revealing an arm covered in tattoos.

Felix grabbed it and shook, offering a smile in return. "Nice to meet you, Lou. Did you ever receive our list of requests for this mission?"

"I didn't. Those bastards at headquarters like to forget to send over the important messages. . . like the ones I need to do my job. Fucking bureaucrats."

One similarity that was pretty much universal across the spectrum of all weapons warehouse operators was their disdain for the organization. It's not that they hated the Road Runners. They simply saw the governing body as too powerful, and never wasted a moment to throw dirt on their names. Commander Briar was the first commander to not receive as much hate, thanks to winning the war, but they didn't love the man, either.

"Never to worry, though," Lou continued. "I've been at this job long enough to know I can't ever rely on getting the information I need. So, I reached out to them this morning. Told them I need weapons ready for the next century's top-ranked agent, and that they better get their shit together. And what do you know? I got a list faxed over within fifteen minutes. Bunch of sorry chumps—no offense if any of them are your friends."

"I'm sure some of them are, but I have no way of knowing who works on these specific requests. That team has hundreds of people."

"Well, you'd think they'd do a better job with so many of them. Enough about that, though. I got everything you need. I've heard some stories about this Angel you're working with in the future. Is she as good as I've heard?"

Even though the weapons warehouse workers were Road Runners and had full access to time travel, few of them exercised that rare gift, and opted to stay in their present time, living a standard, linear life. These weren't people interested in participating in missions themselves, but they still served a critical role in all the mission work carried out by the organization.

"Arielle Lucila? Yeah, she's the real deal. I know it's too early to say, but she could very well go down in our history as one of the best Angels ever. She has that sort of drive about her. All she thinks about is missions and how to complete them. When you talk to her, it's like her mind is elsewhere, even though she's still engaged in your conversation."

"I know the type. I've met enough Angels to understand. Some of them are like robots. Killing machines. I love that about 'em."

Felix studied the tattoos on Lou's arms, most of them tribal designs that led all the way into his sleeves, but he caught the words *Semper Fi* entangled within the design. "You were a Marine?"

Lou let out a soft chuckle. "It's never *were*. We are *always* Marines. I was a young kid out of high school when I fought in Korea."

"I had an uncle in the Marines, so it's always nice to meet you guys."

Lou nodded in appreciation and uncrossed his arms. "Likewise. Let's have a look at your equipment, shall we?"

He pivoted around and led them deeper into the warehouse. Shelves lined the perimeter, reaching as high as the ten-foot ceiling, filled with hundreds of guns of all shapes and sizes. Six rows of tables ran from the front to the back in the middle of the room, and those contained a wider variety of items. Lou took them down a row toward his desk in the back corner, and Felix caught sight of boxes of ammunition, hand grenades, security system parts, and even a table full of swords and machetes.

They reached the desk in the back, where scattered papers covered every inch of its surface. A long, black duffel bag rested on top, and Lou unzipped it, reaching in and pulling out every item on Felix's list.

"Got a nine, AR, butterfly knife, throwing knives, poisons, and the cameras and mics for bugging," Lou said as he studied the objects now splayed atop his paperwork. "And ammo for the guns. Everything look good?"

Felix nodded as he looked up and down at the equipment. "This should do. Can I get a couple of extra pistols? Just something small and easy to conceal."

"Not a problem." Lou shuffled away from his desk and crouched to reach the bottom shelf ten feet away, grunting as he stretched to grab two more guns. "Two extra nines—that way you can use the same ammo. Anything else you can think of?" Lou asked, dropping the firearms into the duffel bag.

Felix shook his head. "I think this is everything. We're staying in Pueblo, so it's not much trouble if I need to come back for more."

"Don't be a stranger. I'm here for you guys and whatever you need. Just call me if anything comes up." Lou reached over his desk and pulled a business card from a stack, handing it to Felix. It had a handwritten name and phone number for Lou.

"I appreciate your help so much," Felix said, sticking out a hand to shake.

"Let's get you packed up," Lou said. "I know there is never a second to waste on your missions. You guys trying to stop another murder?"

"We sure are."

"Well, Godspeed to you all. Good luck out there."

Chapter 18

Selena was the only one without a car, and debated between renting one for herself, waiting for Felix to come back, or figuring out how to get to Mason Gregory's neighborhood on her own. She may have gone through her regular life with the simplicity of punching in an address into her cell phone, but she had also put in the time to study living in different eras, taking retreats of living at least one year in different decades to get a feel for life and how to function like a basic human.

She despised the complexity of such a menial task in 1988, wishing she could open Uber and call for a ride that way. Without knowing how long Felix would be, she had no choice but to head into the wild world of 1988 Pueblo. The Gregory house wasn't too far, but it wasn't a quick stroll through the neighborhood, either.

They had brought an atlas of Colorado and she found it on top of the kitchen table, the book hailing itself for its detailed topographic maps and extensive update through the year of 1987. "Where the hell do we find this shit?" she asked, picking it up and studying it like an ancient relic. She put it back on the table and flipped it open to the table of contents, finding Pueblo, and flipping to the page.

Someone had already highlighted and circled all the important locations for the mission, and made it a simple task for Selena to find the exact route from their house to her destination. "I can walk if I absolutely must," she said, but figured a bus ran up and down the main road outside of the neighborhood. Even catching that would save her twenty minutes. If she arrived five minutes too late and missed Mrs. Gregory leaving the house for whatever reason, it could cause an entirely wasted day. Their missions had virtually no room for error or wasted time.

She memorized the route and wrote the address on a small slip of paper to carry in her pocket. "Time to go," she said, and left the house.

* * *

After a three-minute walk to Buffalo Road, a bustling street with small businesses and evenly-spaced bus stops, Selena only had to wait another five minutes before a bus arrived, headed northbound. She inserted three quarters into the farebox and was on her way, arriving within six minutes to her stop.

All the homes looked similar as she passed them: ranch-style houses with chain-link fences and short driveways that led to the back door. Garages were not common in the area; neither were manicured lawns. Many yards boasted tall weeds or long grass sticking through the fences.

She rounded a corner and turned onto Brush Street, the Gregory residence only two houses down. She walked on the opposite side of the street to avoid being caught snooping.

The Gregory house had an off-white paint job with light green trim. From across the street, Selena saw the front door and two windows on each side. On the left-hand side was the kitchen, a figure moving around freely within, and on the other appeared a living room, as she could see TV antennas standing tall, and a small bookshelf further in the background. The yard was in slightly better shape than most of the ones she had passed, although it had plenty of dirt patches beneath the scattering of children's toys and two plastic cars the little ones surely pedaled around in. A bush in desperate need of trimming sprawled out below the living room window.

Perfect hiding spot, Selena thought, never afraid to hide in shrubbery in the middle of the night. And in front of the living room, she'd have no trouble spying through the window to see what Gregory family life looked like in the evenings.

She had fallen too deep into her thoughts to realize the figure had stopped parading around the kitchen and now stood on the front porch.

"Lindsay," Selena whispered to herself, moving her feet again, seeking a tree to hide behind. According to the mission report, Lindsay Gregory had been married to Mason for seventeen years, in which the couple had one daughter and one son, aged six and three in 1988.

Lindsay stood on the porch, hands on her hips as she studied the lawn, shaking her head before shuffling around to pick up the toys, placing them in a wide plastic chest tucked alongside the house. She was slowly gaining weight these days. That would snowball later with the depression and binge eating following Mason's death. Her long, dirty blond hair, trailed as she whipped around the lawn, tidying it up within a couple of minutes.

She never saw Selena slip behind a van parked on the sidewalk, peering around the back bumper as she crouched. Selena watched as Lindsay finished cleaning and strolled to the side of the house and sat down in her car.

"Fuck!" Selena muttered, standing up while Lindsay backed out of her driveway and took off in the opposite direction. She pulled out the notepad she kept in her back pocket and jotted down that Lindsay drove a maroon Geo Metro, its paint fading, both hubcaps missing from the driver's side of the vehicle. "Dammit!" she cried, frustrated she had no way of keeping up, potentially losing an entire day of spying on the soon-to-be widow.

Where are the kids? she wondered. It was definitely summer break, and the kids weren't of age to be left alone. Maybe Lindsay had just left to pick them up from a summer camp or daycare. Selena had spent plenty of time as a youth in such places, seeing as both her parents were always consumed with work. These were the details left out of mission reports—the holes she had to fill in.

It was almost ten o'clock, so the timing seemed strange if she had left to pick up the kids. Selena would plan to arrive earlier tomorrow, likely before the sun rose, and would certainly rent a car today to avoid any more issues.

A black car crept silently down the street, and Selena's first instinct was to hide behind the van again. She watched as it stopped in front of the Gregory property and sat there for two minutes.

"Felix?" she whispered. She had been too flustered to register the car in front of her, and couldn't help but laugh as she stood up and crossed the street.

Felix had to reach over the empty passenger seat to roll down the window. "Selena?" he asked. "What are you doing? She just left."

"No shit, Sherlock," Selena snapped. "I didn't think I was going to have to follow her already. The reports said she was a stay-at-home mom, so I figured she'd be here most of the time."

"I'm sure she'll be back soon enough. Since you're here, want to stand lookout for me? I can work much faster knowing I'm covered in case she returns."

Selena shrugged, nothing better to do since her target had disappeared. "Alright. You're early, aren't you?"

"I always try to get this part of the work done as soon as possible. I never know how many opportunities I'll get to set up my surveillance."

Selena saw the duffel bag resting on the passenger seat. "Got a gun in there for me?"

"Slow your roll. Yes, I do, but we don't need all that right now. I'm going to park across the street. You can sit in the driver's seat and just watch both directions for Mrs. Gregory. If you see her coming back, honk three times really fast and I'll be out of there."

"Easy enough."

Felix nodded before turning the car around and parking it behind the van where Selena had just hidden. He grabbed the duffel bag and sprinted to the Gregory house without another word.

Chapter 19

Felix didn't waste a second once he stepped foot on the property, bolting around the house, scaling a wobbly wooden fence, and landing in the backyard that had seen even more neglect than the front. He rushed to the back door, relieved the fence was just tall enough to prevent the neighbors from seeing him about to break and enter.

The duffel bag, strapped over his shoulder, clanged against his back while he rummaged through his pants pockets for a lock pick.

"Wait," he whispered to himself, reaching out and turning the doorknob, stomach tightening as the door creaked open into the kitchen. The smaller the town, he had found, the more likely people were to leave their back doors unlocked, especially ones that were fenced off. Even though this was Felix's field of expertise, breaking into homes always made him feel like a criminal.

His heart thrummed, adrenaline flowing through all his limbs as he took his first step inside the house. He had done this same routine at least two hundred times in his young career, but always feared the possibility of the homeowners returning before he finished. He had yet to encounter that scenario, and had no clue how he would react. He didn't carry a weapon when entering a private residence, not wanting a situation to escalate out of control and result in further complications. The lock pick was perhaps the closest thing he had to a weapon, the object nothing more than a dull-tipped screwdriver.

The house was a cramped mess. Piles of mail and bills were stacked on top of the counter next to him. They left pots and pans on the stovetop, the smell of bacon lingering in the air, something guaranteed to make Felix's mouth water, no matter the situation. The family didn't appear to have a dining room, as the table in the kitchen was far too big for the space, allowing little room to navigate around the area. It had six seats, two of which were full with more stacks of papers, these looking like drawings and homework assignments from the kids.

Felix had cameras in his bag, but rarely installed them inside of a target's home. They were twice the size of the miniature microphones he used to bug for sound. He saved the cameras for outside, where they used the views to help learn the schedule of their subjects.

He dashed toward the kitchen sink, finding an elevated cupboard beside it and reaching under to feel for any metal brackets. It had none, so he raised himself up on the sink, flailing for the small domed light fixture above.

"Jackpot," he whispered after feeling the cool touch of metal. He was equipped to plant the bugs on any surface, but using the attached magnets made his life much easier. The bug made a faint clapping sound as it attached to the light, and Felix eased himself down, spinning around to head for the living room.

A raggedy couch and rocking chair were next to each other, facing the old box TV on a small stand across the room. The coffee table in the middle had an ashtray with two cigarette butts left in it, and circular stains scattered across the surface. The living room had plenty of areas for him to plant the bug: the TV, two lamps on either side of the furniture, under the coffee table. He preferred higher elevation, so he decided the lamps would do.

Figuring a majority of the conversations between Mason and Lindsay would come from the living room and bedroom, he planted a bug on both lamps to ensure complete coverage of the space.

An opening from the living room connected to a short hallway, where Felix found two bedrooms and a bathroom. He entered the first bedroom, finding it had two beds on opposite walls. One wall was covered with dinosaur pictures, while the other had princesses and unicorns. A toy chest stood in the middle of the room, its lid open as costumes and toys poured out of it.

Felix expected little useful conversation from the children's room, so he planted one bug on the lamp that stood next to the doorway. He did the same in the bathroom, having to stretch above the sink to secure it to the light fixture.

He continued to the bedroom at the end of the hall, finding it only slightly bigger than the kids' room. The bed had been made, but the comforter showed the ruffled imprint of a body having laid on it earlier. A dresser stood opposite the bed, clothes piled high on it, with more on the floor. They had left the closet doors open, a bottom rack covered in both men's and women's shoes. Suits and dresses hung from the rod, and winter outfits piled on the top shelf, touching the ceiling.

"This family definitely needs some more space," Felix said, and a sick feeling crept into his stomach as he realized they *would* have more space in two weeks. Once Mason was dead. He shook his head and resumed his search for the best spot to plant a bug.

The dresser left a small gap along the bottom just big enough to slip a hand into. Felix dropped to his knees, and that's when a horn started blaring outside.

"Shit," he gasped, all the blood in his body rushing to his head. He already had the bug in hand, but had no time to stick it since it would need glue or tape. He jammed it into the corner, stuffing it behind one of the dresser's legs, ensuring it was out of sight, before jumping to his feet and slinging the duffel bag over his shoulder.

Felix's vision pulsed in sync with each heartbeat. He dashed out of the bedroom and returned to the back door, stepping outside and spinning in a quick circle to gather his surroundings. A dog barked—a horrendous *yap! yap! yap!* from a chihuahua in the yard that backed up to the Gregory residence.

"Shut the fuck up!" Felix hissed toward the fence, to no avail. The world spun in slow motion. He tried to focus on the sounds coming from the front yard, but couldn't hear a damn thing. How he wished he could punt the chihuahua across a football field right now.

He shuffled to the fence, legs tense and ready to sprint, and pressed his face against the coarse wood, fighting for a visual through the thin slots between pickets. The Geo Metro had just turned into the driveway, stopping less than three feet away from where Felix stood.

The rattling engine turned off and the driver's door swung open, prompting Felix to jump backwards, praying his silhouette hadn't been visible through the fence. Lindsay was speaking, and the sound of her voice made Felix's heart stop cold in his chest.

He pivoted around and debated running to the other side of the house. Instead, Lindsay continued speaking, in the distance. And in no ways suspicious. Cell phones were still rare in 1988, so he leaned forward to listen more closely.

"Mommy, I want a peanut butter and jelly sandwich," a little girl's voice said.

"I think we can make that work," Lindsay said, and the sound of their footsteps moved further away as they went to the front door.

Felix froze, calculating the distance from the car to the front door, and also how long it would take him to hop over the fence and dash off the property.

Just go, dammit, he thought, and lunged toward the fence, jumping as high as he could until his fingers grasped the top of it. No one was in sight as he fell down on the other side, landing square on his back, the duffel bag tangled around his arms and neck. Felix hurried to his feet, staying in a crouched position, as the kitchen window faced out the side of the house. If Lindsay went straight to the kitchen sink, she'd spot him.

She didn't, and the moment he heard the front door slam shut, Felix sprinted away from the house.

He reached the sidewalk and never looked back, rushing to Selena in the car around the corner, leaning on the hood to catch his breath.

Selena stepped out. "Well, that was exciting for you," she said with a light chuckle.

Felix shook his head, still panting like a dog. "That was . . . the closest call I've had."

"How much were you able to get done?"

"Bugged all the rooms. Still need to set up the receiver, and tap the phone line. That's all stuff that can be done from outside the house—much less risky. I'm going to have to stay here today, though. I need to at least find a spot in the area to hide the receiver. Within 300 yards of the house."

"How big is it?"

Felix patted the duffel bag where he kept it. "About the size of a shoe box."

"I'll help you look. I'll even drive. We should leave the area for a bit. Got an older woman six houses down working in her front yard. She hasn't looked this way, but might as well play it safe." Selena nodded in the direction, and Felix saw the lady standing near the sidewalk with a water hose in hand.

"Good call. Let's head out."

Chapter 20

While Felix and Selena spent the rest of their day driving around the Gregory neighborhood searching for a hiding spot for the radio receiver (an overgrown bush that separated the neighborhood from an adjoining park that clearly hadn't been attended to in the past year), Arielle fought off the most unbearable waves of boredom she had ever endured.

Boredom was certainly part of the job, especially during the current phase of staking out and following a target, but Arielle typically used that downtime to work on other aspects of the mission—matters that now fell into the hands of Felix and Selena. For the first time during a mission, Arielle had nothing to do but wait for her target to step out of the building he had entered nine hours ago. At one point, she even considered running to a bookstore and returning with a stack of new reads. Her lifestyle had put restraints on her longtime favorite hobby, but if her days looked like this, she just might have a chance to jump back into the imaginative world of books.

The building she had followed Mason to, and remained parked outside of since nine in the morning, stood two stories tall and had CreditConnect posted in big block letters across the top windows. She already knew Mason had worked for the company for the last two years, manning the phones in an account manager role for the credit card processing company. Just as she already knew—or could at least take a highly educated guess—which route he would drive home. You couldn't enter a stakeout without already knowing ninety percent of the information needed. It was the other ten she had set out for, and with that came the waiting game.

After sitting in her car for the entirety of Mason's workday, she shot up in her seat when he finally stepped out of the building at six minutes past five. He walked with a small group of two other women and a man, and Arielle was quick to study any signs of suggestive body language between Mason and the others. He showed none and shuffled to his car after a quick wave to his co-workers, who had split their own ways. A majority of affairs occurred in the workplace, or at least *with* co-workers, and this first outing suggested nothing of the sorts.

"It's never simple," she whispered as she twisted the key in the ignition. She had parked two rows behind Mason, providing a direct line of sight to his car, and also the opportunity to pull out easily and follow him.

She did exactly that as Mason steered his old Civic out of the parking lot and pulled onto the road. Tailing someone in a car was second nature for Arielle, and she did so with the expectation of finding nothing of significance.

For the next fifteen minutes, Arielle followed Mason on the exact route she expected him to take home. He made no stops and followed all traffic laws. When they pulled into his neighborhood, Arielle hung back at least one hundred feet since she lost the concealment of traffic on the main roads. She pulled aside and waited for Mason to coast into the driveway.

It was a hot June evening, and the sun wouldn't quit for another three hours, so Arielle rolled up her windows and blasted the air conditioning, something she couldn't have done all day, as cars from the 1980s were even less fuel-efficient than those from her Original Time. But she couldn't take it anymore, and as she parked across the street from the Gregory residence, her heart froze when she saw Felix in his car a few feet in front of her.

There was no issue with Felix being there, but she expected little overlap with her new teammates while working on missions, especially in the middle of the day. They were to all work during the day, and convene at night, if plausible. He stared at her from his rear-view mirror, and she promptly hopped out of the car and hurried into his passenger seat.

"What are you still doing here?" she asked. "Isn't everything supposed to be in place?"

"Ran into some issues. Almost got caught inside the house. I didn't get the chance to set up the receiver until recently. I wanted to hang out to make sure everything is running smoothly."

Felix raised his left hand that had been tucked along the side of his leg, and revealed a handheld radio receiver. A wire ran from it to his left ear, connecting to a small earphone.

"I see."

In the past, Arielle had been used to just showing up to a mission and having these kinks worked out. She knew how to retrieve the memory chip from a receiver, insert a new one, and take it back to her computer to listen to the footage. While she understood that more went into the process, she had never experienced it firsthand.

Felix pulled the cord out of the headphone jack, allowing the receiver's built-in speaker to flood the car with the voices of Mason and Lindsay. He recoiled at how loud it was, and promptly turned down the volume dial.

"Busy day at work?" Lindsay asked.

Arielle stared at the receiver, not realizing Felix watched her.

"Pretty busy, yeah," Mason said, the first time either had heard their target's voice. He spoke with a slight slur, like he might have a toothpick in his mouth. "How were things around here today?"

"Good. Picked up around the house, got things ready for Amanda's ballet recital Friday night. You told the guys you won't be able to make it to poker night, right?"

"Yes. They actually rescheduled for Saturday night, that way I can go."

Arielle whipped out her notepad to jot down the information about Saturday night. She had an obligation to follow Mason's every single movement if he left the house by himself. A poker game could serve as a cover for lots of things, allowing him privacy for at least three hours at a time. Her face prickled with heat at the thought of getting closer to solving, and hopefully preventing, his murder.

"Oh, good," Lindsay replied. "Amanda is so excited to dance on the big stage."

Mason chuckled. "She's too cute. Just like you."

Lindsay giggled. "Oh, Mase, stop it."

"Just speaking from the heart. What's for dinner tonight? It smells delicious in here."

"Made your favorite: meatloaf with steamed carrots and mashed potatoes."

"You never stop amazing me. How did I get so lucky?"

Arielle and Felix listened for ten more minutes before Felix lowered the volume once the Gregory family all sat down for dinner. He looked at Arielle as she gazed into the distance.

"They sound like a happy, normal family," he said.

Arielle nodded. "That they do. Which only makes his murder more mysterious. He's clearly a good man. A family man who loves his wife and kids. Who would want him dead? *Why*?"

Arielle knew better than to jump to conclusions. She'd seen plenty of instances where the first impressions of her subjects weren't always what they seemed.

"They moved a poker game from Friday to Saturday," she said, and flipped to the front of her notepad where she kept the calendar for June 1988. "That means if the poker game is weekly and returns to its regular schedule, it will fall on the night he's murdered next week. We need to find out where this game is and who plays in it. Then we need to see if we can get Selena a seat at the table. This upcoming Saturday night game is now our top priority."

Chapter 21

By Thursday, June 16, the team was in a groove. All plans centered on the Saturday night poker game where they hoped to find something of substance to aid the mission. On Monday night, the three Angels had met for a late dinner where they discussed their first few days working on the mission. Felix confirmed he had set up the audio and its receiver, and he would drive to the neighborhood to pull the data for them to listen to each night.

Selena rented a car and tailed Lindsay, finding she stopped at a park in the mornings, after dropping off the kids at a summer camp, for a leisurely walk. She was now ready to make her move.

Arielle had two more boring days of sitting in the parking lot of Credit-Connect, using the downtime to outline requests for more information like contacts at the company and the summer camp that they could research. She placed a nightly call to the Road Runners headquarters in 1988 to request the assistance.

While Arielle spent Thursday once more outside the office building, and Felix listened to the prior evening's recording from the Gregory residence, Selena sat on a bench in Ranchero Park, five minutes east of the Gregory house.

It had only taken two days of following Lindsay to learn her daily routine, so Selena could only trust nothing would change by the third day. She dressed in jogging shorts and a tank-top, a water bottle clutched in her grip as she looked both ways at the trail in front of the bench. The trail circled a playground and open fields where kids kicked a soccer ball around, geese waddling around as they picked at the grass.

After fifteen minutes, Lindsay finally appeared in the distance. Selena had watched her enough during the past three days to know exactly what she looked like from afar. Lindsay jogged, still three hundred feet away from where Selena sat on the bench.

Selena scanned the area and saw no potential spectators, so she stood up and started stretching. She always got the slightest of jitters before her initial encounter with a new target. The past had never thrown major roadblocks in her way, but that didn't guarantee it would always be the case.

Her role was strictly grounded in research. Selena was never to tamper directly with the past, but would only unearth the information needed for Arielle to decide what was worth pursuing. She had mastered the art of adapting to her target's personality, needing to develop trust within minutes.

With Lindsay approaching, about fifty feet now, Selena started jogging toward her, the water bottle intentionally loose in her grip. She was within immediate range of Lindsay in a matter of seconds.

Lindsay paid no attention to the woman jogging in her direction, her ponytail bouncing side to side while she kept her head high and eyes focused ahead. Once they were within ten feet of each other, Selena let out a gasp, tossed her water bottle on the trail directly in front of Lindsay's path, and tumbled to the side where she lay on her back in the grass, hands clutched around her ankle as she pretended to writhe in pain.

Selena watched as Lindsay's eyes widened, jaw dropping as her sneakers screeched against the pavement to a sudden stop. "My Lord!" Lindsay cried, rushing to Selena's side. "Are you okay, sweetie?" She crouched down, eyes running up and down Selena's body.

Selena grunted as she sat up, still rubbing her ankle. "I think I rolled my ankle." She clenched her teeth and drew in a sharp breath to sell the faux pain. "I can't believe this happened to me—I used to run track. Now I can't even jog through a park. This is so embarrassing." Selena looked down to avoid eye contact, getting lost in her role and the story she was creating.

"What's your name, hon?" Lindsay asked, placing a gentle hand on Selena's back.

"Selena."

"Nice to meet you, Selena. My name is Lindsay. Everything will be fine—I promise. Worst-case scenario, you'll need to take it easy for the next couple of days. If it's mild, you'll be fine by tonight."

Selena shook her head, mentally returning to the days of her parents' vicious divorce to let tears well up in her eyes. "I don't think I can stand up."

"It's just your ankle that's hurt, right?" Lindsay asked, her voice softening into a natural, motherly tone while her hand continued running up and down Selena's spine.

"Yes, but it hurts so bad."

"Okay, let me help you up. Then we'll be able to tell how serious this is."

Selena nodded as Lindsay took a step back and extended her hand. She grimaced as she reached up to grab it and put all her weight on her supposed good foot.

Lindsay kept her eyes focused on Selena's feet. "You need to put some weight on it—just to see."

Selena nodded, keeping her lips pursed as she gradually shifted her body's weight from her good foot toward the other. She winced, but continued, pleased to have every ounce of Lindsay's concentration. "Okay. I'm on it," she said. "I don't know if I can walk yet."

"That's good," Lindsay said, a smile touching the corners of her mouth. "If you can stand on your own, then it's not too severe. Maybe sit on that bench for a few minutes." Lindsay pointed to the same bench Selena had just left moments earlier. "I'll help you over there."

"Thank you. You really didn't need to do all this."

"Oh, it's nothing. I have two little ones, and they're always getting hurt. This is practically a part of my daily routine." Lindsay giggled at herself, and Selena couldn't help but grin at the joyous sound.

Selena had to work fast in figuring out Lindsay's personality, competency, and overall state of mind. She had studied advanced psychological techniques to pinpoint these traits when meeting new people, but relied more on her instincts and experience after having traveled all over the world since a young age and meeting a wide-range of people. From what she could gather, Lindsay loved life and had a motherly instinct. She cared for others, which meant she saw the good in people, no matter the situation. Lindsay radiated kindness, and it frustrated Selena to think someone would harm such a gentle soul's husband and family life.

Lindsay wrapped an arm around Selena's waist and served as a crutch while they limped toward the bench. "How old are your kids?"

"I have a six-year-old girl, and a three-year-old boy. They are the sweetest kids."

Selena wanted to ask where the boy was the other day while Felix had been bugging their house. "I love kids. Used to babysit in high school. I don't suppose you need a sitter? I'm looking to make some extra money."

"Do you go to college here?"

"No—I graduated last year. Been bouncing around from job to job ever since. Seems like I made more money playing poker games in the dorms than in the real world. So if you know anyone who needs babysitting services or runs a poker game, I'm all ears."

"I wish I could help you, sweetie, but I don't work and have no need for babysitting. If you give me your number, I'll definitely call you if anything comes up on the weekends. My husband and I don't go out too often, but you never know."

"What does your husband do?" Selena asked.

"He works in finance."

They reached the bench, and Lindsay helped Selena sit down, taking a place next to her.

"Thank you for your help. I'm not sure what I would have done if you weren't here."

"Do you not have any friends or family in town?"

"I'm afraid not. All the friends I made in school moved out of Pueblo after graduation. My mom lives in New York. My dad lives in France. No siblings. No grandparents. No cousins."

Lindsay frowned, and Selena knew she had struck an emotional chord. "If you don't mind me asking, what made you want to stay in Pueblo? Was there a boy?"

Selena shook her head, hair falling over her face, and Lindsay immediately reached out to brush it back. "No boy. I like it here. I grew up spending my time between New York City and Paris. I was in such a bubble, I hardly knew smaller towns like this existed."

"We're hardly a small town in Pueblo."

"No, but Pueblo is laid-back. No one worries about having the best fashion, cars, and things. I like living in town even more than on campus. My parents will send me money with a quick phone call, but I'm more interested in making a life on my own. Neither of them will approve of me staying here, so it's not a call I'm going to make."

Lindsay sat back, her folded hands resting atop crossed legs as she stared into the distance. Selena could see the thoughts swimming behind her eyes.

"It sounds like you've had quite the childhood. I can only dream about visiting Paris one day, and you've *lived* there. And now you want to live *here*. I always thought it would be the other way around."

Selena deflated. She needed to make one more push. "Paris is as wonderful as advertised. It is a magical place to visit. But living there is a different story. Same with New York. I guess it's hard for me to pass fair judgment because I was always alone. My parents were always at work—I had to explore the cities on my own or with a babysitter. Looks like I'll have the same experience here in Pueblo, but at least I'm used to it now."

That was as desperate as she could make herself sound without disgusting herself.

After an eternity of a pause, Lindsay finally said, "No, you won't."

"I won't what?" Selena replied, stretching her ankle to give the appearance that she was at least trying to nurse her fake injury.

"You won't have to have that same experience. I won't allow it. You're welcome to dinner any time at our house. If you want to spend time with a family over any of the holidays, just say the word. You're too sweet of a girl to sit by yourself all day."

"Really? You would do that for me?" Selena knew no matter what she said, Lindsay wouldn't back out on her offer. People kind enough to make such an offer in the first place were always true to their word.

"Life is short, sweetie. The older you get, the more you realize that. Once you have kids, forget about it. Time pretty much moves at a sprint once you spend all your time watching your kids grow up. It's important to make the most out of your life, and if I can help you in the slightest way by just providing a loving family you can interact with, then it's the least I can do."

"Lindsay . . . wow. I don't know what to say. This might be the nicest thing anyone has ever done for me. But I can't just impede on your family."

Impede? Selena thought. *I'm going to impede, infiltrate, and find out everything I can to save this woman's family from doom.*

"Not at all. The kids will love you. My husband won't mind. And it was all my idea. Maybe you can come over for dinner sometime soon and meet everyone?"

"I'll need to check my calendar and let you know. Can I call you later today?" Selena was done playing games. She received an invite to the Gregory home for dinner and would do nothing to jeopardize it. She didn't want to jump right into dinner tonight, unless Arielle thought it was a good idea. They still had eight more days until Mason would be found dead.

"Absolutely. Let me write down my phone number for you. If I don't answer, just leave a message and I'll get back."

Selena stood up, standing on her tiptoes. "I think my ankle is already feeling much better. I should be able to make it back to my car. Thank you so much for everything."

"Say no more. Call me, and we'll see each other real soon."

Lindsay reached out and hugged Selena before they parted ways. Selena returned to the trail and walked with her normal stride once Lindsay was out of sight. All she could think on this glorious summer morning was, *I'm in.*

Chapter 22

Arielle sat in her car outside of CreditConnect, nose buried in the newest Stephen King novel, *The Tommyknockers.* She fell into a routine rather quickly, thanks to a firm grasp of Mason's schedule. If he entered the building with his lunch pail in hand, he didn't step foot outside until his shift was over. It was boring, but it made her job simple until they made progress on other fronts.

This morning, she watched him enter with said lunch pail, and promptly reclined her seat to lie back and enjoy the alien horror novel. She left herself at an angle just high enough to see the entrance over the car's dashboard. Anytime the doors swung open, the movement would catch her attention, just in case.

It was 11:30 when her stomach rumbled, the turkey and ham sandwich she had brought weighing on her mind. She adjusted her seat to its upright position and reached into the backseat to grab her brown-bag lunch.

A car blazed into the parking lot; the tires making the faintest of screeches as it turned the corner into the row behind Arielle. It sped down the row, going at least thirty miles per hour, and this prompted Arielle to subconsciously reach under her seat where she kept her loaded pistol. Her fingers brushed the cool steel as she lost sight of the vehicle in the jungle of parked cars.

She debated stepping out for a better view, but decided it was too risky. One rule she followed was to never assume an action was meaningless. Sure, the speeding car was likely someone running late for their shift, but there was always the chance it had something to do with Mason Gregory.

Arielle rolled down her window to better hear outside.

Silence.

She figured the car had found a parking space, and shifted her focus to the office building's entrance, assuming whoever had parked would enter within seconds.

No one ever appeared, and when she heard the steady rhythm of footsteps approach from behind, she whipped out her pistol and raised it in front of her face. She glanced over her shoulder and saw the movement of someone walking down the row behind her car, and remained frozen in her seat, hoping the person would pass.

Instead, they turned into the space where Arielle had parked, prompting her to shove open the door and jump out, gun cocked and ready to blast. "Stop right there!" she shouted.

"What the fuck?!" Selena screamed, jumping back. "What the hell are you *doing?*"

"Selena? What are *you* doing?" Arielle lowered her gun and looked around to make sure no one had spotted their encounter. The coast was clear. "Get in the car. *Now!*"

Selena rolled her eyes and shuffled around Arielle's car, falling into the passenger seat and slamming the door.

"Seriously," Arielle said. "Why are you here?"

"Well, in case you've forgotten, we don't have any cell phones and I need to talk to you. Something major has happened." Selena stared out the windshield, head bobbing from side to side while she spoke.

"With Lindsay?"

Selena nodded. "I befriended her at the park today. She's already invited me over to their house for dinner, and gave me her phone number. I'm in, but I don't know the best day to ask to go over for a visit."

"Wow. You pulled this off after one encounter?"

"Don't act so surprised. You're not the only one who's good at their job."

Arielle bit her lip. Selena seemed to always want to pick a fight with her.

"It's not that I'm surprised you did it—I'm just shocked it happened so fast. A personal dinner invite to their house?"

Selena smirked, reveling in her success. "Yes, and I thought I'd check with our fearless leader how I should schedule this all out."

Condescending bitch, Arielle thought, returning a tight-lipped grin of her own. "Thank you for checking. Follow-up question. Do you think you can get into that poker game on the Friday he gets killed?"

Selena shifted in her seat, finally turning her head to lock eyes with Arielle. "I've been thinking about that on the way over. I think I can, but there are a few factors out of my control."

"Like?"

"For one, we don't know what kind of game this is. It's 1988. They might oppose a woman playing in their poker game. We also don't know who is hosting the game. I have a hunch Mason is involved with some shady people if he ends up murdered. This could be some sort of underground game that is invite-only. Aside from that, we're talking about the night of the murder. Going to that poker game could get some pushback from the past. My presence alone could change the trajectory of the night, so who knows what might come up?"

Arielle nodded in deep thought. Selena had looked at this from all angles, and had valid hesitations. "Okay. Plan the dinner as soon as you feel it's appropriate. You spoke with Lindsay, so I'll trust you to make that call. Let's plan to probe about the poker game, and possibly get an invitation. If we can at least find out where the game is taking place, and the timing of it all, that will help us a ton. Then on the night of, we'll have to make a judgment call if it's safe for you to enter the game, or hang back from the outside."

Selena nodded and looked back at the office building. "Okay. I'll see what I can get lined up."

"Sounds good. What do you have going on the rest of the day?"

"I'll go back home, call Lindsay, and schedule a dinner date. I have some reports to make, then will probably head to the mall. I need a new outfit for going out. Do you want me to wait for you?"

"I'll have to pass. I don't do malls."

"Don't do malls? What does that even mean?"

Arielle raised a hand. "Thank you for the invite."

Selena shrugged. "Suit yourself, but there isn't much to do in this boring town."

Arielle had enough of the attitude. "Look, not everywhere is New York, or Paris. Not everyone gets to live some jet-setting life between big cities. You've lived in Los Angeles, plus those two places. That is not how the rest of the world is. I would think you'd know that by now, after working on so many missions."

"Don't attack me for the life I've led," Selena snapped, her head whipping back as she turned to face Arielle. "I may have lived in some cool places, but my childhood was so fucked-up. Did you enjoy having both of your parents and a happy household growing up? Do you think it was fun being a teenager and having two different lives? School year in New York, and summers in Paris? It wasn't. It was impossible for me to make serious friends in either city, because I always had it in the back of my head that I would just be leaving. It was even harder to date. I tried having boyfriends, and it always completely blew up in my face." Arielle watched as the rage left Selena's face and gave way to pain. Tears streamed down her reddened cheeks. "I've just wanted a normal life, but I have no idea what that means."

Arielle shook her head. "I'm sorry."

"Like hell you are," Selena snarled, the rage apparently not completely vanished.

"No, I am. I'm sorry I've never taken the time to learn your story. I wish I could understand, but you're right. I had a mostly happy life growing up. Maybe I take that for granted."

"And I would think *you* would know how hard some people's lives have been. Everyone in the Road Runners has suffered tragedy, even if it doesn't seem like it on the surface. We all come here to escape our past lives."

"Is that why you joined?"

Selena shrugged. "Who knows? I had a dream life starting in Hollywood. I always think about what things would be like if I stayed. But that's part of life, isn't it? No matter which road you take, you'll always wonder what the other would have been like."

"I don't see it that way. I believe we're always right where we're supposed to be."

"But you wouldn't be where you are without taking a certain path. And that's what drives me crazy about our time travel. We're not able to venture back and see how making a different choice might change our own futures."

Arielle nodded, reflecting. This was something she had thought over plenty of times. She might not have the power to go back and change her own life decisions, but she could very well travel back and stop the shooter from going on his rampage in the mall on that fateful day. Her life would indeed look different. "Maybe we're not supposed to know what life would be like had we made different choices. Maybe we have to trust things work out for the best—even when it doesn't seem like it. You may have not had the ideal childhood growing up, but look at you now. You're incredible at what you do."

Tears returned to Selena's eyes, pooling on the surface but remaining in place. "It's just hard for me to feel accomplished since I can't even share what I do with my parents. I wish I could tell them how well I'm doing without lying about the truth."

"We have to celebrate our successes among ourselves, unfortunately. I know how you feel. I talk with my grandma after each mission and make up stories about the life she thinks I'm living. But that's what we signed up for."

Selena wiped her eyes. "You're right. I should head home. I have to plan out these next few days."

She leaned into her door and opened it before Arielle shot out a hand and grabbed her shoulder. "Hey," Arielle said. "I'm proud of you and all you've done."

Selena gave a tight-lipped grin before stepping out of the car.

Chapter 23

"So what did you get done today, Felix?" Arielle asked as they sat around the dinner table. Felix had prepared a dinner of homemade spaghetti and meatballs once he received word that all three of them would have a rare evening at home together.

"Well, there isn't anything new for me to do. Now my days consist of running over to the receiver, replacing the flash drive, and listening to last night's feed."

"Anything exciting?"

"Not in particular. They had dinner together as a family. Sounds like the girl is in a dance camp for the summer, and the boy goes to daycare at a friend's house. Lindsay left in the morning—for a run around the park, according to Selena. Then she came home, showered, cleaned the kitchen, then headed back out for another hour before returning home with the daughter. They spent a couple of hours together doing crafts, reading books, and watching TV, before she left again to pick up the son. From there, she prepared dinner, they ate, bathed the kids. Lindsay and Mason watched TV after putting the kids in bed and talked about their days. They had sex and called it a night."

Selena giggled. "Enjoy the show, Felix?"

Felix blushed. "No, pervert. It's just audio, and I fast-forward through it."

"You're *such* a professional," Selena teased, shoving a piece of garlic bread into her mouth.

"So, did you schedule a dinner?" Arielle asked, dismissing Selena's immaturity.

Selena nodded, chewing faster to swallow and reply. "Monday night."

"Four days before the murder," Arielle said, looking to the ceiling. "You don't think that's cutting it too close?"

Selena shrugged. "I didn't have much of a choice. That's the first date she offered. What was I supposed to say? 'Can I please come sooner so my friends and I can stop your husband's murder?'" She laughed as she twirled her fork in the pasta.

"Monday it is. Felix, would you be able to wait outside the house that night and listen to the live feed?"

"Why would he need to do that?" Selena asked. "You don't think I can handle it myself?"

"It's not that," Arielle said. "It will be the week of the murder. We'll all need to be ready for resistance from the past. And since we never have a clue what that might look like, I think it would be smart to have help close by, just in case. I might even stop by that night. It will be, at the time, the most important night of this mission. We need to get all the information we can about where Mason will be on the night of the twenty-fourth. Look for notes on their calendar and try to work it into conversation."

Selena nodded. "Of course. Won't be a problem. It's not like Mason knows he's supposed to die that night. Are you going to follow him this Saturday to see where the poker game is?"

"Absolutely. I'm assuming it's in the evening, so if either of you wants to join me, I wouldn't mind some company after sitting in my car alone all week. I don't think we'll have much else to do on a Saturday night."

They poked at their food, neither wanting to volunteer for such a dry task. "I'll go," Felix eventually said.

Arielle smiled in appreciation. "Do we have any thoughts about who might kill Mason? Felix, you've been in their house, and Selena you spent some time with Lindsay. I haven't learned a single thing sitting outside his office building. Maybe we should have gotten you a job there just to see."

Selena shook her head. "It's probably just a boring desk job. I doubt anything going on in there has any ties to his murder. If it had, it probably wouldn't be a cold case. I can say confidently that it is not his wife, either. She seems to love him, and they have a solid relationship. He hasn't stayed late at work so far, right?"

"Nope. The man is like clockwork heading out of that place."

"So, there's definitely not an affair. Eighty-five percent of affairs begin at the workplace. If he was having one, he'd stay late, or at least not go straight home."

"Nothing I've heard on the tapes suggests anything is going on, either," Felix added. "The home life is solid. He's a family man. So we either have a completely random attack, or it's definitely tied to the poker game."

"It's not random," Arielle said. "He had to have been lured to such a remote location. He wouldn't have ended up there by simply driving around. I'm thinking drugs or prostitution were involved, and a deal went wrong."

"This poker game might be a front," Felix said. "Do we know if Lindsay has ever gone to one with him? Even just to hang out with other wives?"

They both looked at Selena, who only shrugged in response.

"I don't know if it's necessarily a front," Arielle said. "But there might be some shady characters who attend. You never know with underground gambling—it can attract all kinds of criminals."

"Yeah," Felix replied. "But those types of games are typically with wealthy people. Drug lords, pimps, that sort of stuff. Hell, professional gamblers. Mason Gregory doesn't exactly radiate that type of vibe. He seems like a guy who plays in friendly twenty-dollar games."

"True. That's why I think we need to all go this Saturday. I want to get the license plate numbers of all the cars in the parking lot, and we can start exploring who is attending this game."

Felix nodded. "We should be able to learn everything we need, short of who actually pulls the trigger."

Selena leaned back and crossed her arms, frowning.

"Something the matter?" Arielle asked.

"I agree we'll gain a lot, but don't you think it's dangerous for us to all be there at the same time? We don't know who we're dealing with. I'd hate for us to end up in a shootout."

Arielle thought back to single-handedly wiping out a dozen members of the Mexican cartel. "I think we can manage it. We've certainly had worse scenarios, and have always come out on top. And now we're a team. If you can find out where the game is played, maybe Felix can bug the place ahead of time."

Felix nodded. "Assuming it can be done, I'd love to."

"I really want as many eyeballs on the place as possible," Arielle continued. "You're right—we *don't* know who we're dealing with. Maybe one of us can keep watch while two of us explore the property. It will be nighttime, I assume, and I know I won't be able to notice everything on my own."

"We'll be there," Felix said, shooting a glance at Selena across the table.

"Yep," she said dismissively.

"Well, that settles it," Arielle said. "I look forward to it. Think we can all learn a lot from each other."

Selena had finished her meal and placed the silverware on top of the empty plate. "Well, if we're done chatting for tonight, I'm gonna head out." She stood and pushed in her chair before grabbing her plate to place in the sink.

"Going to check on Lindsay?" Arielle asked.

"No. Going to a bar."

"Excuse me? We're on a mission. We don't go out and party on missions. This is our work—the whole time."

Selena furrowed her brow. "Maybe *you* don't go out and have fun on missions. But *I* do."

"You can't!"

"Says who? Show me an official rule from the Road Runners that says I can't go to a bar and have a drink to unwind. Show me that and I'll stay."

Arielle clenched her fists under the table, nails digging into her palms. She knew nearly all the official rules the organization had, and there was no such thing preventing Selena from going out in a non-work fashion. "I'm running this mission, and I don't want you going out."

"Well, excuse you," Selena said, putting her hands on her hips, eyes bulging as they focused entirely on Arielle. "You're just the highest-ranking Angel. You don't have control over me. We all report to headquarters. Me and Felix don't work *for* you. If you really have a problem with this, then have Commander Briar call me about it. I was going to invite you, but clearly I forgot you hate fun."

Selena shot a wink at Arielle before pivoting and leaving them alone in the dining room. They listened as her footsteps stomped up the stairs and through the hallway as she entered her bedroom, slamming the door shut for added effect.

Arielle sat with her jaw hanging, Felix avoiding eye contact as he poked at what little food remained on his plate. "What the hell was that?!"

Felix looked up and shrugged.

"Am I in the wrong here?" Arielle asked.

"I'd rather not get involved."

"Just tell me—I need to know these things. I know I can't just command you guys, but am I making an unreasonable request?"

Felix stuffed the last bite of food into his mouth, and over time Arielle would come to realize he did this strategically to allow himself more time to process his thoughts and choose his words. After he swallowed, he said, "I've worked with lots of different Angels, and a lot of them go out during the evenings. It's not a big deal. Everyone is always responsible, and all the mission work still gets done. People have different ways of blowing off steam."

Arielle never partook in such activities like going out to bars. Restaurants were about the extent of her time spent in a social setting. She enjoyed going to the gym, taking hikes in the mountains, and traveling the world for pleasure between missions. She had no problem drinking a dozen piña coladas on the beach while on vacation, but wouldn't dare spend a night out drinking while on a mission. A glass of wine before bed was the most she had ever had while working.

"Do you think she does this often?"

"Selena likes to have a good time. She's also the best at what she does. I don't personally see a reason to argue with her over it. The work will get done at the highest quality you can get, and that's all that matters. Honestly, I think it's all part of her process. She likes going out to the local bars and getting a feel for the town. It helps her better understand how to relate to her targets."

"When did she tell you this?"

"After they assigned us this mission, her and I went to a Rockies game and had some drinks."

"So it's been there from the start. Good to know."

Felix shook his head. "It's not what you think. Selena likes to have fun—that's all there is to it. She doesn't do any hard drugs. Doesn't even get drunk."

"Why are you standing up for her so much?"

"Because no one ever has," Selena said from the entryway.

Felix spun around in his seat, face immediately turning red. "Wh—"

"Thank you," Selena said, a grin taking over her face. "Outside of my mom, I don't think anyone has ever stood up for me. Everyone writes me off as some party girl who can't be taken seriously. Even these fuckers in the Road Runners who rate me as the best actress in the organization don't truly take me serious. So thank you, Felix. Your words mean a lot to me."

"How long have you been standing there?" Arielle asked.

"What, am I not allowed to be stealthy like you? We all go through the same training."

Arielle didn't care if Selena had overheard the conversation, but Selena's ability to slither down the stairs without being heard had caught her off guard.

"I know. And I'm impressed."

"Oh? Well, thanks. I'm heading out now. Don't wait up for me, Mom."

Chapter 24

Selena ended up at the Paris Lounge, a far cry from her previous home. It was a hole-in-the-wall nightclub with cheap drinks, a mediocre DJ, and a sticky dance floor. She had driven over with a smile impossible to wipe away. Despite spending her whole life trying to prove doubters wrong, she often found herself to be her own worst critic. The luxury of her childhood had resulted in things being handed to her for most of her adolescent life, hampering her ability to stand up for herself. It wasn't until joining the Road Runners that she developed this skill, and telling off the great Arielle Lucila had her floating on a cloud.

She had plenty of respect for the Road Runners, and even Arielle, but took pride in knowing she could stand up to them. People would never understand her because she had no desire to live a cookie-cutter life. She had given up all the glory of a Hollywood career to track bad guys for unlimited income and resources. The way she saw it, she was playing with house money for the rest of her life. She had the skills the organization wanted, and therefore, the leverage for whatever pathetic argument might arise regarding her lifestyle.

She was on top of her world, and no one could stop her.

Selena stepped out of her car to find the parking lot jam-packed. She hadn't expected such a sizeable crowd for a Thursday night, but the sign taped to the glass doors at the entrance explained it all: *LADIES' NIGHT THURSDAY! LADIES DRINK FREE.*

She smirked upon reading it, mentally bracing herself for the type of men who were surely lurking inside. The cheapskates always came out to ladies' night, happy to pay the cover charge since they wouldn't have to gamble money on drinks for the women.

Selena's mother had taught her many lessons growing up as an adolescent in New York City, and one of the more important ones was to never let her attention be purchased by a man. "That's how your father landed me, and look where we are now," she'd say begrudgingly. She had heard plenty of stories about how her father picked up her mother with slick talk and expensive rounds of drinks. Charles Nicole had come from money and knew how to use it to get what he wanted, including luring attractive women to his VIP table, where bottle service continued well past two in the morning.

Fortunately, Selena never saw this side of her father. During her summers in Paris, if he wasn't at work, he was with her. They'd see movies, go to fancy dinners and art museums, and do touristy things like visiting the Eiffel Tower and the Louvre. She would see her father's eyes wander whenever they passed a beautiful woman, but he wouldn't so much as speak to one in her presence. Because of that, she always thought of her father as a gentleman, no matter what her mother had to say.

Regardless, her lessons rang loudly in her mind whenever she went out, and now, as she approached the entrance for the Paris Lounge.

The door handles were shaped like the Eiffel Tower and she couldn't help but giggle as she pulled them open. The muffled booming of music became clear as she entered the building where a hostess stood behind a podium, smoking a cigarette. The young woman blew a puff of smoke into the air as Selena approached.

"Just you tonight, hon?" she asked.

"Just me."

"Let me check your ID."

Selena's heart sunk as she fumbled into her pocket. *Did I get a new ID for this mission?*

Other members of the Angels handled hundreds of little details before a mission. Matters like fake IDs, birth certificates, social security cards, and time-appropriate currency were always taken care of. She simply couldn't recall getting those for this mission, but blew a sigh of relief when she pulled the ID out of her wallet and saw an older Colorado driver's license that listed her birth year as 1965.

The hostess checked the ID without a fuss and let Selena pass into the club. The dance floor was strategically placed on the opposite side, two bars along the side walls where crowded lines had already formed, with plenty of women waiting for their free drinks. Tables of men filled the space between the entrance and the dance floor, all eyes scanning the room for their evening's prey.

Selena immediately noticed a couple of men checking her out as she made her way into the mob. She refused to give Arielle the satisfaction of knowing her one rule while on missions: no men. At most, she would flirt for free drinks, but didn't have to worry about that after tumbling into this ladies' night. If things went her way, she'd strike up a conversation with another woman and get a feel for the locals. She loved to dance, and would share one with a man as long as he didn't get too touchy. Otherwise, her plan was always to get a solid buzz to ride out for a couple of hours before sobering up enough to drive home safely.

A man wearing glow sticks as a necklace danced toward Selena as she stood at the back of the line, and started thrusting his hips in her direction. He avoided eye contact and kept a foot of distance between, trying to play it cool.

"No thanks!" Selena shouted over Michael Jackson's "The Way You Make Me Feel" while shaking her head.

The man moved on to the next line of women with no objection. Selena remained six people back in line, watching the bartender pour a line of shots with complete ease. The line moved faster when no payment was involved, and she ordered a vodka soda after another few minutes had passed.

She scanned the room, but found no empty tables, forcing her to stand along the railing that separated the dance floor from the rest of the club. People-watching never got old. She had done it ever since she was a child, and always tried to get inside the minds of those making a fool of themselves—something she attributed to her becoming such a skilled actress.

After making it halfway through her drink, someone tapped her on the shoulder. She turned to see a rather handsome man grinning. He had a strong jaw, and jet-black hair slicked to the side. Beads of sweat decorated his forehead, but his dark eyes drew her in.

"Hey!" he shouted over the music. "I'm Eli."

"Hi," Selena replied, turning her attention back to the dance floor.

Eli had a thick, groomed beard that stood out in contrast to his light complexion. If she wasn't on a mission, she just might have had an interest in conversing.

"I don't mean to intrude," he shouted from behind her, his hot breath blowing in her ear, causing her to recoil. "But you are one of the most beautiful women I've ever seen."

Selena turned over her shoulder and said, "Thank you."

"Are you new to town? I've never seen you here."

"No."

Conversations amid loud club music were already awkward enough, and she knew giving curt responses only made the man feel like more of an asshole. In due time, if he didn't get the hint, he'd ask if they could speak "somewhere more quiet."

"Do you have a boyfriend?" Eli persisted.

"Yes." With that, she turned her head, assuming that was what Eli needed to hear to leave her alone.

"I saw you walk in alone. Is he not here?"

An observer, Selena thought. *He might take a little more work to get rid of.*

"He's not. I'm meeting some girlfriends."

"Can I keep you company until they show up?"

"No thanks, I'm okay."

"Okay. If you change your mind, or if you and your friends want a good time tonight, come find me in the VIP area."

He pointed toward a corner of the bar that had cushioned booths behind a red-velvet rope.

A line right out of my dad's playbook, Selena thought, smirking at her mother's voice warning her in her mind.

"Okay, thanks," she said dismissively.

She saw Eli return to his friends in the VIP section. A strategy she liked to use in these situations was to hide in the bathroom for a couple of minutes. This allowed time for whatever poor soul was trying to hit on her to move on to the next woman and forget all about her.

Selena pushed her way through the crowd to reach the bathrooms in a sectioned off area next to the bar. The small lobby served as a waiting room. The space was dimly lit despite lights running along the baseboards on the wall.

She entered the ladies' room and was relieved to see no long lines inside. A bathroom attendant sat on a stool at the far end of the sinks, handing a woman a clean towel to dry her hands. The attendant looked college-aged and appeared to hate her job—a stern expression was stuck on her face.

Selena shot her a soft smile before stepping into the stall and sitting down on the toilet. She didn't need to go, but just wanted to kill some time and finish her drink in peace. She debated getting one more drink before calling it a night. The club was too crowded. It was impossible to get from one side to the other without catching an elbow in the gut from squeezing through the herd of people. The clubs she used to frequent in Hollywood had limited capacity to keep it comfortable for the patrons inside. Apparently, these smaller towns didn't believe in such things.

She spent a couple of minutes in the stall before stepping out to wash her hands. The attendant slouched on her stool while squirting the soap into Selena's hands and completely avoided eye contact or conversation.

"Hey," Selena said. "Keep your head up. It will get better, I promise."

The attendant finally looked at Selena, and the slightest sign of a grin touched the corner of her lips. "Thank you," she said, just above a whisper.

Selena felt the pain in the girl's voice and wished she could invite her out to the club to chat. She could only hope her few words would help lift her spirits for the rest of the night.

Selena gave the girl a fifty-dollar tip, and that turned the hidden smile into a full-blown grin, revealing pearly teeth. "I can't take this," the girl said, shaking her head. "This is about what I make in a whole night."

"It's yours. Treat yourself to a nice dinner this weekend."

Selena turned and left the bathroom before the girl could say anything else.

She stepped back into the dark lobby, where the crowd had grown even more. A hand grabbed her by the elbow, and Eli's voice and hot breath returned to her ear from behind. "Hello again, beautiful."

She felt his hand run along the small of her back, and she lunged forward to get out of his reach, pivoting to face him. "You can't take a fucking hint, can you?"

"Whoa, I'm just trying to talk to you."

"And I don't *want* to talk to you. Why is that so hard for you to understand? Are you not used to girls being able to resist big muscles and cheap pickup lines? Not everyone likes you. Did that ever occur to you?"

Eli grinned, his teeth glowing in the dim lobby. "Well, damn, baby, you got a mouth on you. I got some ideas for what you can do with it."

"You're fucking gross."

Selena spun back around, and Eli snatched her arm before she could walk away. She wasted no time in swinging her free arm down on his wrist as hard as she could, promptly loosening his grip as Eli grunted and clutched his arm.

"You *bitch!*" he shouted, and Selena shoved through the crowd and toward the exit. Her night was done, once again ruined by a cocky man who couldn't accept rejection.

Once she stepped outside, her mind immediately felt more focused thanks to the silence. Loud music had a way of making everything seem more chaotic, and she already felt more at peace.

She had parked two rows from the back of the lot and rummaged in her pockets for her keys. The music from the club grew loud for a moment as the door opened and closed. She looked over her shoulder to see Eli making a beeline towards her.

"Are you shitting me?!" Selena shouted, hoping to catch any passerby's attention. She had no problem fending for herself, and was hoping to do Eli a favor by letting someone else mitigate the situation.

She saw a group of smokers huddled in the parking lot at a bar across the street, but the traffic on Main Street must have blurred her shouts.

"Are *you* shitting me?" Eli asked, his teeth clenched. "I was just trying to have a polite conversation."

Selena hadn't noticed in the club, but now realized Eli had a solid six inches on her. He was built and could certainly handle his own in a fistfight, assuming he knew how.

"I suggest you go back inside," Selena demanded.

Eli laughed. "You think I'm afraid of you? Just because you're pretty doesn't mean I'm intimidated."

Selena had reached her car and stopped beside the driver-side door, debating if she should attempt to grab the pistol in her glove box. Eli didn't slow at all, and once he was within an arm's reach, he extended his hands toward Selena's shoulders.

She dropped to the ground, catching all her body's weight on her hands, and thrust her feet into Eli's knee, hyper-extending it. He wobbled backwards as he screamed into the night sky, catching himself on the hood of Selena's car.

"You're gonna pay for that," Eli said, the slightest suggestion of fear now weaved into his voice. He gathered his footing and limped toward Selena, pain clearly shooting up his leg with each step.

"Really, dude? Are you just mad you can't get into a bar fight with anyone inside? You're really trying to take it out on me?"

"You should have just come into my booth," Eli said, rearing back a fist and swinging it wildly toward Selena's head. His movement came quicker than she had expected, but she dodged it just in time, the breeze from his errant punch blowing over her face.

This put Eli in a vulnerable position with his entire side and right shoulder suddenly in front of Selena, crouched slightly to protect his busted knee. She grabbed the top of his head and slammed it into her rising knee, connecting squarely with the center of his face.

Blood spurted from his nose as both of Eli's hands shot to it, red streaks running down his hands and arms. He remained on his feet, and this is where his size was working to his advantage. It was going to take even more to get him on the ground.

Not too *much more,* she thought, and swung another kick to his already injured knee. This caused Eli's hands to leave his face and shoot down to his knee as he slowly crumpled to the ground. His face was no longer visible, smeared in the slick darkness of his own blood.

Selena wanted to kick him in the face for good measure, but saw a clear window to get in the car and speed out of the lot. She did so without saying another word, leaving Eli wailing on the ground.

Chapter 25

Friday had passed with no excitement. Arielle sat outside CreditConnect for the last time that week. Felix listened to Thursday's audio recordings from the Gregory household and still found nothing to report. And Selena followed Lindsay from a safe distance, never telling Arielle or Felix what had happened at the Paris Lounge on Thursday night.

Felix had dinner alone on Friday night, while Arielle and Selena followed their targets to the dance recital for Amanda Gregory. They would return later that night to report a typical recital. Mason and Lindsay attended together, and both parents stayed through the duration of the event.

They shifted their focus to Saturday night, when Mason was scheduled to attend the poker game.

On the morning of, Felix woke at six o'clock to get himself ready and prepare a hearty breakfast for the team. He cooked eggs, bacon, pancakes, and prepared a bowl of fruit salad. Arielle studied her map of Pueblo while eating, and Selena brushed up on her poker strategy from a book she had checked out from the library the day before, hoping to land a coveted invite to next week's game.

By eight o'clock, they were all out the door. Selena rode with Felix, and Arielle drove separately to the Gregory neighborhood. They needed the separate vehicles in case Mason or Lindsay left in the middle of the day and had to be followed.

The morning passed without so much as a bird shitting on the Gregory lawn. The front door remained closed, the curtains drawn, and both

Mason's and Lindsay's cars remained in the driveway.

"A lazy Saturday morning," Felix said. "Remember what those were like? I'll bet the kids are watching cartoons and eating cereal in their pajamas."

Felix had parked across the street, two houses down. Arielle took a spot on the other block that ran perpendicular to the Gregory house.

"That seems like a lifetime ago, doesn't it?" Selena replied. "What I'd give to have a day like that."

At noon, Arielle left to grab lunch for everyone, sneakily dropping it on the sidewalk next to Felix's car. It wasn't until two when the front door finally opened, and the two Gregory children played outside on their front lawn. The oldest, Amanda, had fun blasting her little brother with water from the garden hose, and the two played and fought with each other over the next hour. Lindsay had made a brief appearance to mediate a dispute between the kids, but Mason never showed his face.

"Do you think someone picked him up before we even got here?" Selena asked.

"Doubt it. He seems like a guy who sleeps until noon on the weekends. Maybe he's just getting his day started, especially if he has a late night ahead."

"What time do you think he'll leave?"

"Impossible to know. We have to be ready the moment he steps outside."

There was a long pause before Selena spoke again. "Thanks again for standing up for me the other night. It really means a lot. That situation would have been a lot worse if you were attacking me like Arielle."

"Arielle wasn't attacking you. She just has a particular way she likes things done. You challenged that, and she didn't know how to react. You're one of the few people in this world who can say they've startled the great Arielle Lucila."

Selena grinned. "I suppose that's one way of putting it. You're quite the neutral person. A calming presence."

"I just like to have control over my emotions. In this line of work, I've seen far too many people ending up with their lives destroyed, all because their emotions got the best of them. I just try to think slowly and see things from all angles. And that includes different people's perspectives. That other night, I understood perfectly fine where both you and Arielle were coming from. No one was right, no one was wrong."

"I wish I could be more like that. I guess I developed a chip on my shoulder after my parents separated and played tug-o-war with me across the globe."

"If you can recognize *why* you let your emotions run you, then you shouldn't have a problem taking control back from them. It sounds to me like you're very in tune with yourself."

"I guess I'll have to work on it."

They swapped more stories about their childhood for the next three hours. At five o'clock, Mason Gregory appeared for the first time, stepping out of the front door with his keys in hand. His wife and kids had filled the doorway, and he planted kisses on all three of their foreheads before shuffling toward his car in the driveway.

"Shit, it's time!" Felix said, jamming the key into the ignition, but waiting to turn on the car.

Mason pulled out of the driveway, and Felix fired up the engine. Mason turned at the stop sign, and they saw Arielle pull onto the road behind him. She insisted on leading the way, since she already had a feel for Mason's driving style.

"Stay as close to Arielle as you can," Selena said.

Mason took his time exiting the neighborhood, and this caused Arielle and Felix to drive at a painfully slow speed. He could have jogged faster than they were driving.

They followed Mason to the main roads, where he eventually got onto the freeway.

"Where the hell are we going?" Selena asked, but Felix didn't respond. He wouldn't dare break his concentration on the task at hand.

The drive took them through parts of Pueblo none of them had yet visited. After ten minutes on the freeway, they left the Pueblo city limits and were on their way south of town on I-25.

Tailing on the highway was easy, especially since Mason stayed in the middle lane for another ten minutes before getting over to exit at Colorado City.

"Colorado City?" Selena asked. "Do we have anything in our notes about this place?"

"Not ringing a bell," Felix said.

All three vehicles exited, Mason leading the way. Colorado City was deserted compared to Pueblo. They passed a gas station, two campgrounds, and a pizza parlor as they moved deeper into town.

It took them another ten minutes on Highway 165, a county road with trees lining the left and open fields on the right. Everything was spread across the stretch of highway. They passed a bank, grocery store, and even a golf course. The Rocky Mountains glowed a majestic blue, fluffy clouds decorating the horizon above.

Once they reached the other side of town, Mason turned on a side road and drove another mile, passing a handful of barns.

"Where the hell are we going?" Felix asked. Arielle had slowed her pace now that they were isolated on a dirt road. It would be obvious to Mason that he was being followed.

Towering trees lined the sides of the road as far as they could see.

"I'm getting a bad feeling about this," Selena said. "This isn't really a poker game, is it?"

"Let's not jump to conclusions," Felix said, trying to push away his own worries. They were in the middle of the woods. And while they passed some barns, it was clear they were in deep enough isolation where, if something went wrong, no help would come.

The road curved and winded as they continued, and Mason eventually hit his brakes as he slowed to a complete stop. The tree coverage stopped suddenly, prompting Arielle to slam on her brakes as a house came into view, cars piled next to each other in the long driveway that led up to the property. She had remained about 500 feet behind Mason, and that had bought her enough distance to turn around without being noticed.

If he had thought he was being followed, he showed no signs of it, parking his car next to the dozen others.

Felix had stopped the car and waited for Arielle to circle back. She pulled up next to him, facing the other direction, and they both rolled down their windows.

"The house is literally the end of this road," Arielle said. "There are a *lot* of people there. I think we should drive back and pull off the road. Maybe even go all the way back to the highway. When it gets darker, we'll come back."

"Should we just leave, though?" Selena asked. "What if he doesn't stay long?"

"It's a poker game, right? He'll be there at least four hours. That gives us about three hours to kill before the sun goes down. We can probably head over a little sooner. We'll stay right by the turn for this road in case he leaves early. Follow me."

Arielle drove off, leaving Felix and Selena staring at each other.

"Goddammit!" Selena shouted, slamming the dashboard. "We're wasting valuable time. We need to find out who all those people are. One of them is definitely the murderer. To hell with Arielle, let's go."

Felix couldn't have been more grateful to be in the driver's seat. Had the roles been reversed, they would undoubtedly be on their way to crash the party.

"I'm gonna trust Arielle on this one. We need to move in the dark. Besides, more people might show up behind us."

He turned the car around and sped away.

Chapter 26

By 7:30, the sun flirted with the horizon over the mountains, turning the sky a bright orange. What sounded like hundreds of buzzing cicadas reminded Arielle of a distant fire alarm.

"I think it's safe to go," she said from the backseat of Felix's car. They had agreed to drive back to the property together, one less vehicle to worry about when they tried to creep toward the house.

"About time," Selena said from the passenger seat.

They had passed the time by eating a pizza from the parlor. The car reeked of garlic, thanks to Felix insisting on breadsticks with the meal.

"No one has come in or out of this road in the last hour," Selena said. "We should have been in there already."

"Relax," Arielle said calmly. She would no longer let Selena's emotional outbursts get the best of her. Would they get under her skin? Absolutely. But no more letting the young Angel sway her day. "We still need to be careful. There are a lot of people. Some might be hanging out outside. Some might even be leaving. Selena, what do you suggest our cover story be if we get seen?"

Arielle figured if she could get more input from Selena, she might encounter less resistance later on when split-second decisions needed to be made.

Selena pursed her lips. "Since there are three of us, it will need to seem like we were invited. We can say that Mason invited us to the game."

"But we'll be arriving so late," Felix said.

"Then we say we had the wrong time. We thought it started at eight."

Felix snorted. "Wow, you sure can make up a lie on the spot."

"Acting is a weird mix of skill, truth, and lies."

"That should work," Arielle said. "And to be clear, we are *not* going inside the house under any circumstances. Our main goal is to get all the license plate numbers we can. Let our team at HQ do the heavy lifting of finding out who all these people are. We have to avoid being seen, but if we do, we'll stick to these talking points from Selena and get the hell out."

Felix turned on the car and flipped it around to take them back onto the dirt road, into the thick of the woods.

"Any thoughts on who might live out here?" Arielle asked.

"I think Mason just has a rich friend. Not much else to explain it."

"It wasn't a barn like these other properties. It was a regular house. Two stories, big from the glance I got. Not quite a mansion, but pretty damn close."

"Only rich people can afford that much privacy," Selena said. "Doesn't even have a street name. It's just a house in the middle of nowhere."

Darkness crept into the sky, a purple glow clinging to life before the moon and stars took over. The tall trees made it even darker on the road, and Felix turned on the headlights.

They cruised along until Felix recognized the curve in the road where they had stopped earlier. He slowed to a crawl; the gravel crunching beneath the tires.

"Let's creep up to the property," Arielle said. "We might be able to park behind another car and go unnoticed."

Felix obliged, letting the car coast as they rounded the corner and the house came into sight. Cars lined the sides of the driveway, about twenty in total.

"This is quite the crowd," Selena commented. "And house. Wow."

The house was stunning, even at night. It had a white exterior, a four-car garage, and a roundabout near the main entrance. The house was built in an L-shape, so the entrance was out of sight, tucked on the other side of the massive garage.

"Definitely a rich person," Felix said. "Wouldn't be surprised if there's a swimming pool and helicopter pad in the back."

"We're in luck," Arielle said. "I don't see anyone. They're inside or in the backyard. Just park behind the first car you see."

Felix wasted no time pulling to the side of the driveway and parking the car behind a windowless black van.

"Roll the windows down," Arielle said. She wanted to listen to the surroundings and was pleased to find the only sound belonging to crickets. No voices or shouting that might suggest an outdoor party, even from the backyard.

"Everyone have a notepad?" Felix asked, opening the center console to pull his out. "Keep an eye out for motion-sensor lights the closer you get to the house. If one comes on, hide behind a car and wait."

"Good call. Are we all ready?" Arielle asked.

Selena and Felix nodded, opening their doors. Arielle followed suit and welcomed the fresh mountain air, albeit a tad warmer than she preferred.

"You two take the left, I'll take the right," Arielle whispered, pointing across the driveway where more vehicles lined up.

Felix nodded and led the way, with Selena trailing behind him. Arielle started with the black van directly in front of her and crouched down to read the white letters on the license plate. She pulled the notepad from her back pocket and flipped it open to write. Felix and Selena were doing the same, each of them already moving on to their second cars.

Arielle moved on, looking up and scanning the area after each license plate number she had written. As she got closer to the house, she moved slower, more cautiously. Someone could step around the corner at any moment, and she needed to be ready to hide. They had the darkness to their advantage, and they had dressed in black to blend in.

A light glowed from the other side of the garage, presumably from the home's entrance, yet the silence remained thick. The echo of her own footsteps kept making her look over her shoulder, but she pressed forward, nearly to the car parked closest to the house.

"Shit!" Felix gasped from across the way.

Arielle listened as his and Selena's footsteps pattered away from the house, back toward the direction of their car. She saw nothing, but crouched next to the car on her left.

What the hell are they doing? she wondered, and her gut instinct told her to head back. Neither Felix nor Selena would abandon a task for no reason. She pivoted around, taking soft steps to allow her ears to focus on any potential sounds coming from the house.

Practically lunging back to the car, she found Felix and Selena behind the trunk, crouched as low as her. "What's going on?" she demanded.

Felix was panting and held up a finger while catching his breath. "They have cameras. Surveillance cameras on the garage."

"Are you kidding me?!"

"I saw them. I think they caught us."

"How sure are you?"

Selena watched the exchange with worry plastered across her face.

Felix nodded. "I'm very certain."

"Okay, let's—"

A gun fired, cracking the silence like a lightning strike.

Selena shrieked out of reflex.

"Who's out there?" a voice called from the house. "We saw you."

Arielle extended her arms and grabbed Felix and Selena by their shoulders. "We need to get out of here right now," she whispered. "Get in the car and drive like hell. Okay?"

A second gunshot rang out, and Arielle identified it as a shotgun.

"Now!" Arielle snarled, shuffling around the car and diving into the backseat.

The noise level rose as more people stepped outside of the house, chattering. Footsteps marched on the ground like soldiers, just as Felix made his way behind the wheel. Selena moved a step slower, but made it safely inside the car.

"Go!" Arielle shouted as she swung her door closed.

Felix twisted the key into the ignition and spun the car around, flooring the accelerator as dirt flew in every direction.

"Stay low!" Arielle barked, just in time.

The next gunshot blast caught their back window as Felix sped away, shards of glass scattered across the back seat, and in Arielle's hair. Selena screamed, the sound drowned out by the roaring engine and subsequent shots showered in their direction.

None of the other shots landed, and Felix swung around the curve, out of sight from the house.

"Keep going!" Arielle shouted. "They might follow us."

Felix had no intent of stopping and barreled down the dirt road. Arielle sat up and looked through the space where the back window was moments ago. No one was visible. Not yet, at least.

"Ahhhhh!" Felix cried, slamming on the breaks.

Arielle spun around to see a deer in the middle of the road, its head low as it ate something off the ground.

The car slid, tires screeching for an eternity as they inched toward the animal. The stench of burning brake pads filled the car as the rear wheels started drifting at an angle, positioning the car sideways as it continued toward the deer.

For a moment, Arielle saw her life flash before her eyes. And in the deer's eyes. She was on a direct path to the creature, and if they hit it at the wrong angle, they'd be lucky to walk away alive.

Instead, the deer came to its senses and darted into the woods. The car came to a stop inches from where the animal had just stood.

Selena gasped for breath, hands on her chest. "Are you *kidding* me?!" she wheezed.

Felix had his shoulders elevated in a shrug position, arms extended and stiff as he clutched the steering wheel.

Arielle sat up after having been flung around the backseat, and gently touched his shoulders. He was in shock.

"Felix," she said. "You did incredible."

He gulped and shook his head. "I can't believe that just happened. How are we still alive?"

"That was the past, wasn't it?" Selena asked, gaining some control over her breathing.

"It might have been," Arielle said. "Hard to know for certain. It's not like a deer in the woods is uncommon."

"It totally was. We haven't seen a deer this whole time, and *that's* when it shows its face?!"

Arielle sighed, her own tension dissipating. "All that matters is we're still alive."

Chapter 27

"It might have just been a poker game," Felix said as they sat around the table for breakfast the next morning. They had returned home, relieved no one had followed them. Felix had no energy to cook after last night's drama, so they each enjoyed a bowl of Cheerios.

Arielle shook her head. "I don't know. Something just felt *off*. Don't you think?"

Felix shrugged. "I don't usually get this involved in a mission. The whole thing felt off for me. But I'm also used to snooping around someone's house when I know they're not home."

"No one was outside when we got there," Selena said. "It really could have been a poker game inside. I assumed we've already checked out Mason's bank records. Does he have the money hidden somewhere to play in a high stakes game?"

"Why are you so convinced it has to be high stakes?" Arielle asked.

"Selena's right," Felix said. "I used to play in college. Friendly games have people up and out of their seats in the middle of the game. They get snacks, take smoke breaks. It's more of a social gathering than serious poker. You get into hundred-dollar buy-ins, and it's a lot more focused. People are there to win and make money, and couldn't care less about the snack tray in the kitchen."

Selena nodded in agreement. "That's why I ask."

"The Gregorys live paycheck to paycheck," Arielle said. "Unless Mason keeps a stash of cash under his mattress, there are no signs he has extra money for high-stakes gambling. I think we need to stop worrying so much about it, and wait for the results to come back from headquarters. I called in the list of license plate numbers first thing when we got home last night. I let them know it's urgent and to have info sent back by 10 A.M. today."

Felix checked his watch. "That's in half an hour. I didn't realize we slept in so late."

"Time flies when you're surviving," Selena said.

"So how are we supposed to get this information?" Felix asked.

"They're going to call," Arielle said. "Our teams work efficiently across time. All of my communication is with the Denver team here in 1988. I called them last night to relay the license plate numbers. From there, they'll research their existing database, while also sending an agent into the future to run the plates, along with names they find during the initial search. That helps pinpoint if anyone at the poker game either currently has a criminal record, or gets one in the future. That will tell us what kind of trouble we're dealing with. Once they gather all that information, the agent returns to 1988 and will call back with their findings."

"And what time are you heading to the Gregorys'?"

"As soon as I get the call. That's why I told them I need all the info early. I'm leaving at ten, regardless. So if we don't hear before then, you'll need to field the call and take down all the notes."

The phone rang, and all three of their heads shot up like alert cats. "Right on cue," Arielle said, standing to pick up the phone on the kitchen counter.

"Hello?" she answered, grabbing the notepad and pen next to the phone, leaning onto the counter with an elbow while cradling the phone between her head and shoulder.

Felix and Selena watched as Arielle jotted down notes, nodding and offering a brief "Okay" every few seconds.

Selena craned for a better view of the notepad. Her eyes bulged as she turned to Felix and separated her hands a foot apart. "It's long," she whispered.

Felix couldn't see much. He hated when people read over his shoulder and refused to do the same to Arielle.

After three long minutes, Arielle said, "Okay, so around noon?" she checked her watch, then pointed at Felix. "Felix will be here. . . Perfect. Thank you so much."

She hung up and scribbled a few more notes down.

"Well?!" Selena asked impatiently.

Arielle turned to them, notepad in hand. "We have quite the mess. There are a handful of people with backgrounds. Drugs, prostitution, robbery. One man will be on the America's Most Wanted list by 1992 for operating one of the biggest sex trafficking rings in North America. Our team believes the house belongs to him, and that he is already operating the ring here in 1988, although not as grand of a scale as it will become."

"Sex trafficking?" Selena asked. "I don't understand how Mason is tied to all this?"

Arielle pursed her lips. "That's where our mission becomes a bit . . . gray. They are going to keep looking into it, but so far, there is no concrete evidence that Mason *is* involved in the ring."

"Wait," Felix said. "So we're potentially trying to save a sex trafficker? You've got to be shitting me."

"How the hell did our scouting team not catch this sooner?" Selena asked, her tone drifting toward anger.

The scouting teams found the missions for the Angels to work on. They focused on crimes or tragic events that had wide-rippling effects on the community. Scouts worked all throughout time and all across the continent. Once finding a potential event, another team of scouts dug deeper to figure out who was all affected by the event, persons of interest, police reports (if available), and virtually every detail possible to determine if a mission was worth the organization's time.

From there, a panel of Angel Runners reviewed the data and files, and served as the last checks and balances before either throwing out the mission, or pushing it forward for assignment.

"It's too late to dwell on that," Arielle said. "We have to adjust on the fly."

"Adjust?" Felix asked. "I think we need to *abort* this mission. Why should we risk our lives to save a monster?"

Arielle raised a hand. "We have a lot of angles and options to consider. And trust me, aborting the mission is on the table. However, this mission wasn't so much about saving Mason Gregory as it was saving his children's future and the community. And we can't change the mission, either. I know stopping the trafficking altogether seems tempting, but we have no preparation around that."

"What's happening at noon that I need to be here for?" Felix asked.

"Someone is driving down from Denver with complete files on all the people who were at that party last night. Rap sheets, mugshots, addresses. Everything they could get their hands on."

"I'm with Felix," Selena said. "I don't think we should continue."

"Of course. All you two do is side with each other against me. Frankly, I don't give a shit anymore. *I'm* the lead on this mission and *I'll* make the final decisions. If *you* have a problem with that, call Commander Briar and take it up with him."

Arielle returned to the table and sat down, Selena still standing with her jaw hanging open. Felix sat unfazed, staring at the ceiling as if calculating something to say, but coming up with nothing.

"Now, are we ready to talk business?" Arielle asked Selena.

She stood for another twenty seconds, glaring at Arielle, a burst of outrage swimming beneath her surface. Her jaw bulged as it clenched, and she finally gave in, sitting down and pushing her breakfast back to cross her hands on the table.

"Thank you," Arielle said. "I understand there are some strong emotions toward this news. I have the same feelings as you both, but we need to look at the big picture. I'm not ruling out calling off this mission, but I'm also not going to jump to that conclusion. There are a lot of moving parts, and we need to drill them down to weigh the pros and cons. I'm happy to consider your input, but ultimately I will make the last call—probably after a chat with Commander Briar."

"What are we factoring into the decision?" Felix asked.

"A few things. We should all read through the mission report again. We need a deeper understanding of the effects of Mason's death. We know his kids spiral out of control later in life, and that's something that really hurts the community. That's just the future. The immediate aftermath of his murder sends quite the ripple through Pueblo. The problems that stem from this simple murder are much bigger than Mason's family. It has societal impacts."

"That's always been Commander Briar's focus since he defeated the Revolution."

"Exactly. He took a trip into the future and witnessed a dystopian, fascist government running the country. His major focus as Commander has been to learn from that future and understand ways to stop evil from flourishing before it gets the chance. That is literally what drives his every decision. I think we're going to have to stop this murder still, no matter how wrong it may seem. This murder caused division. Some people used it to launch anti-gun campaigns. Others blamed gang activity in the area. There was a day of very heated protests outside of Town Hall. It may seem like a blip on the radar in the grand scheme of things, but enough incidents like this over time, and around the continent, lead to major divisions."

"That's a stretch," Selena said, crossing her arms, a cue Arielle had picked up on: Selena was ready to argue. "The death of a middle-aged account manager from Pueblo, Colorado leads to the rise of fascism? Get real."

"You're thinking too broadly. I've had lots of conversations with Commander Briar about this, and have made the same arguments. The murder itself is insignificant outside of Mason's family and friends. The ripple effect is what we're trying to prevent. The protests may have only been one day, but they were emotionally charged. People dug into their opinions and solidified their stances. In time, these beliefs get passed down to the next generation, and the cycle of division continues and strengthens. Division leads to extremism. I've grown a much deeper appreciation for our work. Sometimes the missions seem ridiculous on the surface, like this one. But it has a much deeper effect. One we can't quite understand. We can only trust the process and keep working. Enough of us Angels influencing the past just might save the future."

Felix nodded. "The future is never safe. Even after what Commander Briar accomplished. The work never ends."

"So we're just trying to make sure people never have arguments again?" Selena asked. "Seems impossible and a tad utopian."

"Not at all. Think of the old assembly line workers who built cars. Many of them had very boring tasks, maybe attaching the mirrors onto the vehicles. Meaningless in itself, but so important to the big picture. If that person skipped a car, that one car could make it out to the road one day and get into a serious accident. I know that's a silly example, but that's exactly what we're doing. Some missions might not feel as important as others, but they all play a role."

"Sounds like we're continuing the mission then."

Arielle stood up. "Most likely. Like I said, let's review things and get on the same page. Understand the driving force behind Commander Briar, because for a mission to be canceled, we would need his approval. I need to get going—I have a long day of sitting outside Mason's house and reading these files. Felix, if you come across anything major in what they're bringing over, bring them to me. Selena, if you can help him read through it all, I'll let you stay home today. No need for two of us to sit outside the house today—I don't expect much action, if any."

"Will do," Felix said.

Selena agreed to the terms, and Arielle left for the rest of the day. The week of the murder was upon them, and with it, plenty of drama awaited.

Chapter 28

Felix enjoyed a lazy Sunday reading through files while the Dodgers played on the TV for background noise. He still had an unpleasant taste in his mouth from the near-death encounter the prior night and had no interest in cooking dinner. The thought of standing in front of the stove seemed so far out of reach, especially with all the reading he had done during the day.

He ordered takeout from a nearby Chinese restaurant.

Selena took some files to her bedroom and agreed to follow Felix's method of sorting the documents into separate piles of importance. There were eighteen total people at the poker game on Saturday night, or rather eighteen vehicles they could pull information on.

Felix made three stacks: urgent, moderate, and insignificant.

When Arielle finally returned shortly after 6:30 that evening, they gathered around the dinner table with takeout boxes and papers scattered about.

It was these moments Felix liked to shine. He'd have Arielle's undivided attention for the next hour as he discussed the day's findings. And there were plenty of juicy details to share.

"So what do we have?" Arielle asked, sitting opposite Felix and Selena.

"Let's start from the top," Felix said, grabbing a stack of papers and tossing them to the center of the table. A portrait of a man with scraggly gray hair and a matching beard stared at the ceiling, his brown eyes bulging, lunacy swimming behind them. "This is Nathan Baldwin. He is the leader of the entire sex trafficking ring, referred to as the 'National in Charge.'"

"These people have official titles?" Arielle asked.

"Sick, isn't it?" Selena replied, shaking her head.

"Yes," Felix continued. "They are highly organized. They have to be, to not get caught. Anyway, Nathan here runs things across the United States. Our team believes he owns the house we were at last night. Nathan will eventually get caught and prosecuted in 1999, ending a fifteen-year operation—he's already been at this since 1984. Being in charge, Nathan makes the most money. By the time he's caught in 1999, he will have accumulated over ten million dollars. We believe he has just become a millionaire now in 1988."

Felix returned to his stack of documents and grabbed the next pile to toss in the center. This one showed a younger man with a long face and droopy eyes, hair freshly buzzed.

"And this is Anton Romanovich. Moved to the U.S. from Russia with his family when he was twelve years old and had a rough time through high school. In and out of juvie, suspended six times in four years. Somehow graduated, but didn't go to college. Spent some time in jail for stealing electronics, and that was the end of his record. We suspect he fell in with these people while in jail and started working with them once he got out. He is the head of the region and oversees Colorado, Wyoming, Nebraska, Kansas, Oklahoma, New Mexico, and Utah. He rents low-priced apartments in all the states mentioned, so we suspect he moves around a lot for the business. He wasn't present during the sting that took place in 1999, so he never gets caught in the future. We believe he is the most likely suspect for killing Mason Gregory, or at least ordering the hit."

"Why so?" Arielle asked.

"That sort of duty would fall within his responsibilities. He's also a ruthless man. Some of the prison records say he was constantly getting in fights, and even paralyzed a man with his bare hands, although there was no direct evidence to link him to it. Just eyewitness accounts. Wouldn't be surprised if that's who was shooting at us last night, but that's just my speculation."

Felix shoved more papers across the table. Multiple photographs of different suspects. "These are everyone else. Nothing too different across these people. Low-level crimes before they joined the operation, some with minimal jail time, some just with fines. Anton and Nathan should be our primary focus, unless Selena found anyone else?"

Selena cleared her throat and rummaged through her stacks, pulling out a candid portrait of a dark-skinned woman who had just stepped out of the backseat of a car. "I came across Cynthia Narine. She runs a brothel in Santa Fe. She's from Trinidad and Tobago, and used to be married to Nathan. She used to help him lure vulnerable homeless women when they were in their earlier days. They've since divorced, but it looks like Nathan keeps her employed. That might be something worth looking into. If he still has feelings for her, we can use that to our advantage."

It relieved Felix to hear Selena talking about the mission in a more serious tone. No one had brought up the possibility of aborting it again.

"Did either of you find any connections between Mason and any of these people?" Arielle asked.

"I did," Selena said, reaching out to flip through the photos on top of her stack. "This guy." She slid the photo forward, a man with a wide grin, glasses, and a receding hairline.

"What is this? Looks like a picture someone takes for their work badge."

"That's exactly what it is. His name is Rusty Kirk. Mason used to work with him at an accounting firm in 1982. Rusty still lives here in Pueblo, and his only job is to manage the books for the operation. He was at the gathering last night, but we believe he's never had any involvement with the actual trafficking portion."

"That's probably how Mason is involved," Arielle said. "Especially if there are no obvious ties, and his name never leaks in the future. Selena, when you go to dinner tomorrow, try to figure out what skills Mason might offer to a group of thugs like this. Rusty is an accountant. We know Mason does account management, but I doubt that's something a trafficking ring would require." She chuckled at the thought. "Especially since we know he doesn't spend a lot of time involved in their scheme. From what we've gathered, it's just a few hours every Friday night."

"Can Mason and Rusty still be taken down if we bust this ring?" Felix asked.

"Absolutely," Selena said. "They have knowledge of what's going on, and can be charged as an accomplice. Not to mention, the other crimes that go along with handling the money for a criminal organization."

"That might be a good place to start," Felix said. "He's probably the easiest person to intimidate within the group. He's just the numbers guy. Wouldn't know what to do if we cornered him."

"Let's slow down," Arielle said. "I know it may seem tempting, but we can't make any plans to break up this ring. This is good information, but not enough to pull something off at such a grand scale. We're not equipped, either. Would need a lot more guns and ammo, and more people. I did some reading today, and I feel comfortable keeping our mission as is."

"Just saving Mason?" Felix asked. "We're not going to influence any of this other mess?"

Arielle tossed her hands in the air. "We can't. We don't understand the consequences if we do. The past is sensitive. We don't even know how much we'd be able to do. This is a trafficking ring that affects thousands of lives over the next decade. It has too wide of a reach. We would get so much resistance from the past. It's too risky."

Felix and Selena nodded. That's what made Arielle the top-ranked Angel. She had a firm grasp on all the factors at play, and knew how to weigh them for any situation, including the random wrenches like this one.

Arielle sifted through the documents and froze, looking up at the other two. "I know who our killer is."

She tossed a vehicle registration form to the center of the table.

"How?" Felix asked, standing up to lean over the table and read the form. It showed a 1967 Camaro registered to one Nathaniel Joseph Baldwin.

"Unless any of these other people own a 1960s muscle car, Nathan is our guy. When I visited the night of the murder, I couldn't completely make out the vehicle, but I'm positive it fell in that range. A 1967 Camaro fits the description perfectly. It was black or a dark blue. We need to find Nathan and confirm what car he's driving."

"We can't go back to that house," Felix said. "Especially after what happened last night."

"I'm not saying we go back, but maybe we wait near that side road for him to come out. Selena, what do you think? We can probably pull you off watching Lindsay after your dinner tomorrow night. I now highly doubt she has any involvement with his death."

Selena licked her lips, and her legs bounced below the table. Felix heard the rapid rhythm of her shoes jackhammering against the hardwood floor. He rarely saw her nervous and understood she was taking a moment to think this through.

"Okay," she finally said. "I can handle that."

"We'll shuffle around our tasks for the week, but I think this is the right call. Tomorrow will still be helpful. Learn everything you can about Mason—there has to be something we're not seeing. I'll still follow him around in case something comes up, otherwise we need to find the right time to intervene with whatever situation comes up between Nathan and Mason. This is finally it. We're in the home stretch."

Chapter 29

Mason Gregory drove home in silence on Monday evening. Fielding sixty phone calls during the day, each about five minutes, made his brain itch with fatigue. *I'm so fucking sick of this job,* he thought. Just a few more years and he'd finally reap some financial benefit from the dirty work he'd been doing on the side.

All he had done was set up private credit card scanners for Nate and the gang to process payments at their brothels all around the country. Transactions went undetected thanks to Mason's knowledge of CreditConnect's system, assigning himself as the lead account manager for a phony business that operated under the name of The Puzzle Piece. On the application, they were a puzzle and board game shop with locations near major cities. In reality, they were a chain of brothels with a constant flow of customers. And girls.

Nate saw himself as a visionary. He wanted to modernize prostitution. And allowing his clients to pay with a credit card provided opportunities for more expansion and better repeat business. Snooping wives would see cash withdrawals on the monthly bank statements and question their cheating husbands. Now they'd see transactions for a game shop. He was even on the hunt for someone who could get him puzzles and board games at a wholesale price. Or less. That way, his clients could return home with proof to match the bank transactions.

What Mason did was highly illegal. A federal felony. But after years at the same company, thanks to a referral from his old friend and co-worker, Rusty Kirk, he had gained the trust of his superiors and got to overlook their more lucrative accounts. He virtually flew under the radar, and at a slow-paced company with towering cubicle walls across the bullpen, Mason had carved out his own little world.

While he had done this shady work for Nate, he had yet to see the financial rewards he had hoped. So far, he received an extra three hundred dollars each month for the last year, enough to buy him into the weekly poker games held at Nate's house. He played a conservative game, never leaving with less than two hundred, sometimes with nearly seven hundred dollars. He'd tell Lindsay he received a cash bonus for outstanding performance at work and take her and the kids out to a fancy dinner in Colorado Springs. She never questioned it.

Nate had promised a raise as soon as the credit card transactions started coming in. Not just a flat raise, but a three percent commission from each transaction. Right now, they were meeting a lot of pushback from clients. They didn't want any paper trail tied to their activities, no matter how much they were promised full discretion and a fake business name to appear on the statements. Nate expected this, but believed the future of money was changing.

"In twenty years," he told Mason at their first meeting, "There won't be any cash or checks. It's all about the plastic." He held up his credit card like it was a literal piece of gold. And Mason believed him.

Rusty cooked the books for Nate, and being an old friend, had no problem sharing numbers with Mason. In 1987, they made two million dollars in revenue. Of that, only five thousand dollars had come in from credit card transactions. Nate was practically losing money by paying Mason the three hundred each month.

Sometimes Mason wondered if he had been conned into the illegal activity. *Invest now and reap the rewards in twenty years!* It was a classic, sleazy sales pitch. But Nate didn't bullshit. Ever. He was a calculated man who studied his numbers closely, but more importantly, studied the world and its economics. If he said everyone would have credit cards by 2007, then that would be true. Mason would be retired by then, and could move to Florida, Arizona, or even Costa Rica if he really wanted.

Assuming Nate's projections came true. As the business grew and more people started using their credit cards, Nate predicted Mason could have north of $800,000 in the bank, off commissions alone, by the year 2010.

Mason daydreamed about this bright future, perhaps the only thing that helped him get through the slog of his workday. "One day, me and Lindsay will sip margaritas on the beach, and never have to check our bank account again," he said to the empty car. "The kids will have their college paid for, and it won't even put a dent in our funds."

The concept had always seemed so absurd. He had to speak it aloud to make sense of it all.

For tonight, he'd push his dreams aside and enjoy dinner with his family, and some new friend Lindsay had met at the park. He hated having company over for dinner. Mason just wanted to come home, enjoy a delicious dinner, and take off his pants to watch TV and enjoy a beer until bed time. It was a routine he appreciated ever since working at CreditConnect. If he didn't have the chance to unwind, he just might implode from the constant nagging and complaints he fielded from his clients.

He often thought of Nate's mansion and fancy cars. His parties with top-shelf booze and the finest women available. The ones he liked to "scout" for his more affluent clients. All was fair game at a Nate Baldwin gathering, but Mason didn't care for the extra-curricular activities. He just wanted to make some extra cash and go back home in peace.

When he pulled into his driveway, he saw a car parked along the sidewalk. Their guest had already arrived, meaning he wouldn't get a single moment to kick back and chat with the kids and Lindsay about their days.

"Please eat and leave," he said as he killed the engine. He hated when guests lingered, especially once the sun went down.

Mason sighed before grabbing his lunch pail and stepped out of the car, trudging up the pathway where he entered the house, the smell of baked chicken oozing into the living room.

"I'm home!" he shouted, and immediately a rumble came from down the hallway as both kids rushed him. Amanda jumped into his arms and David wrapped himself around Mason's leg.

"Hi, Daddy!" Amanda cackled, a wide, toothless grin on her face. She had lost three teeth in the past two months.

"How are you guys?" he asked, putting Amanda down next to her brother. "How was your day?"

"Good," David said, turning and running into the kitchen where Lindsay stood over the stove.

"Good, Daddy," Amanda said. "I went to dance, had lunch with Mommy, and helped her pick up the toys in the yard."

"Very good! Thank you for doing that." They had been working with Amanda on actually telling them about her day, and not giving the simple one-word response like David had.

Amanda skipped away, back down the hallway to her room, where she likely had a meeting of Barbie dolls set up.

Mason turned into the kitchen and stopped when he saw the most beautiful woman he'd ever seen standing next to his wife. She had a slender figure, long brown hair, and an innocent charm behind a shy smile. *She looks like she stepped out of one of those* Swimsuit Edition *magazines*, Mason thought, immediately fantasizing about what lied beneath her clothes.

"Hello," Mason said.

"Hi, hon, have a good day?" Lindsay asked, turning toward him and walking over to give him a kiss. He couldn't keep his eyes off the stranger in his kitchen.

"Yeah, just another day. Who is this?"

"This is the young lady I told you about. Selena. I met her at the park last week."

"Nice to meet you, Mr. Gregory," Selena said, sticking out a hand.

Mason grabbed it, her skin as soft as satin. "Pleasure to meet you. You can call me Mason. No need for formalities."

She grinned and stepped back. "Can I help you set the table?" she asked Lindsay.

"That would be great! Plates and cups are right above you," Lindsay replied, pointing to the cupboard behind Selena. "Dinner's ready, hon. Would you mind getting the kids washed up?"

"Sure," Mason said, suddenly not caring how long their guest wanted to stay tonight. He gathered the kids from their bedrooms and had them wash their hands before taking their places at the dinner table. Lindsay had prepared a feast with baked chicken, steamed veggies, mashed potatoes with gravy, and a small chocolate cake from their local bakery.

"This looks fantastic," he said, sitting down at the head of the table. "You've really outdone yourself, Linds."

Lindsay always put together quality meals, but enjoyed upping her game when company was over. He genuinely believed his wife could open her own restaurant and often encouraged her to. But she believed that would take all the fun out of cooking. They didn't *need* the money to justify the hassle of startup costs to open a new business. Never mind the long hours required to run a restaurant.

Once Lindsay served everyone's food, the kids dove into the mashed potatoes while she and Mason cut up their chicken. Selena watched for a moment before taking her first bite.

"So, Selena, what do you do?" Mason asked.

"I don't have much of a set job. I do some part-time work bartending and babysitting."

"Selena recently graduated from the university and stayed in Pueblo," Lindsay said.

"Wow, I don't think I've ever heard of such a thing," Mason said. "Most of those kids run for the hills when they're done."

Selena shrugged. "I like it here. Pueblo has a certain charm. I grew up living between New York City and Paris."

"Oh, wow, so you come from money?"

"Mason Gregory!" Lindsay gasped, smacking him in the arm. "We don't ask visitors about their finances."

Mason waved his hands over his plate. "My apologies. I didn't mean it like that. It's not every day you meet someone who's lived in such big places."

"No offense taken, Mr. Gregory . . . er, Mason." Selena said, poking at the food on her plate. "My dad has always been rich. My mother not so much. They divorced, my dad moved to Paris, and that's why I spent time in both cities."

"And they're still there?"

Selena nodded. "They like the lives they have. Those places are home for them. I invited my mom to move out here with me. I guess some people just like the chaos of New York."

"Well, from a Pueblo native, welcome to town. Happy to have you."

"I didn't realize you were native to Pueblo. What do you do for work, if you don't mind me asking?"

"Not at all. I work for a company called CreditConnect. It's not the most exciting job, but it pays the bills. I work as an account manager, so do things like customer service, a bit of sales."

"Very nice," Selena said. "I haven't quite figured out what I want to do for a career. I've been doing side jobs ever since college. Even used to make some decent money on the weekends playing poker in the dorms. I was one of the few girls who played. It was so fun taking money from the guys."

"Mason plays every week," Lindsay said. "Maybe he can invite you one of these times."

Mason nearly choked on the piece of chicken in his mouth. While they played poker at their gatherings, it was meant more as a weekly meeting for Nate and all the leadership to get on the same page. They had strict rules about bringing outsiders in. Not even spouses were allowed. Nate understood the delicacy of their work, and while most of the crew didn't have families, he would shuffle things around if it meant keeping the secrecy alive. Just as he had done for Mason this past weekend.

"Oh," Mason said. "We have kind of an exclusive club. I would need to talk to the guys."

Lindsay rolled her eyes. "God forbid a lady tries to play cards with the boys. I'm sure our tiny brains couldn't possibly calculate the odds of hitting a flush."

Selena laughed, and Mason felt like he was being ganged up on. The kids continued eating their food, uninterested in the conversation.

"It's not that I don't want you there," Mason said. "It's not my game. Not my house. If I ever host a game here, you're more than welcome to come."

"Well, thank you," Selena said. "If you get the chance to ask your friends, I'm free this upcoming weekend and would love to play."

"I'll let you know," Mason lied. He already knew the answer without having to ask Nate. In fact, Nate would probably howl like a loon if he brought up this question.

"So, since you work for a credit card company, do you have any sort of accounting background?" Selena asked.

Why is this chick asking me so many questions? he thought.

"No accounting background. I didn't go to college—couldn't afford it. I had to do things the old-fashioned way. Started at entry-level positions and worked my way up."

"What skills did you need to get where you are today?" Selena asked.

"I'm sorry, but why do you have such an interest in my work background?"

"Just curious. I've always enjoyed math. Like I said, I'm still trying to figure things out for my life. I'm trying to see what might be feasible."

Mason took a drink of water, suddenly craving a beer and once more wishing his guest would leave. He didn't care how fun she was to look at. She talked too much.

"Well, I wish I could give you more insight. I don't really have any special skills. I've just learned my jobs on the fly and use that experience whenever I've had to apply for new positions or companies. I have a background in sales, customer service, administrative work, and am learning some new things on computers. None of that compares to a college education, though, so you'll automatically have an advantage whatever you decide. What was your major, anyway?"

"Finance," Selena said, not offering any further details as she shoved food into her mouth.

Mason did the same, grateful for a moment of silence. Lindsay must have sensed the awkward tension because she was the next to speak.

"Who's ready for dessert?"

Chapter 30

Arielle and Felix waited anxiously at home while Selena was at dinner. They tried to pass the time by reading through the files, but concentration proved difficult. Too much was at stake over the dinner. Arielle hyped it up as the night that could swing the entire mission in a different direction.

When they saw the headlights pull into their driveway, they both rushed to the front door like puppies excited to see their owner arrive home.

"What is taking so long?" Felix asked after an entire minute passed and Selena remained in the car. She had cut the headlights, but no other movement came from the car. "Should we check on her?"

The door finally opened and Selena stepped out, and she danced up the pathway to the front door.

"Hey, you two. How are things?" she asked. "Why are you standing at the door?"

"Because we need to hear all about tonight," Arielle said. "What were you doing in the car just now?"

"Relax, *mother*. A good song was on and I wanted to finish listening to it."

"Of course," Felix said, showing a rare glimpse of frustration as he rolled his eyes and tossed his hands in the air.

"You guys need to chill," Selena said. "I didn't get anything that's going to help us."

Arielle's stomach dropped. She had put so much emphasis on this dinner. Such high expectations. *Maybe Selena was the wrong person for the job,* she thought. "You didn't ask about the poker game?"

"Of course I did," Selena said, frowning. "Do you actually think I just went over for dinner to shoot the shit with these people? I tried. And if you'll let me come inside *our* house and sit down, I'd be happy to tell you about it."

Arielle and Felix parted ways to let her pass through, and Selena smirked at Felix as her shoulder brushed his chest on her way to the living room. She found the wine rack and poured a glass of red before taking a seat on the couch.

"Are you coming?" she asked, Arielle and Felix not having moved from the door. They snapped out of their trance, Felix sitting on the opposite end of the couch, Arielle leaning against the wall and crossing her arms. "I probed as much as I could. So much that Mason asked me why I was asking so many questions. I arrived about twenty minutes before him and helped Lindsay in the kitchen. I asked if they had other friends, hoping to get some names we could look up. But she gave me nothing. Said there is a couple from church they like to spend time with."

"Church?" Arielle asked. "They didn't leave the house yesterday?"

Selena shrugged. "I know, but I couldn't act like I knew that. Anyway, when he got home, we had some pleasantries. He couldn't stop checking me out—was kinda weird, seeing as I'm young enough to be his daughter. During dinner, I told them how I used to play poker in college. Lindsay got all excited and told Mason I should join him. He played it off that it wasn't his home to invite someone over. An 'exclusive' game is what he called it."

Arielle laughed. "It's exclusive, all right."

"Then I asked him about his background and work, trying to figure out what the hell this sex ring uses him for. He has no college education, and nothing special on his work resume. Says he's spent his career starting from the bottom and working his way up. Has lots of corporate skills, but nothing I can tell that translates into a criminal operation. After all the probing, it was clear he wanted me out, so Lindsay served dessert and called it a night. Here I am, nowhere further than when I arrived."

Arielle shook her head. "Dammit."

"I'm sorry. I did what I could."

"I'm not upset with you, just the situation. We were really counting on this, and who knows what this may have done to the relationship. They might never have you back if Mason felt uncomfortable."

"Hard to say. Mason hugged me before I left. Maybe he just wanted a reason to touch me, but it felt like we were all on good terms. Just bad, awkward conversation, but I didn't have much choice with only one night to figure out everything. Normally, I'd use the entire two weeks to sprinkle in these types of questions."

Arielle paced back and forth. "We did what we could. We'll have to re-evaluate our strategy for the next mission. But where do you guys suppose we go from here?"

"Arielle," Felix said, standing up, pointing a finger at her. "You need to relax. No, we didn't get the golden ticket we wanted tonight, but we're still in good shape. We know who the killer is."

"To be fair, we don't know with complete certainty. I'm taking a leap of faith with the matching cars. We can't get sloppy and base our actions off an assumption. I've also found it's important to understand the *why* behind a murder like this. It helps pinpoint better times to interrupt the act."

"We're closer than you think. We know Mason's schedule. He doesn't go anywhere besides work and this weekly poker game. He either does all of his duties the night of the poker games, or he does them during work hours."

"It sounds like he has some freedom at work," Selena said. "Or at the very least, he's well respected. This could mean he has some leniency from his superiors should he decide to take time to himself during the day."

Arielle shook her head. "That may be so. But why do something illegal at work? Seems too risky. He's definitely a family man and keeps his wife and kids as his main focus. Do you not agree after having dinner with them?"

"Sure, it *seems* that way, but is he really that dedicated if he's doing this kind of sketchy stuff on the weekends? How could a man with a daughter be involved, in any capacity, with selling off other young women?"

"Money," Felix said. "Money runs the world, don't you know? People will happily throw away their moral compass for a few dollars. We should have had Selena get a job inside his office. Maybe if we could understand what's going on inside that building, we'd know more. Maybe his job status is shaky and he's desperate for cash. Don't forget, we're in an era of raging masculinity. Men don't just go home and tell their wives the income might cease soon. Instead, they make up for the funds any way they can. Gambling, selling drugs, looking for a job during their free time. It doesn't always have to be so drastic. Did he seem secretive at all around Lindsay?"

Selena shook her head. "They were fine. From what I could tell, at least. I didn't exactly have a norm to compare it to. But Mason was engaged in the conversation, didn't seem to be off in his own world."

"Have you tried going into his office, Arielle?" Felix asked.

"Of course. You need a badge to just open the main doors. From what I could see, you need to swipe it again to get through another set."

"Sloppy preparation," Felix said, and Arielle took this personally.

"Excuse me?! I've done nothing but prepare—"

"Not you," Felix cut her off. "The scouting team. *I* can make a fake work badge. Not that difficult. I don't have my machine with me, or else I could have put one together."

"Don't worry about it. We could hack his computer after hours, but we likely wouldn't have a way of knowing if he was in trouble."

Arielle knew they probably could have found this out by hacking his manager's computers and seeing what notes they stored. But there was no point in them dwelling over the matter.

"Let's worry about Friday night," she said. "That's all we can do now."

"What are we supposed to do all week?" Selena asked.

"The same thing we've been doing. Although, I'm serious about taking you off Lindsay. I think that's a waste of time at this point. Maybe a couple of days tailing Nate and another two following Anton."

"That's fine with me, but how close can I realistically get? We know Nate has security cameras outside, and I can't exactly hide across the street like I've been doing with Lindsay. The logistics are going to make it difficult to get much done."

"That's fine. I don't want you approaching him at all. That alone might start the wheels in motion for tampering with the past. Observe. Hang out on that main road and wait for him to leave. Follow him, see where he goes, who he spends time with, that sort of stuff. Same with Anton. Felix, I don't suppose you'd be able to bug their houses."

Felix let out a hearty, almost exaggerated laugh. "Not a chance. I have to know exactly when a subject will be gone, and for how long. That's where good scouting comes into play. If we can get into Mason's office building, I can probably bug that place."

Arielle thought during her pacing. While it seemed productive on the surface, it wouldn't yield any results. Bugging the office would only explain Mason's motivation behind joining the criminal underworld, assuming the issue stemmed from his office job. It had no bearing on his actual murder.

"Let's not worry about the office. We know where Mason is going to be on Friday night. We know some of the people who will be there."

"And what they're capable of," Selena added.

"Indeed. We know where Mason will be murdered. Maybe you can drive the possible routes from Nate's house to the warehouses and look for potential areas we can set up to interfere. Maybe we park on the side of the road and pretend we need help. Those warehouses are kind of in the middle of nowhere."

"I can do that."

"Good. The most important thing is to remain diligent. I'm not expecting too much on this mission, but the days leading up to our targeted event are usually when the past will start intervening. Don't get caught off guard—it can cost you your life."

Chapter 31

Mason hung up his work phone, fuming. How he wanted to rip the cords out of the wall and hurl the damn machine across the office.

That motherfucker, he thought.

Earlier in the day, Mason had pulled up the transactions received by The Puzzle Piece, and to his delight, saw the organization had a monster week. Mason naturally grew excited at the prospect of earning more than three hundred dollars from Nate for the month of June.

Three hundred dollars per week, now that's more like it.

He had wanted to call Nate on his lunch break to let him know the good news, but couldn't contain his excitement that long. He was already spending the money in his mind. At this rate, he might even take the family to Disneyland before school started up, something that had only been a wild fantasy up to this point in their lives.

He called, shared the numbers, and reminded Nate that he waived the processing fees for every transaction that had occurred. Another way to ensure he put more money into Nate's pockets that would eventually come back his way. Nate sounded grateful, but distant.

"That's great, Mase, keep up the good work. You'll see that money in due time. We just have to cover some other charges first."

"Bullshit!" Mason had snapped, cupping his hand over the receiver so his conversation wouldn't carry to his colleagues in the neighboring cubicles. "That's *my* money. We had a deal."

"We *have* a deal. But something has come up and I need to pay some other people. Do you think that bump in sales happened by accident? I have guys on the streets pushing the credit cards. They're the frontline soldiers. They get their money. Then you'll get yours."

"Well, you're not a frontline soldier, and I'm sure you still got paid."

"What the fuck did you say?"

"You heard me. This is complete *bullshit.* I've spent enough time with the others to know that you pay out when the money comes in. Everyone gets their cut. Why am I the only one being fucked over? I got you the credit card machines and watch the accounts every damn day."

"I suggest you watch your mouth, Mason. Don't forget who you're talking to."

"And don't forget who made this all possible."

Those were the last words Mason spoke before slamming the phone down to hang up the call, his body trembled with steaming rage. The stress of doing such illegal activity every single day had long taken its toll on his psyche, but to not receive the financial rewards for doing the dirty work? Now that was a whole new level of fucked-up.

Mason had no options. Nate was the top dog, and whatever he said was final. There was no negotiating with the man, especially over money. If someone had a serious concern and wanted to take up the matter with him, they usually met his revolver.

Mason had heard the stories, and while he didn't know how true they were (he suspected the stories were made up to keep the peasants at bay), he had no plans to find out.

He planted his elbows on his knees and held up his face in the cups of both hands. Next to his computer monitor stood a family portrait. He and Lindsay in the backdrop, Amanda and David with cheesy grins just below them.

"What am I doing?" he whispered to himself. One mistake by anyone within Nate's group, and they could all go under. There were a lot of moving parts, and too much trust to leave with a collective of criminals. The little money he had been receiving so far had made a difference in his family's life, but was it worth it? If Mason went to prison, they'd be left with absolutely nothing. Lindsay didn't have an income. She'd have to find work and cut back on all unnecessary expenses. She would pull Amanda out of her dance classes. David wouldn't get to play baseball next summer. They'd never get to leave the house for pleasure and would be reduced to basic meals. All while Mason rotted away in a jail cell.

Mason's stomach swirled. They made it plenty clear to him when he joined the group that leaving wasn't an option. "When you're with me," Nate had said, slinging an arm over Mason's shoulder. "You're with me for life."

As long as he had been a part of the gang, Mason had yet to see someone leave. No one had even entertained the thought.

"I'm not like these guys," he muttered. Their gatherings brought together drug dealers, murderers, kidnappers. And there were Mason and Rusty—the white-collar workers who ensured things ran smoothly behind the scenes. *Am I closer to a mob leader than a drug runner? Only a few people get to keep their hands clean in groups like this.*

All things considered, he had the cushy job.

Can I actually get out? Or am I really stuck? What would happen if I just stopped showing up to the meetings, or answering my work phone? Will they come to my house? Threaten my family? Would they actually kill me for wanting to return to a normal life?

These thoughts pressed on his conscience, and he grew overwhelmed with the considerations. If he waited for a couple of days to pass—he'd have to wait now, after how he ended his last conversation—would he be able to have a civil conversation with Nate and tell him exactly how he was feeling? He could explain himself from a position of gratitude and regret. Grateful to have received the opportunity for life-changing money, regretful for putting his family in a risky position. He hadn't truly weighed the gravity of the situation from the onset, but things had come into focus. And no, it wasn't because Nate had just stiffed him of the funds he deserved—although that was certainly a factor. He could find work picking up a weekend shift. Hell, CreditConnect might even approve some overtime, and he could get the extra cash that way.

Mason slouched in his seat, his limbs feeling hollowed out while his head spun. The thought of picking up the phone and calling Nate—no matter what mood the man was in—to have this discussion made him nauseous. While he didn't think it likely, it was still *possible* he could end up dead at the close of that phone call.

At least if that happens, Lindsay would collect insurance and have some cushion.

He shook his head free of the morbid thoughts, suddenly concerned about putting together the living will he had long kept on the back burner.

Mason slouched further, on the verge of spilling out from his chair and collapsing under his desk. He had reached a crossroads, and could either commit to leaving the organization or jump all the way in. He supposed Nate would reward him if he showed a little more initiative. *Maybe even a parting gift,* he thought. *A token of appreciation before sailing into the sunset and never looking back.*

He thought of the Selena girl who came over for dinner last night. Maybe she was a godsend to get him out of this mess. She was stunning. Way more attractive than any of the girls they deployed to the brothels and street corners.

Nate had always spoken of expanding the business with a high-end escort service. The girls multi-millionaires would pay up to fifty-thousand dollars to have for one night.

Selena was the perfect candidate. Beautiful. Young. Alone in a city with no family. And she needed money. Nate would know how to convince her. He would sell her on the dream of making twenty-thousand dollars a weekend. And none of it would be a lie. She really would make life-changing money.

"I just have to get her to Nate, and he can seal the deal," Mason muttered under his breath. "Good thing she likes to play poker."

He picked up the phone and dialed Lindsay to ask for Selena's number.

Chapter 32

Felix ordered a meat lover's pizza for dinner on Tuesday night. The stress and pressure of the week were taking their tolls on all three Angels, and cooking no longer seemed a pressing matter. Not after the phone call Felix received earlier in the afternoon.

He expected both Arielle and Selena home by six, as had become the norm since their arrival in 1988 Pueblo. The pizza sat on the dining room table while Felix paced circles around it.

Why would he call here? What does he want?

The front door jiggled and swung open, Arielle stepping into the house. "Dammit!" Felix spat.

"Well, happy Tuesday to you, too," Arielle replied.

"No. It's not you. It's Selena. We need her home ASAP. He called here today asking for her."

Arielle dropped her duffel bag with a loud clatter. "Mason called *here*?!"

"Yeah. He asked who I was, so I said a roommate. I don't know what all Selena has told anyone, so I hope that didn't throw anything off."

"Did he say what he wanted?"

"Nope. Just to relay that he called, and would like her to call him back."

Selena turned into the driveway and Arielle immediately waved her arms, urging her to hurry and come inside.

Selena, who had spent the day trying to follow Nate, didn't waste any time singing in the car this evening, and hurried up the path to meet them. "What's wrong?"

"Mason called for you today," Felix said. "Wants you to call him back."

Selena narrowed her eyes, suspicious. "Just him? Not Lindsay?"

Felix nodded. "It was around two o'clock, so he would have been at work."

"Well, this adds some excitement to my boring-ass day. I sat on that main road all day and no one ever came out. Nate must have not had any business that required him to leave his house. Of course, right?"

"You don't know what this could be about?" Arielle asked, grabbing Selena by the shoulder and forcing her into the kitchen where the phone waited on its cradle.

"No idea. He didn't say anything about reaching out to me. It can't be too secretive—he would have gotten the number from Lindsay. She's the only who has it."

"Then call him. Right now. They're probably having dinner over there, but I don't care. We need to know what he wants."

Felix had never seen Arielle so excited. But it was more of an anxious excitement. Urgency. Borderline chaotic.

"Okay, relax. I'm going." Selena placed her bag on her seat at the kitchen table before picking up and dialing the phone on the counter. "Hi Lindsay, it's Selena. How are you?"

Selena's leg started bouncing while she leaned against the counter. She looked at her friends and mimicked a blabbering mouth with her free hand.

"Well, that's good," she finally said. "Mason called here for me earlier, so I was just returning his message to call back. Is he available? Okay, thank you."

Selena nodded and gave a thumbs up. Mason Gregory was on his way to the phone.

"I'm good, Mason," Selena said after a few seconds. "How are you?"

She nodded her head for about thirty seconds while Mason spoke, then said, "This Friday night? Um, let me check my schedule real quick."

Selena slapped her hand over the receiver and spun around to face Arielle, eyes bulging. "He's inviting me to the poker game on Friday night. What should I do?" she whispered, but the words still spilled out of her mouth like she had no control over them.

"Holy shit!" Felix gasped.

Arielle nodded. "If you're comfortable being there, go for it. We'll be there in case anything goes wrong."

Selena took a moment before uncovering the phone and placing it back to her ear. "Looks like I am available that night. Should I plan to meet you there? . . . Okay, understood. See you then. Thank you."

She hung up the phone and drew in a deep breath. "Alright, guys. I don't know what the hell is going on, but this is really happening. He told me to meet at his house and we can drive over together. Said the house they're going to isn't the easiest place to find." Selena let out a nervous chuckle.

"Look," Arielle said. "I know this is critical to the mission, and being handed to us on a silver platter. But my number one concern on any mission is the safety of our Angels. Knowing what we know about that place, and who all is there, I'm not going to force you to go. I completely understand if you want to call him back tomorrow and make up an excuse. We still know he's going to be there Friday night, regardless if you are. At this point in the mission, that's really all we need to know."

"But we still don't know one-hundred percent for sure who kills him. Or why."

"The *why* doesn't matter anymore. We just need to stop the murder and go back home. I really don't like the way this mission is turning out."

"How is the past going to react to this?" Felix asked. "Selena obviously wasn't there the night Mason was killed. Could her presence lead to some problems?"

"It definitely will," Arielle said. "Be on high alert all week, Selena. Your presence itself could lead to the murder not happening, and the past might push back against that. Might even try to prevent you from showing up. Maybe you should stay home until Friday night. I'll have to think about the best approach for that. But definitely be ready for anything."

Selena gulped and nodded. "Okay, I understand. Would the past have let me come this far, though? Why allow this invite to happen in the first place?"

"We don't have a full understanding of how other people can affect the past. This wasn't a matter of you inviting yourself to the poker game. *Mason* did it. Mason isn't a time traveler, he's living in his original timeline for these events. There have been a few theories. Some argue the regular people can still receive pushback from altering the past. Others say they are protected since they are in their Original Time. I guess we'll have to see what happens with Mason, but that doesn't mean *you* should be any less careful."

"Got it. Okay. I feel alright about this. I'll be ready to enter the belly of the beast. And I'll be damned if anything is going to happen to me."

"You don't suppose . . ." Felix began, but trailed off. He wondered if Mason might try to kidnap Selena, or have the thugs at the poker game kidnap her. They could either want her as a sex slave, or maybe they just wouldn't like if Mason brought a guest along, and wanted to ensure her silence. But they wouldn't ever get away with that with Arielle Lucila on the scene. "Never mind. Do you think Mason asked Nate if he could bring Selena? Or is he planning on just showing up?"

"He said he would ask the host when we talked about it at dinner," Selena said. "I didn't think he actually would, but here we are."

Arielle's brow lowered as she entered deep thought, and Felix could only wonder if she was thinking the same thing he just had.

"Irrelevant," Arielle said. "Let's enjoy some dinner and call it a night. The rest of this week is going to be exhausting."

Chapter 33

Mason hadn't slept six hours combined between Tuesday and Wednesday night. He had mentally committed to the decision to tender his resignation to Nate on Friday evening, and leave him with Selena as a peace offering.

The guilt already pricked at him. He had never committed such a heinous crime against a fellow human being. He thought of his own daughter, and how he might react if she were to go missing one day, forever lost in the underground world of human trafficking. His heart ached, his stomach wrenched, and his limbs shook. He supposed the latter was because of the lack of sleep and amounts of caffeine he had consumed over the past two days to stay a functioning adult.

Mason had debated calling in and taking personal days until this all passed, but decided going to work would be best. Stewing at home wouldn't be any better. Worse, in fact, since Lindsay would prod him and ask him how he was feeling, and probably convince him to not go to the poker game on Friday night. In his current state, he just might agree with that decision, and that would leave him trapped under Nate's thumb for the rest of his miserable life.

At least from work, he could distract himself with tasks, even if that meant mindlessly staring at the screen for hours at a time. He was in his own world—his own personal hell—within the confines of his cubicle. His manager might check in with him a couple of times throughout the day, but he otherwise expected no visitors or distractions.

All alone to swallow this pill like a man, he thought. Mason would never understand the folks within their ring that did this portion of the job for a living. They navigated the streets, scooping up homeless women sleeping on park benches, bringing them to safe houses to get cleaned up and polished to market.

"You'll never have to sleep on a bench again," they'd tell the women. "You'll be in a bed every night, in fact, with a complete stranger. Just spread those legs and we'll change your life forever."

They needed little beyond a sleazy sales pitch when trying to attract women who had absolutely nothing. About ninety percent would join after hearing about the life-altering money they would make on top of the benefits of sleeping in hotel or brothel rooms with a roof and heating. And food. Another five percent would require more convincing, while the last five would still refuse and be released back to the parks they called home.

They rarely forced women into the trade, but sometimes Nate allowed a kidnapping. They typically took these women across the country, far from where they had been captured, in case anyone searched for them. This happened with women who had the highest earning potential. Ones who might qualify for the high-end escort service but couldn't see the exorbitant value they could provide. And earn.

Selena fit this mold, and that was the only reason he thought Nate would let him live.

A knock on the cubicle wall startled Mason from his wandering thoughts, and he jumped in his seat.

"Whoa, sorry to startle you," his manager, Brian Rogers, said with a chuckle. Brian was a tall, heavy man with a thick mustache that often caught the crumbs of his morning doughnuts. Brian was an asshole. "Do you have a minute to chat in my office?"

Under normal circumstances, Mason would have spun into a complete panic attack after hearing these words. But he was already in that phase, so he felt nothing of significance as he stood and said, "Sure."

He had been so consumed with his impending doom that he felt like he was walking in a dream, following Brian down the hallway, passing cubicles where his colleagues continued with their days. Brian led the way, his pudgy ass stretching his slacks to their limits. Mason always thought his boss would sit down one day at a meeting and the button on his pants would burst free, blasting across the room like a rocket ship. The thought brought a much needed grin.

"How's the week going?" Brian grumbled over his shoulder as they stepped into his office. He closed the door behind them once Mason took a seat in front of the cluttered desk.

"It's been fine," Mason replied, now feeling the pressure to act cool. He couldn't recall having made any mistakes in his work.

"Glad to hear. Family okay?" Brian asked as he sat in his office chair, the hinges screeching as they begged for mercy.

"Yes, everyone is doing well."

"That's great. You've been doing great work, and because of that, we want to reward you. We are doing an audit of everyone's accounts and will reassign some of the higher profile ones your way. Companies bringing in at least fifty thousand a month. All the rest in your portfolio will be things of the past."

"*All* the current accounts?" Mason replied, suddenly lightheaded. His secret account was nowhere near earning fifty thousand.

"Yes. We want to maximize the talent on our team, and you have the highest retention rate. Naturally, we want to place the bigger accounts with you."

"Are there any I can ask to keep?"

"I'm sorry, Mason, are you not understanding? You're about to earn at least an extra twenty thousand dollars a year, the way we are looking to structure your portfolio. Why on Earth would you want to keep accounts that will lower that number?"

Mason took a moment to let those words settle in. He had been so focused on working under the radar and keeping things afloat for Nate, that he hadn't realized the quality of work he'd been doing. He had just received a generous opportunity, yet still felt a resistance to jump for joy around Brian's office.

"I don't know what to say."

"You don't need to say anything," Brian replied. "Congratulations. You've earned it. Once the audits are complete, and we confirm everything with your existing accounts is sound, we'll make the announcement next week."

Mason grew queasy. "What does the audit consist of?"

"The usual. A second look at all the numbers to make sure everything lines up. We look for inconsistencies in accounts, fee waivers, cancellation reasons. That's why it can take some time."

Mason became dizzy and worried about standing up. "Okay," he said, the lone word forced. "Thank you. Is there anything else?"

Brian furrowed his brow as he planted his elbows on the desk, studying Mason from behind the glasses perched on his wide nose. "No, that's all. Are you sure everything's okay?"

It was the most concerned, on a personal level, Mason had ever heard Brian sound. He nodded. "Yes. Just a little tired, I suppose."

Mason stood on wobbly legs, reached out a hand and gave the weakest handshake of his life. He mustered a lazy grin before turning and exiting the office, sure to close the door behind him as he hurried down the hall toward the bathrooms.

Mason heaved as he pushed open the bathroom door, grateful to see no one else present as he stumbled into a stall and slammed the door shut, falling to his knees. He caught his reflection in the toilet bowl's water seconds before his guts released the tension and forced vomit of a sickly off-yellow color.

His body shivered while he spat out what remained in his mouth, tears flowing and combining with the mucus pooling on the tip of his nose. The raise, and even the promise of a future fortune from Nate, all seemed irrelevant. Depending on how this audit turned out, there was suddenly an increased chance that Mason was going to prison.

He closed his eyes and pictured it all. Brian receiving a report of the excessive fee waivers applied to The Puzzle Piece. There was a chance Mason would only receive a slap on the wrist, but a closer look at the details was more likely. A full investigation would launch, as CreditConnect needed to ensure no money laundering was taking place. It would only take a matter of days before they discovered The Puzzle Piece wasn't an actual business. The feds would get involved and march into the office building—or Mason's home—to take him away where he'd face a jury on charges of fraud, accessory to sex trafficking, and a slew of other criminal charges.

All for an easy buck, he thought, and puked once more.

He couldn't face a trial. Couldn't face his wife and kids. Couldn't even face himself, if that's how everything played out.

Mason had no chance in prison. He imagined himself in the bright orange jumpsuit, terrified to shower, leave his cell, or take a quiet walk during their outdoor hour. Hopefully, the movies made it seem worse than it really was, but he suspected the reality reflected plenty in the art.

"What the hell am I supposed to do?" Mason moaned, wiping away what he hoped was the last remnants from his insides. His head spun, his stomach now empty.

Do I pack up and move? Do I tell Lindsay?

If he told Lindsay everything that had happened, and she stayed with him, then maybe she would agree to move away. Pack up their bags and disappear into the night before CreditConnect had time to piece it all together. Perhaps his sudden disappearance from work would prevent the audit from even happening. His accounts would all shift to different colleagues in a move that would leave Brian scrambling. This seemed the best scenario to pursue, but was it overreacting?

It was entirely possible they would complete the audit, and nothing would come from it. They might dismiss the fee waivers as something Mason did to accomplish a high retention rate. Hell, they might even adopt the practice, praising him for such a brilliant idea. They might find the waivers and question him about it, and he could try to bullshit his way out of it. He'd seen it plenty of times. Respected employees could get away with more. They wanted him to manage their biggest accounts. There were likely many parts already in motion in the background to make that happen. A minor wrench like the waivers could easily be dismissed to ensure the company's plans moved forward.

Mason stood at a fork in the road, one that determined the rest of his life. The most disturbing part was that his decision didn't guarantee a particular outcome. Both roads could lead to dead ends.

Mason still had a looming conversation with Nate.

I just hope he's willing to listen.

Chapter 34

The three Angels sat around the living room in stunned silence. It was eight o'clock at night. They had just finished a dinner of homemade cheeseburgers, Felix willing to cook the meal he saved for lazy days.

Dinner had gone well. Until the phone rang.

Felix had answered and handed the phone to Selena. She listened for just under a minute, her responses terse as she shook her head. After hanging up, she said, "He just uninvited me from the poker game."

After the phone call, they moved into the living room. Unfinished burgers and dirty dishes remained in the kitchen, scattered between the table and sink. It was the messiest they had ever left the kitchen.

Selena poured them all a glass of wine.

"I should have seen this coming," Arielle said, taking her first sip.

Felix nodded. "We often get tricked into believing the past pushes back with some dramatic event, but that's rarely the case. The past works efficiently. Remember, it wants to maintain its original chain of events. It wants to correct the changes we've made to ensure the same outcomes happen. Selena was never supposed to be at that poker game, so now the past is working to make sure that doesn't happen."

"So if I still go, what will happen?" Selena asked.

"We *can* still go," Arielle said bluntly. "If our goal is to observe the mansion, we shouldn't meet any resistance. Selena wasn't in the house the night of the murder, so that's all the past is reverting to. We still know where the murder will happen. We're going to have to split up. Someone needs to be at that warehouse, waiting to intervene. And whoever we decide that is, will need to be there first thing tomorrow morning. We have to cheat the past, and I'm afraid that's the only way to do it."

"How do we decide?" Felix asked, a tinge of fear in his voice. "It should be you, right, Arielle?"

Arielle knew damn well it should be her. Everyone in the room did. They also didn't know *how* she wanted to play this situation, nor could they.

While her fellow Angels were the best at their given roles, neither of them understood the intricacies of dealing with the past. Neither of them had played out the night of June 24th hundreds of different ways. She was still leading this mission, and would position her team in the best spots for success and safety. She had made enough mistakes in her early days as an Angel to learn how to cheat the past. That's *why* she was the best.

"Felix, you'll be waiting at the warehouse tomorrow."

"What?!" he gasped, jumping off the couch. "Why the hell would you pick me? I don't kill people."

Arielle raised a hand. "Stop worrying. I'll be nearby, but you'll need to step in if something prevents me from getting there. I've already mapped this out. You're decent with a rifle and scope, yes?"

"I, uh, I'm decent, sure. But nowhere good enough to be left with this responsibility. Is this one of those mind games to trick me into some sort of false confidence?"

"I don't play games. You can handle the job. It's that simple."

"Well, do you mind sharing *why*?" Felix scoffed.

Arielle indeed didn't play games, but she utilized strategy. Felix and Selena were now pawns in the chess match she was playing against the past.

"Actually, no."

"Whoa," Selena said, standing beside Felix. "You can't do that. We've been working together this whole time. You can't just decide what to do without discussing."

"I understand your concerns, but you need to understand where I'm coming from. I know what it takes to beat the past. Don't ever mistake who our enemy is. It's not Mason, it's not Nate. It's the past. Every mission, we have to beat the past. I'm putting us all where we need to be, and I just need you to trust me, no matter how little sense it makes to you."

"This is bullshit," Selena snapped. "You're being a dictator." She stomped around the living room, returning to the wine rack and pouring another glass.

"I'm happy to answer any questions *after* the mission, but for now, I need to keep the strategy to myself. Felix, do you have a problem with any of this?"

He had crossed his arms and fell silent while Selena lost her cool, returning to his seat on the couch. He shrugged. "Not much I can do about it. You're in charge, and if we don't comply, I'm sure we'll get banished from the Angels."

"It shouldn't be that way," Selena muttered under her breath.

"Look, guys," Arielle said. "We have structure and protocol. I was afraid of this happening—"

"Then go back to working by yourself," Selena cut in. "Do all the prep work yourself, bug the houses, kill the bad guys. You've never needed us, and you still don't, apparently."

"Selena, sit down and listen!" Arielle shouted. She had never risen her voice toward another Angel.

Selena returned to the couch and sat next to Felix, his eyes bulging as they remained fixed on their leader.

"It's go time," Arielle said, sliding over to stand directly in front of them. "I'm not playing games with either of you. There are a lot of moving parts I need to consider when planning out missions and how to best approach them. I don't have time right now to go over all the little details. We can do that after. I've learned from thousands of these missions and witnessing firsthand what can go wrong. Again, I don't have time to go over the errors I've made in the past. I just need you both to trust that I know what I'm doing. Are we on the same page?"

Felix was the first to nod, and Selena reluctantly gave in a few seconds later.

"Okay, thank you," Arielle said. "Now Felix, you will be at the warehouse tomorrow. You're going to have a boring day, so come to terms with that now. Bring a book. I need you to head there first thing in the morning. The past won't understand your presence there so early in the day, so don't plan on encountering any resistance. You should be able to show up, park among the other vehicles, and hang out all day. I only want you there as a last resort. If things go our way, Selena and I will be there as well. If you don't see us, then you'll need to take the shot. I've circled a perfect hiding place on this map."

Arielle shuffled into the kitchen where she kept the duffel bag, rummaged for her binder, and pulled out a printed map of the area surrounding the warehouse. She tossed it on Felix's lap, and he looked down like it was an ancient scroll.

"Selena. You're going to Nate's house in the morning and will wait along the main road as you've been doing. I'm going to Mason's house and will follow him all day again. Once you see us arrive—I'll leave about a hundred yards between us—follow us down the side road where you and I will pull off to hide. We know where the cameras are now, so we can avoid them. I want you there in case we get caught. Your presence can be a simple explanation, since Mason invited you at one point. I can be your friend you wanted to bring along. This might seem silly, but it *will* work. From there, we will figure out how to proceed. We may try to enter the house, or we might wait outside."

"So you might shoot Nate at his house?" Felix asked.

"Not likely. Way too many people there to try that and expect to outrun them all. Besides, we still need that visual confirmation that Nate is who enters his car and drives to the warehouse. Just another detail we need to confirm before stopping anything."

"And if it's someone else?" Selena asked.

"Then we follow them and still carry out the mission."

"Then why bother? Can't we just blast whoever sits in that car first?"

"Never leave a detail untouched," Arielle said. "We'll stop whoever carries out this murder, regardless of who it is. But we need to make sure our notes and story are all correct. Remember, we have teams that look into the missions long after the fact. If it were to come out later that we stopped the wrong person, that could get very messy for all of us. Possible expulsion from the Angels. You should never act on a whim in these missions."

Felix nodded. "Okay," he said. "I feel better about all this. Still hoping I don't need to pull that trigger tomorrow night."

Arielle shrugged. "Get that out of your head. You need to imagine that you *will* do it. Mentally put yourself in that scenario. Listen to the sounds around you, breathe in the air, feel the rifle in your hands. If you don't do this sort of mental prep, you're doomed to collapse under pressure when the time arises. And I am not trying to do this mission again."

A failed mission would be disastrous. While they could start over, the past pushed back much harder on a second attempt, often making it impossible to change anything. The past, in all its wisdom and glory, strongly believed in the old *Fool me once* proverb.

"So we're good?" Arielle asked.

"As good as can be, I suppose," Felix said.

Selena stared distantly at the wall.

"Selena?" Arielle said.

"We're good."

"Okay, let's call it a night," Arielle said. "Tomorrow will be plenty eventful."

They parted for their rooms in what would be their last night in the house.

Chapter 35

Mason Gregory left his house Friday morning with no idea about the long night that awaited. Perhaps the human soul detected dangers beyond the brain's comprehension. His body felt sick all over, despite having no actual symptoms. After he kissed his wife and kids on the way out, a monsoon of sensations flooded him. He was hungry (he hadn't eaten a complete meal in three days), but also entirely full. He felt both cold and hot. His legs and arms trembled beyond his control. As he drove to work, he swore the car ran on autopilot. He spent the first hour at his desk wondering how he had safely arrived. He couldn't recall putting the key in the ignition or driving on the highway. It was like he had teleported to his desk.

It was a hot summer Friday—scorching, in fact—when he stepped outside of the office building at five o'clock. He released the top button of his collared shirt, its grasp around his neck suffocating. Part of him had expected to be hauled off to prison today. That didn't happen. He still planned to speak with Nate, and while he drove straight to Nate's house after work, a deep worry brewed within his subconscious, wondering if he'd actually survive the night.

I'll still tell him about Selena. If he gets really upset and wants that parting gift, it won't be hard to get her over for the poker game next week.

He mulled over this, but deep down he knew he'd never be able to contribute to a kidnapping. He had mentally checked out of his role with the trafficking ring and wanted nothing further to do with them. Tonight would be the last time ever he saw Nathan Baldwin. He hoped.

His palms sweated as he clutched the steering wheel. Beads formed around his crown. He had survived the day without so much as an encounter with his boss.

He didn't *want* Brian to check on him, but he also wanted to believe his new pay raise might shift their relationship to a more bearable level. As he had learned plenty of times in corporate America, the idea of a company truly caring for its employees was as common as stepping in unicorn shit.

The drive across town, which still felt surreal to him, dragged forever. Traffic was slightly heavier than usual, common for a Friday evening when most workers wasted no time leaving their offices at five sharp to get a start on the weekend. He passed plenty of bars on his way to the highway, many of them with lines out the door, and the outdoor patios jam-packed.

How he wished he had a normal life to do something like that.

He couldn't recall the last time he went out with co-workers for a drink after a long day. It hadn't happened once during his time at CreditConnect. Rusty had made it clear he was to avoid social interactions with any of his colleagues. Workplace friends only increased the odds of his little scheme being noticed. Too many times, those same friends could turn into enemies, and that's when probing into another's work began. A disgruntled colleague was more likely to find out Mason's dirty deeds than management. And if not for the upcoming audit, that logic had proven true over the course of two years. He made zero relationships with those in his office. His colleagues avoided eye contact when passing him in the hall, and had developed the ability to walk right past him as if he didn't exist. Not so much as a grin or subtle head nod to acknowledge him.

Mason expected this of upper management, but grew delighted once colleagues treated him the same way. It meant he closed off any potential relationships from flourishing. No one at the office *hated* him, but they understood he wanted to be left alone.

He came in, did his work, and went home. A typical worker bee that punched in and punched out right on schedule. An ideal employee in the eyes of management. An invisible presence to those in the surrounding cubicles.

None of that mattered as he exited the highway and started his drive through the mountains. His fate waited less than two miles away. It would be hard to get Nate alone, but he hoped to portray a sense of urgency. Their leader was always swarmed by those on his team.

"Can I have a word with you in private?" Mason rehearsed, staring at himself in the rear-view mirror. "Can I have a word with you? In private?" he practiced again, softening his tone. He hoped his calm would rub off on Nate.

His mouth pooled with saliva as he turned off the small highway and onto the private dirt road. The bumps seemed exaggerated as his Civic cruised along, bobbing up and down on the uneven road.

"I can do this. I can walk away from this all and live a normal life. I will get my raise at work and can take the kids to Disneyland with it. I don't need this blood money anymore."

His eyes kept jumping from the rearview and back to the road. He wished he had a mirror to speak in front of. It was a trick he had learned in high school, and one he had used in his professional career. Before any presentation or speech, he'd lock himself in the bathroom and rehearse the entire piece. He didn't know how well that might work. Hell, he didn't even know exactly what he wanted to say to Nate, but wanted to maintain a cool tone.

"Hi, Nate. How's it going?" Mason chuckled, practicing his response to whatever Nate might respond. "Oh, that's good. Can I have a word with you in private?"

Mason shook his head. "Fuck!" It all sounded fake leaving his lips, and he feared the nerves had become too strong. How was Nate supposed to take him seriously if he couldn't even *sound* serious?

He rolled down the window, needing fresh air, not giving a shit about the flying dirt from the road that would soon make its way into the car.

Within a minute, he reached Nate's house, vehicles already lined up and filling the driveway. He parked behind the first car he saw and killed the engine, leaning his head onto the steering wheel to draw in a deep breath.

"Change your life," he whispered. "It's your life, and no one else can control it. You just want out. That's all. He'll understand."

Mason nodded, balling a fist and punching the dashboard. His adrenaline had reached a tipping point, and he needed to let some out.

He stepped out of the car and closed the door, catching his full reflection in the backseat window. Having rarely looked at himself, he wondered when he had aged so much. His five o'clock shadow was peppered with gray. Bags hung under his eyelids, and pimples had sprouted across his cheeks.

I'm in bad shape, he thought, figuring at least some of it had to do with the complete lack of sleep and food over the past couple of days. He didn't feel as tired as he looked, and decided that Nate would take him seriously based on his appearance, no matter how rehearsed his words ended up sounding. He had the look of a man battered by emotional distress.

Mason gulped before turning away from his car and trudging up the driveway. His shoes crunched on the gravel. Birds sung their final evening tunes from high in the surrounding evergreens. But Mason heard none of it. He could only focus on putting one foot in front of the other as he marched to Nate's front door.

The growing commotion of chatter grew louder once he reached the door. Judging by the amount of cars in the driveway, there were already a dozen people inside, drinking and eating to celebrate the end of another week, and the beginning of a new weekend with lots of money to make.

Mason knocked on the door and waited, oblivious to the car pulling up and parking behind his own.

Chapter 36

"He's in," Arielle said.

"What now?" Selena asked.

They parked right behind Mason's Civic, and immediately exited the car, hiding in the confinement of the surrounding woods. They were about one hundred feet away from the house, and both studied the front door through a pair of binoculars.

"Think we can get in there?" Arielle asked.

"What the hell for?!" Selena asked, Arielle waving her hand to hush her.

"Quiet. Someone might hear us."

They both spun around at the sound of an approaching vehicle further down the road. The car parked behind theirs, and a man stepped out wearing a shiny leather jacket, tattoos covering his neck.

"Henry Freeman," Arielle whispered, recognizing the face from the file they had received last week. "I think he does a lot of the questionable business on the streets."

"Why are we dealing with these people?" Selena asked.

Arielle didn't answer, instead focusing on the man entering the house. The door swung inward, and he disappeared inside. She wanted to know if Nate answered his own door during these gatherings, but could never tell from their angle. They had eyes on the cameras and discovered a couple more on the front of the garage that overlooked the front entrance.

"I think if we wait for nightfall, we can sneak in around the back. We'll need a clearer view."

Selena shook her head. Arielle knew this was so far out of her fellow Angel's comfort zone. She was supposed to deal with people in the days before a tragedy, not be thrust into the middle of a dangerous scenario on the night of. In fact, Selena rarely stuck around for the night of the interjection, her work finished well before then. She would hop around from mission to mission, gaining information and developing trust with those involved before disappearing from their lives as quickly as she had arrived.

"But why?" she asked, desperation dripping from her in a *please-don't-make-me-go-in-there* tone. "We can get involved out here. Wait by their cars. Follow them. We have no reason to go in there."

"I'm not saying we kick in the front door for some grand entrance. We can *sneak* in. Snoop around. Imagine listening to the conversations."

"There have to be cameras around back. This place is protected like the White House. Why would he have cameras only in some spots? You saw how fast someone came out last time. Another reason to worry—they might be on high alert this week."

Arielle hadn't considered that. From these people's point of view, someone had snooped around the party only six days ago and got away. With so much at stake, Nate wouldn't spare an expense to ensure his mansion remained safe, his secret concealed.

"You might be right," Arielle said. "We're stuck here until dark. I still say we entertain the thought. In the report, they mentioned there might be girls trapped in the basement. If we can save more lives, then we should. I can't stand the thought of innocent women terrified for their lives down there."

"You're just mentioning this now?"

Arielle shrugged. "It's not part of the mission, but if we can help, then why not? I wish I could say us killing Nate would set them free, but the rest of his crew might have specific plans in place should such a thing happen. Most likely, in fact, and the absolute last thing they'd want are their prisoners to be discovered in the basement."

"Is this why you won't tell us the plans for tonight? Because we would want to help them?"

"No, I'm not telling you in order to keep you alive, and I intend to keep it that way."

* * *

Across town, Felix sat in his car. He had read Michael Crichton's newest book, *Sphere*, to pass the time since he had arrived at eight o'clock in the morning. He had walked over to the sandwich shop a half-mile away where many of the employees from the warehouse enjoyed their midday meal, and took a cold Italian back to his car.

Felix had done a lot of dull work in his time with the Angels, but none of it compared to the torture of sitting in his car for the past nine hours, knowing he still had four more before anything happened. If it did.

He looked into the backseat and saw the blanket draped over the rifle Arielle insisted he bring. Felix spent a couple of hours in the afternoon visualizing the night's events. He wanted to stroll over to the area on the map Arielle had marked for him, but she had given strict instruction to not venture that way until the parking lot had cleared. People might have seen him wandering the area, and that was the last thing they needed if a murder were to occur later.

Felix thought he would have been better utilized bugging Mason's car during the day, or even working on a way to circumvent the cameras at Nate's house, but it became plenty clear Arielle knew exactly what she wanted to happen. By the minute.

"Plan for a late dinner tonight," she had told Felix before they parted ways from the house. "A late dinner in 2022."

He leaned back in his seat and grinned at the thought.

Chapter 37

"Mason, my man!" Nate greeted him, throwing an arm around over his shoulder and pulling him in for a sideways hug. He kept a cigar between his teeth, blowing puffs of smoke toward the ceiling every minute.

Mason found Nate in the dining room where a table had been covered with cheese and fruit platters, and boxes of catered pulled pork and chicken. A typical feast for Nate's weekly gathering.

"How are things?" Nate asked, grabbing another cigar from the counter and offering it to Mason.

Mason waved his hand. "No thanks. Things are good."

"Boy, are they!" Nate cackled. "I know you've seen our numbers from the credit cards. Give us a few more months and you'll be making money you've never dreamed of."

Mason nodded, refusing to show any emotion. He was unable to. He thought he might faint right there on the dining room table. Apparently, Nate was going to pretend their last phone call never happened. Water under the bridge. "Yeah. I've seen. Looks good."

Nate puffed his cigar and craned his neck upward to blow smoke. His eyes returned to Mason and studied him. "Something's the matter with you. Talk to me, Mase. What's on your mind?"

Mason hadn't expected to run into Nate so quickly, let alone be questioned right off the bat. He had budgeted at least twenty minutes to settle in and get mentally ready for the tough conversation.

He looked around for anyone who might have been snooping on their conversation. But the house was too crowded. People were lost in their own discussions. Some shuffled through the dining room to fill their plates, others hovered near the fridge where the beer was kept, and the rest had gathered in the living room where they watched Ozzie Smith and the Cardinals take on Mike Schmidt and the Phillies.

Mason had the exact moment he had wanted.

"C-can we talk in private, Nate?" he asked in a hushed voice. His tone earned a glance from Rusty at the table.

Nate plucked the cigar from his mouth and studied Mason with questioning eyes. "Sure, man. Let's head to my office."

Nate led the way out of the dining room, through the living room, and down a long hallway. They passed three doors before turning into Nate's office, where he closed the door behind them.

The office was a cluttered room with shelves full of books and stacks of paper surrounding a small desk, with more papers spilling over the edges. It reeked of tobacco and marijuana.

"Did something happen at work?" Nate asked, placing his cigar in the ashtray on his desk, leaning against the front of it while Mason stood awkwardly at the door. Putting the cigar down was a sign of concern for someone like Nate. He rarely let a situation change his course of action.

Mason debated telling the truth about the upcoming audit. But that would only lead to more questions. And possibly threats from Nate toward CreditConnect. Threats that could easily become reality.

The audit wasn't the point. He still wanted out.

"Do you ever reflect on your life, Nate?" Mason asked, surprising himself at how calm he sounded. The same couldn't be said for his emotions bouncing all over the walls.

Nate scrunched his face in confusion. "What is this? You have some coming-to-Jesus moment? I sleep at night just fine, if that's what you're getting at."

"No, no. Not you. Me. I've been thinking about *my* life, and what I want from it."

"Are you asking to leave my organization?"

Nate always called his group of criminals an *organization*. He believed he ran a legitimate business, regardless of what society—or the law—had to say.

Mason forced a slow head nod.

"I don't know what you expect me to do," Nate said. "You're kind of a big deal for our operations. Critical, in fact. It's not like you're some street hustler I can replace within the hour."

You sure pay me like one, Mason thought, knowing he'd earn at least a broken jaw if he spoke those words aloud. "I understand that, and I'm willing to hang around to help train whoever you'd like to replace me."

Nate grinned and stood up tall from the desk, tossing his hands in the air. "Well, Mase, we don't exactly let people leave because they feel like it. Sure, I've had some guys with a sick mom or kid who really needed to step away. Those guys leave and never think about us again. But people like you, who want to leave because they think they found their morals." He shook his head. "That's dangerous, you see."

"I just don't want to go any further than I already am," Mason said. "I don't want my family to be at constant risk. I promise you I have no malicious intent for leaving."

Nate chuckled, shaking his head. "That's what they always say, and that's too bad for you. I want to believe you, but I've heard too many horror stories, and been burned too many times in the past. Each time started with a conversation just like this. 'Oh, sorry, Nate, I just want a normal life again.' Then six months later, they're still thinking about how much better they are because of their bullshit morals. And BAM!"

Nate raised his hand and slapped the top of his desk. Pens and paperclips bounced while a couple of sheets of paper fluttered to the floor. "They turn on you. Tell their mutual friends what you do. Tell the police. Then it's *my* problem to figure out how to stay a free man."

"Look, Nate, I understand where you're coming from. But I'm not having some moral objection to our work all of a sudden. I've just been afraid of what happens if we get caught. Any one of us. We're all going down if that happens, and it's not fair to my family. I just want life to be a little more . . . secure."

Nate laughed through his nose and elevated his hands wide apart above his head. "This is as safe as it gets. This house isn't registered on any government document. We are literally off the grid. No one knows about this place except for the people who need to. Do you think I would really expand our business to use credit cards on a whim? Buddy, I've grown. I have people on my payroll for the lone reason of protecting all of us. Lawyers, district attorneys, judges. Why do you think I've been slow to pay you? These guys ain't cheap, but they're worth it in the long run."

"Are you serious? Judges?"

A wide grin took over Nate. "Oh yeah. This is America, man. Land of the greedy, home of the hustlers. Anything in this country can be bought. *Anything.* Sometimes you just need to ask the price."

"Well, then," Mason said. "What's your price?"

Nate's eyelids fluttered as he stared down Mason. "Excuse me?"

"You just said you can buy *anything.* I want to buy my freedom back. What will it cost?"

Confusion gave way to another smile for Nate. "I'm impressed, Mase. You have a hustler's mentality. That's why I'm not setting a price. Not yet. I need to think about it. But I also want *you* to think about it. We're on the verge of big money. Shit, we have the big money already. I just need to pay off these fools and we'll get to pave our own road. Made of gold. Think about what you really want. You and your family will be safe if you stick with me."

"I have a girl," Mason said abruptly.

"I know . . . and a boy, yes?"

"I'm not talking about my kids. I have a girl, and I can get her right in this house if you want her. She's a knockout. A stone cold ten in any book. She's a Killer Whale."

Nate liked to use a ranking system for the girls. It was all based on their earning potential. Puppies were the everyday girls who earned anywhere from twenty-five to one hundred dollars per night. Horses earned around three hundred per night, but usually only worked on weekends. Whales brought in one thousand per night. And Killer Whales could net five thousand dollars or more for one session. So far, Nate had one Whale, and was still on the hunt for his first Killer.

"You sure about that?" Nate asked. "What do you even know about our rankings? It's a lot more than looks."

"I understand. This girl is physically perfect. And her personality matches. She's sweet and gentle, but I get the sense she can lay down the law, if needed. She's everything you'd want in a Killer."

"You got a picture? How can you get her here?"

"No picture. I've only met her once. She finished college and said she's been looking to play in a poker game. Also, she needs money."

Nate pursed his lips and stroked his chin, fumbling with a match to relight his cigar. The mood had shifted for the better, and Mason tasted freedom on the horizon. "And you think she'd be interested? I'm not looking to kidnap some random girl. We don't play that shit anymore."

Mason shrugged. "She sounded desperate for money. No local family. Works multiple jobs. I think she's a prime candidate. And you're the right guy to convince her."

He hadn't meant to stroke Nate's ego, but it seemed to benefit him. The leader of the trafficking ring paced around his desk, cigar fully lit, and faced the wall, turning his back on Mason.

"I'll admit, this is an interesting offer. Are you sure you really want to leave this all behind?"

Mason grew uneasy. Speaking to someone's back was something he couldn't recall having done before. It was odd. Intimidating.

"Yes. I've gone back and forth all week. Ultimately, I decided this is what I want. I understand what I'm walking away from, but I'm thinking long-term. This is the best decision for my family."

Nate nodded slowly, cigar smoke gradually filling the room to create a light haze. "Tell you what. I'll take you up on the offer. Let's meet later tonight. Do you know the warehouses off 40?"

"Yes."

"Meet me at the parking lot outside of the Big Z Home Office warehouse around nine o'clock."

"Tonight?"

"Tonight."

"What about everyone here? We can't just leave."

"They'll be fine. I'm going to give you a generous parting gift, but I can't do it near everyone else here. Have you ever held a briefcase full of cash?"

Mason felt his face flush. This all sounded too good to be true. Not only was Nate open to the idea of him leaving, but he was going to pay a severance package, too? "Can't say I have."

"They're heavier than you think. And I can't just have you lugging it around here. You didn't arrive with a briefcase, and someone will definitely notice. Our guys pay attention to these things."

Mason wanted to ask why they were driving so far. They could have just gone out to the main road and met at a gas station. He didn't want to press the matter—money was on its way, after all. If he needed to drive to Vancouver to pick it up, then that's what he'd do.

"Okay. I'll meet you there."

"Leave here around 8:30. I'll leave at 8:45. Don't tell anyone where we're going, or even that we're meeting. If any of these guys found out what I'm doing for you, all hell would break loose around here." Nate finally turned around, his cigar a small stump between his fingers. "You're a good man, Mason. It's a shame you're leaving."

Chapter 38

"We need to get back to the cars," Arielle said. She checked her watch to find a time of 8:22. "They're going to leave any minute now. I'll follow Mason. You wait around and follow whoever leaves after him."

"Is the car here?" Selena asked. "The one the killer drives?"

"Haven't seen it, but if it's Nathan's, it's probably in the garage."

They had made their way to the opposite side of the property, remaining in the trees and out of sight from the cameras under a powerful glow from the night's full moon. Arielle really wanted to find a way into the house, but from the rear side, they saw through the kitchen window where people kept walking in and out. Some even stepped outside onto the back patio for a quick cigarette break. They stared toward Arielle and Selena, oblivious the two women were there, just waiting to pounce.

Arielle led the way back to their cars, tracing back their earlier steps. Having grown up in Colorado, she'd heard plenty of stories of mountain lions attacking people in the middle of the night. She feared little in this world, especially with her pistol by her side, but something about a wild mountain cat kept her on edge as they navigated the dark woods.

Their shoes crunched on the rocks and twigs, the sound exaggerated amid the silence. But they were far enough from the house to garner any attention. Even if they did, it wouldn't end well if one of them ventured into the woods to confront the Angels.

They reached the cars a couple minutes later, crouching next to the passenger side of Arielle's, staying out of sight from the main road. Mason's car remained in front of theirs.

"I still think we should intervene right now," Selena said. "What if he comes out by himself?"

"If that happens, I'll consider it. But we need to stay hidden."

"How do you think Felix is doing?"

"I'm sure he's fine. He's in a much safer place than us."

Arielle sensed the angst in Selena's voice. Despite all the preparation that went into these missions, it was impossible to avoid the emotional jitters on the day of the big showdown. One mistake could throw all the hard work down the drain. One misstep could result in death. But just as equally, one well-executed plan could change the world for the better. It was a twisted seesaw of good and evil.

"Someone's coming," Arielle whispered, crouching lower. "Stay still."

She had heard the chatter of voices from around the garage, and listened as steady footsteps made their way down the driveway.

Arielle craned her neck enough to make out the figure walking their way and knew it was Mason Gregory. She had watched him enough over the past two weeks to recognize his silhouette against the floodlights pouring from the garage. She turned over her shoulder to Selena behind her. "It's him. He's alone."

She hadn't expected it to be this easy, so Arielle's heart started drumming much quicker. They could grab Mason right now, throw him in the backseat, and drive off. But that still didn't guarantee his survival.

If Mason didn't show, there was no saying what Nate might do for being stood up. The man's life might only be spared for a few extra hours.

These thoughts raced through Arielle's mind as she contemplated her next move. They had a few options to consider, but all required at least having Mason in their possession.

He was fifty feet away when Arielle looked back over her shoulder and nodded. She had no idea if Selena understood that as a cue to make a move right now. At the least, she'd follow her lead.

Once Mason was twenty-five feet away from his car, Arielle stood up, confident the surrounding darkness wouldn't reveal her. She stood in the shadows, watching and waiting. Arielle took one step forward and immediately stopped, collapsing to the ground like she had dropped something important.

"Mason!" a voice shouted from the garage.

Selena remained in her crouched position and helped Arielle get back on her feet.

"Who the hell is that?" Selena whispered.

Mason stopped and turned around. "Rusty? That you?"

"Where you goin', brother?" Rusty called back, trudging down the driveway to meet him.

Arielle couldn't make out his appearance in the night, but could tell he was a tall, skinny man.

"Just calling it an early night," Mason said once Rusty had reached him. They both shuffled toward Mason's car and stopped next to the door.

"Everything alright?" Rusty asked. "You seemed a bit out of sorts today."

"Yeah, everything is wonderful. I'm just tired from work. Been having some long hours at the office. Getting more accounts dumped on me."

"Those fuckers. No one ever said the work was glorious, but you're about to get paid for your efforts. It'll all be worth it in no time."

"I sure hope."

"Alright, amigo, I'll let you get back to it. See you next week."

"See you then."

Mason entered his car and closed the door as Rusty walked away.

"Dammit," Arielle snarled. "Too good to be true."

The engine in front of them fired up, the headlights flashing on.

"We can still try," Selena said.

Arielle rocked her head. "Not while he's in the car. Too dangerous. And he'd be able to honk the horn to get attention. I'll follow. You wait here and follow Nate."

Selena took the instruction in stride and shuffled backwards to be next to her car. Mason had already turned his car around and was on his way down the dirt road.

Arielle dashed around and jumped into her driver's seat, jamming the key into the ignition in one swift motion. Mason had already turned around the curve, which was fine. Arielle kept her headlights off, the moon providing just enough light to see safely.

"You know where he's going. No need to drive like a maniac," she told herself. She often had to recite this reminder because she loved driving fast. Racing lessons were her absolute favorite from her early days of training with the Angel Runners. Driving fast was second nature, a skill she had used plenty of times in the past, but unnecessary in the current moment.

She cleared her mind as she tailed Mason, but more importantly, cleared her soul. Perhaps the biggest advantage Arielle had over her peers was her understanding of time and the universe.

The universe was omniscient. All living creatures were bound to its rules.

We all come from the dirt of this planet Earth, she recalled a philosophy teacher explaining once. *We all return to the dirt at the end of our lives. There has never been an exception to this rule. The Earth floats in the universe, bound by the rules of gravity and physics. Because of this, the universe knows exactly where the Earth will be at any given time. It knows where the moon will be, the precise axis it will be tilted. It even knows when disasters will strike. The universe gives us life. It takes life. The universe understands its living creatures to their very core. And that includes us. There have been plenty of people in our existence who have spoken of being one with nature. Sensing a shift in the world. These people have a unique gift. They can speak the language of the universe, even if not completely fluent. The universe knows what we will do, even before we do it.*

It was this last line that lingered with Arielle for many years since college. A line that has proven itself true over and over. It provided her with an understanding of how to deal with and manage time. No one could master time, as it was part of the grand universe. But they could understand it enough to anticipate its next moves.

That's exactly what she did on her missions. The hardest part of her job—and the thing that made her unlike anyone else in the organization—wasn't her ability to fight, drive, or shoot guns. It was her ability to remove her inner soul's ambitions.

The universe, via time, couldn't put up roadblocks if it didn't know what she had planned. Through all the preparation and reading about her missions and subjects, she had to force the information into her brain while keeping a neutral heart. It was like keeping a secret from the universe. A secret she would later use against time.

She often dropped into recruit training camps to offer words of wisdom. "The universe is the core of existence," she liked to say. "Every living thing, from us humans, to the trees, to the little ants on the sidewalk, are all extensions of the universe. Time is an extension of the universe. Understand this basic principle and you will go far."

Her words always motivated, but she felt no one truly understood her message. It was far from a simple concept to understand, let alone implement. It wasn't something that could be taught. She thought of it more as a sixth sense than anything. She wanted to teach her new teammates about this understanding of the universe. They would need to grasp it if they were to work together long-term. But she couldn't do it ahead of time. Her soul was clear, her mind focused on the task at hand.

Arielle could cheat the past, but she was not immune to its foolery. The bigger the mission, the harder the resistance. For everyday missions like this one, she just might cheat time once more. As far as the universe knew, she was just a girl driving on the highway late at night. It didn't see her as a threat to interject with its plans to kill Mason tonight.

They finally reached the highway, and she grinned as they sped up.

Chapter 39

Just before nine o'clock, Selena watched the garage door creak open, more bright light spilling across the driveway. From her location she could see three sports cars inside, and one black Camaro clearly from the Sixties.

She licked her lips as she watched, legs clenched with anticipation, palms clammy with sweat. It was impossible to get a clear look inside the garage. Doing so would have left her standing in the open, directly between the cameras.

But she saw shadows moving within the light. Tall shadows that stretched twenty feet across the ground.

"Two people?" she whispered, craning her neck over the hood of her car. There had never been a mention of multiple people in any of their reports.

The shadows remained for a couple of minutes, swaying as they clearly carried on a conversation. One shadow disappeared, then the headlights on the Camaro flicked on, the engine roaring into the silent night. The car crept carefully out of the garage, turning wide and slow to avoid hitting any of the cars parked in the surrounding roundabout.

Selena opened her car's passenger door and climbed over to the driver's seat. The Camaro sped away, leaving a long trail of dust that bent around the corner.

"Shit!" Selena gasped, fidgeting with the keys, and eventually dropping them into the dark pit near her feet. "Gah!"

She patted around the floor until finding the keys, drawing a deep breath before guiding the car key into the ignition. *Slow down,* she thought. *The past is going to start fighting.*

Selena got the engine turned on, only to battle with the stick shift. It was stuck in park and wouldn't budge. "What the *fuck?!*" She put all of her force into it, and it finally gave way, dropping straight into drive, where she made a quick U-turn to get on the dirt road.

She wondered what Nate told his guests before leaving. Probably a blanket statement like *I have a quick errand to run. Be back in thirty.* Or her favorite line her dad used to say all the time: *I have business in town. Food is in the fridge. Don't know what time I'll be back.*

She never knew if he really had business, or if that was his cover to meet women during those summer nights in Paris.

Selena floored the accelerator, the Camaro already out of sight on the dirt road ahead. Her car had no business driving at high speeds, and she could only pray a deer wouldn't wander into the middle of the road, as it had done last weekend.

None did, and when she approached the highway a minute later, she saw the Camaro just turning onto it.

Selena had to slam on her brakes just before turning onto the highway, catching the slightest glimpse of a reflector from a cyclist zooming down the street.

"Are you kidding me?!" she shouted. "Who the hell rides their bike in the middle of the night?!"

She gripped the steering wheel tighter, knuckles whitening as her body clenched with frustration. Selena rarely dealt with resistance from the past. Tonight, however, was a different story. She hadn't quite realized all the minor nuances occurring directly resulted from the past pushing back against her. The past sensed her main objective to stop the murder of Mason Gregory, and was throwing out obstacles left and right.

She had only ever heard about the chaos that ensued right before the end of a mission, and now, witnessing it firsthand, she felt completely helpless. And clueless as to how to work around it.

When the bicyclist passed, she had to wait for a semi-truck to steamroll past her.

"Of course!" she grunted, turning onto the highway where she'd remain stuck behind the semi for the next few minutes. The truck belonged to City Supermarket, a regional chain of grocery stores. The trailer's doors had a cartoon banana smiling and giving a thumbs up, next to the words: *Serving the Rocky Mountains since 1947. Count on us!*

The banana and its oversized, cartoonish eyes wouldn't stop staring at Selena.

Creepy-ass fruit!

Selena giggled, briefly wondering if she was losing her mind. She weaved into the opposite lane for a view ahead, but couldn't see in the darkness. These small mountain highways had no street lights, and she knew better than to chance racing around the semi. The road could curve without warning and send her tumbling into a ditch.

Much to her increasing frustration, the semi was driving exactly the speed limit, if not a tad slower. Her left leg bounced as she rode the truck's bumper.

"C'mon, c'mon!" she screamed.

The highway was only one lane, and she remained stuck behind the truck for another seven minutes until they reached the interstate where she could finally get around it and speed up.

The Camaro was long gone. Selena gunned the accelerator, the car's measly engine whining as it flew down the interstate. Traffic was nearly non-existent heading northbound.

Five minutes later, she exited and blazed down the road that led to the warehouse. The only positive out of this drive was that she hadn't seen Arielle anywhere along the way, trusting she had reached their destination safely and on time.

The clock on the radio showed the time was 9:13, leaving less than twenty minutes until the murder. She hadn't achieved a single thing to slow it from happening, watching helplessly as the Camaro gained a head start and never looked back.

Selena pressed down on the accelerator until it touched the floor.

I really hope Arielle and Felix are okay.

Chapter 40

Arielle parked in the lot nearest the warehouse, around the corner and out of sight from Mason. She saw Felix's car parked nearby and him not in it, meaning he had made his way to the spot she marked for him on the map.

Arielle stepped out of her car and tiptoed toward the corner of the building, peering around the edge, hidden in the shadows. She watched Mason's car sitting idle, the parking lights turned on while the engine ran.

Roughly seventy-five feet separated her from Mason's car. She already knew which way the Camaro would pull up from, and could clearly see the light illuminating a ten-foot radius, enough to cover Mason's car and the Camaro once it arrived.

Dressed in black, Arielle could get fairly close, possibly even hide behind the rear of one vehicle once the two men stepped out to have their conversation. They would speak for five minutes before Mason returned to his car. She could step in at any point.

Arielle had put on a utility belt equipped with everything she needed: pistol, baton, flashbangs, pepper spray, and three throwing knives. When dealing with the past, she couldn't solely rely on a single weapon. A gun could jam, the pepper spray could malfunction. She'd even heard stories of batons snapping in half upon initial impact.

The throwing knives were the ace up her sleeve. They were virtually foolproof against the past. They had no mechanical flaws that could be exploited. All Arielle needed was her precision and a powerful throw to make them lethal. She could hit a target from fifty yards away about half the time. She rarely missed under twenty-five yards.

Where she stood was already within her comfort range, but the closer she could get only increased the chances of everything going right.

Arielle stepped away from the building, taking one slow step at a time. She moved in a stealthy crouched position, ready to turn and run if needed. She remained in the shadows, and would for as long as possible. The parking lot had smooth pavement, no crunching steps as she placed her foot down with the gentleness of a cat walking on carpet.

She continued toward the idle car, stopping ten feet away from the outer edge of the light. The Camaro's headlights could easily expose her, but she'd navigate around Mason's car to stay out of their path.

Arielle saw Mason through his windows. He sat forward, drumming his hands on the steering wheel, bobbing his head to the tune of whatever song he had playing on the radio. After having watched him extensively for the past two weeks, this moment caught up to her. Despite what they learned about his involvement with the sex trafficking ring, she saw a man who loved his wife and kids. She didn't know what happened inside his office building, but he punched in and out every day, going through the slog of life to provide for his family. She suspected his involvement with the ring was financially motivated. Even from afar, Mason Gregory seemed a genuine, well-intentioned man. Sometimes good people found themselves in bad situations, and Arielle could only hope their work on this mission would help put Mason back on the right path.

Headlights appeared from the nearby road, zooming toward the lot. It was the Camaro, and Arielle promptly shuffled to position herself more behind Mason's car. Mason killed his engine and turned off the lights, adding to the darkness.

They both waited for the Camaro to park in front of Mason, where it eventually did, cutting its loud engine before it drew any attention.

The doors of both cars opened, Mason stepping out first.

Arielle felt her legs tense. Through it all, this moment in any mission still caused her great anxiety. Her hand subconsciously shot down to her pistol in the holster, gripping the handle.

The Camaro door swung open, and out stepped a tall, skinny man.

"Rusty?!" Mason asked. "What the hell are you doing here? Why are you driving Nate's car?"

Arielle heard the panic in Mason's voice. It was clear he sensed something wrong. She felt it, too. Death was thick in the air, an invisible sensation she had learned to recognize from the day she climbed over her dead family in the mall.

"Hey, Mason, brother. How's it going?"

"I . . . uh. What the hell is going on? We just talked before I left."

"I know. Nate chatted with me right after that. Said you're thinking about leaving us behind." Mason took a step back toward his car, his hand reaching out for the handle. Rusty tossed up his hands. "Easy, brother—I'm just here to talk."

"Why didn't you just talk to me over there?"

"Nate said you'd be here. Told me about the deal he worked out with you. I guess he wanted me to find out how serious you were. Said you have a girl he might be interested in."

Arielle frowned as she stepped left to see around Mason's car. *Who the hell are they talking about?*

She could hear every word of the conversation clearly and wouldn't move an inch. She could take down Rusty with ease from this distance.

"Well, yeah. She's real. Did he think I was making this all up?"

Rusty shrugged. "Not my job to figure out what the boss thinks. When can you get her to us?"

"Wait. Do you have the money?"

Rusty reached into his shirt pocket and pulled out a pack of cigarettes, then sat on the hood of the Camaro. "Want one?"

"Sure," Mason replied quickly, reaching out a hand to grab the cigarette. He leaned toward Rusty to let him light it.

"Have a seat. I'm just here to talk. You're acting too strange."

"Talk about *what?* You and I have nothing to discuss."

"Dammit, Mason, I'm trying to help you. Will you just relax?" Rusty chuckled before taking a long drag, Arielle able to see the orange tip of the cigarette. He blew clouds of smoke into the night sky.

Mason nodded. "Sorry. I've been on edge all week about this."

"I understand. We've probably all gone through similar thoughts, but what can you do about it?"

"Well, I'm leaving. That's what I'm doing about it."

"Sure. But can you really ever leave this life behind? You'll see us, hear about us. We're going to be millionaires. All of us. At some point, you'll realize it was a mistake and want back in."

"Are you supposed to be some sort of last resort?" Mason asked. "Nate sends my closest friend to make this sales pitch so I'll stay? Seems desperate. I understand my value with the credit cards, but I'm sure you guys can find someone to replace me."

"Oh, we will. That's not the point. We can do that, but it's a hassle. Why not just stay on? What's *really* pulling you away?"

"I already explained myself to Nate. Can't you just give me the money and let me move on with my life?"

"That's not what I came to do. I have orders."

"Listen to yourself. You have orders? Is this the military?"

"Look, brother. I grew up with nothing. Lived in a trailer park with my parents and five siblings. That's a lot of nights sleeping on the floor. I came into this opportunity and I'll be damned if I mess it up. I'm just here doing my job. That is all."

"I thought you were my friend."

"You are. But you don't pay my bills. I gotta do what Nate asks."

"Fine. Let's cut through the bullshit, then. There's nothing you can say to convince me to stay. I want out of this life. I'm not going to snitch on you guys. I just want a normal job, and to spend Friday nights at home. That's all there is to it. Can you please pass over the money and be done with it? I'll arrange for the Selena girl to be at the mansion next Friday."

Hearing Selena's name caught Arielle off guard. Maybe Mason was a monster, after all.

"Okay," Rusty said. "Suit yourself. I need to call Nate real quick and confirm he still wants to give you the money."

Mason sighed and threw his hands up. "Are you kidding me?"

"Not at all, brother. I'll be right back—he has one of those fancy phones in his car, so I'll just be a second."

Arielle watched as Rusty turned away and sat back down in the Camaro. She had no idea if the car really had a phone, or if he just said that as an excuse to grab his gun. All she knew was that the next time he appeared, he'd have every intent on shooting Mason Gregory in the head.

Mason remained on the hood of his car for another minute, arms crossed as he stared at the Camaro. He finally gave up, flicked his cigarette butt into the darkness, and returned behind the wheel, never turning the car back on.

Arielle considered causing a distraction. Maybe throwing a rock at Mason's car to get him back outside. But that wouldn't guarantee anything.

Instead, she waited two long minutes before the Camaro's door swung open again. Rusty appeared, no gun in hand. She raised her pistol and waited for Rusty to come around toward Mason, who had just rolled down his window.

"Sorry, brother," Rusty said, his arms twitching. "Nate isn't too happy with you and doesn't want to give you the money."

"Are you kid—"

Arielle pulled the trigger, a slug blasting through Rusty's back and chest. He looked down, blood already forming a dark splotch on his shirt. Rusty clasped his hands over his chest and looked at Mason with bulging eyes. Mason had an equally shocked expression and flailed his hands to open the car door.

"What the fuck?!" he shouted, catching Rusty as he collapsed, easing him toward the ground. Mason spun around, looking everywhere, but was too panicked to let his eyes focus on the woman standing in the shadows.

Arielle stepped forward, no longer concealing her footsteps, entering the glow from the above light.

Mason recoiled when he saw her, backing away from Rusty until he bumped into his car. "Wh-who are you?" he asked between heaves for breath.

"This man was going to kill you," Arielle said, nodding at Rusty's dead body. "He has a gun in his pants. Nate sent him here to kill you."

"Who are you? How do you know this?"

"I guess you can call me a guardian angel. We'll take care of Rusty's body. It'll never be found, and because of that, Nate will leave you alone. He'll know better than to mess with you. Just promise to live a clean life."

Mason nodded, still gasping for air, as the panic had surely taken over all his senses.

"I will."

"Get out of here and don't speak of this night to anyone." Arielle spoke in a threatening tone meant to intimidate, and it worked.

Mason scrambled to his feet and climbed into his car, refusing to break eye contact while turning on the car, fastening his seat belt, and driving away. He drove much faster than she had witnessed over the past two weeks, but seeing his tail lights disappear gave her the sense of accomplishment that always came at the end of a mission.

Applause echoed from the distance, followed by a cheerful whistle. "You go, Arielle!"

It was Selena.

Arielle looked into the void, and after a few seconds saw two figures moving through the dark.

"That was the most impressive thing I've ever seen," Felix said. "How did you do that?"

"Do what?" Arielle couldn't help but smile. She had never performed in front of a live audience before, and the instant praise was gratifying.

"All of it. I was out there in the trees trying to not throw up, and you just creep right up to these guys. Hiding like a ninja."

"And then your patience," Selena said. They all stood under the light, grins wide across each of their faces. "I would have shot him right when he stepped out of the car. But you waited so long. And how the hell did you not get any resistance from the past? It almost took me half an hour to get here because shit kept happening. Barely made it in time to see the show."

Arielle laughed, her body relieved to release the nerves and tension that had built up over the day. "I have a lot to teach you guys. We should get out of here, though. Let's call HQ and tell them to send the clean-up crew." The Road Runners had a team called Housekeeping, and their job was to visit the site after a mission and erase all evidence from existence. "Have them leave the Camaro. That way, the police will find it and trace it all back to Nate. That should be enough to help them bring down the trafficking ring."

"Do you think Mason will be safe?" Selena asked.

"He will be. I told him that once Nate realizes Rusty is missing and never coming back, he won't bother him. I know these types of guys—it's pretty much who I always hunt down. They don't clash with people they consider on their same level. And if it looks like Mason killed the man sent to kill him, *and* made his body disappear . . . he won't hear a peep from Nate. No doubt about it."

Felix wandered toward Rusty's dead body and stood over it, looking down and shaking his head. "I still can't believe it was Rusty this entire time."

Arielle shrugged. "I don't get too surprised any more. Did you know Mason was planning to invite Selena to the poker game next week and offer her to Nate?"

"What?!" Selena gasped.

Arielle nodded. "It's a sick world we live in. Obviously, none of that would have gone according to plan had it played out. But it's safe to say now that Mason won't ever dip his toe into the criminal underworld again. He'll be there for his family, and they won't have to suffer."

"So, what do we do now?" Felix asked, returning to the ladies. Arielle leaned against the lamppost, ready to relax.

"We go to the house and pack, then we go home."

"Such beautiful words have never before been spoken," Selena said, prompting a giddy round of laughter from all three of them. They were slap-happy, delighted to be done with a grueling two-week mission.

"Then it's on to the next mission, right?" Felix said.

"We'll get a couple of days to unwind," Arielle said. "But yes, we'll jump right into preparation for whatever we're doing next. Let's get out of here."

Chapter 41

They had mostly packed before heading out Friday morning, and just had to pick up a couple of things before hitting the road after the mission. They opted to drive to Denver while still in 1988 to avoid the traffic that seemed a constant in 2022. After dropping off Arielle's and Selena's cars at the local rental agency in Pueblo, they all crammed into Felix's car and started the two-hour drive north.

Arielle leaned against the window while they cruised, watching Pueblo disappear. She imagined Housekeeping had already arrived and was preparing to take Rusty Kirk's body into a different year, where they could take their time cremating it and disposing of the ashes.

Another killer off the streets, Arielle thought, still disturbed that Nate lived and continued operating his sex trafficking ring for the time being. Part of her wanted to request a new mission to come back and put him out of business, but she knew that would be shot down. Especially if the Futures Report came back with positive news.

She often forgot just how wide the butterfly effect could spread. Saving Mason and eliminating Rusty could very well have led to Nate's downfall. Not immediately, but eventually.

Once they arrived in Denver, Felix parked at a meter one block away from their future offices and killed the engine. Crime and a massive homeless population still overran downtown in 1988, making it dangerous for anyone to wander the streets in the middle of the night.

"This is it," he said. "Any last errands to run here in 1988 before we head back?"

"Just get me back to my cell phone," Selena said, wasting no time fetching the flask of Juice from her bag. The others followed, and they each raised their flasks before taking the small sip and thinking of their return to the present day.

Within a minute, the world fell dark, and they arrived back in a busy downtown Denver. A warm summer night.

Felix stepped out of the car first and drew in a deep breath. "Missed that modern smog." Arielle and Selena joined him and laughed while they started down the sidewalk in search of a restaurant.

"Look at these beautiful lights!" Selena said, spinning in a circle as she danced down Sixteenth Street mall in downtown Denver. Street lights lined the sidewalks, and music poured out of buildings as the nightlife scene formed. People hurried down the sidewalks while horse-drawn carriages moseyed down the road that was closed to vehicular traffic. The city bustled, and Selena felt right back at home.

"Must have been a Rockies game tonight," Felix said, nodding to a dozen people strolling down the sidewalk in their purple and black attire. "I know we're all starving. Let's go eat."

"Oh, how I've missed it," Selena said. "Look at all these people with a sense of fashion. And they're going to *real* clubs and bars. Not some ghetto hole-in-the-wall."

"Relax, Selena," Arielle said. "You have plenty of time to tear up downtown."

"You have no idea. I'm ready to dance with a man who *knows* how to dance. But first I need a big drink. Maybe you should have one, too, and I can convince you to come out with me."

"Good luck. I'm just ready to crawl into my bed and sleep for two straight days."

"This should do," Felix said, nodding to the restaurant they were approaching. "Mexican sound good?"

"Um, a margarita or four sounds perfect," Selena said. "And they're already dancing!" Her mouth hung open while she led the group into D'Corazon, where half of the restaurant had been transformed into a nightclub for salsa dancing.

Elvis Crespo's voice boomed from the adjoining room while they sat in the dining area and devoured a basket of chips and salsa, margaritas freshly served.

"So, how did you pull it all off?" Selena asked. "I really have to know."

Arielle took a sip from the frozen margarita in front of her and smiled. "It's very complicated, but it's why I didn't want to tell you anything ahead of time. Long story short, the universe knows your intentions. And if you take these missions to heart, it's going to know what you intend to do, and will stop you."

"Are you saying you don't take the missions to heart?" Felix asked, frowning. "I feel like that would come as a surprise if you asked any Road Runner."

"I don't take them to heart. I take them seriously, but they don't consume my soul. I've learned how to separate myself from my work. Kind of like a coroner has to do. We're surrounded by so much doom and death. My God, the whole sex trafficking thing really tried to bother me. I kept thinking about the innocent girls those people were ruining and exploiting. But I couldn't let that be my driving force. Too much emotional investment and you're screwed—my gun would have definitely jammed if I was thinking about those girls."

"So what do you think about?" Felix asked. "Surely you don't just have a blank mind."

Arielle nodded. "I always try for a blank mind, but it's not always possible. I think back to the day I lost my family. The day I survived. It helps keep things in perspective. If I survived that, I can survive anything. Nothing else is really relevant compared to that. At least for me. I'm not even supposed to be here. I'm playing with house money every day."

Selena shook her head. "Don't say things like that, Arielle. That's survivor's guilt talking. You got lucky that day, yes. But you're right where you're supposed to be."

Arielle patted at the tears forming in her eyes.

"Selena's right," Felix said. "You better people's lives. Even if you don't know it. You've turned your tragedy into something beautiful for the world. Because of you, people don't have to suffer through their own grief. The Gregory family won't fall into drugs and addiction. All because of you. I'm sorry you lost your family—I'm not going to pretend I can understand—but you survived. That's the simple fact. You're here, every day, changing lives. I can't speak for Selena, but my life already feels changed after working with you on just this one mission."

Selena nodded in agreement. "It's true."

"Thank you both," Arielle said, her throat tensing with a swell of emotions. "That means a lot. Maybe working together will be good for us all."

Selena grinned. "I'm gonna dare to say it. We just might become friends."

Felix slapped his hands on the table, startling the two women as the silverware and glasses jingled. "Don't say the F-Word!"

Selena burst into laughter, followed by Arielle.

"We can't be *friends*," Selena said, still giggling. "We are colleagues. Teammates. Right, Arielle?"

Arielle smiled, shaking her head as she took another sip of margarita. "I don't put labels on relationships." She pinched her lips shut, trying to not laugh.

"Booooo!" Felix howled through cupped hands over his mouth.

"Weak!" Selena cackled, grabbing a tortilla chip and tossing it at Arielle.

They all burst into more laughter.

"You know what," Selena said. "I'll take it. Don't you remember at the beginning, Felix? Arielle acted like we were going to be business associates for the rest of our lives. I guarantee if we had gone out to this same dinner then, Arielle would have come up with some excuse."

"'Oh, I have too much work to do!'" Felix mocked in his best Arielle impression, batting his eyelashes.

"Woooow!" Arielle said. "You guys are so funny."

"What?" Selena said. "It's not every day you get the number one Angel to *not* deny having new friends."

"She's right," Felix said. "We'll take it. Maybe by the end of the next mission you can say . . . the F-word."

"Maybe," Arielle said, conceding the argument that had spiraled well beyond her control.

They each took sips of their drinks before Felix asked, "When are we going to find out how the mission turned out?"

Arielle stuffed a chip into her mouth, expecting this question to come up, eventually. "I don't do that anymore. We are done. I've been burned too many times in the past. Finding out things turned out the same, or sometimes even worse. That's not common, but after reading a few of those reports, it's just deflating."

"So we'll never know?"

"Do whatever you want. You can get the Futures Report and find out what happened. I'm sure you can look up some of the names on your phone right now—just to see what comes up. But I don't want to hear about any of it."

"Really?" Selena asked. "You're not even a bit curious about what happened to Nate? I hope he got taken down so hard."

"Curious, sure. But what would happen if we found out he never got caught? Maybe he's still in operation today. We already deal with the past enough. No sense in dwelling over it further."

"I'm going to look it up. Later, of course."

"Speaking of later," Felix said. "Any rumblings about the next mission? Just wondering where and when we might be going."

"I haven't even checked my email since we got back," Arielle said, reaching into her pocket to pull out her phone. "I'm sure there's something in there."

Felix and Selena watched in anxious anticipation.

"Well, I have almost 800 unread emails—that will be fun. Let's see."

Arielle scrolled through her crowded inbox until she found a message from the Scouting Department. "Well, this looks interesting."

"What is it?!" Selena pleaded. Felix shifted forward in his seat and drummed his fingers on the table.

"Looks like a local mission in 1991. An unsolved robbery homicide. A bank robbery."

"In Denver?" Selena asked.

"Sure is." Arielle continued to read through the email that provided high-level notes on the potential mission. "Wow. This case had a suspect and a trial, but the jury found him innocent."

"So we're just going back to find out who did it?" Felix asked.

Arielle chuckled. "We're not detectives. We're going back to stop it from happening. Four people died. Two-hundred thousand in cash stolen. Sounds like a fun one."

II

Secrets in the Vault

Arielle Lucila Series, Book 2

Chapter 1

June 16, 1991

The man stared at his blurred reflection in the steel doors, a new life awaiting him on the other side. He faced the freight elevator of the United Bank Tower in downtown Denver, having just paged the guards through the intercom, where he posed as the bank's vice president. They didn't question the ruse, and why would they? Who else could possibly want access to the building on Father's Day at nine o'clock in the morning?

He listened as the gears whirred on the other side of the doors, and tightened his grip on the gun. *It's go time.*

His leg bounced as time seemed to drag. The sounds stopped, and he braced for the doors to open.

Seconds later, they parted, revealing an older bank security guard, coffee cup in hand, not a worry in the world until he looked down and saw the Colt Trooper pointing directly at his chest. He dropped the coffee and reached for his baton.

"Don't even *fucking* think about it," the gunman snarled. "Swing that thing and I'll blast your brains all over this elevator."

The guard—McDowell, according to the name tag clipped to his navy blue uniform jacket—released his grip from the baton and held his hands above his head.

"Better," the man said, looking over his shoulder to make sure no one was around. McDowell had coffee splattered all over his pants, or maybe the dark stain was piss. His eyes bulged with terror, hands trembling in the air. "We're going for a ride. Do you understand?"

McDowell only quivered like he had just stepped into an ice bath.

What a chickenshit!

"I said, do you understand?!" the man shouted, stepping into the elevator, shoving the gun into McDowell's pudgy gut.

"Yes, sir," McDowell said in a wavering, cracking voice.

"Good. Take me to the subbasement, and don't get any cute ideas. This gun will be on you the whole time."

McDowell nodded, but didn't move.

"Push the damn button!" the man barked, whipping McDowell across the face with the revolver. Blood spurted from his nose while he stuck out a wobbly finger and pushed *SB*.

The doors finally closed, and the elevator descended.

"Give me your keycard," the man said, having seen it clipped to McDowell's belt.

"Please," McDowell begged. "Please don't kill me."

"Give me the keycard!"

The elevator stopped, and the man pulled the trigger before the doors opened, knowing the sound wouldn't be heard in the guardroom on the basement level above.

McDowell collapsed to the floor, blood spreading across his chest while his arms lay lifeless by his sides. The keycard lay pinched beneath the guard's dead weight, so the man rolled him over and plucked it off the belt just as the doors opened.

He jumped to the side wall and peered out, relieved to find the coast clear.

The man stepped out and turned left to the lone door next to the elevator, entering a stairwell. He climbed up one flight to the bank's basement level, which was host to the guardroom and vault. He tapped the keycard on the scanner and opened the door, leading out with his firearm in front.

No one heard, he thought, once more relieved to find an empty hallway. The vault waited at the opposite end, but he'd have to pass the guardroom first.

He crossed the hallway and strolled ahead, his baggy sport coat whispering against the concrete walls. Cameras lined the hallway, so he needed to move quickly and with confidence. With a little luck, he could still catch the guards daydreaming before they realized what was happening—his disguise would definitely help.

The man was nearly jogging when he reached the guardroom's door and threw it open, the door banging against the wall and causing the two guards inside to jump up from their desks. He saw another door behind the two men marked as *BATTERY ROOM – CAUTION*.

Both guards whipped out their batons and held them out in front.

The man moved his gun back and forth between the two, letting them know he could take them both out within seconds. The door glided shut behind the man, and that's when he pulled the trigger again.

"Fuck!" the guard on the left shouted, dropping his baton as he clutched his arm.

The man shot the next guard, catching him in the shoulder and sending him tumbling backward. "Get in the battery room!" the shooter yelled. "Hurry!"

The guard who had fallen down crawled toward the battery room's door. The other did not, so the man shot him again, this time in the stomach.

"Right fucking now!"

Both guards pulled themselves toward the battery room, all fight having vanished. The man had made easy work of them and should have an even less difficult time robbing the vault.

He kept his gun fixed on the guards as they first opened the battery room door, still crawling on the floor. The other followed at a much slower pace, bleeding from his stomach. The man kicked this guard in the rear, forcing him face-first into the room, where his colleague grabbed his arms and helped him in. The man stood in the doorway and shot both guards two more times in the head. They lay dead below a row of batteries used to power the bank's computer system.

He reloaded the gun.

The guardroom door swung open, and another guard entered. "What the hell?!"

The man spun around and fired, the first shot errant as the guard dove to the floor. The guard hid on the other side of the desk, and threw his baton over the edge, nearly striking the man in the head, but instead hitting the wall behind him.

"Bad fucking choice!" the man shouted, jumping on top of the desk and shooting downward. He fired six quick rounds, and each hit the guard. The man read the guard's name tag: *Harvey.* "Sorry, Harvey," the man said with a chuckle, reloading the revolver once more with one of the several speedloaders he had stuffed into his coat pockets.

He hopped back down and looked at the ten monitors splayed across the front wall of the guardroom. The vault was indeed open and had six employees inside counting and sorting cash. Not a single one of them seemed perturbed, so he knew none of them had heard the gunfire.

Take your time, he thought. *Clear the evidence.*

Scanning the screens one more time, he found no other guards anywhere else in the banking area. He was all alone with the employees.

He looked down and saw a set of bank keys, slipping them into his pockets. A two-way radio stood on the edge of the desk, and he stuffed that into his other pocket after turning it off. The guard logbook lay open, and he saw a note about a silent alarm going off at 9:20 A.M. from the subbasement stairwell. Wilson Harvey had gone to check it.

He grabbed a handful of the log's pages and ripped them out, stuffing them into the inside pocket of his coat. "What else?" he asked the empty room, scanning the desk for any other clues that he might have left behind. The glimmer of a shell casing caught his eye on the floor, so he spent the next five minutes collecting each spent casing from his rampage.

After collecting the casings, he found a paper grocery bag under the desk, and tossed them into it, bringing the bag with him to the front of the room where he ejected the video tapes for all the active camera feeds, dropping them into the bag. He repeated this process ten times until all footage was officially erased.

Excitement bubbled within the man. He had made it through the hardest part of this robbery, and only had to collect his cash from the white-collar workers in the vault. He'd be home free within the hour.

Brown bag in hand, the man scanned the guardroom behind him, a few splatters of blood soaking into the carpet. Aside from that, he cleaned up the area nicely.

"Sorry, gentlemen," he said. "It wasn't personal."

He turned and left the guardroom, butterflies fluttering in his stomach as he continued down the hall toward the vault. He tapped the keycard to unlock the first door, and stepped in to see the vault wide open, bright light pouring out. Two counters ran the length of the vault, and each had three employees working quietly among themselves, pulling wads of cash out of large black bags, and running them through a counting machine.

All six of the employees were so deep in their work, they never noticed the man creeping toward the vault, arm extended as he held the gun. He rapped the barrel on the vault's door. "How are we all doing?"

A woman in the back gasped and dove to the floor. The two men closest to the entrance casually looked over, then immediately raised their hands. The other three workers, two women and a man, stopped what they were doing and froze, as if they thought maybe the gunman wouldn't see them.

"Let's make this easy," the man said. "And everyone can go home today. I want everyone to close their eyes and get on the ground calmly and quietly. If I see any sudden movements, I will shoot. If I see you reach for any hidden alarms, I will shoot."

Everyone obliged and eased themselves downward. Some covered their eyes with their arms, others simply squinted their eyelids shut. The man nodded toward the gentleman closest to him, presumably the manager, as he wore a suit and tie, while everyone else had dressed more casually for their Sunday morning in the office. "You. Keep your eyes open and load up one of these bags with all the cash you can fit."

The nervous manager nodded slowly and turned around to the counter he was working at, lowering his hands cautiously toward the piles of cash.

He grabbed handfuls at a time and returned them to the black bag.

"What's behind that door?" the man asked, pointing his gun toward another door outside the vault's entrance, just to the side.

"It's a mantrap," the manager said. "Just a different access point to the vault." He continued filling the bag with cash, constantly looking over his shoulder.

"Okay. I want all of you to crawl out of the vault and go behind that door. And drop your keycards before you go in. Let's move, people!"

They all reluctantly crawled along the floor, three of them passing by the manager, who looked down and gulped.

"You're all doing so good," the man said. "Keep this up and we'll all be on our way in no time."

A few minutes passed while they crawled on elbows and knees toward the mantrap, each dropping their keycards by the man's feet as they passed him. "I only see four cards—there should be five."

One man started wailing. "I'm sorry, I forgot."

"No need to cry, cupcake, just toss it this way."

The sobbing man obliged and threw his keycard over his shoulder where it landed close enough to the rest.

"Very good," the man said, picking one off the floor and starting toward the mantrap. He tapped the keycard on the panel and pushed open the door. "Wow, that's a tight fit in there. You guys will be okay, though. In you go."

"You'll never get away with this," one woman muttered under her breath as they formed a line and crawled into the mantrap.

"Excuse you, ma'am. I didn't ask for your thoughts. You'll keep your mouth shut if you know what's best for you."

She said no more and entered the small space. The man backed away from the door, but kept his revolver pointed toward it, backpedaling until he could see the manager more clearly. "How are things going in there?"

"One bag is full, sir."

Oh, he's definitely a bank manager. Even talks like one.

"That's good news. Now bring it out here, drop it on the floor, and join your friends."

The manager did as instructed, carrying the bag in one hand while holding the other above his head. He dropped it on the floor just outside the vault, gave a quick look up and down of the gunman (probably to share details with the police later), and shuffled into the mantrap with the rest of his employees.

"You all have a good day. And thank you for your cooperation."

He pushed the mantrap's door shut, and pulled it to confirm it wouldn't open. Whether going in or out of the door, a keycard was required. He pocketed the one he had already used and left the rest on the floor.

A calming stillness filled the air as he crossed the room and picked up the bag of cash, slinging it over his shoulder. "Money is heavy," he said, and broke into a sprint down the hallway.

He called the freight elevator and anxiously waited for it come to the basement level. Another guard could have been in the bathroom or on a break, and he didn't want to stand inside this building any longer than he needed.

When the elevator doors finally opened, he stepped in, the smell of blood and coffee blending in a nauseating odor. He sent the elevator back up to street level.

The doors parted and revealed the parking garage, the morning sunlight visible just thirty feet away.

"It's now or never." He dashed through the garage, and hooked around the corner of the garage's exit, sprinting down the sidewalk on Lincoln Street. He saw no pedestrians aside from a homeless man rummaging through a nearby trashcan.

This man would get away with this crime for decades to come.

Until one day. . .

Chapter 2

Present day

The trio gathered at the headquarters to meet Commander Briar. After only one mission, the team of Arielle Lucila, Felix Francisco, and Selena Nicole had gained a reputation across the Road Runners organization unparalleled to anything they had seen before.

They were considered a super team. Rock stars. Arielle had already been a celebrity within the group—most top-ranked Angels were—but having worked with Selena and Felix on the last mission, the two had been elevated to a similar status.

"This is crazy," Selena said after they gathered in a private conference room, having pushed through the office where everyone gawked at them, or tried to chat them up as they strolled down the hallway. "Is this what it's always been like for you?" she asked Arielle.

"Not here in Denver. When I've visited offices in different cities, there is a little of it, but today felt like walking down the red carpet."

Felix laughed. "Some guy out there said he wants to do what I do. Can't say I've ever heard that before."

"I don't understand *why* this is happening," Selena said. "Like, it's only been two days since we got back. How does everyone know we even went on a mission together?"

"Remember, we're in a time of peace," Arielle said. "Commander Briar has launched many initiatives to drive engagement from all Road Runners. His focus has been on building a sense of community. Since there is no more war for our internal news to report on, they just talk about the current missions. I think there's a newsletter that goes out once a week, too. And it covers the mission work."

"So it's just a matter of increased visibility?" Felix asked.

"I suppose. I haven't seen what's all been said about us, but clearly we're well-received by the organization."

"It's because we're badasses," Selena said. "I don't mind the fame one bit. It was the life I was going to have, anyway."

The door swung open, and Commander Briar entered. "Good morning, you three. How are things?"

He shuffled around the table and took a seat opposite the three Angels.

"Everything is great, Commander," Arielle said. "Ready for our next mission."

"Always so eager. And how about you two?" He nodded at Felix and Selena. "How are you adjusting to the new life? Have you seen the special report that's been streaming? It's a deep dive into all of your lives."

"Well, that explains it," Felix said. "How did they do that without even talking to us?"

"We're time travelers," Commander Briar said with a light chuckle. "Our team just goes back and follows different parts of your lives. I'm sure they'll be in touch for a live interview in the present time. You three are becoming the face of the organization."

Selena grinned from ear to ear. "Fantastic."

"It's just buzz," the commander said. "Give it a few weeks and it'll die down."

"Unless we keep crushing these missions," Arielle said. "It could get even worse."

"Fine with me. I've been the popular one for long enough. Time for someone else. Now, let's get to business."

Commander Briar turned on the TV hanging on the wall at the front of the meeting room. It revealed a standard PowerPoint, the opening slide reading *Father's Day Massacre*.

"This is a big one," the commander continued. "Not for having a wide reach, but for the popularity this received at the time. On June 16th, 1991, a lone perpetrator entered the United Bank just down the street from us—the Cash Register Building."

The slides changed to show the iconic Denver skyscraper with a roof shaped like a traditional cash register. It quickly changed to show the inside of the bank as it looked in 1991.

"Four guards were killed, and over two hundred thousand dollars were stolen."

The slide changed to show a middle-aged white man with a buzz cut looking into the distance.

"This is Jacob Kennedy. They arrested him on July 4th, 1991 as the primary suspect in this robbery. He was a retired police officer and former guard at the bank. His trial was nationally broadcast, and the jury found him not guilty. He was released, and they never found the money. There were a lot of holes in the prosecution's story, but also in Kennedy's narrative. Personally, I think he did it, but the evidence presented at trial was spotty."

The slide changed to another man, this one a grainy picture. He had large-framed glasses and a receding hairline.

"This is Peter Young. He's another suspect who lived about a half-mile away from the bank. They found some questionable things in his apartment, but nothing connected to the robbery. He also had no alibi. He'll be worth a look when you travel back."

Arielle had opened her notepad and scribbled notes. "When are we expected to start?"

"You'll have some time. There are a lot of moving parts to this one. The scouting team still has about a week's worth of research to do, maybe a little less. Plan for five days at the very least."

"Wow, that's pretty much a vacation," Arielle said.

The commander nodded. "We're trying to put more time between missions. Anything you'll need from us before the mission starts?"

"Actually, yes. I want us to jump in right from day one. I think we could have learned a lot more on the last mission if we had access to the target's workplace. A lot happened inside that building during the daytime, but we had no way in. I want this to be an automatic request for all missions going forward. We need to get Selena inside the building, one way or another. Are we able to do that?"

Commander Briar leaned back and stared into the distance. "I think so. It will vary by mission, and we'll need to find jobs that fly under the radar, but I think we can make it work."

"That's fine. It's not the job so much that matters, but having access to the buildings. Maybe even a custodian-type role would work best. They have access to nearly every part of an office."

"Exactly my thoughts," Commander Briar said. "Everything good safety-wise on the last mission? Because I think this next one will be plenty challenging."

"Yes. We got lucky with the murder being late at night."

"Good. That one was pretty straightforward. A targeted attack. This one, assuming it goes all the way to the day of, won't be so easy. The perp will shoot anyone who tries to intervene."

"Maybe I should be a teller?" Selena asked. "Put me in the front row on the morning of."

Arielle raised her eyebrows, never expecting Selena to put herself in the line of danger. "That won't be necessary. We'll work on finding a good position for you. I wouldn't trust standing at the teller counter. Too much can go wrong."

"If you say so. Are we free to do whatever we want for the next week, then?"

Selena never hesitated to redirect a conversation back to her true agenda.

"Yes, actually," Commander Briar said. "One of our main focuses is to make sure you have time outside of mission work to yourselves. Travel. Relax. Visit family. Whatever you need."

The way the commander was speaking made Arielle uneasy. But she had also been hard-wired from her days in the CIA to work around the clock. She had never minded, especially after losing her family.

"You especially, Arielle," Commander Briar said. "I was looking through your records, and you've never taken off more than three consecutive days. And I'm not sure even those count. I know you take work with you on vacation."

"Commander," she said. "I'm the top Angel. I can't just go off the grid."

He raised a steady hand while shaking his head. "You can. I promise we'll be fine. And if we're not, we know how to get hold of you. We've always been driven by urgency—we had to be, during the war, because any wasted second would cost more Road Runner lives. We're past that now. This time of peace allows us to take a step back and enjoy life. We don't have to complete missions as fast as possible. The past isn't going anywhere. If we can wait a few days to make sure more of our bases are covered, then we'll become even more efficient."

"What's our success rate?" Arielle asked, wondering what the percentage of recent missions had been dubbed as wins by the teams who explored the aftermath.

"98," Commander Briar said. "Was 95 this time last year. We're headed in the right direction, and I just might see if we can push it to 100. Why not?"

A failed mission meant one of two things. Either the Angels in the mission didn't achieve their objective, or the aftermath revealed a situation had reached the same outcome a different way, or ended up worse. Every department pointed fingers at the others when a mission came back as failed.

The prep team received blame for not looking deep enough into the matter. The Angels had to answer questions about what went amiss. Even the clean-up crew took heat for possibly leaving clues behind. Despite the turmoil, the actual cause usually ended up being a bit of everyone's fault. There were far too many moving pieces to pinpoint a specific reason for a mission going awry, so no official blame was ever assigned.

"We can reach 100," Arielle said. "It'll take more work, but we have the right people—we always have."

"I agree. With a year left in my term, and no crises to worry about, this will be my top priority." Commander Briar checked his watch, a flashy Rolex. "I have another appointment to get to. We can circle back once we have all the files from the Scouting team. Otherwise, plan to jump into the mission when you three are ready." He knocked on the table as he stood.

"Thank you, Commander," Felix said.

The commander left the trio alone once more.

Arielle stood up and paced near the television still showing the last slide of Peter Young.

"What's wrong?" Selena asked.

"This just all seems so strange. Less structured. I don't know."

"It's a new level of trust," Felix said. "You already had that respect from leadership, and now all of us do. The commander called us a super team. We're not going to be watched over like a less seasoned team might."

"I get that. I just don't know why all of a sudden... It's never been this way. Not even close."

"You heard him. It's a new era. Things are changing, and it sounds like for the better. You just might find yourself with a little more control over your missions."

Arielle shrugged. "So what are you guys going to do with a week off?"

"Unwind," Felix said. "Might catch a Rockies game, but definitely need to catch up on sleep. Don't feel like I got much on this last mission."

"I'm gonna catch up with some friends," Selena said. "Spend the weekend downtown. Maybe head up to the mountains for a day. How about you?"

"I'll visit my grandma. She's down in New Mexico, and I haven't seen her since last Christmas."

"I'm sure that'll be nice," Felix said. "I lost all of my grandparents by high school, but still remember visiting them every weekend."

"I only have the two on my dad's side, but they live in northern France," Selena said. "I'm not even sure the last time I saw them."

"My abuela is my only living family left," Arielle said. "Well, immediate family. I have some cousins, but none I'm really in contact with."

"Definitely visit her," Felix said. "It'll help you unplug. I dare you to not even take your computer with you."

Arielle laughed. "We'll see about that. Pretty sure my grandma goes to bed around eight o'clock. I'll need *something* to do."

They all shared a laugh at this comment, oblivious to the grueling mission that awaited.

Chapter 3

Arielle arrived in Las Vegas, New Mexico, the next morning. She flew into Santa Fe and rented a car to drive the hour east to her grandmother's hometown.

Las Vegas had a population around 15,000 and sat directly off the interstate. Arielle and her family had made plenty of trips to visit family during summer breaks, where they somehow crammed into the lone guest bedroom available at the house.

Her grandmother still lived in the original house, a small ranch-style home with a white adobe exterior. When Arielle pulled up, she smiled when she saw it all looked the same. Cars lined both sides of Fourth Street. Chain-link fences separated the properties, and the front lawns were dirt or xeriscaped.

Arielle turned her car into the driveway and parked right behind her grandmother's Cadillac.

"Oh, *mija!*" a voice called from the front door, and Arielle stepped out of her car to see her grandma standing on the front step, crouched over with a cane to support her.

"Abuelita!" Arielle called back, running around the car and throwing her arms around her grandma's shoulders. She looked a little older each time Arielle visited. Her once-gray hair was almost completely white, standing out in contrast to her dark skin.

"How are you?" she asked, poking a bony finger into Arielle's gut. "Too skinny. Come inside and let's eat. I made your favorite." She cracked a grin, her lips sunken in, eyes filled with joy.

Arielle followed her inside and let the nostalgia sweep over her. The house had rarely changed over the years, except for when her grandfather had passed away in 2010. The living room and kitchen looked the same as she could remember from her childhood. Magnets covered the fridge, making it impossible to see the color underneath. The smell of green chile and refried beans filled the air, and Arielle's mouth watered.

Two lounge chairs faced the television in the living room, a folding dinner tray standing between them, covered in magazines and newspapers. Family portraits decorated the walls, both in color and black and white. A large crucifix hung above the TV next to a family portrait of Arielle with her parents and brother, the pamphlets from their funerals tucked behind the frame's edges.

Emotions rushed to Arielle's chest and head, and she bit her lip to keep from crying so soon.

"I miss them, too, *hita*. Think about them every day. Do you ever go visit them?"

Arielle nodded. "I try about once a week."

"Oh, good. Keep their graves pretty. They deserve it."

Arielle wanted to change the subject. "What are you cooking, Abuelita?"

"You still like your smothered burritos, yes? I got special hatch chile just for you. You know I can't do all that spicy stuff. Sit down. It's ready."

Arielle shuffled around the kitchen table and sat down in the seat she always used—facing the window that overlooked the front yard. Her grandma pulled out plates from the cupboard and served the food, drowning Arielle's burrito with so much green chile, cheese, and sour cream, that she could barely see underneath it all.

"You been busy, *hita*?" she asked.

Arielle took her first bite and nodded. The flavors brought back so many memories, one of the few things that could tempt her into quitting the Road Runners and spending the rest of her life in Las Vegas.

"Yes, work's been very busy, but it's supposed to lighten up soon."

"That's good. You look tired. You shouldn't work so hard. Go out and enjoy life. Any boys yet?"

Arielle knew the question was coming—it always did. "No boys. I don't have time for a relationship. Not yet, at least." She hadn't introduced a man to her grandma since Kevin in college, not that there had been anyone of substance since then.

"I know you'll find someone. I pray for you every night."

"Thank you, Abuelita." Arielle took another bite and shook her head. She couldn't believe food this delicious wasn't available at restaurants.

"Well, what do you want to do while you're here? How long are you staying?"

"I can stay three days. Honestly, there isn't anything I *need* to do while I'm out here. I have a few days off work and just wanted to get away."

"That's fine. Maybe we can go into town one day."

"How have *you* been, Abuelita? What do you do every day?"

"Oh, the usual. I go to church every morning. Stop at the diner for breakfast. Come home and take a nap. Watch my novelas, then make dinner. After that I take a bath and read for an hour before going to bed."

"Sounds like a nice relaxing routine. Don't mind me if there is anything you need to do while I'm here."

Her grandma shrugged. "It keeps me busy. The days are yours. Have you gone to church?"

Arielle hadn't stepped foot inside a church since her family's funerals. The tragedy had rocked her relationship with God, and witnessing all the nastiness on her mission work didn't exactly restore her faith.

"You have to go to church, *mija*. I know it's hard, but if you talk to God, he'll talk back. He always does."

"I'm not saying I'll never go back, but it's going to take some time."

Her grandma reached out and embraced Arielle's free hand. "I know. And that's why I pray for you. I just want you to find happiness again."

"I am happy."

Her grandma raised her eyebrows. She always could read her grandchildren's emotions, no matter their age, no matter how long it had been since they'd last seen her.

"You're not happy. I can see it in your eyes. You're content, but it can be better, no? Life is too short, *mija*. If it's your job that's not making you happy, go find a new one."

"My job actually treats me pretty well. I make great money, and genuinely enjoy what I do."

"Not just your job. There are lots of factors that go into a happy life. Physical, emotional, spiritual. They all have to be fulfilled. They all take time and attention."

"Abuelita, I promise you I'm doing very well. I'm in the best physical shape of my life. My emotions are fine. And spiritually . . . well, I'm right where I'm comfortable."

"I'm not going to argue. But I know you're not as good as you can be. It's okay to admit you're hurting. I'll never recover from losing your Abuelito, and definitely not from losing your family."

All Arielle needed to hear was the crack in her grandmother's voice, and she let down her guard. The tears she had fought back earlier came roaring back as she broke into a heavy sob and pushed back her plate. She looked up, eyes red and drenched. "I *hate* it," she said. "I hate that this happened to me. I hate that a deranged man gets to live while my family doesn't. I hate God for letting it all happen."

Her grandmother stood up and circled the table, hugging Arielle from behind her shoulders, planting a kiss on the back of her head. "Let it out, *hita*. It's the only way."

Arielle understood she didn't speak of the tragedy enough. She had undergone years of therapy, but a void forever remained. The therapy helped her manage the rage that boiled up when she thought about that day, but the sorrow remained as stiff as it had the first day she returned to her family's empty house.

"I want to kill him," Arielle said under her breath. "I want to kill him twelve times, one for each person he killed. He should have gotten the death penalty. I don't understand why he didn't."

Her grandmother massaged her shoulders. "Don't you wish you could just go back to that day and stop it from happening?"

"Every single day." Arielle's stomach churned at the thought. She really did consider it every day. Her grandmother meant it figuratively, but didn't know how realistic of a possibility it was.

Angels at Arielle's level had few restrictions, but tampering with her own past was one of them. It was highly forbidden for a multitude of reasons. Tampering with one's own past would alter their present timeline. All of the mission work she had done could be wiped out by changing her past. Her very existence could come into doubt.

That's why she only fantasized going to the shooter's prison and killing him in the present day.

"I know everything about him, Abuelita. Nicholas Robert Fenton." The name tasted like dog shit in her mouth. "Born in 1987 in San Diego. Charged with twelve counts of first-degree murder. One hundred and thirteen counts of attempted first-degree murder. Found guilty on all charges. Sentenced to twelve life sentences, plus an additional 2,718 years. Incarcerated at the United States Penitentiary in Allenwood, Pennsylvania. He's in cell D-12."

"Oh, Arielle. It's not good for you to know all this. You're not going to actually kill him. Revenge won't bring our family back, and it won't make you feel any better. You need to erase all that from your head. You're obsessed, and that's unhealthy. I guarantee you he doesn't spend his days thinking about all the people he killed, so neither should you."

"I'm not going to kill him," Arielle said. "But I wouldn't mind having a word."

If Arielle could get inside that prison, then she would absolutely murder him without a second thought. It might not bring her peace, but it would make the world a better place. She could close her eyes and picture his psychotic mugshot that had been all over the news in the weeks following the massacre. How she wanted to wipe that smug grin off his face.

"This is something you're going to have to live with for the rest of your life," her grandma said. "Don't let it control you."

Arielle rarely let the thoughts of killing Nicholas Fenton consume her life. She was much too busy with missions to spend serious time on the subject. It became clear why she avoided taking time off from work. It only offered free time for her to get her emotions riled back up.

Arielle grabbed her napkin and wiped the tears away. "I'm okay, Abuelita. Thank you. I feel much better already."

She stood up and hugged her grandmother, thinking about how good it would feel to one day end the life of Nicholas Fenton.

Chapter 4

Arielle returned to Denver three days later, relaxed and recharged. Her grandmother hadn't pressed her on happiness or other life issues for the rest of her stay. Instead, they chatted about old memories, spent a day in town, and ate loads of food. She was pretty sure she gained five pounds during her quick trip.

Her grandmother had given her a fifty-dollar bill when she left, convinced Arielle was poor and never ate. "Take yourself out somewhere nice," she had said. "And order dessert."

Arielle held the bill in her hand and grinned. She didn't need the money, so she put it in a box she kept with other precious family memories. After each visit she always worried it might be the last time she'd see her grandmother. Abuelita was pushing ninety years, but she was an active woman with lots to look forward to. Arielle felt plenty encouraged after leaving New Mexico.

Arielle had only spent a handful of days at her own house during the past month, having been torn between missions and different trips out of town. The place almost seemed foreign, and she wondered if she should downsize.

She often had this debate with herself, and always talked herself into staying. The house was massive, but maybe one day there would be a family inside of it. Or friends. Working as an Angel for so long often made her feel like a machine. But having a week off had since reminded her what it was like to be a regular 27-year-old. She remembered what free time was like, not having a care in the world.

It almost felt foreign, and part of her felt guilty. She was supposed to be helping people in need, stopping crime, killing bad guys. Not lounging in her bed at eight in the evening.

Her doorbell chimed, and she hopped out of bed, tumbling over the pile of clothes that had been scattered from her trip. She was expecting Selena to pick her up, but not so soon.

She opened the door to find Selena grinning with a bottle of champagne in hand. "Surprise!"

"What are you doing here so early? Is everything okay?" Arielle stepped aside to let Selena enter.

"That question is exactly why I'm here. You worry too much. Let's have some fun. Are you familiar with the term *pregaming*?"

Arielle scoffed. "Selena, stop acting like I'm some old lady. I went to college. I used to party."

Selena looked her up and down. "Sure. And this is also why I'm here. You don't know how to dress for a night out. Don't worry—I'll help you."

Arielle rolled her eyes. "I have plenty of outfits for going out."

Selena stepped further into the living room, looking up at the vaulted ceiling. "Jesus Christ, you live here by yourself? This house in insane. You realize you look like a filthy rich person with your mansion at the top of the hill?"

Arielle shrugged. "I suppose I am filthy rich."

Selena howled laughter. "Quiet confidence. I love it."

"Any Road Runner can make easy money. It's encouraged."

"Oh, I know. And I do. I just don't think I'd ever get so much space for myself. I spend all my money on cars and shoes."

"And that dress? Gucci?"

Selena wore a lacy black dress, nearly see-through to an imaginative eye.

"Wow, you know fashion, too? Maybe we aren't so different after all."

"I keep up," Arielle said. "Went to Fashion Week once in New York. Did you ever go?"

Selena grinned. "More times than I could count. Please, the wealthy go to those things just to make an appearance. I went so many times in Paris with my dad. I've been surrounded by fashion my entire life. But do you know who might know even more about fashion than either of us?"

"Who?"

"Felix. His mother is a fashion designer out in San Fran. Told me he grew up going to fashion shows all the time."

"No shit? Well, looks like we've found something all three of us have in common. Is he still meeting us tonight?"

"Of course. I told him it's a team-building event—which it is. But really we're just going to cut loose before the mission starts. Maybe we can make it a tradition if we keep having these long weeks off in between."

"Maybe. What did you end up doing the last few days?"

"Visited my mom. After hearing about your trip to see your grandma, I thought maybe I should catch up with the one woman who's always had my back."

"Oh? Is she still in New York?"

Selena nodded. "Yeah, and I asked her to move out here to Denver. She told me hell no. She loves the big city too much. I expected that response. My mom tells people she's a native New Yorker, but she's not. Just fell in love with the place and refuses to leave it for anything."

Ariella chuckled. "You do anything fun?"

"Oh, sure. Plenty to do there. Caught a show on Broadway—can't remember the last time I did that. Spent a day at Central Park just talking and catching up. And spent our final day at her apartment, just hanging out and playing board games. I think we both really needed it. I'm glad I went."

"Me too. Glad I'm not alone in feeling weird about having all this time to ourselves."

"Seriously. I can actually go out and have the next day to recover. I feel rejuvenated just thinking about it. Shall we get ready? I'll pour the champagne."

* * *

An hour later they arrived downtown and found Felix sitting at the bar of the very crowded Johnny's Tavern. He had a half-empty beer stein and a basket of hot wings in front of him while he watched baseball on the big screens behind the bartender.

"Hey, you two!" he said, standing up to hug Arielle and Selena.

"Feels like it's been forever," Arielle said. "How has your time off been?"

Felix smiled. "So nice. I've done exactly what I said. Caught the Rockies game yesterday. Been getting a ton of sleep and catching up on shows. It's been so nice to not have to think."

"Yeah, the commander might really be on to something," Selena said. "I almost feel excited to start the next mission."

"You girls already have some drinks?" Felix asked. "I smell it."

Arielle and Selena stared at each other and burst into laughter.

"Yes," Arielle said. "We might have had a bottle of champagne while we got dressed."

"While *you* got dressed," Selena said.

Arielle giggled and threw her arm around Selena. "Right."

Felix looked like he was trying to hold in a laugh. "Is everything okay? I don't think I've ever seen you this way, Arielle."

"What? Tipsy?" Arielle said. "I'm fine. Let's eat."

They found a table near the back corner of the restaurant, and over the next hour chowed down on burgers and appetizers, then shared a slice of chocolate cake smothered in ice cream. They chatted about their past week, mentally bracing for the mission set to begin in exactly two days.

"I did some reading," Arielle started.

"There she is," Felix said with a cheesy grin.

"This mission is quite interesting. Have either of you ever worked on a case like this? Because I don't think I have. Normally, they give us the file with a pretty good understanding of who's behind the crime. This one, though, it sounds like our Advance Team has no idea where to start."

"It's the first one," Felix said. "I chatted with some of the team. Commander Briar wants to expand our range of missions. He's also looking into present-day missions to prevent things from happening in the future. He believes heavily in this one as it removes the prospect of the past pushing back. Imagine the thought of doing a mission and only having to worry about the real-world obstacles."

"Hold on," Selena said. "Why do you know all this stuff? Your team?"

Felix laughed. "We *are* the tech team. We monitor all emails that come in and out of the office. Some are restricted, but this thread between the commander and the Council was not."

"Oooh," Arielle said. "What did the Council say?"

She knew they liked to push back, and sometimes wondered if they just did it for fun.

"They said his initiatives all sound fantastic, but they told him to pick one to focus on. He wants to launch all these new teams and projects, and move people around to fill the voids. They told him no, and he started on this one first. I guess it was a more seamless transition from what we already do."

"But why wouldn't he have told us?" Arielle asked. "Why didn't I realize this?"

"Technically, our last mission was a cold case, at least in the eyes of the local police department and community. This next one, though, is a true cold case, even to us. We're going in blind. Sure, we have a couple of suspects, who may very well end up being our targets, but our Scouting team wasn't able to confirm any details. They were just as confused as the jury, it sounds like."

"So he's easing us into it," Arielle said. "I'm not sure I like it. We're not detectives. I don't know that we're the right team for this experiment."

"What are we, if we're not detectives?" Selena asked. "That's what I've always thought of you as."

"Assassins," Arielle replied calmly. "I'm a trained assassin. And my job is to kill the bad guys."

Felix took a gulp of his beer and gave Arielle a look.

"What?" she asked.

"Commander Briar's been playing you. Remember your mission in Mexico a few weeks ago? The one where you wiped out the cartel?"

"Of course."

"That was part of him wanting to explore a modern-day mission."

Arielle leaned back and touched her fingers to her mouth, thinking. "That son of a bitch. He told me it was because they came across the opportunity and had nothing in the past for me to work on yet."

"Nope. And that's why he sent you by yourself to fend off, what was it, twenty cartel soldiers? He wanted to prove that one Angel could handle a mission like that if they didn't have to factor in the past as another obstacle."

"Well, that just seems reckless."

"But you did it. You were never even in danger. The proof is in the results. I think many Angels don't realize just how good they are at what they do. You've all been conditioned to work around the past, so when the past isn't present it's a walk in the park. Honestly, I'm surprised the commander didn't explore this route first. It's easy."

"So what am I supposed to do now? Pretend I don't know this is all going on?"

"I don't get the sense that it's supposed to be a secret. He just doesn't want to make a big deal out of it. I suppose it's *not* a big deal . . . we're doing the same work, just with an extra step added."

"I wouldn't make anything of it," Selena said. "We can do this the same way."

Arielle considered the comments and agreed. She wouldn't bring up the matter to Commander Briar.

Not yet, at least.

Chapter 5

Later that night, the trio moved from dinner to a busy nightclub. Arielle ordered bottle service so they could have a private area away from the masses.

Music boomed, and Selena found herself back in her element, drifting from their private table to dance on the main floor. She swayed her hips side to side, keeping her drink elevated in one hand, eyes closed while she belted out the words to the newest Ed Sheeran song.

It had been a few weeks (in real time) since she had gone out in downtown Denver, and she didn't want to squander the opportunity. She'd be out until the club closed, even if that meant Arielle and Felix left before her.

However, they surprised her by joining on the dance floor.

"Having a good time?" Arielle shouted over the music.

"You know it!"

Men swarmed around the two of them.

"Do you want me to pretend to be your boyfriend?" Felix asked Arielle.

"No, I'll be fine. Let these boys have their dance."

They stayed on the dance floor for the next ten minutes before settling back at their private table.

"Why don't you dance with any girls out there?" Selena asked Felix while Arielle poured them a fresh round of drinks.

"This isn't really my scene," Felix said. "I don't think I'd ever go home with someone from a nightclub or bar."

"No one said you have to marry the girl," Arielle said with a laugh. "It's just a dance, and you can never see her again."

"Have you met Felix?" Selena asked. "The man doesn't do anything for the sake of doing it. If he's going to invest time in a woman, even a quick dance, there better at least be the opportunity of it being more than that."

Felix nodded.

"You need to loosen up," Arielle said.

Selena broke into a cackle. "Wow, Felix. The queen of serious just told you to loosen up. Who is this woman, and where did she take Arielle Lucila?"

Arielle grinned. "I'm just saying. I understand having rules in life and sticking to them. Like I never accept a drink from a man, no matter what. But if that guy over there in the next booth wanted to come over here and take me to the bar to buy a drink . . . well, I just might say yes."

They followed Arielle's eyes to the man in the pinstriped suit at the neighboring VIP booth.

"Um," Selena said. "That's Javonte Morris, the running back for the Broncos."

"Oh, I know. Isn't he just . . . dreamy?"

"He's been looking this way," Felix said. "When you're not looking."

Arielle shrugged. "Well, the ball's in his court then."

"Oh my God, he's coming!" Selena squealed.

The football player strolled over with a wide grin. His silver chain gleamed in the dim club, matching rings standing out against his dark skin.

"Good evening," he said, towering over all three of them. "Can I buy you folks another bottle?"

"Hi, Mr. Morris," Felix squeaked, standing up and sticking out a hand to shake. "I'm a big fan. Glad to have you in Denver."

"Thank you. I'm enjoying it as well. That's why I bought ownership in this club. Anything at all I can get for you?"

His eyes didn't move from Arielle while he spoke, so she stared right back and replied. "Another Grey Goose would work."

Javonte nodded, the grin having no chance of disappearing from his face. "I can arrange that. Would you three want to come to my suite upstairs? It's quieter so we can actually talk."

"Sure," Arielle said, standing up. Selena and Felix followed, grabbing their cups from the table and trailing behind Javonte.

"I didn't even know this place had an upstairs," Felix said.

"Just be cool," Selena snapped back. "There are probably more famous people there."

They all followed Javonte to a private door with a bouncer standing guard. The bouncer nodded and stepped aside, pushing the door open to reveal a stairwell illuminated with purple lighting. As soon as the door closed behind them it became immediately quieter. Their shoes echoed with each step as they climbed and entered another room roughly the size of the dance floor they had just left.

A bar lined the wall to the right, circular tables and seats scattered across the rest of the space. There were indeed more famous people in this private area, including more Broncos players, a local rapper and his crew, and plenty of beautiful women sprinkled into each of the groups.

"Grab a table," Javonte said, nodding to an open one near the far end of the bar. "I'll grab us some vodka."

They crossed the room, passing the local celebrities. Felix gawked in every direction. When they sat at the table, he leaned forward. "Do you guys realize who all's in this room? This is nuts!"

"I said be cool, Felix," Selena muttered under her breath. "Don't embarrass us."

Javonte returned to the table with bottles of Grey Goose and soda. "Drinks have been served," he said, placing them on the table. He waved a hand toward the bar and the bartender slid over four glasses. "So what's your story? Friends? Siblings?"

"We're friends," Selena said. "By the way, thank you for bringing us up here."

"My pleasure. You looked like you were having a good time. What do you all do for a living?"

They exchanged glances around the table before Arielle spoke first. "We work in finance."

"Very nice. I have a few friends who do that as well. I'm sorry—I just realized I never asked your names."

They shared their names, and Javonte sat down with them at the table.

Selena felt Felix's leg bouncing uncontrollably, so she kicked him in the shin to stop.

"So Javonte, what do you do during the summers?" Selena asked.

"This," he said, raising his hands at the club around them. "I bought ownership in a couple of clubs around town. Seems to be a good investment so far. They always tell us athletes to have a back-up plan. Injuries can strike any time, and a football career can be over just like that." He snapped his thick fingers.

"Wise advice," Arielle said, knowing there were far better business investments than bars and nightclubs.

"I hope you don't mind me being honest," Javonte said to Arielle. "But you are one of the most beautiful women I've ever seen."

"And I'm sure he sees a lot," Felix said. This time Selena's heel jabbed him, prompting him to grimace.

"Excuse our friend, he's a little star-struck," Selena said.

"Nothing to apologize for," Javonte said with his charming grin, returning his attention to Arielle. "Would you be interested in going out to dinner sometime?"

Arielle smiled. "Yes. I would like that."

"I look forward to it," Javonte said, reaching into his suit pocket and pulling out a business card. "I don't start training camp until July, so I'm pretty available until then."

"I can get pretty busy with work—" Arielle began.

"But she'll call you," Selena interrupted, putting her hand on Arielle's back. "I'll make sure of it."

"Well, thank you," Javonte said, tipping back the rest of his drink and standing up. "I'll look forward to your call, but I have to get back to mingling with guests here tonight. Part of the job." He rolled his eyes and smiled. "You're all welcome to stay up here as long as you'd like, and if you need anything, just let Ronnie behind the bar know. He'll take care of you."

They thanked him, and he disappeared to another table, chatting with the rapper.

Felix couldn't stop smiling, even as he sipped from his glass. "So Arielle has a date with Javonte Morris. I'm speechless."

"You're also a clown!" Selena said, slapping Felix on the arm. "Why are you sitting over there acting like a total fanboy?"

"What? He's on my fantasy team. Would you have preferred if I talked to him about that instead?"

Now Selena rolled her eyes.

"You two both need to relax," Arielle said. "I'm glad this played out the way it did. Who knows what will come of the date, but now Selena has a connection in the nightclub industry."

"A *VIP* connection," Selena added.

Arielle smiled and shook her head. "Let's get out of here. I'm getting tired."

Selena wanted to rebuke, but decided the excitement of the last few minutes was enough. She could leave happy knowing the uptight Arielle Lucila had landed a date with a rising football star.

They left the club fifteen minutes later and returned to the warm summer night.

"Is anyone okay to drive?" Felix asked.

Arielle and Selena looked at each other and laughed.

"I'll take that as no," Felix replied, joining in on the laughter. "I guess we need to call for a ride."

"Or we just hang out until we get sober," Selena said. "Let's grab a greasy slice of pizza—that will help speed it up."

"Deal," Arielle said, and started down the sidewalk.

Shouts came from across the street, and they all spun around to see a crowd of people huddling around two men holding their fists up, ready to fight. They were in front of a neighboring bar, Swanky's.

One man shoved the other in the chest, and they both charged at each other.

"Should we go break this up?" Felix asked.

Arielle sighed. "We probably *should*, but do we really need to?"

Fists were being thrown across the street.

"Dammit," Selena said, running across the street in her high heels. She looked over her shoulder to make sure Arielle and Felix were trailing behind her.

The crowd had nearly doubled since the fight started, everyone watching the two drunks swing at each other. One man had blood oozing from his forehead, and the other had a bruise forming around his left eye.

"Stop it!" Selena snarled.

The two men spun around, confused. The one with the swollen eye looked Selena up and down, grinning. "Get out of here, princess—we've got business to handle."

"Excuse me?!" Selena cried, leaning down to take off her heels and toss them aside. "I was just out trying to have a good time with my friends, and now I have to deal with your bullshit!"

She charged the man, who reared back and landed a punch squarely on Selena's stomach. Pain ruptured from her insides and shot all the way throughout her body. She tumbled backward and needed a moment to catch her breath.

She hadn't expected such a forceful punch. This time, she was ready.

"Hey, asshole!" she shouted.

The man turned back around, his eye almost completely shut. "Oh, you want more, bitch? Let's dance."

The man rushed toward her, fist reared back again. Selena dropped to the ground and swung her leg out, connecting with the man's ankles and sending him flailing forward. He landed face down in front of a spectator and hurried back to his feet.

It was too late.

Selena had already lunged his direction and rammed her knee into the man's face, sending a spurt of blood out of his nose. He fell back to the ground, wailing as his hands cupped his nose.

The second man slithered toward Selena and wrapped his arms around her throat. The move caught her off guard, white spots sparkling across her vision. Sensing her strength on its last limb, she raised her right foot and kicked backwards as hard as she could. Her foot skirted to the side of his shin, but she felt it.

One more, she thought, and raised her foot again. This time she landed the blow directly onto his kneecap, bending the knee in the wrong direction.

"Fuck!" the man screamed, hobbling away as he tried to balance himself on the good leg. Selena jumped toward him and swung a fist to the back of his head. The man dropped like a boulder, a nine-millimeter pistol falling out of his waistband.

"Gun!" someone in the crowd shouted, and nearly everyone started running away.

Neither man had attempted to stand up. Selena hunched down with her hands on her knees, panting for breath. Arielle and Felix ran to her.

"I knew we needed to stop it," Selena said. "I saw the gun. His shirt came up after he threw a punch."

"Selena," Arielle said, placing a hand on her back. "That was incredible."

"It really was," Felix said, shock smeared over his face. "You know how to fight like Arielle."

"Not quite," Selena said, standing upright. "Arielle wouldn't have taken that first punch, or been put in a chokehold."

Arielle nodded. "It's true."

They all broke into laughter and left to grab their pizza, supporting a slightly bruised but mostly unscathed Selena between them.

Chapter 6

To Arielle's surprise, after reading through the mission report, she discovered she would leave for her own preliminary mission before the main one started. Their primary target—the man who stood trial, Jacob Kennedy—didn't pass away until 2009.

The Advance Team thought it would be wise to pry information from Kennedy, if possible. Perhaps some questioning two decades after the trial would reveal never-heard-before details. But Arielle would need to rely on her interrogative skills.

They scheduled Arielle to jump back to January 2008 at eight o'clock in the morning.

She drove downtown after an early breakfast, and planned to take her time-traveling Juice from there, since that would put her closer to her 2008 destination in Denver. The office was rather deserted for a Monday morning, but most Road Runners didn't arrive to work until ten. A handful had slept there overnight to monitor events, but the bullpen would soon bustle with the energy of a new day.

Arielle went to the conference room next to the kitchen, placed her luggage next to the door, and took a quick swig of her Juice. She didn't need to bring anything besides the file for the preliminary trip into the past, so tucked the papers into a backpack to sling over her shoulder.

Packing light always makes an easy trip, she thought as she stood in the middle of the room waiting for the past to take her away. All Road Runners were grateful Commander Briar had discovered a new formula for the famous Juice, one that allowed those jumping through time to have their physical bodies transport.

That lone change had removed a lot of hurdles and nuances from the process, making the Angels more efficient. The secret had been in the Book of Time, and had only come into the commander's possession after the war against the Revolution had ended.

Aside from that, everything else about the process remained the same, and Arielle fell into a void of darkness, a sensation of floating on a cloud until she lightly hit the ground in 2008.

The conference room looked mostly the same, only different furniture and technology. Arielle opened the door to peek outside, finding the bullpen emptier than when she had arrived in her present-time.

Still before this place was a headquarters.

The three people in the bullpen didn't pay her any attention. Most Road Runners in the small offices had grown accustomed to people from their future walking out of the conference rooms to go about their business.

A young girl nodded at Arielle, but offered nothing more beyond a polite smile.

Arielle made her way outside, where she had instructions to find a silver Mercedes waiting for her parked on the sidewalk, the keys hidden inside the front wheel.

She found the vehicle and keys without issue and dropped into the driver's seat to open the map provided in her mission report. Jacob Kennedy had never left Denver after receiving a not-guilty verdict in 1992.

Arielle had a map with the route drawn to his house in Golden, about a fifteen-minute drive from the office. All reports suggested that Kennedy rarely left his home in the decades that followed his trial. Kennedy lived like a hermit after having been disowned by his friends and even some family members.

Arielle thought of the darkness surrounding this mission while she drove across town, and how the facts made no sense.

Kennedy had an alibi the morning of the murders and robbery. On their trip to 1991, they would specifically watch for the moment he claimed to have said hello to a neighbor, an act of one of several counterpoints brought up by Kennedy's attorney at trial. On the flip side, he was a former police officer who had investigated crime scenes, and had once worked at the very bank in question as a security guard. No weapon had been found. Neither had the 200,000 dollars of stolen cash. Kennedy's modest life never suggested he had come into extra money at any point since the trial.

As easy as it seemed to place blame on whoever might attract the most suspicion, Arielle had seen plenty of times where the main suspect was indeed innocent. Sometimes people were just in the wrong place at the wrong time and got saddled with the blame.

Arielle turned into Kennedy's neighborhood, a block of single-level homes, all with beautiful, small yards practically on top of each other. The narrow street offered little parking, but she found a space at a house three down from Kennedy's.

Arielle parked and walked up the sloped driveway until stopping in front of Kennedy's house. He had a bright green lawn, even for January, with a long bench on the front porch. A windmill spun near the fence where Arielle stood as she examined the house.

They had studied this moment in time enough to determine Kennedy was home alone.

Arielle strolled right up to the front door and knocked, taking a step back to observe the surrounding neighborhood. Most of the other houses looked the same, and she wondered if this was a retirement community.

The door creaked open, and an old man with a white buzz cut poked his head out. "May I help you?"

"Are you Mr. Kennedy?" Arielle asked, offering a polite smile.

The man looked behind Arielle, his eyes darting in every direction before focusing back on her.

"Who wants to know?" His voice was rough and demanding, obvious hints at his former life as a police sergeant.

"My name is Arielle, sir. I go to college at Metro State. I'm taking a Colorado history class and learned about your trial in 1992. I'm sorry you had to go through that, but I was hoping you might answer a few questions for a paper I'm writing."

"I told you already, I'm innocent!" Kennedy stepped back and slammed the door shut.

Crows cawed from the power line, and Arielle thought they were laughing at her.

The door swung back open, and this time a middle-aged woman appeared, her face tight in a frown. "I'm sorry, young lady. Mr. Kennedy doesn't take questions about his trial anymore."

"I'm sorry if I upset him. I didn't mean any offense. I just genuinely had questions for my paper I'm writing."

"I'm sure that's true, dear, but in the years following the trial, Mr. Kennedy received requests like that every day. And some of them weren't real. The FBI watched his every waking moment. All these years later, I'm sure they've moved on, but it's been a constant hell for Mr. Kennedy. Even if things like this only happen every few years now."

"He still gets people knocking on his door to ask about it?" Arielle asked, faking her surprise.

"*You're* here, aren't you? You kids have your internet and can look up everything. Finding someone's address is pretty easy, from my understanding. What isn't easy is finding information on Mr. Kennedy's trial. It happened before the internet, so I'll tell you what I tell everyone else who comes here. The Denver Public Library is your best bet. They have records of everything from that trial, and might even have video footage of it. That I'm not sure about, since I've heard mixed information. But they'll have your answers. Mr. Kennedy won't."

"May I ask who you are?" Arielle said, almost blurting out that she expected Jacob to be home alone.

"I'm Mr. Kennedy's nurse," the woman replied. "He needs some assistance throughout the day."

How did the team not catch this? Arielle wondered.

"I see," Arielle said. "You know, ma'am, I've been reading so much about this trial and robbery. I, for one, believe Mr. Kennedy is innocent.

Don't get me wrong, there were definitely some things that could *suggest* it was him, but there was far more evidence otherwise. If I can have even five minutes with Mr. Kennedy, I'll be out of your hair."

The nurse studied Arielle with her beady brown eyes, looking her up and down. "Innocent, huh? Well, that's a first. Most people come here trying to find the piece of evidence that makes him guilty."

"Not at all, ma'am. For God's sake, he had an alibi. He chatted with his neighbor that morning of the crime. While it was supposedly happening."

The nurse narrowed her eyes. "You really have been doing your homework. Everyone else says he paid off the neighbor to say those things. Offered her a cut of the stolen money. What do you say to that?"

Arielle shrugged. "I suppose that's possible, but we don't even know what happened to that neighbor. I'm sure if she had come into some extra money, the FBI would have known about it and tied it all back to Mr. Kennedy. But they couldn't. Another reason I believe he's innocent. It's almost impossible to get by the FBI. Beat the police department in court? Sure, that happens. But getting by the FBI monitoring you for *years*? Impossible."

The nurse grinned. "I like your style. What did you say you're going to school for?"

"History. I have a Colorado history class, and we had to choose a topic to investigate and write a term paper about. This one caught my eye."

"I wish you the best of luck, dear, really I do. And I hope you accidentally find something that will truly clear the guilt everyone associates with Mr. Kennedy. I suppose under normal circumstances Mr. Kennedy might actually sit down and chat with you, but this is as far as you'll get these days."

"Why is that?"

"Mr. Kennedy has dementia."

Chapter 7

"I'm glad we don't have to travel anywhere," Felix said. "That's always a nice bonus."

The three had gathered at noon at the headquarters, ready to make their jump back to 1991.

"It's also a bonus knowing what the hell we're doing on a mission," Arielle said. "I traveled to 2008 to try to speak Jacob Kennedy. What a disaster. I don't understand why we're doing this—going in blind. Our own Advance Team can't unearth important details. What makes them think we'll magically do it once we're on the ground?"

"Because we're the best," Felix said. "I told you that already. Do you really think some lower-ranked team could figure this out? If we can't do it, then Commander Briar will write it off as impossible and move on to his next project."

"How are you feeling?" Arielle asked Selena once they settled into a conference room, pointing to her throat that had a light purplish tint of bruising.

"I'm fine," Selena said. "It looks way worse than it feels. In fact, I don't even feel anything."

"You ladies are such badasses," Felix said. "And you don't even know it."

Felix had substantially less combat training compared to Arielle and Selena, and could never break up that fight the way Selena had. He always viewed people with such physical gifts in awe. Being the quiet kid in high school attracted the attention of bullies, but they only ever tried to intimidate him with words. He didn't take them seriously, so their jibes fell flat.

He supposed they left him alone *because* he had no reaction to their cheap insults. *Silence is my greatest weapon,* he reminded himself. The quiet observer rarely got into tussles, whether physical or verbal, no matter how badly he actually wanted to on the inside.

"So did you confront Commander Briar about all these changes?" Selena asked Arielle.

"No, not today. He's in his office, but I figured it's best to just worry about the mission. Did you both have time to review the details?"

Selena and Felix nodded.

"Great. If we're ready then, let's head out."

Arielle stood and shuffled to the front of the room where they had all placed their luggage for the trip into the past. Selena and Felix followed, pulling out their flasks of Juice as they joined by Arielle's side.

"First day of June in 1991, right?" Felix asked.

"Correct." Arielle unscrewed the lid from her flask and took a sip of Juice.

Within seconds all three of them had completed the same act, and sat down on the floor next to their bags.

"See you on the other side," Felix said, grinning.

Selena smacked his arm. "Don't say shit like that."

A minute later, they fell unconscious while their bodies and souls transported through time. The ground rumbled and the quaking didn't cease until they woke up in the same room, finding themselves inside a storage closet.

Felix stood up first and brushed off dust from his pants. "My goodness. The renovations that eventually happen were totally worth it. Look at this dump."

Boxes and furniture filled the dark room.

"They didn't need so much meeting space back in 1991," Arielle said.

"Apparently just storage," Selena said, a bitter countenance as she pulled a cobweb from her hair.

They grabbed their luggage and wheeled it toward the door, Arielle leading the way and opening the door to the office's bullpen. They stepped out to find a much quieter office. A handful of people sat in the bullpen, staring at boxy computers. The room smelled of freshly brewed coffee. File cabinets lined the perimeter, papers gushing out of several of the drawers. The lighting was dim, the walls bare.

"This place is miserable," Selena said under her breath.

"Relax," Arielle said. "Remember, this wasn't a headquarters yet. I think only like fifteen people total work here at the moment."

"Hello?" an older man asked, standing up from his desk in the bullpen. "When are you folks from?"

"2022," Arielle said, moving forward to shake the man's hand.

"Ah, very nice. Welcome. I'm Rich Jenkins, Lead Runner here in Denver."

"Nice to meet you, Rich. We're just on our way, not staying too far from here, actually."

"Wait a minute, are you Arielle Lucila?" Rich had a long, droopy face that perked up at this realization. He had a slight hunch in his back that he forced straight as he looked at Arielle. "I've heard of you. You do great work."

A few other heads in the bullpen looked up after hearing Rich speak, gawking at the trio.

"Thank you, Mr. Jenkins," Arielle said with a smile. "We've got a mission here in 1991."

Arielle studied Rich. He was at least in his late sixties. It was rare to see many older Road Runners. Most Runners retired from the day-to-day grind of working for the organization around the age of fifty. By then, they would have lived an extra thousand years in different eras of time.

While one could never truly quit the Road Runners, the organization allowed people to retire from their responsibilities, while still keeping tabs on them in case any needs arose.

"Well, best of luck to you folks," Rich said. "If you need anything at all, come see me. We keep a decent amount of weapons right here in the office, and have access to the system if you need to look anything up. I can also travel to different years right here from the office to meet with other Road Runners if you need to send a message. This office is the headquarters in 2022, is that right?"

"It is. I may need to send word to our commander, so I'll keep you in the loop."

"I look forward to it," Rich said with a soft grin. "Well, I'll let you get to it. Was nice meeting you all. I'll be here if you need me."

Rich smiled and returned to his desk, walking gingerly with a slight limp.

Arielle looked to the other two and nodded toward the exit.

They followed her and climbed the familiar stairwell upstairs to the marketing office. In 2022, the place bustled with at least thirty Road Runners posing as employees, phones ringing, music blaring. Now, they found only ten people working in sheer silence. Some wore headphones plugged into their portable CD players.

"This place is like a dungeon," Selena said as they passed through the office to step outside for the first time in 1991.

"I see why the office is the way it is," Felix said when they reached the sidewalk. "They need to blend in."

Gone were the restaurants, bars, and sleek office spaces of the time they knew as the present. Instead, they looked around at warehouses and a street lined with semi-trucks delivering goods.

"What the hell?" Selena asked. "Where *is* everything?"

"Have neither of you traveled back in time in Denver?" Arielle asked. "This part of downtown was industrial until they opened the baseball stadium in 1995. Union Station is a few blocks away, and this entire area is a shipping dock for all the goods coming in and out of Denver. The mall is still a few blocks down, but the rest of downtown isn't developed for another few years."

"This doesn't look like a place you should be alone past dark," Felix said, looking up the sidewalk where a man leaned against the building, injecting himself with heroine.

"That's very true," Arielle said.

"I hope we're not staying around here," Selena said, face scrunched in disgust as she looked at the man.

"We're within walking distance, but we'll be at an apartment complex close to the bank. Same building one of our suspects lives in, actually."

Arielle led the way, wheeling her suitcase behind her. Selena and Felix followed, pulling their luggage.

They had a one-mile journey to their apartment building, the arrangements set up in advance for them. On the way, they passed several more homeless people camped out on the deserted sidewalks.

"Go back where you came from!" one man yelled. "I know where you're from. Get the hell out of here!"

He had stood up from the ground, raggedy jacket and pants swaying from his body. His skin had been weathered, his facial hair scruffy. He cracked his lips into a grin, revealing yellowed teeth.

"We're just on our way," Arielle said, walking faster.

"Aren't we all?" the man replied, taking another step toward them.

Felix clutched his bag and ran past Arielle.

The homeless man grabbed his stomach and broke into hysterics. "Buncha pussies! Back when I was in the game, I never had to travel with ladies to stay safe. Good look on you, sissy boy!"

"Let it go," Felix said over his shoulder, knowing Arielle had stopped and wanted to encounter their heckler. "He's delusional."

"I was on my way once," the man said, reaching into his jacket and pulling out a flask, promptly spinning off the cap and taking a swig. He looked up and belched. "Would hate for you three to get stuck in here with me. I'll never get out! If I see you again, *you'll* never get out, either!"

Arielle shook her head and joined Felix and Selena in running away.

The man howled laughter and fell over, kicking his legs in the air while clutching his stomach.

The three Angels reached the next block within seconds, finally out of sight from the homeless man.

"Think he was one of us?" Selena asked.

"Definitely seemed like it," Felix said. "That's why I didn't want a confrontation."

Time travelers who got stuck in the past, typically from losing their Juice and not able to get it replaced, ended up losing their sanity. Many wandered the streets, talking to themselves and anyone else who passed by. Others ended up in a padded room for the rest of their existence in the past.

Making Juice for a specific person required time, and sometimes there wasn't enough to make a new batch before a time traveler overstayed their trip. If you traveled back into the past, you had to return to your present before the past caught up with it.

Commander Briar had hoped to end this matter upon discovering many secrets in the Book of Time, but none were available. This was simply a rule that could not be broken.

"Let's just keep going," Arielle said. "We're almost there."

They had traveled five blocks and were gaining speed. "I can see the apartment building," Selena said, pointing ahead.

The building stood ten stories tall with a beige exterior and steel balconies on the corners of each unit. A crooked sign hung near the complex's front entrance, reading *Mountain View Apartments*.

"We're up on the seventh floor," Arielle said. "Peter Young is on the fifth."

With their destination in sight, the three of them hurried down the sidewalk, escaping the gloom of the suffering downtown area , and stepping into the more residential and business-focused part of town.

They stopped outside of the building, and Arielle unzipped her suitcase and rummaged through it to pull out an envelope full of keys, one for each of them to access the apartment. She unfolded a piece of paper and read from it. "Building code is 4-5-8 to get in. We are apartment number 714."

"I haven't lived in an apartment since college," Felix said, reminiscing. He had lived in the campus dorms during his freshman year and decided it best to live alone off-campus for the rest of his college days.

They walked inside together, the main lobby housing two walls of mailboxes for the residents of the complex. Through another set of double doors was the main hallway, complete with the administrative offices, a rec room, and a swimming pool.

"Place is kind of fancy," Selena said.

"It's considered a luxury apartment in these days," Arielle added. "But really isn't priced like one. It's a hidden gem for sure."

They passed the offices and found the elevators, two shafts available for use. They rode up to the seventh floor and stepped out to a hallway with gaudy carpeting, and cheap art hanging from the walls.

"Not *too* luxurious, I guess," Arielle said with a laugh. "Looks like a hotel up here."

Their door was halfway down the hall, and they stepped into a much more appealing apartment.

The complex only had a handful of three-bedroom units, and they had lucked out being able to secure one. The apartment opened immediately to the kitchen on the right, dining area to the left. On the other side of a bartop counter above the sink was the living room. A hallway broke left, three doors belonging to two bedrooms and a bathroom. The master bedroom was adjoined to the dining area, its door ajar.

"Not bad at all," Felix said. "We own this place?"

"Not exactly," Arielle said. "Well, not right now. The Road Runners will buy the entire building in 1999, needing a central location to keep guests from out of town. Felix, I'm giving you the master bedroom so you can set up all your stuff. We'll actually be able to monitor Peter Young on a direct feed once we can get his place bugged. From my understanding, he's directly two levels below us."

Selena wheeled her suitcase to the hallway and left it there. "So Peter Young is the next likely suspect? But he didn't leave any evidence behind. He worked there, sure, but so did several other people."

Felix moved to the window overlooking the city and mountains. "He may not have left any evidence behind, but he had the perfect view."

He pulled apart the drapes and revealed the towering skyscraper that housed the bank that would be robbed in exactly sixteen days.

274

Chapter 8

As much as they had complained about the Advance Team's shortcomings in preparing for the mission, the reality was they had done superb work. Not understanding who their primary target was proved a critical pain point, but they provided every other shred of information available, plus tools to make their lives easier. Typically, Felix would be the one to get Selena a job within the United Bank building. But the Advance Team had already taken care of that and provided her with a badge and keycard.

Felix reviewed their documents and slid the badge across the table. "You have a job with the cleaning crew. Nine to five, Monday through Friday."

"Wait, am I going to clean toilets?" Selena asked, appalled.

"Probably. You'll need to do whatever your supervisor asks of you. Her name is Olivia Bryant, and she's expecting you Monday for your first shift."

"I'm gonna throw up if I have to clean toilets. You guys, I've never even cleaned one, ever. How am I supposed to do this?"

Arielle laughed. "You better figure it out with all those acting skills. You pour in some cleaner, scrub with a sponge, and be done. Not much to it."

"And if you do throw up," Felix added. "At least you'll already be next to the toilet."

Arielle and Felix broke into laughter, Selena shaking her head. "Not funny."

"Princess Selena has to clean a toilet," Felix said, gasping and placing a hand to his mouth. "Dare I say she might have to . . . mop a floor?"

Arielle slapped her leg as she threw her head back and laughed.

"I'm glad you two are getting a kick out of this. And what will you be doing while I swim in shit all day?"

They regained their composure, Arielle speaking first. "For starters, cleaning is not all you're doing. You need to study the place. Learn where everything is and the best way to access the bank and vault. Take advantage of your first few days and wander into restricted areas. See how far you can get. You'll be able to talk your way out of it. Play the card that you just started, and bat those pretty eyes. The guards won't do anything as long as you seem innocent."

"I'm not worried about that—I can get out of any situation."

"I'll be tailing Jacob Kennedy. He's still our prime target. All reports suggest he got away with it thanks to a botched trial by the prosecution. I don't know—there were a lot of things that make sense for it being him, but also a lot that oppose it."

"And I'm monitoring suspect number two," Felix said. "Peter Young. That will be rather straightforward, since I get to hang out at the apartment all day and listen to his conversations."

"Nothing is straightforward in any mission," Arielle said. "*Especially* this one. Selena, it's important you keep an ear out while you're at the building. Maybe find out where the guards hang out on breaks and try to eavesdrop. There was a suspicion that whoever committed the crime had help from the inside."

Selena nodded while jotting down notes. They each had papers spread across the table in front of them, a cluster of information on all aspects of the mission. "When will you bug Young's apartment?"

"He's off tomorrow, so Tuesday," Felix said. "He works from noon to eight, so I'll be there at about 12:30. Should be a simple place to infiltrate. He lives alone, has no pets. Small one-bedroom apartment." Felix shrugged as if he could do the job in his sleep.

"Is there a reason we didn't try following this guy in a later year?" Selena asked. "If the FBI found nothing on Kennedy, maybe Young had the money all along."

"The Advance Team already looked into it and found nothing. Young dies of a heart attack four months after the trial ended. If he ever had a plan of holding the money to use later, that chance never came."

Felix stood and crossed the room toward the window, looking out at the city. "So crazy that money was never found. If Kennedy had it, he must have buried it somewhere and never went back for it since he had a target on his back. If Young had it, that secret died with him. I know this probably hasn't been a question you've had to answer before, but who do you think did it?"

"Speculation only causes false biases," Arielle said. She took a long drink of water before putting her empty glass on the table. "But I think it was Kennedy."

"Me too," Selena said.

"Interesting. I was thinking Young. Guy gets away with it and never cashed in his prize."

"I just don't feel he was smart enough to get away with it," Arielle said. "Did you watch the clips of his questioning in the courtroom? Dude was dumb as rocks. No way he pulls it off."

"I agree," Selena said. "Kennedy was sharp. If he kept close contact with any of the guards, he could have known enough about the security changes within the building while planning the robbery."

"We have the advantage of looking at the evidence that *didn't* get presented in court," Arielle said. "Did you know they found a box full of fake ID's in Kennedy's house? And they had different names on them."

"How the hell was that not allowed in court?!" Felix asked, spinning around to meet Arielle's gaze.

She shrugged. "Because he had slick lawyers, I suppose. The judge ruled it wasn't relevant to the case because the ID's were never used—that much was confirmed."

"But that shows intent," Felix said. "Why else would he have those?"

"We don't know. And since they didn't admit them as evidence, Kennedy didn't have to answer for them. We don't know when they were created, or why. Maybe there was a legitimate reason, but we'll never know."

"Why do you keep saying we'll never know? You don't seem too hopeful about this mission."

Arielle leaned back and clasped her hands behind her head. "I'm sorry, you two. My head just isn't in this the way it should be. I feel like we're playing against the odds even more than normal. My gut feeling says this mission is a waste of time."

"Nothing we do is a waste of time," Selena said. "Even if the mission ends and we haven't changed anything, it will still be a learning experience."

"We're not paid to learn," Arielle said. "We're here to make the world a better place. Four lives were lost because of this tragedy. Four families broken, on Father's Day."

"Forgive me for maybe sounding too harsh," Felix said. "But I've never understood why it's been our problem to fix things. Life happens. Death happens all the time—tragic, sudden death. Who are we to play God and stop it from occurring?"

"Because we *can*," Arielle said. "There's a reason we never go back and stop a tornado from wiping out a small town. We can't do anything to stop the tornado. If we could, then we'd also have missions like that."

"We could warn the people and guide them out of harm's way."

Arielle shook her head. "The past doesn't allow it—that would be too easy. We could just as easily tell the four victims to call in sick on June 16th. Commander Briar once left a written letter to the principal of a high school trying to warn him about shootings that would occur three years in the future."

"And what happened?"

"The building burned to the ground."

Felix shuffled toward the table and sat back down, staring at his twirling fingers.

"The past will always fight to conserve itself," Arielle continued. "But that doesn't mean we can't change it. We just have to trick it. Remember what I mentioned about needing to block off your intent? The past knows. We play by its rules, but that doesn't mean we can't find loopholes to succeed. In fact, we *have* to. That's the only way."

"I've been practicing that," Selena said. "There are meditative practices that help train your brain to focus on something entirely different while you're doing another thing. Start simple. Paint a wall in your house, but think about cooking dinner while you do it."

"That's exactly it," Arielle said. "That's why I spend so much time learning these missions inside and out before we jump into the past. If I spent as much time studying the reports here instead of at home, it would be impossible to hide my intent while absorbing all that information. But if I do it in my present time, then the past has no way of knowing what I plan to do. A loophole, see? That way when I'm in the grind of a mission, my mind can wander elsewhere, and the knowledge I need for the mission itself is basically second nature."

"I think I'm understanding it a little better," Felix said. "Seems like it takes a lot of time to perfect."

Arielle nodded. "I've done thousands of missions. In the beginning, there were several mistakes. After a couple hundred, I got a better feel for this practice. Haven't looked back since and kept refining it. I suggest we all get a good night's rest. We'll do some light work tomorrow, but the real fun starts on Monday."

Chapter 9

"Two weeks from today, that bank is going to be robbed," Arielle said.

They gathered at The Last Drop, a café directly across the street from the United Bank building, sitting at the outdoor patio for a clear view of the building they would all study over the next fourteen days. Notebooks sat open across the table, cups of coffee and sodas filling the spaces in between. Felix had pushed his notes to the center to make room for a towering plate of nachos.

"You know, Selena," Felix said. "Your badge will work immediately. You can head inside and have a look around."

"No," Arielle said. "That would be suspicious. She doesn't have a work uniform and doesn't even start until Monday. Let's not get ahead of ourselves."

Felix shook his head. "Who robs a bank on Father's Day?"

"Did Kennedy have kids?" Selena asked.

"Yes," Arielle said. "Two adult children. Which means if it was him, he robbed the bank, killed four guards, and returned home for lunch."

"That's absolutely absurd," Felix added. "The crazy thing is that whoever did it is probably sitting at home thinking about it right now. Hell, they could even be in this café watching the building like we are."

Arielle scanned the café , Felix's idea definitely possible. No one who resembled either Jacob Kennedy or Peter Young was in the area.

"I was only kidding," Felix said, offering a grin. "We'd obviously know if either of our targets were sitting at the next table."

"It's a small world," Arielle said. "You never know. Why don't we go have a look around the place?"

"For what?" Felix scooped some beans and chicken and shoved them into his mouth.

"Just to look. It'll be good to have a feel for the block surrounding the building."

They agreed and waited ten minutes while Felix finished his food.

Downtown Denver was deserted on Sunday morning, at least in the bank's area, which was primarily a business district. A young couple jogged past them when they stepped out of the café , and beyond that they didn't see another person within a two-block radius.

They crossed the street and looked up, unable to see the top of the skyscraper and its signature cash register shape.

"Kind of weird, isn't it?" Selena said. "It's just a building to everyone passing by. Even the people inside. But when you know something is going to happen, it has a different energy. Do you guys ever feel that way on some of these missions?"

"I used to," Arielle said. "Not so much anymore. But I still feel it at the mall where I lost my family. Just driving by. It's like I can feel the building staring at me. Watching me. Like it regrets not taking me that day."

Felix and Selena exchanged looks and squirmed.

"What's wrong?" Arielle asked, looking back and forth between them.

Felix looked to Selena, and she spoke. "Nothing's wrong. It's just . . . we never know what to say when you bring up that day."

Arielle scrunched her face. "You don't need to say anything. I never expect you to."

"It's weird for us," Felix said. "I suppose it always has been, and not just with you. Something like ninety-five percent of the current Road Runners entered this life because of some horrific tragedy they endured. Selena and myself are the rare ones who did not. It's such a common question between Road Runners, asking about those past tragedies. It's become as normal as asking someone where their hometown is. And we never know how to reply without sounding arrogant."

"Is this how you feel, too?" Arielle asked Selena.

Her teammate nodded, lips pursed.

"I guess you're right," Arielle said. "I never thought of it that way, but it is something that is discussed rather openly. It's normal to me. I don't *mean* to bring it up so much—it's just part of who I am. Something that has pushed me in life all the way to this point."

"And we get that," Selena said. "Don't take this as us telling you to stop bringing it up—that's not the issue. We just never know if we're supposed to say something back. It's impossible for us to relate. We can only sympathize."

"I appreciate that. And please don't feel pressured to reply. If you want to be silent, that's fine. I guess I talk about it just to let it out. The pain and sorrow never go away. Neither does the fear. My therapist always encouraged me to speak about it whenever the memories of that day pop into my head. Apparently, bottling it all in is no good. Who would've thought?"

"We're here for you," Felix said, extending an arm to grab Arielle's shoulder. She clasped her hand on his, tears welling in her eyes. "I mean it. Even if there isn't something that triggers the memory, and you just want to talk about it. Let us know. We're not your fan club. We're your team. Your *family.* You don't have to act like the top-ranked Angel in front of us. Let it out."

Selena joined and threw an arm around Arielle's other shoulder, the three of them now huddled in a tight group hug.

Arielle let the tears flow. "Thank you," she muttered. "I haven't developed any close relationships with anyone since the shooting. The only person I've been able to talk about it openly with is my abuela. You have no idea how much it means to me. I trust you two, and feel so blessed you've come into my life. I'm sorry if I've ever made your jobs difficult—I know I need to trust you both, but it's hard for me. I always assume something bad will happen if I'm not in control."

They released their embrace, and everyone took a step back, Arielle wiping the tears off her face. She couldn't remember the last time she'd had such an emotional moment away from her grandmother. Felix and Selena stood in front of her, watching her with eyes full of worry. For the first time since joining the Road Runners, she had met someone—in this case, two people—who expected nothing from her. They weren't concerned about discussing a mission, requesting her presence at an event, asking her to teach a course, or just wanting a moment of her time to gush about how great she was.

They were simply present. There for her. No strings attached. It had only taken one complete mission and a couple of days into a second for their collective bond to blossom into a friendship.

Arielle grinned and looked at Felix. "You called us family. I thought we weren't even supposed to be friends."

Felix smiled back. "I guess some things are out of my control."

"Thank you. Really. I haven't had close friends in a long time. I've forgotten what it's like. I've had many roles in my life, but being a friend is one that's been pushed so far back, I don't remember how to do it anymore."

"Don't worry about all that," Selena said. "We'll help you. You know I'll call you out when you get carried away with all that top-ranked Angel crap."

She stepped forward and slapped Arielle on the arm, earning a hearty laugh.

"Thanks, you two. I already feel so much better. Should we head back to the apartment and get ready for tomorrow?"

"There she is," Felix said. "Honestly, I don't mind taking another hour and walking around downtown. When's the last time we got to explore the city? Besides, we're not even done walking around this building."

Arielle nodded. "That sounds great. And yes, we need to check out the building. The freight elevator is near the east entrance—we should start there."

Chapter 10

Selena arrived at the Cash Register Building on Monday morning and met Olivia Bryant, her manager for the next two weeks. Every Monday morning, Olivia hosted a team meeting in the hallway outside the changing rooms for the custodial staff. At seven o'clock, Selena found herself in a huddle of fifteen others, all dressed in the same plain gray uniforms, arms crossed as they listened to Olivia.

"And please welcome our newest teammate, Ms. Selena Nicole," Olivia said, waving Selena to step forward. She did, waving a hand at the group. "Selena comes to us with plenty of experience already, so she'll spend the day with me, more to get familiar with the building. Expect to work with her over the next few months while we reconfigure the rotation. Now, everyone have a good week, and as always, let me know if you need anything."

The huddle dissolved, everyone going their separate ways while Selena remained alongside Olivia.

"You ready?" Olivia asked, placing her hands on her hips. "No break until eleven."

Selena dreaded her day ahead and had to remind herself it was all part of the process. She was inside the building that had so many questions needing an answer. But first, she had to feign interest in scrubbing the toilets and dusting rich executives' offices.

"Absolutely," she said. "How many floors are we doing today?"

"You got it lucky since you're with me. We'll do four. Everyone else pairs off and will handle eight. We budget an hour per floor. If you do well today, you'll jump into that rotation tomorrow."

"And there are how many floors in this building?"

"Fifty-two, if you include the two basement levels. Further down this hall is our break room. That's where you'll want to store any snacks or lunch. I'd say it's fifty-fifty for who eats here and who goes out downtown. You'll have a nine-hour day, with an hour for lunch at one. I tell everyone to always stay in motion. If you're not doing something, then you'll fall behind schedule.

"If that happens, someone else has to pick up your slack. They get a bonus if it comes to that. If everyone hits their allotted floors within the day, the whole team gets a bonus. An extra twenty-five dollars for every day that happens. Might not sound like much, but we get it usually four days out of the week. No one is complaining about an extra hundred bucks. That's an extra two-and-a-half days' worth of pay. Don't be surprised when people start really pushing each other around the holidays. Everyone wants the extra cash."

Selena did the math in her head to find she would make roughly five dollars per hour during her time as a custodian. She couldn't imagine having to live off such low wages, and already admired her new coworkers for their determination.

"Let's get to it," Olivia chirped, leading them down the hall and toward the elevator shaft at the end. Everyone else had already left the area, hard at work for the day ahead. They stepped in, and Olivia pressed the button to take them to twenty-first floor, explaining the building blueprints as they rode up. "We have a pretty simple layout for being such a big building. The bank takes up the first floor, at street level. They also have a vault in the subbasement level where the security office is. If you ever feel uncomfortable during the day, don't call me, call the security team. They'll move much faster. There are phones outside of every door in the stairwell throughout the entire building. They only dial to the security office."

"Why would I not feel comfortable?" Selena asked.

"Child, you are young, pretty, and a cleaner. These corporate men have all sorts of sick fantasies about sleeping with maids. Most of them will just look at you while you clean, but you never know when one might strike up a conversation, or even try to touch you. Just stay alert, and always keep your cart in the doorway so the door can't close."

"I'm sorry, is this a regular thing that happens?"

"I'm not trying to scare you. No, it's not common. We get maybe two incidents a year, but I always remind the women on the team to keep an eye out. Because when these things happen, it's usually the man's word against ours. And who do you think the authorities believe? The millionaire executive, or the minimum-wage janitor?"

"That's so wrong."

"No shit, it's wrong, but that's the world we live in, sweetie. Did things like that not happen at your old job?"

According to the fake resume the Angels had created for her, Selena had cleaned the offices for a music studio in Los Angeles before moving to Denver. "I guess not. At least, not that I realized."

"Well, that's good. I suppose there is some hope for humanity, after all. I find it best to just mind your business while you clean. Most of these people pretend we're invisible, anyway. If you don't already have one, you'll want to get one of those portable CD players. They're a real lifesaver."

The doors parted, and they stepped into a new elevator lobby, this one enclosed with glass walls and formal writing stamped onto the doors welcoming them to the Law Offices of Fields, Mercer, and Wellington.

A closet door was next to the elevators, and Olivia wiggled in a key from her pocket to open it, revealing a cleaning cart fully equipped with a mop, brooms, dustpans, chemical cleaners, rags, and long yellow rubber gloves.

"The carts are on each level of your first assigned floor. You'll start there and work your way up. Return your cart to the floor you found it, and that'll be your day."

Olivia pulled out the bright yellow cart and wheeled it toward the law office's doors, tapping her keycard against the security pad on the wall.

It chimed and flashed a green light, the double doors unlocking with a forceful click.

They entered a lobby where Olivia offered a polite grin to a young blond sitting at the reception desk. The girl was on the phone, but smiled back before returning to her call. She paid no attention to Selena.

"Follow me," Olivia mumbled, turning a corner and hurrying down the hall where the restroom doors waited at the end.

Over the next twenty minutes, the two of them cleaned the men's and women's bathrooms in tandem. Selena took care of the sinks and sweeping the floors, while Olivia cleaned the toilets and followed up with a mop.

"How long have you been working here?" Selena asked.

"Twelve years now," Olivia replied. "It's crazy to think it's been that long. I guess life really can pass by in a blur."

"But do you enjoy it?"

Olivia finished mopping and leaned the mop against the wall, crossing her arms. "No one *enjoys* this work, Selena. You should know that already. I enjoy the steadiness of the job. I know exactly what needs to be done every day. No curveballs, no surprises. Just the same eight hours of work every day of the week."

"I can see the appeal."

"And what about you? You seem too young to be in this kind of job. Most kids out of college will at least attempt to do something significant first, then fall back on a job like this if things didn't work out."

"I didn't go to college," Selena said, having created a persona for the new character she had to portray for the next two weeks. "Barely graduated high school, but somehow did."

"Is your mama a cleaner? I've seen plenty of mother-daughter teams start their own business."

"She was, yes."

"Well, let me tell you this. Find something else to pursue. Especially before you have kids and need to rely on a steady paycheck. Take a chance before it's too late."

"You have kids, I take it?"

"Two boys. Eighth and fifth grade. My husband fell ill . . . twelve years ago. He was unable to work. I found this job and have had it ever since."

"What did you want to do before?"

"I was waiting tables on the weekends to pay my way through college night courses during the week. I wanted to work as a physical therapist, but that requires a complete education and training. Once my husband went down, I became the lone breadwinner for the family. He passed about four years into this job, so I couldn't possibly leave. Two boys require a lot of food, let me tell you."

Olivia chuckled, and Selena grinned. She understood Olivia demanded a certain level of respect from her employees. Many even seemed intimidated. But all Selena saw was a single mother who had given up on her dreams to support her children. A modern-day angel, as her own mom referred to single mothers.

"I have four years until my oldest will start looking at colleges. I save all the bonus money I get and put it into a savings account just for that. It might not be much, but it will help."

They continued talking, leaving the law offices and moving up to the next floor, a telemarketing firm where a bullpen full of men and women with headsets shouted into the phones.

"If you could do anything, what would you do?" Olivia asked.

"I've always wanted to be an actress."

"Well, you moved in the wrong direction. You were already in Holly-wood, weren't you? Don't tell me you left it behind for a boy."

"No, of course not. I just had some personal matters I needed to tend to here in Denver."

"Well, you better get on the plane back to Hollywood whenever it's resolved. Chase that dream. Even if you fail, at least you tried, and you'll never regret it."

Selena sensed a decade's worth of bottled-up emotions swimming beneath Olivia's calm and focused poise. Life had forced her away from her dreams. But Selena could read between the lines. There was a physical therapist hiding inside of Olivia Bryant. An alternate life that never came into fruition. She wondered what would happen if Olivia's husband had never gotten sick and passed away.

"It's been on my mind. I just might go back someday."

Olivia laughed. "Someday never comes, child. Someday is a myth. A lie we tell ourselves to keep going through reality. It's now or never."

She spoke with the grace of someone who had suffered plenty throughout life. It always seemed the kindest and most optimistic people were that way because they had been hardened in the past.

"I hope you get an opportunity again in the future," Selena said. "You deserve the life you want."

Olivia raised an eyebrow. "Maybe when my kids are done with college, I can revisit it. I might be too old of a lady by then to do physical therapy. This line of work definitely takes a toll on your body. We'll see."

They finished cleaning the bathrooms and returned to the elevator to go up to the next floor.

"Do we ever clean the bank? You mentioned the bank vault. I've never seen one of those in real life. Does it look like the ones in the movies?"

"It's just a big door, nothing to get excited about. But yes, we rotate the floors we cover each day. That is one thing we do to mix things up a bit. There isn't much to clean on that level besides the security office. They are nice guys in there, always friendly. Fortunately, their office space is pretty small, because they are messy men. You'll meet them soon enough."

"I look forward to it."

Chapter 11

After an uneventful Monday where Felix wasted a day at the apartment for Peter Young's day off, Tuesday morning brought a fresh excitement.

Young left the building, dressed in his security uniform at exactly 7:45 in the morning. Felix had waited outside the complex to confirm his target was indeed out of the building.

He hurried back in to grab his backpack and promptly went down to the fifth floor, stopping outside of apartment 512 and looking around. An elderly woman moseyed down the hallway, grinning at Felix while he pretended to fumble in his backpack.

"Lost my keys," he said with a light chuckle, and the woman continued toward the elevators without a word.

Instead of keys he pulled out a lock pick and entered the apartment within twenty seconds, closing the door and locking it behind him. He stood with his back against the wall and scanned the apartment.

Young lived a messy life. A recliner faced a TV immediately to Felix's left. What looked like a bedroom nightstand stood next to the recliner, covered with nude magazines, empty beer cans, and an ashtray overflowing with cigarette butts. Behind the recliner was an open kitchen, dirty dishes toppling out of the sink, grease splattered on the wall above the stovetop, and more beer cans.

The apartment reeked of cigarette smoke, and Felix was grateful for it. Surely underneath that stench was something more nauseating, judging by the opened food containers left on the kitchen table.

"How the hell can anyone live like this?" Felix asked himself, suddenly horrified at the prospect of needing to move throughout the apartment.

He took a deep breath and started down the short hallway that branched out to the bathroom and bedroom. Felix skipped the bathroom, refusing to imagine how disgusting it would be, and stepped into a surprisingly cleaner bedroom. The bed hadn't been made, and there was a pile of clothes in front of the closet, but aside from that, he saw no beer cans or cigarettes. The pile of dirty clothes touched the low-hanging shirts inside the closet, mostly work uniforms hanging on the rack.

A nightstand stood next to the bed. Felix shuffled to it and pulled open the top drawer to find a handgun on top of a collection of wrist watches. A telephone sat atop the nightstand, so Felix pulled out his bugging kit and tapped the phone line. He hadn't seen a phone in the living room or kitchen, and assumed this was the only one in the place.

The apartment was cluttered enough to set up hidden cameras and microphones, so Felix took the next hour finding the perfect spots to place them. He stuffed a microphone in the bedroom closet, and snapped another to the clock hanging on the wall in the kitchen. He clipped a camera to the bunny-ear antenna above the TV, plugging in its thin cord to the power strip jammed behind the TV.

The cameras were slightly smaller than a tube of lipstick, and he trusted Young wouldn't recognize them within his mess of a home. And even if he found one, it would be impossible to know for sure what it was.

It would have been more discreet to place hidden microphones inside a lamp or a drawer, but he had the unique opportunity of being able to watch the live-feed from the apartment two floors above.

He hoped to catch Young planning the burglary. Whether it was discreet phone calls, a secret notebook of plans, or even something as full-blown as bank diagrams.

Felix still had two hours left in his allocated time in the apartment and poked around the mess to see if there were already clues left behind.

He pushed aside the dirty magazines in the living room to find a stack of bills underneath.

"Past due," Felix said, picking up the gas bill. It was two weeks late, and beneath it was the electric bill, a month overdue. "This explains the need for money."

Felix took a step back and rubbed his temples, trying to make sense of the late bills. Sure, a security job at the bank wasn't life-changing money, but it should have covered the basic bills. Just where was the man's money going, aside from the liquor store?

Felix dropped the bills back on the table and returned to the bedroom. The robbery suspect had worn a fedora and sunglasses, and that's exactly what Felix hoped to find. The top shelf of the closet was as much of a mess as the floor. Shoe boxes piled atop each other, buried under miscellaneous clothing items like hats, ties, beanies, scarfs, and gloves.

After rummaging through at least a dozen Denver Nuggets and Broncos ballcaps, Felix found two fedoras buried against the back wall. His hands trembled as he pulled out the hats, staring at them like they were the smoking gun in this entire mission.

"Lots of people own fedoras," he reminded himself. "I'm sure Kennedy owns fedoras, too."

Felix studied the hats. Both were gray. One had faint black pinstripes, the other was solid with a black ribbon tied around the base. None of the witnesses had accurately described the fedora worn that day, only that there had been one.

If only he could get into Kennedy's house and confirm what types of hats he owned. Should he not find a fedora in Kennedy's closet, then matters became more interesting. He returned the fedoras and replaced everything how he had found it in the closet. Sunglasses were nowhere to be seen, but could have been in Peter's car, or even on his person. It was summer, after all.

A knock came from the door, and every ounce of Felix's blood froze in its tracks. He spun around from the closet and listened to make sure the doorknob wasn't being twisted or unlocked. His heart drummed in his ears, making the task that much more difficult.

A second knock banged on the door, not soft, not too hard.

Felix crouched as he tiptoed out of the bedroom, staring at the door.

Sweat immediately formed on his palms. These were the situations Felix dreaded. If it had been Arielle in the apartment right now, she would have already identified every possible weapon within arm's reach, and the best places to hide from a potential intruder.

A third knock came, this time accompanied by a deep voice. "You in there, Pete? We don't have time for these games."

Felix held his breath, refusing to emit a single sound and reveal his presence. He thought back to the gun in the nightstand and debated dashing back into the bedroom to get it.

Instead, a sheet of paper slid from under the door, and Felix listened as footsteps trailed away down the hall before stepping forward to read it.

Two dimes by the end of the month. The words were scribbled, barely legible.

"Two dimes?" Felix said aloud, wanting so badly to take the note, but not wanting his fingerprints left on anything. Also, he wouldn't dare remove it. The letter was clearly important and meant for Peter Young. "Holy shit."

Felix was plenty familiar with the world of sports betting, but it took him a moment to remember bookies used the term *dime.*

"Young owes a bookie two thousand dollars by the end of the month. That's where all his money has gone. He has a gambling problem."

Young needed a lump sum of money in a hurry. And what better way to get it than to rob the bank he worked at?

Felix's internal timer had gone off. It was time to leave the apartment. He had done everything he needed and could monitor the activity from the comforts of his living room two floors above.

He stepped around the note and hurried out of the apartment, pulling the door to ensure it shut all the way. As he started toward the stairwell, the man's voice from earlier called out from the opposite end of the hallway. "Who the hell are you?! Come back here!"

Felix jerked his head around, made quick eye contact with a man of at least six and a half feet, dressed in black pants and a matching leather coat, and broke into a sprint toward the stairwell.

It was all he could think of doing, and considering how long the hallways were, and how much space was between the two men, figured it was the right decision. Speed had always been Felix's best weapon, even as far back as high school. Bullies had picked on him for no apparent reason other than being a scrawny, awkward freshman. After one encounter, he simply ran away from the bullies. They could never catch him, unwilling to exert so much physical effort for something hardly worth their time.

By the time Felix reached the door to the stairwell, he looked back to see the man barreling down the hallway, but not even to Peter's door yet. Felix jumped onto the third step and dashed up the stairs until reaching the door to the seventh floor. He swung it open and hurried down the hall to their apartment, gasping for breath as he inserted the key and let himself in.

Felix slammed the door and tossed his backpack on the floor, arms spread as he slid down to the floor, smiling. His legs had once more saved him.

He had just escaped a potentially horrid situation. One thing had become immediately clear, on only their fourth day since arriving in 1991:

The past was already pushing back.

Chapter 12

Arielle sat outside Jacob Kennedy's home on Wednesday for the third day in a row.

So far, each morning saw Kennedy's wife leave around 7:30 A.M. and return home at 4:30 P.M. She apparently hadn't reached the age of retirement like her husband. Arielle considered this another motive for Kennedy to steal the money. Perhaps he stewed all day at home alone, guilty that he spent his days crafting model boats while his wife had to put in actual work. Maybe robbing a bank would allow her to retire.

Get him out of your head, Arielle had to remind herself. She had no proof that he had robbed the place, and just because he had stood trial didn't mean he had committed the crime. She hated this new type of mission. Before, she knew everything about her targets and their involvement with whatever crime had been committed. If she got too hung up on Kennedy as the suspect, she might miss opportunities that suggested otherwise. She needed to control her bias if she wanted any chance of solving this mystery.

Kennedy hadn't so much as stepped foot outside his home on Monday and Tuesday, making this mission that much more difficult. Never mind them not having the chance to bug the place, but Arielle couldn't gain any information if all he did was sit inside. After two excruciating days of boredom, Arielle spun her own theories as she saw him occasionally through the kitchen window, and other times at the dining room table where he worked on the model boats.

She hadn't even seen a clear view of him since arriving in 1991, and she wondered how many more days she could handle of the non-activity before giving up on Kennedy as a suspect. One couldn't rob a bank from their living room.

Finally, on Wednesday morning at exactly 10:41, Jacob Kennedy stepped out of his front door and trudged to his truck in the driveway. Arielle's heart nearly jumped out of her throat as she whipped out her binoculars from her duffel bag on the passenger seat and saw Kennedy live in the flesh for the first time. He had a thick mustache and wore a solid black ballcap low enough to cover his brow. Kennedy dressed in a relaxed summer outfit of jean shorts and a t-shirt decorated with a bald eagle hovering over the American flag.

He slipped behind the wheel of a beaten Ford pickup, and pulled out of the driveway in a hurry.

Arielle turned her car on and flipped it around to follow. She had rented a 1990 Honda Accord for the mission, sure to get black in case she needed to blend in at night. Felix had joined her and rented a Ford Taurus from the same year, leaving them both with transportation for the two weeks they'd spend in the past.

Kennedy drove slow through the neighborhood, and sped up significantly once on the main roads. She followed him for ten minutes and noticed he didn't once violate a traffic law. He finally pulled into a strip mall where he parked in front of a sandwich shop, The Mad Wich.

Kennedy disappeared inside for a few minutes before he reappeared empty-handed and strolled further down to a store called HobbyTown USA. Arielle killed the engine and hopped out of the car, charging toward the store and stepping in.

A bell jingled from above the door, and she looked around to make sure Kennedy hadn't noticed her. He was already down an aisle with boxes of model boat kits.

The shop wasn't too spacious, and only had three aisles, all filled with similar kits for model boats, planes, cars, and helicopters. The aisle aligned with the entrance had a glass counter display with already completed models. Behind it, where only an employee had access, were shelves filled with thumb-sized jars of paint, rubber cement, and paintbrushes in every size imaginable. No one stood at the cash register at the far end of the counter, so Arielle looked toward the back to find Kennedy disappearing behind another door with what must have been an employee.

She went down the aisle with model car kits. The first car she saw was a 1985 Audi Quattro, her father's dream car. He kept posters of the car all throughout the walls in the garage, and many evenings when she'd venture out to tell him dinner was ready, he'd pause from his workbench and nod to the pictures on the wall.

"I'm gonna build that car one day, if I have to," he'd say. "If that's the only way I can get it, I'll build it piece by piece. And I'll leave it for you and your brother when I'm gone. It might not look like much, but those suckers are *fast*."

Arielle never understood her father's obsession with the car, but she planned to one day buy it for him. She never had that chance, nor did he ever build it. Seeing the car brought a rush of memories, and her face prickled with heat as she fought away more emotions. She didn't see Kennedy step out of the back door with the store's associate, the two of them chatting about model boats and sharing a laugh.

They headed directly down the aisle where she stood, and Arielle felt her legs lock as she reached out to grab the car kit.

"Oh, hello, ma'am," the employee said. He was perhaps a decade younger than Kennedy, and offered a warm smile. "Sorry if I kept you waiting. Is there something I can help you with?"

The man stopped next to her while Kennedy walked past, brushing against her shoulder in the narrow aisle.

"I was just looking for something for my dad for Father's Day," Arielle said, glancing over her shoulder to see if Kennedy had any reaction to the mention of the holiday. He did not, and continued out of the building. "I'm really just shopping around to get ideas and prices. These models might be a little out of my budget."

The door closed, and Kennedy was out of view. Arielle shoved the kit back on the shelf and pivoted around, speaking over her shoulder. "I'm so sorry, but something just came up."

The man looked from her and back to the kit, shrugging his shoulders and rubbing his head as Arielle hurried out the door. She looked to Kennedy's truck, didn't see him, then looked to her right just in time to see him step into another business.

Arielle returned to the car and felt her mind spin as she looked up at the sign above the door Kennedy had just entered. "D&D Guns and Ammo," she whispered to herself, slipping behind the steering wheel and grabbing her binoculars. The windows were reflective glass, so she only saw herself. "Dammit!" She punched the steering wheel and tossed the binoculars aside.

She couldn't possibly follow him into the gun shop—that would be too obvious. She had one chance to follow him and wasted it on the craft store, where she didn't learn a single thing about Kennedy or why he went in.

Arielle stewed, legs bouncing, fingers drumming on the steering wheel while she glared at the door, waiting for Kennedy to step back outside.

After five minutes he did, a brown paper bag clutched in his right hand.

"He bought ammo," Arielle said, watching as he returned to the sandwich shop further down the strip.

She couldn't bear the thought of wasting this first opportunity of Kennedy stepping foot outside his house, and reached into her duffel bag, feeling around until her fingers wrapped around a fake FBI badge.

It was a fake badge she carried with her on all missions, just in case the opportunity arose for her to use it. It was a replica of the badges used by the FBI, and rested inside a wallet with a fake FBI identification card. To an average citizen, they'd have no reason to question it. Even most police officers would take one glance at it and believe it was real.

It *was* real, by all definitions. But Arielle was not an actual FBI agent, and that would take time for any authority to figure out.

She stepped out of the car and shuffled toward The Mad Wich, peered through the glass and was pleased to find Kennedy sitting at a table by himself, unwrapping a foot-long sandwich while the brown bag sat on the table opposite him.

Got at least fifteen minutes, she thought, and dashed down the sidewalk, stepping into the gun shop. Rifles covered the walls around the store, while glass counters housed the smaller handguns. More racks stood in the center of the floor containing hunting rifles. Security cameras watched from every corner of the room, and Arielle made sure to keep her head cocked downward.

"Good morning, miss," the clerk said from behind the counter. He was an older man with wavy white hair and a matching goatee. A pair of sunglasses sat atop his head, and he wore a black polo shirt with the company's logo embroidered on it, two pistols overlapping each other, *D&D Guns* curved around the top of the image. "How can I help you today?"

She whipped out her badge, flashed it for two seconds, and tucked it into her back pocket. "I'm agent Lucia Ariano with the FBI. I need to ask some questions about the gentleman who just bought some ammunition from you?" She always used the alias of Lucia Ariano when impersonating an FBI agent. Something about the name felt official, and it cast no doubt when she started questioning people.

The clerk took a step back, and his eyes glanced toward the door. "I'm sorry, what is this about?"

"That man is a suspect in a major crime, and I need to know what exactly he bought."

"Do you have a warrant? And can I see that badge again?"

Arielle reached back and flashed the badge again, this time holding it open a few seconds longer to allow the gentleman to read it. "I'm afraid I don't have a warrant. Just been tailing that man for the past couple of days. Hoping you can help me as a favor."

"The hell I will," the man said, a frown taking over his face. "The government has no right to barge into my store and demand information without a warrant. Come back with a warrant signed by a judge, and *maybe* I'll share information with you."

"Sir, I don't mean any disrespect, but I am not *demanding* anything of you. I'm asking a favor. Think of it as a favor to your country."

"Bullshit! Don't try that slick-talking nonsense on me. A favor to my country is protecting the private information of my fellow citizen. I'm not telling you anything. Please leave my shop, and good luck. Don't step back in here without a warrant. If you do, I'll consider it trespassing, and I know my rights."

"Good day," Arielle said, and turned around to leave.

"Fucking bitch," the man muttered under his breath.

Arielle paused at the door, blood boiling throughout her entire body. She clenched her fists, knowing that turning back around would end horribly. She swallowed her pride and stepped outside, blowing out a long exhale from her mouth.

Few things ruffled Arielle Lucila, but sexist remarks always led to a fury she sometimes couldn't contain. If she had been a man, the clerk might have been more cooperative.

A fucking bitch, she thought, shaking her head. If her mission was to cleanse the world of bigots, she would have turned around and taught the clerk a lesson. But it wasn't.

Arielle gathered her emotions and started back to the sandwich shop when she noticed a pay phone at the end of the sidewalk. She ran past The Mad Wich, glancing to confirm Kennedy was still seated at the table with his sandwich.

A man stood near the pay phone, leaning against the building while smoking a cigarette.

"Excuse me, sir," Arielle said. "Do you have any spare change so I can make a call? It's important, or else I wouldn't ask."

The man plucked the cigarette from his mouth and grinned. He looked a few years older than Arielle, and she hoped he wouldn't start hitting on her. She didn't have time for that shit right now. He pushed himself off the building.

"I work here," he said, gesturing to the building behind him, Arielle realizing it was a laundromat. "I have plenty of change, give me one second."

He nodded and turned around to enter the laundromat, Arielle watching as he moseyed toward the back and out of sight.

After two minutes, Arielle was about to start toward her car when she saw the man's head appear through the window, bobbing up and down as he made his way back outside. He held a hand out, four quarters resting in his palm. "This should be good for a few calls."

"Thank you so much," Arielle said, opening her hand so he could dump the coins.

"Not a problem at all. What's your name? Are you from around here?"

"Just passing by, sorry. I really need to make this call."

The man raised his hands in a *don't-shoot-me* manner and took two steps backward. He pulled out another cigarette and returned to his perch against the laundromat's exterior.

Arielle hurried back to the pay phone and popped in the coins, dialing their apartment phone number. It rang twice before Felix picked up.

"It's me," Arielle said. "How fast can you get to Kennedy's house?"

"Uh, I think it took me fifteen minutes last time."

"Well, drive faster, and get there in ten. I think I can buy us some time—he's not home. Get over there!"

Arielle hung up before Felix could respond, a negotiation tactic she had learned. It created urgency and put tons of pressure on the recipient to make a move. Felix wouldn't argue either way, but hanging up would certainly get him out of his seat faster and into the car.

The smoking man watched Arielle, but she spun around and jogged back to her car before he could say anything else. She opened the passenger door and fumbled through the duffel bag until she pulled out a screwdriver.

Arielle closed the door and shuffled across the lot toward Kennedy's truck, keeping the screwdriver pinned in her armpit, eyes stuck on the sandwich shop's only door to see if Kennedy would step outside. The man continued to smoke his cigarette, intently peering at her.

She reached the truck and decided to first take a quick look through the windows. A soda can sat in the cupholder in an otherwise clean truck. One cigarette butt lay in the ashtray, but it didn't seem he smoked too often—she had yet to see him do it over the past couple of days.

The bed of the truck held a rolled-up tarp, some rope, and a toolbox. Still nothing that suggested he might be in the midst of planning a bank robbery.

Arielle squatted down by the rear passenger tire and looked around to make sure no one could see her. Just as she reared back the screwdriver to plow it into the rubber, a voice shouted.

"Hey! What are you doing?! Get the hell away!"

Arielle looked up to see the gun shop clerk yelling from the door. He had one hand on the pistol on his waist and started toward her.

"Shit!" she cried, standing up and breaking into a sprint toward her car. She nearly dove into the driver's seat, tossed the screwdriver on the duffel bag and jammed the keys into the ignition.

The clerk had stopped at Kennedy's truck for a quick inspection and had only looked back up in Arielle's direction as she peeled out of the parking lot. Smoke flew from the back tires as she burned rubber and jerked the car onto the main road, speeding off with constant looks into the rearview.

"Will he actually follow me?" she said, shaking her head. The clerk hadn't moved with such urgency to suggest he wanted to tail her, but she couldn't show her face at that strip mall again for the rest of the mission. The clerk was already paranoid about their encounter and would surely be waiting to take a shot at the faux FBI agent if he saw her snooping around the property again.

Arielle panted for air, not having had such a close call while doing menial work on a mission. All she wanted to do was pop one of Kennedy's tires to buy Felix some time bugging the house. She had passed a tire shop one block away, and knew he'd have no problem getting it replaced. But she couldn't have slashed it after the clerk saw her. He'd definitely make a call to the police and have people alerted around the strip mall to keep an eye out for the young, suspicious woman who called herself an

FBI agent. He was probably going to call the police, anyway.

Why is this so difficult? she wondered, staring into the rearview. The past was already gearing up for a fight, and it wasn't even the week of the crime yet. Her stomach churned at the thought of how much worse the past might push back as they drew closer to the big day.

Despite the resistance, Arielle held hope. If Kennedy hadn't committed the crime, then the past wouldn't already be pushing so hard.

Chapter 13

Arielle had a rough night after the debacle at the strip mall. She had returned to Kennedy's house and stood watch for a couple more hours. Felix had shown up too late—Kennedy was already back home, too.

They returned to the apartment and Arielle locked herself in her bedroom for the rest of the night, citing a need to review the mission file to understand what was making the initial three days so difficult. She called for a group meeting the next morning over breakfast to discuss their findings so far.

She had never opened the mission file, instead taking a rare moment of defeat as she crawled under her sheets and stared at the ceiling for hours before eventually falling asleep. A heaviness filled her stomach. She didn't want dinner. No TV. No books.

When she woke on Thursday, the sense of dread remained, and she dressed while mentally preparing for another boring day—or perhaps chaos.

She stepped out to the smell of fresh waffles and fruit. Felix had prepared breakfast and was filling the glasses with orange juice when she entered the kitchen. "Good morning, Arielle," he said, offering a warm smile.

"Morning. Selena up yet?"

"I'm here, relax," Selena said, charging out of her room, dressed in her custodial uniform. "Everything okay, Arielle? You seemed off yesterday."

Arielle shuffled toward the table and sat down. "I'm fine. Was just a rough day. And I guess I'm not used to having those."

"Let's talk about it," Felix said, turning off the knobs on the stove before taking his seat at the table. Selena followed suit and promptly took a swig of orange juice. "So what's going on?"

She shook her head as she poked at the whipped cream topping the waffle. "I'm frustrated. I don't enjoy this kind of work—detective work, essentially. We have ten days until the crime and it feels like we've made zero progress. This time is supposed to be spent trying to figure out how to stop it from happening, not *who* did it. Everything I've explained to you about closing off your mind from the past is a lost cause on this mission. I can't close my mind from my intentions, because I don't even know what they are yet. The past is already pushing back. If things had escalated even just a little more yesterday, I would have been shot at."

Arielle balled a fist and slammed it on the table, the plates and silverware clattering.

"Whoa," Selena said. "Take it easy."

"No. I just said I could have been shot. Yesterday. *Ten days* before the crime. Ten days! Bullets! That's not supposed to happen until the day of. Just how ugly is this going to get? I don't understand all the resistance already. Do either of you have anything of substance yet?"

Felix and Selena exchanged glances. "Nothing yet from Young," Felix said. "And you know the drama I had that day. I probably would have been shot, too, if I hung around long enough."

"My point exactly. This is dangerous. We can't do missions like this anymore. What does Young do in his free time?"

"Not much. He eats lots of microwave dinners. Smokes a ton of cigarettes. Drinks beer on his lounger while he watches *Wheel of Fortune* and *Jeopardy* all night. I've watched him for three days, and each day he falls asleep on the lounger. Two nights he woke up and moved to his bed, but the first night he just stayed there. He hasn't made a call beside the pizza he had delivered last night. Hasn't left the place outside of work hours. I don't know, Arielle, but he kind of seems like a waste of time to monitor. At least you got a little more with Kennedy. He went into a gun shop and bought ammo. That's *something*, right?"

Arielle tossed her hands up. "It's more than TV dinners, but it doesn't mean anything. What about you, Selena? Have you crossed paths yet with Young at the bank?"

"Not yet. I've seen some of the other guards, but never Young. We really only see them at the beginning and end of our shifts—we clock in and out near their offices. I won't lie, this work is killing me."

"I know. Sounds like we're all suffering. I'm afraid you have to keep doing this job. Your keycard access to the building is all we need next Sunday. Have you had any luck finding a hiding place?"

"I have a couple spots of interest. The north side of the eighteenth floor is vacant. Open floor space with conference rooms and closets. Plenty of space to hide comfortably."

Arielle wanted a tentative plan for someone on the team to hide out next Saturday night, guaranteeing they would be in the building the morning of the robbery. "Okay, that's good. We'll see how it all plays out. Felix, I might move you to that post if we're certain Young isn't involved. I'll be following Kennedy that morning."

"I don't like that," Felix said. "We're still assuming it was Kennedy. What if it's not? Then you're leaving myself and Selena alone in the building while you're following an innocent man. Seems wasteful."

"None of this is set in stone," Arielle said. "A lot can change in ten days, and it better. Is Young working today?"

Felix shrugged. "We don't know his schedule. He was up this morning, but not dressed yet. Dude sleeps naked, so I'm going to need some serious brainwashing to get that imagery out of my head. I can check back shortly."

Selena fake heaved at the mention of Young walking around naked in his apartment, and this earned light laughter from Arielle.

"Please do," Arielle said. "If he leaves for work, I want you to head straight to Kennedy's house. We can't waste another opportunity. We need the inside of that place at least bugged with mics, preferably cameras if possible. If Kennedy leaves, I'll follow him, and you need to sneak in."

Felix recoiled at the instruction.

"Is something the matter?" Arielle asked. "You've done this plenty of times."

"It's just that you're right. This mission is drastically different. Nothing feels like a normal trip. I can feel the resistance in the air. I'm not comfortable breaking into Kennedy's house, at least forcibly. If the door is unlocked, that's a different story, but if I have to pick a lock or climb through a window. . ." Felix looked into the distance and shivered like he had seen a ghost. "I just don't know, Arielle. My gut is telling me a lot can go wrong. *Horribly* wrong."

Arielle raised her hands. "Let's calm down. Everything is different about this mission, yes, but let's not get ahead of ourselves. Danger is always a risk, no matter how prepared we are. You should remain diligent. You had a close call at the last mission, but got out just fine."

"This time should be easier," Selena said. "We know the schedule for Kennedy's house. Well, his wife's. She leaves at the same time and returns at the same time every day. Once Kennedy leaves, he is the only variable. But Arielle will be on his tail and I'm sure she could buy you some time."

"Of course," Arielle said. "I'm comfortable with that, even if it means parking in front of his house and speaking with him to stall. It's risky, sure, but nothing life-threatening. In fact, the past might not even take issue with the conversation as long as I keep it neutral and boring."

"And your head clear of what we're doing," Felix said, crossing his arms. "You just admitted that hasn't been easy on this mission."

Arielle nodded. "You're right. But this is our job. Don't you remember when they warned you of this in training? They said there will be a time when you become so good at what you do, that it becomes second nature. You'll get so comfortable with your routine that you'll become blinded to the risks that are always present. Then one day, you'll face a challenge that shakes you out of that comfort zone, and you're suddenly scared to do the work you've always done. Looks like we've all arrived at that point with this mission."

"It's true," Selena said, chuckling. "Do you think I planned to clean so many damn toilets in the name of a mission? Hell no. I get high from the chemicals by ten o'clock every morning. I want this mission to end as much as you both. It's just been an awful experience all around."

"Sure, but your life isn't at risk cleaning toilets," Felix said. "I already had an encounter with someone who I'm pretty sure was a bookie. The kind with a jar of thumbs on his desk. And now, we're dealing with Kennedy, who we presume pulled off a bank robbery and *got away with it.*"

Arielle stood up. "Look, this is what we have to do. We know to not put ourselves in harm's way. Go to Kennedy's house and plant some bugs when he leaves. If something arises that prevents you from doing it, then don't do it. Same as every other mission you've ever worked on." She picked up her dishes and dropped them in the sink. "Now, I'm going to his house to do my job. Hopefully something of substance happens today. I'm not having this conversation again. Are we clear?"

Arielle rarely used an authoritative tone with her peers, but it worked when she needed. Felix nodded in silence, glaring at the crumbs left behind on his plate. Selena took her last bite as her eyes dashed back and forth from Felix to Arielle.

"Good," Arielle said. "I'll see you both tonight. Have a good day."

She turned and left the apartment, grabbing her backpack on the way out and slamming the door shut behind her. This was the type of friction she had feared upon learning they would work together permanently as a team. They hadn't encountered many issues on their prior mission, but this one was putting them all to the test. Pushing their limits.

They needed to make progress within the next couple days, or else major problems loomed on the horizon.

Arielle wouldn't dare say it aloud, but she had been thinking of a scenario that rarely happened in her career as an Angel.

Failure.

Chapter 14

A couple hours later, Peter Young left for work. Felix watched the live-feed as Young scampered around the apartment dressed in his security uniform, scarfing down a bowl of cereal, lighting up a cigarette, and hurriedly shaving his face before he dashed out of the building.

Felix felt his gut tighten with dread. He had to head over to Kennedy's house, where—he hoped—his day would pass without having to do anything. He really didn't want to enter Kennedy's home. The whole matter felt off, unlike any other task he'd had to do for the Angels before. For someone who stuck to data and facts, his gut feeling was getting the best of him.

"You'll be fine," he told himself in the bathroom mirror, splashing water on his face. "You have a job to do, and you're the best at it. Go in, plant some mics, and slip out without a problem. Arielle will be nearby if he returns too soon."

Felix gulped, then nodded before leaving the bathroom to retrieve his backpack stuffed with lock picks, microphones, and other accessories needed to bug the Kennedy house.

As he took the stairs to the parking garage, Felix couldn't help but look over his shoulder. He had done just that every time he stepped outside their apartment, worried the monstrous bookie would be back, hunting for Felix now instead of Young.

He'd yet to see anyone knock on Young's door since that day and wondered if the man would stay away since an eyewitness had spotted him.

Or maybe Young told him he's going to rob the bank he works at and will have the money next weekend.

Felix shook the thought away. No one in their right mind would confide in someone that they planned to rob a bank.

He reached his Taurus without a problem and reluctantly pulled it out of the garage and onto the road. Traffic was light as the early morning rush hour had already passed. Business people hurried up and down the sidewalks, briefcases and purses in hand. Felix rolled down his window to let the summer air fill his lungs, drawing in a deep breath as he waited at a red light.

A convertible Mazda pulled up in the lane next to him, an attractive woman smiling as she made direct eye contact. Felix looked away and stared ahead, his face flushing as he felt heat prickle his skin.

"Where you off to, cutie?" the woman called over, and Felix felt her eyes burning into the side of his head.

He worked up the courage to return a grin. "Going to work."

"That's too bad. I'm headed to grab some coffee and would love some company."

Felix hadn't gone on a date with a woman since joining the Road Runners, and the unexpected invite sent his emotions into a whirl. He was intrigued. Not one for spontaneity, Felix supposed his interest only came because he wanted to avoid Kennedy's house. How much did they really *need* to bug the inside of the house?

"The light's about to change," the woman shouted. "You coming or not?"

"I wish I could, but I really have to get to work."

The girl shrugged and sped off as soon as the light turned green.

Dammit, he thought. An opportunity like that would never come again. Felix believed he was attractive, yet did little to highlight that fact. He dressed simple and preferred to blend in with the masses. As a result, women never hit on him, and it had taken him a moment to even realize that was happening at the red light.

Any time he called home, his mother always asked if he was seeing someone yet. And he always disappointed her with a negative response. He loved his work and had no time for extracurricular activities if he wanted to keep his status as the top Angel in his field. On days off, he watched sports and movies, read books, and got in a workout. All his friends were back in San Francisco, so he had virtually no social life in Denver. And he was fine with that.

But he couldn't deny the excitement he had just felt. The flutter in his stomach that came with speaking to someone of the opposite sex. Felix considered the countless possibilities that could come from following the woman to the coffee shop. Her car was still in sight, but he shook his head and continued to Kennedy's house. The fun would have to wait for another day, preferably while not on a mission.

"Was probably just the past trying to stop me."

Felix had heard plenty of stories about the past dropping random people in the middle of a mission to detract from the work. Many time travelers had fallen into the trap, guided by their own lust or overwhelming desire for love, only to find none of it was actually real. Just a thorough distraction.

He cleared his mind over the next ten minutes, and when he arrived at the Kennedy residence, he found Arielle across the street from the house and parked behind her.

She looked at him in the rearview and gave a quick nod, acknowledging his presence. Neither would step out of the car—not on this mission. On prior missions, Felix might have gone and sat with Arielle while they waited for something to happen. This trip into the past had too many unknown factors and risks. They handled every decision with kid gloves to decrease the chances of something going horribly wrong.

Felix looked at Kennedy's house and saw nothing. The two windows revealed empty rooms. Kennedy's truck sat in the driveway. A neighbor three houses down sat on their front porch and watered the lawn, sipping from a mug of coffee. Felix would forever envy people who got to enjoy such simplicity in life. His life as a Road Runner had created a sense of urgency behind every waking moment. He wondered if life would ever slow down enough to sit back and enjoy the fresh morning air without a care in the world.

Suddenly, the front door swung open and Kennedy appeared in the doorway, a backpack slung over his shoulder. He stepped out and drew a deep breath before locking the door and getting into his truck, tossing the backpack on the passenger seat.

Felix looked ahead to Arielle, seeing her strap her seatbelt on, the car rumbling to life in sync with Kennedy's truck. She looked in the rearview and nodded at Felix, instantly sending his stomach into a spiral.

"Shit," he muttered, reclining his seat to stay out of Kennedy's view.

He remained below the window for the next thirty seconds while he listened to the sounds of both vehicles drive off. When he sat back up, the block appeared deserted. The neighbor was no longer watering their lawn. Kennedy's driveway was empty.

Felix sat alone, nothing but his own fear standing between him and the house.

"This is really happening," he told himself, leaning over to grab his duffel bag full of bugging devices. He waited one more minute to make sure Kennedy wasn't returning.

Not a single car came down the block, so Felix opened his door and stepped onto the pavement on wobbly legs.

"It's the same job. Nothing is different. Get out of your head."

He looked both ways and proceeded toward Kennedy's driveway, hurrying to disappear around the side of the house.

Kennedy had clearly locked the front door, so Felix didn't bother trying it—not that he ever attempted to break in through the front. Instead, he circled around to the back, grateful no fence was present.

The backyard hadn't received nearly as much attention as the front. Weeds sprouted throughout the lawn and from the cracks of the concrete patio. A shed stood in the far corner, the door off its hinges and leaning against the exterior. Gardening tools and a lawn mower spilled out from it.

Felix returned his attention to the back door and tried the knob, finding it locked. In a swift motion, he reached into the backpack's side zipper and retrieved his lock pick, stuffing it into the keyhole and twisting until he heard the magical click of the door opening.

He twisted the knob and let the door creak open, revealing the kitchen. He didn't step in right away, always allowing a few seconds to make sure the house was indeed empty and no one came scrambling to close the door. Silence filled the room as he entered and shut the door behind him.

"Anyone home?" he called out, ready to turn and run if a reply came.

But none did, so he stepped through the kitchen, spotting a newspaper open on the table, and clean dishes sitting on a drying rack next to the sink. Felix had been in plenty of homes thanks to his job, and this looked to be one of the cleaner ones.

"Just get in and out," he whispered to himself, taking off his backpack and unzipping it. A quick scan around the kitchen revealed no opportunities to plant a camera. He rarely had the chance to plant one inside a home since the wireless miniature cameras only had batteries with a lifespan of a few hours. The microphones lasted much longer and only activated when sound was audible. The bugs he planted sufficed for the typical two-week missions. The only thing he had to change were the tapes on the receiver he'd hide somewhere outside, preferably in a thick bush.

Felix climbed on top of the counter. His favorite place to plant a bug in the kitchen was the light structure above the sink.

Just as he felt around, the rumble of an engine turned into the driveway outside. "What the hell?" Felix gasped, and jumped down from the sink, failing to have planted the bug.

The kitchen opened to the dining room that faced the front yard, so Felix craned his neck for a view and saw a black car in the driveway. A man had stepped out and gazed at the house.

"Shit!"

Felix pulled the backpack over his shoulder and started for the back door. The man's silhouette appeared through the blinds, and Felix spun around, lunging into the dining room. The back door's knob started turning.

He dashed out of the dining room and down the hallway, hearing the door open and shut. His heart drummed from his stomach to his head. Sweat trickled down his back as he entered the master bedroom and immediately dove under the bed.

Felix tugged on his backpack, twisting and squeezing to make it fit under the bed with him. He gasped for breath while all his senses ran in overdrive, listening attentively as shuffling footsteps approached from the hall.

"Dad?" a man's voice called out. "Are you here?"

Felix cupped his hand over his nose and mouth, his breathing still out of control. His face flushed, arms shuddering, as he scooted further under the bed to stay out of sight from whoever was wandering through the Kennedy household.

Kennedy has a son, Felix reminded himself. *The son was a witness in the trial.*

These thoughts made Felix dizzy. If the son spotted Felix under the bed, that would certainly provoke the past to unleash a fury of vengeance. His breathing remained irregular; he had no choice but to hold his breath once he saw two feet appear in the bedroom doorway.

"Dad?" the voice called again, this time much louder, practically on top of Felix.

He watched the feet shuffle into the room, turning left and stopping in front of the dresser. The feet turned to face the dresser and remained a few seconds while the sound of ruffling papers filled the silence.

Felix wanted desperately to poke his head out to see what was happening, but wouldn't dare take that gamble. He tensed his entire body to stop it from shaking, horrifying thoughts running through his mind.

What if Kennedy's son planned to wait around until his father returned home? If that occurred, what would happen if Kennedy had another stretch of multiple days without leaving the house? Just how the hell was Felix supposed to get out from under the bed without being caught? He imagined the gut-wrenching prospect of somehow ending up stuck under the bed for the next week, starving and thirsty, unable to scurry for the exit.

Don't be dramatic, he told himself. *There will be at least one opportunity to get out of this house today.*

His heart rate had calmed down, his breathing nearly under control. The feet standing at the dresser had turned and started toward the bed, and Felix felt the weight press down on his back as Kennedy's son sat down on the edge. Had this happened even one minute earlier, Felix might have vomited because of his anxiety attack. But now, he was too focused on finding a way out.

Five minutes passed before Kennedy's son finally hopped off the bed and returned to the dresser. Felix heard buttons being pushed and presumed he was dialing a phone. This was confirmed once the man spoke.

"Hey. He's not here. I got here ten minutes ago. His truck wasn't in the driveway."

Now Felix craned his neck for a better listen. He could only hear the crackle of a voice speaking back through the receiver.

"Okay. Will do," Kennedy's son said, and hung up the phone.

Felix suspected whatever was said on the other end of the call would determine if he'd remain under the bed for the foreseeable future, or leave.

Kennedy's son remained at the dresser for two more minutes before straggling out of the room. Felix listened while he took a piss in the bathroom next door and finally made his way out of the house.

When the back door slammed shut, relief immediately flooded over Felix. He waited five more minutes before slithering out from the bed and hurried to the dresser, where he discovered a stack of papers.

On top was an early draft of a living will document. Beneath that was a stack of bills, most of which appeared past due.

Money problems, he thought. *Just like Young.*

Felix had enough. He hadn't wanted to enter this house in the first place and had barely escaped getting caught breaking and entering. He planted no bugs, nor did he care at this point. Someone who didn't live in the house had just let themselves in unannounced—a major red flag for Felix's work, and something he'd never gamble with.

"That's enough of this place," Felix said, zipping up his backpack and bolting for the back door.

Chapter 15

On Friday afternoon, Selena had waited in the bathroom until 5:10. Her shift was over, and she wanted to make sure Olivia left the premises.

She remained in her uniform and felt mentally ready to head down to the basement levels to see what information she could gather about the security office and the vault that belonged to United Bank.

Before stepping out of the restroom, she took a moment in front of the mirrors, splashing water on her face and staring at herself.

"You got this."

Selena might have over-hyped her upcoming task, mainly because she had never dealt with a bank vault before. She imagined the security similar to a Hollywood portrayal. Cameras in every corner, crisscrossed lasers daring someone to trip an alarm that would blare loud enough for everyone between Denver and Dallas to hear.

She knew this vault had nothing remotely close to that type of intense security, but the gravity of her task—and the entire mission—blew things out of proportion within her imagination.

She imagined once she approached the vault, the guards would scream and tackle her. They'd file an official report, call Olivia at home, terminate her employment, and revoke her badge on the spot.

With a quick head shake, Selena left the bathroom on the tenth floor, where she had finished her shift, and caught an elevator to the subbasement level.

When the doors parted, she braced to see any coworkers. The cleaning crew's locker room was in the subbasement level, but she found an empty hallway once she stepped out. Her waiting game had worked, as she figured it would on a Friday afternoon. No one had interest in hanging around to chat—it was time for the weekend.

Cameras covered every floor of the building, and Selena realized she might look suspicious as she stood outside the elevator for an entire minute. She snapped out of her thoughts and started down the hall, opening the doors to a storage closet that housed their cleaning equipment.

She pulled out a cart and loaded it with paper towels, a bottle of glass cleaner, a broom, and a vacuum, figuring these options would appear standard to the security team who would soon see her outside of their office. Selena tucked her shirt back into her pants and made sure all of her buttons were in their proper places.

The subbasement level rarely had traffic outside of the cleaning crew and maintenance workers. Security never had a reason to come down since the area had restricted access. The main basement was one level up, and that's where the security team had their office a few steps away from the bank's vault.

With the cart loaded, she pushed it down the hallway to the elevators and called a car. The motor hummed, and Selena's guts tightened while she waited.

"Give your best performance," she whispered to herself. "That's all you can do. You're a seasoned cleaner just doing her job."

The elevator doors parted, and she stepped in, a musty smell filling the small space. She rode it up one level and stepped out to another empty hallway.

The area mirrored the subbasement level. Concrete floors and walls. No attempt at a single decoration. The lighting, however, was much brighter. A couple of doors stood closed along the walls, presumably more storage space.

Selena started forward, making a concentrated effort to move at a normal pace down the hall. Her eyes stayed ahead, waiting for someone to step out of the security office and send her back.

But no one did, and within a quick minute, she stood directly outside the security office.

The door was solid, but the walls were glass, giving Selena a clear view inside. From the door, she tipped her head enough to look inside and saw two guards sitting behind a desk, monitors glowing on their faces, showing multiple angles from around the entire building.

Selena pulled her cart into the middle of the hallway and grabbed the broom to sweep the floor. She kept her head cocked low, but high enough to see inside the security office.

From what she could gather, more than half of the monitors showed the bank. She saw the bank lobby, the teller windows, the nearby vault, and a short hallway that led to different bankers' offices. The other views showed different areas of the building, office workers heading out for the day, others getting started for a night shift.

If their focus is the bank, how the hell did it get robbed so quickly and easily? she wondered. *And with the vault right in front of them?!*

Selena swept the broom further down the hall, now in plain sight of the security guards if they simply looked out their windows. She looked ahead toward the vault at the end of the hallway, its circular door closed, containing hoards of cash within its impenetrable steel walls.

She hesitated to get any closer, instead studying the area from afar. There was no barrier between herself and the vault, and she found this peculiar. If a robber were to get on this specific floor—not something that proved too difficult of a task for someone smart enough to rob a bank—they would face no further resistance beyond the security office. The vault had its complex locking devices installed, but the ease of being able to walk right up to it seemed an irresponsible move on the bank designer's behalf.

This bank had a mantrap to the side of the vault, presumably as a second access point. But the main entrance stood unimpeded.

Whoever designed this bank and its vault must have been asleep at the wheel, Selena thought. On the day of the robbery, the vault had been open because employees were inside. If the robber knew the vault would be open—which Selena didn't believe was a coincidence—then that removed the only true barrier between the robber and a vault full of cash. All the robber needed to do was get past the security team.

Selena placed her broom on the cart and grabbed the glass cleaner and paper towels. She shuffled right up to the security office windows and sprayed the liquid, promptly wiping it clean.

This caught the guards' attention, and one of them stood up, waving to Selena. He made his way to the door, and Selena's heart drummed while he pulled it open.

"Evening," the man said, poking his head out. "I think somebody already came by this morning to clean our office."

Selena saw the name badge clipped to his shirt. *McDowell.* She recognized the name from the mission reports. Bill McDowell was the guard who would end up being shot in the elevator that the robber used to enter the building. A heavyset man with lots of stubble on his face, McDowell watched Selena curiously.

"Oh?" she said. "I wasn't aware of that. My supervisor asked me to come down here to sweep, mop, and clean the windows. I can go back to make sure."

"Don't worry about it," McDowell said. "Just thought I'd save you time, but if that's what they asked you to do, carry on. Did you need to clean inside of our office?"

Selena nearly started drooling at the invitation to step inside the security office and promptly nodded. "Yes, if that's okay."

"Of course. It's the end of our shift—not a lot going on."

McDowell pulled the door open all the way and stepped aside to allow Selena room to enter.

"Do you mind if I put my cart in the doorway?" Selena asked. "Would make it easier for me to not have to go in and out."

"Be my guest," McDowell said with a warm smile. Selena guessed the man was in his late fifties thanks to the streaks of gray in his hair and stubble. He had a soothing gentleness when he spoke, and this immediately put Selena at ease as she wheeled in her cart.

Another guard sat behind the desk, digging into a bag of potato chips.

"That's Dawkins," McDowell said. "And I'm Bill McDowell. Are you new here? I don't think I've seen you before."

Bill returned to his seat next to Dawkins and leaned back, arms crossed over his chest. Dawkins was closer to Selena's age and struggling to keep his eyes off of her.

"I am," Selena said.

Selena grabbed the broom again and started sweeping around the office, glancing up every few seconds to absorb the views and surroundings within the room. A macabre sense of destiny filled the air, as if the past had made its presence known, daring Selena to try something that would change the course of the murders set to occur in just nine days.

Below the highest monitors hanging on the wall opposite their desk, Selena saw the direct, clear view they had of the vault. Anyone in the security office would have no problem seeing any activity or motion that took place in the vault area. She studied the two dozen screens. They cut to different angles every few seconds, but she found it odd that over an entire minute, not once did she see outside the building.

She had so many questions she wanted to ask about their processes, but knew it would only raise suspicions if the new custodian took a sudden interest in the building's security.

Selena swept closer to the desk, her eyes falling on the log sheet that appeared to track each guard's shifts, duties, and incidents that arose. The log separated two smaller monitors that stood on the desk, each connected to a keyboard the guards could control, presumably to choose which camera they wanted to view.

"How are you liking it here?" McDowell asked, breaking the awkward silence. Dawkins remained involved with his potato chips, his eyes peering out from the mop of messy black hair tousled over his forehead.

"It's been good so far," Selena said. "Can't complain. Everyone on the team has been really nice."

"You let us know if you need help. All the phones in the stairwells call right down here. Sometimes new hires have their keycards set up wrong and can't get into every room they need. If you come across that, just give us a buzz and we'll get you in. Right, Dawkins?"

McDowell let out a hearty chuckle as he leaned over and clapped a hand on his young colleague's back.

"Yes, sir," Dawkins mumbled, face flushing red as he avoided eye contact with Selena.

"Well, I appreciate that," Selena said, putting the broom back onto her cart. "It looks pretty clean in here already. I'll get out of your way."

She offered a wide grin before pushing the cart back into the hallway and letting the door close behind her. Selena tried to avoid getting emotionally vested in her missions, but once she was free from the security office, she knew one thing.

I don't want Bill McDowell to die.

Chapter 16

"Let's discuss our findings from the week," Arielle said on Saturday morning as they gathered around the breakfast table. Felix had whipped up some pancakes and sliced bananas for them to enjoy.

They had Young under surveillance, and Arielle would drive to Kennedy's house later in the morning.

"For starters," Felix said. "I don't think Peter Young is involved. The guy does *nothing*. We're a week in, and all he does is watch TV, eat, and sleep. He's like a house cat."

Selena giggled at this.

"We can't rule him out, though," Arielle said. "There's a chance he's planning everything while at work. Why not? Everything he needs to know is right in front of him there. The bankers' routines, the security schedule, building access, and knowing all of the escape routes. He can literally walk the different routes he might want to take on his way out. He's still a prime suspect for us. Have you seen him at work yet, Selena?"

Selena shook her head, drawing a circle on the table with her finger. "Yesterday was the first time I got to venture down to the security office. There were only two guards in there. He could have been off already, or doing his rounds somewhere else in the building."

"And what about Kennedy?" Felix asked Arielle. "It doesn't seem like we're gaining traction with him, either."

"Because we're not," she replied. "He at least does things, and has occasionally left the house. That day I followed him was to the shooting range. Naturally, I thought that was some big revelation. He wanted to practice shooting, right? When I followed him inside, though, he was shooting with a hunting rifle—not at all the gun that was used in the robbery. Hunting season isn't for another five months, so he must just be staying sharp. No signs of him preparing for a robbery."

"Forgive me for not knowing this," Selena said. "But what exactly would that preparation look like?"

"Well, visits to the site ahead of time. Which hasn't happened. Trips to the shooting range—if he was using the appropriate guns. That's probably the extent of what we'd be able to see from outside his home. As far as within, he could study blueprints of the building, maps of the surrounding area, suspicious conversations with his wife—assuming it's a secret from her."

"There's so much that can go on inside that house," Felix said. "Every step of preparation, in fact. The guy is home alone all day. He can literally spend eight hours plotting this robbery, all to have his notes and plans packed away before his wife gets home."

"But you didn't see anything like that, right?" Arielle asked.

"No. But I wasn't exactly on the hunt for that sort of thing. I was in the kitchen and the master bedroom. Didn't see anything in either spot. But there were stairs to the basement. A whole other world I didn't get to explore."

"We need to get back into that house."

Felix shook his head vehemently. "Don't count on it. After that last encounter—I refuse to step back inside."

"That reminds me. Did we ever hear about Kennedy's son? I still wonder what he was doing there."

"They found nothing of substance. Completely clean background from now until the end of his life. Was never mentioned in the trial outside of his testimony that Kennedy had lunch with his kids on that Sunday. Never had a sudden spike of money."

Arielle crossed her arms, staring to the ceiling in deep thought and frustration. "I just don't get it. He goes there, calling for Kennedy. No answer. Calls someone from the house phone and tells them Kennedy's not home. Why would he need to call someone to tell them that? It sounds so suspicious—I can't wrap my head around it."

"There can be a lot of moving parts to a robbery. Young could have the security aspect under wraps. Kennedy's son could have been involved in the preparation or aftermath of the robbery. They could have paid off the next-door neighbor to serve as an alibi."

"Sure, but for $200,000? The more people involved, the less money Kennedy would get to keep."

"Don't look too deep into the amount that was robbed. I highly doubt they planned to only steal $200,000. I'm betting they got cold feet and bailed sooner than they wanted. There was how much in the vault? Something like three million dollars?"

Arielle nodded. "You're right. And this feels like it's becoming a mission where we will find nothing out until the morning of. And it fucking disturbs me—this is not how I work."

She felt the rage steaming within, but refused to show her frustration through any emotion. If her team sensed the doom she was experiencing, the wheels would fall off this mission within hours. They looked to her for confidence, and she needed to exude that at all times. It was her burden to shoulder—part of the territory as the top-ranked Angel.

They must have sensed something, however, as both Felix and Selena sat in silence, poking at their food, looking down at their plates to avoid eye contact.

"Look, Arielle," Selena said. "Don't think you're alone in this. We've never dealt with a mission like this, either. We're all reacting to whatever each day brings us."

Arielle clenched her teeth behind sealed lips. While she appreciated Selena's attempt to ease her concerns, she hated that someone else had to step in to console her. That was supposed to be her job.

She gulped before replying. "What did you see in the security office last night?"

Selena looked across the table to Felix, who nodded silently in response.

"Not much to speak of. I met one of the victims. He's a really nice guy.

Their office overlooks the vault. They have monitors that cover every inch of the building. However, I didn't see any that showed views from outside the building. They might exist, but I didn't see them while I was in there."

Arielle stood from her seat and circled the table to lean against the counter. Her frustration was reaching its limits with this mission, and she could no longer sit still while they lost at every turn. "I'm going to sleep on this decision over the weekend. But I think we need to attack this mission with more intensity. Nothing is going to just fall into our lap on this one—we need to force the past to reveal at least one of the cards it's playing in this game."

"Won't that be dangerous?" Felix asked, leaning forward. Arielle had grabbed his attention, and she knew she would. Felix liked to play things safe, and the mere mention of potential danger usually spun his worries out of control.

"I don't think dangerous is the right word," Arielle said. "Our lives won't be at risk—I'd never do that. But there may be risks. Some gambles. For one, I want Selena to encounter Young while at work. We have to force the issue. Try to get close to him. Talk to him while he's in the security office. See what sort of papers he has nearby that might suggest he's involved. Like I said, this won't pose a threat to your life, but it could result in losing your job."

"Do we know for sure what shifts he works?" Selena asked. "I'd be able to plan my day better to make this happen."

"We have one week of data," Felix said. "We can use it to guess, but security jobs like this can vary from week to week. It's actually quite rare for a guard to have a set schedule. They'll rotate who is working on weekends and graveyard shifts."

"I might be able to find out," Selena said. "There was another guard in there when I stopped by. Someone our age. Wouldn't stop checking me out."

"Use that," Arielle said in a serious tone. "We need to pull out all the stops we can. Felix, I think you should go back into Young's apartment one more time. This time to look for clues."

"Yeah, but the last time I was in there the mob came knocking at the door."

"That wasn't the mob. You'll be fine. Once you know he's gone for the workday, you can take your time. No need to answer the door if someone comes knocking. Just go about your business."

"And does this mean you're going to knock on Kennedy's door to have a chat?" Selena asked.

Arielle scrunched her brow in thought. "I might. I've been thinking of what I can possibly do to get in there. Pose as a salesperson? A maintenance worker?"

"But why?" Felix asked. "It's not like you'd be able to just snoop around the house while he's home. If he thought you were up to something, this guy might shoot you."

"Maybe I can distract while you rummage through his things."

"Excuse me?!" Felix gasped, standing up to meet Arielle's eye level. "I already told you, I'm not going back in there."

"Well, I might need you to. But I'd be there too."

Felix sat back down, shaking his head. "You're being reckless, Arielle."

"Reckless? They gave us a mission to play detective. We are *not* detectives. The commander is being reckless by giving us this mission."

"That doesn't mean we have to play with fire. You do know that it's okay to fail sometimes, right? We can treat this mission like we would any other, and if it doesn't work out, then we tell the commander our work style doesn't fit this type of mission. And guess what? We won't get missions like these again."

They sat in silence for a few seconds, staring at each other.

Selena spoke next. "He's right, Arielle. If we succeed on this mission, we'll just keep getting assigned more like it."

"I'm afraid I'm just not wired that way," Arielle said. "We were given a mission to complete, and that's what we're going to do. I'm not going to give up on it because it's too hard, or to avoid future ones. I have a standard of work to uphold, and I hope you'll join me in completing this."

Now Selena stood and circled the table to stand directly in front of Arielle. She reached out and grabbed both of her shoulders. "We will always have your back. But we need you to run your ideas by us. You're flustered. We see it. We won't tell anyone. But this means you might not make the best decisions. Lean on us. Trust us to help you complete a mission."

Tears welled in Arielle's eyes, and she looked at Selena through blurred vision. This was only their second mission working together, and she already saw the growth in both Selena and Felix. They were confident in themselves and their small team. They were holding Arielle accountable while also taking a weight off her shoulders.

She didn't wipe the tears away, instead letting them streak down her face. "I'm scared. I'm worried we're going to fail. I've never felt so lost since I've become an Angel."

Felix stood and joined them to make a huddle around Arielle. "You're losing sight of yourself. You've put too much pressure to live up to your reputation. Yes, this mission is hard and has so many unique challenges." Felix pointed his index finger and jammed it into Arielle's chest. "You're Arielle fucking Lucila. You don't live up to your reputation. Your reputation lives up to you. Stop overthinking everything, and do what comes naturally. *That's* what makes you the best."

Selena wiped away Arielle's tears. "Clear your mind. Hit the reset button. And we can all discuss how next week will look. We have eight more days to figure this out. We will succeed."

"Thank you," Arielle whispered, stretching her back to stand up tall, her confidence slowly returning. She knew exactly what needed to happen next.

Chapter 17

Selena insisted on joining Arielle outside Kennedy's house on Sunday morning. She had originally proposed they all take the day off and spend it downtown. There was a chalk art festival just south of the Sixteenth Street Mall, with vendors selling food, clothes, and random goods.

Arielle, unsurprisingly, refused to blow off a whole day while on a mission. She claimed that if nothing of significance was happening at Kennedy's house by two o'clock, they could head back downtown for the festivitics.

Selena didn't believe her. She had already come to know Arielle well enough to see through the thinly veiled lie. It was no different than a parent telling their nagging child "we'll see" to mollify them.

Felix remained at the apartment, another slow day of watching Peter Young lounge around in his underwear. At least he wore that much.

It was ten o'clock when they turned onto Kennedy's block and parked across the street from his house.

"Well, what do you know?" Selena said. "They're sitting in the dining room having breakfast. A late breakfast, at that. Riveting stuff."

Arielle shook her head. "If you only knew. This is maybe the most action I've seen all week. Mostly it has only been dinner when I've seen them together. I sat out here yesterday for eight hours, all while Kennedy was nowhere to be seen, and Mrs. Kennedy cleaned every nook and cranny of the house."

"So another day of wasted time? Got it."

Arielle laughed, a bit of lunacy swimming beneath its surface. "You don't get it. This is the work I do. It's not anything new. Sure, this mission might move slower than normal, but if you really break down all the missions I've worked on in the past, it's probably sixty to seventy percent just sitting around. Everyone thinks my job is to break into buildings and shoot the bad guys—which it is—but it's just not that way all the time. There's a certain buildup to get to that point."

"Then what separates you from the pack?" Selena asked. "I'm sure your counterparts face the same struggles."

"They do. The difference is I fill that downtime with knowledge. A lot of the others will just sit there all day. Maybe knit a blanket, or something to pass the time. I learn everything I can about the mission. The file is my bible, and I study it until I know every little detail inside. There is always something overlooked that can change the entire trajectory for a mission."

"Then why haven't you been doing that for this one?"

Selena saw those words sting Arielle. She knew their leader was dealing with plenty of doubt—and confidence issues—regarding this mission. She didn't mean for her words to sound so cold, and could only brace for Arielle's response.

Arielle looked forward through the windshield, gazing into the distance. The Kennedys could have been on the moon right now, for all she knew. After thirty seconds of silence, all she did was shrug. "I don't know. I've tried. Don't get me wrong. But when I read this file, it's like the words just run together. The images all look both familiar and foreign."

"Do you think it's the past?"

"It could be. But this mission . . . it just hasn't been simple. We don't even know who pulls the trigger. There's a chance it's neither Kennedy nor Young. We have no idea."

"But why does it matter? We can still show up ready to stop the crime from happening. We don't *need* to know who it is."

"But we do. We can't take gambles. There could be multiple people involved. Decoys. I know it sounds absurd, but things like that really happen. We could end up killing a—somewhat—innocent person. And besides, the mission instructions are to find out who committed the crime. It doesn't actually say to stop it from happening. Legally, we're not bound to do anything the Commander says, but rather what's in writing on our official mission reports. And it's plain as day on the second line of the document. 'Objective: To identify the persons responsible for the acts of violence at the United Bank Robbery on June 16, 1991, also known as the Father's Day Massacre.' And that's it. Nothing about stopping it."

Arielle held her gaze out the windshield, despite Selena whipping her head around toward her. "Are you saying what I think you're saying?"

"What? That we only need to observe who does it and not worry about stepping into the line of danger?" Arielle paused, leaving Selena in unnecessary suspense. "Sure I've thought about it, but can I actually just sit by while a crook murders four innocent people? Can any of us justify doing that if we're already here?"

Selena hadn't yet considered that angle.

Did they have a moral obligation to prevent the murders from happening, simply because they knew they would occur? The Road Runners had authorized hundreds of missions deemed 'observational' in the past, strictly to watch and learn what had happened at critical historical events. They knew what would happen while in the moment, yet never made moves to interfere. And these were crimes much more horrific than the one they were dealing with.

"Do you think there's something bigger at play?" Selena asked.

Arielle finally broke her long-distance gaze and met Selena's eyes. "I've thought about it. It's possible. Commander Briar could be seeing how we act under these circumstances, but that doesn't seem like him. He's very transparent about everything we do. He's not one to play mind games. Which is why I think this just slipped through the cracks. It's either a miscommunication or a misunderstanding. The commander reviews dozens of mission reports each day. Did this small detail just slip by him?"

"That seems more likely. Especially with everything else he has going on."

Silence fell over the car while they both looked to the Kennedy house, surprised to see Jacob standing in the open front door, giving his wife a kiss, keys in hand.

"What?!" Selena gasped. "Where's he going?"

Arielle fired up the engine. "This is why I come on the weekends. He's off to somewhere by himself."

After a minute, they had followed Kennedy onto the main road. All Arielle could do was pray that he was going to do something related to the robbery. She couldn't bear the thought of another wasted day.

"Any idea where he might be headed?" Selena asked as they stopped two cars behind him at a red light.

"So far, it's the same direction he went that day I followed him to the gun shop and sandwich place. But he could be going anywhere. It's almost eleven o'clock."

They followed him through the light Sunday traffic for another ten minutes before he turned into the parking lot belonging to Mad Shot Sports Bar. The bar had a sign hanging over its entrance portraying an angry, cartoonish dog shooting a basketball. Arielle giggled at the sight.

"A *sports bar*?" Selena questioned, looking around to make sure there wasn't any other business. "Seems strange for a man who never leaves the house. And on a Sunday morning in June? There aren't even sports on yet."

"Guess we need to follow him in to see what he's doing here. Keep in mind, liquor stores are closed on Sundays. That law wasn't changed until much later. He could just be getting his fix for the day."

Kennedy parked in the front row, only three other cars in the lot. Arielle took her time turning in and parking on the side of the building, out of sight from Kennedy.

The bar had a brick exterior and only one window on the side, in which hung a Denver Broncos Budweiser neon light. A dumpster stood next to a side door that presumably led to the bar's kitchen.

Arielle and Selena stepped out, and Arielle looked through the window, but couldn't see much through the neon light.

"Do we need disguises?" Selena asked.

"For what? He doesn't know who we are."

"I always use disguises. Just in case. You never know when he might recognize you elsewhere."

Selena's approach on missions was to never be spotted. And if she was, to look as bland as possible. They were both dressed in jeans and t-shirts, a fortunate happening that would help them blend in inside the bar. She retreated to the car and leaned in to open her backpack on the floor. She returned with two pairs of sunglasses, handing one to Arielle.

"Wear sunglasses inside a bar?" Arielle asked. "I feel like that will make us stand out more."

"Oh, we're already going to stand out. I guarantee you the only men inside there are like Kennedy. Middle-aged and boring. We're young and hot. They're going to be looking at us. Might as well hide our faces best we can."

Selena rarely had trouble understanding how to best adapt to her settings, given the location and year, and this time proved no different. Morning trips to the sports bar, outside of football season, never garnered attention from the younger, college crowd.

"If you say so," Arielle said, slipping the sunglasses over her eyes, tossing her hair back.

"Let's go," Selena said, rounding the corner toward the entrance. She paused before opening the door, turning to Arielle. "We need to go to the opposite side of the room. If he's to the left, we go right. If he's at the front, we hang back."

Arielle nodded, and Selena pulled open the door, the scent of beer and fried chicken immediately rushing them. The bar was practically empty. Several men sat at a table along the left side of the room, next to a pair of pool tables. And Kennedy sat at the bar toward the front, minding his business while the bartender filled a couple of steins full of beer. Four TVs were mounted above the bar, two showing a golf tournament, while the other two showed the pre-game talk for the Yankees and Orioles game about to begin.

Classic rock played through the speakers, not too loud to drown out conversation, but not subtle, either. Selena led them to a table in the corner to their right, giving a direct view of Kennedy's back. He'd have no reason to turn all the way around to look at them. As Selena predicted, the two men, who had just received their beers from the bartender, stopped their conversation to admire the two women who had just entered the building.

The bartender, an older gentleman with wavy gray hair, approached them and placed two menus on the table. "Good morning, ladies. Can I get you anything to drink?"

"Tequila sunrise," Selena said without hesitation, immediately grinning at Arielle, as she knew the alcohol order would bother her.

Arielle looked down to the menu. "I'll just have water. . . while I think about it."

"You got it," the bartender said, nodding before returning to his post to make their drinks.

Arielle said nothing about Selena's order, too focused on Kennedy. She held up her menu to glance over the top in his direction.

They sat across from each other, both able to see Kennedy through the sides of their vision. "What's he doing?" Selena asked.

"He's watching baseball. Doesn't even have a drink or food in front of him."

"Do you think he really came here just to watch baseball?"

Arielle shrugged, putting the menu down. "So far it seems like it. But we'll stay to see. I can't say I'm interested in spending all day in this bar watching sports."

They spent the next fifteen minutes watching Kennedy watch baseball. Selena sipped her drink and ordered a round of hot wings, claiming it would help them blend in more.

That's when another man stepped into the building and made his way straight to the bar. He wore raggedy jeans and had a cigarette stuck between his lips.

"Is that who I think it is?" Arielle asked, unable to look away.

Selena had tracked the man from the moment he stepped in. She knew exactly who it was. "Yes. It's Peter Young."

Chapter 18

They never went to the downtown festival on Sunday. Instead, they had spent the rest of the afternoon at Mad Shot Sports Bar, conversing with Felix, who had shown up just after Young.

This surprise meeting between the two suspects injected fresh energy into the stalled mission. They spent Sunday evening reviewing all the potential crossover between Young and Kennedy.

On Monday morning, Selena rolled out of bed ready to attack the day. She had every intent on bumping into Young at the office. She still wasn't sure what she wanted to get out of the encounter, but knew initiating the contact would at least open up fresh possibilities with six days until the robbery.

As the day progressed, anxiety mounted.

Olivia had a strict rule about the cleaning crew not interacting with anyone else in the building. They were to move in the background unnoticed. If she were to find out Selena was stopping by the security office, it would result in a reprimand. And that the security office wasn't part of her cleaning schedule, which just might lead to more suspicions. Ones she couldn't currently afford.

Selena arrived at seven o'clock on Monday morning, an hour before her scheduled start time. Not even Young had left for the office yet. She took her time changing in the locker room, and browsing the day's schedule, pinpointing exactly where Olivia would be at certain times of the day.

Olivia worked the lower floors, including the basement, but would be done with those before lunchtime. The highest she went in the building was the sixth floor, where she'd be around three in the afternoon. That's when Selena planned to head down to the basement and pretend to clean around the security office again. She gave herself a twenty-minute window to meet Young and then return to the twenty-third floor where she was assigned.

Cleaning office after office helped the day pass. She had bought a portable CD player from the thrift store and chose Mariah Carey's self-titled debut album to listen to on repeat. After lunch, she couldn't take any more, and ditched the music.

When the clock struck 2:50, she rolled her cart into a storage closet on the twenty-third floor and took the long elevator ride down to the basement level.

She had no nerves this time, confidence shooting through her veins as the elevator doors parted. Selena wasted no time marching down the hall, swinging open the storage closet doors, pulling out the cart, and continuing down the hallway toward the vault and security office.

No sign of Olivia or any coworkers. She was home free.

She grabbed the broom first and started sweeping the area outside of the security door. She leaned over to peek in and saw Young sitting behind the desk next to McDowell and Dawkins, the two she had met during her last venture to the basement.

"I'm in," she whispered, cracking a wide grin as she knocked on the door.

McDowell was sitting nearest the door, and opened it. "Selena? Good to see you again. What brings you down this way?"

"Oh," Selena said, cocking an eyebrow. "Was someone already down here? My schedule says to clean the security room at three."

"Someone was in earlier in the morning," McDowell said. "But there's no harm in having it extra clean, I suppose."

He chuckled and stepped aside.

"Thank you."

Selena entered the office and saw Dawkins look at her before jerking his head away. Young stared ahead at the monitors like a mindless zombie.

McDowell returned to his seat and shoved an elbow into Dawkins's side.

"You guys having a good day?" Selena asked, pulling out a duster and running it over the front of their desk.

"No complaints here to start the week," McDowell said. "But I'm sure that will change by Friday."

"Dawkins, right?" Selena asked the young guard, his face flushing immediately.

He nodded. "You can call me Brian."

"Good to see you again." She turned her attention to Young, who had finally broken his gaze from the monitors thanks to Selena impeding his view. "I don't believe we've met. I'm Selena. New to the cleaning crew."

Young stood up and stuck out a lazy hand. "Peter. Nice to meet you."

His hand was clammy, Selena glad for a quick handshake. Seeing him up close for the first time completed the puzzle of the man they had been watching on the live-feed. He had a scraggly mustache, fuzz on his cheeks, and a slightly lazy eye. He had a toothpick in his mouth that kept moving from side to side.

"We were talking about going out for drinks after work today," Dawkins said. "Would you be interested?"

Selena looked around to make sure he was talking to her. "Today?"

"I know it's a Monday, but we work such weird schedules. We hardly know what day it is anymore."

"You're all going?" Selena asked, looking around the room to McDowell and Young.

Both men nodded, McDowell grinning. "Us old-timers don't go out too often. Ain't that right, Pete?"

Young cracked a faint smile, finally plucking out the toothpick. "No, we don't. But what the hell? I don't mind having a good time."

"Count me in," Selena said. This trip to the basement couldn't have gone any better. "I get off at five."

"So do we," Dawkins said. "Well, more like 5:15. Gotta wait for the next crew to show up and get settled. We're just going across the street to The Last Drop. Do you know it?"

"I do. I thought it was just a café , though."

"They have a full bar. Quiet evening crowds. Just how these old guys like."

Dawkins winked at McDowell who returned a chuckle.

"Sounds like a good time. I'll see you there at 5:15."

Selena gave a quick sweep over the floor, not forgetting she needed it to look like she really needed to clean their office. Within two minutes, she bid them farewell and left their office.

Her mind flooded with the possibilities of what this evening out with the security team could mean for the mission. She'd even have time to run back to the apartment after work and let Felix know what was going on.

She was on the cusp of discovering just how much Young was involved in the robbery.

Chapter 19

Selena had wasted no time when the clock struck five o'clock. She had already packed up and stored her cart before heading down to clock out for the day. Olivia had commented on her quick and impressive work, but more importantly, had no idea about Selena's brief meeting with the security team.

Olivia had tried to strike up a conversation, but with the clock reading 5:05, she had less than ten minutes to get out of the building before the security team left from their shift to head across the street.

Feeling somewhat rude, she had bolted out of the locker room and building and ran to their apartment where she changed into a fresh pair of jeans and a new blouse. As long as she could keep Dawkins interested, she'd have more opportunities to get close to Young, even if only for the rest of the week.

She let Felix know her plans, and he vowed to head down to the café as soon as Arielle arrived home, typically around 5:30.

Selena left a frazzled Felix without another word. She hurried back toward the office and stopped in front of the café at exactly 5:28.

The front exterior was all glass, decorated with markings advertising their morning happy hour for coffee and their evening happy hour at the bar—a detail she hadn't noticed the day they first came. Through it, she saw a group of men huddled around a standing table in the back corner.

"Play it cool and be natural." She always offered a few words of encouragement to herself.

She headed straight back to the table where Dawkins and McDowell conversed over a couple mugs of beer. They had changed out of their security uniforms, both men wearing jeans and button-up shirts. She found Dawkins rather handsome now that she saw him in the real world, and he must have felt the same, as he couldn't look away.

"Selena!" McDowell greeted. Two other men had stood at the table on the opposite side of her friends, and they spun around. "Let me introduce you. These are a couple other guys from the team. You might see them around. This is Harvey and Sid."

"You can call me Wilson," the one called Harvey explained. "Bill here refuses to call anyone by their first name."

McDowell shrugged. "It's a military thing, I guess."

"Wilson Harvey," Selena said, more to herself. The name was another one of the victims in the robbery.

"I know. Two first names. Or two last names. Whichever you prefer. My parents must have been drunk when they named me."

"That explains so much," McDowell said, and the entire table howled in laughter.

Wilson looked to be in his early forties. He pushed six feet, and seemed to keep in good shape judging by the muscles bulging beneath his skin-tight t-shirt.

"And I'm Hassan Siddiqui," the one called Sid said, stepping forward to shake Selena's hand. He was close to Selena's age. "Sid for short. I guess my Pakistani name is too much for Bill to say."

This earned another round of laughter as the men all took drinks from tall beer steins.

"Well, it's nice to meet you both. Thank you for having me. I haven't had much of a social life since I moved to Denver."

"We're happy to have you," McDowell said. "Aren't we, Dawkins?"

Dawkins immediately turned red and started shaking his head. McDowell couldn't have made it any more obvious. This was all some sort of setup for Dawkins to spend time with the new cleaning girl outside of work.

"Wasn't that other guy I met today coming?" Selena asked, taking the spotlight off Dawkins. "I think his name was Peter."

"Pete? Yeah, he'll be here. He was still wrapping some things up. Might even head home for a second—he doesn't live too far from here, actually."

Oh, I know, Selena thought, the anticipation brewing.

"He's probably pre-gaming at his apartment so he doesn't have to spend any money here," Wilson said. "Pete is a bit of a cheap-ass."

They all howled again, clearly growing more tipsy with each passing moment.

"And to think it's only two-dollar beers. He'll still bitch about it being watered down or something."

"Stop it," McDowell said, nodding toward the entrance. "He's coming."

Peter Young entered the café and shuffled to the back corner where his colleagues waited. He had a cigarette pinched between his lips as he walked up with a crooked smile. Selena made a mental to note to ask Felix if Young was a chain-smoker.

"How's it going?" Young asked, squeezing in at the table between McDowell and Harvey.

"We're doing just fine," McDowell said. "Get yourself a beer—it's happy hour."

"Oh? How much?" Young raised an eyebrow as he reached into his jeans pocket for his wallet.

"Two bucks until six o'clock. Still have a half hour."

Young nodded, satisfied, and pulled out a five-dollar bill before strolling over to the bar.

Everyone else at the table stared around at each other, holding their laughs in.

Selena saw the door swing open from the corner of her eye, Felix appearing in the entryway for a moment before scurrying to the opposite corner of the room, grabbing a corner booth with way too much space for himself.

A minute later, Young returned with two beers, handing one to Selena. "Saw you didn't have anything yet."

"Oh," Selena said, surprised. "Thank you, Peter. That's very nice of you."

He killed his cigarette on the table's ashtray and nodded, expressionless.

Young looked toward the entrance and waved, causing everyone else to look.

"Well, I'll be damned," McDowell said, a wide grin consuming his face. "Is that who I think it is?"

Selena froze in place while Jacob Kennedy made his way toward their table, her heart pounding against her chest like a vicious thunderstorm.

"Gave him a call," Young said. "Told him we'd be here for a bit."

McDowell opened his arms and threw an embrace around Kennedy. "It's so good to see you, Kennedy. How's the retired life treating you?"

McDowell hung back to allow Kennedy space at the table while he shook hands with everyone, pausing at Selena. "And who might you be?" Kennedy asked her, his voice deep and somewhat lazy.

"Hello. I'm Selena. Started working at the building with these guys—cleaning crew."

"Well, nice to meet you," Kennedy said, his push-broom mustache hiding a faint grin. He took a step back to speak to the table more easily. "And retirement has been everything I could have hoped for."

"You still making those model boats?" McDowell asked.

"Every day," Kennedy said, sticking his thumbs into his belt loops, a small gut protruding over his waistband. "If I didn't have those boats, I might go crazy. Not sure what else I'd do."

"Still refuse to take up golf?"

"Eh, not for me. I go to the shooting range now and again, but outside of that, I clean around the house, work on my boats, and read some books."

"Reading, huh? You hated doing that when you worked with us."

Kennedy shrugged. "Had good company, I guess. The wife still goes to work—she'll retire at the end of the year—so it's pretty quiet at home all day."

"Let me grab you a beer," McDowell said.

Kennedy raised a hand, shaking his head. "Not drinking much these days. Tried it a few times at the start of retirement, and realized how shitty it makes me feel. Tell me what you guys have been up to, huh?"

The group of guards started discussing and griping about their jobs. The noise drowned into the background for Selena as she looked around the circle, completely out of her element.

That's when she looked toward the corner booth for Felix, and instead saw Arielle stepping through the entrance.

Arielle scanned the café , spotting Kennedy and Young together, then bulged her eyes upon seeing Selena in the middle of the gathering. They locked eyes, Arielle speaking through their stare as if saying, *What the hell are you doing?!*

Selena looked away, grinning and nodding to blend in with the conversation she knew nothing about, then looked back at Arielle to nod toward the restrooms behind the rowdy group of men.

"Excuse me, gentlemen," Selena said, putting her beer on the table. McDowell smiled at her, and no one else seemed to notice her slip away and head into the ladies' room. Before she stepped in, she looked over her shoulder to confirm Arielle was on her way.

Selena made her way to the sink and checked herself in the mirror, brushing back a couple of frizzy hairs that had come undone from her ponytail during the workday. A few seconds later, Arielle entered the restroom, closing the door shut behind her.

"Selena?" she asked in a loud whisper. "What the hell is going on?" She joined Selena at the sink, leaning against the counter as they locked eyes.

"Things escalated quickly today," Selena replied. "I went down to the security office to meet Young—which I did. But then the other guys invited me out for drinks. Young apparently invited Kennedy, and here we are."

Arielle bit her bottom lip, something Selena noticed she did when she became flustered, assuming she didn't have any gum to chomp on. "This is so dangerous. Do you understand that?"

"Of course. It's not like I planned for this to happen. The only reason I accepted the invitation was because Young said he was coming. Thought I'd get to know him a little better. Never expected Kennedy to just show up like this."

Arielle drew in a deep breath. "Tread carefully. Normally I'd say you need to bail right now, but both me and Felix are here, and we'll keep a close eye in case anything goes wrong."

"I can handle this," Selena said with complete confidence. "I won't speak to Kennedy unless spoken to. I'll blend in and just try to listen."

"Be aware of everything. If you stand in the wrong spot, it can prevent a conversation from happening, and the past could start pushing back. If you say the wrong thing and change the subject—the same thing can happen."

"I got it. I'll be a fly on the wall. Did something happen today at Kennedy's house?"

"Of course not. Just another slow day. Until he left. Imagine my surprise when I followed him all the way here, right across from the bank. We should keep a close eye on him once he leaves here."

"That will need to be you or Felix. I can't just leave whenever Kennedy decides—that will look suspicious."

"You could leave early. I honestly doubt Kennedy is going to say anything about his plans to rob the bank where all these men work."

Selena shook her head. "I'm going out there and will be totally natural. I trust my instincts to guide me. If I need to leave, then I will. If not, I'm staying."

"Just don't get drunk."

Selena rolled her eyes. "Did that really need to be said? You still don't trust me, do you?"

"I trust you fine. Just reminding you what the focus is on tonight. No mistakes."

"I'm going back out there. See you at home, *Mother*."

Selena stormed away from the sink and left the bathroom before Arielle could say anything else. She really was sick of Arielle's assumptions that she lacked self-control.

When she returned to the table, the group of guards seemed to have a more focused discussion. Selena stepped up next to McDowell, who stood behind the small huddle, but was still involved in the conversation.

"I heard they took your guns away," Kennedy said. "Seems wild to do that for a security team guarding a bank. Do they just expect you to fight off people with your fists?"

McDowell laughed as he shook his head. "Don't even get me started. We still have batons, but that's about it. I'm not sure what they expect us to do if someone holds up the bank? Throw the baton at them?"

Everyone laughed. Except for Kennedy. His eyes narrowed on McDowell. "Why did they change that?" he asked. His tone didn't have a hint of the amusement as his peers.

McDowell shrugged. "No idea. Policy change is all they told us. Probably some dirty liberal who thinks guns are the devil."

This earned more laughter. Still nothing from Kennedy.

Selena took a step sideways to get out of Kennedy's line of vision. The amount of concentration she could see in his eyes was alarming, especially considering the conversation. She couldn't risk him getting distracted by seeing her. His dials were clearly in motion, and that realization wrapped a fist of dread around her soul.

Gone was the joy Kennedy had when he stepped into the café and saw all of his old friends. Instead, Selena saw the same blank expression that she had become familiar with from the mission report. The same distant stare as Kennedy's mugshot and candid photos from his trial.

"Well, that's too bad," Kennedy said, breaking out of his trance and standing tall. "You boys stay safe over there. Glad I left before they changed that policy—probably would have pushed me to quit."

"We'll be fine," McDowell said. "It's nothing I'm worried about. Police are only five minutes away. Now that I think about it, maybe it's just a liability thing. Don't wanna pay extra insurance if one of us gets shot, so they want us to hide with everyone else."

"Defeats the purpose of having security, I suppose," Kennedy said. "I should get going, though. Said I'd make it home for a late dinner. Can't piss off the missus."

"Wouldn't dream of it," McDowell said. "Take care of yourself."

They all slapped Kennedy on the back as he made his rounds to say goodbye. He shook hands with Young and appeared to whisper something to his friend before they parted and Kennedy exited the café . He said nothing to Selena, or even acknowledged her on the way out. She was completely fine with it.

Selena looked up to see Arielle trailing behind Kennedy, Felix remaining in the booth as he kept a close eye on Young.

It has to be Kennedy.

Chapter 20

They all convened at home by nine o'clock on Monday night. Selena had been the last to arrive, caught up in a conversation with Dawkins about their lives and childhoods. She had no pressure to follow either Kennedy or Young, and they both left once the bartender told them they were getting ready to close. Dawkins gave Selena his phone number, so for the rest of the week, she had an insider on the security team.

Arielle urged Selena to take advantage. Perhaps call Dawkins one night and see what he knew about Kennedy and Young.

Selena didn't plan to stop by the security offices anymore, deeming it too risky. Eventually, she'd get found out, and still needed to ensure access to the building over the weekend.

All the doubt that had hung over their mission like a dark cloud had given way to hope. Arielle moved and spoke with purpose, as she had always done while leading a mission. On Tuesday morning, before her and Selena headed out for the day, they gathered in the kitchen for a quick cup of coffee.

"We have five days between us and the robbery," Arielle said. "What are your thoughts?"

Selena spoke first. "I think they're both involved. Young is in the building every day. He knows exactly what's going on with the bankers, their schedules and routines, and same with security. The robbery was pulled off too cleanly for the robber to not have known all the little details. He's relaying the information. Kennedy already knew about the guns being taken away from the security team. Who else would he have heard that from?"

"I'm not sure," Felix said. "I feel like they would see each other more often. And he's yet to make a call to Kennedy from his apartment phone. In fact, he still hasn't called anyone besides takeout from restaurants. I don't exactly see him as the brightest bulb. The times he's left the apartment has been to the liquor stores and grocery store. Twice a week, he heads down to the gas stations and buys lottery tickets. He's never used a pay phone. So he's calling Kennedy from the office—which would be even dumber than calling him from home—or they set plans for their next meeting each time they're together."

Arielle paced circles, the coffee no longer appealing as her mind had drifted. "It's impossible to say. Kennedy is definitely the brains behind the operation. I'm sure he's told Young to not make any calls to his house. He's a retired cop—he knows what sort of evidence can come up later in a trial."

"She's right," Selena said. "There's no way he just went in to this based on memory of the building."

"He has a map of the building's interior layout," Felix said. "That is something they give to each security guard upon hiring them. He was familiar with the layout after working there and had a map to study during all this time. I've read all the details about the trial. He has the map, a box of various bullets, and even fake ID cards with different aliases—the judge blocked these from being shared during the trial. But it seems like he was planning to run away and start a new life. Why else would someone need all that?"

"And what was revealed about Young during the trial?" Arielle asked.

"Young testified as a witness in the trial. The defense even tried to position him as a possible suspect. Well, he *was* a suspect in the beginning of the investigation before they arrested Kennedy."

Arielle sat down at the table, planted her elbows on the surface, and rubbed her temples. "I can see both sides of the argument. My gut tells me Young is involved in some capacity. We've never seen him mingle with anyone else, but he's gone out with Kennedy twice in the two weeks leading up to the robbery. I can't discount that as a coincidence. At the same time, the two of them never stepped aside for a private conversation at the café . They hung out with the group the whole time."

"You didn't see the look in Kennedy's eyes," Selena said. "When he started asking about the change in gun policy within the security department, his mood completely changed. I could feel it. Almost wondered if I was feeling the past brewing its sick plans right along with him. I trust my gut feeling."

"We should've gone to that trial," Felix said. "I'm not sure anyone on the Advance Team considered it. I think they just gathered newspaper reports that covered it. We should have had someone in that courtroom for the duration. We'd know a lot more."

"We can't dwell on that," Arielle said. "Besides, I think I'm understanding this mission a little better, and why it's been so difficult. I haven't been able to block my mind from the past because we don't know all the facts. And this isn't a mission where we're trying to stop something from happening. Instead, it's grounded in knowledge. We want to learn the truth, and the past knows that. It's blocking us from knowing the truth. This case becomes cold after Kennedy walks, and the identity of the killer is never known. Young dies four months after the verdict, and Kennedy lives shrouded in privacy for the rest of his life. Knowledge of who is responsible can change the lives for dozens of people involved. The detectives, the judges, the jury, the families of the victims and Kennedy. This has a wider reach than we initially realized. Young could have done it and taken the secret to his grave. Same with Kennedy."

Arielle stood up rummaged a drawer for a pack of gum, promptly popping two pieces into her mouth. "There's something we need to do this week," she said, shifting her focus to Felix. "You're going back into Kennedy's house."

Chapter 21

Felix woke up Wednesday morning after a rough night of sleep and immediately ran to the toilet. He thought he was going to vomit, but nothing came up. Arielle allowed him all of Tuesday to process and plan for a day inside Kennedy's home on Wednesday.

He protested the decision, but Arielle assured him his safety. She had plans to lure Kennedy out of the house and make it a seamless process for Felix.

That didn't matter, as he couldn't shake the overwhelming feeling that the past would push back and something would go horribly wrong.

After ten minutes of hugging the toilet with no action, he pulled himself to his bedroom to get dressed, slipping into his all-black attire reserved for when he had to break into a stranger's home.

He had insisted on returning to Young's apartment to poke around more—he'd feel safer being in the same building. But Arielle had only crossed her arms and shook her head. "You'll be doing that later this week. Tomorrow is about Kennedy."

She then went into a rant about growing as an Angel. How taking chances was the only way to expand one's abilities and horizons. She was once a timid Angel, playing it safe and taking every caution in the book. It wasn't until she started taking chances that she saw her rank climb the charts.

Her intended motivational speech fell upon deaf ears, however. Felix had no interest in climbing the charts, content with his present role and ranking. He was the best at what he did. And while entering a target's home to plant bugs was part of his job, he felt this upcoming task was far out of the realm of his day-to-day.

Once ready for his assignment, he headed downstairs where Arielle had started the coffeepot and had a box of doughnuts on the table. Selena sat, crumbs already sprinkled across the napkin she had laid out.

"Good morning, Felix," Selena said, looking up from her food. "How are you feeling?"

"I've been a lot better. I rarely have trouble sleeping, but last night was a disaster."

"You have no reason to be nervous," Arielle said. "I know this is intimidating, but I think you're making it out to be something bigger than it is. I will keep Kennedy away. Trust me."

"Kennedy wasn't the problem last time, remember? His son just let himself into the house. So we know for sure his wife and son have access to the house. Who else? Doesn't he have a daughter, too?"

"You're thinking too much. We're running out of time, and we need answers. The closer we get to the day of the robbery—which is only four more days, by the way—the harder it will be to get anything done. You hid just fine last time, so be ready to do the same if someone shows up again."

Felix shook his head and bit his lip. He already knew he wasn't going to change the situation. He was going into Kennedy's house today, and could only hope he'd come back out alive. He had debated traveling back to his present time to call Commander Briar, but already knew he would side with Arielle.

"Do I still really have to drive myself?" Felix asked. "I don't exactly feel in the best mental state to drive a car."

Arielle's lips parted, and she let her jaw hang for about ten seconds before replying. "We need to speak in private. Right now." She looked to Selena, who glared back before standing and retreating to her bedroom. The walls were thin in this apartment, and she'd likely still be able to hear whatever Arielle had to say.

Arielle waited until Selena closed her door, then spoke. "Look, Felix.

I know you don't want to do this—it's clear. But we need this. I think entering Kennedy's home while he's gone is a less dangerous task than following him, as I've been doing. Not because Kennedy has been a threat to anyone, but being closer to a subject while in the past can lead to more opportunities for push back. There may be some resistance getting into his house, but I consider it low risk."

"Bull," Felix said. "You just said yesterday how us seeking information is what the past will push against. How is me going into Kennedy's house not that?"

"Yes, that's still true. But it's still nowhere near as high of a risk as if we were trying to stop this robbery from happening. I'm still going back and forth on if we should try that or not."

"Well, it won't be me or Selena stopping this robbery. That's *your* job." Felix felt his heart drumming. He never raised his voice toward authority figures.

"Of course that's my job. And so is deciding how to best use our team to solve this mission. That includes you going into Kennedy's house to poke around. I'm not going to let anything bad happen to you."

Felix tossed his hands in the air. "Fine. I'll go pretend I'm a spy and do a job that is way over my head."

"Dammit, Felix, it isn't." Arielle balled a fist and slammed it on the kitchen table. "Do you know what your problem is? You have no faith in yourself. You are by far one of the smartest people in our entire organization, but you'd never know it from speaking with you. We don't have time to dive into why you have so much self-doubt at this moment, but you need to kick all those negative voices in your head to the curb.

"Honestly, with some combat training, you'd be right up there on the charts with me. I consider you smarter than me. You think fast on your feet and can adapt to any situation. You've proven it repeatedly through all your work with the Road Runners. So stop feeding me your nonsense about how badly this part of the mission will go. I'm not even asking you to take anything from Kennedy's house. Just walk around, see what clues there might be, and report back to me. That's it."

Arielle panted for breath after her rant, her face having turned a soft shade of red.

"Okay," Felix said after a minute. "I'll do this. Let's go."

He didn't wait for a response or reaction from Arielle, grabbing his keys and leaving. Felix had battled self-doubt for most of his life, never believing he was good enough, despite what the rest of the world had to say. He had discussed this matter with a Road Runner therapist during his climb to the highest-ranked Angel on the technology side.

A belief that he wasn't deserving of such an accolade plagued him to the point of his quality of work suffering. Felix had a difficult time getting out of his own head and trusting his natural skills to lead the way. He had an education like no one else in the Road Runners, and an understanding of technologies from all eras of time unmatched by anyone.

Yet he still never felt good enough. His therapist had once suggested he inflicted this doubt upon himself, because of guilt from leaving his parents behind to run the fashion boutique in San Francisco. They had done so much for Felix's education, and he fled right after graduating college. His parents had never brought up the matter, either, claiming to be fine with his decision to start a life of his own, wherever that should be. He manifested the shame on his own and supposed that was why it seemed impossible to shake free from his psyche.

Once Felix reached his car parked in the underground garage, Arielle bolted out of the stairwell door and hurried toward him.

"Wait!" she shouted.

He stopped before pulling open his car door.

Arielle needed a moment and leaned against Felix's car to catch her breath. "What's going on? You can't just leave like that."

"Sorry. But I'm ready to get this over with. You're right, Arielle. I can do this, and I apologize for acting like a frightened child. There's just a lot on my mind, I guess, and it was clouding my vision. Let's knock the rest of this mission out so we can go back home. I'm gonna need a few days off before the next one."

"Is everything okay?"

Felix shrugged. "I honestly don't know, and that's the problem. I call my parents and chat with them between missions, but I don't know the last time I've gone out to see them in person. I need to go to San Fran when we get back."

He shook his head, letting it hang low. Arielle reached out and placed a hand on his shoulder.

"Look, Felix, I get it. I visit my grandmother when I can. Our lifestyle makes it hard to maintain relationships outside of the Road Runners. But if you need time away, then take it. I wish you would have just come and talked to me. I assumed you were just being difficult about all of this."

"I would have if I had known what was bothering me. I think I'm a little homesick."

"Well, you know what's wrong, which means we can help you. I'll fly you to San Fran on my jet right when we get back, that way you don't have to deal with booking a flight or any of that hassle."

"Thanks . . . That's really kind of you."

"It's the least I can do."

"Let's get out of here before I change my mind," Felix said with a crooked grin.

The two hugged before getting into their separate cars and leaving the for Kennedys' house.

Chapter 22

Felix stood on the back porch of Kennedy's house, hand shaking as he stuck the lock pick into the doorknob, letting himself in.

Arielle had driven ahead to Kennedy's favorite shooting range and paid for a one-hour time slot. She then called him from a gas station pay phone, posing as the shooting range to remind him of his scheduled appointment, something he quickly disputed, then agreed to go after learning it was already paid for. She had no idea if the plan would work, but Felix had waited in his car across the street and watched as Kennedy pulled out and left, Arielle appearing from around the corner to follow him, shooting Felix a thumbs up before they disappeared from the block.

Felix had no idea what she had done and only watched in amazement. She had told him he'd have at least ninety minutes in the house alone. He planned to use exactly one hour to snoop around and then get the hell out.

When he let himself into the house, Felix found the place even more disorganized than last time, perhaps because Kennedy had left in a hurry. Dirty dishes filled the sink, the scent of toast filled the air, and a jug of orange juice sat on the counter.

Felix wanted to take no chances this time, bolting the back door's lock to ensure he'd hear someone fidgeting with it should they show up again. He checked the front door to find it already bolted and felt more at ease knowing he'd have some warning before someone barged in, unannounced.

He wanted to spend a majority of his time in the basement, where they suspected Kennedy was planning the robbery in private, away from his wife. But first, he strolled into the master bedroom and slipped on a pair of rubber gloves before touching anything.

The bedroom had been picked up, the bed tidy, dirty clothes out of sight. Felix shuffled toward the dresser where Kennedy's son had stood during the suspicious phone call.

Last time, he had only seen a handful of utility bills, but rummaging through the pile, he found a stack of past due bills for water, cable, phone, and electricity. The Kennedys were at least three months behind on their bills, totaling around seven hundred dollars. Felix didn't think too much of it—that certainly wasn't enough to justify robbing a bank—until he found the next bill underneath. It was for a Visa credit card and had an outstanding balance of twenty-one thousand dollars, also three months past due, which meant it had likely accrued more interest since the bill had been delivered.

"Jackpot," Felix muttered under his breath.

He placed the bills back how he had found them and continued down the dresser, finding loose jewelry, receipts, books, and a few CD cases scattered in a mess. Felix crossed the room and opened Kennedy's nightstand drawer, which he assumed was his thanks to the magazine on top with model boats on the cover. Inside the drawer was a couple of hundred dollars in cash—and a handgun.

Felix picked up and examined the Colt .45. He put it back and pulled out a notepad from his back pocket to jot down his findings in the bedroom. He couldn't remember the gun used in the robbery, and would cross-reference that fact when he got back to the apartment.

Out of due diligence, he checked Mrs. Kennedy's nightstand drawer and found nothing of significance, then proceeded out of the bedroom and down the hall toward the stairwell leading to the basement. From the main level's landing he could see out the front window, and confirmed he was still alone.

Felix started down the dim stairs, refusing to turn on any lights. When he reached the bottom, the musty smell of rarely used basements filled his nose. A quick glance around suggested the place was mainly used for storage. Boxes and bins piled from the floor to the ceiling all around the perimeter. It was an open floor space, no walls or partitions. The only spot along the perimeter that didn't have boxes was the washing machine and dryer. A box of detergent stood atop the dryer, its lid flipped open, a pile of clothes stacked next to it.

A square table was on the other side of the basement, directly below a hanging light, covered in newspaper and miniature bottles of paint.

"This is where you do your boats," Felix said, shuffling toward the table. Only the tools were present on the table: paint bottles, brushes, tweezers. No boat, however.

Felix found this peculiar and rummaged through the box on the floor underneath the table. He saw two unopened boat kits, and more paint bottles. If Kennedy spent all of his time in the house, shouldn't he have at least been in the middle of a new boat project? It was possible he had just finished one and was taking a break.

"Or he's been too busy planning something else," Felix whispered. He looked around and saw no finished boats, either. That wasn't as odd—they were likely elsewhere in the house to be displayed, considering no one came down to the basement.

As much as Felix wanted to believe there were clues tying Kennedy to the robbery, he'd yet to find anything of true substance.

He checked his watch to find only twenty-five minutes had passed. He had plenty of time left to raid the basement, and intended on using every second.

"Okay. If I were planning a bank robbery in this basement, how would I do it?" Felix asked himself, pulling out the chair at the table and sitting down. He propped his elbows and looked around the room from Kennedy's angle. He had a clear view of the stairs and could easily see if someone was coming down. The table had likely been set up that way if Kennedy wanted to keep his secret under wraps from his wife. The box of boat materials was under the table so he could quickly pull it out and give the appearance of working on a model.

"If I had papers scattered on the table and needed to put them away in a hurry, I would just dump them into the box. . . but they can't stay there."

Felix looked straight ahead, where two boxes stared back at him. They were unmarked, despite all the other surrounding boxes having labels on them like *photo albums, kids' trophies, memorabilia.*

The boxes were on the opposite side of the laundry machines, sandwiched between others. Dust covered everything except for these two boxes. From the seated position, if someone were to come down and talk to Kennedy at the table, the boxes would be to that person's back, out of sight.

"Easy to get to while still hidden," Felix muttered, feeling his stomach tighten as he stood up, unable to break his stare from the two boxes.

He shuffled to the wall and pulled the box on the left, flipping open the flaps that served as a lid. "What the hell?"

The box was heavier than he expected, and now he saw why. Filled from the bottom to top were pornographic magazines and VHS tapes. Felix, suddenly feeling the urge to take a shower, shoved the box back into its place. Judging by the lack of dust on that box, Felix concluded Kennedy enjoyed pleasuring himself during his trips to the basement.

"Ooookay," he said, turning his attention to the box on the right, quickly accepting he might not find the smoking gun they were all hoping for.

The next box felt even heavier, so Felix braced himself for more dirty magazines as he opened the top.

What he found froze his heart mid-beat.

Felix crouched to sift through the contents. There was a smaller box inside, about the size of a shoebox, filled with an assortment of ammunition of all different colors, shapes, and sizes. He found a gun, another Colt, but one he presumed carried .38 caliber rounds, most of which were in the ammunition box.

A manila folder was pinned against the box by the ammunition, and Felix plucked it out, finding the word *PLANS* scribbled on one side. He flipped open the folder and floor plans of the United Bank building spilled out. They showed the layout of the basement, subbasement, and main levels. The page on top showed the vault area and its proximity to the security office.

What Felix found most odd was nothing drawn on the floorplans. If Kennedy were truly planning to rob the place, wouldn't he have at the very least drawn a preferred route in and out of the building? Or did he know the place well enough to not feel the need to do that?

Felix placed everything back into the folder before returning it to its proper place in the box. Below the gun was a stack of plastic cards all tied together with a rubber band. He pulled these out and flipped the stack over, finding the top card as a Colorado driver's license with Kennedy's portrait, but a name of Lucas Reynolds.

"Here they are."

He snapped off the rubber band to see the other cards, finding four more driver's licenses: two more from Colorado, one from Texas, one from California. They all had Kennedy's same portrait, but different names. The man was also Kenny Pearson, Joshua Wilson, Charles Wallace, and Ethan Miller.

Felix wrote these names down in his notepad and would research them later. These were the pieces of evidence the judge ruled to keep out of the trial.

"He's planning on running and hiding. That's the only explanation for this many fake IDs."

Felix wrapped them all back in the rubber band and dropped them into the box. He pushed everything around. He found nothing else and closed the box back up.

When he picked it up off the table and spun around to put it back in its place, a booming knock came from the front door upstairs. Felix dropped the box out of shock. His heart jumped all the way to his throat, limbs stiffening as he found it nearly impossible to move.

This is the moment you knew was coming, he thought.

A second knock followed, just as loud and aggressive as the first. He felt better knowing it was someone who couldn't let themselves into the house, or else they wouldn't have knocked again.

Felix debated taking the gun out of the box and going upstairs, but didn't want to risk something happening to the potential murder weapon—that would surely throw a wrench in the past's plans to carry out the attack.

Instead, he remained frozen in the basement, grateful it had no windows to the world outside. If needed, the basement was probably the best place to hide in the entire house. He could move a stack of boxes and hide behind them. The room was such a mess; he doubted Kennedy noticed if anything was out of place—beside his own boxes that he seemed to frequently access.

Felix waited five minutes before finally grabbing the box and putting it back, and starting up the stairs. He had wanted to poke around more of the house, but the loud knocking had thrown out all of those desires. It was time to get out.

When he reached the top landing, adrenaline blasting through his body like a broken water pipe, he scanned the area to make sure no one had discreetly slipped into the house. Besides his heart drumming in his ears, the house was silent. He tiptoed toward the dining-room window and craned his neck for an angle at the front door.

No one was there. Whoever had knocked had already given up and left.

He dashed through the house, stopping at the back door to peer out the window that stood inches above his line of sight. Once he saw no one, he stepped out and sprinted alongside the house toward the front.

His car sat across the street and he blazed directly toward it, jumping in and closing the door as he panted for air.

I made it.

Felix let out a nervous laugh as he turned on the car and sped away.

Chapter 23

Later that night, the team gathered for dinner a few minutes past seven. Felix ordered a pizza, citing he was too eager to share his findings to cook a meal.

"Our guy can shoot," Arielle said, starting the conversation once they were all seated and had grabbed a slice. "I booked his time at the shooting range and grabbed a bay for myself four spots down. After seeing the clinic he put on, I'm convinced it's him. Keep in mind, the robber fired eighteen rounds that day, and all but one found their target."

Felix nodded, shifting forward in his seat and pushing back his plate he had yet to touch. "It's gotta be him. For starters, him and his wife are over twenty-thousand dollars in debt. So there's a motive. He had a gun in his nightstand drawer—probably for protection—but he had another in a box in their basement. And I'm pretty sure that box is dedicated to his robbery plans."

"Why do you say that?" Selena asked.

"Well, there was the gun, a box of bullets, five fake IDs. But the biggest giveaway of all . . . he has the floorplans to the bank, including the vault. Combine all of that. What do you get? Someone looking to rob a bank. Case closed—you can thank me later."

Felix chuckled, clearly satisfied with himself.

Arielle shook her head, promptly wiping away Felix's cheesy grin. "I'm afraid it's not that straightforward. A gun and bullets mean nothing. He goes to the shooting range often. What type of gun was it? Because according to the notes from the trial, a .38 Colt Trooper was used during the robbery. Silver revolver with a wooden handle."

Felix nodded. "That was it."

"And the fake IDs are definitely suspicious, but they don't guarantee anything. He never used them, according to the court documents. I'm not dismissing Kennedy as the main suspect, but we still have nothing definitive. These findings make things lean toward Kennedy, but we have one more suspect to check. Felix, you're going into Young's apartment tomorrow for another look around."

"I expected as much," he replied, crossing his arms.

Arielle waited for another outburst, but none came. Felix must have gained some serious confidence after his venture into Kennedy's house. "By the end of tomorrow, we should have a good idea who we want to narrow our focus on. There's still a chance—likely, perhaps—that we'll have to tail both Kennedy and Young on Sunday morning. But if we find nothing of importance in Young's house tomorrow, then we're moving all-in on Kennedy."

"And we're positive it can't be anyone else besides those two?" Selena asked.

Arielle scrunched her face. "There isn't anyone else of interest. Why do you ask?"

Selena shrugged. "There are many people who work in that building. Even just the security team. I'm not saying anyone specifically, but I feel like there can be more moving parts to this than we realized. This could be a coordinated effort involving multiple people wanting to split the heist."

"What, you think your boyfriend is involved?" Felix asked, his grin returning.

Selena rolled her eyes. "You're hilarious. No, I don't think Dawkins is, but he might have information that can help. I'm debating if I should call him tomorrow night to talk on the phone, or invite him to go out somewhere. Just him and I."

"Definitely on the phone," Arielle said. "If you go out, he's going to think it's a date, and that adds a whole other dynamic."

"Right, but if he thinks it's a date, he might be more willing to talk about anything, including his coworkers. That topic might be of no interest if we're on the phone."

Felix chimed in. "I think the phone is better, too. It reduces the risks. The past will still try to fight back as we get this information. Worst-case scenario, if you're home on the phone, the call will drop. Who knows what might happen if you're out and about."

"Very good point," Arielle said. "Just because today ran smoothly doesn't mean that will hold up. Every day closer to the robbery is more opportunity for chaos. You should make the call from right here."

Selena finished the crust from her first slice, nodding as she brushed the crumbs off her fingertips.

"Okay. Phone call it is."

"It'll be like high school," Felix said. "You can talk on the phone for five hours until someone falls asleep. No one wants to hang up first."

Selena crumbled up her napkin and chucked it across the table to drill Felix in the face. Everyone burst out in laughter.

Arielle was glad to see such free flowing conversation from her team. They were comfortable. They trusted each other. And that would only pay dividends in the long run.

"Did you see any guns in Young's apartment?" Arielle asked, bringing the focus back to the group.

"He had one in his nightstand—that seems to be a thing with these security guards. It wasn't a Colt, though, so no match to the gun used in the robbery."

"But he is a gun owner—that's what I was more curious to know. I wonder why he's never gone shooting with Kennedy. It's clear they have a solid friendship."

"Can't be seen together in that type of setting," Felix said. "Kennedy knows how to cover his bases—you keep forgetting that. He's too smart to get caught, and that's why he never was, even after being arrested and put on trial."

"Do you think we'll have to stay afterwards to find out who did it?"

Selena asked. "Like you said, the mission isn't to stop this robbery from happening, it's strictly to find out who did it."

"I've been mulling that over," Arielle said. "There's a chance we'll stay until Monday. It's hard to say how Sunday will play out. We know the route the robber will use when running out of the building, but after that we don't know where he goes. Does he get in a car and drive away? Is someone else waiting for him in a car? There could be some sort of handoff—maybe Kennedy gives the money to Young and they go their separate ways.

"Let's keep in mind, Kennedy isn't arrested until three weeks after the robbery. By Sunday night, no one has a clue he might be a suspect. I'd love to find out where the money is hidden. Assuming Kennedy did it, he has a three-week window to hide the cash, dispose of the gun and everything else he took from the security office. That's a long time."

"Are you saying we stay even longer than Monday?" Felix asked, raising an eyebrow.

Arielle shifted in her seat, crossing one leg over the other as she looked to the ceiling. "Are you not curious? We're already here. Why not plan on seeing where the money is? Who knows, we might find that out on Sunday and can leave then. I just want to go back with all the information we can get. Most importantly, who did it and where that money is stashed."

Felix raised his hands defensively. "I'm all for staying. I guess we're just a little surprised about your change of heart. Just last week you were ready to bail on this mission. Now you want to stay beyond the robbery."

Selena nodded to support Felix's statement.

"Well," Arielle said. "I let the logistics of the mission cloud not only my vision, but my passion. I put too much stress on myself trying to make this mission fit the mold of prior ones. I might have been a little offended that we received a mission that didn't require us to disrupt the robbery. A slap in the face is how I first took it. Usually new Angels get missions where they go back in time just to learn something and report the findings. But I've since seen why they chose us for this one. It's complex and messy, and I'm still not sure how clear of an answer we'll get once it's all over. So thank you both."

"What did we do?" Selena asked, shooting a puzzled look to Felix.

"You both kept your head down and worked, despite my feelings. It would have been easy for you to agree with me and lose interest in the mission. I wouldn't have been able to blame you if it came to that, since I was the one spewing the disgust. But you ignored me and kept at it. We wouldn't be anywhere close to where we are today without that. So I thank you. And I owe you."

"You don't owe us anything," Felix said. "But you *could* buy that first round of margaritas when we get back home."

Selena nodded, a wide grin taking over her face at the mention of a margarita.

"Margaritas, huh?" Arielle asked. "Do we have a new tradition now, after missions?"

"I suppose we do," Selena said. "D'Corazon after each mission sounds just fine to me."

"Consider it done," Arielle said. "Now let's get some rest. Tomorrow should be another fun day."

Chapter 24

Felix was awake first on Thursday morning. They had three more days until the robbery, and two candidates: one a clear front runner, the second not as obvious. The goal for today was to cross Young off the list so they could narrow their focus strictly on Kennedy. At least, that was Felix's goal.

He had woken at six-thirty, a half hour before Young typically got out of bed to start his workday. Today was no different, so Felix used the extra time to prepare a full breakfast for himself and the ladies. Eggs, bacon, toast, sliced fruit. He didn't care how loud the bacon sizzled in the stillness of the early morning; the smell was the perfect jump-start for the day.

By seven-thirty, everyone had eaten, dressed, and left the apartment building, including Peter Young. Felix hung around until eight, just to make sure Young didn't return for any reason. Once deciding it was safe, he left the apartment and took the stairs down to the fifth floor.

The hallway was abandoned, minus a mother dragging a whiny child from their apartment, a baseball bag slung over the kid's shoulder.

Once they cleared out, Felix marched up to apartment 512, reached into his pocket for his trusty lock pick, jamming it into the keyhole and twisting until he heard the satisfactory *click* of success. He had this part of the process down to a basic instinct after having done it so many times. He spent less than three seconds in front of the apartment door before disappearing inside and closing it behind him.

Young's living quarters didn't look too different compared to last time, but Felix could also take his time on this trip.

The aroma of coffee filled the small apartment, the abandoned coffeepot sitting on the counter next to the sink, still filled with dishes to the brim. Felix had watched Young enough to know the man only washed a dish when he needed to use it. He'd even used a dirty plate on various occasions, something that made Felix gag each time he saw it.

He went to the bedroom first. Again, nothing looked different from last time. Clothes remained on the floor in front of the closet, its doors wide open. Felix shuffled to the nightstand, slipped on a pair of rubber gloves, and opened the drawer, seeing the pistol still in place.

"A Ruger P89 or 90," Felix said, pulling out his notebook to write the model. It was not the gun used in the robbery, and this satisfied Felix. One more piece of evidence that suggested Young hadn't carried out the attacks.

He closed the drawer and turned his attention to the dresser near the bedroom's doorway. On top was scattered change, old receipts, pens, blank notepads, and three pairs of sunglasses.

The robber had worn sunglasses, and one pair looked like the same style seen in all the pictures and sketches that would show up during the trial. Felix noted this finding in his notepad, discouraged by the potential clue. Nearly everyone in town owned a pair of sunglasses, so it wasn't exactly a smoking gun, either.

He then started going through the dresser's three drawers, each filled to the brim with unfolded clothes, underwear, and socks. Nothing of significance.

Felix spent the next fifteen minutes doing the same thing in the closet, with much more of a mess to sift through. He found a shoebox filled with old pictures of Young and a blond woman of around the same age, presumably an old girlfriend, judging by the obvious signs of affection. Besides that, he found nothing.

Relieved all signs still pointed to Kennedy, Felix returned to the living room. His gaze fell on the closet doors near the apartment's entrance, and that's when his gut wrenched, a sense of dread drenching him like a bucket of ice water.

The closet had a pair of bi-fold doors with a grab handle on each. A set of handcuffs clasped around each handle to prevent the doors from opening. Felix had no idea if those handcuffs had been hanging there on his last visit—it seemed like a detail he wouldn't have missed, but he hadn't exactly been scanning the room for such things.

The cuffs gleamed in the dim light coming through the shaded window overlooking downtown. Felix approached, fishing out his lock pick that would work easily on a pair of handcuffs.

He had them unlocked within seconds, leaving them hanging from one handle.

When he pulled the doors open, the dread kicked into a higher gear. He had found a hidden treasure of incriminating evidence all piled up within the closet.

Unlike Kennedy's organized box of goods, Young had stuff all over the place, scattered about the floor and on top of boxes. The first things he found were three sandwich bags full of ammunition. Upon closer examination, he deemed them as .38 and .357 caliber. On the closet's top shelf lay a revolver, and he pulled it down to find it fully loaded.

"Shit," Felix muttered. After twenty minutes of hope and optimism, Young remained a primary suspect, perhaps even more so than Kennedy, once Felix continued digging through the closet.

He flipped open the top box's lid and found a police scanner and two speedloaders that fit the revolver above. This discovery was perhaps the most alarming, seeing as the robber had fired eighteen rounds from a revolver in fairly rapid succession. One loaded revolver plus two speedloaders equaled eighteen rounds and allowed the shooter to reload in seconds. Sprawled on the bottom of the box were five different police badges, each for a different department from around the state.

They looked and felt real, but Felix wasn't versed enough in police badges to know an obvious fake. He took a moment to write his findings in the notebook before closing the box and opening a second.

In the next one, he discovered two batons and four grenades, prompting him to close the box and leave it untouched. The last thing he needed to tempt the past with was an opportunity to blow the entire apartment complex to the moon.

A small notebook, roughly four by six inches, lay on the floor between the tower of boxes. Felix squatted down to pick it up, a title scrawled in sloppy handwriting: *Confidential need to know only.*

The first few pages had disturbing drawings of gravestones, including one for Young himself. After flipping a couple of pages, it became clear Young meant the drawing to be a cemetery. There were dozens of names, none of which Felix recognized aside from Young. Certainly no names that had any ties to the robbery.

Chickenscratch began on page six, and with it, a new thread of evidence Felix couldn't deny, including a disclaimer at the top of the page:

Warning—these entries are blunt and brutal. Sensitive psyches are advised to stop now. If you are emotionally unstable, close this journal immediately. There is one caveat—my deepest secrets are not revealed here. You'll never know a damn thing. I trust no one.

Reading this caused gooseflesh to overtake all of Felix. He shook his head and continued on:

If you're reading this, then I'm already rotting underground. A fitting end to a lame attempt at life. However, it was not as lame as you detectives and police officers. I have a question for you all. How can you be so pathetic? Your investigative abilities—if you can call them that—are at best guesswork and pure luck. How does the old saying go? You have done too little too late!

To wrongfully accuse a man is a level of cowardice I can't begin to comprehend. How low must one go to simply pin fault on another human being without having all the facts? I'm not saying I lived a perfect life. Far from it. I've done both good and bad in this world. But I never committed the crime you supposedly believe I did. That reminds me of my mortal flaw—I never forget who screwed me over. And guess what? I have another flaw! I am patient to a fault. I believe in getting even. I have the patience to do just that. Even if I have to wait 50 years, I will get even. That's a promise.

The last time I stole money was when I was eight years old. I wanted a

Superman comic so bad from our neighbor's yard sale. My mom said no, but I snuck into her bedroom and took the two dollars anyway. And guess what? I felt guilty. So much that after a week, I confessed what I did. I got quite the ass-whooping that night, but that doesn't upset me. It was deserved.

What isn't deserved, however, is having to go through a bullshit trial for being accused of robbing an ATM. How stupid do you take me for? You actually think I would openly rob an ATM at my place of employment? With all of the cameras around? None of which showed me doing anything even remotely close to robbing a machine.

This may all be a part of your lame job, but that one accusation has ruined my life. Even after being found INNOCENT, do you know how the public treats someone who had to stand trial for such a crime? Like a fucking PARASITE.

And it's funny, because there are TWO actual parasites, and they both work for United Bank: Tom Trawinski and Alvin Lasch. If you open the dictionary to the word 'asshole', you'll find a picture of these two scumbags. These are by far the worst employers I have ever worked for, and I've worked for some shady people. They tried to lock me up for something I didn't do.

Lying Tom can burn in hell. It WILL happen. The Lord will have his way with men like Tom. He's the one who should be in the federal pen raking rocks with a 16-pound hammer. Not me. Alvin, too. These men are a disgrace to humanity and society.

Felix snapped the notebook shut and looked around the apartment. He felt like he had fallen into a trap by reading the lunacy penned by Young. There were plenty more pages to read, and Young seemed nowhere close to finished with his rantings.

One notebook had just swerved this entire mission into a different direction. A shift was underway, and Felix couldn't help but wonder if the past had placed that notebook in the closet to distract them from Kennedy.

"Or this is real, and Young did it. We have the rest of today, all of tomorrow, and all of Saturday. Two and a half days until the morning of the robbery."

He stood in the closet for five more minutes, playing through all scenarios, trying to think about what Arielle might have done if she was standing in the closet right now.

"I'm going for it," he said, and stuck the notebook in his pocket before leaving the apartment.

Chapter 25

Felix had fought off an excessively trembling body for the two hours after he returned home with Young's notebook. He felt like he had just committed a major felony, one that could lock him up for years. He could only hope the past didn't have that sort of appetite for justice.

During the first hour in the safety of his apartment, Felix had put the notebook on the kitchen table and sat there staring at it. He never opened it or touched it, treating it like a lethal bug that could end his life with one drop of venom.

He didn't understand the past on the complex level that Arielle did, so he wasn't sure what to expect as far as a time range for something to happen. Would someone come knocking on his door, accusing him of being inside an apartment that wasn't his? Or perhaps nothing would happen until Young returned home and discovered his notebook missing.

Felix took a gamble and believed Young wouldn't seek the notebook over the next two and a half days. By now he had over ten days of live and recorded footage of Young in his apartment, and he hadn't once seen him open those closet doors. In fact, he pulled up a recording from last week, curious to see if the handcuffs had always been clasped around the closet's door handles. Sure enough, they were, and he beat himself up for missing such a detail. Felix prided himself on his keen observation skills, and this felt like a blunder that should have never happened.

He didn't dwell on it for too long. The handcuffs would have become obvious had Young actually used the closet. Instead, they blended into the backdrop, no different from the black-and-white poster of Marilyn

Monroe hanging in the living room.

After that first hour had passed, Felix worked up the courage to open the notebook and resume reading. By five-thirty in the evening, the notebook was stuffed with different colored sticky notes on what seemed like every page. He had paced circles around their living room, and continued doing just that while he waited for Selena and Arielle to arrive.

At 5:50, Arielle finally stepped through the door. She looked to the kitchen, saw nothing cooking, then to Felix, who had beads of sweat forming on his forehead, and finally down to the notebook clutched in his grip.

"Is everything okay?" she asked. "Where's Selena?"

Felix shrugged. As much as he had been watching the clock, it hadn't occurred to him that Selena should have been home already. His stomach dropped to his knees as he couldn't help wonder if his stealing of the notebook had led to something bad happening to Selena. He wanted to spew out hundreds of words at a time, but didn't know where to start.

"Felix?" Arielle said, dropping her backpack by the door and crossing into the living room. "You don't look too well. What happened today?"

Felix nodded, a lump suddenly forming in his throat. He had no idea why he had become so nervous to speak to Arielle about his findings. He supposed part of it was knowing drastic changes might need to be implemented with less than three days remaining.

"Sorry," he finally managed. "I don't know where Selena is. Did she maybe go out with that guy, after all?"

This drew a look of concern from Arielle, her eyes glancing to Selena's open bedroom door, as if she were in there and no one knew it. She checked her watch and shook her head. "If she's not here by six, we'll need to go for a walk and see if we can find her."

"Oh my God!" Felix gasped, causing Arielle to take a cautious step backwards. "Young should be home, and I haven't even thought to check."

He smacked a hand on his forehead and dashed into his bedroom where he kept his laptop on the bed. He had become so convinced that Young was the robber, that he forgot his main job was to watch the angry, isolated man.

When he flipped open his laptop, the feed showed Young in his typical position on the recliner, a microwave dinner on his lap while he flipped mindlessly through the TV channels. The handcuffs remained on the closet doors.

"Okay," Felix said. "We're okay."

Arielle came into his bedroom and tossed her hands in the air. "What's going on? Seriously—tell me right now."

Felix jumped off his bed and pushed past Arielle back out to the living room where he had tossed the notebook on the couch. He held it up like an all-powerful relic. A book from the heavens that contained every answer to life's greatest questions. "Before I start, did you find anything on Kennedy today?"

Arielle shook her head. "Wish I could call it a productive day, but he did nothing. Never once stepped out of the house."

"Can't say I'm surprised." Felix could feel the words coming out faster than normal, and attempted to slow himself down. "I have in my hands a journal belonging to Peter Young. It is loaded with the thoughts of a madman who wants *revenge* on United Bank!"

Arielle's jaw dropped as she stared at the journal. "Felix, do you know how dangerous having that in your possession is? You need to put it back."

"I thought this through. I think we'll be okay for the night. I can take it back in the morning—I can't in this instant, obviously. But at least we'll have it for the entire night to pick it apart and see what else we can find. Young has one twisted mind. The guy is a nutjob!"

Felix recapped what he had read, getting Arielle caught up with what he referred to as the "heavy details."

"Do we know if those two guys still work there?" Arielle asked. "Trawinski and Lasch."

"No clue. We'll have to see what Selena can find about those names. But it gets more interesting." Felix thumbed the journal open and ran a finger down the page, reading the entry aloud. "'This whole process has been bad enough, but the most humiliating part was having to ask my dad for money to pay for the lawyers. Ten thousand dollars. I barely make that in a year, and now my dad resents me for having to borrow it. On top of that, my dad actually believes I robbed that ATM.

"'He worked at a bank his entire life, and insists I'm guilty. My dad was my best friend in this world, and I've lost that relationship because of this false accusation. My life has been completely ruined, and that leaves me only one option. My accusers will be judged by a higher authority, and I hope He has mercy on them. I will not.'"

Felix closed the journal, keeping a thumb between the pages to save his spot. "This paints a pretty obvious picture, don't you think?"

Arielle nodded. "It's hard to argue his motive."

"It sounds like he had a pretty up-and-down relationship with his dad. Says he was his best friend, but also goes on about how it all soured after this accusation. I can't help but wonder if Father's Day was chosen on purpose because of that, as some sort of sick way to prove something to his father."

"What was the timing of all this?"

"It sounds like Young was arrested for this ATM robbery in May 1990, was acquitted by the fall, and his father passed away in January 1991. It really was a rough stretch for him."

Arielle sat down at the kitchen table, pale. "Great work, Felix. I think we were all ready to dismiss Young, but now we can't. Even if he isn't the one who directly robs the place, he *has* to be involved somehow, right?"

"I believe so. Between the handful of meetings with Kennedy, and learning about all of this pent-up hatred for the exact bank that will be robbed . . . how can we believe otherwise?"

Arielle checked her watch and stood up. "It's 6:10. We need to go make sure Selena is okay. We're going to have a long night digging through this journal." She chuckled as she shook her head. "Good call on taking it. I probably would've done the same thing."

"Thanks. Let's go. I want to come back as soon as possible to finish going through this notebook."

Chapter 26

Selena changed her plans in the middle of the day, opting to ask Dawkins out to drinks and dinner after work. Just the two of them, she had emphasized during a quick trip down to the security office during her lunch break. Dawkins eagerly agreed.

At 5:15, Selena changed into a pair of jeans and a crop top. She figured that would distract Dawkins just enough to let his guard down and speak openly about his colleagues.

It worked immediately. When she stepped out of the locker room, Dawkins was already waiting in the hallway, having changed into jeans and a button-up. His eyes immediately fell to her exposed abdomen as he did a double take.

"You look incredible," he said, unable to keep a grin off his face.

"Oh, this old thing?" Selena teased, putting her hands on her hips and batting her eyebrows.

Dawkins cackled. "Shall we head over?"

"Please. I'm starving."

They shared the details of their day with each other as they walked down the hallway, took the elevator up to the street level, and strolled across the street toward the café.

A few people hustled up and down the streets of downtown Denver, most clearly leaving work. It was a warm summer evening, and the heat seemed to radiate off the concrete. Selena's mouth watered at the thought of a cold drink.

Once they entered the café, the bartender waved them over to sit in a booth along the window. They looked out and had a clear view of their office building immediately across Seventeenth Street.

"Always a good feeling to get out of that place," Selena said. "Don't you agree?"

"It's not that bad. You don't like your job?"

Selena shrugged. She'd never had a regular nine-to-five type of job, and only knew how people talked about them from what she had seen on TV. "It pays the bills, but it's not exactly what I want to do."

Dawkins laughed. "Well, I don't suppose too many people are doing what they *truly* want to do. I don't see myself being a security guard for the rest of my life."

"You want to become a cop?"

Dawkins shook his head. "Nah. I know that's the stereotype with guards, especially in our building. Everyone is a former cop, wants to be a cop, or failed in the police academy. If I can be honest, I'm not entirely sure what I want to do for a career. What about you?"

"Acting has always been my passion. It's something I've done since I was a little girl. I *wanted* to be in school plays and all that stuff. I know I just moved here, but I want to go to Hollywood and take my shot."

Dawkins nodded, clearly impressed. A server came over and Dawkins ordered a couple of appetizers for them to munch on. Selena was sure to order a frozen margarita.

"That's impressive," he said. "Why not go for it, right? What do you have to lose? You can always find different jobs to the pay the bills, but you don't get a second chance at life. Chase your dreams while you can."

Selena smiled. A genuine smile. Brian Dawkins sat across from her in the booth, oblivious that she had come from the year 2022. She had planned on toying with him to get new information about his colleagues, but she suddenly found herself drawn into his natural charm.

He had a true interest in her, paying full attention while he spoke, gazing at her with welcoming eyes.

Selena had to shake herself out of the trance and remember what she came to do. "That's a nice thought. So you don't like your job too much, either?"

"I actually enjoy it. It keeps me in shape and has lots of downtime. Being such a massive building, I must walk at least five miles a day during sweeps. But there's also three hours of just hanging out. I can read books, do a crossword. Hell, might even bring in an actual jigsaw puzzle one day." He laughed while the server returned with a basket of French fries and a plate of chicken wings. "Please, help yourself."

Selena grabbed a fistful of fries. "How are your coworkers? You all seemed like a pretty tight bunch that day we were here for drinks."

"They're good guys. I don't really see any of us staying friends beyond this job, but I suppose we keep each other company while we're there." He gave a subconscious nod toward the building.

Selena could tell he wasn't going to elaborate anymore, so she needed to force the matter. "Well, they seemed like a fun group to me. What was the younger guy's name? Sid?"

Dawkins nodded after taking a bite of chicken. "Sid. He's a really cool dude. Probably my closest friend at work since we're both younger."

"And I know all about Bill. He's probably the nicest person I've met since I started working there."

"Bill is the man. He looks out for everyone. He's not a supervisor, but he acts like one. Which is good for us. He keeps everything running smoothly, so the higher-ups never come down to check on us. They just see the work getting done every day and don't question it. But it's all Bill's doing."

"Who was that other guy? Kind of chubby, wears those big glasses?"

"Peter Young. He's . . . interesting."

Selena sat forward. "How so?"

"How much time do you have?" Dawkins asked, letting out a chuckle.

To hear about Young, I have all the time in the world.

"That bad?" Selena asked. "We haven't even ordered dinner yet, so why don't you tell me about him. He's seemed really distant in the couple times I've encountered him."

Dawkins waved over their server so they could order their entrées. He asked for a steak, medium-rare. And Selena ordered a chicken sandwich with extra tater tots on the side.

"Distant?" Dawkins asked when they resumed their conversation. "That would be a compliment. That guy gives me the fucking creeps."

Selena placed her hand on her bouncing knee to keep it under control. She couldn't help but sense something valuable coming her way. "The creeps? I don't know if I'd go that far."

"That's because you don't have to sit in a room with him all day. He speaks to no one. He might say hello at the beginning of a shift, and goodbye at the end. But that's a big maybe. Outside of that, he just sits there all day in silence. He can clearly hear the conversations we have in the office, but he never chimes in. He'll occasionally read a book, but most the time it's like he's staring into space. Like no one is home inside."

"Do you think he's okay? Does he need mental help?"

"Hard to say. Bill has told us he wasn't always this way. I guess last year one of the ATMs was robbed. Something like $30,000 was stolen. The guards used to refill the machines on the weekends—we don't anymore, because of this. But Peter was arrested and had to stand trial. They blamed him for it, even though there was no actual proof. The video footage was spotty—the lights had been turned off in the room—and all they could make out was the general body outline of the robber. They felt Peter was the closest fit, but it honestly could have been anyone. There were four guards on duty at the time of the robbery, and since it was a Sunday, it clearly had to be an inside job since the building was closed and locked to the public. There was no evidence of breaking and entering. Nothing even reported on the security log that entire day."

Dawkins leaned back and raised his eyebrows, proud of himself for having remembered so many details about Young's story.

"And he still works there?" Selena asked. "How is that even possible?"

"He was suspended during the trial, obviously. But after they found him not guilty, he returned to work. Because of the verdict, the bank had no grounds for terminating his employment—he was an innocent man in the eyes of the law. Everyone thought he would quit, anyway. Who would want to work for a company that falsely accused you of robbing them?"

"But he didn't."

"Exactly. And no one knows why. It's not like security jobs are hard to find. You can get one almost anywhere. Everyone knows he hates upper management. But he comes in, does his job, and goes home without saying a word. We've speculated he does this to keep his job. It's fair to think the company would jump at the slightest of opportunities to fire him, so he makes it impossible by being a virtual robot."

"Were you working there when this all happened?" Selena asked. The server had brought their dinner, but she didn't even notice, too enthralled by the story involving one of their main suspects.

"I wasn't," Dawkins said. He noticed his sizzling steak and wasted no time grabbing his utensils to dig in. "I started maybe a month after Peter's trial had ended, but it was still such a hot story around the security office that I heard all about it."

"Why do you think he stayed?" What Selena really wanted to ask was if Dawkins thought Young was planning some sort of revenge. Whether that was by robbing the bank or murdering everyone who falsely accused him. But that seemed too specific of a question, and she didn't want to seem *too* interested in this story.

"Hard to say, but I think it's because of the location. He lives walking distance from here, and I know he has some medical conditions where he shouldn't drive long distances. Even though he drives all the way out to Flagler to visit his mom."

Selena was taking mental notes and filed this tidbit away to revisit later. "Okay, so this is all really interesting, but if he's such a closed-off person, why did he come out with you guys?"

After washing a bite of steak down with a swig of beer, Dawkins asked, "Why are you so curious about Peter Young? Shouldn't we be talking about you and me?"

Dawkins raised a fair point, and Selena had to remind herself that she was on a date with this handsome source of information. She cracked a soft grin, hoping it appeared seductive. "I'm sorry, but this is something

I've always done. It's part of my desire to act, I guess. I've always tried to get inside the mind of interesting people. *Different* people. What makes them tick, you know? There will be plenty of time for us, but I want to hear how this all ends."

Dawkins let out a chuckle. "Well, if you insist. I mean the story itself is over, but sure, let's keep talking about Peter Young. It's romantic."

Selena laughed and nodded for him to continue.

"Okay, so the only reason Peter came out with us is because his friend showed up. Jake Kennedy. He used to work on the security team—also before I had started. I don't know much about Jake besides that. I've only met him a couple of times, but he seems like a nice enough guy. Rumor has it that he helped Young rob that ATM, but Jake wasn't even working there at that point—he had retired. So unless he came to work with Peter that morning, that story makes no sense. Someone would have definitely mentioned a non-employee being in the building at the time of a robbery."

"Hmm, that is strange, but I guess everyone has friends, right? Even someone like Young."

"I suppose they do."

"It's crazy to think a guard on the inside robbed the ATM. Or do things like that happen more often than I realize?"

Dawkins looked around before leaning forward over his plate, speaking in a hushed tone. "We talk about it all the time. How easy it would be to rob a bank, especially ours. Wouldn't take a genius to figure it out." He leaned back and spoke in a normal tone again. "We're not exactly known for having the best security detail at our bank. Quite the opposite, in fact. We have access to the vault, know the coverage from the cameras, the schedules of when the vault will be open. We don't have guns, so I'm not sure how they honestly expect us to stop anyone if they were to come in with a gun. I mean, if Peter robbed that ATM, he got away with it! In the middle of a Sunday afternoon. No clear footage, no fingerprints. Nothing. A quick five-minute job that had no chance of being traced to anyone. It's a joke."

Selena took a bite and chewed on it excessively. She had learned this trick from Felix, who never hesitated shoving food in into his mouth to buy himself a few more seconds to think and process information before replying.

"Well, I'm sorry to hear you can't do your job well," she said. "Sounds like if they asked us to clean the floors and leave us with no mops."

Dawkins laughed. "That would be quite the task."

"Do they not think your bank has a high risk of being robbed? I just don't understand why they would disarm security guards who protect a vault full of cash."

"I wish I knew their logic behind that decision. They must suppose the vault is safe since it's two levels below the actual bank. Even if a robber were to hold up the tellers, it's pretty much impossible for them to get down to the vault. And if they did, they wouldn't have enough time to take the money and escape before the police arrive. And this is all assuming the vault is even open. So, no, I don't particularly consider our bank at a high risk to get robbed."

This confirmed essentially everyone's belief that it had to be an inside job. But who was the insider? Kennedy didn't work there. Young did. The two seemed to still have a tight bond, and both had a motive: revenge for Young, and clearing a mountain of debt for Kennedy.

They had spent their time trying to pin the robbery on one of the two, when it was clearly becoming obvious that they were working together.

Selena had heard enough, satisfied with the evening's findings. "That's all fascinating to me. I just hope you never get robbed."

Chapter 27

When Arielle and Felix arrived at the Last Drop, they spotted Selena and Dawkins sitting in a window booth and had to stop to turn around, instead crossing the street to watch them from a distance.

Arielle figured Selena was fine, but they wanted to keep a close eye, just in case. She assumed Selena was trying to prod information from Dawkins, and didn't want the past to unleash its fury.

That it had thrown no obstacles their way yet made Arielle uneasy. Even with all the facts and evidence they had accumulated, something still felt off. With only two full days before the robbery, they had officially entered the home stretch.

"Doesn't this seem like a waste of time?" Felix asked after they sat on a sidewalk bench just out of sight from the café . "We have a notebook we can examine together that has everything but a confession in it."

"We'll head back soon. Who knows how long Selena will be? This guy doesn't seem to pose a threat. I'm sure Selena is playing him like a fiddle."

"How do you trust your instincts so easily? You've taken, what, two looks at that guy and can already tell he's harmless?"

"Instincts develop the more you do something. Do you know how many people I've had to watch from a distance? For *weeks* on end. Trying to analyze and figure out their next moves. Besides, we have research on everyone involved. This Dawkins guy comes from a loving family, private education, and the worst thing on his record is a speeding ticket for driving ten miles over the limit. I know that doesn't mean anything definitive, but it's not exactly a recipe for concern, either."

"I guess that makes sense."

"Let's head back. I don't think there's anything here for us."

Arielle stood up, then Felix, who turned around to look at the bank building behind him. "Don't you want to go in there?"

Arielle grinned. "Of course, but it's too risky now. Selena gets to have all the fun inside."

"We should at least plan what we're trying to do on Sunday morning, no?"

Arielle crossed her arms and turned around to face the bank. "We can make a tentative plan, I suppose. Follow me."

Arielle led them toward the intersection of Seventeenth Avenue and Lincoln Street, breaking right to walk along the west side of the Cash Register Building on Lincoln.

A bridge connected the skyscraper to a small parking garage across the street. They passed under it and walked the rest of the block until reaching another parking garage for employees of the building. Next to that was an entrance for freight deliveries and armored vehicles that delivered cash to the bank.

The security gates had been lowered to block entry after hours, but Arielle reached out and grasped the gate, peering through the slots for a look inside the garage. "It's kind of dark, but you can barely see the silver of the elevator doors along the back wall."

Felix stepped next to Arielle and squinted as he looked. "I see it."

"So, all we know is the robber entered the building through that elevator. He called security posing as the vice president of the bank, asking to be let in."

"Wait, these gates were open on a Sunday?"

Arielle nodded. "Cash delivery day for the bank. That's why the vault was open and there were employees working. So the robber would have strolled in through the open gate, pretended to be the VP, and everything spiraled from there."

Felix looked around and pointed to a security camera mounted high on the column next to them. "No footage of the robber walking in that morning?"

Arielle shook her head. "Tapes were swiped from the security room, remember? All the tapes that would have shown the robber's path throughout the attack. A clear inside job—it was done with too much attention to the little details." Arielle stepped back and looked around, brushing her chin with a finger. "What we still don't know is which way the robber escaped. We can assume he left the same way he came in, but if he had someone else driving a getaway car, it could have been any of the exits, even on the other side of the building."

"I've studied the layout and I don't think that makes sense. He would have covered a ton of ground to run to the other side of the building, and I'm thinking he wanted to get out as fast as possible. I think he took the stairs. There were no logs of a keycard being used during the robber's departure, and those are the only doors that don't require one since they can't open from the outside."

"Excellent point." Arielle stepped even further back, wanting to absorb the building and its surroundings. "I've had similar suspicions, but that makes sense, especially if you've examined the security and layout."

Felix stepped back to join her, looking up toward the top of the skyscraper, which was out of sight. "I don't have any proof of this, but it's my best educated guess. There might be another possibility we're not even aware of. Selena might know better, having been in there."

Footsteps approached from their right, and Arielle saw Felix's eyes bulge. She looked over to see Selena and Dawkins within twenty feet of them, continuing to stroll closer.

Selena had been laughing and abruptly stopped when she realized who was standing on the sidewalk in front of her. She locked eyes with Arielle first, pursing her lips and narrowing her eyes. Arielle interpreted it as *Don't say a word, everything is fine.*

Arielle grabbed Felix by the shoulder and pulled him away to walk back toward the café .

"What are you doing?" he muttered under his breath, looking over his shoulder to see Selena and Dawkins disappear into the parking garage.

"Relax. She's fine. I think he's giving her a ride home."

Arielle sped up, nearly in a power-walk, and Felix had to jog to keep up. "So, we're just going home?" he asked.

"Yes, it might be a stretch, but let's try to beat them there."

Arielle debated seeking a cab, but figured it would take too long to track one down. It was roughly a fifteen-minute walk back to the apartment complex from the café, and she figured they could make it in ten minutes if they jogged.

She didn't ask Felix, knowing an argument would ensue, so she started running.

"Wait!" he shouted, and she only looked over her shoulder with a wide grin.

"Keep up!"

Felix tossed his hands in the air before gathering the courage to jog as well. Arielle knew he'd be fine. Felix kept in good enough shape to handle a simple run through downtown on a warm night.

After two blocks, they didn't have to deal with any traffic lights and pedestrian crossings. Each block had stop signs instead, which they promptly ran straight through. She knew driving from the bank to their apartment would take less than five minutes, but she was counting on added time for Selena and Dawkins to find his car and drive out of the garage. If they were lucky, he might have even needed to run inside the building to grab something before leaving. In that case, they would definitely beat them back.

That wasn't the case, however, as they found Dawkins and Selena already parked in front of the complex when they rounded the corner. Felix gasped for air, placing both hands behind his head as he stared at the sky.

Arielle had seen Selena's silhouette through the car window and ducked behind another car two spaces back. Felix crouched next to her. "What are we doing?"

"They're right there," she whispered, cocking her head in their direction. Arielle stood taller, but not completely straight. They had the advantage of the rapidly growing darkness with each passing minute. The sun would be completely gone within the next half hour. She saw their heads bobbing in conversation for the next three minutes before Selena finally stepped out of the car and closed the door behind her, waving to Dawkins, who turned his car around and drove away.

"Selena!" Arielle shouted, stepping back onto the sidewalk.

Selena spun around, startled. Once she saw Arielle and Felix approaching, she grinned while shaking her head.

"What the hell? Were you guys following me all night?" Selena asked, tossing her hands in the air.

"Actually, no," Arielle said. "We were worried when you didn't come home, but figured you might have gone out with Dawkins. Thanks for telling us about the change in plans."

"Sorry. It just sort of happened. I had every intent on making the phone call tonight, but trust me, this turned out even better than I imagined. I learned so much tonight, my head is spinning."

"Well?" Felix asked.

Selena frowned and looked around. "Well, nothing. We're not talking about it out here. Let's go inside."

She didn't wait for the other two and pivoted around to walk back inside the complex. Arielle and Felix followed her all the way up to their apartment, no one speaking a word as they clung to the thick anticipation.

Once they stepped in and closed the door, Selena let the words fly like air out of a popped balloon. "I think Young and Kennedy are in cahoots. Dawkins said all the guards joke about how easy it would be to rob the place. Young stood trial for robbing an ATM *in the same bank!* There wasn't enough proof to find him guilty, but Dawkins said he changed after that trial. Speaks to no one, and only went out that other night because Kennedy was there. I'm convinced it's both of them."

"That lines up with what I found in his notebook," Felix said, hurrying to the table where he had left it, and holding it up for Selena like a prized possession.

"I'm not quite there yet," Arielle said. "I can see the obvious connections, but let's remember Young testified at Kennedy's trial. Young wasn't working when the robbery happened. He had no alibi, but his keycard never registered on Sunday morning, either. If he truly has a role in all of this, then he either did the robbery—which eliminates Kennedy from the picture, because Kennedy had no way of working things from the inside—or all of his work is happening right now."

"Not entirely true," Felix said. "Kennedy could still be the brains behind all of this. He could make the exact plans for Young to follow without having to get his hands dirty. In fact, that could explain why he eventually gets off—because there was no physical evidence tying Kennedy to the crime."

"This is tricky, and I don't know that we'll get our answers before Sunday morning. All we can do at this point is keep this knowledge in the back of our minds while we work through these next couple of days. Buckle up—it's going to be a bumpy ride to Sunday."

Chapter 28

On Friday morning, Selena left for work an hour earlier than scheduled. Over the past week she had scouted potential areas where she could hide Saturday night.

With fifty floors in the skyscraper, she had plenty of options, but wanted to position herself to minimize potential roadblocks that might spring up on Sunday morning. She had discovered multiple vacant office spaces throughout the building, simply by learning which floors were skipped on her cleaning route.

The only problem she faced was the distance from these floors to the basement level where the robbery would occur. She couldn't risk being spotted on security footage on the morning of the robbery, running through the halls at hours when no cleaning crew was present. Especially if they had to stay beyond Sunday to solve this crime. Selena's idea of a good time was the end-of-mission margaritas waiting back in 2022. Not running from the authorities because they spotted her on camera hours before the bank was held up.

"What if I stay in the basement?" she asked the empty locker room. She had initially dismissed this idea as lunacy. While she wanted to be close for the moment of the robbery, she didn't want to risk the chance of being seen by any of the guards roaming the basement and subbasement levels. That was a recipe for the past to unleash the wrath of hell to protect the robbery.

The locker room wouldn't suffice, however. Aside from the lockers—which she could squeeze into if absolutely forced—there was a shower in one corner, and nothing else beside the benches in between.

The restrooms were further down the hall, and while she could guarantee privacy over Saturday night—none of the guards were women—she couldn't quite wrap her mind around the idea of sitting in a stall for fifteen hours.

Selena had changed into her uniform for the workday, and still had fifty minutes to spare before the start of her shift, so she stepped out into the hallway and strolled down to the storage room.

She inserted her key and pushed the door open. *No keycard needed for this door,* she thought, already giving the room an advantage. No keycard meant no trail of her movement throughout the building. The door closed behind her and she bolted it locked.

Selena flicked on the light switch to reveal a space that would certainly work. The room was approximately fifteen by fifteen feet. Filing cabinets lined the back wall, covered in dust. Boxes lay scattered across the floor, but could easily be moved to create a makeshift hiding spot. Old signage that once belonged to the businesses in the building leaned stacked against the wall to Selena's right, not taking up too much space.

Upon first examination, the room was crowded, but with time to spare, she could set it up in a reasonable manner to hang out for several hours on Saturday night.

The only problem was the concrete floor.

It was cold, and a draft seeped from somewhere she couldn't locate. It wouldn't be the most comfortable place to hang out for an extended time, but it beat sitting in a bathroom stall.

"This will have to do," Selena said to the empty room, already imagining how she wanted to arrange everything for her stay.

She planned to arrive at the building on Saturday around five o'clock in the evening. From there, she'd head to the locker room to change into her work uniform, to at least give the appearance she was there for her job. The cleaning crew didn't work Saturdays regularly, but sometimes were asked to come in. This hadn't happened in her brief time with the company, but it gave her an excuse if she needed to make up a lie on the

spot.

Once dressed, she'd go straight into the storage room where she'd remain behind the locked door until Sunday morning. She could only hope whoever was working security at the time wouldn't pay attention, and leave her in peace.

Selena had a lot of factors to juggle without worrying about how the past might respond to her presence. She had to plan her meals for all of Saturday, timing them so she could use the restroom before leaving for the office. She wouldn't be able to step out of the storage room to use the building's facilities.

A big breakfast on Saturday morning would have to hold her over for twenty-four hours until she could slip out of the office on Sunday morning. Her stomach churned just thinking of the starvation she'd face by Saturday night, alone in a dusty room with nothing to eat.

"I can handle a one-day fast. People do it all the time." She spoke the words into existence, hoping to fuel her confidence in the matter.

She'd bring a backpack filled with a small pillow and sheets. There was no reason for her to stay awake the entire time, and she could even sleep overnight if she wanted. That would help pass the time—and hopefully some of the hunger pangs.

Selena studied the room once more, trying to figure out the best place to sleep, when a knock boomed from the door. Her muscles tensed as adrenaline kicked in. She had seen no one since arriving this morning.

The room fell silent, and she glared at the door. A second knock came. Louder and heavier, dust puffing from the hinges.

Just open it. It's Friday morning. You're working today. It's not like you're doing anything wrong.

Selena shuffled toward the door, confidence building with each step. A knock boomed one more time as she reached for the handle and pulled open the door.

"Dawkins?"

Her date from last night stood in the hallway, grinning from ear to ear with a cup of coffee in each hand.

"I really wish you'd start calling me Brian," he said. "This whole Dawkins thing makes it feel like you're one of the guys."

Dawkins extended one coffee to Selena, who quickly grabbed it and took a sip.

"What are you doing? Why were you knocking on the door like the police? I thought you didn't have work today."

He threw his head back to laugh. "Happy to see you too, Selena. I was supposed to be off today, but was asked to come in. There was a message waiting on my machine after I got home last night. Someone called out, and apparently that's my problem. So here I am, working overtime."

Dawkins drank his coffee and moved back to allow Selena to step out of the storage room. "And I could ask you the same question. What are you doing in this room?" He peered over her shoulder.

Selena stepped out and closed the door behind her. "Was looking for some extra bottles of glass cleaner. Olivia asked me to grab them yesterday, and I forgot. Thought I'd sneak in early to get them."

Dawkins looked Selena up and down. "Well, where are they?"

Selena shrugged. "She told me they were in this storage closet, but I couldn't find them. She must have meant another one. I'll have to look around."

"That makes sense why you were in there so long."

"I'm sorry, were you watching me?"

Dawkins smiled. "Well, I saw you and watched you go in there. Got a little worried—wasn't sure why you'd be in there so long. And what if I was watching you? Can you blame me? I sort of like you."

Selena didn't need to act. Her cheeks really flushed. "Well," she said, grinning. "You shouldn't abuse your power to stalk me. I'm just here for work."

"Of course. My apologies, Ms. Nicole. I won't let it happen again."

Tension filled the airwaves between them, and part of Selena wanted to pull Dawkins into that storage room and rip his shirt off. She couldn't deny he possessed a certain charm, and wondered how a long-distance relationship might work through time.

Selena shook her head, still unable to wipe the smile off her face. She knew this was probably just the past playing tricks with her—likely, in fact. Fortunately, she knew better and took another drink of coffee. If Dawkins still treated her this way once the mission was over, then she'd reconsider. For now, she had to take everything that happened over the next three days with a grain of salt.

"I want to see you again," Dawkins said, his smile fading to a more serious expression. "I really like spending time with you."

Time, Selena thought. *The one thing in my life that has no real way of being measured.*

"I had a great night, too. I'm pretty busy this weekend, though. Might not be free until next weekend."

"You didn't like the weeknight date after work? We can even go further from this place. Maybe catch a movie or something. That new Robin Hood movie with Kevin Costner comes out this weekend—looks pretty kick-ass."

"That could be fun. I'll have to let you know. What do you have going on this weekend?"

"Well, I've already been told I might have to work tomorrow morning for a few hours, so we'll see. If not, I'll probably head up to the mountains and hike. Sunday I'll probably go golfing. It's Father's Day, you know. My dad and I used to golf together, but he lives in California and wasn't able to make it out here. And I certainly can't fly there on this minimum wage job. So I'll call him in the morning and head out to the course to commemorate the day."

"That's really sweet of you." Everything Dawkins said made Selena like him a little more. "We should probably get back to work—I still have to find this glass cleaner before Olivia gets here."

Dawkins tugged his sleeve to check his watch. "I guess we should. Don't be a stranger if you're down here in the basement again. I'll be here until four."

They stood in silence, and Selena sensed his urge to hug her, possibly even kiss her. She wanted to give in, but gave a quick nod before taking another sip.

Dawkins offered an awkward grin before turning down the hall toward the security office. "I'll see you later."

"Have a good day."

Selena finished her coffee before returning to the locker room to kill a few minutes before her shift officially started. If everything played out smoothly this weekend, she planned to ask Dawkins out on that date for next weekend. She could figure out the logistics later.

Chapter 29

Across town, Arielle sat in her car, witnessing a typical Friday morning for Jacob Kennedy. He had breakfast with his wife and saw her out the door by 7:45. As usual, Kennedy spent the next half hour getting dressed and ready for the day.

Today, however, he didn't retreat to his model boats. He grabbed his keys and bolted out of the front door. He peeked into the bed of his truck and vanished to his backyard for a couple of minutes before returning with a three-foot gardening shovel, tossing it into the back, and getting behind the wheel.

Arielle snapped her hand to the ignition and turned on her car, not expecting to be leaving so soon. She felt a distant flutter in her stomach, as part of her believed Kennedy was about to do something directly related to the robbery.

She followed him out of the neighborhood as he made his way toward westbound Sixth Avenue, a state highway that ran from Denver to the mountains west of Golden. In her few trips following Kennedy, he had yet to get on the highway.

They drove for fifteen minutes while Arielle remained five car-lengths behind, entering the foothills of the Rocky Mountains. Arielle studied what she could of Kennedy from such a distance. He maintained a speed five miles over the limit, not once looking around as he sped down the highway that eventually merged into I-70.

He knew exactly where he was going.

Engulfed with dark green trees to the left, and an elevated view over a valley to the right, Kennedy took Exit 253, the sign identifying it as Moss Rock Road. No vehicles were between Arielle and Kennedy when they got on the ramp, so she had to lower her speed to keep a safe distance.

Kennedy reached a stop sign and took a right onto Stapleton Road, a hairpin curve that headed back west on a dirt road. Because of the change in direction, Kennedy and Arielle momentarily faced each other from opposite sides of a median. He had apparently slipped on a ballcap, keeping it cocked low to cover his eyes. She could only see his thick mustache protruding from beneath it.

She followed him for another half-mile as the road wound deeper into the foothills, before he pulled off to a parking lot with a sign welcoming them to Beaver Brook Trailhead.

"He's going on a hike?" Arielle asked herself, trying to remember what type of shoes she had seen Kennedy wearing when he stepped out. She was fairly sure they were the usual mud-caked tennis shoes he had worn most of the time, but now had her doubts.

The parking lot was a single row of thirty spaces. There were already twelve other cars parked from the early risers looking to beat the heat for their morning hikes.

Kennedy parked in the very first spot, directly in front of a shed-like structure that housed the restrooms. Arielle saw the lot had two entrances, and drove around to the other side, parking in a middle spot where she could see the tail end of Kennedy's truck sticking out.

She killed her engine and rolled down her driver's side window, the fresh air coating her lungs and hitting her with nostalgia that brought her back to the many times her family would spend weekends camping in the mountains.

She could smell the succulent scent of meat sizzling on the grill while her dad tended to it, tongs in one hand, a beer in the other. Her mom would be inside their camper, preparing side dishes while she danced and hummed along to Vicente Fernández pouring out of their old stereo. Arielle and her brother would spend this time chasing butterflies or skipping rocks across the lake.

Tears welled in Arielle's eyes, the memories growing to a near unbearable level.

The slam of a door snapped Arielle out of her trance, bringing her back to the present—well, 1991 present—and she spun around to see Kennedy trudging from the parking lot toward the thick clump of trees in the opposite direction of the hiking trail.

"Where the hell are you going?" she whispered, opening her car door and staying crouched low. She looked around and saw no one else in the immediate vicinity.

Kennedy had reached Stapleton Road, the shovel clutched in his grip as he looked both ways before crossing.

Arielle ran toward where his truck was parked and had a clear view of Kennedy as he jogged into the thick evergreens. The trees essentially served as a wall, blocking out all views from anyone driving by or hiking the trail.

Kennedy was out of sight in a matter of seconds, and Arielle broke into a sprint to cross Stapleton Road, looking back over her shoulder once more to make sure no one was watching her.

Hundreds of evergreens towered over her, creating a maze-like sensation to search for Kennedy. She tried using her ears, but a gentle breeze mixed with chirping birds made it impossible to hear anything else.

Arielle zigged and zagged through the woods, careful to not step on any sticks that might snap and draw attention. She moved from one tree to the next, making her way deeper into the mountain, praying she'd be able to find her way out.

Fortunately, the space started clearing after fifty yards, and that's when she spotted Kennedy in an open clearing, strolling toward a lone evergreen, not another of its tree brethren within a hundred feet.

"Oh my God," Arielle said, placing her fingers to her lips as she watched Kennedy. "This is where he hides the money."

She couldn't move. She didn't *want* to move. This was history in the making.

Kennedy circled the tree twice, patting the earth with his shovel before deciding on a spot where he began digging. Arielle stayed within the trees, watching like a distant eagle.

The accused robber had found the perfect hiding spot out of sight from society. It was his own private corner of the world. The amount of people who pushed their way through the patch of woods to come out on this other side were certainly less than a handful. People driving by probably assumed the evergreens stretched for miles along the mountainside. Why would they ever stop and venture into it? And the hikers who climbed the trail across the road? Why would they wander into the woods when they had the safety of a footpath, a restroom, and even a couple of picnic tables at their disposal?

Arielle wondered how Kennedy stumbled across this site, and how many times he had been up here already. This was his first visit since she had arrived in 1991, and this meant the robbery had definitely been planned for an extended time.

She sat down between two trees, their sprawling pines concealing her from Kennedy should he look back. He dug for a half hour before stopping, tossing the shovel to the ground, and throwing his hands behind his head while he gasped for air. Kennedy didn't exercise, from what Arielle had witnessed, and this task was surely putting a strain on his body. Five minutes passed while he caught his breath, then he picked up the shovel and dug for another thirty minutes.

A mound of dirt stood about two feet high, and Arielle assumed the hole Kennedy had dug was around three feet deep. He huffed and puffed as he circled his finished product, examining the hole from every angle.

Kennedy never once looked over his shoulder. He had complete confidence in the privacy of this location. If someone wandered back in this direction, he was already a quarter of the way to having a full grave dug and had a weapon in hand.

This intrigued Arielle, slipping a dark thought into her mind.

She could make Kennedy disappear right now. She had her throwing knives in the car, and could get close enough to use them before Kennedy realized what was happening. Even with her bare hands, she was confident she could take him down despite his shovel. And in the middle of nowhere, with no people in sight, how could the past push back and cause resistance?

The mission could end today, and they wouldn't even have to worry about burying his body. They had a crew that would come clean up the mess and make it look like no one had ever set foot on the other side of the woods.

She watched him, mentally calculating how long it would take her to run up from behind him and end his life.

"But I can't," she told herself.

And she wouldn't.

Even with the obvious evidence standing right in front of her, none of this confirmed Kennedy was the actual robber. It still could have been Young who carried out the murders, and maybe Kennedy had dug this hole to play his role in the cause.

At this moment, Arielle was ninety-eight percent sure Kennedy was the one responsible, just as the FBI had been when it originally happened. But ninety-eight was not one hundred, and that lingering two percent was filled with possibilities they could only hope to eliminate by Sunday morning.

At the very least, they could plan to have someone monitor this location on Sunday. She presumed the robber would head straight here to hide the money and get it off the grid, with plans to dig it out later.

Once Kennedy had recovered his breath, and spent a couple minutes massaging his legs, he clutched the shovel and started back toward the trees. Arielle debated running to the hole to see exactly how deep it was, even potentially filling it back in to throw a wrench into the plans.

As tempting as it was, she opted to follow Kennedy. He moved with too much purpose to ignore, and she wondered if he might head somewhere else in relation to the robbery.

Kennedy bolted into the woods, and Arielle made her way to trail his path, sure to keep a safe distance. Once they broke free on the other side of the evergreens, Arielle went right to cross the street, not wanting to be directly behind Kennedy while he tossed the shovel into the bed of his truck. She crouched as she crossed Stapleton Road, lurking behind the parked cars as she spied on Kennedy.

He wasted no time getting behind the wheel and backing his truck out of the parking spot. Arielle had to dash to her car to keep up, panic settling in as she thought he might get away.

Fortunately, Kennedy had to stop at the exit to wait for a car to pass before turning onto the road. This bought Arielle just enough time to gain ground.

Kennedy sped away. Arielle's engine roared as she tried to keep up, not putting too much pressure on herself, as Kennedy would have two stop signs before getting back onto the highway.

When he reached the first, he stopped for an excessive amount of time. No other vehicles were present to prevent him from driving forward, yet he remained.

Arielle started slowing down well before reaching him, but couldn't come to a complete stop at such a far distance. That would look suspicious if Kennedy was paying attention to what was happening behind him.

Once she was within three car lengths of his truck, he turned left without using a turn signal—the first time she had witnessed him violate a traffic law—and sped toward the next stop sign only one hundred feet away.

He again waited at the stop sign, and Arielle's entire body tensed when she pulled up behind his truck waiting to turn onto the highway.

Kennedy wasn't looking around for other cars. His eyes were glued to his rearview mirror, locked into a stare-down with Arielle.

This standoff felt like an eternity for Arielle, her heart drumming up to her throat. But it was only five seconds before Kennedy looked away, turned left, and floored his accelerator as he got on the highway.

Arielle remained frozen in her car, fingers squeezing the steering wheel as her knuckles turned white. Kennedy was gone, out of sight, but his presence lingered.

A horn honked from behind, making Arielle gasp as she snapped back into reality. A car had pulled up behind her. They drove around, flipping Arielle the bird as they passed and skidded onto the on-ramp.

"Did that really just happen?" Arielle asked her empty car. She hardly noticed the rude driver, still trying to process her encounter with Jacob Kennedy.

She drove ahead, not turning onto the highway, instead pulling to the side of the parallel frontage road that had hardly any traffic. Thoughts tumbled throughout her mind, and she felt helpless trying to grasp one to focus on.

Was he really looking at me? Was it just a coincidence that he looked up and we locked eyes? Did he recognize me? Do I need to stop following him? What will happen if he sees me again?

Arielle fought to slow down her mind, making a checklist of all the points she had just mulled over.

"He *was* looking at me. That wasn't a mistake."

Arielle's mouth grew incredibly dry, and she rummaged through her backpack for an emergency water bottle she kept stashed. She unscrewed the cap and nearly chugged the entire bottle.

"He *knew* I was following him. That's the only explanation for why he stopped and waited *twice.* He wanted to look me in the eye to tell me he knew I was there. I wonder if he saw me hiding in the woods."

The possibility made her queasy. If that was the case, Kennedy might already have plans for a backup location to hide the money.

She shook her head, disgusted with herself for somehow getting caught. She didn't even understand how it had happened. Five cars were between them during the entire drive over on the highway.

Could he have noticed the same car parked across the street every day? It was never even directly in front of his house, and he never looked out the window.

"Fuck!" Arielle shouted, balling up a fist and punching the steering wheel. The car's horn let out a subtle squeak. "Friday morning and this mission is *fucked.*"

She put her car back into drive and turned around to get on the highway, fuming.

One thing's for sure, she thought. *I can't go anywhere near Jacob Kennedy for the rest of this mission.*

Chapter 30

Felix spent his Friday morning reading through the rest of Peter Young's disturbing diary. The man was a lunatic—there was no way around that fact. He had a dark obsession with revenge, not just on the bank that had wronged him, but toward everyone who had ever maltreated him throughout his life.

He even mentioned elementary school bullies he hoped would "have maggots crawling over their skeletons as they rotted in the soil."

Mentally, Felix had gone through such a dark tunnel from reading these sinister rantings that he needed a break after a couple hours. So he went outside for a walk around the neighborhood before the heat became too unbearable. It was only eleven o'clock when he stepped outside and saw Arielle shuffling down the sidewalk with her head hung low.

Felix paused for a moment, at first not sure that it was actually Arielle, then once realizing it was, debating if he should approach her. For all he knew, she was working the mission and wouldn't welcome his interruption. She also never returned to the apartment during the day.

Judging by her slouched shoulders and lethargic pace, he figured something had gone wrong.

"Arielle?" he called out, startling her into a more upright position. She frowned as puzzlement mixed with her apparent anguish.

"Felix? What are you doing out here?"

"Well, I spend my days here. What are *you* doing here?" Once they met in front of the apartment building's entrance, Felix saw Arielle's eyes were red and puffy. "What's wrong?!"

Traffic passed on the road while a group of middle schoolers started skipping down the sidewalk. Arielle looked over her shoulder to them before returning a depressing gaze to Felix.

"I messed up," she said, an octave above a whisper. She bobbed her head up and down in a subtle nod. "We're screwed."

"We're not," Felix said. "I just came out to walk around the block. Join me."

He turned around to face the same direction as Arielle and started walking. After a couple of steps, she finally joined him. He allowed the tension to linger, waiting for Arielle to speak first. Once they reached the corner of the block, she did.

"Kennedy saw me," she said. "I've played it over a hundred times already, and he definitely looked right at me. He knew I was following him, so he stared me down so that I'd stop. And it worked. Here I am."

Arielle tossed her hands in the air before sharing with Felix the full story of what had just happened in the foothills.

"I can follow him," Felix said.

"No. That's not the point. None of us can follow him anymore. This all proves he's been suspicious. We shouldn't even drive down his block anymore. Tomorrow might be the most crucial day in figuring out how this all plays out, and now we have to sit here and hope we catch something on Young. Speaking of, he's off work today, right? Has he done anything?"

"Not yet. He didn't get out of bed until 9:30. Took a shower and made some bacon and eggs. Ate in front of the TV as he always does. Had no vibes of someone preparing to rob a bank in two days."

Arielle shook her head. "It doesn't make sense. Young's involved. I have a hard time believing otherwise. Do we know if he works tomorrow?"

"We don't know."

Arielle rubbed her temples as they continued their lap around the neighborhood block. "I just can't believe we're in this situation. Kennedy can be doing *anything* related to the robbery today, and we have no way of finding out."

"Swap cars with me," Felix said.

"Kennedy's still going to be paranoid. Especially now. I'm worried he'll recognize my face. What if he tells Young about me following him? What if he knows more about us than we want to believe is possible. He could know we're living in the same building as Young."

"Remember, he's in his Original Time. Why would he have any reason to suspect someone is following him for a crime that hasn't happened yet? That's just not how any of it works. And he knows that, being a retired cop and all. Honestly, Arielle, *you* sound a little paranoid."

Felix watched as Arielle chewed on this thought.

"I'm not going to say it's impossible that it was all a coincidence. But I also trust my gut. He was looking *at* me. Intentionally. Was it because he recognized me, or was he just having some fun with the car driving behind him? Both seem like logical explanations, but also illogical. I don't know."

"I'm telling you—go back. Take my car. Hide further down the block. Ten houses down if you need to. And if he leaves and you need to tail him again, stay even further back. You might lose him because of it, but at least you're trying. Because sitting here with me all day will guarantee you find nothing of use."

"I'm afraid, Felix. Just . . . don't tell anyone I said that."

"Afraid of failing this mission? Since when? This mission is a joke. We could have just as easily showed up on the day of and chased whoever comes running out of the bank with the bag of money. All we need to know is who did it—we don't need to stop it. Did you forget that?"

"Of course not. I've done this long enough to know it wouldn't be that simple. I don't know if this incident with Kennedy is part of the past pushing back—I think it is, but we can't truly know for sure. Sunday morning won't be easy. I suggest you come to terms with that now."

"It's all about spacing. You need to have more faith in our team. I've been studying the map of the bank, the layout of the street blocks, and all possible escape routes. There are three of us to cover the perimeter—"

"Plan for just you and I. Selena will be inside, and we can't guarantee she'll be able to get out before the robbery happens."

"Fine. Two of us is still enough to cover the west side of the building. All common sense points to the robber exiting the same way he entered. Besides, we're going to know early Sunday morning how involved Young is. The first timestamp, according to the old police reports, shows that the robber called the security team from the freight elevator at 9:14 A.M. If Young is still sitting in his underwear by nine o'clock, then we can rule him out."

"I have to go to Kennedy's house that morning, no matter how risky it is. We have to have a visual on him."

"I've already mapped out your morning," Felix said as they rounded the complex's northwest corner and started back toward the main entrance. "It takes eighteen minutes to drive from Kennedy's house to the bank. The latest Kennedy can leave his house is 8:55 to fall into the timeline of events. I'd say you should plan to leave there by 8:50 if it doesn't appear he's leaving. That will give you five minutes to spare."

"I'll need more than five minutes if the past is going to push back."

"I can be down at the bank, so don't worry. If Young isn't showing any signs of movement by nine o'clock, I'm zooming over there."

Arielle shook her head, and Felix was relieved to see her mental dials cranking once again. "We're close enough to ditch the car. Walk—that's gonna be your best bet. I'll be there with the car to chase down whoever drives off."

"Walk? That doesn't seem like the right call at all. You know I'm one of the top drivers in the Road Runners, right?"

"That's not the point. Just trust me, okay?" Arielle paused and looked up at the sky for wisdom. "I'll be there. You can hop into my car and we'll be ready for anything."

Felix nodded. They reached the entrance. "Okay, that's reasonable."

"Thank you. Let's go inside and figure out the rest of the day."

Chapter 31

After much debate, Arielle agreed to let Felix go to Kennedy's house on Friday evening. He vowed to park at the far end of the block, opposite the house, and watch from a distance with a pair of binoculars.

Felix stopped at a McDonald's on his way to grab a couple of burgers for his stakeout. He was surprised to have kept his nerves at bay, but that was mostly thanks to his strong belief that Young was responsible for everything about to unfold. He expected the night at Kennedy's house to pass without excitement.

And that's exactly what happened for the first four hours of excruciating boredom. When Felix had turned onto Juniper Street at 4:15, Kennedy's truck wasn't even parked in the driveway. No one was home, and the temptation to go back in and properly bug the house swelled to an uncomfortable level, but he had strict orders from Arielle to not so much as approach the house.

While her decisions didn't always make sense, he trusted them. Arielle never made an order for the sake of making one. There was guaranteed to be a long, thought-out reason behind it with factors Felix had yet to experience during his time with the Road Runners. Arielle had amassed wisdom from thousands of missions, and had no reason to lead them astray.

Felix had settled into his spot at the far end of the block, an open grassy field to his left as he faced the house. He had killed the engine and sat in silence, eating his burgers while he waited for something to happen.

Some kids had come to the field and tossed a baseball around. Couples went out for evening walks with their dogs on long leashes, holding hands as they strolled down the sidewalk to enjoy the first night of the weekend.

It was absurd to think a potential bank robber and murderer lived among such regular people.

When the sun started setting, the kids who had played baseball earlier ran their equipment home and returned with even more kids, nearly all dressed in black. It wasn't long until a very intense game of hide-and-seek kicked off across the neighborhood.

Kennedy still wasn't home, and not so much as a light was turned on inside or outside the house.

"Where's his wife?" Felix asked aloud.

She could have met him wherever he was once she got off work. Or Kennedy could be out with friends—or accomplices—while his wife went to a happy hour with coworkers that was stretching well past dinnertime.

By 8:30 the sun had set, the hide-and-seek game in full swing with kids scattered all about the neighborhood. None of them paid Felix any attention, assuming they even noticed him. Although, one kid hid behind his rear bumper for a couple of minutes before making a mad dash to the lone tree standing in the center of the grass field.

Headlights appeared at the far end of the block, snapping Felix out of the lull he had fallen into. The lights seemed to glare into his soul before they turned into Kennedy's driveway.

The sounds of the screaming, energetic kids drowned into background noise as Felix pulled out his binoculars. The street lamps cast an orange glow up and down the block, and provided just enough light for the binoculars to pick up Kennedy's moving silhouette as he moved from the truck toward his front door. He had what looked like a plastic grocery bag clutched in his grip.

Two kids were down near his house, and Kennedy waved at them. They appeared to stop and say something in return, but Felix didn't have a clear enough view to be sure.

Kennedy disappeared into his home, and Felix stepped out of the car.

There were at least twenty kids scattered about the block, and it provided him enough cover as he crossed the street and started toward Kennedy's house. The porch light had been turned on, as was the dining room, where he saw Kennedy sitting at the table, head planted in his hands.

"Long day of planning the robbery?" Felix whispered under his breath, taking cautious steps as he stood in front of Kennedy's house. His truck was within range, so he hurried along the sidewalk until planting himself behind the bed of the truck, out of sight from Kennedy in the dining room.

Felix looked around to confirm none of the kids were paying him any attention. He stood on his tiptoes to get a better view and looked into the truck bed, finding a mud-caked shovel, a five-gallon container of water, and a pair of dirty boots.

He reached in, briefly wanting to steal the boots for further examination, when a woman's voice called out from behind.

"Hey! Get the hell out of my truck!"

Felix spun around, stomach already leaping into his throat, and saw Kennedy's wife parked in the middle of the street, window rolled down, jaw hanging open. They locked eyes for a millisecond before Felix pivoted and sprinted away.

"Get back here!"

Felix had already passed four houses when he looked over his shoulder and saw the car creeping down the block to follow him.

"Shit!" he gasped between breaths, lungs burning with each heave of air he took in.

He had no chance of outrunning a car and needed to get crafty. He didn't want to risk Mrs. Kennedy finding out what kind of car he drove, either, so getting back into his vehicle and speeding away wasn't an option.

A Rottweiler rushed the chain-link fence of one house Felix ran past, snarling and barking to cause all the attention in the neighborhood to shift to the man running through the night. Even the kids fell silent and turned their attention to the unfolding scene.

Felix approached the end of the block where the road curved left to exit the neighborhood. He'd have no chance of escaping that way, and couldn't risk hiding in someone's backyard. There were already too many eyes on him.

Mrs. Kennedy was still about five houses down, likely afraid to speed because of all the kids running around, so Felix took the chance to bolt to his right and cross the street, running right by his car as he stepped onto the grassy field.

A handful of kids stood frozen at the tree serving as their "home base" and gawked as the grown man ran in their direction.

"Get out of here, mister!" one kid shouted, a boy who couldn't have been older than ten years old.

Felix sprinted past the tree, paying the kids no attention, a decision he believed was the reason he didn't end up with a mob chasing him. From where he had parked his car earlier, Felix wasn't able to see where the field ended. Now, he saw its outer perimeter still fifty yards ahead, where it backed up to a ditch filled with tall, yellow weeds. On the other side of the ditch was a paved pathway that wove into another neighborhood.

Felix reached the ditch and stopped to turn around. The ground had sloped just enough where he could still see the top of the tree, but none of the kids under it. He tried to listen for their voices, to see if they were following him, but he couldn't hear anything over his heavy pants for breath. He had just sprinted the length of nearly three soccer fields, his legs and lungs happy to punish him for it.

Seeing how tall the weeds were, Felix stepped into the ditch to let them conceal him even more. He crouched, breathing in heavy amounts of pollen and whatever particles were floating in the air, burning his nose and throat.

He crouched lower, knowing he only needed to pass five minutes before he could safely step out. The kids might still be outside playing late into the night—it was a Friday night, after all—but he presumed Mrs. Kennedy wouldn't expel too much effort chasing down someone who hadn't even taken anything from the truck.

Unless she gets Jacob, and he comes searching with his gun.

The thought made Felix dizzy. The four and a half hours of boredom had caused him to get greedy. He hadn't planned on approaching Kennedy's house at all. But once he saw Kennedy arrive home, all that boredom swirling around in his mind made him want to make his wasted time worthwhile. What would it hurt by just walking by the house? The neighborhood was plenty busy and Kennedy wouldn't have noticed.

Felix didn't know how good of a look Mrs. Kennedy had gotten of him. It was dark, sure, but there was enough light to make out a face—he had seen hers just fine, even if for a quick second. He hadn't worn a disguise. Even a pair of sunglasses, or a hat, would have made him difficult to identify.

Something slithered against Felix's ankle, prompting him to look down, his blood instantly freezing in his veins. He had long suffered from a severe case of ophidiophobia, and seeing the garter snake swirl in a circular motion around his ankle instantly made his head spin while a heaviness pressed down on his back.

"My God," he whispered, unable to look away from the snake that was at least twenty inches long. "The only poisonous snakes in Colorado are rattlesnakes. This is a Garter snake. No poison—hardly any venom."

Part of a therapy to overcome his fear of snakes was familiarizing himself with all the snakes he might encounter in his line of work across North America. Garter snakes posed no threats, their venom causing redness around a bite mark, at worst. Knowing this still didn't help, Felix growing more nauseous with each passing second.

His body broke into chills as beads of sweat formed on his forehead. He focused on taking deep breaths and swallowing large pools of saliva to keep his dinner down. The snake refused to leave him alone, satisfied to keep circling his ankle as the world spun.

Felix ran out of spit to swallow, his lips and tongue turning dry as dirt. His balance wavered, and he started flailing his arms. "I'm not gonna make it. Dear God, please don't let me die in this ditch."

The snake opened its mouth and sunk its fangs into Felix's calf in one swift motion. Felix couldn't shriek, his jaw locking into place as his entire body tensed at the sharp pain exploding up his leg.

He felt the warm stream of blood oozing toward his ankle, soaking into his sock. That's when he took three drunken steps backward to get out of the ditch, and fainted on the grass.

Chapter 32

Arielle and Selena were already on their way by 8:15.

Selena had arrived home shortly after six, having taken an hour after her shift to head back to the storage room to move some boxes around. She created a fort that would conceal her presence if someone wandered into the storage room on Saturday, an event she considered unlikely.

They discussed dinner plans for when Felix arrived, but when they hadn't heard from him by 7:30, Arielle grew concerned. They spent the next half hour debating what to do. Selena argued Felix had likely found something of interest and didn't want to leave.

Arielle knew the games the past liked to play. If Felix had found something crucial to the mission, the more reason for the past to resist him from gaining and sharing that knowledge.

Arielle had moved Felix's laptop onto the dining room table, where they watched Young devour an entire pizza by himself, something Selena had deemed "both disgusting and impressive."

At eight o'clock, Selena surrendered her position. Felix wasn't one to stay out past dark, and she acknowledged the possibility that something indeed could have gone wrong.

They took the next fifteen minutes changing into all-black attire, loading their pistols, and slipping into bulletproof vests. Just in case.

Selena told Arielle to stop overreacting, but she refused to cave. You could never be too cautious when dealing with a stubborn past.

"Young's not doing anything," Arielle said before they left the apartment. "The guy is a total bum. I'm thinking it's impossible for him to be involved in any capacity with this robbery. He just sits there all day and night, drinking beer and eating junk food. No wonder he dies from a heart attack next year."

They checked the monitor to find Young passed out in his recliner, jaw hanging open while he held a beer can in one hand and a cigarette spewed tiny streams of smoke from the ashtray on his side table.

"I have to agree," Selena said, nodding to the screen. "Does anyone really believe that man had such a major impact on the world?" She chuckled as they turned away and left the apartment.

They took Arielle's car and sped across town to Golden. Selena outlined her plans for tomorrow during the twenty-minute drive, and Arielle grew impressed with how thoroughly Selena had plotted out her part of the mission.

Not only did the young actress have a solid plan in place for a seamless execution, she had also pinpointed potential vulnerabilities and had backup plans around those. Hearing it all, Arielle wouldn't have planned it any differently.

They reached Juniper Street by 8:40.

Arielle turned onto the block from the west, the opposite end of Kennedy's house.

"Look!" Selena shouted, pointing across Arielle's body. "It's Felix's car."

"Shit," Arielle muttered under her breath, slowing down and swerving across the road to park right behind it. "He's not in it."

Silence filled the car once Arielle killed the engine. Neither of them knew what to do or say, looking around for any signs that might provide a clue.

"Think those kids saw him?" Selena finally asked, nodding toward the group of kids huddled near the lone tree standing in the grass field.

There were only eight kids remaining from the big game of hide-and-seek that had just ended minutes ago when Mrs. Kennedy chased down the man running from her house.

"There's a good chance," Arielle said. "We might need to ask them, but let's get out and look around first. Don't want to seem too suspicious if we don't have to."

Selena reached out and pressed her arm against Arielle to pin her back in her seat. "You're not suggesting we go down to Kennedy's house, are you? Which one is it?"

Arielle nodded in the direction. "That one with the pickup truck in the driveway."

They stared at it, seeing the glow of lights through the house's windows.

"They're home," Selena said. "You don't think Felix went over there and tried to sneak in or something?"

"I highly doubt that, but he may have drifted that direction, and who knows what might have happened. I could see him wanting a closer look. He might be in their backyard hiding. Hopefully that's all it is."

Arielle opened her door, and Selena followed suit. The kids were watching, studying them from a distance.

"I think they saw Felix," Selena said. "Why would they be staring at us like that?"

"Don't think too much into it. We're strangers in their neighborhood—they're probably just being nosy."

It was natural for people to gawk at an unknown person, but they usually returned to their own business after a few seconds. A minute passed, and the kids were still gazing at them.

"What do we do?" Selena whispered as she came around to meet Arielle on the sidewalk.

"Act natural. Let's stay on this side of the street and walk down a few houses. Keep an eye on these kids. If they follow us, then something is definitely going on and we might need to bail."

"We can't just leave Felix."

"That's not what I said. We just might need to leave this neighborhood. We can drive around to the next block and try to sneak our way back. I'd never leave an Angel behind—you should know that by now."

Arielle started forward, taking long, confident steps. She knew plenty well how to act like she belonged. Any sign of doubt, even from a distance, would only further raise suspicions from the attentive kids.

After fifty feet, they reached the edge of the field that gave way to houses and yards for the rest of the block. Once they passed the first house, Arielle stopped and turned around. Selena was only several paces behind and nearly crashed into her.

"Are they following?" Selena asked, refusing to look back at the same time.

Arielle shook her head. "I don't see any of them. Let's keep going—we might be in the clear."

Arielle didn't know what to think. Something in the air felt off, and she had no way of knowing if it was her instincts or the past trying to interfere. After passing two more houses, she continued down the sidewalk with an occasional glance over the shoulder. Still no kids visible. They remained in the field, minding their business.

"I think we're clear," she said to Selena. "Let's stop across from Kennedy's house and see what's going on. Do *not* cross the street and step onto his property."

"Don't worry about me—I have no interest in that."

They arrived after a minute. The living room and dining room lights were both on, but no one was visible through the windows. For the first time that Arielle could recall since observing the house every day, the curtains were drawn shut. Her first thought was that Kennedy was planning the robbery at the dining room table. Why would he have the sudden desire for privacy?

"Arielle, get down!" Selena gasped, pulling Arielle's arm as she crouched behind a car parked along the sidewalk.

A police cruiser had just turned onto the block from the end they had come. It crept at a painfully slow pace, and didn't stop until it parked right in front of Kennedy's house.

"What's going on?" Selena whispered, but Arielle didn't respond. She held her gaze to the police car and watched two officers step out and trudge up the pathway, knocking on the front door. The car's emergency signals remained off and the two officers didn't appear in any hurry.

Arielle assumed their visit wasn't for anything too serious.

Mrs. Kennedy opened the door, dressed in a flowing nightgown. Jacob appeared in the doorway next to her a few seconds later.

Despite the near silence that had fallen over the neighborhood, they were too far to pick up on any of the words being spoken. Mrs. Kennedy did most of the talking, at first pointing to the truck in the driveway, then swinging her arm around to point all the way to the end of the block. Where they had parked. Where the kids were loitering in the field.

"Don't move," Arielle muttered. "Not 'til they're completely gone."

They waited another couple of minutes for the conversation to end. Kennedy shook the hands of both officers, and Arielle presumed he had shared his ex-profession with the two gentlemen standing on his front step.

"Let's see where they go," Arielle said in a hushed tone. "They might give us an idea what happened."

The cops returned to their vehicle and immediately flipped it around, driving back the same way they had come. Arielle saw Mrs. Kennedy watching from the window, holding the curtains apart for a clear view of the far end of the block.

As tempting as it was to drift back that direction for a better look, Arielle and Selena remained grounded in their positions. If Mrs. Kennedy saw two women lurking across the street, there was no saying what might happen. For now, they had the concealment of the dark, out of range from the street lamps.

The officers stopped their car directly next to Arielle's, prompting her heart to race. Would they snoop around the vehicles parked along the street? Did Mrs. Kennedy identify Felix's car as one she hadn't seen before? This could lead to complications, and might even leave them stranded in the neighborhood.

But they never gave a second look toward any of the vehicles. Instead, the two officers whipped out their flashlights and shone them at the kids, sauntering over to them with the continued carelessness of a walk through the park.

The kids huddled around the cops, and the group chatted for three minutes.

The tallest kid in the group kept pointing a lanky finger to the distance behind them. The officers looked in that direction multiple times, shining their flashlights.

"This has to involve Felix, right?" Selena asked.

"It definitely *feels* like it. The good news is I don't think he's hurt. There would probably be more urgency if that was the case. I think he was snooping around the Kennedys' house and got caught. He must have made a run for it, and it seems to be beyond that tree where they're all hanging out."

"How are we supposed to find him? He could be hiding anywhere, or could have run two miles away. I don't see Felix as one to take the risk of hiding in a bush to watch what's happening. He'll put his head down and keep running until he can't."

"I agree. We need these cops to leave, and possibly the kids. Who knows what they might say if they see us."

"We can't sit here. The police will make rounds through this neighborhood all night now."

"I think we're fine. Look." Arielle nodded to the group of kids. The two officers had started back toward their car, some kids following close behind, others branching off in their own direction. "Cops broke up the party. Probably don't want any of the kids outside if they think something's going on. We just got really lucky."

They watched for the next few minutes while everyone dispersed to their homes. The police were the last to leave, but did so without wandering deeper into the field.

The neighborhood fell silent aside from the chirping crickets.

"I think we're clear," Arielle said. "Let's go."

Chapter 33

They shuffled toward the field, opting to walk at a normal pace. Moving too fast or slow, or even staying crouched while they scampered down the sidewalk, would only make them look suspicious.

Fortunately, they only needed to worry about their appearance underneath the street lamps. Otherwise, their black attire helped them blend into the shadows.

Once they reached the field, they felt exposed outside of the coverage of surrounding houses. Surely anyone peeping from their front windows would spot them standing in the field.

"We need to move fast," Arielle stated the obvious.

She broke into a near sprint, Selena following close behind. The field stretched about fifty yards along the nearest home's property before reaching a concrete path. Arielle stopped at the path, well out of sight from the neighborhood.

Both directions led to different neighborhoods, and it was impossible to know which way Felix might have run. She decided left, since that was more toward where the tall kid had pointed.

"You sure about this?" Selena asked. "He could be nowhere near here. He might have even circled the area and arrived back to his car."

"Well, we're parked behind him, so he'll know we're looking for him. He's plenty observant to realize that."

"Maybe. He also gets flustered really easy. I can't imagine how his mind is right now. He might have tunnel vision to his car just to get out of here as fast as he can."

Arielle had already considered this possibility, and it didn't bother her. Felix getting home safely was the only concern. And if he did that while they were out looking for him, then so be it. "You know this is all the past. It has to be."

"I wondered that, but wasn't sure. How do you know?"

"It started this morning when I was following Kennedy into the mountains. I'm pretty sure it's been a domino effect since then. We were so close to finding that concrete evidence tying it all to Kennedy. And the past just won't let us. I was ninety-eight percent sure Kennedy is responsible as of this afternoon. I'm gonna say ninety-nine."

"What's holding back the last one percent?"

"Seeing the proof with my eyes. *Everything* points to Kennedy. Here we are two nights away from the robbery, on Kennedy's block, and we're going the opposite direction from his house. That's no accident."

"You don't think Felix just made a bad decision and got caught too close?"

"Well, sure, but that's not really the point. I've been sitting across from Kennedy's house for two weeks now, and I've yet to have anything like this happen."

They walked in silence for the next thirty seconds before Selena spoke. "I'm terrified for tomorrow. Just thought you should know that."

"Why? You have a really sound plan."

"I'm worried I'm going to get caught. I went into that storage room this morning just to look around, and Dawkins saw me go in from the security camera. He just came right up and started knocking on the door. How can I expect to waltz in there tomorrow evening and act like everything is normal? My crew doesn't work weekends. The guards know that. They'll see me and wonder. And there's nothing stopping them from coming into that storage room to see what I'm up to. It's not like there's a lot of activity in the building to distract them on a Saturday. They'll probably notice every person who walks into the building."

"That's probably true, but we have to take the chance they'll forget all about you once you disappear from the cameras. If you get caught and kicked out of the building—which I don't think they'll do—then you'll come home and we can figure it out from there. Besides, the building is massive. There might be more going on than you realize. And if not, their boredom just might be the reason you're able to slip in undetected. I'm sure some of these guys fall asleep at the wheel on the weekends."

Selena let out a nervous laugh. "I'm not going to count on *that*, but hopefully you're right."

"Look, Selena, I know this mission has been all over the place. But you've both stepped up to the occasion. For someone who has worked on hundreds of missions by myself, I think it's safe to say this would be a guaranteed failure if I were here on my own. You've both stepped out of your comfort zones, and I'm grateful for it.

"Look at what we're doing, looking for Felix. Would you have thought for a moment, at the beginning of this mission, that he would have even dared stepped out of the apartment?"

"You're wearing off on us more than you realize. Once we got past the intimidation of working with you, it's become impossible to not match your passion."

Arielle shrugged. "I don't do anything special—I just get the work done. That's all I've ever done."

Selena chuckled. "It's so much more than that. Anyone can clock in, do the work, and clock out. This is your life. There is no clocking out with you, and that's why you're the best. Me and Felix see that, and want it. We want to be the best, too."

"And you are both the best at what you do."

"Yes, but there's another level above that, and that's what we've never realized until working with you. The best will come and go—there's always someone to fill that spot. You're already greater than that, though. You're a . . . legend. You have this mythical perception that people just don't understand. And they never will, unless they get to work directly with you."

Arielle stopped and turned to face Selena. "Where is all of this coming from? You never sing praises to anyone, and you just showered me in them."

Selena looked down, embarrassed. "I guess I've never praised anyone because I've never been grateful to have anyone in my life—besides my mom, of course. And I'll admit, I came into this team closed-minded and skeptical. I thought you were overhyped and overrated. Just some bossy bitch—sorry—who wouldn't care about me. But I was so wrong. You've brought so much clarity and structure to my life with just these two missions we've done together. I've always felt like I've been wandering through life with no direction, but I finally know where I want to go. What I want to make out of my life."

"And what's that?"

"A legacy." Arielle noticed Selena's bottom lip trembling. "That's the difference between you and everyone else. Your name is going to remain in discussions long after you retire from the Angels, long after the day you die. I know that might sound weird to hear, but it's beautiful. Powerful. You've changed this organization and the world for the better, and nothing can take that away from you. I'm going to pursue my dream of one day winning an Oscar, even if it exhausts me to death. I want that to be my legacy."

Arielle smiled. "And I'll be right there in the front row to hear your acceptance speech. Now, shall we get back to finding Felix?"

A subtle grin touched the corners of Selena's mouth as she nodded.

They continued forward, and only after a dozen steps, Arielle came to a sudden halt, sticking out an arm in front of Selena. "Is that him?"

She pointed toward a ditch filled with tall weeds.

Selena squinted her eyes. "Is that a body on the ground?"

That's all Arielle needed to hear before dashing toward the lump. The body lay on the edge of the ditch, limbs splayed out in every direction.

"It's him!" Arielle shouted once she was within range to make out Felix's face, crouching by his side. "Holy shit!"

Selena caught up, and they each grabbed Felix from under his arms and pulled him completely out of the ditch and onto the grass.

"Felix!" Arielle shouted, squatting over his stomach so she could shake him by the shoulders. "Felix, wake up!"

His head rolled from side to side while she shook him. Arielle eased him back to the ground and stepped to the side, planting her knees into the earth and pressing her ear to his chest.

"He's breathing! Thank God, he's breathing!"

Tears had welled in her eyes and she wiped them away before sitting back up into a kneeling position at his side.

"What do we do?" Selena asked, panic completely overtaking her voice.

Arielle didn't hear Selena and kept nudging Felix in the side. "Wake up, dammit. Wake up, Felix!"

Felix moaned like a teenager refusing to wake up during summer break.

"Yes!" Arielle shouted. "C'mon!" She grabbed his head and rocked it.

"He has blood on his leg," Selena said, pointing to the dark splotches that had long dried up.

Felix moaned again, this time his eyelids fluttering as he attempted to come back to consciousness.

"Felix," Selena said in a nearly normal tone. "We're here. Wake up."

A few seconds passed as he bobbed his head from side to side, and he finally opened his eyes all the way. He looked to Arielle, then to Selena, then to the stars high above. "Jesus," he whispered.

"What happened?" Arielle asked. "Why are you bleeding?"

She scooted down to his ankle for a closer examination, but it was too dark, and the blood was too dry and caked on the skin to see a wound.

"Help me up," Felix said, his voice cracking before he cleared his throat. "Please."

He lifted his head off the ground, looking down at his feet.

Arielle and Selena grabbed him by the arms and pulled him into a seated position. He swayed for a moment before finding his balance, and planted his hands in the grass to keep from tipping back.

Felix drew a deep breath. "I was hiding in this ditch and got bit by a snake."

"What?!" Arielle gasped. "Do we need to get you to a hospital? Was it venomous?"

Felix closed his eyes and tilted his head back, clearly dreading his next words. "No . . . I sort of have a . . . phobia. I fainted from panic. The snake wasn't poisonous."

"Are you serious? How do you know that?"

"I know almost everything you can about snakes. I knew the snake wasn't harmful before it bit me. But once it happened, my mind just couldn't process it and shut down entirely. I haven't been this close to a snake in years, and just seeing its fangs sink into my leg sent me into a shock I've never experienced before."

"Christ, Felix. We thought you were in serious trouble when we saw you on the ground next to a ditch. I thought the worst had happened."

"So you're totally fine?" Selena asked.

Felix nodded. "I could use a bandage maybe, but yeah, I'll be good."

"Good," Arielle exhaled in relief. "Now, can you tell us what the hell happened? There were cops looking around the neighborhood. Had a chat with the Kennedys, and they kept pointing this way. I think your position behind this ditch saved you, or else they would have seen you from that tree where the kids were playing."

Felix recounted the events that had led up to him being caught by Mrs. Kennedy and having to run for his life.

"Why the hell would you step on Kennedy's property?" Arielle asked. "That's reckless at this point in the mission."

"I don't know what came over me. I got greedy, I guess. It was dark, the block was busy with kids, Kennedy was clearly inside his house, relaxing. It's not like I haven't had stealth training—I break into people's houses regularly. It was just terrible timing on my part."

"This could have ended so much worse," Arielle said in a rather motherly tone—the old *not angry, but disappointed.*

"You're telling me. All I was imagining was Jacob Kennedy hunting me down with one of his guns. And the worst part is I got nothing out of all this. Didn't learn a damn thing to help the mission. A completely wasted evening."

"Nothing is ever a waste," Arielle said. "This is just one more reinforcement that Kennedy is responsible. The past wouldn't have thrown all this your way unless you were close to finding something out."

"Now we'll never know," Felix said, finally getting to his feet, brushing off his shorts and legs.

"You're fine, and that's all that matters. We need to get back home, and prepare for what lies ahead."

Chapter 34

On Saturday morning, Arielle had originally planned to start the day at six o'clock. After last night's events, however, she told everyone to sleep until eight. They were already running on fumes and needed to muster all the energy they could for the final two days of the mission.

They gathered in the kitchen around 8:15, Felix with his laptop open to a live-feed of Peter Young's apartment, where the security guard remained in bed.

"Morning," Selena said as she made her way to the refrigerator to pull out all the fruit they had.

"Good morning," Arielle said. "How's everyone doing?"

Felix yawned and stretched his arms above his head. "Slept like a boulder. Really. I don't think I made a single movement all night. How about you?"

"I had a hard time falling asleep," Arielle said. "But still got about seven hours. I'll take it. What are you doing, Selena?"

She had chopped up fruit and tossed it all into a bowl. "Everything I'm going to eat for the day needs to happen within the next hour. I'm going to fill up on fruit and veggies, take a laxative at one, and be cleared out before I head to the office at four. I *refuse* to shit in a corner of that storage room like a zoo animal. Not happening."

"And water?" Arielle asked.

"I'm going to drink as much as I can before noon. It should all be out of me by four. I'm pretty hydrated, so not too worried about going thirsty while I'm in there."

"And you're going to pee in a corner of the room? Your body isn't going to make it that whole time, even if you stopped drinking right now."

"I'm allowing myself one pee while I'm in there. There's a bucket I can use. Otherwise, I'm going to do some exercises to sweat out some of the water. That should help reduce the urge. I've studied all of this to understand what needs to happen—I'm not too worried about it."

"You're taking snacks to have toward the end of your stay, right?" Arielle asked. Her phrasing made it sound like Selena was about to check into a luxurious package at the Brown Palace Hotel instead of a dusty storage room.

"Yep. I have applesauce, cans of soup, pudding, and chocolate bars. All low-risk for choking hazards—I don't trust the past."

"Very good. To be fair, I've never heard of the past actually killing someone—that would create a change in a timeline elsewhere—but I appreciate the thought you put into it."

Felix chuckled. "Well, if there were ever a time for the past to start killing, it would definitely be this mission."

"Thanks a lot," Selena said. "Death is exactly what I wanted to hear about this morning."

"You know we don't mean it like that," Felix replied, guilt immediately seeping into his voice.

"Of course, but I have to give you a hard time for it." Selena grinned while she shook her head and started popping grapes into her mouth.

"So," Felix said. "Are we even going to bother going near Kennedy's house today?"

Arielle rubbed her forehead. That same question had kept her up at night. "We kind of need to."

"I'm not going back," Felix said sternly. "I mean it."

"I'm not expecting you to. I'll go—I just don't know when, or for how long I should stay. I'll need to think about it. I can't just sit here all day and do nothing."

"You can, though," Selena said. "No one would fault you. We've done everything we can. It all boils down to tomorrow morning."

"She's right," Felix said. "Weigh the possibility of you actually finding something useful against the risk of going near his house again. If you ask me, it's not worth it."

"But it's the day before the robbery. If there were ever an opportunity to find something, it's gotta be today. I'm going, even if just for a couple hours."

Felix shook his head. "I know we can't tell you what to do, but I think you're making a mistake, Arielle. At least reconsider. Please."

"I've done plenty of thinking. I'll head there and park where you did last night. But I'm not going to step out of the car, no matter what I might see. And I'm sure the past will try to tempt me in plenty of ways."

"You think the past pulled me out of the car last night?" Felix asked, his face looking like he had just eaten something sour.

"Well, sure. You had no plans of going anywhere near Kennedy's house, but you did. I'm not saying the past can physically move you, but I believe it could have set up things to drive that temptation."

"That's lovely," Selena said, stuffing more fruit into her mouth and washing it down with a gulp of water.

"We just need to be extra aware. Our plans today can get tossed out the window in a split second. It's like I was telling Selena last night—we have to be ready to go with the flow."

"That should be easy for me today," Felix said. "I'm not leaving this apartment for anything."

Arielle checked her watch. "That's fine with me. In fact, we should plan for an early dinner so we can get to bed around eight. I want to head over to Kennedy's at six tomorrow morning, in case I run into obstacles."

"All while I'm having the time of my life," Selena said, grinning, "Just make sure we grab some margaritas when this mission's over."

"Oh, we most certainly will. Let's gear up for today."

Chapter 35

Arielle left at noon, sure to give Selena a long, tight hug before departing. As much as everyone liked to worry about the prospects of the day, Arielle trusted their hard work and knowledge would keep everyone out of harm's way. Felix's placement had virtually no risk, and Selena was low-risk, at least for tonight.

Arielle had the most to worry about. She'd been in countless of these high-pressure situations before and had learned how to navigate through the minefield of obstacles and temptations the past would throw her way.

She would not make eye contact with Jacob Kennedy. She was mainly hanging around his block to follow him in case he left. Should he stay home all day, that was fine with her.

During her drive across town, Arielle thought back to the prior missions that had been as difficult as this one. Saving a high school baseball team from a fatal bus accident. Preventing the kidnapping of a judge's daughter. Countless missions of blowing up their old rival's properties as part of their decades-long war in the underground world of time travel.

But I'm better now compared to back then, Arielle thought.

By the time she turned onto Juniper Street, confidence had swelled within Arielle. But not the type of confidence that would make her do something stupid like park across from Kennedy's house again.

No.

Confidence in her ability to stay disciplined. The past would continue its games to preserve itself, and she was ready for it.

Arielle parked her car in the exact spot Felix had just last night. She hadn't realized how much stress the darkness had caused them, finding the neighborhood peaceful under the afternoon sun. There were no kids playing in the field—the forecast called for ninety-eight degrees of brutal sunshine. Arielle felt the heat already brewing.

A gentleman six houses down from Kennedy washed his truck in the driveway, a cigar pinched between his lips, a bucket full of ice and beer bottles sitting on his front porch, rock music blaring from a boom box stationed on a table in his open garage.

Arielle studied the man, trying to figure out if he had noticed her. He seemed off in his own dimension, banging his head to the music, taking puffs from his cigar without a care in the world.

Over the next hour, the truck was clean, the cigar spent, the beer gone, and the man returned inside. A few people had emerged from their homes, families stuffing into their cars to drive off for whatever weekend events awaited. A teenage couple set up a picnic under the lone tree in the field, enjoying sandwiches and an extended make-out session under the shade.

Seeing it made Arielle think about Kevin. And his opioid addiction.

If I had just seen the signs sooner.

Arielle shook her head free of the self-inflicted blame. Fortunately, she was on high alert since waking up this morning, and was ready for anything that might throw her off her game. Who knows if that couple really had a picnic in the Original timeline, or if the past had placed them there to spark emotional vulnerability within her.

For added assurance, Arielle locked her door and reached over the passenger seat to lock the other. One more step to keep her inside the car should she decide, against her will, to step out.

Another hour passed. The couple had vanished back toward the path where she and Selena had found Felix just hours earlier.

It was 2:15 and Arielle felt satisfied with making it to the halfway point of her stakeout without seeing Jacob Kennedy.

At 2:18, a car turned onto Juniper Street and parked in front of Kennedy's house, the driver remaining in the car while the engine kept running, faint clouds of exhaust puffing out of the muffler.

The car was a light brown Nissan Sentra, probably an '88 or '89 model. It had parked with its rear facing Arielle, so even through a pair of binoculars, she couldn't make out the driver. She could, however, read the license plate, a California tag she jotted down to call in later.

"Who the hell are you?"

Kennedy appeared from his front door, dressed in gym shorts and a raggedy t-shirt, clearly without plans to leave his house. He waved at the car before making his way down the path, where he squatted to poke his head through the open passenger-side window.

Arielle held her gaze through the binoculars, unable to see much thanks to a brutal glare off the car's back window. The figure in the driver's seat wore a ball cap, so she figured it was likely a man—thought she couldn't confirm this with confidence.

She watched for ten minutes while the two talked, wondering what they would have to speak about for so long, and why the driver never stepped out. Kennedy's head bobbed every few seconds, and hc only stood up once to stretch his back before squatting back down to lean in through the window.

After those ten minutes passed, Kennedy returned inside, but the car and driver remained. Arielle wanted nothing more than to drive by to see who was in the car. She felt like a caged lioness salivating over a piece of meat just outside of paw's reach. There had been too many close calls in the past couple of days to justify driving down the block right now. With her luck, Kennedy would step outside again right when she was in front of the house, and recognize her car from yesterday.

Kennedy returned outside after a couple minutes, this time with a brown paper bag clutched in his hand.

Arielle returned to her binoculars to watch Kennedy hand the bag over to the driver. They chatted for a few more seconds before the car took off and Kennedy waved them farewell.

Don't do it, Arielle told herself, her hand having subconsciously moved to the key she left in the ignition. *The past wants you to follow that car—don't fall for it. It was probably just one of his kids.*

"He wouldn't have his own son wait in the car. That was a suspicious conversation and delivery of that brown bag."

Every cell in her body burned with overwhelming curiosity. She knew if she followed that car out of the neighborhood to find out who was driving, everything would fall into place and make sense. She also knew it would expose her to highly risky matters once back on the road. The best she could do was hope the encounter had no relation to the pending robbery.

"Dammit!" she screamed, and punched her steering wheel. She could count on one hand how many times she had felt completely helpless while on a mission. And this was one of the worst instances.

Arielle lifted the lid to the center console and rummaged through the car's paperwork until she found the packet of gum she had tossed in there on the first day. She never would let a car she was driving go without an emergency pack, and she popped two sticks into her mouth.

She still had ninety minutes until four o'clock, when she had vowed to leave to meet Felix at the apartment for an early dinner.

The thought of sitting in the car for another hour and a half shredded her psyche, knowing the car that drove away had some sort of tie to the robbery.

She watched Kennedy return inside the house and close the door, leaving the neighborhood motionless under the baking sun. Arielle threw her head back and silently screamed.

Chapter 36

While Arielle spent the next ninety minutes stewing in her car, Felix watched Young on his laptop while Selena flushed out her insides in preparation for her long night ahead.

She stepped out of the bathroom and joined Felix at the dining room table, floorplans of the bank's basement and subbasement levels splayed out.

"Still doing nothing?" Selena asked.

"Honestly, it's incredible the man isn't 600 pounds. He does *nothing*. It's really looking like he has no involvement. He should be doing something today if he was, right?"

Selena shrugged. Diving into the mind of a potential bank robber was not something she had ever considered. Then again, if she had ever been asked to portray a bank robber, she'd have no choice, but that opportunity had yet to arise. "I suppose we'll know tomorrow morning just how involved he is."

Selena had her own growing suspicions about the mission, but had opted to keep them to herself. While it may have been risky to keep her thoughts to herself, she wanted to practice the skill that Arielle had taught them about withholding that information from the past. But would there ever be a right time for such an attempt? Her theories had formulated over the past few days, and so far nothing had happened out of the ordinary aside from Dawkins spotting her in the storage room early that morning—something she chalked up to his evolving infatuation with her.

"He's involved in some capacity," Felix said. "How else do you explain the secret meetings with Kennedy?"

"They weren't really that secret, though. Sitting at a sports bar is hardly a place to discuss a private matter like bank-robbing plans. Maybe they genuinely wanted to hang out and have some drinks. Think about it—the past didn't even resist you taking his notebook. That alone makes me think he's not involved."

"Unless the notebook has nothing to do with this. He could have made those ramblings months ago and not touched it since. I've yet to see him open that closet door during this whole time. I suppose that would be too much work for him."

Selena heard the frustration in Felix's voice. "You're just feeling helpless after what happened last night. It doesn't help that Young gives you nothing of substance. Just stay patient and trust that we're all in the right places. We have less than twenty-four hours until this robbery. Eliminating a suspect is just as important as anything else. If you have to spend all day watching Young eat himself within an inch of his life, then so be it. If we can cross his name off the list, then it's worth it—because he's still very much a serious suspect."

Felix rolled his eyes and nodded toward the monitor that showed an empty living room. Young had disappeared into the bathroom after slipping into a robe. "At least he takes showers."

"I know what you're thinking, and it's not true."

"Oh? What am I thinking, Selena?" Felix spoke in a mocking tone before clenching his jaw shut.

"You think you're a failure because of last night. You're beating yourself up way too much. You're alive and well, and that's all that matters."

Selena saw the sides of his jaws bulging out as he clenched tighter. She was right, and Felix knew it. She could see the confirmation in his eyes.

"I *am* a failure. This has got to be my worst mission ever. I've been in Kennedy's house twice and haven't been able to set up any successful monitoring. That's literally my only job. I've been watching Young for two weeks and haven't learned a damn thing outside of his notebook. And even that's been as useful as a drop of water in the middle of a desert. I'm afraid of getting kicked off this team for failing to do my job. These last two missions have been so high-pressure working with Arielle."

"And whose fault is that? Arielle doesn't really put pressure on us. It sounds like you're putting it on yourself. Guess what? This has probably been the worst mission for all of us. Even Arielle. She's lost and confused on this one, even if she doesn't seem like it."

"Did she tell you that?"

"Not verbatim, but yes. And if this mission ends in failure, it's going to be on us as a team. No one is going to individually get thrown under the bus. We've all had some shortcomings along the way—it will be impossible to pinpoint the fault on any one of us."

Felix fell silent while he doodled on the table with his finger. Selena knew this was his way of processing everything she had just said. After a minute, he spoke. "Are you ready for tonight?"

"I am. I finished a gallon of water by noon, and should pee out the last of it by four." Selena checked her watch. "About another hour. Then I'll be on my way. Got my backpack loaded with the snacks I'll need, and two blankets. I'm going to roll one into a pillow—figured that would be easier than squeezing a pillow in. And I'm going to stop at the store on my way to grab some sleeping pills."

"Is that a good idea? What if you sleep longer than you should?"

Selena raised a calming hand. "I'm gonna take this pill at, like, six o'clock tonight. And on an empty stomach, it's going to process through my body much faster. At worst, I'll sleep until three in the morning. But I'll wake up with plenty of energy and be ready for all the action at nine."

"And what exactly are you planning on doing? You can't just pop out of the room and scare the robber—you'll get shot."

"I'm aware. I'm not planning on stepping foot outside of that room until the robber is in the vault. I'll have the door propped open an inch or two and will just be watching through the crack. Just trying to see if I can make out who it is. That's all Arielle asked me to do. Once the robber is out of sight, I'm going to sprint the other way."

"Seems like a lot of work for something that probably won't yield any results. The robber is in a disguise. How are you supposed to see anything looking through a cracked open door?"

"Well, the good thing is I've spent time in person with Kennedy and Young. Most of the security team, in fact. Arielle is relying on my instincts to pinpoint the robber."

"That sounds like nonsense."

"But it's not. You can sense someone's presence. Kennedy definitely had a strong presence that night at the bar. Besides, even if it's just through a door, I'll have a much better idea of the robber's size and build. Kennedy and Young have two very different bodies—it shouldn't be that hard to tell who is who." Selena checked her watch. "I'm gonna get going."

She stood up and left Felix at the table to stare mindlessly at his laptop showing Young's empty living room. He'd plan to sit there until Arielle arrived home.

It only took Selena five minutes to use the restroom one final time and gather her backpack full of goodies for the long night ahead. She slung it over her shoulder and returned to Felix. "I'll see you in the morning, okay? Don't be so worried about me."

"I worry about all of us—you should know that by now."

"Of course, and we appreciate that. But just rest assured, I'll be fine. I'm not taking any risks. Hell, I might get caught and end up back here in a couple hours—that's still a very real possibility."

"I won't hold my breath."

Selena left the apartment and started on her usual route she had been taking to the office every morning. Around the midpoint was a convenience store where she planned to stop for sleeping pills.

Once she reached the store, she found the place swarmed with six police cars, all lights flashing under the afternoon sun. This same area was where the scenic views of the natural beauty surrounding the neighborhood started giving way to the jungle of concrete that was downtown Denver. A laundromat was next to the convenience store, and that's where she was forced to stop behind a police car serving as a barricade.

Three people huddled outside the laundromat entrance, all facing the scene with arms folded over their chests.

"What's going on?" Selena asked.

"I guess a homeless man walked into the store with a gun," a middle-aged woman said. She stepped forward, brushing back sandy hair behind her ears. "Tried holding up the place. The owner refused to open the cash register and ducked a couple of shots. Grabbed his shotgun, and the two got into a shootout. Cops said the bum ended up shooting himself."

The woman paused and shook her head. "I feel so bad for Bohdan—he's the owner. Must be so shaken up."

"Do things like this happen often around here?" Selena asked.

"No. Not at all. For a big city, it's pretty safe. In this part, at least. That's why this makes no sense. I suppose the world grows a little madder each day."

"I stop here almost every day on my way to work. Was just on my way and was going to grab something. Can't believe this is happening."

"You must have an angel looking after you. That's what I think. If you came a few minutes earlier, you would've been caught in the middle of this. Lord knows what could've happened."

An angel looking after me, or the past? Selena thought. Someone would have tried to draw a parallel, even if the homeless man had taken his own life and couldn't have possibly been involved in the bank robbery. *That's how I know this whole thing is from the past. But why? The past doesn't want me to sleep this evening.*

"Well, thank you for filling me in," Selena said. "I still need to get to work. Hope you all have a better rest of the day. Glad you're okay."

"Me too, hon. See you around."

Selena crossed the street to get around the patrol cars. She craned her neck for a look inside the store, but could only see huddles of police officers through the windows.

Dread settled into Selena's gut. She had left the apartment with so much optimism about their final leg of this grueling mission. She had a plan that would work, dammit, but matters were already getting pushed off-course thanks to the past's interference. If this much could happen before she even arrived at the office, what might await during the evening ahead?

Selena walked the rest of the way to the office, glancing over her shoulder every few seconds, paranoid that the past itself might jump out from a corner and suck her very existence away.

Once she reached the building, enough negativity had consumed her mind. She tapped her badge to the card reader and stepped inside.

Chapter 37

Only ten minutes after Selena had left, Peter Young emerged from the shower, clean and dressed in a pair of jean shorts and a raggedy Metallica t-shirt.

Felix was grateful, seeing as Young typically paraded around his apartment naked after bathing. Some times for an entire hour.

When Young grabbed his wallet and stuffed it into his rear pocket, Felix jumped out of his seat. He hadn't expected Young to leave the apartment.

Felix didn't even have his shoes on, scrambling to find them in his bedroom before dashing back to his computer to see Young still in the kitchen, helping himself to a can of Coke.

"C'mon, you son of a bitch. Where are you going?"

Young placed the can on the counter, patted his pockets, and left the apartment. Felix noticed he didn't grab the car keys hanging on a hook next to the door, meaning Young was going somewhere on foot.

Felix grabbed his pistol and tucked it into the back of his waistband. He rarely carried a weapon while on missions, but he no longer felt safe and was in no position to take any chances.

He dashed out of the apartment and sprinted to the stairwell, knowing Young had never taken the stairs and always opted for the elevator. This would buy him just enough time to get outside first.

He hurried down the stairs, swinging around the corners and nearly sliding off balance a few times. But he reached the first level in record speed and made a mad dash for the building's exit. The elevator chimed right as he passed it, but he was out of sight before the doors parted.

Felix scampered around the sidewalk, panting for breath like an exhausted dog, while he searched for somewhere to hide and wait. Not knowing which way Young planned to go, Felix started walking down the sidewalk to look natural. There was no one else outside the apartment, and Young would likely notice a shady character hiding behind a trash can or tree.

Felix went south, and after ten paces heard the complex's doors close. He took three more steps before taking a casual look over his shoulder, seeing Young headed north. He sighed relief. Being in front of Young would have been awkward to finagle his way back behind him. This way allowed him the ease of simply turning around to follow Young and stay a safe distance behind.

He spun around and didn't need to hurry. Young moved at the pace one would expect of an obese middle-aged man with heart problems. *No way this guy robs the bank,* Felix thought. A bank robber would need to be a lot quicker on their feet. Even if Young could break into a sprint, how far could he reasonably run before stopping to catch his breath?

Young moved with no urgency, kept his gaze forward as he unknowingly led Felix four blocks to the nearest gas station. He cut through the lot and rounded the small building where a pay phone stood next to an outdoor storage bin of windshield wiper fluid.

"Shit," Felix muttered under his breath. The pay phone was too out in the open for him to sneak behind Young to listen to his phone call. The best he could do was stand around the corner and hope he could hear it.

Young picked up the phone off the receiver and popped coins into the slot, promptly dialing a phone number he appeared to have memorized. Felix inched his way to the corner, peeking around the brick exterior of the building where he saw Young facing his direction. He didn't notice Felix, however, so he quickly retreated out of sight.

"Dammit." Felix truly had no angle and already knew he was too far away—about thirty feet—to hear the conversation clearly. It didn't help that the occasional vehicle hummed by and drowned out the silence.

He peeked again, seeing the bin of wiper fluid bottles only ten feet away from Young at the pay phone. Young was talking. Felix could hear the mumble of his distant voice, but couldn't make out anything.

"Please don't let anything bad happen to me," Felix whispered, then stepped out from the corner, strolling calmly toward the bin of fluid. How he wished the bin was full of something that required more inspection. All the bottles of fluid were the same, so he couldn't justify standing there for over fifteen seconds. When he reached the bin, Young's voice became plenty clear.

"Everything is set," Young said. "You're clear."

Young paused when Felix reached into the bin and pulled out a bottle of fluid. Felix's heart froze as he pretended to read the bottle's label, paranoid Young had stopped talking because of his presence. He couldn't bring himself to look over to see what Young was doing. What if Young recognized him from the apartment?

Don't be a fool. He's never seen your face. You're just paranoid. Like always.

Relief flooded over Felix when Young spoke again, no suspicion in his voice. "Sounds good. It's been a pleasure. Good luck."

Felix sensed the conversation coming to its brief close and rushed away with the bottle of fluid in hand. Realizing he'd have Young behind him now, he went inside the store and disappeared down the candy aisle, keeping his eyes glued to the window, waiting for Young. The phone call must have not ended as soon as he thought, as a whole minute passed before Young walked by the window, returning the way he had come.

Felix went to the cashier and placed the fluid on the counter. "Sorry. Decided I don't need this."

He bolted out to find Young already crossing the street to return to the apartment. He wished he would have stayed longer reading the bottle's label, but he thought his head might explode with panic had he remained another second. There were thousands of possibilities for the words he heard from Young's mouth, and he kept repeating them in his head.

Everything is set. You're clear. It's been a pleasure. Good luck.

Those words could have easily been related to a potential bank robbery as they could have been intended for a friend or family member. They were nothing of substance, but Felix already felt the dials turning in his mind to crack the code. These words were just another puzzle he needed to figure out. And even though he knew they would likely lead nowhere, he wouldn't be able to help but stew over them for the rest of the evening. Fortunately, the robbery occurred the following morning, so this puzzle had a short window of relevance.

Everything is set.

Felix mulled over this phrase, figuring things might make more sense if he broke Young's words into smaller pieces. Was everything set for the robbery in the morning? If that was the case, then surely he had spoken with the robber. Why would someone who owns a home phone need to stop at a pay phone to make a call a mere four blocks away? That alone made it seem like a sensitive matter, and not just a discussion about dinner plans.

You're clear.

They had long suspected Young's involvement stemmed as an insider with the security team. What he might have cleared was the lingering question that needed an answer. Young didn't work during the robbery, nor did he today. If he made any type of preparation at the bank, it would have been completed on Friday. But what could he have done?

He could have taken the tapes out with no one realizing in time before the robbery. Felix didn't know how often such a task was the norm for the security crew.

He could have left the vault unlocked, but was that even possible? Standard bank security systems cued an alarm if the vault was left unlocked for a particular amount of time.

Felix shook his head, hoping the answer would fall into his mind, but no mission was ever that convenient.

It's been a pleasure.

This line from Young might have been the most troubling to peg. Would someone really say that with such normalcy under the circumstances? It was definitely possible, especially if the person was expecting a large sum of money to arrive because of the fruits of their illegal labor. *Thirty-*

thousand dollars, Felix thought. *To take out some tapes and leave a door unlocked? I'd definitely give that proposition some thought.*

Felix never had issues remembering his humble roots of his family scrapping together enough money for meals, no matter what his bank account said these days, courtesy of the Road Runners. Thirty-thousand dollars for a blue-collar worker could change their life tremendously. What Peter Young would do with all that money was another question. Drink it away? Eat it away? He'd probably go to Vegas and get the best of both worlds, plus an opportunity to donate it to a charming casino.

Good luck.

The last phrase from Young before he hung up. The one that stirred those damned butterflies in Felix's stomach. The one that suggested more was to come. You didn't wish someone good luck for something they had already accomplished.

Felix had gained too much ground on Young during his mental calculations, and was glad he regained some focus in time to slow down once they reached the corner of the apartment complex.

He stopped and watched Young return inside, oblivious to the man from the future following him. Felix no longer felt the urgency to watch Young's every move. All he could do at this point in the mission was gamble on the knowledge they had available. Despite the horrific notebook and violent rantings of Peter Young, those last two words he had spoken summed everything up.

The call was made at a public pay phone. No home call log that could be pulled up in court.

Good luck.

It was as open-ended as it was definitive. Those two words implied Young was done with his part, and Godspeed to whoever was stepping into that bank in the morning, armed and ready.

Felix returned inside the apartment complex, a stale odor seeming to linger in the lobby, with one thought swelling in his mind.

Young isn't our guy.

Chapter 38

Whatever fear had lingered in Selena during her walk into the office—never mind the stress that had accumulated after seeing her favorite local convenience store barricaded by local police—vanished once she pulled open the door and stepped into a deserted lobby.

Employees sometimes took the freight elevator—the same one the robber would use the next morning—but it wasn't required. As a member of the cleaning crew, Selena had a master key to get into the building from any door.

She figured the skyscraper's main entrance might draw the attention of the security team, but they'd quickly dismiss her presence once they realized who she was.

Okay, she thought. *I'm in the building.*

She strolled across the lobby, its marble floors finely polished, the leftover lemony scent still present. A pair of couches surrounded a small coffee table in front of the main reception desk—staffed by security guards during the weekdays. Fake plants lined the windows in the lobby, providing just enough privacy from any wandering eyes roaming down the sidewalks outside.

To Selena's right was the glass wall and door that customers used to enter the bank. Selena went forward to the main elevators and pushed the down button. This task could take an entire two minutes during the bustle of the work week, but a door opened immediately.

Selena stepped in and took the elevator down to the subbasement level.

She stepped out, further relieved to find the long hallway also abandoned. The locker room waited roughly fifty feet ahead, and she felt her feet floating across the dust-covered concrete floor as she thought she had a clear path.

If the past had ever wanted to toy with her, it did so when a guard stepped out of a side room and started down the hall toward Selena.

Time screeched to a halt as her temples pounded with adrenaline. And fear.

Selena squinted for a clearer view of the guard, but still didn't recognize him. The two kept closing in on each other, Selena bracing for the worst.

Act normal. You're working today. You belong here. Hold your ground, no matter what he says.

Selena rarely had issues sticking to her guns, but something about this entire situation felt off. She wasn't herself. Was a lack of confidence something the past could plant into one's mind? Arielle had mentioned the past had never actually killed someone, but that didn't mean it couldn't render someone useless on a mission by rewiring their brain.

You're overthinking. Just shut up and handle this.

The two were within ten feet of each other, Selena now confident she had never seen this older gentleman before. He was at least seventy with snow-white hair protruding from a solid black ball cap, the word *SECURITY* embroidered across the center. He walked with a slight hitch in his step, as if he had a bad knee.

Is the weekend crew like the junior varsity team around here? Selena thought. No wonder the place got robbed. They left this poor old man, who would struggle to chase down a turtle should one decide to empty the vault, without a gun. What exactly did the security team think he could do to fend off an actual armed robber?

"Good afternoon, doll," he said with a lopsided grin, voice gentle and warm. "You're working today?"

"Hello, sir," Selena said, calculating every word and how it might be received before it left her lips. "Yes. Would much rather be out with my friends tonight, but here I am."

"Ah, yes. Saturday night. Not exactly a nightclub here, is it?" he asked, and let out a hearty chuckle. "Don't work yourself too hard, you hear?"

"I won't. Have a good evening."

"You too, doll. Take care."

Selena hadn't noticed it, but the old man never actually stopped walking. She had, but he kept moving along at his ginger pace, not a single plan of stopping his momentum.

She couldn't help but smile as she looked over her shoulder to see him inching his way toward the elevator she had just come from.

"See," Selena whispered to herself. "Nothing to worry about."

She pressed forward to the locker room and slipped in before anyone else spotted her. She flipped the light switch to blast the long fluorescent bulb above, buzzing a bit too loudly for her liking.

Selena sat down on the bench for a moment to make sure her thoughts were really as calm as she had thought. She wasn't lying to herself, and truly felt at peace after her encounter with the guard.

Is the past throwing me a bone? Is there a depth to it—that it doesn't want such bad things to happen to innocent people? Could the past actually be rooting for us to succeed, while still doing its due diligence for appearances?

She laughed at the thought. Of course none of that was true. The past wasn't a human with emotions. The past was an extension of time, which was an extension of the universe. And the universe simply *existed*. It didn't care if you were Mother Teresa or Adolf Hitler—what you did during your time in the universe was your business.

"Then let's own this moment," she said to help snap her focus back into place.

Selena pulled her t-shirt over her head and stepped up to open her locker. When she saw a small gift box inside, propped on top of her folded uniform pants, her blood froze.

What the hell is that? Who's it from?

Any tranquility she had composed within quickly vanished, her mind racing like a bat out of hell.

This is it, she thought. *This is the past finally waiting for its chance to make me turn around.*

Her thoughts quickly moved into paranoia—the box was a bomb planted by the robber, in her locker, of course—then moved into a panicking logic. *Someone knows all of our plans and is sending a message to stop. We were the ones being watched this whole time. That's the punchline the past has been waiting oh-so-patiently to deliver.*

That thought seemed a stretch, but not one she wanted to rule out completely.

Then she moved into a more reasonable logic.

Dawkins.

The guy clearly had feelings for her, even after a faux date. Dawkins had access to the women's locker room after hours, and could even find out which locker belonged to Selena. The box inside her locker was solid red with a black bow tied across the top of the lid. It was square-shaped, and no bigger than six inches on the sides.

A romantic gesture? she wondered, part of her hoping it was true, the other still sensing a trap.

She debated touching it. More harm than good could come from it. Opening the box might very well lead to the mission unraveling, and it seemed an unnecessary risk to take at this stage. She was in the building, only spotted by one guard who had likely already dismissed their encounter.

"One more step and I'm where I'll need to be for the rest of the mission."

Selena at least wanted to know what was in the box, and the thought of leaving it behind completely untouched and returning home after the mission would eat at her for the rest of her life. The box could be tied to the mission, or have no relevance to their work at all.

She needed to move the box, as it rested on top of her folded uniform pants.

Selena reached out with a trembling hand, forcing herself to get the shaking under control. If there was a miniature bomb inside the box, her nerves would certainly do no favors when handling the package.

She picked it up carefully and noted how light it felt between her fingers.

Selena didn't dare shake the package, instead placing it gently on the bench behind her. She gawked at the box through the entirety of her changing outfits, refusing to break eye contact.

Once dressed in her work uniform, Selena stuffed her clothes into the top of her backpack and looked into her locker. All that hung was a second uniform shirt—one she'd never wear again.

It finally occurred to her, that even if they were still in 1991 on Monday morning, Selena wouldn't be coming into work. The whole building would be a crime scene—work would definitely be called off for at least a week while the authorities gathered evidence from every square inch of the skyscraper.

I'm not coming back here. Ever.

The reality was both calming and unsettling—mainly because of the mystery package. If she left it in the locker, they would discover it on Sunday afternoon. Selena already expected her name to float around during the investigation, seeing as she was a staff member who would essentially disappear from the face of the planet after the crime.

Perhaps the legend would change after their involvement. Maybe Selena's name would long stand as a mystery suspect for the bank robbery, assuming it all went through as it originally had. How else could anyone explain her brief employment for only two weeks before a robbery, followed by her vanishing act?

The thought sent chills down her back. Being accused of a bank robbery was no light accusation. A charge like that, even if unproven or lacking a shred of evidence, could tarnish one's name and reputation.

"But I don't exist in this timeline," she whispered.

Living the life of a time traveler, always in different years, made it hard for Selena to remember the simple fact that she wasn't on the grid during most missions she worked. If the authorities wanted to stress over her name after this robbery, it would only be a waste of time. While her name was real, her social security, ID's, and any other form of identification they might try to research were all false.

The realization always left her humbled. If Selena disappeared entirely, who would notice? Her parents, after a few weeks of no calls. Arielle and Felix, certainly, and the rest of the Road Runners organization. But who else of actual significance?

She was renowned in the time travel world, but what about the real world? The world everyone else lived in. The one where achievements were celebrated—across the globe, sometimes.

They might complete this mission and have all the answers to the questions that went unsolved for decades. Selena might even end up being the one directly responsible for discovering who the monster was behind the robbery and murders. But what did it mean for her? A quick pat on the back and a follow-up assignment to get back into the past.

This constant lifestyle of hustle and bustle didn't bother her too often, but now and then these same thoughts forced their way into her mind and planted themselves there for anywhere from a couple days to two weeks. More often than not, these thoughts caused her a severe bout of depression that led to hiding in her house, lazing around in her pajamas while every ounce of motivation to exist drained from her body like a hidden waterline leak.

She didn't quite feel that level of self-hatred creeping in yet, and it could all vanish after the mission was complete—that had happened more than once.

Selena closed her eyes and imagined the glamorous life of a Hollywood star. Galas, award shows, flashy outfits, handsome actors, and a life traveling the world doing what she loved more than anything. Buried in the depth of these missions, her dreams felt like they lived on a different planet entirely.

One day, I'll chase it all. I'll have it all.

She stuffed the mystery box into her backpack and left the locker room behind for the last time, heading for the storage closet on the basement level above.

Chapter 39

Arielle arrived back at the apartment about fifteen minutes after Felix had returned. She found him sitting at the dining room table, laptop flipped open to the live-feed of their suspect.

"How'd it go today?" she asked, pulling out the seat next to him. The laptop was pushed back, a glass of lemonade standing in the space between Felix and the computer. His focus was on the liquid ring that had formed around the base of the glass. He traced the fluid with his finger in a circular motion.

Felix explained everything that had happened, building up to his convincing proposal that Young's involvement did not carry into the day of the crime on Sunday.

Arielle shared the few details she had on the random visitor who had stopped by Kennedy's house. She pulled out the note with the car's license plate as a reminder to call it in. It could sometimes take hours to get a result back, even for the top-ranked Angel. While her requests took priority over many other Angels, she couldn't jump to the top of the line, no matter how urgent the information might be.

"So what are we supposed to plan for in the morning?" Felix asked.

Arielle shrugged. "The same plan we've had all along, I suppose. I agree with you about Young not being further involved, but we can't take that leap of faith without concrete evidence. You'll still need to keep your eyes on him in the morning before making your way to the bank. I wouldn't put too much weight on it, though. Maybe plan to leave around 8:30, assuming he shows no activity."

Felix nodded, his eyes quickly dashing to the screen that showed Young in his typical spot on the recliner. "Okay. And you're still going to Kennedy's house?"

"I'll be there around seven, ready to watch anything that might happen. From a distance, of course."

"And you're going to follow him? Won't tomorrow be the riskiest day to do that, considering everything that's happened already?"

Arielle nodded. "It sure is, but it's what we're here for. Sometimes you have to push fear and worry aside and just get the job done."

Felix allowed a moment of silence before speaking. "That doesn't mean you should risk your life for the job. Past all the glitz and glamour of being the top-ranked Angel, you're just a person doing a job. If you die tomorrow, I'm sure there will be a week of festivities to celebrate your life and achievements within the Road Runners. But then what? The number-two Angel becomes number one. Everyone shifts up a spot, then life goes on. No matter how much you accomplish in this role, you're only going to be a name in the history books. And only for the Road Runners, at that. I hope you keep this kind of perspective."

"I do," Arielle said. And she did, to an extent. Her biggest fear was dying before her grandmother. She couldn't bear the thought of leaving her closest relative alone in the world. She may have not had as many opportunities to visit her abuela as she'd like, but the thought of her grandmother somehow being the last member of the family left seemed a torturous way to end her final days on the planet. Would the Road Runners even inform her grandmother if Arielle passed away? Or would they would leave her to count the final days wondering why Arielle stopped reaching out and visiting? "I know I talk a big game, but I really proceed with caution. I'm not reckless, and I always weigh the potential death traps that can happen. I suppose I've just been doing this long enough, where it all comes natural to me now."

"Don't let that comfort twist into your downfall. That same story has been repeated plenty of times throughout history. Comfort leads to letting your guard down. Thinking you're invincible is probably the deadliest belief someone can have."

"I don't think that at all."

"Really? Who's the number-two ranked Angel behind you?"

Arielle bit her bottom lip. Why did Felix seem so hell-bent on pushing her buttons?

"Marcus Conners," she said confidently.

Felix shook his head. "He hasn't been number two for at least six months. Has it really been that long since you've looked?"

"I don't see how that's relevant."

"But it is. Don't get me wrong—I'm not one who puts a ton of stock into rankings of any sort. However, if I was, say, in the top ten, you can bet I'd be looking at those rankings daily, trying to understand how to move up and also how to avoid falling down the list. Someone who hasn't looked at the list in six months means they're comfortable with where they are and don't have a worry in the world about falling down the list."

Arielle sat up straight. "Wait, are you saying that someone is closing in on me? Who's in second?"

"None of that matters. That's beside the point. You can look that up after the mission."

"What happened to Marcus?"

Arielle had met Marcus Conners on multiple occasions, often to swap strategic ideas. The Angels at the top of the charts never worked together, the organization preferring to keep the talent dispersed evenly across multiple teams.

"Marcus suffered a serious injury on a mission. Tore an ACL, Achilles tendon, broken ribs, and messed up his spine. He's no longer in the top 100 while he's been in an intensive recovery."

Now Arielle stood up, and Felix joined her, the two looking like they might be about to break into fisticuffs instead of a heated discussion. "How did I not hear about this?!"

"Because you don't care. You're not worried about those below you on the rankings. They shared this information in the weekly emails from the Commander's office."

Arielle wouldn't admit it to Felix—at least not right now—but she rarely opened those weekly emails. They provided high-level happenings and occasionally spotlighted a Road Runner for some achievement. She thought of it more as a basic newsletter with information she never found interesting.

"I care. That's not fair of you to say I don't."

"I'm not saying you don't care about Marcus—of course you do. But you live so focused in your own world, that you're not aware of everything else happening outside of it. You might call that tunnel vision, but I see it as a dangerous level of comfort. You like it in your world. Nothing bad can happen to you in it. You control every aspect of your own universe. And you're certainly not worried about some other Angel barging in and taking your place on the throne. Why would you? It's *your* world."

Arielle felt a pang in her stomach that she wasn't sure was hunger or anxiety. "Why are you saying all this? I don't understand why tonight, of all nights, you'd want to plant this in my head?"

"I say it because I care about you. It's weird. I consider you pretty humble. But that doesn't mean your awareness is where it should be. Maybe your humble when dealing with others, but hold yourself on a pedestal within your own mind."

"I hold myself to high standards. I wouldn't say it's a pedestal."

"Whatever it is, it's good to be reminded of the big picture some times. I'd hate to see your downfall. You've done a lot for me and Selena, and we're in this for the long haul. But our team can't succeed if you make a mistake that costs everything."

Arielle's throat tensed shut. Part of her wanted to cry. The other part wanted to scream. "Thank you," she muttered, taking a big gulp to open up her throat. "I've never had someone care for me within the Road Runners the way you and Selena have. I'll be the first to admit how skeptical I was hearing about the plans for these permanent teams. But I'm glad it happened."

Felix grinned. "Our team is going places. It's only a matter of time before they rank the teams instead of the individual Angels. I wonder where we'll end up on that list." Felix looked to the ceiling and stroked his chin to feign deep thought.

This earned a giggle from Arielle, who felt a sense of relief she hadn't known she needed. A weight was lifted off her shoulders. Her team had her back through everything. An unconditional love she had never felt from anyone besides her family and Kevin, once upon a time. It had been building up over the past few weeks, but Arielle now fully believed that it was okay to *not* be alone in the Road Runners.

"Thank you, Felix. For all of your words. I needed to hear all of that. You're exactly what this team needs. A calm, unbiased perspective on everything we do. It's invaluable."

Felix held his tight-lipped grin, never one to enjoy a shower of compliments in any setting. He checked his watch. "We need to have dinner and get some sleep. Tomorrow's the big day."

Chapter 40

Arielle woke up on Sunday morning at 5:06, twenty-four minutes before her alarm, feet hitting the ground with a nervous anticipation of the day ahead.

She had broken her own rule last night, consuming two glasses of wine after dinner. But she needed it. She was in sync with her mind and body, her thoughts out of control. Without the wine, she probably would have been awake until midnight, likely later. With it, she lay down and dozed off minutes before eight o'clock.

Arielle had passed the time by packing her suitcase while she sipped on the wine. She had encouraged Felix to do the same. If all went smoothly this morning, they would return to the apartment, grab their bags, and never look back. Felix offered to pack Selena's bag as best he could. They had taken a peek into her bedroom to find clothes tossed all over the place and toiletries scattered across her nightstand. Arielle was grateful Felix bit the bullet to clean up her mess—doing so would have caused her serious stress.

Arielle fought off jitters while she dressed for the morning. It was nothing new—she typically experienced some level of nerves on the morning of the ultimate showdown. Thankfully, her anxiety didn't stem from a lack of belief in her abilities, but rather from the unknown. Would all their hard work over the past two weeks pay off? This mission, in particular, had brought up more doubts than most in the past.

Arielle could count on one hand how many times she had started the final day of a mission with no clue how it might turn out. Today was one of them.

Jacob Kennedy, Peter Young, now an outsider they were previously unaware of. Who slips into the bank and kills four people?

While Kennedy was still the obvious suspect, difficulty in finding concrete evidence made Arielle wary of fully committing to him.

Once her bag was packed, she left it on the foot of the bed. Arielle had dressed in her standard mission-day attire of black spandex over her entire body. She put a pair of athletic pants over, along with a baggy jacket that would allow room for a bulletproof vest underneath, should she desire.

She headed downstairs to find Felix at the kitchen table, laptop open, a glass of orange juice in front of him.

"Good morning," Arielle said. "Any action yet?"

Felix shook his head, an elevated level of seriousness consuming him. It was go-time, and Felix Francisco wasn't one to fuck around. "He's sleeping. I went back and checked the footage. He stayed up until 1:30 last night, watching late night television shows while he dozed in and out. Slammed six beers between ten and midnight."

"Doesn't sound like someone who needs to be awake early on Sunday morning."

"Not at all. He's gotta be passed out drunk still. I'm not counting on seeing a trace of him."

"It just doesn't make sense."

"We'll have a better idea by the end of the day."

"No breakfast this morning?" Arielle asked, nodding to the glass of juice.

Felix laughed through his nose. "A bit early, no? If you want something, I can make some toast real quick. I know you're trying to get out the door."

"Don't worry about it, I'll grab a banana on my way out." Arielle would have plenty of time to eat once she arrived at Kennedy's neighborhood. She didn't exactly expect an eventful morning until around eight o'clock. Before leaving, she filled a short glass of water, chugging it instantly. "I'll see you down at the bank around nine o'clock. . . assuming Young really isn't involved today."

Felix glanced at the screen still showing a dormant living room. "Yes. I'll be there."

Arielle nodded, the tension heavy in the air. It didn't need to be said, but they both understood the risks they would all endure throughout the morning. Felix's words from last night still lingered heavily on Arielle's mind, and she felt obligated to proceed with an extra level of caution.

"I'll see you soon."

Chapter 41

As Arielle drove across town, Selena awoke from a long night of tossing and turning. The lack of sleeping pills proved costly. Aside from an already flustered mind, Selena endured drastic temperature changes within the storage room throughout the night. From too hot to cold, her blanket ended up twisted into a spiral. Even with the makeshift pillow and blankets, sleeping on the concrete floor left her with plenty of back and neckaches by the time she woke up.

Shortly before four o'clock, she heard what she thought was a buzzing sound. An alarm blared for only a couple of minutes before cutting off.

Was that something with the robbery? An early setup?

It was possible the entire security team was in on the heist, each with a role to play to ensure a smooth robbery. But that didn't explain how four guards wound up dead before lunchtime. Unless the robber reconsidered before entering the bank. Killing off accomplices only made the surviving participants richer with a bigger cut of the money. This also seemed likely, but Selena sensed herself slipping down a dangerous rabbit hole of unproven theories. She shook her head free of all the thoughts, focusing on her simple task of keeping an eye out for the moments following nine o'clock.

On a positive note, her planning around food and drink was correct. Even upon waking, she had no urge to relieve her bowels or bladder. With her body tense and sore, Selena spent twenty minutes doing yoga stretches. The area had remained quiet all night, not that it mattered. She calculated roughly five hours of actual sleep.

I've done a lot bigger tasks on a lot less sleep before, she thought once she added up the time.

She had slept in her work uniform overnight and now changed into her mission outfit—nearly the same thing as Arielle—and stuffed a black ski mask into her back pocket. That was only to be worn if she felt in danger of being seen by security.

After stretching, Selena rummaged through her backpack for a pack of pudding, her stomach growling the instant her eyes fell on it. It wouldn't fill her by any means, but she welcomed any small boost of energy. She peeled the lid off, licking the chocolate goo before folding it into itself, and dug in with the plastic spoon she had brought.

Footsteps clopped down the hallway, freezing her for a moment until they continued past the storage room. Selena had to remind herself that she was on the security team's floor, and they still had a job to do. There was probably someone walking around overnight, but she had either been too occupied or sleeping to notice. In just a few hours she'd listen to Bill McDowell's final march to his death in the elevator.

I wonder if that's him, she thought. He would likely start his shift around this time, according to their notes.

Selena still had her nagging suspicions about the mission, and thankfully the distractions throughout the night helped keep those thoughts at bay. It was a lot harder than it sounded, keeping her mind oblivious to its own thoughts, but Arielle insisted this was the skill that made her great.

From Selena's viewpoint, she was perhaps the safest one on the mission thanks to her hiding spot. Aside from someone barging into the storage room, there was little the past could do to interfere with her snooping.

She checked her watch to find a time of 5:45, less than four hours until the robbery. If there were happenings within the bank from any potential insiders, those would unfold in the coming minutes.

"Today's the day," she whispered as she rolled up the blankets and stuffed them into the backpack. She had pulled out all the snacks and replaced them on top for easy access. Her stomach spun after the measly pudding it received, clearly desperate for more.

She originally planned to hold the door open while peering out, but with plenty of time to kill, Selena searched the storage room for something to ease that task.

She sifted through cleaning supplies, both old and new. Old radios the security team likely used in the past. Boxes of uniforms. Light bulbs. Toilet plungers. She even found a dusty six-pack of beer bottles.

Selena considered using the toilet plunger's handle to prop the door ajar, but thought it might leave the crack *too* open—it was an inch in diameter. When she found a pyramid of six small paint buckets hiding in the corner, she immediately rummaged the pile of supplies. Paint trays and rolling brushes were well in stock, and when she found the stirring sticks, she had exactly what she needed.

"Need to test it out," she said, grabbing three of the sticks and holding them together in a tight bundle about half an inch thick.

Selena shuffled toward the door, examining the sticks for any cracks and vulnerabilities that might prove them ineffective. She even gave them a slight bend to make sure they were sturdy.

The door handle stared at her, prompting a hesitation. The latch made an audible clicking sound when turning the knob and would surely catch the attention of anyone in the hallway. That was why she needed to have the door propped open before the robber arrived. Silence was the most critical aspect of remaining hidden.

She pulled the door handle, its click echoing around the storage room. She hadn't even pulled the door open, waiting for a reaction from the other side.

None came, so she squatted down, keeping a tight grip on the handle so the latch wouldn't pop back into place and make her do this all again. Her arm wavered as she pulled the door open, an intense focus on not pulling too quickly.

With two inches of space, she saw the cold grayness of the hallway's concrete floor. In just a few hours, a robber would make his way down that very concrete, one murder already under his belt, as he sought the vault.

Selena slid the bundle of stirring sticks into position, standing them vertically inside the doorjamb. Once placed, she inched the door closed, keeping her finger between the gap to hold up the sticks. When the door touched the sticks, the gap it left was just wide enough to pull her finger out.

"Holy shit," Selena whispered, standing up. "It worked."

She took a step back and crossed her arms, admiring her work. The door was ajar by the half-inch provided by the sticks. She stepped forward and pressed her face against the door, one eye peering through the small crack.

The hallway was still empty, but all that mattered was that she could see it. Knowing the robber would come from the left side of the hall, she'd have a clear view of most of his trek from the elevator.

Her only concern was not knowing how the door looked from the outside. There was still a little over three hours to kill, and if any of the guards ventured down the hall, would they notice the door slightly open?

Selena returned to her backpack, and sat on top of it, anticipation growing heavier with each passing second.

We're almost there.

Chapter 42

At 6:17 A.M., Arielle arrived to Juniper Street an hour earlier than planned, the neighborhood silent and still. A light fog lingered over the grassy field. The clouds glowed in a purplish haze, sunrise only thirty minutes away.

She parked next to the field, facing Kennedy's house at the opposite end of the block. If Jacob Kennedy didn't step foot outside of his home before 8:57—the absolute latest time he could leave to arrive at the bank by 9:14—where would that leave them?

Arielle braced for both possibilities and was equally prepared for either outcome. She expected Kennedy to step outside sometime between 8:30 and 8:45, leaving time for a leisurely drive across town. Kennedy had so far proven himself a patient driver who followed the law—not surprising for a former police officer.

Once he got in his truck, Arielle's job was pretty straightforward: follow Kennedy to the bank and watch him call for the security team to let him in.

What she *didn't* have planned was the decision to spring into action or not. The mission called for only finding out who was responsible for the robbery. Unlike the hundreds of missions she had completed before, they did not ask her to intervene and prevent the tragedy from happening. However, that didn't mean she would pass the opportunity if it presented itself. Nor did the mission report say anywhere that she *shouldn't* intervene. It was a loophole. One she could only presume Commander Briar had left open on purpose.

Arielle didn't have her usual slew of weapons as she did when preparing to stop a heinous crime. She had only her pistol and a couple of throwing knives.

She needed to shake off the thoughts. Even if the mission would be deemed a success for the elementary task of finding out who the robber is, walking away without trying to stop four murders from happening went against every grain of Arielle's instincts.

But there she sat, still without enough proof to definitively say Kennedy was responsible for the morning's robbery. Had that been the case, she would interfere right now. Every Angel was to never act off an assumption.

Interfering with the past was delicate business, and every move should be pre-meditated and calculated to avoid problems. Arielle had once tested the boundaries of this theory on one of her early missions, and paid dearly.

It was a situation not too different from the one currently in front of her. She had to stop a liquor store robbery, and had narrowed down the suspects to two potential men. One she deemed less likely to be the culprit based on a minimal amount of evidence. She went with her gut feeling, and sat outside the wrong house the night of the robbery. The suspect she had become so convinced was responsible ended up spending his entire night at home, drinking a bottle of wine while watching soccer on TV.

By the time Arielle realized he had no plans of robbery, she hurried to the store, much too late. They marked the mission as a failure and assigned her to work with a special team who dissected every step of her mission to determine where things went wrong.

Failing a mission wasn't a call for punishment by the organization—dozens of failed missions occurred on a weekly basis—but Arielle beat herself up over the fiasco, vowing to never trust something as abstract as a gut feeling again. Perhaps the misstep had made her too literal of a person since then, but she only failed two missions in the years since, both extremely complicated matters with several factors beyond her control.

With Young all but eliminated as a serious suspect, Arielle still refused to go all-in on Kennedy. They lacked that final piece of the puzzle to fuel complete confidence in her decisions.

She ate her banana while passing the time. At 7:08, the front door of Kennedy's house swung open, and out he stepped, dressed in raggedy shorts, a t-shirt, and a pair of white sneakers with green grass stains smeared across the bottom. He had his hands on his hips as he examined the front yard, drawing in a deep breath full of the fresh morning air.

"What the hell?" Arielle asked as she watched him trudge along the house, disappearing into the backyard for several minutes before returning with a lawn mower. The echoes of that past failed mission rang loudly in her mind. "Why would someone planning to rob a bank worry about cutting his grass before leaving?"

The task, though normal for a warm summer morning, made absolutely no sense in the thick of their investigation. She wanted to drive off to find a pay phone to call Felix to alert him of the unfolding matter. However, Kennedy still had ninety minutes before needing to leave. Even if the chore made little sense at the moment, Kennedy could still be right on schedule for the robbery.

Maybe he's doing it to distract his mind, Arielle thought. She had fallen victim to mindless housecleaning in the days leading up to a big mission, all to keep her mind occupied. Sitting in a room and dwelling on an intimidating task had only ever driven her mad. And she had done hundreds of missions.

It would be Kennedy's first robbery, making it highly unlikely he was numb to the dangerous undertaking. There had to be a healthy amount of nerves consuming him. He was still human, after all.

But the more she watched him, the less she believed he would soon drive to the bank. Before he started on the lawn, Kennedy reached into the passenger side of his truck, popped a cigarette into his mouth, and lit it up. Only after a couple of drags was he satisfied enough to rev up the mower.

Is he just preparing the lawn for a relaxed Father's Day with his family?

The possibility had certainly crossed her mind, but she didn't rule out the chance of Kennedy being twisted enough to rob the bank in the morning, stash the money in a hiding spot—presumably the hole he dug in the mountains—then return home by lunchtime to spend the rest of the holiday with his family.

She had been in this business long enough to know some people simply lacked souls. And sometimes those same people hid behind seemingly normal lives.

For the next fifteen minutes, she watched Kennedy go up and down the front lawn, cutting the grass in near-perfect lines. When he finished, he went to the backyard and did the same. Arielle could only hear the humming of the motor while he was in the back for another fifteen minutes.

When the motor fell silent, Arielle saw the time was 7:43. Kennedy still had an hour before leaving for the bank. That thought quickly vanished when he returned to the front yard with a gas-powered lawn trimmer.

"Are you kidding me?" Arielle whined from the car.

She crossed her arms, shaking her head as she watched him landscape the front lawn. There was still time for him to pack everything away and head to the bank, but the window was closing.

Just when she thought it couldn't get any stranger, Kennedy's next-door neighbor stepped outside. She was a woman perhaps slightly younger than Kennedy, pink curlers in her hair, a long teal bathrobe swaying at her ankles with each step. She had walked out of her house and waved to Kennedy before shuffling over to their shared fence.

Kennedy killed the trimmer and met her. They conversed for a minute, swapping laughs as Kennedy stood with his arms crossed over his chest. The neighbor returned to her pathway and strolled to the sidewalk where she picked up the Sunday morning newspaper and returned inside.

Kennedy studied his lawn before taking the trimmer to the backyard. Arielle listened to the piercing roar of its motor for about five minutes before the neighborhood fell back under the blanket of silence.

That was his alibi, she thought. The mission files had mentioned he had an alibi in court who testified that they had seen Kennedy working on his lawn in the morning. Even wished him a happy Father's Day like a caring neighbor would do. Either the woman had no sense of time, or she was in on the secret. Kennedy could have easily offered his neighbor some money to testify in his favor in court. But was that agreement already in place before this morning, or had it just happened?

"Stop it," Arielle told herself. *You're letting your mind drift all over the place. An agreement like that would have been settled indoors. It's not something you casually mention to your neighbor while you're mowing the lawn.*

The frustrations swirling around the mission seemed to reach a boiling point for Arielle at this precise moment. She wanted to scream. She wanted to sprint down the street and attack Jacob Kennedy, barge into the house and get all the missing answers.

Why is the truth refusing to show itself? she wondered. The past was winning this battle, and easily. Nothing pissed off the top-ranked Angel more than a lack of knowledge.

Kennedy finally returned from the backyard at 7:56 and moseyed back into the house without a single shred of urgency. The realization that Kennedy might not be responsible made Arielle sick to her stomach.

She had thirty long minutes ahead until she'd find out for sure if Kennedy would head off to the bank.

Chapter 43

At eight o'clock, Felix dressed in his uniform. Peter Young remained asleep, not so much as stirring in bed.

Felix would give the man until 8:30 to show any sign of life. He could technically wait longer, mathematically speaking, but if Young wasn't out of bed by 8:30, the odds were entirely against his involvement in the day's events.

Felix was already convinced of this. Watching Young snooze the morning away only cemented this belief. If Young was involved, it wouldn't have been so easy to take his notebook. The live-feed wouldn't have been running flawlessly this entire time. There were virtually no obstacles for his spying on Young.

"Listen to the past," Arielle had told them one night.

And that's exactly what he was doing. All the resistance so far had surrounded Jacob Kennedy and his house. Kennedy dug a mysterious hole in the middle of nowhere. Kennedy had bank floor plans in his basement. Plus guns and ammo.

But Young had to be involved, at least to a degree. He had the thirst for revenge. The police scanner. And he was the other half of the private meetings with Kennedy. It seemed impossible for someone as lazy as Young to be the mastermind behind the operation, but any other explanations otherwise were becoming less likely. Could someone who crafted such a brilliant robbery scheme simply sleep in the morning of the big day?

Felix had to remind himself that people were unfathomably complex.

Just because *he* wouldn't dare get caught sleeping had he planned a robbery of his own, didn't mean other people thought the same way. In fact, this very mission proved just that.

"We all live in our own little worlds," Felix said to the empty apartment. "All trying to do what we think is right, no matter how far off course that might actually be. The world is an odd, robust jumble of chaos. Where everything makes perfect sense, yet somehow makes absolutely no sense, all at the same time."

It was 8:15, and still nothing from Young's bedroom. Setting up in this apartment complex had now seemed like a mistake. They would have been better off trying to buy a house on Kennedy's block, or at least somewhere in his neighborhood. Felix didn't want to write off Young as a waste of time, but felt their efforts could have been better spent pursuing someone else of interest.

Felix's stomach growled. He hadn't eaten breakfast—his mind was too occupied. Even after their prior mission working together, he still hadn't grown used to remaining involved on the day of an actual crime. The days of bouncing from mission to mission, setting up surveillance, and disappearing were over.

"I'm a full-fledged Angel," he muttered. He played an important role in today's events, no matter how irrelevant Young had become in the past few hours.

By 8:20, Felix lugged the suitcases out of everyone's rooms and parked them next to the kitchen table, where he had spent what felt like the last three years of his life sitting and watching Young do absolutely nothing. At least he'd have a scar from the snake bite to remind him of the lone exciting moment on this mission.

If all went smoothly, the team would be back in this apartment by ten o'clock to grab their bags and return home to the present. No one had said it aloud, but it had become clear all three of them longed for that moment. This mission had emotionally drained each of them, every day somehow more complex than the prior.

At 8:25, Felix rummaged through his backpack for his pistol. He hated pulling it out, a reason he thoroughly enjoyed his old mission work of never needing it. But he was an Angel, and every Angel was trained in the fine arts of firearms. Preferring peaceful resolutions, Felix rarely took his weapon with him, even when breaking into random people's homes.

Today, however, he tucked it into the back of his waistband. He also despised this move, likening it to something criminals did. But he couldn't simply walk around with the gun on his hip holster, not when he'd be feet away from a robbery in progress. Preparing a mission, even something as gutsy as breaking and entering to set up bugs and cameras, posed little risk if he had a trusted schedule to follow.

The day of an actual crime was an entirely different beast. They had to factor the past and its wrath. After two weeks in the past, minor things had changed, trajectories moved, and there was no predicting how the crime would ultimately unfold. Felix understood this elevated risk, and that's why he carried his pistol.

Everything functioned at a high-risk, high-reward level for the entire day of a crime. And this fine Father's Day would prove no different.

The clock struck 8:30, and Young remained snoring.

Felix shook his head. "Unbelievable."

As much as he knew this moment would come, it didn't disappoint him any less. It was officially safe to eliminate Peter Young from consideration as a suspect for the Father's Day Massacre.

"Off we go," Felix said, slamming the laptop shut and quickly shoving it into his suitcase.

He hurried out of the apartment building, nothing but the gun tucked into his waistband. He was to meet Arielle at the west side of the bank, where they would watch the area for the robber to arrive.

When he stepped outside, he found the weather perfect. The morning sunlight kissed the nearby skyscrapers. A couple strode down the sidewalk with their dog leading the way. Birds sung cheery tunes over the quiet neighborhood while a father and his young boy sat on their porch across the street, watering their lawn without a worry.

The calming utopia of the world made Felix that much more uneasy, knowing what was about to unfold just a half-mile away.

He started down the block, having budgeted twenty-minutes to walk to the bank. After three blocks, he had already passed a half-dozen people out for a morning jog through the neighborhood.

Just try to look normal, he told himself, the biggest secret in the world wanting to burst out of him as he attempted to take regular strides. He even offered a small grin to one jogger, who paid him no attention.

Felix was ready to cross one more block when he saw a car swerving across the intersection. His legs immediately locked, mind kicking into high-gear as he watched the vehicle jerk left to right as it made its way down the road at a lethal pace. They were still in the neighborhood, the posted speed limit at twenty-five miles per hour. Felix figured the car was going at least double.

"Hey! Watch out!" a voice shouted from across the intersection, fear suddenly growing heavy in the air.

Felix remained stuck in a virtual staredown with the berserk car veering toward him. The thought of death numbed his entire body. He tasted the saliva flooding the back of his mouth, thick as his throat clenched shut.

Is this really how it ends? Felix thought. *Some drunk driver is going to crash into me. Poof! Drive home safe, folks.*

The sensation of facing death straight on rattled Felix. In a matter of seconds, hundreds of thousands of memories flooded his thoughts, each one of them crystal clear for the millisecond they displayed in his mind. The human brain was not built to process thoughts at such a deadly velocity.

The car strayed right—Felix's left—then skidded back left, smoke puffing from the screeching rear tires as the car lurched onto the sidewalk, narrowly missing a telephone pole before connecting squarely with a fire hydrant. The hydrant split the car's front end directly down the middle of the hood. More smoke oozed from the wrecked engine, spreading a thin, transparent fog across the neighborhood block.

Felix felt and heard his heart pounding in his ears. He hadn't even realized he'd been holding his breath, panting as he recovered.

Water erupted into the sky. It fell on the crashed car, the driver leaning head first into the steering wheel, not moving.

"Holy shit!" Felix cried, taking a step forward, then stopping. His basic instincts were to run over and help the driver get out of the car before it became flooded from the hydrant water. But in that moment, he understood that if he approached the vehicle, he'd be stuck as a witness for this chaotic accident.

Exactly what the past wants, he thought. There was someone on the sidewalk further down the block, where the car had come from, who could likely testify they had seen the car swerving across the road, but they didn't have the up-close look at its final resting place on the hydrant.

Homes lined the block, and one resident stepped out to see all the commotion. It was only a matter of time before more followed suit. Felix returned his attention to the car, the street now with a half-inch layer of water pooling across it, and looked at what he assumed was a dead body behind the wheel. The driver still hadn't moved despite the amplified white noise of water crashing onto the car's hood.

Dread ballooned inside Felix as he knew what he had to do. It was going to look cowardly, but he started running across the intersection, leaving the scene behind.

"Hey!" the man who had stepped onto his porch shouted. "Hey, stop!"

Felix kept his head forward, running at a brisk pace, the back of his mind so badly wanting to turn around to help. He didn't even look at the man through the corner of his eyes, hearing the terror in his voice.

"Hey!" the man insisted. "What happened?! You can't just leave the scene of a crime!"

It's not a crime. It's an accident.

Felix had to assure himself of this simple fact. It's not like an innocent bystander had been harmed. Just the driver, who could have been drunk or suicidal, for all Felix knew. Perhaps he could send in an anonymous letter to the police station explaining what he had witnessed. It wasn't his fault he had to run to learn the truth about a decades-old cold case.

The adrenaline remained steady throughout his body as he dashed through the neighborhood. The shouting man's voice had continued but faded into obscurity.

Sirens wailed in the distance, followed by flashing police lights coming from the direction Felix was running. The police cars were about two blocks down, probably a few hundred yards away from where the bank was about to get robbed.

Felix reached the next intersection and broke left. He ran halfway down the block, another quiet neighborhood minding its business. He still panted as his lungs tried to catch up from the excitement. Once he heard the cop cars zoom by behind him, he stopped to let out an exaggerated sigh of relief.

Good one, past, he thought, trying to brush aside the overwhelming fear he had just endured and refocus on the task at hand. He was still three blocks away from the bank and had to make up for lost time.

Felix checked his watch to find the setback had only cost him ten minutes, including the small detour he was now taking. The skyscraper stood tall in the distance, its cash-register-shaped roof seeming to pull Felix toward it, daring him to intervene with the past's disturbing plans.

He put his head down and ran the rest of the way.

Chapter 44

It was perhaps the longest thirty minutes of Arielle's life, waiting for Kennedy to step out and get in his truck. And she had once sat frozen in time during Commander Briar's mission to confront Chris Speidel.

At exactly 8:40, Jacob Kennedy reappeared in his doorway. This time he wasn't examining the lawn or taking in a lungful of fresh air. He went straight to his truck after closing the door behind him. No goodbye kiss to his wife, at least not from the doorway. He no longer moved with the casualness he had displayed all morning. He moved with purpose, taking shorter, confident steps toward his truck.

Kennedy sat down behind the wheel and fired up the engine within seconds.

This is it, Arielle thought, relieved all of her doubt was vanishing. She could see his thick mustache through her binoculars. The only things missing were the sunglasses and fedora.

Kennedy pulled out of the driveway and drove away from where Arielle sat at the other end of the block. She flipped her car around and circled around the block to find Kennedy turning right toward the eastbound Sixth Avenue on-ramp that would take him downtown.

Arielle felt no pressure to keep up with Kennedy as he drove—she already knew where he was going. And with how much time remained before the bank was to be robbed, she doubted he'd have time to stop anywhere else before. She kept the most distance she had compared to any of the other stalking during the mission. But Kennedy always remained in sight.

She expected little resistance from the past. Her tricks of masking her intentions weren't even needed, because she truly didn't know what she would end up doing once they arrived at the bank.

Every move, every decision felt so delicate. Like a child holding a newborn chick in the palm of their hand, terrified of crushing or dropping the fragile creature. Arielle felt this same sensation as she followed Kennedy across town for the next twenty minutes. Every touch on the brakes, every turn signal, every lane change were treated with an exaggerated caution.

It was easy. Kennedy drove as he had been—committing zero violations. When they exited the highway, arriving downtown, he even slowed down in anticipation of the light turning yellow. Traffic had been light, but enough cars had gathered at the stoplight for Arielle to remain six vehicles behind Kennedy. He had no angle of making eye contact with her from his position at the front of the line.

When the light turned green, he took his time proceeding forward, the tall buildings of the downtown skyline directly in front of them as they turned onto Lincoln Street.

Tension crept into Arielle's body, starting in her arms, forcing her to tighten her grip on the steering wheel. *This is really happening. We're two miles away from the bank. It's Kennedy.*

She felt an odd sense of glee. Perhaps relief. While the odds and little evidence they had found had all pointed to Kennedy as their main suspect, there had been plenty of doubt around that theory.

Each block they drove killed that doubt one piece at a time, until they finally arrived at the corner of Seventeenth and Sherman. Kennedy sat at the red light, his turn signal flashing on the left.

Arielle pulled over before turning onto Seventeenth, wanting to keep a safe distance behind Kennedy. Downtown was deserted, not another vehicle visible in their immediate vicinity. They were smothered in the shadows of the concrete jungle blocking the still-rising sun.

At 8:59, the traffic light flashed green and Kennedy turned left. Arielle crept forward, taking her time to reach the same light Kennedy had just left. In time-sensitive matters, she liked to keep a mental count of the passing seconds—because even one second could change the outcome of an entire mission.

She wanted thirty seconds between herself and Kennedy, so she didn't even touch the accelerator, letting the car coast up to the light at a mere five miles per hour. The light turned red, and she happily stopped, spotting Kennedy's truck parked on the curb right in front of the bank's main entrance. To the right, she saw Felix hustling down the sidewalk, stopping in front of the Last Drop's front doors. There were a handful of cars parked at the meters in front of the diner, the place bustling with a breakfast crowd full of families and fathers to kick off the day's festivities.

Felix saw Arielle and tossed his hands in the air in a *what-am-I-supposed-to-do* manner. Arielle rolled down her window and waved him over. He clasped his hands behind his head and stood tall, drawing in a deep breath before jogging toward the intersection. The light was about to turn green, but there was no one behind Arielle, so she waited for Felix, tossing her backpack into the rear to clear the passenger seat.

Felix reached the car and pulled open the door, huffing and puffing like he had just run a marathon. "You . . . will not believe . . . the morning I've had," he said between gasps for air.

"Shhh!" Arielle pressed her finger against her lips. "He's right there." She nodded to the left. "I'm not sure of the best place to park so we can still see him and he won't notice us."

"Why is he in front of the main doors? The robber didn't escape through there."

They sat through the green light and watched it turn yellow, then red again. Arielle hoped Kennedy wasn't noticing them sit through two green lights. Ideally, he had bigger things to worry about.

Arielle tapped the clock on the car's radio. It read 9:02. "He still has twelve minutes before he's set to call security from the freight elevator. Maybe he's going to pull up closer that way."

The entrance to the building's parking garage, where the freight elevator was, stood open halfway up the block on Sherman, between

Seventeenth and Eighteenth. Arielle could see where it normally had the drop-down fence was now a dark, open space. *He knew it would be open today.*

Arielle shook her head. Felix looked around. "Park in front of the diner," he said.

"But I won't be able to turn around and follow him up Sherman from there. Once I pass this light, I'd have to circle completely around the building to get back here. It's all one-way streets."

Felix rolled his eyes and stretched his hand to Arielle's shoulder. "If I can survive a near-death experience this morning, I think you can handle making an illegal U-turn to get back on Sherman. It's not exactly rush hour out here." He chuckled and leaned back in his seat, still breathing heavily.

"Excuse me. . . Near-death? What—"

Felix raised a finger. "We'll discuss it later. Kennedy's on the move."

Arielle swung her attention back to Kennedy's truck, now treading up the street toward the parking garage. The light turned green and Arielle drove forward, parking in the first spot on the corner of the intersection in front of the diner. She still had a clear view of Sherman Street and could see Kennedy's truck. The brake lights were on as he stopped in front of the parking garage entrance.

"It's 9:10, and he still isn't making a move," Arielle said, brow scrunching while she gazed out the window.

"9:14 is the time of the first call to security, right?"

"Correct."

The brake lights flicked off, and the truck rocked as if Kennedy had put it into park.

"Who's that?" Felix asked, leaning over the center console to watch over Arielle's shoulder.

Arielle didn't know what he was talking about at first, then noticed a figure walking down the sidewalk toward Kennedy's truck. She reached back into her bag and whipped out the binoculars. "It's the robber!" she gasped. "I don't understand."

She saw a man dressed in a fedora and sunglasses, a thick mustache above his lip. He looked a lot like Kennedy. Granted, the disguise left plenty to the imagination. The mustache was Kennedy's signature, yet Kennedy remained behind the wheel.

The man hustled and made no eye contact with Kennedy's truck before turning into the parking garage. Just as he did, the truck came back to life and veered off, turning right on Eighteenth Street and out of sight from Arielle and Felix.

"What the *hell* is going on?" Arielle asked. "Who do we follow?"

"Well, we can't exactly follow the robber. He's on his way—it's too late."

Arielle knew this, but that voice in her inner psyche screamed at her to disrupt the robber before he lay a finger on the intercom. "Hang on," she said, throwing the car into reverse and peeling backwards to face northbound on Sherman Street.

In one swift motion, she flung the gear into drive and floored the accelerator. The move might have been exaggerated, considering she came right back to a screeching halt after a half block, but the adrenaline was overflowing her senses.

When they came to their stop outside of the garage entrance, Arielle noticed Felix's hand white-knuckling the grab handle above his head, legs fully extended as if he had been slamming on an imaginary giant brake pedal. The little color he normally had in his face had vanished, his lips pressed tightly into a ghastly paleness.

Arielle craned her neck to see Kennedy around the corner, but he remained out of sight. She had a second to decide what benefited the mission more: tailing Kennedy or the robber.

"Felix, snap out of it!" Arielle slapped her friend square in the chest.

He jolted back to focus. Whatever had happened to him earlier clearly had some lingering effects. He looked down at his locked knees and pushed his shins down to force a bend in the legs. "I think Kennedy is the getaway driver," he said in a distant tone. Felix might not have appeared fully there, but even through the tension, his mind remained focused on the mission, putting together all the pieces of this troubling puzzle.

Arielle agreed. It explained Kennedy disappearing around the corner and not approaching the garage entrance. "Young's at home, right?"

The clock showed 9:12. They had less than two minutes to decide their next move.

"I can't say if he's still home right now, but he's not here. I know that much. He still wasn't out of bed when I left."

"So who the hell just walked into the garage?"

Felix shrugged.

9:13.

Arielle opened her door, stepping one foot out before Felix grabbed her arm. "What are you doing?!"

"I have to. I can't just sit here and hope Selena gets a better view than us. I need to at least try."

She could feel Felix's hand trembling beneath his tight grip. He held her arm like a scared child not wanting to let their parent go. And he surely didn't want to be left alone outside of an unfolding bank robbery.

Arielle looked at the clock, knowing only seconds stood between the robber's finger and the call button that would change everything. "I have to do this."

Felix's grip weakened. He nodded, staring absently toward the floor. "Just keep a safe distance."

"Of course." Arielle stepped all the way out and closed the door behind her. Downtown was eerily silent, the air still. Somewhere around the corner, Jacob Kennedy waited in his truck. That no longer seemed like a priority now that she took silent steps toward the garage entrance.

The clock struck 9:14 in her mind as she entered the garage, the disguised robber just having pressed the call button.

Everything was right on schedule.

Chapter 45

About forty feet remained between Arielle and the robber. He had his back to her, a long jacket swaying to his knees. The fedora was parked so low on his head that she couldn't quite make out the color of his hair. The lighting in the garage wasn't the best, either, adding to her difficulties.

She crept toward the first parked car she saw and crouched behind the rear wheel. The robber wouldn't see her if he turned around, but the garage was quiet enough to hear his echoing voice as he spoke into the call box.

"Hello," the robber said, his voice unrecognizable. It sounded as if it were being disguised. Like someone younger was trying to sound older by deepening their tone. "This is Robert Caldwell. I've lost my keycard and need to get up to my office. Will you be able to let me in?"

Arielle nodded, satisfied she could hear everything. Robert Caldwell was the bank's vice president. Even during Kennedy's trial, they mentioned the robber had used this alias to gain entrance. So far, everything was on track with how it had originally played out. Their tampering with the past had changed nothing.

"Good morning, Mr. Caldwell," a voice crackled from the intercom. "We're sorry to hear that. We'll be right there to let you in. Should be about one minute."

"Thank you," the robber replied, taking a step back and swaying from side to side while waiting.

The urge to sprint forward and take him down had reached its peak. If only this mission hadn't proven so difficult up to this point, Arielle just might have done it. Her inner motivator had given way to another voice telling her it was a bad idea. There was simply too much ground to cover to hope the robber wouldn't turn around and see her.

Instead, she pulled out her gun, cocked it, and waited.

The guard coming down the elevator would be Bill McDowell. If Arielle didn't stop this from proceeding, Bill would be dead within the next two minutes.

She lined up a shot and pulled the trigger.

The gun made a faint clicking sound, but nothing else happened. Arielle clenched her jaw, half expecting this to happen. It wouldn't be the first time the past had conveniently jammed her gun, and it wouldn't be the last. Changing the past could never be that simple.

The elevator chimed, its doors parting to show a relaxed Bill McDowell with a coffee cup in hand, face scrunching in confusion when he first saw the man standing outside the elevator.

Arielle hadn't noticed from her angle, but the robber had already pulled out his gun and extended it toward McDowell.

The security guard dropped his coffee cup, the hot liquid splattering across the elevator floor, as he whipped his hand to the baton handle on his security belt.

"Don't even *fucking* think about it!" the robber shouted. "Swing that thing and I'll blast your brains all over this elevator."

McDowell obliged, dropping the baton and raising his open hands above his head.

"Better," the robber said, looking over his shoulder and making direct eye contact with Arielle Lucila through his sunglasses. She had no way of knowing his expression behind the disguise, but he suddenly shoved McDowell toward the back of the elevator and hurried inside.

"Stop!" Arielle shouted, stepping out from behind the car. Her hands flailed to her utility belt, grasping one of her throwing knives.

The robber frantically pushed the button to close the elevator doors, and they took their time gliding shut. Arielle flung the knife, watching it clang against the steel elevator doors, the black sunglasses watching her through the crack just before they shut.

She raced to the elevator, sure to pick up her knife.

A muffled bang rang out from the other side of the door, and she knew Bill McDowell was now the first victim.

"Fuck!" Arielle screamed, punching the elevator door. She had waited perhaps two seconds too long, assuming her knife would have even landed successfully on the robber. She clenched her fists, fighting every urge to press the call button to alert the rest of the security team of what was unfolding. But she had already decided beforehand that would be the wrong decision. Doing so would likely lead to the police getting called already, leaving Selena trapped inside where they would soon sweep the building.

After one more punch on the elevator's doors, Arielle spun around and fled the scene. Felix remained in the car, leaning out the passenger-side window, gawking toward the garage entrance.

Arielle ran to him. "He's in."

"Did you see who it was?" Felix asked, his eyes studying Arielle for any clue.

Arielle pursed her lips and shook her head. "No one I could recognize through the disguise. It's *not* Young or Kennedy—that much we know."

"What do we do?"

Arielle placed her hands on her hips and looked to the clear skies. "I have no idea. We can't exactly get into the building at this point. That elevator was our only way in."

"So we just sit here and wait for Selena to come out? Does she even know which side of the building we're on?"

"I told her where we'd be. She's going to take the stairwell that comes out next to the freight elevator—no keycards needed for her to exit."

"Can we not get that door pried open?"

"You want to pry open a door during a bank robbery? You're smarter than that, Felix."

Arielle learned that Felix's mind worked in overdrive and could some-times overlook common sense.

He leaned back. "So we sit and wait. Welcome to my world."

As much as Arielle hated hearing it, he was right. All other options had vanished as soon as those elevator doors closed. Whether that was bad timing or an act of the past, she'd never know. It was a moment that would haunt her over the next few weeks as she digested the happenings of the mission.

Defeated, Arielle circled the car and returned to her seat behind the wheel, where the helplessness would eat at her for the next fifteen minutes.

"It all comes down to Selena."

Chapter 46

Selena had been glued to the storage room's door from the moment her watch struck nine o'clock. She needed to know all movements that had taken place in the minutes leading up to the robbery.

When Bill McDowell had meandered by, on his way to the elevator, Selena felt a gnawing in the depths of her soul. Watching a man go unknowingly to his death was not something she was used to. Much like Felix, she typically did her work before the day of a crime—or she at least had no reason to be present during the act.

Even her involvement in their prior mission working together didn't involve her coming this close to the action. She and Felix had the luxury of watching Arielle take care of business from a distance.

Seeing McDowell sparked feelings she had never faced before. While most missions involved a death, she had never gone through seeing it all play out.

Only days ago she was at the diner chatting with McDowell, getting to know the kind and decent human being he was. Before that, he had welcomed her with open arms into the security office when she had lied about needing to clean their space. He was a trusting man who saw the best in people.

As he took his final walk to the elevator, she knew with confidence that he believed the bank's vice president really was outside and had forgotten his keycard. He hadn't once considered a potential threat waiting for him outside. If he had, he wouldn't have moved with a calming casualness down the hallway.

Even as a spectator, Selena felt like everything was going to be alright. And that was all thanks to McDowell's presence, despite what lied ahead for his own fate.

In the seconds she had to process all these thoughts, and her personal tug-o-war of jumping out of the room or not, she understood just what made Arielle stick out from the rest. With enough practice anyone could elevate their skills of driving, shooting, and even espionage to match Arielle's level. It was her decision making that separated her from the pack.

Every mission was a series of decisions that needed to be made, based on the information available, while also factoring how the past might play into the equation.

Selena had nowhere near the knowledge of the past and its stubbornness as Arielle, but she suspected if she had leapt out of the storage room to stop McDowell from continuing to his death, there would certainly be hell to pay.

She further understood Arielle's unbreakable discipline. Any person with a normally functioning conscience would justify jumping out and stopping an innocent man from his brutal murder. But that was why the Road Runners didn't recruit the average Joe off the street. Knowledge and discipline was the combination they looked for in recruits. Anyone with those two intangible skills could be groomed for any role the organization desired.

Now, in the thick of the most critical moment of the mission, Selena had to dig deep within herself to tap into that same discipline. It was unlike anything she had emotionally experienced before in her life.

Dedication can often be confused with discipline. Staying up late to cram in a study session while friends were out partying on a Friday night was dedication. Forcing herself to *not* stop McDowell—something she believed was absolutely the right thing to do—was a level of discipline she hoped to never face again. The mission was bigger than herself and her personal desires.

Making that type of decision was sick. And wrong. And flat-out excruciating.

But once McDowell passed, and she realized she couldn't undo her decision, she could move forward with the next phase of the mission: waiting once more.

McDowell left, which only meant the robber would return minutes later.

Selena mentally prepared for the moment. Spending the last seventeen hours in solitude left her on an island of wonder. The lack of communication had proven troublesome. It was entirely possible that Arielle and Felix had already figured everything out, but they had no way of relaying that information to Selena within the building. They had floated the idea of Selena carrying a radio, but they all agreed the risk outweighed the reward. If one wandering security guard heard the crackle of a radio, all plans would collapse within moments.

All she could trust was they hadn't solved the mystery yet, and she needed to follow through with her task. Identify the robber and get the hell out. Don't wait around for the fireworks to begin. She knew the exact route she needed to take out of the building.

Her job was easy, yet extremely difficult at the same time. Selena hadn't anticipated all the added stress that had already presented itself. And she only hoped more wouldn't come once the robber started his journey down the hallway. She had plenty of doubt.

Her heart started beating faster than its normal pace, and she leaned into the meditation practices she had long mastered to attempt getting it back under control. It was 9:19 according to her watch, and she had expected the robber to appear at any second.

Perhaps Arielle and Felix had prevented any of it from unfolding. Despite what the mission report called for, she knew Arielle was incapable of resisting the urge to stop the robbery from happening. And knowing Arielle, she just might have pulled it off.

All that hope vanished, however, when Selena heard the distant chime of the elevator doors parting at the far end of the hallway. Every muscle in her body tightened, her breath held in an overwhelmingly anxious anticipation.

The world fell still and silent, and she focused her hearing on the approaching footsteps.

Who am I kidding? she thought. *I'm not Arielle. I don't know what I'm listening for. A footstep is a footstep.*

Arielle likely could tell the height and weight of a person by the simple sound of their footsteps.

That didn't stop Selena from at least trying. The footsteps sounded heavy. They already knew the robber was a man. So that's what she envisioned while listening. She tried to keep Kennedy and Young out of her thoughts, wanting as neutral of an eye as she could have. The robber would be in full disguise, and she'd have a second, maybe two, to process everything through the sliver of the cracked-open door.

Over the past week, she had counted the amount of steps from the elevator to the storage room multiple times. Arielle had offered her this tip to anticipate exactly when the robber might appear. That decision was paying off huge dividends.

She had run this experiment using different strides each time, not knowing how long of a step the robber had. She found a range of twenty-eight to thirty-six steps.

The robber had already taken sixteen since she heard the elevator doors open, give or take a couple. The steps neither slow nor fast.

By the twenty-fifth step, Selena crouched, sure to remain below the robber's line of vision should he glance toward the door. What she saw froze her blood.

It can't be, she thought.

The robber wore the attire she had expected: sunglasses, fedora. And the mustache.

Only the mustache didn't look real. Even in those few seconds, she clearly saw it was slightly off-center, like an amateur makeup artist had glued it on.

The mustache, however, was only a distraction. She immediately recognized the robber's body. Tall, yes, but slightly slender. Way too thin to pass as Young or Kennedy. What stood out the clearest was his chin, the only part of his face she could truly see.

She had stared at that face for hours not too many days ago. And the chin connected with a chiseled jawline she found rather irresistible.

It can't be.

Once those two seconds passed, she could only see the back of the robber, and that only made things worse. She knew, without a doubt, the man behind the disguise was Brian Dawkins.

Just days ago she had plotted out a complex plan to continue a potential relationship with the young security guard from California. Now her body broke into gooseflesh. The idea she had even sat with him through a whole dinner made her sick to her stomach.

Selena had actually suspected Dawkins had some minimal involvement after their dinner. He had freely admitted he wouldn't be working during the robbery, and that alone had propelled him as a suspect in her eyes. All the chatter he had offered about how the guards discussed the ease of robbing the bank had turned the dials for her to consider it all a team effort.

Now she dreaded she hadn't shared these thoughts with Arielle and Felix. Compared to them, she felt intellectually out of place. She doubted herself, didn't trust her own instincts. All out of fear of being wrong.

With this revelation, Selena felt a weight of responsibility for letting it all reach this point. She should have trusted her gut. Maybe she could have veered Dawkins off the path that led him to breaking into his own bank and murdering four of his colleagues. She had long considered herself a sound judge of character, but knowing a cold-blooded killer had slipped right through her filters made her doubt everything she knew.

Selena picked up her backpack and slung it over her shoulders. It was time to leave and never look back.

Dawkins was no longer in her line of sight through the cracked door, so she pulled it open all the way, staying low to catch the paint stirrers before they clanged to the ground. She stuffed them into her back pocket, not wanting to leave anything behind that had her fingerprints on it, and stepped out to the hallway.

She let the door glide shut, bracing it with her arm so the latch clicked as faintly as possible. It was quiet enough, and Dawkins continued down the hall where he'd soon enter the guardroom and shoot the poor souls who had no idea what was coming.

I can't just sit here and let him do it. This is all my fault.

She knew it wasn't what the mission called for. Nor was it necessarily the smartest thing to do, but the guilt was already eating at her, and she needed to rein it in as best she could.

Selena dashed toward the elevator, not caring how loud her footsteps might have been. The forty steps between her and the elevator dissipated in seconds. The door to the stairwell stood immediately next to the elevators.

She pushed open the door and spun around to hold it open with her back, and shouted down the hall.

"Dawkins!"

The robber froze and pivoted in a swift motion.

Selena would never see the emotion swimming behind those sunglasses, but she could only imagine how startled he must have been. He said nothing, didn't move, and they had a stare down that felt like several minutes, despite only being a few seconds.

"Don't do it!" Selena shouted, her words echoing down the empty hallway, bouncing all around them. She saw the gun in his hand, but it never wavered. He wouldn't dare harm Selena. Would he?

"Hey!" a voice hollered from the far end.

A guard had stepped out of the office, baton elevated as he charged toward Dawkins.

If only Selena had called out Dawkins's name later, she might have saved the guard's life.

Instead, Dawkins swiveled around and promptly shot the guard square in his forehead. The guard went from a crouched, running position to looking like someone had electrocuted him, limbs jolting out in every direction. The baton flew from his grip and clattered on the ground, rolling in a circle before coming to a complete stop a few feet from the security office door.

Oh my God! Selena thought. *I just changed the past.*

And she had.

Two guards were supposed to have been killed in the security office, while a third would later enter, oblivious, and also get shot in the open doorway. Now, a guard lay dead in the middle of the hallway, and Dawkins broke into a sprint toward the security room.

Before he reached it, the other guard who had been inside stepped out. Dawkins lunged toward him, whipping him across the face with his gun to send him spiraling to the ground. Once down, Dawkins hovered over him and shot him twice in the back.

The guard lay lifeless as Dawkins entered the security office, its door unable to close shut as it rested against the dead man's splayed out feet.

Selena's legs locked. She had never seen someone get murdered, and she had just witnessed two within seconds of each other. She knew Dawkins entered the guardroom to strip away all evidence. But she wondered if he would still go through the same process once he knew someone had seen him. And not just anyone, but Selena, who knew exactly who he was.

Selena debated following him down the hallway, only because she couldn't help but wonder if the changes she had just made in the past would cause Dawkins to kill all of the employees in the vault. Originally, he had not, sparing six lives while he robbed the vault. Why, they never understood, and Selena hoped that would still be the case.

Dawkins was rattled, however, and sure to lash out by any means necessary to spare himself being caught and arrested. Selena thought she might vomit, the mixture of death and guilt becoming too much for her to handle.

Run, the voice in her mind pleaded. *Run before you get sucked into this. Run before you become a suspect. Run before it's too late.*

Once more fighting her own will, Selena turned and dashed up the stairwell. Her hurried footsteps echoed, the door closing shut with an aggressive bang that made Selena squeal. She tripped twice on her way up the stairs, legs shaking out of control as they had turned to Jell-O.

She caught herself both times, hands clutching the steps ahead to keep her face from slamming into them. By the time she reached the top landing and flung open the door to the parking garage, Selena was nearly hyperventilating.

The cool air of the outdoors, albeit dank within the garage, injected Selena with rays of hope. She was free from the storage room.

She hadn't realized how bothersome the isolation had been until she took that first step outside. Death had been on her mind plenty during her stay in the basement, and she couldn't help but wonder if she would spend her final moments staring at its gray ceiling.

She had a new sense of life and hope, plus a greater appreciation for her work as an Angel Runner. It wasn't the great Arielle Lucila, or even the brilliant Felix Francisco, who had learned who the killer was. It was Selena Nicole. The vibrant actress-turned-Angel who had no faith in herself to perform at the highest level for her secret organization.

All the self-doubt that had brewed over the past decade of her life had taken a huge blow today. Selena smiled, proud of herself—something she couldn't recall having ever felt.

She looked around the parking garage, saw no one, and let the door close behind her. There was no going back into the building to stop whatever mayhem might unfold, and she had to be okay with that.

Selena bolted out of the garage to search for Arielle and Felix.

Chapter 47

Arielle sat like a statue behind the wheel, refusing to break her gaze from the garage. Every second that Selena hadn't appeared made Arielle grow a little more nauseous.

She had been beating herself up ever since returning to the car, and now wondered if her actions changed how everything was playing out inside. It was possible Selena was in danger because of Arielle's actions, but she had no way of knowing. All she could do was trust the past to keep things as close to the same trajectory as the Original timeline.

Hearing the gunshot blast that killed McDowell was both a tough blow to take, but also relieving. McDowell was supposed to die in that elevator, so everything had remained in place up to that point. Arielle might have been more worried had she not heard the weapon discharge.

Felix had been rambling about all the facts they had come across during the last two weeks, trying to make sense of who the killer could be if it wasn't Kennedy or Young. He ran through every name of the security guards who worked in the bank. He had even entertained the idea that Kennedy was working with someone else on the outside. Young covered matters from the inside, Kennedy was the mastermind (and getaway driver), while a third-party had been hired to do the dirty work. The actual robber could have been anyone, in that case, and they were only hurting their cause by assuming it was someone who worked inside the bank.

His voice droned into the background for Arielle. She had given up trying to identify the robber through the little evidence they had. If it had been that easy, they wouldn't be sitting outside the bank while murders occurred just inside.

No, she wouldn't dwell anymore on what they could have done differently, or who the robber was. That ship had sailed.

The elevator ride from the garage to the basement only took thirty seconds, according to Selena. To walk from the elevator door to the security office was roughly another forty-five seconds, possibly a minute if the robber was taking his sweet time.

Selena was to exit the storage room once the robber entered the guardroom.

That was all she needed to do. The whole thing should have taken less than two minutes once the robber descended in the elevator.

When the clock struck 9:21, five minutes had passed, and Arielle could only assume things were not playing out as they had originally.

There was still no reason to believe Selena was in any true danger. She was hidden, out of sight from the robber. Even if the other guards on duty had somehow realized what was playing out and confronted the robber at the elevator, Selena would still be safe within the confines of the storage room.

Maybe she's just needing to wait it out a little longer than planned.

By 9:23, Arielle fought the urge to find any way she could to get inside the building, no matter how reckless of a decision that might be.

That's when Selena spilled out of the garage, head spinning around frantically in every direction. Felix finally stopped talking and stuck his hand out the window, waving it silently.

Selena scanned over the car twice before seeing Felix, and dashed toward them, practically jumping into the back seat.

"We need to get out of here!" Selena wheezed through sharp gasps for breath. "GO!"

Arielle fired up the engine and sped away, no questions asked. They reached the end of the Lincoln block, screeching to stop at the red light. She looked right, as was Felix, and they both spotted Kennedy sitting in his truck further down Eighteenth Avenue.

"He's right there!" Felix cried.

Arielle looked both directions. She could only turn left onto Eighteenth, as it was a one-way street that ran east to west. Kennedy was parked facing them, the correct direction. Not seeing any cars, she floored the accelerator and blazed through the red light, flying up Lincoln and taking a sharp right on Nineteenth Avenue. Selena tumbled around the backseat like a bowling ball, banging on one door before being flung to the other.

Nineteenth allowed two-way traffic, and Arielle blew by the couple cars present as she approached Sherman Street, again turning hard enough to flip the vehicle, had it been an SUV. Sherman was clear, so she gunned the car to return to Eighteenth in record time. Kennedy remained parked in his same spot as she approached the intersection.

The block between Sherman and Lincoln was less than three-hundred feet, and Kennedy was parked at the midpoint. Arielle turned the car onto Eighteenth and pulled over immediately, staying roughly one-hundred feet behind Kennedy. They were certainly close enough to be noticed by Kennedy, but he didn't appear to pay them any attention.

"Okay," Arielle said, as if she had just completed a menial task. "Tell us what happened in there."

Selena recapped the uneventful night, sure to mention the guard who had seen her upon arrival.

"Is he going to remember your face?" Arielle asked.

"Hell if I know. He looked straight at me, but didn't really stare at me, if that makes sense."

"Shit. The police will seek anyone who was in the building over the weekend. If this guard mentions seeing you, it's going to make you a suspect. They'll find out easily enough that you weren't supposed to be there."

"Well, the good news out of all this is that we can leave. Dawkins is the robber."

Selena said this in an almost uninterested tone.

Felix spun around in his seat to face Selena. "Dawkins?! Are you certain?"

Selena nodded. "The one person I ended up spending the most time with on this mission. I could tell it was him, even through the disguise. I called out his name." She lowered her head as if ashamed to admit this.

"You *what?!*" Arielle spun around, taking her eyes off Kennedy's truck. "You tinkered with the past by doing that."

Selena nodded, keeping her head low. "I know," she whispered. "I shouldn't have done that. But I had to be certain, you know? What if I was wrong?"

"You can still be wrong," Arielle said. "I'm sure he turned around not because of the name you said, but because you said anything at all. Selena, what happened?"

She finally looked up, shaking her head, tears welling on the surface of her eyes. "The other guard came out of the office. Dawkins shot him. Then he shot the other. I left before seeing what would happen to the fourth."

"Holy shit," Arielle said, turning back forward and rubbing the sides of her head. "Okay. We're okay. Right?"

Arielle knew she wouldn't have botched this part of the mission had she been the one inside the bank. But was it truly a mistake? Selena discovered the robber's identity—that was the goal. But Arielle would have saved as many lives as she could, given the opportunity.

The robber, presumed to be Dawkins, appeared at the far end of the block ahead of them. He had run to the corner of the intersection, looking from left to right until he saw Kennedy's truck. The sunglasses, fedora, and mustache all remained.

Arielle saw him, but Felix was the one who shouted, "There he is!"

All eyes in the car narrowed on Dawkins, scampering down the sidewalk like a panicked zombie.

"He doesn't have a bag of money," Arielle said, pulling up her binoculars for a better look. Now that she had Dawkins in her mind, she could definitely see the resemblance on the little she could see of the bottom half of his face.

"Where's the money?" Felix asked, squinting as Dawkins had run into the street, making a direct line for Kennedy's truck. "It's supposed to be in a large black bag, right?"

Dawkins had nothing but the clothes on his back, and presumably a gun hidden somewhere within the layers.

"It's not there," Selena said, a hint of relief slipping into her voice.

"So, the robbery didn't happen?" Felix asked.

Dawkins reached Kennedy's truck and leaped into the passenger seat. Kennedy sped away immediately. Arielle dropped her hand onto the gear, but didn't move further.

"What are you doing?" Felix asked, urgency clinging to every word. "Aren't we going to follow them?"

Police sirens wailed in the distance.

"No," Arielle said. "We're not."

"What?!" Felix and Selena cried in harmony.

"The mission is done," Arielle said, still refusing to move the car. "We got what we needed. There's nothing more we *need* to do. Trust me, I'd love to follow those two wherever they're going, and beat the shit out of them. But what does that accomplish? It only gets us further tangled in this mess—and this has been a *messy* mission. I had my chance to stop it all, and that failed. The dead are already dead. Nothing we can change about that. Let's stop while we're ahead. When anyone looks back to this mission, all they'll see is that we accomplished what was asked. A success."

"We can't just leave without knowing what happened in there," Selena said.

"I agree. Let's head back to the apartment to get our things, and we can watch the news. It shouldn't take long for this to become a breaking story. I'd say as long as we leave the apartment by noon, we shouldn't have anything to worry about. Can we all agree on that?"

"You really don't want to know where Kennedy and Dawkins are going?" Felix asked, his mouth still agape from amazement.

"Sure, but it's not worth putting us at risk. We know they're *not* going to that hole he dug in the mountains—they have no money to hide. They're probably just going somewhere to get cleaned up and hideout for the rest of the day. Dawkins is about to be wanted for at least three murders."

Arielle finally moved the car into gear and drove forward, the sirens growing louder as they approached the building. She circled the block once more to get back east, leaving the Cash Register Building in the rear-view mirror.

Chapter 48

They practically barged into their apartment, Arielle and Selena rolling their eyes while Felix struggled with the key getting the door unlocked.

"Put the TV on!" Selena commanded as soon they stepped inside.

The suitcases had already been lined up neatly next to the kitchen table, courtesy of Felix. He hurried to the TV, which he couldn't recall having been turned on at all during this mission, and pressed the power button. It turned on to Channel Four; the feed distorted. Felix adjusted the antennas above the box until it showed a clear image of two news anchors, a man and woman, with sorrow splayed across their faces. A headline flashed across the bottom: *BREAKING NEWS: FOUR DEAD IN ATTEMPTED ROBBERY AT UNITED BANK.*

"Four dead," Arielle said, crossing her arms as she stood in front of the TV, mesmerized.

Selena watched her, worried Arielle might still hang on to the fact that she had shouted Dawkins's name.

The woman anchor spoke in a concerned tone. "We've just been informed that three of the deceased were security guards for the building. The fourth was a bank employee. There was a small group of employees there to count and sort money that had arrived earlier this morning, something they did every two Sundays. The rest survived, along with a fourth guard who heard the gunfire and immediately phoned the police. The security company had revoked the possession of firearms from their guards a year ago."

"They haven't said anything about missing money," Felix said, stroking his chin.

"The money isn't important," Arielle said. "The same amount of lives were lost."

"Don't sound so down about it," Selena said. "Like you've said, our goal was never to stop the murders. Unfortunately, we have the same amount of victims. On the flip side, it won't become a cold case. We know Dawkins was behind that disguise. What do we do now with that information?"

Arielle turned the volume down on the TV, standing in front of it as she faced Felix and Selena. "We don't have to do anything. We'll hand over our findings to HQ, and they'll take it from there. I'd assume they'll have someone from this era worry about finding the best way to deliver that information to the authorities. But you're right, Selena. Justice will be served to all three men involved. Kennedy, Young, Dawkins. They're toast. Possibly even other guards who could have been involved—we don't know."

"I can't wait to read the Futures Report on this one," Felix said, his eyes still drawn to the TV that was showing different pictures of the interior and exterior of the United Bank.

"I wish we could know how Dawkins originally did it," Selena added. "How did he get away with it forever? How come his name was *never* mentioned in any of the investigation?"

"I'm surprised Kennedy never outed him," Arielle said. "They could have sentenced Kennedy to death had the trial played out differently. And he, what, followed some code of not ratting out his accomplice?"

"He had to have felt very confident about the lack of evidence in the trial," Felix said. "I looked through those trial notes. The prosecution's case was suspect. A real stretch of the imagination."

"It's not like Kennedy was innocent," Arielle argued. "Can't exactly say the prosecution was far off—they just had the guy running everything behind the scenes, not the one who pulled the trigger."

"Could Kennedy have planned to be found not guilty to get money?" Selena asked.

"I don't think you get compensated for time in jail," Arielle said.

Selena shook her head. "Not money from the state. Money from everything that probably followed the trial. Think about it. You stand trial for one of the biggest crimes in Denver history. You're found not guilty and released. You don't think people are going to throw whatever they can at you for an interview? Something like this can turn you into a local celebrity—if not more. If Kennedy was smart enough to plan this whole thing and not get caught, then I'm sure he was smart enough to think this through before throwing Dawkins under the bus. Kennedy had some serious debt and needed a way out. The money was never found originally. Maybe Dawkins ran off with all of it, never to be heard from again. Kennedy still could have understood the opportunities that awaited after an acquittal."

"That seems like such a huge risk for something that wasn't guaranteed. He couldn't know for sure how the trial would go. And if his idea failed, he faced death. I can't think of a reasonable person who would literally risk their life for a few thousand dollars."

"Reasonable people don't orchestrate bank robberies."

"You guys are arguing about nothing," Felix interrupted. "Look."

He nodded to the TV that showed a police officer speaking in front of the bank. Arielle turned around and raised the volume.

"We believe this was an inside job," the officer said. "It was all very calculated. The perpetrator knew exactly where he was going. Took the videotapes from the security room, ripped pages out of the security log book, and exited the building without any hesitation. We have not discovered any money missing, although we believe it was intended to be a robbery. The employees working in the vault heard gunfire and immediately hid the money they were counting. Five of them hid in a mantrap, but the sixth remained in the vault. The perpetrator shot this employee and escaped without any cash."

"See, Selena," Felix said. "You did make a positive impact. The gunshots occurred in the hallway because of you. You alerted those employees. Now, you couldn't control what happened after that, but you gave them an opportunity to get to safety. Be proud of what you accomplished."

Arielle nodded silently, Selena waiting for her potential praise. But none came. Instead, she turned the TV off. "I've told you both I have no interest in the Futures Reports, or seeing how things turned out. I'll admit, I had plenty of curiosity, and that's why we watched the news. But this mission is over, and I need you to trust me. I've played this game before. Selena, you're probably going to dwell over these murders for the next few weeks. You'll feed yourself a ton of guilt because four murders still happened. This is not healthy for you. I suggest you remove this mission from your memory as soon as possible. Start preparing for whatever the next one is. Are you satisfied with how this all turned out?"

"Yes."

"Good, then just leave it at that. With all the resources we have as an organization, not enough care and attention are given to our mental health. Especially us Angels. We witness death, evil. We experience the most drastic swings of emotions: hope, doubt, fear, guilt. If I can be open, I'm feeling a little of all that right now. It's impossible to reasonably process it all."

"But we accomplished what we needed," Selena said. "Why such a range of emotions?"

"It's not so black and white. I've seen Angels go into some dark depressions, even after a successful mission. The problem with what we do is that there is always something we look back on and think we could have done better. Obviously with this mission, we'd have loved to save all the lives lost. We could have, had we known Dawkins was our guy from the beginning."

"You can say that again." Selena still wasn't ready to admit to her team that she had suspected him for some time, and if being honest with herself, wasn't sure she ever would. Perhaps that was exactly the type of negative dwelling that led to mental health issues for Angels.

"All I'm saying is to not overlook how much these missions can eat at you." Arielle strolled away from the TV and grabbed her suitcase, pulling it toward the apartment door. "We face a dark road after each mission, and I'm so glad to have you both in my life to vent to about it. I've always gone into these strange moods in the few days between missions where I feel kind of empty. Unfulfilled. I haven't been able to put a finger on it until recently, and now that we all have each other as a tight-knit team, I encourage we all openly share our feelings to prevent any dark thoughts."

"What are you saying?" Felix asked. "Dark thoughts? Like suicide?"

Arielle shook her head. "No, not to that extreme. But I can totally see how people fall into that. For me, it's been more like thoughts of running away. Hiding from the world. Sometimes I wish I could hit the restart button on my life and do it all over again. I still have a lot of emotional scars I'm dealing with. Between losing my family and the love of my life . . ."

Selena crossed the room and threw her arms around Arielle, who was crying. "You don't need to hold anything in."

The scene unfolding in their borrowed apartment was becoming rather intense for Selena. She had come from a family who refused to show emotion, so she'd always thought that was just how people were. She expected nothing different from the most intimidating figure in their time travel universe, but over their last two missions working together, Selena had learned that emotions were far more complex than she ever understood.

She had always seen Arielle as a confident, powerful woman who had it all. Ask anyone within the Road Runners and they would likely all share the same opinion. Arielle sat on a pedestal. She set the bar others tried to reach. But now, getting to know the person—the human—behind the façade of power and greatness, Selena saw a strong but insecure person dealing with trauma that might never stop haunting her. Yet, Arielle still powered through it all with grace and an unwavering will for the success that had built up her image over the years.

Tears rolled down Arielle's cheeks as she stepped out of Selena's embrace. "I've always prided myself on being a loner. Completely independent. I didn't need help from anyone for anything. Losing everyone important in your life will have that effect. I figured I was meant to be alone in this world.

"I had long given up hope of finding anyone I could trust. Be vulnerable with. But it's you two. And I'm never letting you go."

Felix and Selena exchanged a look once Arielle's head hung low, and both encircled her, each grabbing an arm. "Are you saying we're friends?" Felix asked, causing a muffled laugh through tears from Arielle.

"I'm so impressed with you both," Arielle said, regaining her composure. "And you're not just phenomenal at your work, you're incredible human beings. You two carried this mission. You both risked so much to see this through, all while I was wasting my time following Kennedy's every move. Selena, why didn't you tell us you thought Dawkins was involved?"

The question caught Selena completely off guard, and she felt her face flush. "H-how did you know?"

Arielle cracked a grin, wiping away the tears with her sleeve. "I piece things together. Even when it seems like I'm doing nothing, like those brutal days spent outside of Kennedy's house, I'm always thinking. I think about everything. It was clear you had taken an interest in Dawkins, but I wasn't sure why. Possibly romantic, but unlikely. Maybe it was because he was one of the few people who actually spoke to you at the office. I don't know. But after you went on that date with him, I started piecing it together. You didn't have much to say that night. I could tell you were hiding something. Then yesterday, when I saw that California plate outside of Kennedy's house, it all made sense. I still didn't know how much to believe, so I wanted to see it play out."

"Play out?" Selena asked, her jaw remaining open for a few seconds. "What if I got hurt?"

"I trusted you. I had complete faith in you to follow your hunch and see it through. And you were right. I still don't know why you kept it a secret, and I don't expect an explanation. But next time, share your thoughts—they matter."

Selena's face remained red, but relief flooded through her just the same.

"Well, that was a lot to unpack in the last few minutes," Felix said. "We should probably get going. We have a date at D'Corazon. If I recall correctly, we deemed it as a post-mission ritual now."

"You mean margarita time?" Selena teased. "Absolutely."

They all grabbed their suitcases and lugged them out the door, leaving the 1991 apartment behind forever.

Chapter 49

Instead of risking a trip across town amid an attempted bank robbery, they opted to step outside the apartment building where they waited for complete isolation before taking their swigs of Juice and jumping forward to 2022.

The apartment complex remained behind them, a whole new facelift given to it in the thirty years that had passed. Peter Young was long gone.

"This walk kind of sucked last time," Selena said. "We can call a Lyft to give us a ride."

She wasted no time powering her cell phone back on after it had been a useless piece of plastic for the last two weeks. She licked her lips like a ravenous dog in anxious anticipation as the screen flashed on.

Felix laughed. "Right back to our lazy ways, I see. Why not walk? It's a beautiful day."

That it had been.

"Well, sure, we can walk, Felix, but that means more time until we get those celebratory margaritas."

Arielle chuckled. "I have to agree with Selena on this one. If this mission hadn't been so grueling, maybe we'd walk. But I'd rather get to those margs and bowls of chips and salsa as quickly as we can."

Felix shrugged. "If you say so. I guess I find a quiet walk through nature more calming than a loud restaurant."

Selena tossed her hands up to gesture around them. "Bro, this is downtown Denver. There's nothing quiet or nature about this place."

"You know what I mean," Felix said, shaking his head in defeat while

Selena called the Lyft.

They only had to wait a couple of minutes for a car to arrive, followed by a ten-minute drive through the heart of downtown to their final destination at D'Corazon.

It was 12:15 and the streets of downtown bustled with a heavy crowd for the lunch hour. A line filed out of D'Corazon's door, and Selena moaned when she saw it.

"Relax," Arielle said. "It's lunch, not dinner. People are in and out fast."

"Should we take our bags back to headquarters and come back?" Felix asked. "It's only three blocks down."

"I'd rather not," Arielle said. "If we show up there, who knows how long we'll get stuck in some conversation about the mission. I'd rather just wait it out here and deal with all that after."

Their wait only ended up being fifteen minutes, where they passed the time watching the hordes of business people hustling up and down the sidewalk of Blake Street. Cars sat at a standstill on the road, adding extra heat to an already sweltering day.

Arielle looked at her team. Felix yawned. Selena gazed mindlessly into the distance. They were beat.

Once they settled at a table near the back of the restaurant, Arielle asked, "What are you two planning to do with your time off?"

"Sleep," Felix said with a laugh. "I'm going home after this, getting into bed, and will wake up whenever my body so desires."

"I haven't thought about it yet," Selena said. "Definitely going to shut myself inside my house for the rest of the day. But maybe a trip somewhere tomorrow. I could use a couple days on a beach with drinks being delivered around the clock. You're more than welcome to join me."

"I'll consider it," Arielle said. "I need to touch base with Commander Briar to see what we have coming up next. And I'm going to have a long talk with him about never assigning a mission like this again."

"Good luck with that," Felix said. "We completed the mission. The bottom line is it was a success. They won't care about all the trouble we had—that's just part of the mission, they'll say. If anything, I think we'll get *more* missions like this."

"All I can do is try. He listens to me. If I voice this concern, it'll at least be taken under consideration."

"Arielle standing up to the commander," Selena said, grinning. "That's so . . . Arielle."

They all broke into laughter, a server finally coming to take their drink order. Selena ordered a round of strawberry-mango margaritas for the three of them.

"You're going to get a big boost in the rankings," Felix added. "It'll further cement your place at the top."

"I'm sure Arielle is just fine with her ranking," Selena said. "What are you planning on doing with your time off, anyway—assuming you don't join me on the beach?"

Arielle sat back and crossed her arms. "I don't know. I wasn't planning on leaving town, but maybe I should. Especially since the mission was in Denver. Would be nice to go somewhere else, even for a few days."

"Are you going to call Javonte?" Selena asked, shooting a devilish smirk across the table.

Arielle blushed. "Haven't decided yet. Maybe I will."

"Well, he is an NFL player. I'm sure he can afford to join you on a trip at the last minute."

"Unless he has training camp," Felix added. "That's more important."

Selena rolled her eyes. "I'm sure he can take a weekend off. I think you should call him. No harm in seeing where it might go."

"I don't know," Arielle said. "I've been thinking it over, and I don't think he's my type. A professional athlete. Aren't they just looking for trophy wives?"

"You don't think he can handle you," Selena said.

Arielle grinned. "Well, I could probably kick his ass and make him cry if I wanted to. Can a macho football player be okay with having a woman like that in his life? Besides, I probably shouldn't see someone in the public eye. I don't exactly live a life I can flaunt around. It's still top-secret. Keep in mind, I haven't dated anyone since becoming a Road Runner. I don't know how it would work with someone on the outside."

"Sounds like a romance story waiting to happen."

The margaritas arrived and everyone wasted no time in pulling theirs in and chugging long sips from the orange-and-red concoction.

Arielle pushed her drink back, satisfied. "A romance? Not likely. But I feel ready for something more in my life. Maybe not a relationship. Perhaps a new hobby. Maybe even a dog."

"Well, jeez," Selena said, sarcasm clinging to every word. "Why date an NFL running back when you can adopt a dog?"

"I think that's wise," Felix said. "We're all still young and crushing our careers—our lives, I suppose. I've never considered the complications that come with dating a non-Road Runner. The Bylaws clearly state that we can only share our secret with spouses and children. You'd essentially have to date someone, go through an engagement and wedding, then drop the bomb on them. That doesn't seem like a great way to kick off a marriage, but what do I know?"

"You guys are too serious," Selena said. "Who said anything about engagements and weddings? I just suggested it for Arielle to have some fun, not to marry the guy. You can have a handsome, athletic man on your arm. Get suite tickets to the games every Sunday, eat at the fanciest restaurants in Denver. And, yes, maybe go on some obnoxious vacation with the guy in paradise."

"I can already do all of that stuff myself," Arielle said, shrugging.

"Suit yourself. I wouldn't pass up the opportunity, but I suppose we're all different."

"I don't know why you're so concerned about this, Selena," Felix said. "Don't you have something you were going to show us from the mission?"

Selena's eyes bulged as she sat up straight. "Oh my God, I almost forgot. Yes, I need to open it here with you both."

"The present from the locker room?" Arielle asked. "Who do you think it's from?"

"I'm pretty sure it's from Dawkins. I don't know who else it could be."

"Well, that's disturbing," Felix said. "Let's see it."

Selena reached under the table and pulled her backpack onto her lap, unzipping it with vigor and dropping the gift on the table before shoving the bag back underneath.

"What would he have given you?" Felix asked.

"No clue, but I wouldn't have gotten it until Monday, the day after the robbery—assuming the cleaning crew would even be allowed in the building."

"They definitely would not."

"Enough," Arielle said. "Open it."

Selena nodded, fingers crawling over the box and pulling at the seams. She tore the gift wrap completely off to reveal a box of chocolates, frowning in confusion as she flipped it over and found a folded piece of paper taped to the bottom of the box.

She pulled it off, opened it, and started reading.

"Selena. You have been such a wonderful addition to our team. I know this isn't fun work, so here is a little something to show my appreciation for everything you have done in your first few weeks. Looking forward to working with you. Olivia."

Tears welled in Selena's eyes.

"Olivia?" Felix asked. "Your boss from the cleaning crew?"

Selena nodded, wiping away tears. "I don't know why that hit me so hard. I wasn't expecting that."

"It's because you've touched someone," Arielle said. "And they showed you appreciation. Few people do that, but it seems you left quite the impression on Olivia."

Selena smiled, unable to look away from the gift.

"We may not get much visible appreciation," Arielle said. "Not in this sort of sentimental way, at least. But it's what we do. We touch lives. We help people. Many of them will never know it."

"I'm understanding that," Felix said. "I've never felt my work has made a huge difference, but seeing it all in motion has shown me that every little detail matters."

"We should never feel like we're just going through the motions of some job," Arielle said. "Our missions aren't busywork. They serve a purpose. Even when it doesn't feel like it. Even if they fail. They aim to make the world a better place."

"I feel awful," Selena said. "Olivia will never hear from me again. I'm just vanishing from her timeline."

"You're probably going to be a suspect for a little while because of it," Arielle explained. "The chatter will eventually die down once they find zero evidence linking you to anything, but rumors will fly. It's impossible to say what will happen to your reputation."

"Just until they pin it all on Kennedy and Dawkins," Felix added. "Once they have those two in prison, everyone will forget your name."

"Except Dawkins," Selena said.

"Doesn't matter. Them being locked up will clear your name."

"We're wasting our breath," Arielle said, taking a sip of her drink. "This is all speculation—don't play that game. Wait for the Futures Report and see exactly what happened. And leave me out of it—I don't care. We're here, back on our home turf in our Original Time. Let's celebrate what we accomplished, relax, and prepare for the next one."

"Cheers to that," Selena said, raising her glass. "God knows the world still needs plenty of cleaning up."

III

Dirty Money

Arielle Lucila Series, Book 3

Chapter 1

July 22, 2017

The bold-lettered headline jumped off the cover of the *Seattle Times*: MOTHER KILLS TWO CHILDREN IN MURDER-SUICIDE.

Adam Marshall thought it was a twisted prank when he received the newspaper in his prison cell in Herlong, California, over six hundred miles from his hometown of Seattle.

The photo accompanying the article was a recent family picture of the mother and two children. Grins wide, teeth pearly-white, and no obvious concern about their father rotting away in a prison cell for a crime he never committed.

It was no prank—the newspaper was as real as the concrete walls around him. Hot tears rolled down Adam's face and splashed onto the page as he mentally inserted himself into the family portrait. Where he *should* have been.

Ten minutes passed before emotions got the best of Adam, prompting him to expel the contents of his stomach into his cell's metallic toilet.

"You okay in there, Marshall?" a voice called from the other side of the wall. It was his neighbor, PJ Phillips, serving a ten-year sentence for tax evasion.

"I'm fine!" Adam replied quickly, wiping the puke from his lips with a square of toilet paper before flushing it all away.

Adam was far from fine. Being falsely sentenced and imprisoned had taken its toll on his mental health, but reading the news that had broken out of Seattle sent his mind into a deranged tailspin. Would the headline exist if none of this bullshit had happened? Adam had been an involved father, there every day for his children. Never missing a baseball game or dance recital. Never too busy with work to cower behind the excuse so many parents used to get out of such events.

Rage intertwined with an overwhelming grief he'd never experienced before. If he could just lower his head and plow through the wall like a wild rhinoceros (and take out that cocksucking Warden Burke in the process), he might find some peace of mind.

Instead, he sat helpless on the ground, back against the wall while his hands trembled the newspaper. He was never getting out of this hell. Even at thirty-two years old, with eighteen years remaining in his twenty-year sentence, the duration seemed an eternity.

Adam *needed* to be home. He could close his eyes and smell the coffee brewing in the kitchen before heading out for work, Emily finishing up the dishes after feeding the kids breakfast. Jaxson's school was on his way to work, so he dropped him off every morning, leaving his son at the door with words of encouragement and a kiss on the forehead. He could still imagine that youthful scent between his lips if he tried hard enough.

That lifetime, though only three years in the past, had seemed another century entirely. Sometimes Adam wondered if it had ever been real. How could he go from having his dream job, house, and family to sitting in a six-by-nine prison cell, counting down every single day of a twenty-year sentence? Most people didn't know how many days were in twenty years, but Adam knew the precise answer: 7,305.

The only shining light was knowing he'd see his family a couple times during the kids' summer break, and that they'd be waiting for him after all of those days had passed. Emily had believed him when he explained himself, and she still had. Or else she wouldn't have kept visiting every summer. She knew the man he was, and couldn't connect the dots that tied him to the money laundering accusation. Adam had never even fully understood what money laundering *was*, let alone how to commit the crime.

Now Adam had none of that to look forward to. What would his life look like when he took his first step back into freedom as a 49-year-old man in 2035? He'd be utterly alone. His parents might have passed on by then—they were already in their mid-sixties. His three siblings had disowned him after the guilty verdict and hadn't so much as sent a letter during his first few years in prison. Friendships had already started dissipating once he had kids, and the few that remained surely wouldn't survive a two-decade absence.

Adam had these thoughts swirling in his mind as he read the article over and over, hoping by some miracle there was fine print deeming it a fake story.

Emily had shot each child in the head while they slept before turning the gun on herself, the reporter explained. Jaxson was their oldest, a seven-year-old boy who loved sports and playing with his little sister, Tegan. She was five and loved to dance and sing all over the house.

And Emily was the love of his life. A caring wife and mother who always put everyone else before herself.

Adam struggled to piece the story together. Where did Emily get a gun from? They had never kept one in the house. Who showed her how to use it? Did they know what she had planned on doing? Was it even a plan at all, or a crime in the heat of the moment?

He figured she would have gotten a gun since she served as the sole protector of the house. But they lived in a safe neighborhood. The worst crimes around were teenagers shoplifting from the mall. Did something happen that would have sparked her desire to have extra protection at home? He'd never know.

Adam brushed his thumb over Emily's face in the newspaper. "What happened?" he whispered. "What drove you to this?"

A lump bubbled in Adam's throat as a fresh wave of tears overtook him. He tried to put himself in his wife's shoes and imagine how awful life must have become for her to end it for all of them. It had to be tied to Adam's absence, and the thought sent sharp pangs of guilt throughout his body. Guilt for something he *didn't* do.

Adam imagined the night of the deaths in his mind, his fists balled up, fingernails drawing blood from his palms as he imagined his wife murdering their children in their sleep.

He never understood how miserable it must have been for his family. Emily had mentioned nothing on their visits—only talking about the good things happening in their lives. He never considered his family just might have it worse in their struggle to continue their life together without Adam in it.

His life was straightforward. Swallow watered-down eggs for breakfast. Scrub the prison floors. Receive a two-minute shower. Sit in his cell for two hours before having another shitty meal for lunch. An hour outside. An hour inside reading. Scrubbing the floors again. More time in the cell. Another shitty meal for dinner. Back to the cell for the rest of the night.

It was the same monotonous routine every single day. He had been told of new chores after a few years, but none had come yet. They planned out his life until his release. Emily and the kids had to scramble to establish a new routine while being shackled to the story of their father caught in one of the biggest money laundering schemes in recorded history.

They had it much worse than Adam.

He closed his eyes, and everything that led to this came flooding back to his mind.

He saw himself applying for the job at WonderHome. Interviewing with the CEO and other executives. Receiving an offer letter. His first day on the job as a full-time personal assistant with a major salary. He remembered how on top of the world he had felt through it all. He *was* happy, in the truest sense of the word. All until the day the FBI barged into their offices and went straight to his desk. He could see the agent who had spoken to him, hiding behind a pair of sunglasses while two other agents yanked Adam's arms behind his back to arrest him.

The panic and confusion that had consumed him in that moment still hadn't left to this day. He saw the jail cell. The hours of interrogation by so many attorneys and legal experts. He remembered the courtroom. The jury. The district attorney and his team who were so hell-bent on sending Adam to prison. And the judge. The *fucking* judge who never allowed an objection from Adam's defense team, but always did for the opposition. He remembered the smug look the judge gave him while reading the twenty-year sentence aloud, and the way he waved his hand to dismiss him from the courtroom like he was nothing but a nuisance who had wasted tax dollars and time.

Adam opened his eyes. His family was gone. That was the reality of where this fucked-up road had led him. He'd remain stuck for the next eighteen years in prison, wishing he could just go back and stop it all from happening.

Chapter 2

Present day

Arielle Lucila tipped back the final remains of her second glass of wine.

She sat at a table for two in a dimly lit corner of one of Denver's finest restaurants, the Palace Arms. She had agreed to a date night with Javonte Morris, a running back for the Denver Broncos, who had been pursuing a night out with the top-ranked Angel ever since they met at a nightclub he partially owned.

They had already enjoyed a lavish dinner with the finest cuts of steaks, lobster, and a banana mousse dessert that she would surely think about long after they left.

The temptation remained for a third glass of wine. Conversation had flowed smoothly, especially for her first real date since college. Following the end of her long-term relationship, Arielle had given little consideration to jumping back into the dating world, and dove all the way into her career as an assassin for the time-traveling society known as the Road Runners.

Men had approached her plenty of times over the years, but none had ever caught her attention like Javonte. He had a quiet confidence, and despite his face being broadcast across the country every Sunday during football season, Javonte admitted to preferring a low-key lifestyle away from the cameras and glamour most superstar athletes flocked to.

"So, what did you think about dinner?" Javonte asked, cracking a childish grin as he leaned back and crossed his arms. Even in the poor lighting, his diamond-encrusted necklace and bracelet sparkled blindingly. Arielle estimated the two pieces were worth around $75,000. But athletes had their salaries publicized and debated by all those who cared. And Javonte was currently on year three of a $30 million contract.

That was something else that drew Arielle to him. They both had virtually unlimited funds, yet neither of them acted like the rich snobs sitting at the other tables in the restaurant.

Arielle smiled, poking around the remaining mousse on her plate. "I'll admit I had a great time tonight."

Javonte clapped his hands, drawing attention from the other diners. Some scoffed at the abrupt loud noise, while others gawked in amazement that they were sitting in the same room as a future Broncos legend. "I told you we'd have a good time. All I wanted was a chance."

"Yes, I know," Arielle replied, face breaking out into a full grin. "You were right."

"It doesn't have to stop, either. Do you want to go to my club? We have one of the best DJs in Denver spinning tonight."

Part of Arielle wanted to—the spontaneity of the wine made her feel laid-back for once.

"I wish, but I promised my friend I'd meet her for drinks after our date."

Javonte raised both hands, gesturing to her to say no more. "You gotta talk with your girl about how the date went. I get it. If you two are looking for something to do later, you should still stop by. If not, when can I see you again?"

Arielle had been bracing for this question all night. It had become inevitable that they were connecting and their relationship wouldn't end after one date.

"I'll have to let you know," Arielle said. "Work is about to get pretty busy—I'm talking long hours around the clock. We don't all get to spend our days running around with a ball."

"Oh, hell no!" Javonte howled, clutching his gut. "Shots fired!"

Arielle had told him she worked in the district attorney's office. It was her go-to occupation of choice when she had to lie, seeing as the job could require upward of eighty hours per week and leave her the opportunity for abrupt phone calls that would "call" her into the office. And she had read enough Grisham novels to feel confident in bullshitting her way through a conversation about the law, if required.

"Okay," Javonte said, leaning forward. "You know where I'll be. Hit me up when you're ready to go out again. Now let's get you out of here."

He rose from his seat, and Arielle couldn't help but admire her date. Six feet tall, two hundred and fifteen pounds of pure muscle wrapped inside an Armani suit.

Damn, she thought, wishing she hadn't confirmed the plans with Selena.

Arielle joined his side, and now that the running back was standing—and towering above the room—everyone took notice and gazed while the couple strolled out of the restaurant, arms intertwined.

"So, where are you off to?" Javonte asked.

"Not sure yet," Arielle said. "Selena hasn't let me know where. I need to call her."

"You sure like to live on the edge. Wandering downtown without a plan in the world. I don't think I could ever do that—I need some structure in my day."

Arielle giggled. "I'm the same way, actually, but Selena couldn't be any more opposite. Knowing her, she's dancing on top of a bar right now, gathering a crowd, and that's why she hasn't let me know where to meet yet."

Javonte laughed. "Sounds like a fun friend. I suppose we all need one in our life, right? Well, whatever you end up doing, I hope you have a good time. I'll be waiting for your call."

He released his arm from Arielle's, his fingers brushing over forearm in a subtle gesture that sent goosebumps up her back.

"Thank you for tonight," she said. "I really needed that."

"The pleasure was all mine. Now go have a fun night with Selena."

Javonte offered one last grin as he turned and started down the sidewalk.

Selena was at the bar across the street from the restaurant they had just left, probably on her second margarita. Arielle knew this, but didn't want Javonte to think they were being watched on their date—not that they were. Arielle had suggested the bar for Selena for the sake of having as short of a walk as possible after the date.

She waited for Javonte to disappear before crossing the street and stepping into La Loma, an upscale Mexican eatery that touted over one hundred tequila choices. Arielle pushed her way through the crowded lobby and found Selena sitting at the bar, her purse saving the open seat next to her.

Selena sat half-facing the bar and entryway, grinning and waving as Arielle approached.

"Well, you look like you had a nice time," Selena said, the two hugging before Arielle took her seat. "I don't think I've ever seen such a big smile on your face."

Arielle nodded, pleased to find a frozen strawberry margarita already waiting for her. "It went way better than I was expecting. He really is a nice guy, not into the fame and all that."

Selena squealed before taking a long sip of her drink. "Tell me all about it."

Arielle spent the next ten minutes recapping the date, Selena eager for every detail, devouring an entire basket of chips and salsa while she listened.

"So, when's the next date?" Selena asked.

"You sound just like him," Arielle said with a light chuckle. "I don't know yet. We're about to start that mission, so probably after that. Depends if I go visit my grandma after the mission—I haven't decided yet."

"Well, don't make him wait too long. He may be humble and all that, but he *is* an NFL player and nightclub owner. It's not exactly a struggle for him to find other women if he never hears from you."

"I know that, but why does there have to be so much pressure? What does a second date mean? At what point does it transition from dating into an exclusive relationship? I enjoyed the night out with Javonte, but this is the part I was dreading. Why does dating have to be so complicated?"

Selena reached out and placed her hand on top of Arielle's. "It's only as complicated as you make it. Be upfront from the beginning. Tell Javonte how slow or fast you want things to go. If he can't accept your requests, you can try to compromise or just move on."

"But I don't even know what I want. I'm not opposed to being in a serious relationship—I was ready to marry Kevin, after all—but at this point in my life, I honestly don't understand where a boyfriend even fits into my schedule."

Selena had ordered two tequila shots that the bartender now placed in front of them. She grabbed one and held it up. "Arielle, you need to get out of your head. Not every aspect of your life has to be planned to the finest detail. Sometimes you just need to jump into the deep end, start swimming, and see where you end up. Some things in life can't be planned. You don't think Javonte has a busy schedule? He's a professional athlete. He has practice, workouts, trainings, film sessions, charity events, and tons of travel. Plus, he's a business owner. He's just as busy as you, but look, you both cut time out of your schedules to have dinner tonight."

"That was just dinner, though. I can make meal plans any time. Being in a relationship is a lot more than having dinner together. He'd want me at his games, probably even some of the road ones. He'll want me to join him at some of those charity events. I can't be that type of girlfriend."

"Did he tell you that's what he's looking for?" Selena asked. Arielle grabbed her shot glass reluctantly and tapped it against Selena's before they both downed the tequila.

"Well, no, but—"

"But nothing. *Talk to him.* You're playing mind games with yourself because you don't actually know what he wants. You're making assumptions. He might be totally fine with you having a busy schedule and only seeing you every couple of days. That's just how some relationships are. Do you think Beyonce sits around at home all day waiting for Jay-Z to come home, dinner cooked and served on the table? Hell no! They are both busy individuals, and they make it work, even if that means going weeks without seeing each other. Just stop trying to plan everything, and *talk to Javonte*."

Arielle rubbed her forehead. The margarita and tequila shot were mixing with all the wine to give her a headache. "Okay. I'll talk to him and see where he stands with things."

Selena clapped her hands together. "Thank you. Now that I've helped you sort out your love life, have you heard anything about the next mission?"

"Not yet. I only ever get a list of the potential missions we can go on—usually twenty or so—but I don't find out until we meet with Commander Briar. He has the final say on what's assigned to us."

"Well, I can't wait for Monday morning to find out. I'm still riding a high from the last one. I still can't believe how that all went down."

"Believe it. You won that mission for us. *You* were the hero."

"And you made sure everyone knows about it—thank you for that. It was nuts seeing my name in the rankings. Top 300, sure, but it's not something I ever thought would happen. Top-ranked actress is still mine, but we're never expected to crack the overall rankings—that's for Angels like you."

"There was a time when a woman would never be considered for a chance of ranking. Now there are four of us in the top ten alone, and I don't know how many others in the top 300. Expectations are just other people drawing their boundaries for you. Who gives a shit what they say? Just go out there and do your best. That's all we can do."

Selena nodded. "Then I guess we'll keep climbing the ranks." She raised her glass, and Arielle clinked hers against it before they finished their drinks.

"Have you heard from Felix at all?" Arielle asked.

"I know he's alive and well," Selena said with a chuckle. "You know how he is. Been at home since the last mission ended. Pretty sure he locks himself in his basement to play his video games and watch sports—assuming he isn't going out to the games in person."

Arielle laughed. "We all have our ways of unwinding. I had promised him a trip to see his parents before we start the next mission. I'm not sure if he remembers that, but I'm still going to do it. We'll take my jet if you want to come with us a couple days before the mission starts. If not, you can just meet us wherever we end up going."

"You think we're finally leaving Colorado for a mission?"

"Oh, I insisted on it. We need a change of scenery every now and then. We're supposed to cover all of North America. I requested tropical locations in Costa Rica and Guatemala, but I'm sure we'll end up nowhere near there."

"Well, that would be a fun time!"

"Exactly. I think that's why they usually send Angels over the age of forty to handle the missions down there. I guess they don't fully trust us rowdy twenty-somethings to get the job done with all the temptation in places like that."

"Sounds like ageism to me."

"You can take that up with Commander Briar, if you'd like. Don't expect to make any progress."

Arielle stood up from the bar, swaying so slightly.

"You're ready to leave already?" Selena asked, an offense taken in her voice.

"Yes. I've had way too much to drink. You forget I don't do this often...it just hit me. I really need to lie down."

Selena giggled as she stood to join Arielle. "See, they can send you to Miami in the middle of spring break. What are they afraid is going to happen? You'll have a rager on the beach and pass out by eight o'clock?"

Arielle howled laughter, the booze exaggerating the humor in every-thing. "I just need to get to bed. I'll see you on Monday?"

"Can't wait."

Chapter 3

By Monday morning, Arielle felt like herself again. She wouldn't call Sunday a hangover day—she didn't have a headache or nausea—but she hadn't quite felt like herself, opting to spend the day in her pajamas to binge-watch game shows.

She couldn't remember the last time she had a lazy day like that, and was understanding the benefits of relaxation in between missions. It had only been a month since the recent shift to more work-life balance. She had grown so used to feeding a constant urge to do something, that a day of true leisure (she couldn't even recall if she brushed her teeth in the morning) seemed like a betrayal to her inner workaholic.

When she sprung out of bed on Monday, however, she had never felt so mentally or physically ready to start a new mission. It had only been a week since they returned from the last one, but her mind was so *clear*. Focused.

She had become used to transitioning from one mission to the next, sometimes with mere hours in between. Now, she had time to actually decompress from the last mission and start the next one with a clean palette.

Their meeting was set with Commander Briar for 10 A.M. While getting dressed, Arielle thought back to how skeptical they had all been before their first mission together. It was a new process for all of them having to work with the same dedicated team, and while Arielle knew she wouldn't have issues with her direct mission work, she had doubts on how the team dynamics would play out, especially with a loose cannon like Selena

Nicole.

Two missions later, she and Selena were practically best friends, and Felix fit in perfectly when the trio were together. That initial angst had given way to excitement as they stared down their third mission together. Everyone understood each other's strengths and weaknesses, and how to make it all gel together.

By the time she arrived downtown, parking her BMW in front of the familiar marketing firm that housed the Road Runners' headquarters in its basement, Arielle stepped onto the sidewalk feeling like a new era had arrived in her career.

The calendar had flipped to August, and they only had a few weeks left of the blistering heat before autumn took hold. Arielle stood on the sunny sidewalk, drawing in a deep breath of the crisp morning air. She was still on top of her game and didn't even consider herself close to reaching her prime. She had more room to grow as an Angel, and now she had a team eager to rise with her.

Commander Briar had been right. These new teams were truly for the best. They would need to prove themselves on more missions, but Arielle already believed they could handle a mission of any magnitude thrown their way. No matter what the commander assigned them today, they'd take the files, make a plan, and execute it. Then it was back to another week off.

"Arielle!" Felix shouted from down the sidewalk, jogging toward her with a wide grin smacked across his face. They embraced, and Arielle immediately noticed a similar wave of energy emitting from Felix. The last mission had taken an intense toll on him, and Arielle wondered if that had driven Felix into hiding upon their return home. Whatever he had done worked, apparently.

"How are you doing?" Arielle asked.

"Never been better." Optimism clung to each word. "I wasn't quite ready to come here today, at least last night. But when I woke up today, I was a little excited. Is this how it's always felt for you doing missions, being the best and all?"

Arielle laughed. "Being the best doesn't make any of this more or less fun. If anything, it has made it more routine. Trust me, I've had plenty of missions where I needed to drag myself to come here. I think the time off played a huge factor in how we're all feeling. Me and Selena were just talking the other night how we're excited to start this next mission, too."

"Well, if we're already on the same page, I'd hate to be the poor soul on the other end of this mission. You ready to go in?"

"Let's do it."

They climbed the short flight of steps and entered the marketing office, the place abuzz with agents on the phone and the *click-clack* of fingers banging on keyboards. The employees were all part of the Road Runners organization, their lone job being to operate a legitimate marketing firm. The last Arielle had heard, Commander Briar had implemented new leadership to make the company a reliable source of income for the organization.

The vibes were plenty different from the prior times Arielle had strolled through, back when they were simply going through the motions to keep the company afloat.

No one even paid them any attention as Arielle and Felix strolled to the manager's office in the back. When they stepped in, they found the typically forgotten office space completely remodeled with updated furniture, motivational artwork, and a fancy coffee machine in the corner.

Before, the room had been more like a closet, considering its rear door led down to the basement where the headquarters lay hidden.

"Like what I've done with the place?" a woman asked from behind, startling Arielle and Felix as they admired the new office.

They spun around to a short, pudgy woman, likely in her mid-thirties with reddish-brown hair brushed as straight as the bristles on a brand-new broom. She smiled at the two Angels, looking back and forth between them. Her eyes lit up when she realized who was standing in her office.

"Arielle Lucila and Felix Francisco?!" she squealed. The professional tone she had just used gave way to one of a teenage girl giddy to meet her crush from her favorite boy band. "They told me you'd be here at some point. Obviously, Denver is your home base. I'm just so . . . honored."

"It's nice to meet you," Arielle said, sticking out a hand. "What's your name?"

"I'm so sorry," the woman gasped, her cheeks flushing red. "I'm Jackie Monaghan, and I run this office now."

"I'm impressed, Jackie," Arielle said. "You did all this in a week? It's a whole new mood out there. Not to mention in here."

Jackie grinned, her face still red. "Why, thank you. A week in real time, maybe. Commander Briar hired me and asked for immediate results and an overhaul. So, naturally, I took our staff into the past where I could train them for a month, and brought them back the following day ready to hit the ground running. I might have scheduled all the contractors to come in while I was in the past, too." She grinned, satisfied with her recap of events.

Felix nodded. "That's actually really efficient."

"I suppose that's why Commander Briar picked me. Why waste my precious time on Earth doing any task in the present when I can go back a week and do it then, and only miss ten minutes in the present? I don't see why more people don't think this way."

"What did you do before taking over this role?"

"I was in the accounting department for the Road Runners. My efficiency was through the roof, and that gained me some attention." Jackie shrugged, her face finally returning to its normal pale tone. "I'd leave most days by lunchtime, sometimes earlier, with all of my work done for the day."

"Doesn't that get exhausting?" Felix asked. "And confusing?"

"Not at all. Hard to be exhausted when I get to take a nap every single day. One perk of being done so early. As for confusing—no. I keep tons of spreadsheets and checklists. It might seem intense to an outsider, but it's all very organized when I look at it."

"We just might have to get you on our team," Felix joked.

Jackie's eyes bulged, completely missing the sarcasm in Felix's statement.

"Don't listen to him," Arielle said, smacking Felix on the arm. "We don't have any openings right now—not that it's even up to us."

"Well, if that time ever comes, you know where to find me."

"Yeah, wandering around last week," Felix said, sparking a round of laughter.

"It was a pleasure meeting you, Jackie," Arielle said. "But we really need to be heading down to meet with the commander now. If you'll excuse us."

"Of course. Don't mind me. Best of luck to you on your next mission."

Arielle and Felix made their way past Jackie's desk and pulled open the door to welcome the usual mustiness that accompanied the dim, somewhat creepy stairwell that led downstairs.

When they started down and the door closed behind them, Felix said, "Well, she was interesting."

"I liked her. She has a ton of confidence, but a strange way of expressing it. Seems like she's already made an impact, so I'm sure the commander loves her already."

They reached the bottom landing and pushed open the door, Arielle bracing for what other changes they might have made in the short week since she'd last been down in the headquarters.

To her delight, nothing had changed. The bullpen bustled with chaos, always reminding her of how movies portrayed the stock exchange, with everyone shouting over each other, although not *as* loud.

This small corner of the world, buried beneath downtown Denver, ran operations affecting hundreds of millions of lives across North America. It was both intimidating and peaceful to Arielle, and she could never help but smile when she felt the energy the headquarters provided. Commander Briar wouldn't remain in his position forever, and she only hoped the next commander opted to keep the organization's main office in Denver.

"Good morning, you two," said a man sitting to their left at the corner desk, directly across from Commander Briar's office. It was Elijah Ward, the commander's assistant.

Chairs stood against the wall across from Elijah, giving the commander's office an official waiting area for visitors.

"Good morning, Elijah," Arielle said. "How are things?"

"Better now that you're here, darling."

Elijah rose from his seat and came around to give Arielle a hug. The two had gotten to know each other over the years. Elijah had left his home in Toronto after a messy divorce with his ex-husband, and ended up in Denver, where he took the first job he could find at the Road Runners office before it had become the headquarters. Commander Briar promoted Elijah to be his assistant shortly after the war against the Revolution ended.

"I like what you've done with the place," Arielle said. "Both down here and upstairs."

"Isn't Jackie just the best? She's made my life much easier, which has allowed me to do more of the things I've been putting off down here. HQ is about to get a massive overhaul as well, but we can only do it in small portions, obviously."

"Well, I look forward to it. Is the commander ready for us?"

"Give him about five minutes, and he'll see you. Hi, Felix." Elijah shot a wink at Felix before pivoting and returning to his desk, making Felix blush.

Arielle took a seat against the wall, Felix joining her. He leaned over and whispered, "Does he know I don't swing that way? He's always winking at me."

Arielle grinned, shaking her head. "I don't think he cares," she whispered back. "If he thinks you're cute, that's all there is to it. He's a real jokester, too, so it's impossible for me to know if he's being serious or just messing with you."

Felix shook his head, smiling to himself, when Commander Briar's door swung open, their leader strolling out with complete casualness. He grinned upon seeing Arielle and Felix, the two of them promptly standing up to greet him.

"Nice work on that last mission," Commander Briar said, shaking hands with both. "Selena isn't here yet?"

"I'm here!" Selena called out from behind, the entrance door closing behind her as she shuffled down the short hallway to meet them.

"Great, you're all here," Commander Briar said. "I have a pretty loaded morning, so I'd love to get started. Let's head into my office."

The commander spun around and returned to his office, the three Angels trailing behind him. Three chairs were positioned in front of his oversized desk, the commander taking his seat behind a thick file stuffed with papers.

"Before we discuss the next mission," he said, interlocking his fingers beneath his chin. "I want to hear your concerns about the last one. I know you got the job done, but it wasn't the cleanest of missions. What were some issues you ran into?"

Felix and Selena both looked to Arielle, happy to defer. They may have all been on the same team, but neither of them had reached a level of comfort in having these types of conversations with the leader of their organization. Arielle expected as much, and cleared her throat before speaking.

"I think the biggest issue we ran into was the setup of the entire mission. We understand there will always be some level of investigating that needs to be done, but this one seemed like we had to figure out the whole story. It made it difficult for us to really set a plan, and it felt like we were constantly chasing a moving target. We're not detectives, but the mission felt like one that should have had one. We don't know how to follow clues and build a case."

Commander Briar raised his hand, nodding. "I knew I'd hear all about this, eventually. From the day I assigned this mission to you. You have all the skills a good detective has. The only difference is that you've been used to using those skills to navigate around the past. Sure, we can line up a ton of missions with everything laid out. You'll just need to show up and know how to carry out the assassination without the past interfering. That alone is detective work—identifying problems and inconsistencies, opportunities for failure, your target's schedule and whereabouts.

"What we've found through recent studies is that there is less resistance from the past when our Angels go into missions having to figure things out on their own. The past knows everything, so it knows when you arrive with a plan, no matter how well you've masked your intentions. What it doesn't know is what you will figure out when starting from a virtually clean slate upon your arrival."

"So you're going to deliberately withhold information from us?" Arielle asked. "To make the mission easier?"

"Not easier," the commander replied firmly. "*Safer*. See, we've already had a few dozen missions done with this new team structure. And while they have successfully completed most, we've had an increase in concerns from the Angels. What you're telling me about your last mission is on par with what we've been hearing. It has elevated the danger since we launched these teams."

Arielle's stomach sunk. The Road Runners loved to experiment with many matters. An increased risk to any member would typically end an experiment. They didn't gamble with their members' lives, and she feared the new team structure might vanish as quickly as it had formed.

Commander Briar must have sensed her unease, saying, "But never fear, we're making adjustments. When I read Felix had been bitten by a snake in your post-mission report, I knew something was wrong. Granted, that could have been a total fluke occurrence, but I think we all know better. Especially considering *when* it happened during the mission."

"So our missions are going to become more *difficult*?" Selena asked. Felix had let his eyes wander into space, likely thinking back to the traumatizing night he had to deal with the snakebite.

Commander Briar lowered his hands to his desk and leaned forward. "I can't make a blanket statement like all missions will be more difficult. Some might be. Some might be easier. We can't really judge that yet. But our top priority is your safety, so I can say all missions should have less risk involved. More work once you're in the past, but not necessarily harder to complete our objectives."

He leaned back as the office fell silent, Arielle noticing the fatigue swimming behind the commander's eyes. An exhaustion she hadn't seen on him since the last days of the war.

"What do you guys think?" Selena asked her fellow Angels.

Felix shrugged. "I suppose it's like anything else. We just have to go out and see how it all plays out. You know less danger is okay in my book, even if it requires we have to worry about more details once we arrive. I think we'll manage."

All eyes in the room turned to Arielle, who had remained silent during the commander's explanation. She wasn't fond of the idea of having more to do after arriving in the past, but knew an argument over safety would be one she'd never win.

"Let's try it," she said. "I am curious, though—what will happen to the Advance Team that does all the research ahead of time?"

"Nothing different for them," Commander Briar said. "They will conduct the preliminary research ahead of time. The only difference is that you may see less information in your reports from them. Expect them to be a lot more high-level than the tons of details you're used to."

"So they'll be withholding information that could be beneficial."

"That is correct, Ms. Lucila. My team members, with the help of the Lieutenant Commander, have been working to find the sweet spot for how much information to give, and how it affects the risk associated with each mission. They believe they have found the breakeven point, and that's why I'm coming to you with all of this today. We would never test these things on our best-performing team—your missions are already risky enough. But they have enough of a sample size to feel confident in your next mission and what is provided to you in the Advance Team's report."

Arielle pursed her lips. She could recall only a handful of times where the commander had called her *Ms. Lucila*. The two had a strong relationship, but the formality of this address reminded everyone in the room who was in charge.

She nodded. "Okay. We'll report back with any concerns after the mission. Now, can we talk about what our next mission is?"

Chapter 4

The tension had grown heavy in Commander Briar's office, and he promptly called for a quick five-minute break before they jumped into the details for their upcoming mission.

The commander stepped out and disappeared to the kitchen.

"Are you okay?" Selena asked Arielle.

"Yep," Arielle said, her jaw clenching. She knew they wired the office with listening devices and wouldn't dare peep another word about her disgust concerning the recent changes. She already had her frustrations with playing detective on the last mission, having insisted she would speak with Commander Briar about never receiving missions like it again. Instead, this was going to become the new normal.

The thought of going into a mission with less information made Arielle's blood boil. She had grown accustomed to absorbing as many details as possible before taking a trip through time. The uncertainty she had felt during multiple points on the last mission was nothing she wanted to experience again. Now she didn't have a choice.

Felix and Selena took Arielle's one-word response as the obvious clue she didn't want to discuss the matter. They sat in silence until the commander returned and closed the door behind him.

"All right," he said as he settled into his seat, acting as if everything was fine. He opened the file that had been on his desk since they arrived and turned it around to face the three Angels.

They saw a newspaper clipping from a July 2017 edition of the *Seattle Times*. The headline read: MOTHER KILLS TWO CHILDREN IN MURDER-

SUICIDE. A portrait below showed a woman with a young boy and girl.

"Meet the Marshall family," Commander Briar said, pushing the clipping forward. "The mother is Emily. Son is Jaxson. Daughter is Tegan. As you can see, these three had a night from hell a few years ago. Our goal is to stop this tragedy from happening. However, we strongly believe stopping it has nothing to do with interfering directly with the family."

The commander ruffled through the stack of papers to fish out a mug shot of a man in his early thirties. He dropped it on top of the newspaper clipping, the man's green eyes staring at all three Angels with a desperation swimming behind them.

"This is the father, Adam Marshall. The murder-suicide occurred in May 2017. Before that, the FBI arrested Adam in 2014 for suspicion of money laundering. They sentenced him to twenty years in prison in June 2015. Adam has insisted on his innocence to this day, and many believe him. All the money laundering was through the company he worked for, WonderHome, Inc."

"The real estate site?" Arielle asked. "Why didn't we hear about this? They're the biggest online real estate marketplace in the country."

"Exactly," Commander Briar said. "That's where it doesn't add up. The laundering scheme was all done within WonderHome's infrastructure, but everything was only under Adam's name."

"So they framed him," Selena said, always eager to jump to a conclusion.

"Not exactly. It's entirely possible that he pulled this off on his own, and that he is indeed guilty. He worked directly for the company's CEO, so he had access to nearly every aspect of the company. His name is on all documents related to the laundering. No one else. His trial was a mess of pointing fingers. He said the company set him up. The company said they had no knowledge of what he was doing—which could be true since he only had one person, the CEO, overlooking his work. And we know a CEO won't spend their time monitoring their assistant."

"So why do the Road Runners think he's innocent?" Arielle asked.

"As our Advance Team dug deeper into this tragedy's past, they came across deposition interviews with Mr. Marshall. Several on our team believe he didn't understand what money laundering even was, let alone how to pull off a scheme of this magnitude."

"And that never came up in court?"

"Of course, but the prosecution just powered through, saying he was playing dumb. And why not? They had all the evidence they needed to put him away. It was a slam-dunk case, and they won with no issues. It was definitely an inside job, but it seems too big for one person to handle. He had to have someone helping him. I find it impossible that he didn't. We're talking *millions* of dollars. It could have been someone higher up in the company that kept their hands clean. Or maybe a colleague. A fellow assistant from another department. What we don't know is how happy Mr. Marshall was at his place of employment. Did something happen that could have sparked a thirst for revenge? That's what we'll need you to find out."

Commander Briar sat back and crossed his arms, waiting for one of the Angels to speak.

"If I may be honest, Commander," Arielle said. "The Mason Gregory mission had a lot of happenings inside his employer's offices, but we didn't have any way in. I wasted so many hours sitting in my car and staring at the outside of the office building."

The commander opened his mouth to speak, but Felix cut him off. "That won't happen again. Whoever needs to get inside the office will get inside. I'll see to it."

Felix spoke with a tinge of disdain, clearly still displeased with himself for the error he had made on the team's first mission together.

"This doesn't sound like a two-week mission," Arielle said.

"It's not. You'll be traveling back to mid-2013 in Seattle and staying for at least eight months. The goal is to get at least one of you employed by the company before they hire Mr. Marshall. It can even be all of you—that part is up to you to figure out, along with what might be the best position to fill to keep a close eye on Mr. Marshall. He was only with the company for six months before his arrest."

"I am *not* cleaning toilets again," Selena said, earning a light chuckle from Felix.

"I wouldn't worry about that, Ms. Nicole," Commander Briar said. "This will be a focus on the other end of the corporate ladder. The executives. The suits. Whatever you kids like to call them these days."

"Heartless sharks," Arielle muttered under her breath. "Eight months, though. Seems excessive."

Commander Briar raised a steady hand. "Missions will get longer, but it's lightening the workload. We've heard loud and clear from several Angels that the constant grind of going two or three weeks straight is taking its toll. I understand the simple necessities in life, like eating and sleeping, come at a premium during your missions. Just because you're in the past and not aging doesn't mean these things have no effect on you. You're still a human, and I'd like to apologize for the lifestyle you've had to endure."

"It's honestly never bothered me," Arielle said.

"Speak for yourself, *numero uno*," Selena said. "I, for one, am grateful, Commander. So thank you. When you say the missions will run longer, are you implying we'll have actual free time during the trips into the past?"

"That is the intent, but your schedule is ultimately up to Arielle. There shouldn't be a need to follow around your target every waking moment of the day. Especially on this mission, since most of the action is going to occur at the workplace, Monday through Friday. You might have to use a couple of weekends to get some matters sorted, or do additional tailing, but only if you suspect someone. Live in Seattle. Enjoy your time there, and you'll be mentally ready for the work as it comes."

"Why does it seem like there are so many changes?" Arielle asked. "Don't get me wrong, they seem for the better, mostly, but there are so many things in motion."

"We're in a time of peace, and it's my priority to make the lives easier for every Road Runner. I want to take advantage of that luxury. We're time travelers. There's no reason for us to rush through anything, or ever feel crunched for time. So what, live eight months in the past? You're still only losing ten minutes from today. We are running a mission per week for each team of Angels. In real time, you are losing ten minutes per week for working a mission. The teams in Europe are doing one mission each month, and their success rate is virtually perfect."

"One a month?" Selena gasped. "I could chase my Hollywood dreams on that schedule."

"Exactly. And my goal is for us to reach that level, but that's a matter of having more Angels recruited and trained, because we'll still need to cover the same amount of missions. Having more teams affords everyone more flexibility. I don't know if that will happen during my term as commander, but I will certainly get the ball rolling before I leave. As an organization, we owe it to our members for sticking through that war. It was all-hands-on-deck for too many years. Extreme levels of stress. Loss of family and friends. I want to reward our members by giving them their lives back—it's the least we can do."

"It definitely feels like the general mood is shifting across the Road Runners," Arielle said. "So whatever you guys are doing is working."

Commander Briar stood up and closed the file, pushing it into Arielle's lap. "I never wanted to be the commander. They forced this whole candidacy onto me because I could resist the freezing of time. But now that I look back, the Road Runners saved me from myself. Before any of this time travel business, I was in a dark place. I had been battling depression for two decades. Burying my pain in booze, pills, and junk food. I had even stuck a pistol in my mouth every year on the anniversary of my sweet Izzy's disappearance. Sure, I had my issues at the beginning, being recruited by Chris Speidel. Then his daughter was playing mind with games with me. But it was the Road Runners who ultimately brought me in and turned my life around. And this was *during* the war. We all deserve sunshine after the darkness, and I want to leave that opportunity as my legacy long after I'm gone. I want the Road Runners to be fun again, if they ever were."

Tears welled in Arielle's eyes. She had lived through the darkest points in the war. As the commander had just mentioned, she had lost friends at the hands of the Revolution. Even during her climb to the organization's top-ranked Angel, the life of a Road Runner constantly orbited around stress. The good had finally arrived out of the mess, and she could now clearly see what was driving Commander Briar as he stared down the final year of his term.

Arielle rose to her feet, Felix and Selena following suit. She stuck her hand across the commander's desk, and he grabbed it to shake. "I don't know if you hear this enough," Arielle said, "But thank you for risking your life to save us all."

He offered a tight-lipped grin, gulping down what Arielle believed was the urge to cry.

"Now," she continued. "If you'll excuse us. We have a mission to do."

Chapter 5

The trio agreed to depart Wednesday morning, leaving the rest of Monday and all of Tuesday to pack and prepare. Since they were traveling not too far into the past, the Road Runners had already worked many logistics out, and the three Angels simply needed to show up.

Arielle kept a three-week rotation of clothes she packed for every mission. For this one, she packed and an extra week's worth, limiting her having to do laundry to once a month while on the mission.

She packed within an hour of arriving back home from headquarters and promptly left for the cemetery across town where her family had been laid to rest. She tried to visit their graves once a month to keep the flowers and display tidy.

When she reached the site—three graves belonging to her mother, father, and brother all next to each other—she sat on the grass in front of the middle gravestone, her mother's.

"Hi, guys," she said, staring at all three graves. A towering oak tree showered her with shade on a hot, sunny day. Birds chirped from high up, while a trio of squirrels chased each other up the tree trunk. Arielle realized in this moment just how far out of touch she had fallen from nature.

She kicked off her flip-flops, letting the blades of grass caress her feet, and drew in a deep breath of air. It had been weeks—hell, years—of being constantly in motion. Never having a moment to sit down and enjoy the little pleasures of the world. Though she was surrounded by the deceased, she felt the calming presence of the cemetery and its beauty.

Perfect landscaping, bright flowers as far as she could see, and even a maintenance worker stopping to eat his lunch at a table in the distance. Life was happening all around her, yet Arielle felt like a stranger. A misfit. Wasn't she supposed to be doing something besides killing a few minutes sitting in the grass?

"I don't remember who I am," she finally said to her family. "Ever since I lost the three of you, I've kept myself constantly busy. It started as a way of coping with the loss. A way to distract myself from feeling the pain. But over the years, I'm afraid I got used to it. If I'm ever not in motion, I just feel . . . empty."

The three gravestones stared back, silent. Arielle felt her family's presence. She had lost her faith in any sort of religion after the incident that took her family, but she still believed in the afterlife. It wasn't a stretch for her to believe the spirits of her parents and brother visited her at this moment.

Normally, she had to fight off tears when speaking to the gravestones. Today, however, was different. She felt warmth within her soul. She felt connected to everything around her.

"I'm going to have a lot more free time soon," she continued. "And I don't know what I'm supposed to do with it. Maybe I'll finally get the time to properly grieve losing you three. I've been thinking about it a lot lately. Many people believe we're supposed to power through grief and not let it slow down our lives. Bury our pain with work or hobbies. But that does nothing. It's been seven years since you've been gone, and the pain is still here. The grief is still waiting. It doesn't just go away with time. It waits until you stare it down and confront it. That's the only way to truly get *through* it. I'm going to have some dark days ahead as I come to terms with all of this, but I suppose I need it."

Tears welled in Arielle's eyes, but not from sorrow. She still felt plenty of peace within. Her tears came from a place of fear of the unknowing. She had never confronted these emotions swirling around her family's death. Sure, they'd creep up from time to time and she'd have a good cry in the shower. But she'd never tried to work through them. Whether that meant locking herself in a dark bedroom for a week, eating gallons of ice cream, or just *feeling* the emotions to their core.

Her schedule had been deliberately jam-packed since she buried the three people she loved the most. She wasn't even tired after seven years of a constant grind, but knew that was all changing beyond her control. Improved mental health was clearly at the top of Commander Briar's agenda, and perhaps he was on to something.

Arielle would face her demons within the next year, whether or not she liked it. And while it would be torturous to go through, it could only leave her in a better mental state at the end.

Her cell phone rang, causing Arielle to jump from the ground. She had fallen so deep into herself that the obnoxious chime coming from her pocket had startled her back to reality.

She had no plans of answering until she saw *Abuela* on the caller ID.

"Hello?" she answered.

"Mi hita, how are you?" her grandmother replied, the worry evident in her voice. "Is everything okay?"

"Yes, Abuela, why do you ask?"

"I don't know. Sometimes I get strange feelings. I thought I should reach out to make sure you're okay."

Chills broke out across Arielle's back. Her grandmother had always had an ability to sense different things about the family—either good or bad. The morning of the mall shooting, she had called to make sure everything was okay. At the time, it was. Little did any of them know what would unfold later that afternoon. Arielle often thought back to that phone call and wondered how it all worked. Did her grandma sense things that weren't quite clear? Was it like reading something in a language she couldn't understand? She was the complete opposite of Arielle, someone in total sync with the universe and its ways. Arielle often wondered if her abuela knew about the time-traveling life she lived, but kept quiet.

"What are you up to, mi amor?"

Arielle gulped. It was impossible to lie to her grandmother for a multitude of reasons. "I'm . . . at the cemetery."

"Ay, gracias a Dios," she replied, instant relief flooding through the phone line. "No wonder I felt something. You're all together right now."

Hearing her grandmother say this with such confidence opened the floodgates. She hadn't been wrong about feeling her family's presence. If her grandma could sense it 600 miles away, then it wasn't some part of her imagination.

"I'm having a hard time right now, Abuela," Arielle said through intense sobbing. She rose to her feet, blood rushing to her head and making her dizzy. "Some days I just can't handle it. I *need* them here with me. I want to share my life with them. They were always there, and one day that just stopped."

"I miss them too, hita. And there is nothing wrong with having these feelings. Your abuelo has been gone for twelve years now, and I still have days like this. We can't erase the memories or the connection we had with our loved ones. It's just impossible."

Arielle couldn't speak, and started crying harder. It felt like the world was pouring sorrow on her. She missed her grandfather, too. Missed the family trips to New Mexico to visit her grandparents when they were the happiest couple she had known. She missed her life the way it had been.

Arielle had never felt so far from being the top-ranked Angel than she did right now. None of her status or achievements mattered, because she had no one to share them with. Celebrating with yourself got old real quick.

"How are *you?*" Arielle asked, when the tears subsided. "Have things been going okay since I last visited?"

"Nothing has changed here. Same routine. You don't have to worry about me. It's you I worry about."

"I'm fine—I promise. I'm just a little . . . at a crossroads, I guess."

"Are you finally leaving this job that takes all your time?"

Arielle let out a laugh, grateful for a different sound than the heavy crying. "No, Abuela, I love my job. It's probably the only steady thing in my life."

"It's the *only* thing in your life. You need to go out and have more fun."

"That's exactly what's coming, and I don't know what to do for fun. I can definitely travel the world, but I already do a lot of that for work."

"I don't know what to tell you, but I'm sure you'll figure it out. I know you don't want to go to church, but do you pray?"

Arielle remained silent. She couldn't recall the last time she said a prayer, and knew her grandmother would scold her if that was her response. Her silence said enough.

"Well, hita, you need to pray again. Just try it. That's all I ask."

"I can do that. I need to try *something*."

"If it works, great. If not, then at least you tried."

"Thank you, Abuela. I didn't know I needed this phone call, but I'm glad it happened."

"Don't you ever hesitate to call me. It doesn't need to be for any reason."

"I know. I have to get going, but we'll talk again soon. I love you."

They hung up, and Arielle left the cemetery, eager for the mission to begin.

Chapter 6

On Wednesday morning, Felix sprung out of bed and dressed within minutes. He hadn't expected Arielle to follow through on her promise to take him to visit his parents before starting their next mission. People as busy as Arielle said a lot of things, and while their intentions were pure, something always seemed to come up in their schedules. Especially Arielle. She was always in demand. Needed at some meeting at headquarters. Or called on to write a report.

But when she called late Tuesday night to confirm the next morning's flight details, he understood nothing could change that. Arielle had looped in the trip to San Francisco as part of the mission, meaning on paper, the mission had officially begun and they could distract none of the three Angels to tend to something else.

He had been antsy about his parents meeting Arielle and Selena, not sure how to best explain his relationship with the two attractive women. Surely his mom would have lots of questions, while his dad would sneak in a suggestive wink at every opportunity, figuring his son had found himself in a love triangle worthy of the gods.

Felix would explain the situation for what it was—a work trip with colleagues—but his parents would still jump to their own conclusions. They couldn't help themselves. Regardless of what they believed, he knew they would welcome his new friends into the Francisco household with the warmness that always filled his childhood home.

Felix pushed these thoughts aside as he pulled into the hangar where Arielle's personal jet awaited. The top-ranked Angel had their own jet to use for personal or Road Runner business. With this being their first mission out of town, it was Felix's first time riding on the luxurious airliner.

He parked in the lot and stepped out to a row of at least a dozen different jets, all different sizes. He saw Arielle and Selena walking together, stopping in the middle of the row where a mobile flight of steps had been set up to reach a medium-sized white jet's entrance. "A1" decorated the jet's tail, presumably to signify the top-ranked Angel.

The two turned around and waved at him, waiting for Felix to catch up. They had their suitcases, two each, while Felix pulled his lone one behind him.

"Good morning, Felix," Arielle said once he had finally approached them at the base of the stairs. "Excited for the trip?"

"More than you know." They each took turns giving him a hug when the jet's pilot appeared from the open doorway. He was a muscular, middle-aged gentleman with a chiseled jawline and a perfect balance of gray hairs streaked into what was once all black.

"Peter!" Arielle greeted him as he descended the steps, throwing her arms around him.

Peter was in complete pilot's attire, and Felix appreciated the professional touch. He'd ridden on the commander's jet a few times, and the pilots had always looked like some random shmuck off the street, despite their credentials.

"Meet my friends and new teammates," Arielle said. "We'll be doing all missions together from now on. This is Felix Francisco and Selena Nicole."

"A pleasure to meet you both," Peter replied, taking off his hat to greet them, and offering a firm handshake to Felix.

"This is Captain Peter Holland," Arielle continued the introduction. "He was a fighter pilot in the United States Air Force for fifteen years. There is no one better to fly us around North America."

The captain smiled. "It's true. This jet might not be equipped to fight off enemies, but if something ever arises, I know how to get us to safety.

Not that it's an issue anymore, since the war ended." He pulled up his sleeve to check a shiny Rolex. "We should get ready for takeoff. Can get you there a few minutes earlier than planned."

The pilot offered a grin that reminded Felix a bit too much of George Clooney, before he spun around to grab both of Arielle's bags and starting up the stairs.

"You get your own luggage service?" Selena asked, putting her hands on her hips. "Don't they know you can kill anyone with your bare hands? You hardly need—"

Arielle shot up her hand. "That's enough. He'll come back for all of our bags. No need to get all fired up about my perks."

Felix thought it odd that the pilot of a private jet would be the one to load luggage. But he was a Road Runner, and probably made an exorbitant amount of money to do just that. Within one minute, Peter hustled back down the stairs, grabbed Selena's two bags, and took them up.

Arielle led them up the stairs, where Felix had insisted he'd carry his own suitcase. When they reached the top and entered the jet, Selena cried out, "Are you kidding me?!"

Felix was the last to enter and immediately understood Selena's surprise. The inside looked something out of a Hollywood movie.

Four regular airline seats were behind the cockpit, all facing the front. Behind those, however, were two couches lining the opposite sides of the walls, centered around a long glass table with a lounge chair on each end. Everything was decorated a simple black and white, minus the light gray carpet. Toward the back of the jet was a fully stocked bar with trays of appetizers placed on the counter. A woman dressed in a flight attendant uniform had just finished putting the final touches on a plate of bruschetta.

"Welcome aboard," she greeted, coming around the bar. "How are you today, Arielle?"

"Good to see you again, Octavia. I'm doing wonderful. I'd like for you to meet Felix and Selena. The three of us are working as a team on all missions going forward, so you'll be seeing them around a lot more."

"A pleasure meeting you," Octavia said, offering a hand to each of them. After the pleasantries were out of the way, she snapped back into focus. "It looks like a three-hour flight today. Appetizers are all served on the bar. Lunch will be a prime rib coupled with fresh asparagus, mashed potatoes, and garlic butter mushrooms. I will serve it thirty minutes after takeoff. If any of you would like a drink from the bar, just let me know, and I can bring that out to you."

She offered a soft grin before disappearing through a door behind the bar.

"What's back there?" Selena asked.

"A small kitchen," Arielle said. "A closet with cleaning supplies. And maybe a bedroom."

Selena slapped her leg. "You have a bed on your own private jet? Get out!"

Arielle shrugged. This had been her norm for the past couple of years. "Flights are the one place I can get reliable sleep."

"Apparently," Selena said. "Private chef cooking prime rib and serving it to you all before nap time. Why have you never mentioned any of this to us?"

"It's not that big of a deal," Arielle said. "I don't need to flaunt all this stuff. Honestly, it's kind of embarrassing, but this is what they gave me when I reached the top spot. This is how I get around to each mission."

Selena shook her head. "You know my dad is rich. I've been on yachts off the coast of France, and a couple of private charters, but I've never seen anything like this. You're up here living like a Bond villain."

"I don't know," Felix said. "I think a Bond villain would be incredibly jealous of this jet."

They all shared a laugh before Arielle rose from her seat and led the way to the bar to make a plate of appetizers. Felix followed suit, both starving and eager to see what kind of fine dining they served on this luxurious airliner. Besides the bruschetta, he found a tray of shrimp, another with at least a dozen fresh cheeses, and bacon-wrapped figs. He grabbed two of each before returning to his seat.

After ten minutes passed with them ordering a round of drinks and starting on their appetizers, the jet had taken off. Once they reached a cruising elevation and things had settled down while Octavia prepared their table for lunch, Arielle said, "I want to brainstorm for this mission. Nothing formal. Let's just talk out some ideas for how to best approach this one."

"Before we do," Selena said. "I have to admit, I don't fully understand what money laundering is. It has to do with hiding money, is that right?"

"I wouldn't call it hiding money," Felix said. "It's more like disguising money. Basically when criminals get their hands on money illegally, they will funnel it through a legitimate means to make it appear legal."

"How on Earth do you make it *appear* legal?"

"There are a few ways. Some run the money through businesses, either fake or real. They'll use the dirty to 'buy' goods, funneling that money to the business without ever receiving the goods they supposedly purchased. It's even more common with cash-heavy businesses. Think of car washes or strip clubs, places that deposit a lot of cash every day. Banks have no way of knowing if that cash is legal or not. This is the way the mob used to operate out of the back of restaurants before everyone started paying with credit cards. It was just another front to funnel money through."

"So we're getting involved with some pretty high-level criminal activity?"

"Absolutely. Money laundering is probably the most serious white-collar crime. Just based on what we know about the company we're dealing with, I'm willing to bet they laundered the money through real estate transactions. This is done when real estate is purchased with cash—the dirty money—then quickly sold. It's my understanding that WonderHome launched a new division of their business that deals specifically with purchasing and reselling property all around the country. They positioned themselves as the real estate experts in the nation, and no one ever questioned it. Say if you or I started flipping houses every other week, the feds would target us. But if a billion-dollar company is flipping dozens of houses every day, well, that's just part of their business, right?"

"It's always the corporations who can get away with whatever they want," Arielle said. "As long as they keep raking in the billions, no one ever thinks of questioning *why* they're earning so much money. Instead, they just get glorified by society, especially the poor, yet most of the time there are plenty of shady dealings behind the scenes. It doesn't make sense."

"And we're sure we have to deal with this money laundering and not the murder-suicide directly?" Selena asked. "I'm sure there are other opportunities where we could intervene to prevent the tragedy from happening. I mean, who would you rather take a risk with? A stressed-out mother with a gun, or a billionaire with their entire livelihood on the line? Who do you think has the resources to make a problem disappear with a quick signature on a check?"

"I've read through the initial report," Arielle said. "The issue with stopping the murders from happening is that we don't know if that will just delay them from occurring at a later time. Removing the *cause* of them is a guaranteed way to ensure neither of those children ever turns up dead."

"And what if we find out Adam Marshall really was guilty?" Selena asked. "Are we supposed to just let him free so his family never suffers? He still needs to face his own justice."

Arielle nodded. "That's something we'll have to deal with it as it comes up. But I don't think they would have ever assigned this mission if they didn't have a sound reason to believe he was innocent. Now, let's talk strategy. We need to infiltrate this company and pose as employees. Thoughts?"

Felix smiled, a certain dark satisfaction swimming behind it. "Easy. I can craft some resumes to get you both jobs in the company. Which departments do you think would be best?"

"Definitely HR," Arielle said. "They'll have the most oversight into all the departments and happenings. And those people love to gossip. Maybe we get Selena in there to start, then she can help get me hired in a different department. I don't see a reason for you to work for the company, Felix. We'll need someone on the outside still."

"Definitely," Felix said. "What if you took a job with IT or the software engineers? That would help me have easier access to hack into the company's system. We'll be able to see emails, authorized users, and really anything we want. That's probably our best play. Do you think you can pull that off?"

Arielle shrugged. "Acting has never been something I've needed to do on missions. But I guess there is a first time for everything. I don't have IT knowledge, though, so I'm not sure how I can exactly fake my way through this."

"Even easier," Felix said, his smile widening. He was growing pleased with his ability to mold this mission to his vision, and Arielle seemed to go along with it. "I can give you a small earpiece to speak to you. I can walk you through any sort of IT issue that may arise. We even have special glasses and necklaces equipped with hidden cameras, so I can know exactly what you're looking at. And it's all very easy to turn on and off, so you can only use when needed throughout the day."

Arielle put her elbow on the table and propped up her chin with a fist, staring into the distance. Felix recognized the look as her deep thought, something they had all gotten familiar with in such a short time.

"You know," she said. "It's just possible that between having us in HR and IT, we might prevent Adam from ever being hired by WonderHome. We can manipulate things like his application, interview schedule, whatever we need to make him seem like a poor candidate. If it works, it saves us a ton of work, and we can be out of there in less than a month."

Selena laughed. "You know it's never that easy."

"Oh, I'm aware it's unlikely to work. Pulling that off would drastically change Adam's timeline. But it's still worth trying."

"I agree," Felix said. "There is a lot we can try to prevent him from getting that job. All it takes is one action for him to get rejected, and we're in the clear. And we'll have time. It's not like you're both going to get hired and jump right into your roles. You'll have orientation and training to go through. A couple weeks, at least, until you're both on your own. During that time, I can see how we can make Adam look like a terrible candidate."

"Sabotage," Selena said with a crooked grin. "Makes us seem like the criminals."

"I don't think the Marshall family would agree with that statement if this all works out," Arielle said.

Octavia returned from the kitchen with a tray full of their lunch plates.

"Lunch is served," she said.

"I like what we've come up with," Arielle said. "We can flesh it out some more once we get to Seattle. But first, let's eat and get ready to meet the Francisco family."

Chapter 7

They landed in San Francisco two hours later, stomachs full and satisfied.

"Beautiful day," Arielle said once they descended the steps from the jet. "I've always loved the weather in San Fran. It's usually just the right temperature."

As with anything else on a mission, a town car had been arranged to take them from the hangar to the Francisco house, driven by a Road Runner who barely spoke to the three Angels riding in the back seat.

"I've never been here," Selena said, eyes glued out the window. "Are we going to do any touristy things?"

"That's up to Felix's family," Arielle said. "If they want to, sure. If they want some alone time with Felix, you and I can go sightseeing."

"I want to see the famous Golden Gate Bridge. And ride on a trolley. And visit Alcatraz."

Felix giggled. "So many things to do in this city, and you want to go where all the other people spend their time."

"I didn't grow up here, asshole," Selena said, reaching across Arielle to smack Felix on his arm. "I want to see those things. Maybe if you invited us out here more, we could go do more stuff that you locals love."

"You two need to relax," Arielle cut in. "We're here for two days, and the priority is for Felix to spend time with his family. If seeing these things is that important to you, Selena, we'll make it happen. Can we try to have two days without bickering before the mission? Please."

They drove through downtown San Francisco and made their way to the neighborhood of Nob Hill.

"What kind of neighborhood is this?" Arielle asked. "Half the buildings look modern and almost luxurious, and the other half are covered in graffiti."

"It used to be a really shady neighborhood," Felix said. "But over the past five years, it's gone through a lot of changes. It's actually becoming more of an affluent neighborhood. Think of it like Five Points in Denver. In a couple more years, people will have no idea these blocks used to be filled with drug dealers and murderers. I know because we lived in this area when I was a kid. Was never allowed to be outside past sunset. My parents have since moved to a different block and are in a much nicer apartment now."

"I'll say," Selena said when the car pulled over in front of a tri-level apartment building painted a light shade of blue with white trim around the curved windows. People jogged up and down the sloped sidewalks, parents pushed their babies in strollers, while couples walked their dogs.

It was a crowded intersection on California Street and Leavenworth, but one that felt entirely safe from its troubled past.

They gathered their luggage on the sidewalk and waited for Felix to guide them into the building, punching in a code on a keypad to jolt the door unlocked.

"We have to go up to the third floor," he said, barreling down the hallway toward the elevator at the opposite end. Arielle hardly had a moment to admire the artwork hanging on the main level's walls. Paintings of San Francisco landmarks like Fisherman's Wharf, Golden Gate Park, and a massive one that overlooked the bay.

The elevator doors parted immediately after Felix pushed the button, and they crammed into it with their bags.

"Tight squeeze, I know," he said. "The buildings may have been remodeled, but they couldn't make them any bigger."

They reached the third floor, and the doors opened to a mini hallway, one door on each side, marked 301 and 302. Felix strolled up to 301 and knocked with a heavy fist.

His parents must have been waiting by the door because it opened within three seconds, his mother appearing in the doorway with the widest grin smacked across her face.

"Oh, Felix!" she cried, stepping into the hallway and throwing her arms around her son. She planted multiple kisses on his cheeks, his face promptly flushing red. "How I've missed you. How *we've* missed you. Please come in, all of you. And you two must be Arielle and Selena?" She released Felix from her grasp and stuck out a hand to Selena.

"I'm Selena. A pleasure to meet you, Mrs. Francisco."

"Call me Elise—I insist."

Elise had wavy brown hair that ran just past her shoulders, a slightly overweight frame, and was at least six inches shorter than her six-foot son. Her face had minimal signs of aging to go along with the warm smile she couldn't erase.

"And you must be Arielle," she said, moving her attention after Selena slipped into the apartment behind Felix.

"Yes, ma'am, it's so great to finally meet you. Felix has told us so much about your family."

Elise looked over her shoulder to confirm Felix was out of range, and whispered to Arielle. "He doesn't know it, but his sisters are on their way right now. It will be the first time we're all together, outside of Christmas, in years."

Arielle heard the pure joy emanating from Felix's mother, and it struck a sharp pain in her heart. She had heard that same tone plenty of times from her own mother whenever they had family visit from out of town. A glee that couldn't be matched by anything else in the world. The unconditional love for family.

Elise guided Arielle into the apartment where her husband stood behind the island-style kitchen counter, slicing up a watermelon, while Felix threw an arm around him and showed a rare, joyous grin.

"Selena," Elise said. "Arielle. This is my husband, Benji."

"My goodness," Benji said, looking Arielle and Selena up and down. "Fantastic work, son!"

Felix flushed again.

Elise hurried around the counter and smacked her husband on the chest. "Those are his coworkers, you dirty man!"

Benji howled with laughter, grabbing his gut that had seen its share of beer over the years. "I know, my love. I just can't pass up a chance to poke fun."

Elise rolled her eyes as she slung her arm around Benji's back. "Forgive my husband. His sense of humor has no limits. You'll get used to it."

"I mean no disrespect," Benji said, coming around the counter to shake hands with Arielle and Selena. "I've been the class clown my whole life. It's a role I've earned, and love to own it. That said, if I ever say something offensive, just call me out. You kids these days have so many rules—I can't keep up. I'd hate to be a comedian the way everyone gets offended by everything. Ooh, would you ladies like to go to a comedy club while you're here?"

"Enough," Elise said. "Let them settle in. My goodness, they still have their suitcases. Come, let me show you to your room."

The kitchen had white granite counters running in a U-shape around the island in the middle, stainless steel appliances, and at least a dozen cupboards and cabinets to keep everything perfectly organized. The kitchen opened up to the living room, where a TV mounted on the wall took up every inch of space above a fireplace. Behind the L-shaped couch facing the TV was a long wooden dining table that seated sixteen, with an elevated view of the window overlooking the peaceful neighborhood below.

On the other side of the entrance was a hallway that stretched down to the master bedroom at the end, a bathroom next to it.

"This place has two floors?" Arielle asked.

A stairwell ran down from the hallway across from the bathroom door.

"Yes," Elise said. "And that's where you'll be staying. Downstairs there are two more bedrooms and a bathroom. Come!"

Arielle and Selena grabbed their suitcases and followed Elise down the stairs where a smaller living room separated the two bedrooms.

"You two don't mind sharing a room?" Elise asked. "Otherwise Felix will have to sleep on the couch in the living room."

"Not at all," Arielle said. "Are your daughters not going to need a place to stay?"

Selena's head whipped around to Arielle at the mention of Felix's sisters, and she gave a satisfied grin. They were both anxious to dig deeper into the mystery known as Felix Francisco, and who better to give insight than his siblings?

"Oh, no, they live just outside of town and will drive back home." Elise led them into the bedroom with a queen-sized bed positioned in the corner and closed the door behind her. "I need to ask you both something," she said, just above a whisper. "You work with Felix pretty regularly? You know him well?"

Arielle and Selena looked at each other, unsure where the conversation was going.

"Yeah," Selena said. "The three of us spend a lot of time together. Our job requires a ton of teamwork and travel."

"I'd say we know him as much as he lets us," Arielle added. "We've gotten to know him pretty decently, but I feel there is still so much we don't know."

Elise nodded, sitting on the foot of the bed as she stared at the floor. "Does he seem emotionally stable, would you say?"

Selena shrugged. "Well, he rarely shows emotion, and we have a pretty stressful job. He stays calm under pressure. But I don't know if that's stability or if he's just hiding his true feelings. He's impossible to read sometimes."

"That's my Felix. He's always been so focused. He has tunnel vision with the things he cares about in life. Rarely gets distracted by outside matters. We had him seen by behavioral experts when he was a teenager. We worried something was wrong because he never showed emotion. He gets excited about baseball and whatever projects he works on, but that's really it. But everyone we spoke with said he is completely normal. Does he have friends? Does he go on dates?"

Now Arielle shrugged. "He doesn't mention friends to us, but we have no idea what he does during his time away from work. He's gone out with us a couple of times outside of work, and he always seems to enjoy himself. As far as his romantic life, I have no idea. He's never mentioned anyone. Has he to you, Selena?"

Selena shook her head. "No. I actually went to a baseball game with him when we first met. He told me many things about his life, but he never mentioned a girlfriend or anything like that."

"Keep in mind," Arielle said. "The people in our line of work spend a lot of their time on the job. I just went on my first date in years the other day, in fact."

It occurred to Arielle that she had no clue what Felix had told his parents he did for work. Every Angel had a lie they told to their loved ones, needing to keep the truth concealed. If Elise prodded into that, Arielle wasn't sure how they'd pivot out of the conversation.

"Okay, that's good," Elisa said. "As long as he's fine. I always worry about him. We're going to deliver some big news later once his sisters get here. It might shake him up because I know how much he hates change."

"Oh," Arielle said. "Do you need me and Selena to leave? Totally understand if you need some private family time."

"Not at all." Elise stood from the bed. "No one is dying—nothing that serious. But I know it will bother Felix, even if he doesn't show it. I'll let you two get settled in for now. Come back upstairs whenever you're ready. I think Benji is going to make some margaritas soon."

"Now we're talking," Selena said with a wide smile.

Elise grinned back before she left the bedroom, leaving Arielle and Selena to worry about the Francisco family's impending news.

Chapter 8

They returned upstairs fifteen minutes later to find Benji back at the kitchen island, this time with a blender, a bucket of ice, three bottles of tequila, orange juice, lime juice, and a gallon of margarita mix.

A platter with crackers and cheeses sat on the front ledge of the island, where Felix and his mother had gathered around.

"Hope you ladies like margaritas," Benji said as he combined the ingredients in the blender. "I may or may not make them a *little* stronger than what you get at the bars."

"I can vouch for that," Felix said. "And yes, we all drink margaritas at our favorite spot in Denver after we finish our . . . projects."

"We love a good marg," Arielle said. "Felix, can we speak with you really quickly? It's about work."

Felix looked at them with a puzzled stare. "Okay?"

He shoved a cheese cube into his mouth before leading them to the balcony outside. The space had a patio table, a cornhole setup, a tall smoker, and a barbecue grill. All with a majestic view overlooking downtown San Francisco.

"Is something wrong?" Felix asked.

"No," Arielle said. "We just need to know what you've told your parents you do for work. Your mom was asking questions when she took us to our room. She didn't ask any specifics, but it would have gotten messy if she did."

"I didn't even think of that," Felix said, shaking his head. "All they know is that I work as a software consultant for top businesses in Denver.

They don't even fully understand what that means, so I doubt you'll get specific questions about our work."

"Okay, good," Arielle said. "That's all we needed to know."

"What do you think about my parents?"

"They're awesome," Selena said. "So chill and fun. And your dad makes homemade margaritas. I can stay here as long as we need."

Arielle saw the apartment's front door open, two women who closely resembled Felix stepping in with their hands tossed in the air as they skipped into the kitchen.

"Looks like everyone is here now," she said, nodding toward the scene unfolding behind Felix's back.

He scrunched his brow in confusion before turning around. "Holy shit!" His jaw hung open while his sisters barged through the sliding patio door, howling like loons as they smothered their brother with hugs.

"I thought you both weren't going to make it," Felix said.

"That was a lie," said the older sister. "We just said that so we could surprise you. We wouldn't miss this for the world. So, who are your friends?"

The two sisters pivoted around to face Arielle and Selena, looking them each up and down.

"This is Arielle and Selena," Felix said. "My friends and coworkers. We're heading to Seattle to work on a project in a couple of days."

"Well, it's nice to meet you," the older sister said, stepping forward and hugging Arielle. "I'm Clara."

The younger sister did the same thing. "And I'm Sarah. It's nice meeting you."

They took a step back and the three Francisco siblings stood together, their resemblances to one another clear as day in the afternoon sunshine.

Clara was a few inches shorter than Felix, her sandy hair tied into a long, swaying ponytail. Sarah stood even shorter than Clara, with much darker hair cut to shoulder-length.

All three shared the same light brown eyes.

"So you're only here until tomorrow?" Sarah asked Felix.

He nodded. "We leave tomorrow night. We have the company jet, so we can leave whenever we want."

"Well, aren't you fancy," Clara said. "A private company jet. Look at you, little bro, doing big things."

It had been obvious to Arielle that Felix and his sisters had grown up in a humble environment. Felix had mentioned his mother's fashion boutique being highly lucrative and successful. Yet, outside of a beautiful apartment, they showed little signs of a family sitting on a fortune.

The patio door slid open again, and Benji popped out to announce that all margaritas had been served.

They retreated inside, where seven margarita glasses waited on the kitchen island.

"I'd like to make a toast," Benji said once everyone had grabbed their drink. He raised his glass in the air. "To family. We are so blessed to have everyone under the same roof. It's a treat that your mother and I never take for granted. And to Felix's new friends. We welcome you to our home and our family. *Salud!*"

Everyone raised their glasses, clinking them against one another before taking their first sips.

"Mr. Francisco," Selena said. "These are incredible. What is your secret?"

"Why, thank you. I add a little more orange juice than normal, and less margarita mix. And double the tequila." He cackled as he said this, taking a long drink from his glass.

Elise slipped in beside Benji and wrapped her arm around his back. "Your father is right. Days like this are the ones I'll remember forever." Tears welled in her eyes.

"Mom, what's wrong?" Clara asked, her face shifting from a wide grin into a concerned frown within seconds.

"It's nothing," Elise said, shaking her head. She looked at Benji. "I don't think I can do this."

Benji rubbed his hand up and down her back. "It's okay, my love." He turned to the rest of the room, focusing on his three children standing next to each other. "Your mother and I have an announcement to make. It's her announcement, so I'm going to let her tell you. But I want you to know it is something we both discussed together. This was not her decision—it's both of ours. You may like it, you may not. But I'm incredibly proud of your mother and would do anything to support her. I hope you can do the same, because this was not easy."

Arielle looked to her left to see the three siblings swaying in nervous anticipation. To her right, Selena was doing the same thing, as if she had been a part of the family her whole life.

"What is it, Mom?" Sarah asked. "Tell us."

Elise stepped forward, taking a deep breath. "Your father and I are moving to New York City. My fashion business is doing so well, and I've come into an opportunity to open a boutique in New York. Our plan is to get it going and run it for at least five years. We figure that will be enough to allow us to step back and retire."

The apartment fell completely silent as tears welled in Elise's eyes.

"It's not forever," Benji reiterated. "Your mother is still being humble. She has made it to the top. It's not just the boutique. They have invited her to New York Fashion Week, Paris Fashion Week, and Milan Fashion Week."

"Mom, that's fantastic news!" Sarah said, running around the island to hug her mother. "Why would you be so worried about telling us this?"

"Because San Francisco is our home," Elise said, hugging Benji and Sarah at the same time. "Our dreams became a reality here. Our life is here. When we moved to this country from Colombia, we chose San Francisco because we thought the opportunities would be best. It's hard to just leave it all behind."

Felix shook his head, tears streaming down his face as he joined his little sister hugging his mother. "It hurts. I can't lie. But you made it, Mom. You were right when you chose San Francisco. The opportunities here are exactly what have led to this moment. Now you get to grow even more. The entire world is going to know your name. I'll miss coming here for the holidays, but I'm so, so proud of you."

Felix buried his face into his mom's chest and let out uncontrollable sobs.

Clara remained silent as tears streamed down her face, her arms crossed to hug herself. Benji shuffled over to embrace her and wiped the tears off her cheeks.

"It's going to be okay," he whispered.

Arielle and Selena exchanged glances before taking silent steps backward. Arielle wanted to drop and crawl all the way downstairs to hide in the bedroom, but that would only make the situation more awkward.

Instead, they stood like mannequins, refusing to move another inch to not draw any attention. After everyone had hugged and wiped their tears away, Elise faced Arielle and Selena. "I'm sorry to have done this in front of you. We wanted to tell everyone at the beginning of our gathering rather than waiting until the end. I'm sorry if it was weird for you both."

"Not at all," Arielle lied. "Congratulations on your new opportunity—it sounds like a lot of fun."

"Yes, congratulations," Selena said. "If you're up to it, I can connect you with my parents. My mom lives in New York, and my dad lives in Paris. They can definitely show you around."

"That would be fantastic!" Elise cried, strolling around the island to give Selena a hug. "I've been to New York a few times, but know nothing about living there."

"I can vouch for it. It's a wonderful place to live, especially since you're used to living in a big city. You'll have no problems adjusting. There's just a lot more people and places, but you'll learn your way around in no time."

"See," Benji said, both daughters now in his embrace. "Everything is going to be fine. And we have every intent on returning here to retire. In fact, we're not even going to sell this apartment. We'll rent it out, or leave it available for any of you three to use should you wish."

"I love you all so much," Elise said. "Your father is right. We've made it. And I couldn't have done it without all of you. I've never forgotten all the help you kids did in the first days of opening my boutique here."

The family all huddled around Elise, hugging her as the last tears made their rounds. Arielle watched Felix, worried the drastic change would distract him from his work on the upcoming mission.

Chapter 9

Friday morning saw the Angels return to Arielle's private jet. They had agreed to stay Thursday night at the Francisco house instead of catching a flight in the late hours.

The rest of their stay with Felix's family passed rather quickly. They ended up finishing the two pitchers of margaritas Benji had made before going out for dinner downtown, followed by a visit to their favorite ice cream shop, Wicked Scoops.

On Thursday, Arielle insisted on taking Selena out to all the touristy sightseeing she had wanted to do. This left the Francisco family alone with each other on Felix's last day in town. They visited Alcatraz, the Golden Gate Bridge, Fisherman's Wharf, and even stopped by the Mrs. Doubtfire house, where Robin Williams had once hosted a birthday party for the ages.

It left the two of them drained, part of the reason they opted to go to sleep later that evening instead of hustling back across town to catch a flight.

For now, they soared high above the coast, making their way to the Pacific Northwest.

"How are you feeling?" Arielle asked Felix once they had taken off and settled into the flight.

"I'm okay," he replied. "It was tough news to hear at first, and I'm obviously not thrilled about it. But they seem pretty set on returning home after a few years. I just hope that stays true."

"It sounds like your sisters are going to run the apartment as a vacation rental," Arielle said. "I overheard them talking in the next room when I was trying to fall asleep last night."

Felix nodded. "It should do really well. I guess we'll have a place to stay if we're ever back in town. It'll be weird. I associate San Fran with my parents and childhood. I remember when I was young, my mom didn't even know what she wanted to do with her life. All she did was work random jobs to keep food on the table. So did my dad. But it wasn't until she got a job cleaning up a local fashion boutique that something awoke within her. The owner let her take the scrap materials home, and she'd sit at the kitchen table of our cramped little apartment, trying new things with the materials. And the rest is history. My sisters and I have had all the success, and I know that's all our parents wanted when they moved to the States. As much as the change hurts, I'm just happy to see my mom accomplish something for herself."

"And not just anything," Arielle added. "Something *major*."

"I noticed your older sister didn't have much to say," Selena said.

"She's taking it the hardest," Felix said. "She got engaged last year, and is planning on having kids soon. My parents ranted and raved about how they'll get to be involved grandparents, since they don't live too far. That all just changed with the announcement. Clara won't move to New York, and I'm sure she's feeling a little abandoned by all of this. She'll be okay, though. Her fiancé has family in town, and by the time they get married and start having kids, there won't be much time left before my parents plan on returning."

Arielle sensed through his tone that Felix really was fine. His parents had softened the blow of the news with their promises to return. Benji refused to die in New York, and said he would crawl back through broken glass to San Francisco if it was the last thing he ever did.

"That's great. Are we feeling ready for this mission?" she asked both of them.

"I'm very ready," Felix said to Arielle's delight. "I have so many missteps from the last one that I want to redeem. This one will go much smoother. I actually spent an hour getting things started last night."

"Way to pull an Arielle," Selena said with a laugh.

"Wasn't much," Felix said. "Just started on your resumes so you can get hired sooner than later. The first thing I want to do when we get there is send in your job applications. Is there a particular date we are trying to go back to, and is there a reason? I ask, because I've been experimenting with the best approach. If we're putting Selena in the HR Department, it could be as simple as having her delete Adam's application from the system as soon as it comes in. Or would it make more sense if she was still a new hire in her ramp-up period, or someone more seasoned with a few months of work under her belt?"

"I see where you're coming from," Arielle said. "But I don't want to spend an extra six months, or even three months, on top of what has already been scheduled. It's just not efficient because you and I would have nothing to do for all that time until Adam even applies. We wouldn't make much progress trying to intervene with him so early. Even if we found a way, the past will still work to correct itself if given enough time. Because I've also thought about going back way before any of this is happening, finding a management role at some other company, and hiring Adam before he ever applies at WonderHome. There are just too many factors at play to ensure that would even work, and I'd hate to waste our time. Let's focus on what we can with WonderHome. Besides, if he really is innocent, we want to take them down. Because if it's not Adam, it will just be someone else later on, and who knows how *that* will all play out?"

"Do we have a backup plan in case I get fired?" Selena asked. "I mean, we are planning on doing some pretty questionable things within the company. It'd be foolish to just assume we don't get caught."

"You'll be doing that dirty work," Arielle said. "So you will be at the highest risk. But honestly, I'm not worried about it. Companies don't fire someone for making a mistake or two, and that's why it's important that we frame everything as a mistake on your end. The accidental deletion of Adam's application, or whatever else we come up with. I'll be in the company and blending more into the background. Even if you end up getting fired, or our plans simply don't work, I'll still be there. I'd love to get a bug planted in the CEO's office, but that is something incredibly risky and grounds for immediate termination if we get caught. We'll get a feel for things once we're hired, so we'll see."

"Only need two minutes to plant a bug," Felix said. "And putting one underneath a desk is very easy. You can probably do it in thirty seconds, actually. All you have to do is make sure no one sees you enter the office, and you'll be done. I'd say I'll do it, but if I were to get caught, well that's a legit crime. Trespassing. If one of you does it as an employee, you can at least make up something on the spot for why you're in there. Might face some discipline and questioning, but nothing that should land you in handcuffs."

"Gee," Selena said. "Thanks for really selling us on doing this part of the job."

They shared a quick laugh.

"We're almost there," Felix said, nodding toward the open window behind the couch.

Below the jet, the clouds formed a white sheet as far as they could see. Protruding through the clouds, however, was the snow-capped top of Mount Rainier. Its sheer size made the summit appear like a palace atop the clouds, a final destination at the end of an epic journey.

And it was.

Arielle loved to hike the challenging mountains in Colorado and other states. Mount Rainier had killed plenty of people who had tried to reach its top, but that didn't stop her from fantasizing about the accomplishment.

She had gone on plenty of hikes with her family as a child, though her parents and brother lost interest in the hobby. But not Arielle. She viewed hiking as the ultimate workout, as it challenged her mind, body, and soul all at the same time. Nothing else provided her with the same type of physical and mental therapy as climbing to the top of a mountain and reaping the reward of a sublime view of nature available only to those willing to make the sacrifice.

"So what touristy things are you going to make us do, Selena?" Felix asked, a grin spreading across his face.

Selena rolled her eyes. "I'm a world traveler. I'm sorry if you can't handle that I like to see everything I can, even if that includes touristy things. But since you asked, I want to go to the original Starbucks, the Space Needle, and Pike's Place Market. And let me guess, you want to go to a baseball game?"

Felix nodded. "Of course. I've been out here a couple of times during the offseason, so haven't been able to catch a Mariners game, but it looks like I'll finally get the chance. And to be fair, I'd also like to go to the Space Needle. I've been to it, but have never gone to the top. Pike's Place is a really cool spot, and the Starbucks is just another Starbucks. Nothing special about it."

Arielle laughed. "I was afraid this might happen working on a longer mission. Let's set some ground rules. Just because we're going to be together for six months on this mission doesn't mean we have to spend every waking moment together. If Felix wants to go to a baseball game by himself, he can. If Selena wants to parade through Pike's Place and catch the fish out of the air, she can. We'll still do lots of things together, but don't feel like you're bonded to the mission. There will be lots of downtime. On the flip side, when it's time to work, I expect no distractions. All business from there on out. Are we clear?"

"Yes, *Mother*," Selena said, earning a shake of the head from Arielle.

They shared a laugh before Peter announced the jet's descent would begin in approximately twenty minutes.

Chapter 10

Selena didn't get the same excitement about starting new missions as the other two. Even as a Road Runner who had earned a most luxurious lifestyle, missions still felt like work. Something she *needed* to do, rather than wanted to do. Arielle and Felix identified their work as part of themselves, while Selena still dreamed of a career in Hollywood.

The recent changes to their time off between missions had rekindled her hopes. Weeks, possibly months, between missions would allow her to chase her dreams, and she planned to pursue them with the same ferocity she had while attending Julliard.

For now, the dream would have to wait for another day.

At least I don't lose time once we travel back, she thought, grateful she could do all this work for the Angels and hardly have any days pass in her real life.

When they touched down in Seattle, Selena felt the first rush of being on this trip. She had never spent time in the Emerald City and looked forward to exploring everything it offered. And with actual free time built into their schedule, she had a vacation sensation as they jammed into the town car that would take them to their new home during the mission.

"So, I didn't get to have any seafood while in San Fran," Selena said. "We need to make that happen tonight. I've already looked it up and there are a couple of fine dining spots overlooking the beach."

"You'll need to see if they exist in 2013," Arielle said. "When we get to the house, I want to jump back from there. No reason not to."

She spoke while scrolling through a block of text on her cell phone, not even looking up. It was the mission report, and Selena assumed she was confirming the exact date they were to jump back to in 2013.

"Good idea," Selena said. "Our phones should still work when we jump back, right? Thank God for a mission where I get to keep my phone."

"We may need to get new phones while we're here," Felix said. "The same cell towers might not exist. It's fifty-fifty, I'd say, based on other missions I've gone on."

The thought of spending her first couple hours in a new city and year at a cell phone store made Selena queasy. She just wanted to get out into the world and not worry about all the logistics.

"Well, let's hope it works."

"Okay," Arielle said. "We'll be going back to October 16, 2013. Adam applies for the job on November 17. That leaves us one month to apply, interview, and get accepted into our new roles. Felix, do you think that's enough time?"

"It should be. I'm going to make your resumes strong enough to grab their attention right away." He pulled up an image of the 2013 calendar he had already saved on his cell phone. "That's a Wednesday. We can submit the applications the same day we arrive, and I'll bet we get a call back before the weekend. I've worked with a lot of tech companies, and they usually move pretty fast. They'll probably book an interview for the following week, potentially a second one the week after that, and you'll be hired before November. Your first days will probably be on November 4 or 11, which still leaves us plenty of time before Adam applies on Sunday, November 17. Might not get to prevent his application from being seen, but we don't know for sure how long training will even be."

"I would think a job in HR is less time in the classroom and more hands-on," Arielle said.

"Not necessarily. HR deals with a lot of legal matters. Labor laws, insurance policies, hiring practices. It could very well be as much time in a classroom as any other."

They turned away from the skyscrapers of downtown and headed east, where cedar and maple trees lined the residential blocks.

"We're not staying in downtown?" Selena asked.

"Afraid it's not ideal for this mission," Felix said. "The only places we own are apartments in the big buildings. We need to get in and out quickly if needed, and waiting for an elevator to run twenty levels up and down isn't the way to do that. We're close to downtown, though, maybe a ten-minute drive. And I've spoken with the team who maintains our properties, and asked if they could leave us two cars. I may have accidentally launched a new initiative, as the Road Runners are now in the business of buying cars to keep at each property we own."

"One less thing for us to worry about," Arielle said. "It's really smart, actually. Sounds like something Commander Briar would have approved in a heartbeat."

Selena saw the GPS tracker standing on the dashboard, showing they had two minutes until their destination.

Not too far at all, she thought. Selena would have downtime and wanted nothing more than to explore Seattle's night life. A quick drive downtown would make that task much easier.

"Besides," Felix said. "Look at this neighborhood. The trees literally run the entire length of the blocks. So much privacy. Our house is on a big corner lot, but you can hardly see any of it passing by. And the house is incredible."

"Who maintains these homes all over the continent?" Arielle asked. "I guess I'm not familiar with that process at all."

"The Road Runners have an entire property management department. They hire contractors, cleaners, whatever is needed to update the properties as needed, depending on the year the mission will take place. It's almost like being a set designer in Hollywood. They can make any property fit its surroundings. If we were traveling back a century, they would make the house looked like it belonged in that era. It's all quite fascinating how they go about it."

"Sounds like it takes a lot of time."

"It does. I'd bet this mission we're on has been on the Commander's desk for at least the last six months while details get sorted out. It's also why we have multiple properties in each city, because there will always be at least one going under renovation."

"I'd bet Jackie's method of traveling back a week to get all the work done will become the new norm for everyone across the organization. Even I've been thinking of ways we can implement that practice."

Felix nodded. "Keep an eye on her. I hear her name come up all the time in different meetings. She's going to advance through the ranks real quick."

The town car turned onto a neighborhood block and immediately stopped in front of the first house on their right.

"We have arrived, folks," the driver said. She had remained silent ever since they left the airport. They instructed drivers to do just that when transporting Angels to the official start of a mission. The rule had been in place as long as Selena could remember, meant to allow time for mission discussion without distraction.

The driver opened her door and hurried around to the trunk, where she pulled out their luggage and lined up their bags on the sidewalk.

The three Angels joined her outside, finding the street narrow as cars lined both sides in makeshift parking spots. Only a handful of the properties had driveways. A Nissan Altima and a Toyota Camry, both gray, were parked in front of their house.

"I believe these are our cars for the mission," Felix said, studying them.

Arielle tipped and thanked the driver before she left them alone.

Slanted rays of sunshine fought through the trees towering over the neighborhood.

"You really can't see much," Arielle said.

"Only about half of each house," Felix said. "If that."

They grabbed their luggage and turned around to face their home for the next several months. Two droopy cedar trees stood across from each other, a walkway running up the center from the sidewalk to a flight of a dozen steps toward the front entrance.

"Everything is so *green*," Selena said.

Bushes, landscaping rocks, and flowers filled the small hills on each side of the stairs. A half dozen of plotted pants decorated the steps that led up to a busy front patio filled with three tables, six chairs, and a swinging bench. Two white pillars towered from the ground to the house's roof two levels above.

"Why do we have to spend all the winter here?" Selena cried. "I bet hanging out on this patio is absolutely stunning in the summer. Well, it *is*—look at it now."

Birds sung their late-morning tunes from high in the trees. Squirrels played on the branches. And despite being less than two miles from the bustling downtown, the area had a serenity matched by being alone in the wilderness.

"Let's go inside," Felix said, starting up the stairs, lugging his heavy suitcase behind.

He reached the front door and pushed it open. They followed him into a foyer complete with a coat closet, a staircase that led upstairs, and a long hallway running to the back of the house. To the right was a family room, complete with a mounted TV, coffee table, a couch, and three lounge chairs. To the left was a living room with two couches centered around another coffee table, this one with a pile of board games. A full bookshelf stood in the corner, two landscape paintings serving as the decoration.

"All of the bedrooms are upstairs," Felix said. "Let's check out the rest of the place."

He started down the hallway, passing by a door that concealed the main level's bathroom, and ended in a kitchen and dining area that spanned the entire width of the house. A dining table was on their left, leaving the rest of the space open for a kitchen that would make a chef drool.

That's exactly what they found Felix doing, his mouth hanging open as he looked around a shiny kitchen made almost entirely of marble. The floor, countertops, and cabinets all glimmered as they blended seamlessly into one another. A sliding glass door revealed a back patio overlooking an even more lush backyard, complete with a grill and a firepit.

"Okay," Selena said. "This place really is amazing. I'll have no problem calling it home for the next eight months, even if most of our time here is in the winter."

"I don't mean to burst your bubble," Arielle said, shuffling into the kitchen. "But the house is probably not going to look like this in 2013 when we go back. This is what it looks like today. Should we head into the living room to do this?"

"Let's go."

Chapter 11

October 16, 2013

They gathered in the living room, having wheeled their luggage with them to ensure it traveled into the past after they took their Juice.

Arielle and Selena took opposite ends of one couch, while Felix took the other to himself.

"This mission is going to be very different," Arielle said, rummaging in her suitcase for her flask of Juice. The other two did the same. "We've obviously done the whole roommate thing on past missions, but those have only been for two weeks at a time. And we were in Colorado for both. This time we're going to learn a lot more about each other, especially with all the downtime we'll have between mission work."

"What are you getting at?" Selena asked.

"I don't want us to lose sight of our cohesiveness as a team. We really are great together, and I'd hate to see anything break up that chemistry. Eight months is a long time. By the end of the mission, we just might become more of a family. And that doesn't mean it's all glamorous. Families fight with each other. They grow resentful. It is possible to spend too much time with the same people, that you get sick of each other, and that can spiral into hatred. Possibly to the point of never speaking to each other. I've seen it happen within my family, and others' families. Maintaining our team dynamic might be the most difficult part of this mission."

"I'm not worried about it," Felix said. "You laid out the perfect ground rules during the flight. If anyone needs their alone time, they are welcome to it. Personally, that's how I recharge: locked in my room, playing some video games or watching TV. Selena likes to go out and party to recharge. Two very different approaches, but it's what works for us."

"And what about you, Arielle?" Selena asked. "What do you do to unwind?"

Arielle rolled her head to look at the young actress who had once made her life a living hell, but had now become like a little sister. She shrugged. "I wish I knew. Usually I travel between missions, but it's been such a long time since I've had a mission with actual downtime during it. I'm so behind on TV shows—I don't even know what's out these days. And there are so many streaming platforms. How the hell does anyone keep up? I used to read for pleasure. Maybe I'll get some books. I also like hiking, and I'm sure there are some good trails further out from the city, if any of you'd like to join."

"I'll pass on the hike," Selena said. "I love the outdoors, but climbing up a mountain? Ugh, just shoot me now!"

They all broke into laughter.

"I'll go on a hike with you," Felix said. "I've never done one before. I suppose it wouldn't hurt to try."

"Well, thank you. I'd appreciate the company."

"Let's go back already," Selena cried. "The anticipation is killing me. Do you guys still get butterflies before taking a sip?"

Felix let out a nervous laugh. "Always."

No one quite understood how the Juice worked. All they knew was that the Road Runners had obtained the official formula to make the liquid from the Book of Time after the war. The secrets in the potion were passed down centuries, dating back to Chronos, and were altered over the years to achieve a seamless, time travel perfection.

There had never been a case of the Juice not working, or having a malfunction of any sorts, but any Road Runner who took that fateful sip always had a gnawing doubt in the back of their mind that it would all go haywire, leaving them trapped in the past—or future—forever.

It was no different from riding an airplane. Sure, the odds were nearly non-existent of being on a plane that crashes, but the possibility always looms in the back of your mind. And when those wheels touch down at the destination city, the relief always floods over your system. Another successful trip.

"The nerves never go away," Arielle said. "Now let's get down to business."

All Angels traveled with a small flask of their Juice, each with a larger bottle kept at their home or office.

"To October 16, 2013," Arielle said, raising her flask as if proposing a toast.

The others raised theirs and repeated the date, and all three took a sip no more than a standard wine sampling, and screwed the lids back onto their flasks.

"Everyone, touch your luggage," Arielle said. Anything that was in contact with a time traveler during the transition through time would come with them.

The transition felt like a light intoxication. Arielle grew lightheaded, and saw Felix and Selena bobbing their heads slowly from side to side, as if they were listening to a smooth jazz record.

After the lightheadedness passed, she fell asleep, but not unconscious, unable to physically open her eyelids. She could only trust Selena and Felix had reached the same stage, but it didn't really matter. They would all end up at the same place within seconds of each other.

Arielle swam in the void. Darkness consuming her entirety as her mind and soul blasted through the realms of time. She always thought of this stage as what it must feel like to die and assumed that was why everyone had the nerves they did after taking the sip of Juice. Silence complemented the blackness, regardless of what was happening in the world outside of her body. She floated through time and space—though not able to confirm this—a wandering soul looking for its host in whatever dimension they had been destined to go to.

The Juice truly was a miracle. A potion that bent reality in every sense.

It was always during the suspenseful minute between two timelines that she felt genuine appreciation for the life she had.

The end of the transition concluded with what felt like a slap on the chest, as if someone had grabbed hold of her soul and was trying to smack it back into her body.

Her eyes shot open to see the same living room they were just sitting in from nine years into the future.

She had arrived in 2013.

Selena and Felix both stirred back awake, happy to once again have arrived safely.

The furniture in the living room remained the same, likely done intentionally as most Road Runners opted to drink their Juice from a particular, safe area.

"We made it," Selena said, rolling her neck in circles as if she had just woken from an uncomfortable plane ride instead of bounding through the dimensions of time.

"Welcome to 2013," Arielle said, standing up and wheeling her suitcase back toward the stairs. "Doesn't look like much changed around here."

The aesthetics were all different. The kitchen had granite instead of marble, downgraded appliances, but it remained large and plentiful with all the equipment.

"Dammit," Felix said. "Cell phones aren't working. I'll need to buy some burner phones today if we plan on applying for your jobs. We *need* to do all that before anything. Do we still have cars outside?"

He rose from the couch and hurried to the window, sliding the curtain aside. Selena followed, bringing her suitcase with her.

"There are two cars still," Felix said. "I think they're the same ones—they're just brand-new in 2013, because they look a lot shinier than what we just left."

"Keys are supposed to be in the master bedroom nightstand," Arielle said, recalling this specific instruction from the briefing. "Let's take fifteen minutes to get settled into our bedrooms, then I want to have a quick meeting to discuss a tentative schedule for the mission before you leave for the store, Felix."

* * *

They gathered at the dining room table where Arielle laid out the mission files, along with her planner and calendar.

"Everything good in your rooms?" she asked.

"One of the bigger rooms I've had on a mission," Selena said. "Can't complain, especially for how long we'll be here."

"I have an incredible view of all the trees in the neighborhood," Felix said with a laugh. "If I didn't know better, I might think we were living in the jungle."

"This is definitely different from the last two missions," Arielle said. "To be fair, I've done a mission in the jungle before, and I don't recommend it. Lots of creatures to worry about, on top of the past. It wasn't fun in the least bit. But, I'm glad to hear everything is good here. I want to spend the rest of the day just getting familiar with the area. Maybe we can drive the route to the WonderHome office. First, I want a general schedule. And I'm sure it will change since we can't quite predict when WonderHome will call us for interviews."

She shuffled through the papers until finding a list of important dates for the mission and flipped open her 2013 planner to October.

"All right, we are here on Wednesday, October 16," she said, circling the date. "Selena and I are going to submit our applications to WonderHome today. And you think it will be a couple of days until they reach out to us, Felix?"

Felix nodded. "I've made your resumes so strong that you should both move to the top of their lists. I'd be surprised if they sit on your application beyond the weekend. But what do I know about recruiting for a major corporation?"

"Let's say Monday at the latest," Arielle continued, circling the twenty-first on the calendar. "They'll call us by then to set up an interview either later next week, or the week after. For the sake of our planning, let's assume everything falls later. That way it's easier to move things up instead of pushing them back."

Arielle had gained her organization skills from her mother, and couldn't help but feel her presence now that the calendar was open amid a scatter of documents. She remembered plenty of times seeing her mother doing the same thing at their kitchen table, whether it was planning for the annual family vacation, tax preparation, or something as simple as a trip to the grocery store. Her mother never left the house unprepared.

"We're not going in completely guessing," Felix said, leaning over Arielle's shoulder to view the list of critical dates. "We know Adam applies on November 17, and reports to the office for his first day of training on December 2. That's only two weeks from application to the first day. They move fast."

"True," Arielle agreed. "It's also for a higher priority position, so I don't want to base everything off that. But, yes, they can move through the hiring process at a brisk pace. All that said, our goal is to be in a position at the company where Selena can influence the recruiting process. Ideally, she'll be the one who receives the application on Monday morning of November 18 and can remove it from the system before anyone else sees it. And even if not, she can hopefully have some say over the interviewing process."

"We should still try to intervene on Adam's end," Felix said. "If you're able to get to a point where you're working on your own, Arielle, you might get me the info I need to hack into the company's system. We can change the date and time of the interview, change Adam's contact information. Anything to make him *not* receive communication from the company. It would be better if I did this and tried to make it look like a technical glitch. Because there won't be a valid reason if we were to have Selena update those details in the system, since they could likely trace that back to her."

"So I'm basically going in there and acting like a complete dumbass for my few first days, aren't I?" Selena asked.

"Precisely," Felix said. "But don't act too dumb. We still need you there for the long haul. Being in HR will get you access to all the happenings around the company. Since we don't know how wide this scheme is, we'll need ears open across all the departments."

"Yes," Arielle said. "Let's not get fired in the first month. We'll need to be ready to adjust our plans, too. If Selena gets caught, or ends up on some sort of probation, we need to plan around that so she doesn't lose her job. I can shoulder more of the responsibility, as much as I can from my role. We should focus on preventing Adam's hiring, or getting him terminated from the company as soon as possible. He gets arrested on May 23, 2014, so let's set a target date for the first of May to have him removed. If we can't by then, everything will be in motion and out of our control."

"Then it will be dangerous for everything we try," Selena said, leaning back in her seat across from Arielle.

She never read the full mission reports. Arielle knew this. But she also had a mind like a sponge. After two missions of working together, Arielle knew Selena was absorbing all the information being presented, even the dates, and wouldn't have to look any of it up again. It was a gift she admired, no different from the servers at restaurants who could memorize all the orders for a party of fifteen, including who didn't want onions on their burger.

"Exactly," Arielle said. "We have enough time. I'm going to tail Adam for the next week. We'll see how interesting it is. I'm bailing if it means sitting outside of an office or house all day like the two last missions. But I mainly want to get a feel for the guy. Who does he spend time with during the week? Weekends? You never know where a helpful detail can come into play."

Selena and Felix clung to every word. Even after two missions working exclusively with Arielle, they still had a hunger to learn her thought processes behind every decision.

"And that's why I'm going to head over to his house right now," Arielle continued. "Selena, would you like to come?"

Chapter 12

Adam Marshall had just arrived home from work. At noon. On a Wednesday.

His usually green eyes were bloodshot red from the tears of rage he had cried during the drive from downtown back to his home in the suburbs. His oldest son, Jaxson, was away at his second month of preschool. But his wife, Emily, remained home with their one-year-old daughter, Tegan.

How he wished he could have come home to an empty house. Adam didn't want to cry in front of his daughter, even if she had no means of understanding the situation. He had already called Emily to inform her they had fired him from his job, the second time in as many years that a company had done so.

The last time was a matter of the company moving to Montana. Adam didn't beat himself up too much over that job loss, because who the fuck wanted to live in Montana?

This time, however, his blood boiled at the mere thought of how things unfolded. He pulled into his driveway, killed the engine, then returned his death grip to the steering wheel, knuckles turning the color of freshly fallen snow.

Fired for doing a good deed, he thought, teeth gritted while he stared at the front of his house. They had packed his box of belongings while he sat in a conference room with his manager and a Human Resources representative as they delivered the final blow. The box now sat on the passenger seat, an apron, name tag, and various family pictures spilling over the edge.

"Those motherfuckers," he said, finally stepping out of the car, leaving the box behind. He could get it later. He didn't want to look like too much of a loser when he entered the house.

Adam followed the pathway from his car to the front door, passing the lawn covered in a fresh blanket of brown and yellow leaves, crunching the few that hadn't been swept off the concrete. They decorated their front yard for Halloween, an inflatable vampire and Frankenstein monster facing off in front of the maple tree that stood guard within their picket fence.

They had moved into this new house in the months before Tegan was born, excited at the opportunity to live in a better neighborhood with better schools thanks to Adam's new, higher-paying job as a grocery store manager at the local chain, Emerald Grocery. They hired him to run the chain's busiest store in downtown Seattle, a twenty-minute drive from his new home in Bellevue.

The tire swing dangling from the maple tree provided the daily reminder that Adam had achieved life's greatest dream of becoming a middle-class father. Every day was damn near the same thing. Wake up to get himself and Jaxson fed and dressed. Start the coffee for Emily—he didn't drink that caffeinated shit. Kiss his wife and daughter goodbye before leaving to drop Jaxson off at preschool, to then drive across two bridges full of traffic to make it downtown before nine o'clock.

And that had only been the last two months since Jaxson started at the Loving Hands Preschool and Child Care Center, where the other parents stuck their noses in the air at the thought of their children having to mingle with the son of a grocer.

These thoughts zipped through his mind as he reached the front door and pushed it open, dragging himself through the doorway where he tossed his keys on top of the small table that collected junk mail and whatever sloppy art Jaxson brought home from school each day.

Adam heard the TV playing the Baby Channel, an odd-looking puppet counting to ten in its high-pitched voice.

A hallway ran from the front door to the living room straight ahead, the kitchen and dining rooms off to the left through their own entryway. Emily appeared at the end of the hall, her lips pursed into a frown as she shuffled down the hardwood toward Adam.

"I'm sorry, babe," she said, planting a kiss on his lips that he didn't bother returning. The shame phase was already taking hold. Emily worked so hard to keep the house clean and proper, all while taking care of Tegan. That was their agreement when they found out Emily was pregnant for the second time. Adam insisted they could make it work for Emily to continue her career as a dental hygienist. She didn't need to give it all up to be a stay-at-home mother.

But Emily had insisted. She wanted to spend her time with the kids and be present in their lives as much as possible before they were both in school. At that point, she planned to return to her career, or possibly look into something new.

Today felt like they were back at square one.

"Let's talk about it," she said, running a hand up and down his back, guiding him down the hallway where he stole a quick glance of Tegan bouncing wildly in her jungle-themed baby jumper, the puppet on the TV now reviewing the colors of the rainbow.

More shame pounded within Adam's chest upon seeing his little girl.

How could I let everyone in my life down with one stupid decision?

Emily sat down at the dining table, her yoga pants highlighting her curvy lower half. She had added a daily exercise routine into her schedule six months earlier, and the results had led to a definite increase in Adam's libido.

"What happened?" she asked in a hushed voice, as if Tegan were snooping on their conversation from the other room.

Adam shook his head, shoulders slouched as he settled in the chair next to Emily. "I'm still trying to understand that myself. You know how the store partners with different non-profits to take the extra food that gets close to expiring."

"Right. And they take it to different shelters and soup kitchens."

"Exactly. Well, two weeks ago, we had a *ton* of food that needed to go. Like, double the normal amount. I called up the usual companies we work with and told them to invite any others we don't work with to come and get some food. They did, but even after all that, there was still enough food left over to send to probably five different companies. But no more were coming. So at the end of that day, I told the staff to take whatever they'd like home. It was all piled up separately in the back, where it wouldn't get mixed up with anything new coming in. And that's why I was fired."

Adam leaned back, fists clenched underneath the table, as he shook his head some more. He could feel his face turning red. He'd punch a hole in the wall if it wouldn't be his problem to repair, and now regretted not doing just that on his way out of the store earlier this morning.

"What?!" Emily cried. "How is that even a fireable offense?"

Adam shrugged. "The word of me allowing this made its way up to corporate. They said I was supposed to throw the food out, and that by allowing the staff to take it home, they considered it theft. Like, I know the rules and that's what we normally do. But there were at least fifty boxes of cereal, hundreds of cans of food, fresh fruit, veggies. It could have fed us for five months, at least. I couldn't just throw all that in the dumpster."

"Of course not," Emily said, reaching for Adam's hand, which promptly uncurled and allowed the caress from his wife. "Is there anything you can do, legally?"

Adam shook his head, tears welled in his eyes. "It's a clear rule written out in our policies and procedures. I'd have no legal ground to stand on."

"Who do you think did it? Did someone have it out for you?"

Adam shrugged. "Doesn't matter. I suppose there is always someone who doesn't like the manager, if not multiple people. Honestly, I doubt it was even told to corporate by some malicious intent. I'm betting word just got out and reached someone higher up. The corporate suits—now those people are always looking for someone breaking a rule to make an example out of."

"Did you even get a chance to defend yourself?"

"Not much I could say in defense, because this was a clear rule violation. All I told them before I left was 'Based on how this all played out, one of us is going to hell for how this is being handled, and it's not me.'"

Emily threw her head back and let out a laugh. "You really said that?!"

Adam cracked a smile, his first of the morning. "I did. I was, and am, so pissed off about all this. Like, can you even believe it? I got fired for giving food to my staff that makes twelve dollars an hour instead of throwing it all in a dumpster."

Adam needed to say this out loud to make it feel more real. He laughed, continuing to shake his head. "Like, are you kidding me? After all we've gone through with these stupid jobs, and this is how it ends. I'm thinking I'm just not cut out for a job in corporate America. But what the hell else can I do? We have kids to feed and put through this expensive preschool. The last box isn't even unpacked in our house. I can't just take on a loan to start a new business. Most take five years before you'll even see a profit. Plus, I'd never be home."

Adam was rambling, and this prompted Emily to stand up and hug him from behind his shoulders, kissing the top of his head. "Relax, babe. Everything is going to be okay. It's always worked out before. There are thousands of jobs out there. Maybe you just haven't found that right one yet."

"Clearly."

"Why don't we go out to lunch?" Emily asked. "Let's take your mind off of all this. You pick the spot. We'll go relax with Tegan and unwind the rest of the day. And tomorrow, you can start a search for the next job."

Adam stood up and turned around to face his wife, sliding his arms around her waist and pulling her in tight. "I love you. You're the best."

They kissed, oblivious to the car parked outside with two time travelers from the future.

Chapter 13

October 17, 2013

The next morning, the three Angels gathered in the kitchen for a late breakfast. No one had gone grocery shopping yet, so Selena ran out for a box of doughnuts from Mighty-O Donuts two blocks down.

Arielle and Selena had spent the rest of the prior day following Adam and his family as they went to lunch at a 60s-themed diner. They even went inside to have lunch for themselves and enjoy the food and atmosphere. After lunch, the Marshalls returned home for a couple hours before Adam returned outside to pick up their son from preschool. Once they returned, no one stepped out for the rest of the evening when Arielle called it a day at five o'clock.

Felix didn't return home until a few minutes after Arielle and Selena had arrived back. His day had comprised of a prolonged visit to the Seattle weapons warehouse where he stocked up on the three Angels' usual requests. What took him longer than normal was the extended discussion he had with the warehouse operator about the best equipment Felix would need for hacking into a database for a company as grand as WonderHome.

Felix didn't bring his own equipment because it was against the Road Runners' bylaws, and likely wouldn't work, anyway. Every mission in the past required him to figure out how to best perform his job with the equipment available in that year.

He then had to stop at the Road Runners' Seattle office to print documents he needed for the mission. After that, he went to buy three cell phones they could use for the next six months. That process took nearly three hours before Felix left the Sprint Wireless, cussing under his breath.

"Sorry about last night," Felix said. "I just had so much to do still and wasted all the day doing errands. I got our phones, but I'd love to hear about what you found out following Adam."

"Well, it just so happens yesterday was the day he got fired from his job," Arielle said. "Or at least that's what it sounded like. We were three tables down from them at the diner and could only pick up bits and pieces. It explains him arriving home in the middle of the morning and the box of belongings we saw in the passenger seat of his car."

"They seem to have a strong family life," Selena added. "Obviously, we only observed half a day, but everyone seemed happy with each other, especially considering he just lost his job."

"I want to go back this morning to confirm. If he's home all day, it'll be safe to assume he lost his job."

"Isn't it possible he's just on vacation?" Felix asked. "And maybe he brought a box home of stuff."

"It's possible, sure. But the box had things like family pictures, a stapler, a calculator...all the things you'd expect to see for someone having packed their desk in a hurry. And it was all just thrown in there."

They munched on their doughnuts and coffee, taking a moment to process their findings.

"Sooooo," Selena said. "You have a phone?"

Felix chuckled. "Yes, Selena, I got us smart phones to use for the rest of the mission. I was about to buy the burner phones, but already started hearing your voice in my head. Complaining about how they didn't have the internet, and *how on Earth* would you ever manage six months without social media."

"Hey," Selena snapped back. "It's 2013. Facebook is actually cool."

"Oh, jeez," Arielle said, joining the laughter.

"All jokes aside," Felix said. "We needed smart phones for this mission.

Burners don't have cameras on them—I thought they did. It will make our work a lot easier if you're both able to take pictures on your phone and text them to me. Especially you, Arielle, since you'll be sending me things to help hack into WonderHome's system."

"Works for me," Selena said. "So, where are the phones?"

Felix cracked a sly grin and stood up to reach into his pockets, pulling out three different cell phones.

"You had them this whole time?!" Selena gasped, standing up to smack Felix.

He howled with amusement as he laid them out on the table.

"I couldn't resist seeing that look on your face," Felix said. "And it was worth it, even if my arm doesn't think so." He smiled as he rubbed where Selena had just whacked him. *She packs a mean punch.*

"It's so nice having a smart phone on a mission," Arielle said. "It's been a while since I've had a mission with one. Were you able to apply for those jobs last night?"

Felix nodded. "I was up later than I wanted to be, but it got done. I needed these phones first, because hopefully they'll call today. That would be most ideal."

"Less than twenty-four hours after applying?" Selena asked. "Dream on."

"Not for me to say," Felix replied. "I also created a shared drive for us to swap documents—and uploaded both of your resumes. I suggest you review those now, because you'll need to speak about it whenever they call. Which will hopefully be today."

He shot those final two words directly at Selena, who only grinned in response while she searched through her new phone for the faux resume.

"I have three years of experience as a software engineer with Twitter?" Arielle asked.

"It shows you have experience from one of the biggest tech companies in the world," Felix explained. "I thought all of this out. The timing puts you there during Twitter's biggest years of growth, and by now in 2013, it would perfectly explain why you're looking to leave your job. They've grown too much. A lot has changed with the company culture. It's not the same place as when you started. Honestly, we can plug in any of the big social media companies if you'd like, and it will be the same story. Facebook, Instagram, LinkedIn. You name it."

"No, Twitter is fine," Arielle said. "And thank you for such attention to detail. You've never even worked a corporate job. How do you know what all goes into this?"

Felix smiled. "I know you don't think anyone could do as much research as you, but I do. I love reading about these things because it's all foreign to me. And besides, if I want to create a billion dollar company one day, I'm going to need a full understanding of every aspect within a healthy functioning organization. I'm actually a little excited about this mission."

"You're such a nerd," Selena said. "And so am I, apparently. I have a master's degree in Human Resources Management? That sounds like the worst six years of life one could waste."

Felix laughed. "You're going to do great. I uploaded some material for you to read as well. So you can sound like you have that master's degree."

Selena shook her head and muttered under her breath, "At least it's not cleaning toilets again."

"And same for you, Arielle," Felix continued. "You'll see that you're proficient in JavaScript, TypeScript, HTML, and CSS, among a few other things. I sent you a cheat sheet to understand what all of that means."

"Are these the things that come up in regular conversation?" Arielle asked. "Like outside of work?"

"I'm afraid so. I found a message board run by software engineers, and even the off-topic threads always circle back to software stuff. If Selena thinks she's a nerd, then you're Urkel. It doesn't get any geekier than a room full of software engineers."

"If you need any acting lessons," Selena said, shifting her voice to become high-pitched and nasally. "Just let me know!" She pushed an imaginary pair of glasses up the bridge of her nose and snorted, earning raucous laughter from around the table.

"Wow," Arielle said. "So that's what they taught you at Julliard."

"What can I say? I can pull off any role," Selena replied, still laughing.

"Well, let's not do that voice in your interview and you should be fine," Felix said, still grinning. "Your resume shows you as educated but disciplined. You worked in the HR departments for both Wal-Mart and Shutterfly. This shows you have both tech-industry experience along with major corporation exposure. I read a lot of blogs about what qualifications recruiters look for in both of your positions. For HR in tech companies, it's that combo."

"You're setting us up for success," Arielle said. "It's like we're counting cards and flipping the script on the house."

"And I love that," Felix said. "I do know how to count cards, actually. Only used that gift to make a couple hundred dollars here and there. I don't want to do anything that will get noticed. Would hate to end up in a back alley getting my kneecaps bashed in."

Arielle and Selena looked at him, astonished. "Is that really what happens?" Selena asked.

"It's a serious offense. It's one of those things that isn't illegal, but highly frowned upon. Casinos don't actually have someone to break your knees if they catch you. They just ask you to leave. That's all they really can do, since there isn't a law."

"Good to know," Arielle said. "Don't ever sit down at a blackjack table with Felix."

He grinned proudly. "You should be so lucky. I think you're both set for the day, though. I have some things I need to get set up on my computer, then I'll be free in the afternoon. You should both read as much as possible from the documents I shared. We're in this for the long haul—it's important you know your jobs like you really have been doing them for the past few years."

"Sounds good," Arielle said. "I'm going to head back to the Marshall house, and will read while I wait for something to happen."

Chapter 14

October 21, 2013

They didn't receive the call from WonderHome before the weekend, like Felix had hoped. Arielle and Selena had to calm him down, as he grew antsy during Friday afternoon when no calls came through. He started to doubt the resumes he submitted, and was already thinking of the next steps to get them into that office building.

After they stressed that these things could take two weeks sometimes, they had a relaxing weekend of grocery shopping, a few dinners out downtown, and a rainy Sunday exploring the city.

Arielle had spent a couple of hours on Thursday and Friday morning outside of the Marshall house to find nothing of significance. She confirmed Adam had indeed lost his job after a closer examination of the box that remained in his passenger seat. She saw memos on the company letterhead for Emerald Grocery, plus the termination letter that had fallen to the car's floor.

Monday morning, however, the Angels relaxed until they had something to do. Following Adam was a waste of time so early, especially since they didn't have plans to bug his house. Not yet.

Selena was the first to receive the phone call that sparked everything else. It was a few minutes past ten o'clock. Felix had loaded the dishwasher with their plates and glasses from breakfast. Arielle was up in her bedroom reading more about software engineering. Selena was sitting at the kitchen table, chatting with Felix in between dishes, when the phone rang.

His head immediately whipped over. No one else had their phone numbers aside from each other.

"It's them!" he gasped, shuffling over to confirm the 206 area code on the caller ID.

"Calm down," Selena said, raising a hand. "I can't do this if you're going to jump all over me."

She stood up and answered the call, glaring at Felix. "Hello?"

Selena couldn't remember the last time butterflies flapped around her stomach, but they returned in a hurry once she pressed the phone to her ear. She knew how to act, but could she truly bullshit her way past a corporate recruiter to land a job she had no experience in doing? Would Felix's resume actually work? There were too many factors out of her control, and she supposed that was why the insects did cartwheels within her stomach.

"Hello," a woman's voice replied. "I'm looking for Ms. Selena Nicole."

"This is her."

Felix stopped doing the dishes but remained at the sink, leaning against the counter as he observed Selena kick off their first task of the mission.

"Hi, Ms. Nicole. My name is Janina Victoria with WonderHome. I was wondering if you had a couple of minutes to chat about your application to work with our People Operations team."

"I sure do. Did you say People Operations?"

Selena pictured a room full of surgeons operating on several bodies, and almost laughed out loud.

"Yes, that is what we call what is traditionally known as *human resources*. You'll probably hear a lot of newer companies call their HR departments People Operations instead. POPS, for short."

"Interesting."

"I see you've worked with Shutterfly and Wal-Mart. They probably still used the HR label. We felt *human resources* was an antiquated term and wanted something more modernized."

Selena had to turn on her acting skills. The phone call was already starting to drag, so she let out a hearty laugh. "Well, thank you for explaining. I was wondering what job I applied for. Threw me for a curve there."

Janina laughed through the phone, and Selena figured she couldn't be more than a few years older than her, judging by her voice.

"No worries at all," Janina said, a new cheeriness slipping into her voice. "It will take a few years for POPS to become the new norm, so I guess we'll just have to keep explaining. Now, I'd love to talk about your background because it sounds like a perfect fit for the type of candidate we're looking to hire."

"Oh?" Selena played dumb, feeling in complete control now that she understood how to best reflect the recruiter on the other end of the line. Plus, she had actually taken a couple hours the night before—on a Sunday night!—to read the notes Felix had provided. He had even outlined some potential questions and answers for this very phone call she found herself on. "Well, I'm thrilled to hear that."

"As are we. So it looks like you've been able to gain a lot of experience in a short matter of time. You graduated college in 2008 and went straight into the HR department at Wal-Mart. What did you do for them, exactly?"

"A little of everything," Selena said, smirking because she felt like a student taking a test with the answer key hidden up her sleeve. "One of my professors had a connection with their main corporate office and got me a job with similar responsibilities as an intern, but with a full-time salary and benefits. I look back and credit my three years there as the real education. I worked with the benefits team, recruiting, analytics, talent development, and improving the workplace culture."

"Very impressive," Janina said, the distant clacking of a keyboard as she took notes. "And that led you to Shutterfly?"

"Yes. As much as I loved what I was doing at Wal-Mart, I couldn't handle living in Arkansas. I need interaction with people. Diversity. Things to do on the weekends besides town fairs and museums. I applied for several jobs in California, Florida, even New York. Shutterfly called first and offered me a job, so I was on my way."

"Well, Seattle is definitely going through some serious growth and changes. Lots of run-down places have been upgraded and are now bustling with young professionals. And it looks like you focused primarily on recruiting during your time at Shutterfly?"

"Yes. They had me start as a sales recruiter and eventually branched out as a senior recruiter for other departments."

"And why are you looking to leave, if you don't mind me asking?"

Selena indeed didn't mind her asking, because Felix had already provided a response to this question. *How does he do it?*

"If I may be honest," Selena said, lowering her voice as if telling a secret. "I think I've hit my ceiling here. I'm still in the senior recruiter role and there doesn't look to be any opportunity to move up any time soon. The company isn't growing, and because of that I'm just kind of stuck behind my director, and she is stuck behind the VP. I believe my only opportunity for growth can come with a bigger company like WonderHome."

"That is certainly possible here," Janina said, her perkiness remaining high. "We don't do things the traditional way. If we were to hire you, you'd become familiar with all facets of our department before deciding where you might best fit. Recruiting is what we need, and clearly what you have the skill set for, but if something else were to catch your eye, we wouldn't stop you from pursuing that instead."

"That's great to know. I really have been enjoying my time as a recruiter. I find it incredibly challenging. Like, how do you really know if the candidate is going to be as good as they look on paper? Or even after the interviews? Sometimes it's a complete miss, but that's what I've come to understand. Some people are simply good at interviewing and suck at their job. And vice versa."

Janina laughed at this, and Selena took it as some sort of inside joke only HR workers understood. She laughed back, not sure what else to say.

"I'm really impressed," Janina said. "Hope you're not one of those candidates who is only good at interviewing." She cackled again, and Selena once more returned the sentiment.

"Not at all. I'm just as good in person." Selena couldn't resist throwing in some of her own personality now that it sounded like the call was going to lead to an interview.

"What do you think about us flying you out here for an interview?" Janina asked. "We'll cover your flight and stay for two nights. One day to interview and see our offices. And another to explore the city and see if it lives up to your standards."

"That would be fantastic. When would that be?"

Felix pumped a fist into the air and hurried to the stairs to call up for Arielle before returning to watch the rest of Selena's conversation like a proud coach.

"Would you be able to take this Thursday and Friday off from work? I can even see about adding a third night if you'd like to fly in Wednesday evening."

"That shouldn't be a problem. I have so much PTO."

"Fantastic. I'll send you an email right now. If you can let me know by this afternoon for sure that this week will work, and what day you'd like to fly out here, we can get everything booked for you."

"Thank you so much, Janina. I can't wait to meet you in person."

They hung up, and Selena looked at Felix with a tight-lipped grin. Arielle barged into the kitchen. "What's going on?" she asked, looking back and forth between the two of them.

Felix gestured toward Selena to explain.

"I have an interview with WonderHome this Thursday."

"That's great!" Arielle cried. "So they just called you, I take it?"

"Sure did. And the phone interview couldn't have gone any better, thanks to Felix. Every question she asked me was on the list he made. I hope you studied yours."

"Of course."

"And if you get Janina on the phone, you'll need to be a bit more enthusiastic than your normal self."

Arielle scoffed while the other two broke into laughter. "I know how to sound enthusiastic."

"Yeah, about staying up until two in the morning to read mission reports. Janina is definitely one of those girls who keeps the energy up all day. Probably partied like crazy in college and joined a sorority."

"Way to stereotype," Arielle said, crossing her arms.

"I'll make you a bet. A hundred dollars. I'll get Janina out for drinks after we work there, and I'll get her to tell me all about her sorority days."

"I'm not making that bet."

They all knew Selena had an uncanny ability to read people, even through a brief conversation over the phone.

"That's what I thought."

"All that matters is the first step has finally fallen into place," Felix said.

"And now step two is," Arielle said, pulling her buzzing cell phone out of her pocket. "It's them."

Felix grinned. "Let's do it again. Good luck."

Chapter 15

October 24, 2013

Arielle and Selena each had their first in-person interviews scheduled for Thursday morning.

Arielle's call with Janina had gone just as smoothly as Selena's. Wanting to avoid appearing too similar to her colleague, Arielle had informed Janina that she had just moved to Seattle in pursuit of a new opportunity.

Meanwhile, Selena left them Wednesday night to check into her free hotel across from the skyscraper that housed the WonderHome corporate offices.

"Hotels are relaxing," she had explained to Felix, who asked why she'd leave when they had a perfectly suitable house. "Think about it, a hotel is a place where someone comes into your room, makes your bed, cleans your bathroom, and makes sure everything is fully stocked. Every day. Why would I pass that up? Plus, they gave me a daily stipend of one hundred dollars to feed myself."

Arielle left early Thursday morning to meet Selena at her hotel room so they could get ready together. Selena had all the knowledge on makeup and clothing, and had grabbed everything they needed while on a mini-shopping spree with the free money WonderHome had given her.

Arielle arrived at a hotel room that looked partly like a salon. Makeup brushes lay spread out on the counter next to the TV, jars of nail polish and mascara peppered in between containers of lipstick and powder. Hair brushes, clips, and a blow-dryer were all set up in the bathroom. And on the bed were two outfits complete with boxes of brand-new shoes beneath each.

"Wow, Selena," Arielle said, stuffing her keys into her pocket because she didn't want to lose them in the mess. "Do you think all of this is necessary? I mean, they think they flew you out here. I'd say they are more than interested in hiring you."

"That's a shocking question coming from you," Selena fired back. "Do you think we should risk not getting these jobs by just coasting through the interview?"

"Fair. But damn, this just seems like a lot of stuff."

"Not like I won't wear my makeup again. Can't speak for you, though."

Arielle ignored the cheap shot. "So what all do we have going on this morning?"

It was 8:30 when she arrived at the Seattle Union Hotel, a twenty-one-story building two blocks away from the office. Selena's room was on the fifteenth floor and had a breathtaking view overlooking Elliott Bay and the Seattle Great Wheel. Selena's interview was scheduled for ten o'clock sharp, with Arielle's following half an hour after that.

"We're going all-out for these interviews," Selena said. "We need to wow everyone we meet, leave an impression, and become truly unforgettable. Just playing the odds, I'm probably going to interview with mostly women, and you with mostly men. That's why I got you a pair of heels and an outfit that will show off those calves you work so hard on."

"Heels? I couldn't tell you the last time I've worn heels. I hope you didn't get them too tall. Would hate to fall on my face."

Selena laughed. "That will definitely accomplish our three objectives. You'll be fine—they're two-inch heels."

Arielle rarely dressed up. Her date with Javonte had been the most effort she had put into an outfit in years, and even that one didn't have heels. Walking down the sidewalks in a pair of heels just might be the most troublesome part of this mission for the top-ranked Angel, and the thought made her snicker.

"So I get to show skin, and you'll be in a pantsuit?" Arielle asked.

"God no," Selena snapped. "I would never do that to myself. I got a new blouse and skirt with a little slit on the knees. And of course new heels. But I don't need to make anyone drool."

"Neither do I."

"But it'll help. I've already looked up the people we're most likely going to meet today. The manager of the software engineers is a middle-aged man. How many women do you think even apply for this job to begin with? I'm sure these guys would love some eye candy."

"Pigs."

"I know they're pigs, but that's what we need to appeal to. This is corporate America. Anything that can make these old guys' days at the office more enjoyable. Combine your looks with your resume and smooth-talking. You're automatically in."

Arielle shook her head, but knew Selena was right. She'd have to swallow her pride—taking down the patriarchy would have to wait another day. "Fine. Doll me up."

The words felt gross leaving her mouth, but she had never seen such a cunning smile spread across Selena's face. A crazed look like she had been waiting for this moment her entire life.

Selena pulled out the chair parked beneath the TV counter and spun it around. "Have a seat."

* * *

At 9:30, Arielle and Selena stepped outside the hotel, dressed and ready for their interviews. Selena had even gone as far as buying a purse for Arielle, a $500 purchase from the Coach store a few blocks down in the fashion district. Arielle never carried a purse on missions, so Selena justified the splurge, citing she wanted the purse back after the interviews if Arielle didn't want to keep it (she didn't).

A two-block stroll through downtown had never felt so long. Arielle had to concentrate on each step, wary of cracks her heel could slip into and cause a rolled ankle.

Selena walked with much more confidence and ease, smiling back at the few businessmen who couldn't help but admire the two women who looked ready to overthrow a CEO.

"See," Selena said. "We're already getting checked out. Corporate America is too predictable."

Despite feeling like a drunken baby learning how to take its first steps, Arielle breathed a sigh of relief when they reached the entrance to the Wilson Investments Center, a skyscraper spanning forty-two floors, home to nearly every financial firm in Seattle, plus other major corporations like WonderHome and Nordstrom.

They looked up the glass exterior, unable to see anywhere near the top of the building.

"Okay," Selena said. "From here, we need to go on our own. We don't want them to think we know each other."

One thing that all three Angels had agreed on was Arielle and Selena should avoid crossing paths as much as possible while at the office. They were going to be digging into highly illegal activity, and if things took a turn, it could be catastrophic if the company made a connection between the two of them.

"Of course," Arielle said. "Thirtieth floor, yeah?"

Selena nodded. "I'll head up first. You can probably head up in about twenty minutes, just to play it safe."

"Deal. Good luck."

They shared a brief hug before Selena continued into the building, leaving Arielle alone outside. There was a waiting area in the main lobby, complete with lounge chairs and coffee tables, but she didn't want to sit around. The anticipation was already growing heavily on her mind. She had been up past midnight studying her resume and all of Felix's notes. He really had done a masterful job in preparing them to land these jobs.

Instead, she found a Target across the street with a Starbucks logo plastered across the window. She'd spend the next half hour there until heading up for the interview, wondering how it was playing out for Selena.

Chapter 16

Thirty floors up, Selena stepped into the WonderHome lobby. The company logo filled up the entire wall behind the reception desk, its letters massive and bubbly, except for the H that was shaped like a house.

A young blond woman, likely fresh out of college, sat behind the desk, a man of similar age with spiky black hair leaning against the desk as he spoke close to her.

The woman noticed Selena and turned on her most welcoming smile. The man looked over his shoulder, gave the woman a pat on her shoulder as he mumbled something before disappearing down a long hallway.

"Hello," the woman said, standing up. "Are you here for an interview?"

Selena noticed the nameplate on the desk. Becca Faulkner.

"Yes. I believe I'm meeting with Janina Victoria."

"Oh, Nina? She's the best."

Selena immediately heard the Valley girl accent in Becca's speech. The slightly higher pitch with a hint of ditzy optimism toward everything in life. "She is *totally* the best," Selena said, immediately jumping into a mocking impression of the unsuspecting receptionist.

"Let me take you back," Becca said. "Do you need a drink or snack? We have coffee, water, soda."

"Just water is good. Thank you."

Becca reached under her desk and pulled out a water bottle from a mini refrigerator. "This way." She turned and started down the long hallway with doors to five different conference rooms before opening up to a bigger space Selena couldn't quite see.

Becca turned into the middle door, a conference room with an oval-shaped table in the middle that seated at least six people. "Nina will be about five minutes. Let us know if you need anything else. And good luck."

"Thank you," Selena replied as Becca left the room and closed the door. *We'll be seeing plenty of each other soon enough.*

Selena had studied her notes late into the night as well, but she didn't require as many times through the documents as Arielle. She absorbed information quickly, and now played it all back in her mind. The phone interview was one thing, but she now had to keep up the in-person charm while recalling a faux background working in Human Resources. Plus, she needed to be ready to adjust her personality depending on who else walked through that door. Not everyone would be as cheery and positive as Janina.

Selena chugged her water while waiting, and a knock came at exactly the five-minute mark, the door swinging open to reveal a wide-grinning Janina.

"Selena?" she asked, chomping on a piece of gum.

"Yes." Selena rose and stuck out her hand. "It's so nice to finally meet you."

"You have no idea." Janina closed the door and pulled out the seat across from Selena, speaking in a hushed voice. "You are my godsend. I've been having the hardest time filling this role, but your application came through and I knew it was exactly what we've been looking for. Are you ready to interview?"

Selena's heart raced a little faster. She wasn't entirely thrilled at the idea of Janina having likely already talked her up to the others she would interview with this morning. She didn't know what expectations were already set based on these behind-the-scenes conversations. If they already had Selena on some sort of pedestal, it could only increase the chances of her bombing the interview before it even happened.

Instead of sharing these thoughts, she only smiled and nodded. "I'm very ready. What does the schedule look like?"

"You'll be interviewing with the manager of our POPS department, Susie Foster, and her boss, the Vice President of POPS, Amara Edwards. They are both incredible women and have made our department the best by far. I'll let them know you're here and ready. I have to go get another interview started, but I'll be back as soon as you're done chatting with them."

The other interview was Arielle, likely sitting in the lobby not knowing what to say to a girl like Becca. A light smile touched Selena's lips as she thought about it, holding in her laughter.

"Thank you for everything. I won't let you down." Selena said this more to build her own confidence. The WonderHome office had a more laid-back vibe than a typical corporate setting. This made her more relaxed than she had expected, and she needed to be on her game, ready to focus and adapt to whoever walked through the door next.

Janina left Selena alone for another five minutes, where she stared at the wall to rush through her last moments of recalling her made-up resume.

When the next knock came on the door, Selena felt as if the floodlights lit up the stage she was about to perform on. *Let's do this.*

The door opened and two women stepped in, immediately causing a panic for Selena. She hadn't understood the schedule as meeting with both of them at the same time. This complicated her plans for adapting to her interviewer, but she appreciated the challenge just the same.

"Hello, Selena," the first woman through the door said, approaching the table with her arm extended for a handshake. She was in her forties, possibly early fifties, judging by the soft wrinkles touching her hazel eyes. Reddish-blond hair flowed beyond the boxy shoulder pads of her purple blazer. "I'm Susie Foster, manager of the People Operations team here at WonderHome. It's a pleasure to meet you."

"Likewise," Selena said, standing to shake both women's hands.

"And I'm Amara Edwards," said the other woman. "Vice President of People Operations."

Amara had an intimidating presence, and Selena couldn't quite pinpoint what it was. Perhaps she was already jumping to conclusions that Amara was involved in the money laundering scheme. They had figured it likely for any member of the executive team to have involvement, yet Amara didn't seem like one to take shit from anyone. She sat down and brushed back her long braids behind her ears, slipping on a pair of glasses as she studied a copy of Selena's resume.

"You have an impressive background," Susie said, taking the seat next to Amara, and opening a folder with a blank sheet of paper on one side, and the resume on the other. She clicked her pen and started writing on the blank paper. "And for such a young age, to have had these jobs."

Selena grinned, feeling for the mood. Both women were older than her, that much was obvious, but did that mean they were necessarily old-school in their thinking? They worked at WonderHome, and this place was very much setting the trends for future corporate America. "I've always been a bit of an old soul," Selena said, dipping her toe into this approach. "Before I even graduated, I started looking for jobs. But not just any entry-level job I could find. I wanted to find a company that could be home for a long time."

"Tell us what happened that caused you to leave both Wal-Mart and Shutterfly," Amara said, scratching down notes of her own.

"I hit a wall at both places. I'm a very driven person with a constant need for growth and improvement. Honestly, I think my age held me back at those two places. I reached a point where I was ready to step into roles with more responsibilities, but they never entertained the thought, no matter how much of a top-performer I proved to be. That's why I'm hoping to work with WonderHome. I understand the company is a lot more open to advancing the careers of those who deserve it, even if it means in a different department. You invest in your people, and that's all I want. I even heard you have a girl who is a director, and she's only twenty-six."

Amara and Susie looked at each other and smiled. "You've done your research," Susie said. "And yes, that is true. She is the director of our public relations department, and has been in the role for about six months."

Selena felt she was taking the correct approach, so sat back, crossed her arms, and shook her head. "A 26-year-old *woman.* Director at a major corporation. That's all I need to know about this place."

"Now, Ms. Nicole," Amara said, shifting in her seat to cross one leg over the other. "You understand you won't be jumping into a higher role, right? I wouldn't exactly call this recruiting position an entry-level job, but it's just above that."

"Absolutely," Selena said, sitting forward. "Clearly, I don't have any type of leadership background because of the way I've been held back. I tried shopping around for managerial jobs, but it became obvious I'd have no chance without it on my resume. All I'm hoping for is an opportunity to prove myself and get that chance. And I know that can take time, but like I mentioned, I want a company I can be with for the long haul to do just that."

"Have you been to Seattle before?" Amara asked, leaning back. The question softened the tension that seemed to linger in the room during any type of interview.

"I've visited a bit," Selena said. "I really enjoy this city. So much to do and see."

"That's good. Some people think working downtown is a chore, but I believe if you love the city, then it provides a certain energy to your day."

"I couldn't agree more. I actually grew up in Manhattan, so I'm used to life in a big city. That's why Bentonville was a bit of a culture shock for me when I was working at Wal-Mart's corporate office."

"I'm sure it was," Susie said with a chuckle. She exchanged glances with Amara, who nodded silently as if they were having a telepathic conversation. "We think you're a great fit for this job, Selena. With that, we'd love to end this interview and have you sit with our team for a few hours, if you feel up to it."

"We know this isn't quite the norm," Amara said. "But we like to do things differently. So many candidates look good on paper, but that doesn't always translate to real life. We'd love to see how you fit in with our team."

"So, like job shadowing?" Selena asked.

"Exactly," Amara replied. "You'll gain some insight into what your day-to-day would look like. And while it's not a *major* factor in our decision, we listen to feedback from our existing team on what they think about the potential of working with you."

"Let's do it," Selena said, taking the lead by standing up.

A screeching, sharp blare sounded from the hallway, repeating three times. Five seconds of silence followed, then the trio of blares repeated.

Amara and Susie looked at each, brows furrowed.

"Fire alarm?" Susie asked. "We're not scheduled for a fire drill."

"No," Amara replied, rising slowly out of her seat, appearing unsure if she actually wanted to stand up. "Excuse me."

Amara left the conference room, the obvious scream of the fire alarm even louder for the moment the door was open. Selena saw the strobing light that accompanied the sound.

"I'm sure it's just a mistake," Susie said, offering a forced grin. "Gotta love a fire drill, right?"

Selena smiled in return, nodding her head. The sound screeched throughout the room, making it nearly impossible to hear Susie's words clearly.

A minute later, Amara threw open the door, a light haze appearing the hallway behind her. "We need to go. Smoke is coming from the kitchen."

Susie jumped out of her seat, and Selena followed them into the hallway, where several employees were starting their trek from the other side of the office.

Selena had been in plenty of fire drills, but never in a real scenario where everyone followed the protocol. It surprised her to find everyone walking calmly toward the stairwell in a single-file line. A few people had backpacks and purses slung over their shoulders, but no one else appeared concerned with grabbing personal items from their desks.

Wow, she thought. *All the training really becomes ingrained in our minds.*

She checked her watch to find the time was 10:40. Arielle should have been in her interview, but she didn't see her in the hall. Selena couldn't exactly ask Amara and Susie about her friend, either, and could only trust she was okay.

"Let's go, Selena," Susie said, tapping her on the arm to snap her out of her trance. "We have thirty flights of stairs to go down."

Chapter 17

Ten minutes later, they stepped outside the skyscraper, the sidewalks and streets flooded with the thousands of employees who had their days interrupted. Three firetrucks barricaded the street from traffic, allowing everyone room to gawk at the building, many looking up for any sign of a fire.

The building stood undisturbed, and if it weren't for the massive crowd outside, anyone passing by would have no idea of the chaos unfolding inside. People in bright orange vests scattered among the gathering, hoisting up signs with their company names or logos on them.

Selena had stayed with Susie and Amara, and followed them over to Janina, who was holding the WonderHome sign, their employees gathering around while a man stood on his tiptoes, checking off names on a clipboard as he matched their faces in the crowd.

At least seventy people had encircled Janina, and Selena couldn't find Arielle anywhere.

Knowing her, she went to stop the fire.

A tap on the shoulder proved otherwise, as Selena spun around to see her fellow Angel. She took a step back, Susie and Amara not noticing as they had become engulfed with helping make sure everything was going as it should.

"Were you in your interview?" Selena asked, just above a whisper.

Arielle nodded. "I think this happened because of us. The past knows. Were you thinking about the mission already?"

Selena was about to say no when she remembered she *had* thought of how Amara might be part of the scheme. "Nothing major. And it wasn't even for that long."

"Dammit, Selena," Arielle said through gritted teeth, like a mother trying to scold their child in public. "Come with me."

Arielle grabbed Selena by her forearm and pulled her through the crowd, not stopping until they reach an open space away from the WonderHome employees.

"What the *hell*?" Selena cried, ripping her arm free from Arielle's grip. "You can't just—"

"No!" Arielle barked. "We're on a mission. I can do whatever I need to make sure it doesn't get messed up before we even start."

Selena was plenty familiar with Arielle's tones, but had never heard this one with such harshness swimming behind each word.

"What were you thinking about?" Arielle demanded. "I need to know."

Selena looked over her shoulder to make sure her interviewers were not within ear's reach. "All I was wondering about was if the VP of People Ops had any involvement with the laundering. That's it. The thought left as quickly as it came because they started interviewing me. I swear."

Arielle's face softened at this. "Okay. That's not bad."

"That's not bad?! You make a scene, just to tell me *that's not bad*?! What the hell, Arielle? How do I know it wasn't *you* having thoughts about the mission?"

"Because I wasn't—"

"Bullshit! You can't help yourself. You probably asked to use the restroom and were already snooping around the office. I know how you are."

"I did that, sure, but my mind was clear."

Selena's jaw dropped. "Unbelievable. On second thought, no, it's completely believable. You're a junkie for this stuff. We can't just turn our brains off from the mission, no matter how good you think you are at doing it. *You* still have a subconscious, remember?" Selena balled a fist and knocked it on her head to prove her point.

"Selena, enough. You're the one making a scene. We still have these jobs in the bag. Be smart."

Selena pursed her lips tight enough to turn them white. She wished nothing more than to blast her fists through Arielle's face.

"I'm sorry I jumped to conclusions," Arielle said. "I just can't imagine it's a coincidence that this is happening the day we're here to interview. Maybe this really happened in the original timeline—we have no way of knowing for sure."

"Don't ever come at me like that again," Selena said, sure to emphasize the disgust in her voice. "If you do, I'm requesting a transfer to a new team."

"I said I'm sorry. My emotions got the best of me. If I can be honest, when I saw the smoke up there, I thought the entire mission was about to go to shit. What if the office burned down? I never know how strong the past will push back against our work."

Selena shook her head. She hadn't even considered the ramifications of a fire in WonderHome office, and how it could alter their mission before they even secured their jobs with the company. "That doesn't excuse the way you acted."

"I know. Never again. I promise."

They looked around, the crowd seeming to grow with each passing second.

"So, how was your interview going before this happened?" Arielle asked.

Plenty of distance was now between them and the WonderHome employees, the space having filled up with at least another hundred people.

"It was going so well," Selena said. "They were about to have me sit with the team. I know I haven't done many interviews in my life, but it really sounded like they were ready to offer me a job on the spot. Did your interview even get to begin?"

"Well, that's great news. And yes, mine was about fifteen minutes in with the manager of engineering. We started early since everyone was ready. It was going as well as I could have hoped. The terminology still feels foreign to me, but I talked my way through the questions well enough. I'm not sure how this fire drill is going to alter our plans for the rest of the week."

"Why don't we go check with our interviewers and see what they say? The hotel is only two blocks away. We can hang out there and wait for all of this to die down. Pike's Place is probably going to be overcrowded now because of this, *and* it's almost lunchtime."

They agreed and fought their way through the crowd.

* * *

"Do you really not feel any type of anxiety around all of this?" Arielle asked.

WonderHome had advised them both to remain on standby for the rest of the afternoon. They had no clue when the building would become available again, if at all. But if so, they wanted to resume the interviews as soon as possible.

Arielle and Selena returned to the hotel, where they ordered lunch to the room. Selena flipped through the channels before landing on reruns of a game show called *The Weakest Link*.

"Honestly," Selena said. "No. I like the pace of this mission. It hardly feels like work, and more like adjusting my life to a new routine. I'm loving all the free time."

"Sure it's nice. But we've already been here for more than a week, and it doesn't really feel like anything is in motion. And then today with the fire alarm... Maybe I'm being paranoid, but I feel like it's a bad omen."

"Omen?" Selena asked. "I never took you as someone who believed in omens. You're always spewing facts and science. Are you allowed to believe in something as supernatural as an omen?"

Arielle laughed. "Selena. We're time travelers. You need to give me some credit. I believe in a lot more than you might think. Now, would I base a critical decision on something as abstract as an omen? Of course not. But there's a time and a place for such discussions."

Selena studied Arielle. "If you say so. All I know is that we're going to get those jobs. If it takes an extra day because of this fire alarm, then so be it. We still have over a month until Adam Marshall submits his application, so I don't see what there is to even be worried about."

"I know. I just prefer knowing exactly what is going to happen on each day of a mission. The typical two-week missions are perfect for scheduling everything out."

Selena had ordered a French dip sandwich and let it soak in the beef *jus* before taking a bite. Arielle poked at her tomato soup.

"If they ask, I'm voting for more missions like this," Selena said. "I haven't felt a single drop of stress since we've been here."

Arielle's phone buzzed, and she grabbed it out of her pocket. "It's them." She answered and listened attentively, nodding while someone spoke on the other end. "Okay, I can plan for that. Thank you, and I'll see you soon."

"Well?" Selena asked, not giving Arielle a second after hanging up the call.

"Interview is back on for this afternoon. Two o'clock, which gives us an hour—I'm assuming you'll get a call shortly. You won't believe what the cause of the fire was."

"Did it come from WonderHome?"

"Sure did. Someone left the foil over their plate and ran it in the microwave. I guess it started sparking, and the food caught on fire with the paper plate. An entire skyscraper had to empty in the middle of a workday because someone doesn't know the basics of reheating their food."

Selena snorted laughter, clutching her stomach. "I wish I could say I had more faith in humanity, but we've all seen the future."

Arielle shook her head. "Unreal. I'd say that was the past that made that happen, but now I don't know. Just plain old stupidity, I suppose."

Selena's phone rang. "I guess it was only a hiccup. Everything is falling right back into place. Let's seal the deal this afternoon."

Chapter 18

October 28, 2013

They had both finished their formal interviews on Thursday after much laughter about the aluminum-wrapped lunch plate heard 'round the world. Friday, they both returned for additional job shadowing, where the staff was still abuzz regarding the fire.

Someone named Mick had apparently started it. "Classic Mick," one engineer had joked.

"Mick's such a sweet guy," Janina had explained to Selena. "But he's so fucking dumb sometimes. Like, who breaks a vending machine by ordering too many things? Mick. No one else."

The mood was light around the office on that Friday, giving Arielle and Selena a truer sense of their future coworkers. Bottles of wine and cans of beer were cracked open later in the afternoon, all noted as part of the typical end-of-week routine before different cliques made their way downtown for happy hour.

As much as Selena had wanted to join, Arielle warned against it. No good would come from joining the alcohol-filled ramblings and gossip. Not until they were officially on the books as employees.

One thing at a time, Arielle repeated all throughout Friday in random text messages she had kept sending to Selena and Felix throughout the day. She had heard the rumblings of happy hour and after-hours gatherings early in the morning and knew she had to put out that flame right away. Even Felix was growing frustrated with the slow-moving pace of the mission. Arielle had no choice but to emphasize how long of a process this would be.

They survived the weekend.

Selena went out Friday and Saturday night, exploring the city. Felix locked himself in his room all day Saturday, and planted himself on the couch on Sunday, where he watched a full slate of football games. He could have already known the results, so Arielle wondered why he opted to waste a day in such a manner.

But with no mission work to complete, she had no say in the matter. Even Arielle enjoyed a quiet Saturday shopping at the local mall, grabbing a couple of books to read for the inevitable downtime that would come.

On Monday morning, Arielle and Selena woke early with eager anticipation for the phone calls that would land them coveted access to the WonderHome office as employees.

They still had nothing to actually *do*. No interview. No job shadowing. No mission documents to read. And it drove Arielle antsy.

"When are you expecting a call?" Felix asked. In a rare instance, he was last to arrive in the kitchen, helping himself to a cup of coffee.

"They said they wanted to finalize a decision Monday morning and inform the candidates immediately," Selena said.

Felix nodded. "Probably an hour for them to chat about it and come to an agreement. Then maybe another hour for the offer letters to be prepared. They won't jump right into a meeting first thing on a Monday morning. Maybe nine o'clock. I'd say you'll get the call around eleven."

Even after a weekend locked in his virtual cave, Felix came out of hibernation sharp and calculated as always.

"What's on tap for this week?" Selena asked.

"Until you start training at WonderHome," Felix said. "A lot of nothing."

"We can try to check in with Adam," Arielle said. "Not saying we need to spend all day sitting outside his house, but maybe find an opportunity to bump into him outside of home. Were you going to see about hacking into his home computer?"

Felix nodded. "Honestly, it shouldn't be that hard, but we want to be careful. Keep in mind, the FBI will investigate Adam sometime within the next seven months. The last thing we want is our fingerprints all over his cyber data. They would know someone was in there illegally, and could likely pinpoint it back to us—well, *me.* I'm not worried about the ramifications because we can just disappear, but it opens the possibility of the mission being cut short, interfered with, or drastically changing the timeline of events."

"Why didn't you tell me any of this sooner?" Arielle asked.

"Well, because we don't need to worry about hacking into his personal computer, assuming either of you land the job with WonderHome. That's where our focus needs to be. Nothing in his trial notes suggests any of his wrongdoing occurred from a personal computer. They tied everything to his work accounts. The only thing we might gain from hacking his home computer is trying to sabotage his application. The risk doesn't outweigh the reward."

Arielle nodded, stroking her chin. "Okay. We can put that on the back burner for now and fall back on it as a last resort. You really will have a quiet week."

"We all will. But I'm not done, either. You've both never had jobs in the fields you're about to undertake, so I've been drafting up more material for you to read and get familiar with. More of a deep dive into the basics of each job. You'll need to sound a little more versed once you actually start training."

"Oh, joy," Selena said in a monotone. "More dry reading. That's my favorite part of this job."

They all laughed, enjoying a quiet morning while they waited for the phone to ring.

* * *

Felix wasn't far off. WonderHome called Arielle first at 11:26, followed by another call to Selena ten minutes later. They offered both of them jobs, with a start date set for the following Monday, the fourth of November.

With that, the Angels found themselves eager to plot out the rest of the month's events. According to Janina, the first three days of training were an orientation for all new hires to attend together. Arielle and Selena would be together during this time. After that, everyone would be with their own departments for job-specific training for the rest of that first week, and all the second week.

They hung a calendar on the side of the cabinets nearest the dining table in the kitchen. They circled November 17 in a bright red marker, signifying the day Adam applied to WonderHome. Being a Sunday, this meant they would review his application on Monday the eighteenth.

"Selena, that has to be you," Arielle said.

They had converted the dining table into a temporary workspace. Papers lay scattered about the table, three laptops flipped open with more documents on their screens. A container of lemonade stood in the center of the table, each Angel with a full glass in front of them.

"It's impossible to know if I'll be doing actual work by then," Selena said.

"It doesn't matter. If you have to go in an hour early, then so be it. We need to find that application and remove it from the database before anyone realizes it was there. Training will be over by then—that much we know. You can play it off as just coming in early for your first official day on the job and wanting to get settled and sorted out. If anything, you'll just look even more impressive. All I'm saying is we can plan for this, but be ready to adjust on the fly."

"Okay, I can do that," Selena said.

"Now, let's assume this plan doesn't work out for us. We know Adam's first day of training is on December second. This tells us he's going to follow a similar schedule to what we just had. He'll have to interview during that week of the seventeenth—most likely toward the end, like us. Then he'll be notified that he received the job the following week, before

Thanksgiving, so he can start the following Monday."

"Aww, we're going to celebrate Thanksgiving together," Selena said, a genuine smile spreading across her face.

"A Thanksgiving that already happened," Felix murmured, earning the usual smack from Selena.

"Yes, I know," Arielle said. "We'll have a few holidays we get to celebrate together, even if it's just a replay of the past. That will be a whole other discussion. Now, for those two weeks between the application being submitted and Adam starting at WonderHome, I want us to take an aggressive approach. If we can do anything to prevent him from starting, we can call this mission good and go home. Leave it for the Futures team to figure out how everything unfolds from there."

"Remind us what the mission report says our objective is," Felix said.

Arielle pursed her lips. She knew Felix had the answer right in front of him, most likely, but wanted to hear her say it out loud. He had his little ways of keeping checks and balances on Arielle when her ambition could rise above what was actually necessary.

"Of course." Arielle shuffled through her papers to find the hard copy of the mission report assigned to them from Commander Briar. "The mission is to prevent the arrest and prosecution of Adam Marshall."

"Exactly," Felix snapped back. "There are no shortcuts on this mission. Even if we somehow stop him from getting this job, how do we know that stops him from being arrested? The past will still try to correct itself, so we have to stay until the day of his eventual arrest, regardless of what happens. That's the only way we can go back and say with confidence that we completed the mission. May 23, 2014. Buckle up because that's how long we'll be here for—no way around it."

Arielle grinned. She wasn't actually thinking of leaving the mission early, but planned to run the possibility by Commander Briar should they prevent Adam's hiring within the next month. Regardless, she said what she said, and Felix called her out.

"Thank you, Felix. How can we intervene with Adam during this two-week time frame? It sounds like hacking his computer won't be happening. Is there any way of intercepting communication between WonderHome and Adam? We can pose as a different company offering him a job with hopes of it leading to him declining the job offer from WonderHome. We can physically try to intervene with him on the days he's set to drive to the WonderHome office for his interviews."

"Those all sound like good ideas," Selena said. "If I'm not able to scrape him from the WonderHome database, I'll at least have access to the schedule for his interviews. Even his initial phone interview."

"It may be way out of your comfort zone," Arielle said. "But you need to be aggressive during that first week on the job. Possibly even towards the end of training. Insist that you get hands-on experience at every turn possible. Force the matter. Hell, see if you can be the one does the phone interview with Adam. We need to hit that two-week window with everything we can. I'll be doing the same in whatever capacity I can manage from my role, but mine is focused more on the long-term. You can make the most impact right out of the gate."

"Arielle's right," Felix said. "Even if we can throw things off in the slightest, maybe it can change the trajectory. A six-month mission is more like moving a cruise liner—one degree can make a world of difference, and you won't know until much later how much of a difference it was."

Selena leaned back in her seat, appearing to sulk in her stress as she stared at the floor below the table.

"We know you can do it," Arielle said. "And *you* should know that, too. After our last mission, how could you possibly have any doubt in yourself?"

Selena looked up, a seriousness swimming in her eyes Arielle had never seen. Gone were the childish antics and games she seemed to always play. Selena might never admit it, but Arielle knew their last mission had elevated Selena to new heights. New confidence. A stronger appreciation for their work. It was these characteristics that transformed an Angel Runner into a force to be reckoned with. If Selena would just lean into her new self, it would only be a matter of time until she climbed the rankings and would come knocking on Arielle's door in the top spot.

She looked Arielle directly in the eyes, and Arielle felt her presence expand within the kitchen. With just two words they all understood a new chapter was underway for Selena Nicole.

"I'm ready."

Chapter 19

November 4, 2013

The week passed in a blur. With Selena locked into her new role, Arielle encouraged her to use the past week to unwind. Clear the mind.

Once they both started work, their life in 2013 would change for the remainder of their stay. Even with weekends off from WonderHome, the mission would weigh heavy on their minds and consume their every waking moment.

Selena didn't believe this was entirely true, at least for herself. She knew how to turn her mind on and off from whatever it needed to focus on. If she had to grind through five days at the office to be rewarded with a relaxing weekend at the end, WonderHome and Adam Marshall would be the last things on her mind on Saturday mornings.

All three gathered in the kitchen before Arielle and Selena were set to leave for their first day of training at WonderHome.

"I forgot to ask," Felix said to Selena, "Aren't they under the impression that you were working and living in California at the time of your interview? How did you explain moving here so quickly?"

Selena ate a croissant with a glass of orange juice and nodded while she finished the bite in her mouth. "They didn't ask anything about my living arrangements. And I don't think they can, aside from the address I'll need to provide them today. If it comes up, I'll just tell them I'm living with a relative for now, and that I packed up in a week—small apartment, not a lot of stuff. As for my job, I already told them I gave my two weeks' notice, and that Shutterfly told me to make the end of October my last day. From what I read, that's fairly common. A lot of these companies don't actually make you wait out those two weeks anymore."

"From what you read?" Felix sneered. "You keep saying that."

"And we love it," Arielle interjected, joining in on the fun by smacking Felix on his arm.

"What the hell?!" he gasped, rubbing the area. "I didn't sign up to be smacked around like I'm your little brother."

Arielle and Selena exchanged glances before bursting into laughter, Felix unable to resist and eventually joining them. "We just might keep it up until we get that dinner invite back in our real life," Selena said.

Felix sighed. "You act like we never have a meal together. All we do is have nearly every single meal together on missions. Six months of it coming up."

Selena shook her head vigorously. "The missions don't count. We want a dinner off the clock with you. At your place."

"I think Selena just wants to see where you live," Arielle said.

"I do. I have so many questions and theories."

Felix laughed and took a sip of coffee. "Theories, huh? Am I really that mysterious to you?"

"Well, duh," Selena said. "You fall off the map after our missions and come out of the woodwork just in time for the next one. I can't even find you in the Road Runners database because all of your information is hidden."

Felix threw his head back and enjoyed a round of laughter to himself. "Impressive. You tried to look me up. Guess it was a good thing I blocked my data from appearing, or else I'd have Selena showing up on my doorstep with a bottle of vodka ready to party every weekend."

Arielle laughed, and that earned her a smack from Selena, making Arielle lose all control.

The mood was easygoing, and even Selena couldn't help but smile.

"Okay," Arielle said. "We can pick this up later. We need to get going for our first day of work."

They all stood from the table and made their way to the front door.

"Don't go sleeping all day now," Arielle said to Felix, who only responded with a shake of the head.

"Good luck!" he called out when they reached the car on the sidewalk. Arielle and Selena got into the car, Arielle behind the wheel.

"He really is like a little brother," Selena said. "He's older than me, but he still has that sort of way about him, you know?"

"I almost feel bad for him," Arielle said. "He grew up as the middle child between two sisters, only to end up working with us. I guess it's a dynamic in his life he just can't escape. He's a good guy, though. Obviously, he can get along with us well *because* of the siblings he grew up with."

"I really do just want to see his house. Don't you? He seems like a guy who has movie posters for decorations in all the rooms. And you know his gaming setup is *out of this world.* I'm just intrigued."

"There will be plenty of time for that when we get back. It's time to focus on today."

Always right back to business, Selena thought. Arielle couldn't help herself when it came to her work. She was someone who couldn't turn it off and on like Selena. Arielle was simply always *on.* Like that damn bunny from those battery commercials, Arielle would spend her entire day banging on a drum if that was what the mission called for.

"Of course," Selena said.

For a Monday morning, traffic was light beneath the gloomy skies. Rain had fallen overnight, leaving the roads shiny and full of puddles in the sporadic potholes.

"How do you think these two weeks of training will go?" Arielle asked. "What's your angle?"

Selena understood how deeply Arielle thought about her work. Before working with the top-ranked Angel, Selena jumped into missions with a set agenda. She understood the character she would portray and executed that performance with near perfection. And it had always been enough to succeed. But after doing it about fifty times, the routine grew repetitive. Selena would show up to go through the motions. And she was a fantastic actress, so no one ever realized how little passion she was putting into her work.

Working with Arielle had changed her outlook. Arielle drilled as deep as possible into the work ahead.

What's my angle?

Before, Selena would have said her angle was exactly what it said on the mission report: to portray a new employee at WonderHome and use her position on the recruiting team to interfere with Adam's application. Plain and simple.

That answer would never fly with Arielle, however, and she understood why. Succeeding at so many high-intensity missions required a deeper understanding. Selena had accidentally developed a relationship with Brian Dawkins on their last mission, but understood how to properly use that to their advantage when it came to the mission. How could she replicate that type of work on every mission going forward?

"I think my best angle is to befriend as many of my coworkers as possible," Selena said. "I need to develop trust with them, and that starts with the job. Show I'm reliable with my work and not some pushover, then people will be more open to trusting me outside of the office."

Arielle nodded. Selena had found her way onto the same train of thought as their leader. "And then what? How are you going to tie all of that together for the mission?"

She's challenging me? Teaching me?

Selena had to stop to think. Perhaps that was the point.

"I'm . . . not sure."

"And that's fine. But you'll need to consider it. I can't know for sure, but I have a feeling this mission is going to be won outside of the workplace. Someone in that building knows about the money laundering, even if it's ultimately not Adam. And because of that, people will *not* discuss the matter within the office walls. Maybe an occasional meeting in the CEO's office with a select few, but you won't be in there. Look for loose lips at a happy hour. Trust your coworkers who develop a healthy relationship with you. But always be wary of those who have something to gain by your failure—they'll always be your demise in the corporate world."

They reached downtown, traffic coming to a stop as the next six blocks ahead were a row of red lights.

"How do you know so much about everything?" Selena asked, Arielle whipping her head around to look at her, eyebrows drawn in with confusion.

"I don't know everything."

"I didn't say you know everything. But you definitely know a bit *about* everything. Like you haven't had a corporate job, so how do you know how it all works with the happy hours, and who to trust or not trust?"

A light smile touched the corners of Arielle's mouth as she returned her attention to the road. "I've never told anyone this. Can you keep it a secret?"

Selena's stomach tightened like a wrung-out cloth. She was no gossip queen, but could she handle a secret from the great Arielle Lucila? Her curiosity throbbed like a stubbed toe, however. She *needed* to know. "Okay. I got you."

Arielle cleared her throat. "The tragedy with my family is the root of everything for me. After I officially became a Road Runner, I went through some really dark days. The grief never ends and can sneak up on you when you least expect. I thought I was doing myself a favor by joining this new organization, and couldn't believe all the opportunities that lay ahead with time travel.

"I was in the middle of training when a nasty bout of depression completely knocked my life off the rails. They don't mention this part of my story when they run articles or specials about my rise to the top, because I vehemently told them to never discuss this part of my life. I didn't leave my house for a week. I ate maybe five times total during that week. Didn't bathe, brush my teeth. Anything. I contemplated suicide, even went as far as preparing for it. Wrote a letter, bought a bottle of painkillers. Have you ever looked in the mirror and had no idea who was looking back? That can twist your mind into some really dark corners you don't even realize live within you."

Selena sat up, incredibly uncomfortable by Arielle's secret story. She didn't know what to say, and questioned Arielle's ability to tell it so calmly as they made their way through traffic.

"I never could bring myself to do it. Deep down, I knew the pain would last forever, but not the depression. Life would continue one day. And with those endless possibilities given to me by the Road Runners, why would I take the emergency exit before seeing what potential it all had? I think people take their own lives not so much out of disgust toward their current life, but out of hope that whatever happens next is better. It can't be worse, right? Just my thoughts. But for me, I didn't have to see what happened next. I had something so unique. I could live a different life in a different era, and so I did."

"Wait," Selena said. "So you used time travel as a sort of therapy?"

"I wouldn't call it therapy, per se. Therapy is working on and improving yourself. I absolutely hated my life, and wanted to immerse myself in someone else's life. I had a three-day stretch of time travel you wouldn't believe. If we only lose ten minutes in our real time for each trip into the past, then I'll let you do the math. I'd travel back, live a whole new life—I spent at least five years on each trip—then come back and immediately jump to another time to do it again. I'm talking mere seconds in between trips. There are 1,440 minutes in a day, and I did this for three straight days."

Selena looked at the car's ceiling and did the math in her head. "That's over 400 trips."

Arielle nodded. "I honestly lost count once I got into the triple digits, but I estimate I lived around 425 different lives during those three days. Name a job, and I've probably done it."

They pulled into the underground parking garage below the office building, Arielle wasting no time parking in the first open space she found, killing the engine.

"Looking back," Arielle continued. "Living all those lives is definitely the reason I've become who I am today, but that's not what I was ultimately seeking. I was just someone with no direction. And if you can't understand yourself—your true self to the core—then I suppose you'll just always wander through life. Lost. I had to live over 400 other lives to understand my life was unique. When I returned from what ended up being my last trip during those wild three days, it was that sort of feeling when you finish a good book. Like you're snapped back into reality and aren't sure what to do with yourself. It took me a few more days, but the most important lesson I learned was that no matter who you are, no matter your background, your family, your financial situation, or your job—everyone suffers through tragedy of some sort. It's universal. Sure, you might feel special, or that your tragedy is worse if it makes the national news, but that's not really the case. There were dozens of instances during those other lives where I read stories about entire families being lost in car accidents. Different method from my tragedy, but the same result."

"So you realizing that you're *not* unique . . . is what *makes* you unique?" Selena asked, not entirely following Arielle's logic of how it all tied together.

Arielle nodded, a long tear creating a stream down her cheek. "We're all unique in certain ways, but also the same in many others. This realization saved my life, and all I wanted to do was repay the Road Runners for the opportunity. It was at that moment I dedicated my life to the organization and helping in any capacity. I literally owe them my life. It's hard for us time travelers to think about our own deaths, because that can feel centuries away, but something in my gut tells me I'll lose mine defending the Road Runners." She paused and wiped away the tear. "And I wouldn't want it any other way."

The tension had grown as heavy as a boulder sitting on both of their shoulders. Selena could only shake her head, now having an even deeper understanding of what made Arielle tick. It was disturbing, but somehow beautiful when looking at it from the outside. She had so many questions she wanted to ask, but time was up on this conversation. They pulled into the office's parking garage.

"Gather yourself, Selena," Arielle said, unbuckling her seat belt. "We don't want to be late on our first day."

634

Chapter 20

The WonderHome office brimmed with excitement when Arielle and Selena entered the lobby. They had staggered their entries apart by a minute, still needing to keep their connection a private matter.

They had set a round table next to the reception desk, where Becca stood guard over plastic champagne flutes filled with mimosas. A dozen employees gathered in the lobby, most with the angst a child might feel on the first day of school. Nervous laughter, awkward smiles and handshakes, and attire to impress on their first day in a new environment.

Arielle knew by tomorrow they would all come in dressed casually.

"Welcome to your first day at WonderHome," Becca said, a wide grin as she handed mimosas to everyone in the lobby. "No, this is not how we'll greet you every day, but we wanted to make your first day special, especially since this is a larger new-hire class with fourteen of you."

Friendly laughter peppered across the room.

Arielle and Selena took opposite ends of the lobby and exchanged a hasty glance. Even after spilling her secret truth, Arielle fell right back into mission mode the second she had entered the elevator from the garage. It was freeing to share that dark part of her life that she hadn't even mentioned to her grandmother. Her therapist knew about the hundreds of trips throughout time, but still didn't have all the details—not that Arielle could remember the minuscule after hopping through so many worlds.

She shared this with Selena for both of their sakes. She hadn't realized the relief that swept over her. But her primary aim was to motivate Selena.

She saw something in the actress she was certain Selena had yet to see in herself. The potential to be the best. Some people just needed a shove in the right direction to realize their full abilities, and with Selena getting a taste of success from their prior mission, Arielle saw this opportunity as paramount to capitalize on Selena's growth as a person *and* an Angel.

A lanky man made his way to the front of the room, standing next to Becca, where he took a long sip from his mimosa. He wore a button-up, baggy black jeans, and a solid blue baseball cap.

"I'd like to introduce you all to Kurt Brennan," Becca said. "Kurt has been our lead trainer for two years now. You'll be spending most of the next two weeks in a classroom with him and your fellow new hires. Kurt."

Becca stepped back, and Kurt gave her a cordial nod before facing the crowd. "I'd like to extend the welcome. You're all joining an absolutely booming company. We are number one in the industry and plan to stay that way for many years to come. Each of you will help lift WonderHome to the next level. If you're ready to jump into our training for today, please follow me down this hall to the conference room we'll call home for the next couple of weeks."

Just like that, the party had ended.

Time for business.

Arielle pulled out her cell phone, where she had created a new notes document to jot down any remarks throughout the day. She typed in Kurt's name and role. This early in the mission, anyone could be a suspect for the eventual fraud accusations that would fall upon Adam Marshall. She also put down Becca's name, but highly doubted she had any involvement.

The group of new hires formed a line to follow Kurt down the narrow hallway. They passed the conference rooms where they had attended interviews two weeks prior, and stopped in the kitchen area, home to the famous microwave fire that had halted everyone's life.

"This is our kitchen," Kurt said. "The fridges and cabinets are always stocked, and you're welcome to help yourself to anything you'd like."

The counters in the kitchen formed an L shape that connected with the wall that had four different refrigerators—one for drinks, one for beer, one for cold snacks like yogurt and cheese sticks, and one for general use by the employees to store their lunches brought from home. Toasters, mini-ovens, and coffee machines stood across the countertops, cupboards both above and below with a wide range of snacks and fruit.

One of the new employees gleefully took charge and stepped forward, helping himself to a bottled coffee from the fridge and a banana from one of the far cupboards.

"Don't be shy," Kurt reiterated. "I'll give you a couple of minutes before we head back to train."

Small chatter broke out as everyone studied the options. Arielle knew this sort of downtime was critical to building rapport with her fellow employees, but she didn't want to waste time on people who would have no relevance to their mission.

So she approached Kurt, who had been left alone while everyone else hunted for morning snacks. He leaned against the wall in the hallway, scrolling on his cell phone.

"Hello, Kurt," she said. "My name is Arielle."

He offered a polite grin before stuffing his phone into his pocket and shaking her hand. "Nice to meet you, Arielle. Software engineer, yeah?"

"That's correct. I'm so excited to be joining WonderHome. You've been here for two years?"

"I've actually been with the company for eight years and have bounced around so many departments, but I feel more at home doing orientation. I think that's why they asked me to train, because I've done a little bit of everything."

Kurt let out a chuckle. He stood a hefty six-four, and had a welcoming presence, like a man-sized teddy bear.

"Eight years," Arielle repeated. "That's impressive. Many people don't stay that long at tech companies."

"I know. I was here when you could still call us a start-up. It's truly bonkers to look back and see how much this place has grown. The entire company used to be on just this floor. Now we have four floors—looking to expand to five with the creation of our new real estate team."

Arielle's heart skipped a beat. The laundering scheme took place with real estate transactions, all of which were initially processed by the company's widely-touted real estate team.

"I've heard about that new department. How does that work, exactly?"

"We'll dive into all of that in training. Nine out of the fourteen new hires are on the real estate team. The company is really pushing to get it going. They think it might even become the biggest part of the business."

The chatter from the group had slowed, so Kurt called for attention and continued down the hallway, everyone following where they saw the main bullpen to the left.

"This is our sales team," Kurt explained as he stopped in front of a door. "The heartbeat of the company. They make thousands of phone calls from here every single day to realtors around the country, hoping to earn their business. We have one new sales rep joining this new class, correct?"

A skinny woman raised her hand with an appreciative smile.

"Well, this will be your home after training, so buckle up."

The bullpen bustled with chaos. Nearly every visible employee was on the phone, speaking into their headsets as they either paced in circles or reclined in their seats, feet up on the desks. Arielle had gotten to know sales team members plenty of times throughout her trips through time, and appreciated the wide scale of personality types that succeeded in the cutthroat role.

"Let's head in," Kurt said, opening the door he had stopped in front of, holding it while the new hires made their way inside the conference room.

Four rows of tables spanned the length of the room. They set computers and name placards up at each seat.

"Please find your place and get settled in," Kurt said, closing the door behind him and strolling to a podium at the front corner of the room. He tapped on his computer, causing a projector to hum to life, blasting the white wall with a giant WonderHome logo. "Before we jump into training, I need to take a roll call. Just raise your hand when I call your name, please."

Everyone took a minute to find their spots. Arielle was at the end of the front row, Selena positioned in the row immediately behind her.

"Ben Burke. Real estate team."

A scrawny young man raised his hand with a crooked smile.

"Angeline Caldwell, real estate."

A middle-aged woman raised her hand and nodded at Kurt.

"Julia Ellis, sales."

The skinny woman from outside raised her hand.

"Rodney Perry, real estate."

"Present," Rodney said, booming loud and proud, earning a grin from Kurt.

"Oscar Harper, real estate."

An older man, seemingly of retirement age, raised his hand.

"Arielle, we just met," Kurt said, shooting a quick glance at her. "Daniel Mills, customer service."

Daniel looked fresh out of college and was the only one who cared to follow WonderHome casual dress code.

"Selena Nicole, recruiting."

Arielle turned around to act like Selena was a stranger, shooting over a sly grin.

"Amina Newman, real estate."

Amina looked exhausted, but raised her hand with the same excitement as everyone else.

"Ruby Osborne, customer service."

Ruby looked like the loving grandmother who kept snacks in her purse.

"I'm going to run down the last four on this list since they are all on the real estate team. Noah Pearson, Israel Pitts, Anna Roberts, and Leon Stone."

The four raised their hands in rapid succession. Arielle had written everyone's names and departments on her cell phone. The real estate team might be worth befriending, and that all started here in the training class.

"All right," Kurt continued. "There will be plenty of time to get to know each other, but I want to start with a brief history of the company and how we ended up where we are today."

The projection gave way to a picture of a man with two thumbs up in what appeared to be the kitchen area they had just left.

"This is our founder, Peter Howard. He started WonderHome in 2004 after struggling to find a home to buy after graduating from college. He felt there was too much disorganized, overwhelming information and envisioned a way of streamlining all that data to live in one place. That led to the birth of WonderHome. Since our founding we have worked with over 50,000 real estate agents and brokers and have contributed to hundreds of thousands of relationships between those realtors and homebuyers across the United States. We are a company on the verge of going public on the New York Stock Exchange, and that is very much the goal as we look to add a new stream of income with our new real estate team. Before I get into that, was anyone already familiar with Peter and the founding of this company?"

They all looked around at each other in silence.

"That's okay. I was just curious. Peter still serves on the board of directors, but has taken a much smaller role in the day-to-day operations to pursue other business ventures. Our leadership team has some of the best talent you can find and is well equipped to take us to that next level."

The screen changed to show the main five officers for WonderHome, complete with their portrait and names. Arielle gave up on the cell phone and started scribbling in the notebook provided to each employee. She'd get information written more swiftly this way, and wouldn't give off the appearance of disinterest by typing on her phone.

CEO, President, COO, CFO, CTO. One of these people definitely knows about the laundering, if not all of them.

Arielle had brushed up on corporate money laundering schemes throughout American history. Nearly every single case had people involved at the top. Lower-level employees couldn't pull off such matters on their own, plenty of checks and balances hanging over their heads. But who would check the CFO? The CEO, perhaps?

For money laundering to work, it seemed necessary for the Chief Financial Officer to be involved. They overlooked everything money related, so if the books needed some fudging, that would ultimately end up on their desk.

Landon Greene.

The portrait of the WonderHome CFO showed a smiling man of around fifty. Light brown wavy hair, a thick jaw at the bottom of a long, droopy face. Arielle stared into the dark brown eyes of his photo, trying to dig into his soul. She had seen it plenty of times throughout her career. The most innocent-looking people committed the worst crimes.

Are you our guy? Arielle wondered, the slide changing to give way to the WonderHome website's home page.

A knock came on the door before it swung open, a woman entering with a wide grin. Arielle's heart froze as she recognized the face from the screen they had just been looking at.

"Well, this is quite the surprise," Kurt said. "And what timing. I was just showing our new class our leadership team. Everyone, please welcome our CEO, Michelle Garrison."

Chapter 21

Selena burned her gaze into the back of Arielle's head. While the CEO crossed the room, Arielle turned around, her eyes bulging as they locked with Selena's for a split second.

It didn't need to be said—they both understood the importance and suspicion of Michelle Garrison. All their strategies centered on the company's executive team, and it was natural to suspect the highest-ranking officer the most.

"Good morning, everyone," Michelle said, taking center stage at the front of the room. "Kurt, I hope you don't mind me stopping in. I just got in for the day and remembered we had a new class starting. Did they get you all mimosas and breakfast?"

Everyone nodded. The mood had shifted from the light playfulness Kurt had orchestrated to a much heavier one. Michelle had done nothing besides smile and speak in a soft tone since entering the room, yet her presence remained plenty intimidating.

"I wanted to extend a welcome on behalf of the entire company. We are entering a new era at WonderHome, and it should thrill you to join the team at such an explosive time."

Selena studied Michelle. They already knew she was forty-eight; however, not a single gray hair appeared in the sandy blond, and Selena wondered if she ever let her roots grow out enough for anyone to see the natural sign of aging. Michelle had plenty of money, over sixty million dollars, according to a 2010 article in Forbes highlighting the country's top female executives. And it showed.

She kept in great shape, curves highlighted by a gray Alexander McQueen suit. Pearls hung around her neck, two flashy rings on each hand, but none on the ring fingers. Freshly manicured nails and teeth that clearly had seen their fair share of artificial whitening.

Probably drives a Mercedes, Selena thought, suddenly wondering if they should have taken a different approach to get close to Michelle Garrison. The Road Runners had money, and any of the three Angels on this mission could have used that to their advantage. Michelle probably hung out at high-end restaurants with her fellow rich friends, where they all stuffed their faces and laughed about how great their lives were.

Arielle raised her hand, and Selena felt her stomach drop to her knees. Was asking a question not something that could alter the past? What kind of resistance could hit them again? Surely not another microwave fire.

Michelle pointed at Arielle. "Yes, ma'am, a question?"

"It's nice to meet you, Ms. Garrison," Arielle said. "I've heard a lot about the new real estate team WonderHome is putting together. Almost all of this class is working on that team. What can you tell us about it?"

"I'd be happy to." Michelle's grin widened as she paced softly. A couple steps to the left, a couple to the right. It reminded Selena of an attorney delivering closing remarks to a jury, the movement intentional to keep the audience engaged. "We've been in this industry for a long time now. We have all the contacts, we know all the systems, we are essentially a database with all the knowledge. The wizards who crunch all of our numbers—shout-out to Accounting—came to me with an idea that I thought could revolutionize the company. We spend a lot of money trying to acquire real estate agents to market with WonderHome. And that will continue. It's still the forefront of our business and will be for several years to come. But where we have found opportunity is by entering the real estate arena directly.

"We can take some of the money from customer acquisition expenses, and instead use *that* to hire our realtors. We'll be hiring some who are already licensed, and others who are looking to earn their license. It's more cost-effective to hire a realtor directly than trying to get their business. And once we have a realtor, they can go out and make multiple transactions on behalf of WonderHome. We will be directly involved in buying and selling homes. Homeowners can hire WonderHome to sell their properties, and we take a cut of the closing costs. Our agents will keep an eye out for properties that can be flipped for a profit. It's going to open the floodgates on an additional stream of revenue."

"So WonderHome is becoming a broker?" Ben Burke asked from the back row.

"In a sense, yes."

"What do realtors think about this? Surely they will see you as competition instead of a partner in their business."

"RE/MAX has over 100,000 real estate agents. Our goal is to hire 10,000 across the country over the next two years. We're not cutting into anyone's opportunities. A RE/MAX agent doesn't go out into the world seeking properties to flip—unless they do that in their free time. They don't do it on behalf of their brokerage. We will pay our realtors a generous salary. They won't work on commission. They will scout the country for real estate opportunities that can bring in revenue for WonderHome. There is no brokerage that exists, at least on a large scale, that does what we do. This is only going to bring more traffic to our site. I say it will increase the opportunities for agents who market with us. If we have our own properties listed on the site, and an interested buyer comes along, they still need an agent to work with, and they can choose from the pool of agents who market with WonderHome. At the moment, we don't have plans to have our agents work with potential home buyers—*that* would create competition with other realtors. We want to remain in the background of these transactions as much as possible, and will deploy our realtors to buy properties to flip. Does that make sense?"

Michelle looked between Ben and Arielle, who both nodded back. She pulled up her sleeve to reveal a purple Cartier watch.

Selena shook her head. While everyone else in the office wore jeans and T-shirts, Michelle strolled in wearing at least $25,000 worth of clothes and accessories.

"I'm afraid that's all I have time for this morning," Michelle said. "I need to stop now, or I'll talk about our new real estate for the rest of the day."

I'm sure you would.

"Again, welcome to WonderHome, and I can't wait to work with you. Kurt, you can have your class back now."

This earned laughter across the room as Michelle made her way out the door, the stench of her perfume lingering well after the fact.

"Well, there you have it," Kurt said, standing at the front of the room with hands clasped in front of his belly. "That's our CEO. Michelle is a woman of grand passion and intensity. Once she believes in something, there is no stopping her. That's why we all believe so strongly in the direction the company is headed. Now, shall we get back into our training?"

Kurt continued with their originally planned material, but Selena's mind drifted away. She felt there was something with Michelle Garrison worth a deeper exploration. She couldn't wait to follow her.

Chapter 22

November 8, 2013

At the end of their first week of training, Arielle and Selena needed nothing more than to tend to their overworked minds. They had agreed to take the training as seriously as any other employee. They would be with the company for at least six months, and part of that responsibility was simply not getting fired for incompetence.

Despite sitting three feet apart all week, they communicated strictly via text messages, and rarely swapped words in the office. When Arielle asked Selena if she wanted to pick up dinner on the way home, it blindsided her when Selena wanted to keep working on the mission.

I want to follow Michelle, Selena's text message read. *I know there is SOMETHING tied to her. Want to know more.*

Arielle agreed to join her and sent a message to Felix, letting him know they would arrive later than originally planned. He had already been enjoying a quiet week at home, working on research and preparing for the later phases of the mission, and wouldn't mind a bit more time to himself.

They staggered to the garage, where Arielle arrived at the car first, Selena a couple of minutes behind as she waited for the next elevator.

The week had been nothing short of mentally exhausting. They knew more than any reasonable person needed to know about the history of WonderHome.

Selena arrived at the car and opened the door, tossing her bag onto the passenger seat, but remaining outside. "C'mon. Let's go."

"Oh? Where are we going?"

"Where are *you* going?" Selena asked. "I said we need to follow Michelle. She's still in the office."

"And how do you plan on following her? You can't just sit outside her office and wait for her to leave."

Selena sat down in the car and closed the door, tossing her bag into the back seat. "This has been eating at me all week—"

"So, more secrets you've been keeping to yourself? We've talked about this."

"No secrets. I don't have any information—just a feeling that we need to follow her. We talked about her passion for this new real estate team on Monday night. I know you sense her involvement."

"Of course. And I don't mind following her around, but we need to have a plan. We can't just wing it on a mission like this. What will you say if you get too close and she recognizes you?"

"That's why you're here. Those things never happen to you. Sneaky little ninja."

Arielle laughed. They were both slaphappy after the long week.

"And why did you wait until today? We could have been following her all week."

"I know you're into that boring stuff of watching people eat their dinner and wash their dishes. But I want something of actual substance. It's Friday. She's a filthy rich, single executive. She's not going home after work—she's going out to blow off some steam. We'll be able to see where she hangs out, who she's with, what kind of *activities* she's into."

Selena tapped her finger to her nose, prompting an eye roll from Arielle. "I've told you, not every executive does cocaine."

"We'll just have to see for ourselves."

As much as Selena's theories could seem incredibly off-the-wall, Arielle knew this was right up her alley of expertise. Raucous nightlife, chaotic clubs, swanky bars, lavish gatherings. You name it, Selena loved all that shit and would see things Arielle simply couldn't. It was her love language.

Always ready to cover all the bases, Arielle wanted to ask Selena about the possibility of Michelle staying in the office late. She had seen plenty of executives keep bottles of booze in a desk drawer—or even out in the open in a fancy canteen—all to enjoy a happy hour with their inner-circle before leaving for home.

But Selena had determination in her eyes, and it was obvious she was sensing *something*. Perhaps it was good to have someone on the team who followed their gut.

"Okay," Arielle said. "If you want my opinion, I think we should split up. We don't know if she's going out here by the office, or driving somewhere else. The weather is a factor, and today is pretty cold, so I wouldn't be surprised if she opts to drive where she's going instead of walking four or five blocks through downtown. As you mentioned, she's loaded—probably pays for valet wherever she goes."

"How does it work if we're split? If she drives off, I can't get back to the car in time if you need to follow her."

"I know. I'll follow, in that case, and let you know where we end up. You can catch a Lyft to meet me. That said, I think you should go back into the office. Try to follow her from there. There's a bathroom outside the elevator lobby on the thirty-fourth floor—that's where her office is. If you wait outside that bathroom door, you'll be able to spot Michelle once she exits her office further down the hallway. It's a long hall, so I doubt she'd even notice you at the far end. That gives you a moment to slip into the bathroom, wait about twenty seconds, and step back out to catch an elevator at the same time as her. You'll know from there if she's going to the garage or street level."

"Brilliant. Okay, I'm going in. Will text you."

Chapter 23

Training had ended at four o'clock that afternoon, and to Arielle's delight, Selena had texted her at 4:55 that Michelle was heading out for the day. She passed the hour listening to the spotty radio reception from the garage. Pharrell Williams sang about getting lucky when the messages started pouring in from Selena:

On her way.

In the bathroom.

She's in the bathroom. I'm hiding in stall.

Two minutes passed until the next message.

In the elevator with her.

STREET LEVEL!

The texts stopped for two minutes—it could sometimes take an entire five minutes to ride the elevator thirty floors down, especially around this time when everyone in the building was heading out.

Street level meant Michelle was indeed going to brave the cold weather and trek through downtown, so Arielle hopped out of the car and used the stairs to reach the building's main lobby where dozens of people bustled on their way out.

Arielle headed outside, waiting under an overhang until Selena texted her again.

Heading outside. Staying behind her.

Arielle turned her back from the building's main entrance. She had spoken to Michelle in the training class and couldn't risk being recognized. It wasn't raining for the first time all week, but she wished terribly to have an umbrella right about now. She was left no choice but to look over her shoulder every couple of seconds.

Michelle stepped out, a long black wool coat concealing what was surely another expensive outfit underneath. She was talking on her cell phone, a relief to Arielle. Michelle looked right in Arielle's direction before turning the opposite way down the sidewalk with the rest of the professionals stampeding to happy hour.

Selena bolted out of the building just as Arielle had started to follow. They nearly crashed into each other, both having kept their eyes glued to their target.

"Did she see you?" Selena asked.

"No. How was the elevator ride?"

"Fine. I'm not sure she even saw me. Six other people were all crammed into it."

"Perfect."

Michelle walked at a brisk pace. Arielle and Selena had both worn jeans, and the cold autumn air whipped at their ankles as they hurried down the sidewalk to keep up. They passed Pike's Place Market, where hordes of people stood in the street. Fortunately, downtown was pretty crowded as far as they could see, even after going two blocks, where Michelle gained speed on a downhill slope.

"My God," Selena gasped. "I've never seen someone put their head down and just power walk through a city like this."

They were passing multiple people trying to keep up with the speedy CEO. Two more blocks later, they paused across the street from a bar called Red, a café and wine bar with a half-dozen people in business attire waiting in the short line outside.

Within a minute, the line dissipated as everyone made their way in.

"We're going in, right?" Selena asked.

"Of course. We just need to be careful. I highly doubt she'll recognize us, but you never know."

"Yeah, because *someone* just had to ask the CEO a question that sent her on a rant. Way to be."

"Hey, we learned a lot. Michelle is *clearly* involved with that department."

"No shit. Let's just go in, please. I can't stand out here all day. And doesn't a drink sound nice about now?"

Arielle rolled her eyes and started across the street, Selena eager to follow. They wasted no time stepping into the bar, Selena's eyes lighting up as they peered around.

"Holy shit," Selena muttered, eyes wide like a child who just woke up in the North Pole. "Their wine rack goes all the way to the ceiling."

Arielle followed the towering wine rack as it indeed had a dozen shelves that touched the ceiling. A staircase spiraled around the rack for easy access. Selena squealed beside her.

"Calm down before they kick us out," Arielle said under her breath, throwing an elbow into Selena's side. "Act like you belong."

The bar was definitely for the wealthy professional demographic, ranging in all ages. Mostly everyone wore fine attire, businessmen with their ties loosened as they blew off steam and business women with their blazers unbuttoned.

"Do you even see her?" Arielle asked, craning her neck. They were still in line to check in for a table.

People packed into the bar, not an open seat visible from where they stood. A bar top circled around the great tower of wine, tables and booths filling the rest of the space as far back as they could see.

"She's upstairs." Selena nodded toward the second level, across the back wall.

Arielle spotted Michelle sitting at a round table with a group of other people.

They reached the host stand where a young man with frosted pink hair greeted them. "Just the two of you queens today?" he asked.

"Yes," Arielle said. "Any chance we can sit upstairs?"

He leaned forward on the stand and whispered, "I'm not supposed to let anyone sit up there who isn't one of our high-roller regulars." He rolled his eyes. "But if you promise to not bother any of those people, I can find you ladies a table."

"You're the best," Selena said.

"Girl, I know it," the host said, batting his eyebrows at them. "And if anyone asks why you're sitting up there, you can tell them that Rolando sent you—and Rolando doesn't give a shit!" Rolando chuckled at himself, causing Arielle and Selena to break into laughter. "Y'all follow me now."

They followed Rolando around the bar, where they climbed a flight of stairs to the bar's exclusive second level. He looked back as they weaved through a couple of tables and rolled his eyes again. He put them at a table along the rail overlooking the rest of the bar below, sliding two menus onto the table.

"You ladies enjoy your drinks," he said, grinning as he spun around and disappearing before Arielle or Selena could thank him.

They sat in the center of the upstairs area, and Michelle Garrison was only two tables down, ordering from a server. Arielle faced her table, Selena with her back to it.

Selena looked down at the menu and asked, "Who's all sitting with her?"

Arielle had a much better view of Michelle's company at the table, but scrunched her brow as she tried to recognize any faces. "I honestly don't see anyone with her from WonderHome. At least not from the executive team."

"I guess that makes sense. If she was coming with someone from work, they would have walked over here together."

"It's a weird mix at her table. Six total people. Her plus two guys that look to be in their twenties or early thirties. A man and woman who look around her same age. And a younger woman who might have come with the other two guys."

Selena looked over her shoulder, trying to play it cool, whipping her head back around to Arielle. "I don't recognize anyone there, either. But we're in the VIP section. They could all have developed some sort of friendship at this bar. The host said up here is for the high-roller regulars."

"They certainly look comfortable, like they've known each other for a while."

Arielle watched as everyone at Michelle's table raised a shot glass in the air, toasting to the weekend ahead. They down their shots and returned to their conversation, occasional laughter rippling around the group.

"Can you take pictures of them?" Selena asked. "Here. Take a picture of me." She grabbed her glass of water and raised it.

Arielle nodded and rummaged through her small purse for her cell phone, pulling it out and promptly snapping pictures of Michelle's table in the background while Selena pretended to pose. "Okay, we're good. I can see all of them except for the young woman. Her back is to us."

"Good. Let's just keep an eye and be ready. We need to follow Michelle's every move."

They ordered wine, Arielle stopping after the first glass while Selena opted for a second. They mimicked whatever happened at Michelle's table, so when that group ordered a round of appetizers, so did Arielle and Selena.

Two hours passed where they kept ordering appetizers, eventually becoming too full to keep eating. Arielle had let Felix know they wouldn't be home for dinner and he shouldn't wait up. He responded with a thumbs-up emoji.

Seven o'clock passed when Michelle's table finally threw in the towel and asked for their check. Arielle paid her and Selena's tab without even seeing the bill, needing to be ready to get up and leave as soon as Michelle did.

Michelle slipped into her jacket and stood up with the rest of the group. They all shared hugs before departing. Michelle stayed at the back of the line with one of the young men. Selena watched the group descend the stairs.

"What's happening?" Selena whispered, tipping back her glass of wine to kill off the final remains.

Arielle shrugged, her eyes glued to the impromptu private conversation. Michelle reached her hand up and stroked the man on his cheek before starting down the stairs, leaving the man a few steps behind.

"Act natural," Arielle said.

They rose and put on their jackets before Michelle had reached the bottom landing. They hurried through the crowded dining area and nearly ran down the steps, fighting through one more herd when Michelle stepped outside of the bar.

Arielle and Selena stepped outside and saw Michelle crossing the street. Arielle kept her gaze on the man who chased after Michelle. She reached out and grabbed Selena's arm. "Wait."

"Michelle!" the man shouted, dashing across the street toward her. "Michelle!"

"What the hell?" Selena asked as they started taking a couple of steps toward the unfolding scene.

Michelle stopped and turned around, remaining in place as she waited for the man to reach her. When he did, he crouched to plant his hands on his knees while catching his breath.

After a few seconds, he stood up and started speaking with Michelle again. She had her arms crossed to keep warm. She nodded, then the man threw his arms around Michelle and pulled her in close, where they shoved their tongues down each other's throats.

"Oh my God!" Selena cried. "What the fuck is *happening*?!"

"Uhhhh," was all Arielle could muster, unable to look away from the powerhouse CEO making out with a man at least twenty years her junior.

Selena started laughing. "This is great!"

Her words fell on deaf ears for Arielle as she kept watching them. The two kept their mouths interlocked for at least thirty seconds, the man running his hand up and down the small of Michelle's back. They finally broke apart and promptly grabbed each other's hands, continuing down the sidewalk.

Selena was still laughing. Louder, with an odd sense of joy.

"What the hell is wrong with you?" Arielle asked. "Do we need to keep following them?"

"I think we've seen enough. I can't believe my eyes. All I had was a feeling, and it was right!"

"About *what*?!" Arielle asked, growing frustrated.

"That she was in to younger guys. I originally thought maybe it was rich men, but it's *young* men. Of course."

This was all coming out of nowhere. Selena had shared none of these thoughts before, and Arielle still didn't understand the relevance. "What—"

"Don't worry about it. I know how we can easily get into Michelle's house."

Chapter 24

November 10, 2013

Selena had shared her idea with Arielle during their walk back to the car on Friday evening. While Arielle thought it was a stretch, she still agreed to it. They'd need cooperation from Felix, however, and didn't know how he'd respond to such a request.

Rather than giving him a full weekend to dwell on the matter, Arielle suggested they discuss it with Felix on Sunday night, leaving him a full week to prepare should he agree.

Arielle knew he wouldn't be open to the plan right off the bat, but believed they could convince him. They let him watch his football games all of Sunday, until dinnertime when Selena ordered takeout from a local Chinese restaurant.

"Week two on the job coming up," Felix said as they settled around the table. "What do you two have planned?"

"A few things," Arielle said, exchanging a quick glance with Selena. Neither of them expected the topic to come up so soon. "A week from tonight, Adam Marshall will apply to WonderHome. I'd still like to see what kind of interference is possible to prevent that from happening, but I understand it's a long shot."

"Do you think you'll be getting access to the WonderHome system?" Felix asked. "Because I came up with an idea. It's not guaranteed to work if we have to wait until next Monday, but if Selena works in the recruiting system this week, we might be able to stop the application from even happening."

Arielle had a particular way she wanted tonight's conversation to go, and it was already on a complete detour. She wanted to dictate the topics and present the grand idea. Instead, Felix had jumped right into mission-talk and now had his own ideas. She needed to reminder herself that her team was collaborative. And while she had the authority to make final decisions, Felix and Selena wouldn't accept such things without a discussion. Slowly, they had evolved into a singular unit. Anything that involved one of them on a mission now involved all.

"Okay, what is it?" Selena asked, stuffing a bite of chicken fried rice into her mouth.

"I'm thinking we apply for Adam. I can dumb down his resume and set up a dummy e-mail address for him to receive correspondence. And I can communicate directly back to the company *as* Adam. As of this week, they have no idea who he is. Ideally, they can reject his application, and that way when he applies on Sunday, it will look like he's being greedy, and possibly a liar, since they'll see a different resume."

"That's actually a fantastic idea," Arielle said. "Let's try it. But what is the relevance of Selena having access this week? It sounds like this can all take care of itself."

Felix laughed. "I thought you knew better than that, Arielle. We're dancing with the past. I've been trying to understand it at the level you do. I doubt I'm anywhere near that point, but I have some new confidence. This mission isn't about WonderHome or Adam Marshall and his dead family. It's about the past. We have our objectives we want to accomplish, and we need to work around the past to achieve them. That's it, plain and simple."

Arielle nodded. The week off hadn't been a total waste for Felix. Quite the contrary. Much like Selena, he had grown. Elevated his skills and understanding of their work to the next level.

"But you're right," Felix continued. "It's not mandatory for Selena to have access for this to work, but if she does, I see it as one less possible barrier. We still don't know what happens when this application comes into recruiting. They might call him to ask questions about his resume. Maybe they'll think he's a good fit for another team. Who knows? If Selena can intercept the application and reject it right away, that would be ideal. That way, it's in the system that they already turned him down before his real application comes through on Sunday night. And Selena will have actual ground to stand on, saying Adam does not look like a good fit for the job."

Selena nodded along. "I see. I think it's a wonderful idea, too. All they told me on Friday was this next week will be more hands-on."

"Same for me," Arielle said. "However, I know I'll be working out of a sandbox version of our systems—all dummy accounts. If recruiting does the same thing, none of this will pan out how we want."

Felix shrugged. "All we can do is try and see what happens. Hopefully, it's a quick, automated rejection."

The conversation calmed down, and they ate in silence for the next minute.

"We have an idea, too," Arielle finally said to break the silence. On cue, Selena cracked open a can of beer and took a long swig.

"We?" Felix asked.

"The idea came to Selena after what we saw on Friday evening at the happy hour."

Felix stared back and forth between the two. "I thought you said it was a normal happy hour."

"Selena, please explain." Arielle stuffed food into her mouth, grinning across the table.

"All right, thanks Arielle," Selena said. "So, the happy hour was normal. What we didn't tell you was what happened after. Michelle was with a group of people inside the bar, and when they all left, a younger man chased her down outside and they started making out."

"And you left that out why?" Felix asked. "What does that have to do with anything?"

"Well, my idea came from seeing that, but I needed to check on some things over this weekend. If you didn't notice, I've been on my phone a lot."

"You're *always* on your phone." Felix would never resist a chance to call out Selena.

She glared at him, a smirk touching her mouth. "Anyway. My idea is for the long term, assuming we're not able to prevent Adam from getting hired on. We need to do anything we can to get close enough to Michelle to find out who really should go down for the crime. When I saw her with that guy, it made me curious. So I spent all weekend browsing about a hundred different dating apps and sites. I found Michelle on two of them. Cougar Love and Elite Bonding."

Felix started laughing. "She thinks of herself as a cougar. Too funny!"

They all laughed. Arielle was relieved to hear Felix still in a light mood, and wondered if he really didn't see where this was going.

"Yes. So Cougar Love is exactly what it sounds like—older women looking for younger men. And then Elite Bonding is a dating app for executives and professionals. Or just rich people. Because of this, we know exactly what she is looking for. And we can deliver it to her on a silver platter."

Felix had been grinning and nodding along, even after Selena finished speaking, and left the three of them in an awkward silence. Both Arielle and Selena held steady gazes toward Felix, neither wanting to come out and say exactly what Selena's grand idea was.

Thirty seconds passed, and Felix's grin faded, a tinge of panic slipping into his eyes. "Wait," he said, then gulped. "No, no, no. I don't think so. You're nuts, no, out of your mind. That's it. You're out of your *fucking* mind if you think I'm doing this."

He let out a nervous laugh and swung his head around to Arielle.

"We only want to discuss it," Arielle said.

Felix smiled, a somewhat manic look as he realized the walls closing in around him. "Cool. I don't. So how about that? This is definitely not part of my job. Not in the slightest."

"Hold on now, Felix," Arielle said. "You don't even know what we're suggesting."

"Of course I do! You want to prop me up as some rich professional on these dating apps. Try to land a date and develop a relationship to spy on her. Right?"

Selena pursed her lips before saying, "More or less, yes."

"Exactly. And I'm not an actor like the talented Selena Nicole, so you know I'll just botch this. How can you even expect me to understand how to date an older woman? That's just . . . wrong. She's only a couple of years younger than my mom."

"Okay, just slow down," Arielle said, frustration slipping in her voice. "One thing at a time. Selena will prepare you for everything on the acting front, including your outfits."

Felix threw his head back and laughed. "I've seen how the rich people dress at my mom's boutique, remember? I don't need help on that front."

Arielle gritted her teeth. Felix was normally open-minded and willing to at least hear out someone's idea, but he now was being hostile and interrupting everything she said. He was acting like Selena, and it caught Arielle completely off guard.

"Okay, dress yourself," Arielle said. "Selena will still help with how you can approach this."

"The hell she will."

"What the fuck, Felix?!" Arielle shouted and slammed a fist on the table. After the brief rattle of their silverware and glasses, the room fell deathly silent. "Why are you being like this?"

Felix raised his eyebrows and let out an exaggerated laugh. "*Me?* You think *I'm* the one at fault? I'm just trying to stand up for myself. Like Arielle Lucila would. This shit is not my job. I stay behind the scenes. If you want me to break into her house and plant a bug, then just say so, but all of this is grossly unnecessary. I can do my job without having to speak to a single one of these people."

"I'm not trying to force you into anything. I was only trying to have a discussion. If you really don't want to, that's fine. We'll find another option, but hear me out. Okay?"

Felix rolled his eyes and crossed his arms, leaning back in his seat.

"Whatever you say, Arielle. It's your world and we just live in it. I'm sure you have all the perfect words to convince me to do this. So let's hear it."

"First off, our roles are evolving on this team. I'm not one for acting, but here I am about to start a second week of pretending to be someone I'm not. This is not the way I wanted things, but it's what the mission calls for. The way it looks, more missions are going to look like this. We're all going to need to be more involved than our main roles. We have to really get into the mission and immerse ourselves in the world around our targets, all while keeping a safe distance to not piss off the past. And so far, I'd say we have it figured out. It was a smooth first week at WonderHome. Our presence hasn't altered anything."

"Okay," Felix said in a calmer tone. "But how is me dating Michelle Garrison not going to have an effect? Messing with someone's love life has always proven costly in this line of work. Just ask our dear commander."

"We're not expecting you to marry the woman. Just go on a couple of dates and see what happens. I don't expect you to do anything physically that you're not comfortable with. This would be strictly to see what kind of information you might pry from her. If it looks like there's nothing, then call off the relationship. No harm done. And if you don't want to do this, I can submit a request to the Road Runner offices here in Seattle for another actor who can help, but you'll miss out on what can be a big boost in your ranking."

Arielle knew Felix didn't care about the rankings—few of those in his role did—but knew he wouldn't like the thought of having a third party come in to do what he was being asked. That wouldn't look good on the final mission report, which was read by several people across the organization, Commander Briar included.

"You would bring someone else in?" Felix asked, his tone now the complete opposite of the outburst he had moments ago.

"Yes, Felix. This is a brilliant idea that I'd like to see play out. It opens up so many possibilities for us to get close to who we believe is the brains behind the laundering. Besides, you'll get to pick the mind of a highly successful executive. You want to be a billionaire one day, so maybe she's worth talking to."

Selena cleared her throat after taking another drink of beer. "And I'll be here every step of the way. You'll be prepared for whatever comes up. Just trust me. Trust *us*. We know this is so far out of your comfort zone, but is that not the only way to grow? By doing something out of your norm. If either of us could do this, we would. But we're not young millionaire men."

Felix balled a fist and gently touched it to his lips, staring at the table with an intensity they were all feeling.

"You don't need to decide right at this moment," Arielle said. "Take a couple of days to think it over. All I really need is some notice if I need to bring another actor on or not. Deal?"

Felix drew a deep breath and took his time blowing it out of his mouth. He pursed his lips and shook his head. "I'll think about it."

Chapter 25

November 13, 2013

On Wednesday morning, Felix informed Arielle that he would do it. She responded to the news with a big hug and a promise that he wouldn't regret it.

Felix didn't really *want* to pretend to date Michelle, but he couldn't bear the thought of a fourth person coming to live with them so deep into the mission. He respected the dynamic of their trio. It worked. Everything ran smoothly the way it was. And with little work to do until Arielle could lend him access to WonderHome's systems, Felix would have to spend his free time brushing up on how to act like a young, rich executive to court one of the most successful women in the world.

If he viewed it as a challenge with certain levels of achievement, the whole thing became easier to swallow.

Felix spent Wednesday morning in his bedroom, working on a jigsaw puzzle of the Seattle skyline that he had purchased a couple of weeks ago.

He had spent Monday and Tuesday crafting and polishing a resume to submit on behalf of Adam Marshall. He pulled as much information as he could find online, which was plenty for this purpose. His education background and prior jobs were all listed in Adam's LinkedIn profile. Felix copied it all over and weakened a resume that was rather impressive. He wondered why Adam would settle for a job that was essentially Michelle's servant in the first place.

He sent Selena and Arielle a text message to inform them he'd submit the application later that afternoon. Everything was uploaded and filled out on WonderHome's hiring page—he just needed to click "submit".

Selena had believed she would be in front of her work computer during the entirety of Wednesday afternoon. What she'd have access to was still in question, but it was their best shot to push this attempt of sabotage through.

Until then, Felix did the unbearable and created profiles on the two dating apps where he planned to connect with Michelle. A big part of him was hoping her profiles were inactive. Perhaps she had accounts on these sites, but hadn't logged in to use them in months. That would throw a wrench in this absurd idea and get him off the hook.

Selena had prepared notes for him to create his profiles, including taking a couple of pictures using his phone to upload to the dating sites. She once again stressed the importance of creating a backstory for the character he would portray while on dates with Michelle.

A knot formed in Felix's stomach. He didn't want to do any of this. None of it fueled his passion like hacking into a computer system did. Even the mindless busywork that went into preparing for a mission—things like getting fake ID's and paperwork sorted out, drawing routes on maps and circling key locations—were more appealing than creating a dating profile where he would be hunted by what society referred to as cougars.

"So fucking weird and wrong," he whispered to himself.

His oldest sister, Clara, had once brought home a man fifteen years older than her, and that led to nothing but a dramatic outburst from both of his parents. One of which Felix and his younger sister, Sarah, enjoyed watching. Clara had always been the golden child. Never in trouble, never even *suspected* of wrongdoing. Felix couldn't recall a time they had ever grounded Clara, and truly believed if she wasn't an adult at the time of this incident, their father would have sent her to her bedroom to "think about what she had done."

The thought made Felix giggle to this day, and eased his mind as he re-focused on the disturbing task before him. It took him half an hour to get his profile up and verified on Elite Bonding, positioning himself as a corporate executive currently working for Starbucks. They were a large enough company that if Michelle tried to look up their employee roster online, she'd get nowhere quickly. He listed his title as the Head of Research and Development.

Selena had brought home a suit and tie for Felix to wear for his profile picture, eventually snapping a portrait that could serve as a professional headshot. She encouraged Felix to upload the picture and create a fake profile on LinkedIn because "any executive worth their weight is on that site."

That much was true, and to make things appear legitimate, Felix called in a favor to his colleagues to create fake corporate Starbucks employee accounts to connect with on the platform. He had done all this on Tuesday when he had secretly moved forward with Arielle's plan before informing her.

All he had left to do was upload his new portrait, and everything would be in motion.

The morning had passed, which meant Felix could finally submit the application left open on his computer for Adam Marshall. Deep down, he knew this plan had little chance of working, but for his own sake of not having to pursue a date with Michelle, he prayed it would.

"I guess there's only one way to find out," he said, and clicked on *SUBMIT*.

Chapter 26

November 17, 2013

"I have news!" Emily Marshall said as she entered the kitchen on Sunday evening. The Marshalls had finished a dinner of grilled cheese sandwiches and tomato soup, where Adam remained to clean up the aftermath, a mountain of dishes piling out of the sink.

The kids were off to their rooms to get ready for bedtime.

"What kind of news?" Adam asked, picking at a piece of melted cheese stuck on one plate.

"I've been putting out some feelers for jobs you might be interested in," Emily said, leaning against the counter next to Adam, cell phone in hand.

"I have a friend who knows the CEO for WonderHome. They have lots of jobs posted, but there's one they're having trouble filling: an administrative assistant."

Adam laughed. "An *assistant*? Em, I was just a store manager for a major grocery store. I think I can find something a little more within my qualifications."

"I knew you'd say that, but hear me out." Emily turned her attention to read from her phone. "They're looking for someone who has great organizational skills, understands complex problem-solving, and can make quick and difficult decisions on the fly. Doesn't managing a store require all of that? I'd say you qualify based on that alone."

"Well, sure, but that doesn't mean I *want* to be someone's assistant.

I've gotten used to calling the shots at work. I can't imagine it any other way."

"I get that, but this isn't just being anyone's assistant. It's the *CEO's* assistant. You don't think you'll have some pull for that reason alone?"

"I guess, but where is the opportunity for growth? Not like I can get promoted to CEO."

"Babe, have you really become this close-minded since you lost your job? Think bigger. No, you won't get promoted to CEO, but put in a couple years as her assistant, and you'll have every door in the company open to you. You'll literally have the most important person in the company to vouch for you. Do you think some hiring manager will just ignore their own CEO recommending you for a job? Not at all."

"But I've never done anything remotely close to being an assistant. So I'll handle paperwork and fetch this lady's coffee every day? Like, I get the opportunity is more than it seems, but I can't see myself committing to this type of work."

"What if I told you it pays more than you were making before?"

Adam laughed again, turning off the sink and turning his full attention to his wife. "Then I'd say you're high. No way in hell an assistant job pays more."

"*CEO's* assistant. You know this lady is worth hundreds of millions of dollars, right?"

"You know I don't follow all that stuff. So what does it pay?"

"Well, for the right candidate, the pay will start at $100,000 and could go as high as $125,000."

"Uh, what the fuck? Excuse me?" A giddy smile spread across Emily's face as she looked up from her phone. "You're joking."

"I'm not. This is very real. Look!"

Emily held up her phone, the job application on the screen.

"You think I have a chance at this job?" Adam asked. "Which friend has this connection?"

"Emma, from the Pilates studio. She said she'll put in a good word for you. And from what it sounds like, she goes back a long way with Michelle

Garrison."

Emily let the moment hang in the air between them, and she watched as Adam looked up at the ceiling, then down to the floor as the gears in his mind twisted into motion.

I can't just become this lady's assistant, he thought. *For that much money, she's definitely looking for someone specific.*

"Well?" Emily asked, her eyes bulging. She had surely recognized the look on his face as his acceptance. Spend enough of your life with someone, and they'll know what you're thinking before even you do.

"This is an interesting opportunity. But am I a sellout? Because I promise you, if it paid the same as my old job, there is no way in hell I'd be doing this."

Now Emily let out a laugh. "A sellout? Adam, it's a good-paying job at a top-tier company that will open up so many opportunities for your future. How is showing interest in that being a sellout? You would work directly with a multi-millionaire. We'll get invited to her house, meet her friends and family, and build connections that way. The opportunities from this go way beyond the walls of WonderHome. And that money is just the salary. Emma told me Michelle gave her last assistant a $25,000 Christmas bonus, plus an all-expenses-paid trip to the Caribbean for their family. You can stand there and wrestle with some moral decision that doesn't really exist. Or you can apply for this job that can change our lives."

She was right. If Adam applied for this job, their lives would be unrecognizable this time next year. Thanksgiving was less than two weeks away, which meant Adam's in-laws were heading to Seattle in the next ten days, a thought that deserved its own throbbing headache. They would cram into this house that didn't have enough space. They would dirty the place with their inability to discipline the kids in the slightest, letting them run wild and overriding whatever Adam and Emily said.

Between his mother-in-law's nonsensical opinions about everything and his father-in-law hogging the remote—*who the fuck pauses live sports?!*—it was no wonder Adam drank himself into oblivion at Thanksgiving dinner.

But with an alternative lifestyle driven by a fatter bank account, that could all change. They could be the ones taking the trip to visit the in-laws in Oregon. They could book hotel rooms and not have to be around the in-laws every waking second of the day. And just maybe, Adam could watch Thanksgiving football games in peace without the nagging about how violent a sport it was from his mother-in-law.

Maybe we just take a cruise next year and deal with none of it.

The thought sent a flutter into Adam's chest.

"I suppose there is a lot we could get done with that kind of money," he said.

Emily nodded. "We've been talking about finishing the basement, remodeling the kitchen, and building that shed in the backyard. We'd finally get to look at all of that."

Adam could sense the angst radiating from his wife. She desperately wanted him to apply for this job. He drew a deep breath for dramatics. It was a rare occasion for Adam to hold so much influence over his wife, and he wanted to drag the moment out as long as he could, returning his stare to the ceiling as he blew out the air.

"Oh my, God, Adam!" She finally caved. "Apply for this job before I do."

Adam broke into howling laughter, clenching his stomach. "Okay, okay. One question though—will you still love me when I'm an administrative assistant?"

Emily bit her bottom lip and punched him playfully on the arm. Adam had known Emily equally well, and knew that lip bite signified a moment of fierce attraction. Send in this job application tonight and he'd almost certainly get lucky after the kids were asleep.

He couldn't pass up a slam dunk of an opportunity. "Okay. I'll apply right now if you finish the dishes."

Emily squealed and clapped her hands, jumping like a teenage girl who just met her boy band crush. "Deal."

She planted a wet kiss on his lips and slipped into the space between him and the sink, her ass brushing against his crotch.

It's so on, Adam thought, running his hands down her sides before he pulled away. "Okay. Can you send me that link to apply?"

"Already did five minutes ago," she said with a chuckle.

"Ahh, so this was all an act. You already knew I was going to apply."

"Maybe." She threw a grin over her shoulder. "Now go get it done."

Adam obliged, shuffling out of the kitchen and down the hallway where they kept a room that was half office, half guest space with a futon and a nightstand crammed next to the computer desk and bookshelf.

Seeing that futon just reminded Adam that his in-laws were coming, and it was indeed urgent he apply for and get this job.

"Okay, let's do this," Adam said, turning on his computer and waiting for it to load. The older models were nowhere near as fast as the computers he had the privilege of using at his grocery store office.

After a couple of minutes, all was set. He opened the application and read through it, finding his past job experience somehow aligned perfectly with the role. He'd been applying to multiple jobs over the past week, never feeling truly inspired by any of the companies he had been researching.

But they knew WonderHome around Seattle as the ultimate company one could work for. With his resume already updated and ready to go, he attached it to the application, filled out his information, and submitted.

He leaned back and smiled, staring at the screen with the most hope he had felt in weeks. "I have a good feeling about this."

Chapter 27

November 20, 2013

By Wednesday morning, they were certain they had pulled off the impossible. The week prior, Selena had found her way into the recruiting system and marked Adam's fake application as rejected because of substandard qualifications. On Monday morning, she had done the same thing with Adam's actual application.

She removed both applications from the shared recruiting inbox, placed into the vast folder where tens of thousands of rejected applications fell victim during the year.

Arielle had made plans for them to potentially leave the mission early, assuming Adam never received contact from WonderHome through the end of 2013. They would spot check the next six months to see that Adam remained away from the company to pursue other opportunities. If so, that should have been enough to clear him from the illegal activity that would eventually befall him and lead to the death of his family.

Selena rode high on cloud nine, believing she had once again done the dirty work behind the scenes to close out another successful mission. Felix was the lone skeptic, urging them to at least wait out the week before planning a victory lap.

When Selena's manager, Susie, called her into her office just before lunch on Wednesday, all of Felix's doubt and warnings immediately rushed to the front of Selena's mind.

Shit, she thought.

The training class had ended last Friday, and all the new hires got a couple of hours that afternoon to set up their new desks and finally mingle with their department colleagues. Recruiting was a small team of five, and all five of Selena's coworkers exchanged glances when Susie had stuck her head out of her office door across the hall, adding to Selena's paranoia.

Shit, shit, shit. Play it cool. You're new. It was an honest mistake.

The fluids in her stomach drained and seemed to pool in her wobbly knees as she stood from her desk and grabbed her water bottle.

It could just be a check-in. I am new, after all. Not everything has to be doom and gloom when your boss asks to speak with you in private.

Selena entered Susie's office, where her manager had returned to the seat behind her desk.

"Please close the door behind you and have a seat," Susie said.

Shiiiit.

Selena could immediately tell from Susie's tone a serious conversation was underway. Susie kept a lone goldfish in a round glass tank on the ledge of the window behind her. Selena watched it swim laps around a miniature castle, then looked out to the window to the skyscrapers of Seattle.

"How have your first couple of weeks been?" Susie asked, leaning back and softening her tone. "You getting settled in?"

"Yes," Selena said. "I've loved every minute so far. I'm definitely happy and see myself being with WonderHome for a very long time."

Susie smiled, looking at the empty space on her desk before making eye contact with her new employee. "That's great. We always love to hear that. And I'll say, you are quite popular already with your new teammates. They've had nothing but praise for how fast of a learner you are. Same from Kurt—thinks you'll go very far here."

But? Selena wanted to ask. Susie trailed off and let them sit in uncomfortable silence for a fifteen second period that felt more like five minutes.

"Well, that's great," Selena finally said. "I like them all, too. Great group on this team. One of the best I've worked with."

"Glad to hear it. Part of being new is obviously having your work spot-checked for quality purposes. We came across something that caught our attention."

The room started spinning around Selena. This wasn't even her real job. She was playing make believe. Why did she feel so nauseous all the sudden?

I can't get fired, right? It's not that serious of an offense.

"Oh?" Selena said, fighting with every cell in her body to sound in control of her emotions. "Did I make a mistake on something?"

"Yes. Does the name Adam Marshall ring a bell?"

Fuck. It's okay, play it off. Talk your way out of this.

Selena looked up to feign deep thought and avoid eye contact with Susie, who was staring her down.

"Adam Marshall," she said to herself. The name tasted dirty in her mouth, like speaking it while in the past would somehow unravel the very fabric of reality. "Oh! The guy who submitted his application twice and changed all the information. Yes, what was the matter?"

"It appears you marked his initial application as rejected, then quickly rejected the second one that came in without giving due diligence. That isn't something you should even do yet. You'll need more time getting familiar with the team's processes now that you're out of training. Probably another couple of weeks. Did someone tell you to mark those as rejected?"

Selena couldn't lie. Throwing out someone else's name would only make this situation messier. "No, it was all me. I'm sorry if I got ahead of myself. That application came in and I clearly saw it wasn't a good fit. A grocery store worker as the assistant to Michelle seemed like a stretch, so I marked it as rejected. Then the second application came through again from the same guy, but his resume was completely different. I've seen that old trick before and knew he was certainly lying about the details on the new one."

"Okay. And I can agree with him not being qualified based on the first application, but he's actually a direct referral from someone Michelle trusts very much. Because of that, we had to dig around to find his application and that's when we saw it in the rejected folder. We also called the candidate, and he said he never sent two applications. We told him about the first one that came in, and he swore up and down it was not him. A coincidence, he said, because the email address provided wasn't even his, and that's all appeared true so far."

"I see," Selena said, genuine worry spreading across her face. This failed plan dealt too closely with Michelle. *Fly too close to the sun and get your wings burned off.*

"I can excuse the mistake because I understand your thought process behind it. But you still shouldn't even be clicking on anything in our applications queue. Look around it to get familiar, sure, but this could have been a costly mistake that Michelle would have seen through directly. Fortunately, she had only emailed inquiring about the applicant's status, and we could get it all corrected without her knowing."

"I'm so sorry, Susie. I won't do anything like that again."

Susie raised a hand. "Nothing to apologize for. Just wanted to bring this to your attention. And honestly, if this candidate wasn't a direct referral from the CEO, this wouldn't have even been an issue. One thing you'll learn is that we don't have a ton of involvement with recruiting for the executive team. They will ultimately hire who they want. They interview their candidates directly. We set up the scheduling and initial communication for these roles. The executives take care of the rest."

"I guess that makes sense. What can we possibly know about being Michelle's personal assistant, right?"

Susie rolled her eyes. "Sounds like a nightmare, if you ask me. Not because Michelle is hard to work for, but it can be some serious pressure to work that closely with the CEO. It's more demanding than people might realize."

"I'm sure it is."

Susie leaned forward. "Between you and me, I'd bet my entire salary that this Adam Marshall guy gets the job."

Hearing this from the manager of recruiting sent a nasty jolt throughout Selena's body. After all that, Adam still emerged as the favorite to land the coveted job that would change his family's life forever. The past really didn't care what came its way—it would always preserve itself.

"How can you be so sure?"

"We have had this job listed for two months. We've received lots of qualified applications, but Michelle has brushed them all aside, claiming she's looking for someone who can shake things up. I don't know what that means exactly, but this Adam guy is the first direct referral from Michelle. That she reached out to us tells me he's already her favorite. Besides, he's a man younger than Michelle. Her last two assistants have been younger men—she's just into that, I suppose. I think she gets some sort of kick out of the reversal of the gender stereotypes by having a male assistant. And they're always so handsome, I'll give her that. Michelle gets credit for a lot of things, but she doesn't get enough love for the giant middle finger she throws up to the patriarchy."

Susie laughed, and Selena joined her, sensing the drastic shift of the mood in the room.

"What did this Adam guy do to you, anyway?" Susie asked, the question catching Selena off guard.

"Excuse me?"

"Well, his is the only application you did anything to in the system. If I didn't know any better, I'd think you were trying to make sure he didn't get hired here."

"Ha!" The sound escaped Selena's throat, and she wasn't sure if it was real or not. "No, of course not."

"Well good. Because he's most likely going to work here, and he'll have some serious pull. Would hate to be off to a weird start with the big boss's number two."

Selena forced a wide smile. "No, we can't have that."

Chapter 28

November 25, 2013

"They're officially hiring him," Selena said.

The three Angels gathered for dinner on Monday night. Felix spent the weekend preparing for this possibility, expanding his profiles on the two dating apps to position himself as appealing as possible to Michelle.

Arielle and Selena had spent a portion of Saturday tailing Michelle, finding nothing of significance. The CEO spent her morning at the gym, followed by a trip to the spa and a solo lunch at a local barbecue restaurant called Flamin' Dave's. When she returned home after lunch and didn't reappear for an hour, they called it a day.

On Sunday, they followed the Marshall family around, hoping to hear any insight about his potential job. WonderHome hadn't made a final decision until Monday morning, so the status was still up in the air while Arielle and Selena followed them. Their morning started with an early mass, where the two Angels sat in the back pew. Being in church for an hour caused Arielle plenty of guilt, but she could finally tell her abuelita she had finally gone to mass—she didn't need to know that it was actually for work.

After mass, they went down the street to a Denny's, where the family devoured pancakes, eggs, and bacon. A trip to the grocery store followed, the Marshalls seeming to genuinely enjoy each other's company while they loaded their cart with groceries for the week ahead, the two kids sitting in the cart and making up games to pass the boredom. Arielle grew sickened imagining how this family's fate would play out if they weren't able to stop Adam from getting involved in the messy world of money laundering.

They never heard Adam mention a peep about the WonderHome job to his wife, and once more gave up on the cause when the Marshalls returned home for a lazy Sunday afternoon lounging around the house, the wind howling outside all day, blowing red and yellow leaves in violent swirls around the neighborhood.

By the time the three Angels convened for dinner on Monday night, Adam had received his offer letter from WonderHome, and they had officially failed to prevent his hiring. A solemn mood hung over the dining room where Felix had served a dinner of baked chicken, mashed potatoes, and asparagus.

"Well, we weren't entirely positive we were going to stop him from getting hired," Felix said. "Too many moving parts. Maybe if we have arrived earlier, we could have had more influence on that part of the process."

"I don't think it matters," Arielle said. "It was always going to be a tall task. Adam getting hired has such a long ripple effect on several other things that happen over the next six months. Things we're not even aware of yet. We're going to have to chip away at it like always."

"Were you involved in any of the hiring process?" Felix asked Selena.

She shook her head. "Nope. I think after my blunder with his application, they really might have suspected me of something. They let me nowhere near his application after I cleared my name."

"Again, nothing I'm worried about," Arielle said. "He's hired, starting on December second, after the Thanksgiving break. Everything is right on schedule, and we both have our jobs. I should have some free rein after the break as well, and we can really get into the thick of WonderHome and hopefully figure out what's going on behind the scenes. For now, we need to look at the next steps. Felix, your profiles are ready?"

Felix nodded. "Sure are. I analyzed some of the more appealing accounts and mimicked them."

"Perfect. Now is probably the time to engage on the app until you connect with Michelle. If you can get a date lined up before the new year, that would be ideal. If you can get into a somewhat regular schedule of dates with her by February or March, that will give us our best shot of at least trying to get some information out of her."

Felix nodded quietly as he took a bite of potatoes.

"Think this is going down to the wire again?" Selena asked.

"I hope not, but we have to plan for it, just in case. While Felix works on Michelle, you'll need to keep your ears open for any happenings involving the executive team. And I'll be trying to monitor their emails and phone calls as best I can. I'm still not sure what checks and balances exist in my department. I don't know if anyone will watch what I'm doing, so I'll be playing it carefully in the beginning. As for Adam, I want to be ready to pounce on any mistake he makes. We need to get him written up for as many things as we can humanly justify. Make his file look like a disaster and make his life hell. Just maybe we can drive him to quit."

"Be careful if you're getting involved in that personally," Felix said. "Who do you think the CEO is going to trust more, her handpicked assistant, or the recruiter who 'accidentally' deleted Adam's application?"

"That's a good point," Arielle said. "We all need to be more diligent than usual. As Felix mentioned, when we first started brainstorming, the FBI will be in the WonderHome system at some point. We can't leave any virtual fingerprints that show our involvement. That would force us to dip out of this mission before having time to execute our work. We just need to take everything one day at a time."

"Should be easy," Selena said. "My team is getting Wednesday off, so that's a long five-day weekend for me starting tomorrow night. Might go out and find a ladies' night somewhere after work if either of you wants to join me."

Arielle had come a long way since their first mission of working together. Before, she would have lost her mind at such a prospect. Now she understood this was just part of Selena. She worked hard and played harder. But it all made her function at her best level when it came down to mission work.

"We'll see about that," Arielle said with a grin. "Some of us work for a living around here."

They all howled with amusement and finished dinner, unaware of the obstacles that lay ahead.

Chapter 29

December 2, 2013

The following Monday, the calendar flipped to the second day of December. Arielle was up earlier than normal, as was Selena. It was the biggest day of the mission so far—Adam's first day at WonderHome.

The two were out the door fifteen minutes earlier than normal, eager to arrive at the office. Arielle earned more freedom within her role and planned to see what all she could get for Felix to hack into the company's internal systems.

Felix had connected with Michelle on the Elite Bonding app, swapping multiple messages with her over the Thanksgiving weekend. Their first date was scheduled for December 14, a moment Felix was already dreading, yet preparing for in his usual professional manner.

Overall, Arielle was pleased with their current standing on the mission and hoped the week would bring further momentum. She let her team know this during their Sunday night dinner, which was the Thanksgiving leftovers they had ordered for the holiday.

When they arrived at the quiet office, Selena and Arielle parted ways as they had been doing since their interviews. As far as anyone was concerned, Arielle and Selena were complete strangers, despite being in the same training class.

They had already set the main lobby up to welcome yet another new hire class. Becca was finishing her preparations for the mimosas, silently minding her business with a pair of headphones strapped over her head.

Selena arrived at her desk to find Janina already at work. She sat on the endcap where she could easily be reached by anyone on the team.

"Good morning, Selena, how was your Thanksgiving?" Janina asked, leaning back in her seat.

"It was good and relaxing, can't complain. How was yours?"

"Oh, flew down to San Diego to spend the weekend with my family. It was a good time. Plenty of food and drink. I still feel full from that Thursday night dinner."

Janina laughed, much too early for Selena's liking.

"I hear that," Selena said. "Hard to come back to such a busy week."

"Ugh, I know. Most companies get to relax between Thanksgiving and Christmas. But not us. It's all because of this new real estate team. We're going to be pretty steady with new hires until next summer. I'll need your help with some things today—time to show you the ropes for new hire classes, anyway."

"Oh?" Selena replied, her anticipation promptly shooting through the roof. She just might get to dip her toes back into the lake that was the Adam Marshall mystery. "What all does that entail?"

"Essentially processing them as employees within the system. They should have all submitted their important documents to us—driver's license, social security cards, et cetera—but after Kurt takes roll call later this morning, he'll give us the list of everyone who actually showed up, and we can begin processing once we know they're actually here."

"Do people really accept a job and not show up for it?" Selena asked, genuinely puzzled at such a sentiment.

"It happens more than you might think. Not *too* often at WonderHome, but I'd say maybe one person out of every three hiring classes will just go MIA and never show. We don't like to assume the worst about people and do our diligence in trying to get in touch. I think some people find a job they like better and don't have the courtesy to let us know. I have a feeling it might start happening a little more with all these realtors we're hiring. Real estate, in general, is a competitive job market with lots of bouncing around to different brokerages."

"That's nuts. I couldn't imagine just blowing off a job, especially at a place like this."

Janina laughed. "Oh yeah. Us in the world of recruiting like to think there's a special place in hell for these people. But what can you do? Life is too short to get hung up on the negative, don't you think?"

"Indeed it is."

"Do you want to get started? There are supposed to be eight new employees showing up today, so what I like to do is get a head start and get all of their profiles open."

"I'd love to!" Selena said, certain her early morning enthusiasm came across in a positive light for her team lead. In reality, she was just excited to dig deeper into Adam Marshall's file and understand what she might manipulate further down the road.

Janina rolled her chair into the aisle of desks and parked it next to Selena. For the next five minutes, she directed her through the system where they converted applicants to employees. They poked around the database, Janina showing her the different tools and options available, along with brief explanations when each might be used.

After the impromptu training session, they made their way down the list of the new hires who would stroll into the lobby in mere minutes. Each profile had a checklist on the side for any outstanding documents. All new hires still needed their pictures taken for their work badges, something Janina said she would handle later in the morning.

"Is that not something I can do?" Selena asked.

"One thing at a time," Janina said with a laugh. "I'm sure you can handle taking a picture, but that's not the issue. I just don't like to throw too many things out to the newbies on my team. I'll take the pictures and let you upload them. By the new year, you'll be comfortable enough where I'll let you take care of the whole process."

It seemed trivial, but that was also why Selena needed to let it go. All she really wanted was a chance to speak to Adam Marshall.

I'll get my chance, she told herself. *Just stay patient. It's only his first day.*

Patience, however, was far from her strong suit.

"Do we go out there to meet the new class once they arrive?" she asked.

A crooked grin spread across Janina's face. "You just want a mimosa, don't you? No need to lie about meeting the new hires. You work in POPs—you can get a mimosa without asking."

Selena let out a hearty laugh. "Guilty," she said, suddenly giddy. She would absolutely wander out to the lobby for the morning celebration. And she would meet Adam Marshall.

"They should actually start arriving in the next ten minutes," Janina said, standing up from her chair and rolling it back to her desk. "Keep getting those profiles ready so we can just click 'enter' once we know they've shown up."

"Will do."

Selena focused on her work, saving Adam's profile last.

* * *

At five minutes to eight, Selena locked her computer screen after jotting down all of Adam's information she could fit onto both sides of a sticky note. She had his prior work experience, address, emergency contacts, social security number, and both his cell phone and home phone numbers. It was a virtual gold mine that she wasn't even sure Felix could do anything with. But in the name of sabotage to save an innocent family, all was fair game.

The POPs department sat down the hallway in the opposite direction from the training room and the rowdy sales floor. Even from there, in the glorious silence, the noise level carried down the hall and sent a flutter into Selena's stomach.

She sent a text message to Arielle: *New hires in the lobby. I'm going to say hello. Not sure if you can?*

She didn't expect Arielle to join her. No one else from any other department outside of POPS was even told of the morning event. A software engineer showing up for a mimosa would certainly look out of place, but it was still worth a shot.

A couple other of Selena's teammates had shown up and were getting settled in for the morning. Selena took advantage and bolted away before they could suck her into the usual morning chitchat.

She hurried down the hall and found the small crowd gathering around Becca's desk just as they had on Arielle and Selena's first day. This time, there were boxes of doughnuts and croissants to complement the table filled with mimosas. For a class of only eight new hires, there were already a dozen people gathered in the lobby, a handful of faces Selena didn't recognize.

But she saw the only one that mattered. The face she could close her eyes and see thanks to his mugshot being drilled into her head like a piercing migraine.

Adam Marshall stood nearest the drink table, mimosa in hand as he engaged in conversation with another new hire. He had dressed for success, as they say in the tech world. A navy blue suit jacket, unbuttoned to show an eggshell dress shirt underneath. Dark blue jeans and a laptop bag slung over one shoulder completed his ensemble.

He's kinda good-looking, Selena thought, her only other reference being his raggedy, shocked and surprised mugshot.

Adam wore his hair in short messy spikes, a new look from what they had seen in their prior days following him.

New haircut for a new job, Selena thought, now taking slow steps toward the mimosa table. She studied him, then looked away, not wanting him to sense her gawking.

When she reached the mimosas, she grabbed one, keeping her back to Adam and the other man he was speaking with. From what she could gather, they were talking about the Seahawks game that was scheduled for Monday Night Football later that evening. The other man was bragging about how he had scored some tickets to the game, convinced the team was going to win the Super Bowl (which they would).

Selena spun around, taking a sip, but getting their attention and stopping their conversation. They stared at her, saw her badge dangling from her waistband, and knew she was not part of the new class.

"Hello, guys," Selena said, immediately trying to get a feel for how she should act. Friendly and open was the safest bet for the current situation. "Welcome to WonderHome. Are you both part of the new class starting today?"

"Yes," the man said, sticking out a hand to Selena. "My name is Shane Lawrence."

"Nice to meet you, Shane," Selena replied, shaking his hand.

"And I'm Adam Marshall." He offered a charming grin, and Selena immediately thought back to the prior mission and how she had caught feelings for Brian Dawkins while working in the past. Then she remembered how fucked-up that all turned out and erased any budding attraction.

"Adam, nice to meet you," she said, shaking his hand. When they touched, she felt that sensation of destiny looking over them. As of this moment, she could look him in the eye and tell him exactly how his future would play out. Of course, he'd laugh at her and probably report her to the authorities for some type of mental illness. "And what role are you gentlemen taking on at WonderHome?"

Gentlemen? Who the fuck am I?

"I'm merely a new sales rep," Shane said. "I guess we can't all hit the big time right out of the gate like Adam."

"Oh?" Selena said, playing dumb and turning her attention to Adam.

He blushed and stuffed his free hand deep into his pocket, where he was surely fidgeting with his fingers.

"I'm going to be the assistant to Michelle Garrison," he said, promptly taking a long swig from his mimosa to avoid saying anything further.

"That's right!" Selena cried, hoping to ease his tension. "I forgot we were expecting her new assistant this week. How exciting!"

He grinned, and she couldn't read if he was truly embarrassed or simply holding back his joy.

"So what do you do?" Shane asked Selena, crossing his arms and shifting his weight back on his heel.

"Apologies. My name is Selena Nicole, and I work in recruiting. I just started here last month, so I'm still pretty new myself."

"Selena? I don't believe we spoke throughout any of the hiring process," Shane replied.

It had become clear Adam was happy to let his colleague take on the brunt of the speaking. Every new class had that one yapper who just needed to make their presence known.

Fucking kiss-ass, Selena thought.

"No, you probably would've spoken with my lead, Janina. I've been working on things more behind the scenes. Processing applications, scheduling interviews. Things like that."

"Ahh, that's right. Janina is who I spoke with on the phone."

A moment of silence hung between them, and Selena took the chance to change the subject.

"So Adam, how do you know Michelle? It's my understanding not just anyone can score an interview with her, let alone get hired on."

"It's crazy," he said, adjusting the strap on his shoulder. "I had never met her until the day of my interview. My wife has a friend who is good friends with Michelle. She heard I was looking for work and threw my name into the hat. I honestly can't believe how fast it all came together."

"Classic friend-of-a-friend situation, am I right?" Shane said, chuckling and bumping his elbow into Adam's arm.

I'd love to punch this guy square in the jaw, Selena thought, knowing she could make him cry. *Classic douchebag-on-the-floor situation, am I right?*

Selena saw Susie and Amara enter the lobby together and knew this conversation had seconds remaining.

"Well," she said. "It was nice meeting you both. I need to make my rounds, but I look forward to seeing you guys around the office."

Not so much you, Shane, she thought, grinning as she shook both of their hands once more.

"Likewise," Adam said. "Looking forward to it."

Chapter 30

December 14, 2013

Over the following two weeks, Adam Marshall settled in the new routine of his life, reporting every morning to the office at eight o'clock sharp, and leaving around five in the afternoon.

For Arielle and Selena, they found tailing Adam at the office wasn't as simple as they had hoped. With Selena on the thirty-first floor, Arielle on the thirty-second, and Michelle and Adam up on the thirty-fourth, the logistics complicated matters beyond their control.

Arielle never had business on the executive floor. And Selena could only justify a trip up there once a week. That did little to allow them insight into Adam and Michelle's world.

Arielle had gradually brought home information to Felix with hopes of hacking into the WonderHome systems. One issue, however, was Arielle's security clearance. She had access to most facets of the company, but not all. She could mainly deal with day-to-day operations that affected employees across the company. This would only help to an extent. What they really wanted was the access to read emails, private chat messages, and bank account information. Not even Arielle's direct manager had access to these things, and it was her understanding that only the Chief Technology Officer had the coveted blanket clearance for all tech matters, with a handful of others having a variety of levels of access in between.

Felix spent many nights of those first two weeks of December trying to break ground, running into one obstacle after another. It neither fazed nor surprised him. This was a company worth just over four billion dollars, and they had obviously not spared a penny in the cybersecurity budget.

Arielle had even requested access to work from home, citing the need in case issues arrived in the middle of the night or over weekends. Besides, most others in her department had similar access. She was approved by her manager, but the final approval needed to make its way up to the CTO, who could take weeks, possibly months to get around to such a trivial request.

Felix believed having that VPN access at home would open more possibilities for him, but he would continue forward just the same until then.

Today, however, none of that mattered.

Felix had a Saturday night dinner date with Michelle Garrison, and all worries about hacking came to a screeching halt. He understood algorithms well enough to manipulate the dating app to finally show him Michelle after hours of mindless swiping. He had sent her the initial default message of interest when she popped up on his screen over Thanksgiving weekend. And by Sunday morning, Michelle replied with *Hello there ;)*

Seeing the message made him want to vomit. A winky face? From a middle-aged woman? Felix had dealt with enough emojis and what he considered childish games throughout college, to the point he gave up on even trying to date.

Most of the women he went to classes with were wise beyond their years. Strong, independent, brilliant, and often fierce. Yet, for some reason, in the name of dating, those same women resorted to the same antics of playing mind games and refusing to be straightforward with their intentions.

Felix figured no matter how intelligent a person was, they couldn't outrun their age. He has planned to wait until his thirties to start his search for a life partner, but the reply from the WonderHome CEO gave him second thoughts about that as well.

Michelle advertised herself on the executive app as a hard-working CEO looking for someone who could "appreciate" her lifestyle. Her portrait looked like a professional headshot, the kind she might put on the company's online directory. She listed her city as Medina.

Medina was home to the wealthiest residents of Seattle. Bill Gates, Jeff Bezos, and a handful of athletes called Medina home. An eight-figure salary was basically the minimum requirement to live in the lavish city overlooking Lake Washington.

Felix felt incredibly in way over his head.

"Do I try to go back to her place tonight?" Felix asked, the question tasting like dogshit on his tongue. Arielle and Selena had posted up in his bedroom to help him get dressed for the date, making sure the outfit would precisely portray him as a young, rich executive.

"Slow down, cowboy," Selena said, working on Felix's necktie. She had taken full control over all wardrobe decisions and dressed Felix in an all-white suit from Armani, shoes from Dolce & Gabbana, and even the necktie was over two hundred dollars from Gucci. When Felix had asked Selena why it was necessary to buy such excessive clothing, she explained that Michelle would expect nothing less. *We're in this to win it,* she had said. *If you want to get a suit from the mall, then this date will be the last. If we want to infiltrate this woman's life, you need to play the game by her rules.*

Arielle laughed. "Going back to her place tonight is entirely up to her. If it does, you need to make it clear you're not interested in sex, yet still be receptive to the invitation. Does that make sense?"

"Of course it doesn't make sense," Felix said. "I don't play these mind games. I just say how I feel."

"Oh, we know," Selena said. "So whenever you're with Michelle during these coming months, you need to be less Felix and more of a rich asshole."

"How do you know she likes assholes?" Felix snapped. "Not all rich people are assholes. Hell, I'm rich and I'm not an asshole."

Selena smiled. "Because I looked up that guy she was out with when we followed her. Sergios Vascou. Moved to Seattle after working on Wall Street for three years. Still in finance, and still a piece of shit. You should see this guy's social media. Different women every weekend. Always at a nightclub popping bottles. Even saw a picture where he forgot to wipe the coke off his nose. Young, rich, and stupid. Doesn't know what to do with all that money, so he tries giving it away to strippers and bartenders."

"Look at you," Arielle said. "Doing the snooping work Felix usually handles."

Selena laughed. "Anyone can look up an account on Facebook. Don't patronize me. The point is, Felix, Michelle likes rich men."

"Clearly. We're having dinner at Birelis. I looked at their menu and read reviews. Dinner for two comes out to a thousand dollars on average. Why in the world do people live like this?"

"Because they can," Selena said. "And it's fun to do on occasion. And choosing Birelis is just a test. I've done some more reading—what can I say, I have at least two hours of downtime during my workday—and something people do on this Elite Bonding app is choose the expensive restaurants to make sure their match is legit. Apparently some people can fake their way onto the app and show up to the first date in a beat-up car, wearing jeans and a T-shirt."

Felix couldn't help but laugh. "That actually sounds like a fantastic prank to pull on the elite class."

Selena shook her head. "Well, these people don't think so. As you can guess, some of their users got together and did what any rich American does when they don't get their way. They filed a lawsuit against Elite Bonding."

Felix and Arielle both burst into raucous laughter.

"Naturally," Selena continued. "That failed. So the users have sort of adopted this method on their own. It was typically men who were pulling this prank, so the women will make the reservations and arrive at the restaurant first. They'll instruct the host as to who they are expecting, and only if they are dressed the part will the host bring them back to the table, and the date can officially begin."

"What?!" Arielle cried, sitting on the foot of Felix's bed and grabbing her stomach as she continued laughing. "Is this for real? Or is this just something one person has done and wrote an article about?"

"Oh, it's very real. There are message boards and Facebook pages dedicated to this particular demographic, and this method is used by nearly everyone. Even the men understand this is the norm if they are serious about advancing to the actual date."

Felix shook his head. "Only you and your love for this kind of gossip could have figured all this out. I guess we owe you some thanks."

Selena stepped back from Felix, brushing his shoulders as she looked him up and down. "Please. I'm only getting you through the door. It's *your* job to take it from there."

Arielle rose from the bed and stood next to Selena. "Wow, you do good work. Felix, you look like you could get any woman in the world right now, if you really wanted."

Felix immediately blushed. He wasn't used to compliments like that. When he looked in the mirror, he was always satisfied with who he saw. Not ugly. Not sexy. Just a normal guy. But that was only his perception, and he understood how other people saw him was beyond his control. Arielle's compliment was intimidating. Because for the first time in his post-college life, he looked in the mirror and couldn't believe his eyes.

He looked ready to go head-to-head with James Bond, and the sensation was overwhelming.

"Thank you," he whispered under his breath. Selena and Arielle exchanged wide grins. "As long as this helps with Michelle, I guess it's okay."

Selena clapped him on the back. "This is more than okay. You, sir, could walk into a *GQ* photoshoot right now and no one would think any differently."

Felix pulled at his lapel to tighten the suit jacket more snugly around his shoulders. "Okay, let's get this date over with."

Chapter 31

The three Angels had more money than they knew what to do with. They knew better than to blow it all on cheap entertainment. For this portion of the mission, they found it extremely unlikely the Road Runners would reimburse them for a limo for Felix's date, so Arielle picked up the tab.

Before the limousine had arrived, Arielle stressed the importance of the evening ahead. Under no circumstance was Felix to bring Michelle back to their house. She would take one look at their middle-class neighborhood and leave back to her castle in Medina.

Selena had coached Felix as much as she could about how to proceed through the date, covering topics like best appetizers, wines, entrees, and desserts. Plus topics of conversation to avoid, which ones to dive deeper into, and how to best use his posture and body language to portray interest in Michelle.

By the time Felix fell into the silence of the limo, promptly trying to make sense of why anyone in the world would pay for a limo for a solo ride to a dinner date, his head spun with a clutter of reminders that he hoped to deploy during dinner.

The limo had a soft purple glow from a hidden light tucked somewhere along the edges of the ceiling. A bucket of ice with a bottle of champagne sat unattended on the rear seat, so Felix kicked back, put his feet up on the empty, stretched-out bench in front of him, and poured himself a glass.

The driver kept the glass divider up, something Felix was grateful for. He had enough on his mind and couldn't possibly bear the awkward small talk. Perhaps the driver was equally uncomfortable, surely not having driven solo passengers frequently.

Felix spent the twenty-minute drive across town, mentally running down the list Selena had jammed into his mind. She had offered to use his bugging equipment to guide him through the date, but he dismissed that notion immediately. He may have not had the most experience dating rich women, but he was confident to execute this plan without a hitch. The champagne helped soothe his nerves, so he poured a second glass, knowing it would be his last. A bottle of wine was surely in the cards for dinner, and he needed to pace himself. Getting sloppy was the last thing this mission needed, but he also had to push aside what Selena had called his *inner Felix.*

"How do you stop being yourself?" he asked the empty limo, leaning his head back to relax, the champagne bubbles still exploding in his throat. "There is no such thing as hiding from yourself. We are who we are, to the core."

Felix understood this just fine, but further appreciated the stakes that lie ahead. His job with the Angels had always been to make life easier for the lead Angel assigned to a mission. This staged date with Michelle was no different. If it went poorly, they'd have to dig elsewhere to find the truth about who was responsible for the laundering scheme. Even Felix believed Michelle had involvement. But to what extent?

While the topic wouldn't come up on a first date, Felix planned to poke around as best he could to pull information out of the CEO.

The limo came to a last stop, the glow from a nearby street lamp shining over the vehicle, resting in front of Birelis.

The restaurant was hidden behind lush foliage, sitting atop a hill overlooking the west coast of Lake Union. The surrounding area felt like they had entered a forbidden forest, tucked away somewhere off the map where you could only find if you knew the exact route.

The limo's door opened, a man in a tuxedo and white-gloved hands standing guard outside. He was not the limo driver.

Felix slid over, letting his feet lead the way out, and when his shoes touched the pavement the man said, "Welcome to Birelis, sir. We hope you have a most pleasant dining experience this evening."

"Thank you," Felix said, reaching into his jacket to produce a twenty-dollar bill he slid into the man's gloved hand. Selena had explained how any person who helped in even the slightest way, such as opening his door and greeting him, expected a tip.

Twenty bucks for opening a door and saying hello, Felix thought. *I've clearly been in the wrong profession.*

Once outside, Felix realized it wasn't a street lamp they parked under, but a covered entryway for the restaurant. There were no street lights as far as he could see from their perch on the hill. A couple of boats had their lights beaming out on the lake, but were far enough to not disrupt the secluded ambiance of Birelis.

It feels like we're all alone in the world, Felix thought. The surroundings were pitch-black thanks to the towering trees. And completely silent, the subtle putter from the limo's exhaust providing the only audible sound within a half-mile radius.

The man stuck out his arm toward a red velvet carpet running from the limo to the restaurant's entrance. Classical music played somewhere from a hidden speaker. Two valet workers stood off to the side, speaking to a customer at the podium. Felix walked on the carpet where another tux-wearing man opened the door for him.

I'm not giving him a twenty, Felix thought, heart drumming in his chest as he passed by and nodded a thank you.

He stepped into the waiting area, where a smiling college-aged woman stood behind the host stand. "Good evening, sir," she said warmly. "Do you have a reservation tonight?"

Felix looked around, blown away by the interior layout. Chandeliers hung from the ceiling, each spaced ten feet apart, dimly lit. They looked to be made of pure crystal. The dining room was crowded, yet the usual bustle of chatter was non-existent.

People were still talking, yet it seemed like they were all whispering. It reminded Felix more of those few minutes in church right before mass starts. *Where the hell am I?*

The room was so dim, he couldn't clearly see where it ended. It just gradually got darker, despite the chandeliers glowing gently above.

"Sir?" the young woman asked.

Felix snapped back to the reality before him. His palms immediately started sweating, and he could feel the moisture forming in his underarms. Selena had been sure to stuff a handkerchief into Felix's suit pocket, and he promptly whipped it out to wipe the sweat from his brow.

"I'm sorry," he said, just now realizing the beauty of the woman trying to get his attention. If he didn't feel like he was about to faint, he just might have talked to her about what she liked to do in her free time. "First time here." He let out an awkward laugh as he stuffed the handkerchief back into its place.

The woman maintained her charming smile throughout the entire exchange. "I understand, sir. We have a beautiful dining room. Breathtaking, some might say. Did you have a reservation?"

"Not me personally, but I am meeting someone. Michelle Garrison."

The hostess looked Felix up and down, gave a nod of approval, and said, "Please follow me. Ms. Garrison is already seated."

That was it, Felix thought. *The nod meant I pass the test. I'm dressed well enough.*

While everything about this evening, and the process leading up to it, seemed like utter bullshit to Felix, Selena had once again proven she knew her stuff. Perhaps better than anyone else.

Felix gulped as he followed the woman through the dining room, wiping his hands on his pants to get them as dry as possible. The last thing he needed was to greet Michelle with his nervous sweat.

All tables had small fishbowls as their centerpieces, candles somehow floating on the surface while little betta fish swam laps underneath. Their table for the night was positioned along the wall at the centerpoint of the restaurant. Far from the kitchen. Far from the entrance where the chilly breeze would whip across them each time the door opened.

There sat Michelle Garrison, hands folded on the table, a glass of red wine directly in front of her.

"Ms. Garrison," the hostess said. "Your company."

She bowed out without another word, leaving Felix standing there like a dumbstruck buffoon trying to figure out what to do next.

"Felix?" Michelle asked, standing up. She wore a form-fitting black dress that sparkled even in the dim light, flowing loosely at her ankles, an opening that revealed a teasing sliver of her tanned left leg.

"Michelle," he replied, stretching out his hand. She shook it and pulled him in to plant a soft kiss on his cheek.

"I'm so glad we could get together tonight," she said, returning to her seat.

Felix hurried across the table to help push her chair in.

"Oh," she said. "Such a gentleman. Not many like you these days."

Felix was struggling to flip the mental switch and become someone else he had no interest in being. He pressed through and gave it his best shot.

"Thank you," he said, immediately regretting his response. *What the hell am I thanking her for?*

Michelle giggled as Felix got himself situated across the table. "I've ordered us a bottle of Chateau Margaux. Would you like a glass now?"

Felix had no idea what that meant. "Sounds perfect. Thank you."

Michelle raised a hand and pointed to Felix, nodding to someone off in the distance. Felix was becoming hyper-aware of his surroundings, his mind racing just beyond his grasp of control.

"So Michelle," he said, hoping his acting could distract his panicking thoughts. "Are you *the* Michelle Garrison?"

Fuck, that was a stupid question.

But she didn't seem to mind, laughing it off and taking a sip from her wineglass. Felix noticed the red lipstick stains stuck on the brim of the glass, something that had always grossed him out.

"You're funny," she said. "But if you're being serious, then yes, I am Michelle Garrison, CEO of WonderHome."

Felix had played out how this date would unfold at least a dozen times.

He assumed Michelle would be an intense personality. Even Arielle and Selena agreed with this sentiment, as was the word around the office. But outside of that skyscraper, Felix was seeing Michelle in a different light. And it made sense. She had a persona to maintain while at work. She was the big boss no one could push around. Her employees could never see the way her bottom lip quivered when she was attracted to a man. Or the way her foot bounced underneath the table as she fought the same nerves as Felix—albeit for much different reasons.

"That's incredible," Felix said. "How are you liking it?"

Michelle studied Felix with a gaze of intense curiosity, and he didn't know how to interpret it. Was he saying something out of the ordinary? Did people at this particular level of employment—and society, for that matter—*not* discuss their jobs? Felix found it unlikely, and Selena had mentioned nothing of the sorts. Chatting about work was perhaps the most universal of conversation starters after the weather.

"I like it a lot," Michelle said. "It's an incredibly stressful role, but so rewarding at the same time. I have a wonderful team and it trickles all the way down to our most entry-level positions. Have you ever done anything in a leadership type of role? What is it you do exactly for Starbucks?"

"I'm a senior director in our communications department. I have a small team that reports to me, but we mainly overlook press releases and social media response. I enjoy it. Starbucks takes good care of us."

"Do you work much with Howard?"

Howard? Felix thought, soon realizing she must have meant the CEO, Howard Schultz.

"Not really, honestly. I'm two levels below him. I report directly to the VP of communications, who works with Howard."

"I'll have to mention your name to him the next time I see him."

Felix's heart returned to its violent thumping. He *hated* living this lie. Of course all the CEO's in Seattle knew each other. Michelle probably had Bill Gates' number stored in her phone, and that thought was all he needed to keep pushing through. If he could actually stretch this date into them regularly seeing each other, it was only a matter of time before he found himself with an opportunity to meet one of his idols.

"That's not necessary," Felix said with a chuckle, sounding more nervous than he intended.

"Enough about our work life," Michelle said excitedly. "I want to know about you as a person."

Felix noticed her finger running along the brim of her wineglass in slow, steady circles. She kept biting her bottom lip and her foot beneath the table wouldn't stop bouncing. He could feel the subtle motion inches away from his own feet.

She's actually into me, he thought, feeling both relief and dread at the idea.

And stress.

Chapter 32

December 20, 2013

"We have to capitalize on tonight," Arielle said, driving her and Selena across town for the WonderHome holiday party. "We didn't even know about this party during our planning. It feels like a gift being dropped into our lap."

It was the Friday evening before WonderHome would shut down for the entire week following the Christmas holiday. Felix was still struggling to hack into the company's system, but he remained persistent, confident a breakthrough loomed around the corner.

Tonight, however, was the holiday party set to take place at the Washington State Convention Center, where they would welcome over 1,000 guests. The company flew in their employees from all around the country for the celebration, and plus-ones were welcome.

"And if we have some fun along the way, that'll be fine, too," Selena said. She had unsurprisingly volunteered to get the outfits for the occasion, giddy to have a night out in a fancy dress. "It has an open bar."

"Just work your magic," Arielle said. "You're going to have an easier time than me. No one outside of my department even knows who I am. We don't work directly with too many others. But you seem to know everyone, so you need to play that card and get a conversation going with Adam."

"We can figure that out. It's a big party, lots of people and movement.

I feel like I can strike up a conversation with anyone there tonight, even Michelle."

"Did you find it weird that she wants to see Felix again, but didn't ask him to be her date for the party?"

"Not at all. Someone of Michelle's status won't bring a date unless it's serious. Now, if she shows up with someone else, then we'll have some issues to address. But I would bet she's going to arrive solo and leave that way. No CEO wants to take any chance of a potential scandal or rumors. She's smart—she knows how to play this game."

"True. I think we need to strike up a conversation with Adam's wife. She might relay valuable information without even realizing it."

They had agreed tonight would be appropriate to be seen together in front of their coworkers. Few people would recognize Arielle thanks to her low-profile job, and most would assume she was simply Selena's friend.

"Don't you think this is weird? We're going to mingle with our subject and his wife. Like, we know this woman is going to kill her kids one day. Does that not bother you?"

"Well, no, not really. Because we're going to stop all that from happening. One thing I've learned in this line of work is that people aren't purely evil. I've seen my share of evil and those who hurt others for sheer amusement, but ninety percent of the rest are just good people being pulled into bad situations. I guarantee you when we meet Adam's wife, she will probably be someone you'll want to be friends with. The demons that plague her in the future don't even exist yet."

Selena nodded. "We're here."

They pulled into the convention center's parking garage, where they got into line for the valet parking, another tab picked up by WonderHome. The company spent just under three million dollars on the holiday party, not sparing a dime to provide the ultimate evening as a thank-you for the employees' hard work during the year.

Five minutes later, Arielle and Selena rode the elevator up from the garage, the doors opening to an obnoxiously elegant showcase of holiday festivities.

"Are those real people?" Selena asked as they stepped out of the elevator and started toward the long line forming at the check-in table. She nodded upward, where three people dressed as angels were hanging from the ceiling, floating with the grace of acrobats.

"What the hell?" Arielle replied. "Yeah, those are definitely real people."

Selena laughed, shaking her head. "Well, I'm glad we decided to not bring Felix as a date. He'd have a heart attack if he saw this."

They stood in line, mesmerized by the angels twirling their arms and legs in such slow, smooth motions that Arielle kept second-guessing if they really were humans or some sort of advanced mechanical robot. By the time they reached the check-in desk ten minutes later, they looked back to see the line wrapping around a corner, out of sight.

"Oh. My. God!" Becca cried. She had been manning the line at the check-in, eyes lighting up. "Selena and Arielle, you two are *fucking* hot! You look like supermodels. I've always known you're both pretty, but you know, it's at work. Arielle, look at your calves. Holy shit! Selena, you go on with your bad little body."

Arielle laughed, blushing. She had been hit on by plenty of men, but couldn't recall having ever received such an aggressive compliment from a woman. Plus, Becca was clearly beyond the point of tipsy, booze radiating from her breath.

"Why, thank you," Arielle said. "You look gorgeous tonight, too."

Becca batted her eyes at them before turning her attention to the list of names in front of her, crossing off Arielle and Selena. "You two are all set. We have an open bar, dance floor, silent disco, and games. Enjoy yourselves tonight. We also have free Ubers at the end of the party if you need transportation getting home safely."

"Thanks, Becca, we'll see you in there."

They continued beyond the check-in, handing their jackets off to a young man running a coat check station, and stepped into the grand ballroom.

There was a circular bar in the center of the room, a dozen bartenders hustling to serve the long lines forming. Against the wall nearest the entrance stood a photobooth station with two thirty-foot tall snowflakes on either side of equally massive letters that spelled out WonderHome. A replica of Santa Claus in his sleigh hung from the ceiling, being pulled by all the mythical reindeer. The dance floor far was along the back wall, where the booming of music and flashing lights lit up the otherwise dim ballroom.

To the left was the silent disco, a dance floor full of people wearing headphones with flashing lights. Beside them was a pool table, ping-pong, giant Jenga, and a miniature bowling alley.

"Seriously," Selena said. "Where are we? I feel like a little kid walking into Chuck E. Cheese for the first time."

Arielle laughed. "I don't know, but I think we're going to have some fun tonight. Look, our guy is here."

She nodded toward the bar where Adam and his wife were standing with Michelle and a small group from the executive team. They all had a shot glass in hand and were toasting before slamming them back.

Selena grinned. "When the CEO is doing shots, it's about to get rowdy up in here. Let's go."

Selena marched toward the bar, pulling Arielle by the wrist.

"Selena, what are you doing?" Arielle muttered under her breath.

"Just trust me, okay?"

Selena took them straight to the huddle formed around Michelle.

"Are we already doing shots?!" Selena asked, planting herself next to Adam. He shuffled aside to allow room for Arielle to join the circle.

"Selena!" Amara, the vice president of POPS cried out, reaching across the circle to hug her department's newest hire. "You look incredible. Everyone, Selena Nicole is the newest addition to our recruiting team. She has hit the ground running in her role, and we couldn't be any more excited to have her on the team. I think she has a long career ahead with WonderHome."

Arielle remained by Selena's side, feeling invisible, but not completely caring as she scanned the surrounding faces.

Michelle Garrison, CEO. Landon Greene, CFO, plus his wife. Raj Kalan, President of WonderHome, plus his wife. Mila Bachman, CMO, plus her wife. Adam and Emily Marshall.

"Well good," Landon said. "Maybe she can work her way up and take your job, Amara, so you can finally take that vacation."

They all burst into laughter, except for Arielle and Selena, who had clearly missed the inside joke.

The executives kept laughing and carried on a separate conversation. Arielle turned to Adam on her right. "You guys been here a while already?" she asked.

"No, just a few minutes, actually," Adam said. "We had a little too much fun at dinner before, though. When the CEO tells you to order whatever you want, what else can you do?"

He let out a nervous chuckle.

"Very true," Arielle replied, forcing a grin, pleased to know Adam was already being invited to such social events with his new boss. "I'm sorry, but I don't believe we've met before. I'm Arielle Lucila, and I work in software engineering."

"Oh!" Adam cried, sticking out his hand. "I'm Adam. I was just hired as Michelle's assistant."

"Congratulations."

"Thank you. And this is my wife, Emily." Adam half turned and pulled Emily by the waist to be at his side. She offered a polite smile before sticking out her hand.

"Nice to meet you," she said. "This is quite the party!"

"I'll say." Arielle looked over her shoulder to see Selena chatting with her VP, and couldn't help but feel a sense of pride in how confident the young actress had been in forcing this situation. No dancing around the subject, just walk up and start. Arielle felt relaxation spread over her, knowing she was in the driver's seat with the Marshalls now only speaking with her. "So you're new to WonderHome, but are you new to Seattle?"

"Far from it," Adam said. "I'm a Seattle native, and Emily has lived here since she was six, so practically a native, too."

"Oh, how cool! And how long have you been married?"

"Five years in April," Emily said proudly.

"That's great. Do you have any kids?" Arielle knew the usual checklist of topics people asked upon first meeting.

"A three-year-old boy and an eighteen-month-old girl," Emily said.

"She's one," Adam cut in, grinning. "Eighteen months is one and a half."

Emily laughed and playfully smacked Adam on his chest.

Arielle thought they were very much in love. They each kept a hand on one another, whether it was holding hands, an arm around the waist, or a caress on the back. They were in constant physical contact.

Arielle's heart ached. She hoped this hadn't been the case, as if them hating each other would somehow lessen the mounting pressure to complete their mission. But here they stood, just five months until they would arrest Adam and throw their life into shambles.

"Excuse me," Adam said. "I'm gonna get another drink. Do you ladies want anything? It's on the house."

He laughed, delighted with himself, and clearly tipsy.

"Oh, stop it, babe," Emily said, finally releasing her grip from Adam's back. "I'll have another vodka cranberry."

"I'll do the same," Arielle said. "Thank you."

Adam nodded before disappearing to the growing lines at the bar. Arielle saw Selena still consumed in the tight huddle of executives.

Now, Arielle had Emily Marshall alone, not another soul in the universe to speak with.

"So, Emily, how is Adam liking the new job? Honestly."

Emily looked around. "What do you mean? Every day he comes home and raves about working for WonderHome."

"Sure, the company is great. But what about his actual role? I've heard some horror stories about working directly for Michelle. She's intense. Cutthroat."

"You know, he's mentioned that he's seen that side of her, but never directed toward him. I suppose that's because he's getting his work done on time and correctly."

"Well, that's good. As long as Michelle is happy, then I suppose he'll be happy, too."

"Indeed. I think what he's enjoyed the most is he's doing meaningful work. He thought being the assistant would be more like a paid internship—getting coffee, booking appointments, that sort of stuff. But so far, the work has been whatever they need help with. He feels like the position is more of a tryout for a consistent role doing something else. But so far, he's enjoying dipping his toe in all the different departments."

Arielle could sense the excitement radiating from Emily. She was a proud wife who absolutely adored her husband. Thanks to her research, Arielle had already known about the struggles Adam had run into holding down various jobs. With his wife now in front of her, she heard the relief in her voice, like Adam had finally found that job and company he could spend the rest of his life with.

Adam had reached the bar and was ordering their drinks. She needed to speed this conversation up before he returned and veered their discussion in another direction.

"That's good to know," Arielle said. "I'll have to keep an eye out for him. Do you know if he does anything with the new real estate team?"

She felt this was the best opportunity to ask, and braced for the answer, the room seeming to fall silent as she shifted all of her focus to Emily's response.

"The real estate team? My goodness, that's been the main part of his job since he started."

Chapter 33

December 31, 2013

"Oh, my God," Felix cried out from the living room couch. "I'm in!"

It took until the last day of 2013, but Felix had finally broken through WonderHome's security.

The holiday party ended up a bust for Arielle and Selena. Shortly after Adam had returned with drinks, the group of executives had excused themselves from the small gathering, and disappeared through a door that Arielle assumed was a private meeting room for the upper echelon of the company to mingle in privacy, away from the noise and annoying lower-level employees.

Arielle's conversation with Emily Marshall had been the last of their interaction with that group.

"We know he's working on the real estate matters," Arielle had said during their ride back home after the party ended. "It wasn't a complete waste of time—we still learned something."

With the party landing on Friday evening, and the company closing their offices for the following week for Christmas, Arielle and Selena had gone a full ten days without going to work.

Felix, meanwhile, insisted Arielle take over the duties he normally handled while they were at work—cleaning, cooking, grocery shopping, and whatever else needed to be done around the house. Felix was close. He had known it. Sifting through thousands of lines of coding, trying tens of thousands of different passwords, and just wishing on a prayer to get into the system had pushed him to the brink of near madness.

Never mind the looming second date he had coming up with Michelle after the new year on Saturday.

"What?!" Arielle cried out, jumping up from her seat in the dining room. Selena lazed on the love seat in the living room, mesmerized by an all-day countdown of 2013's top music videos on the TV.

"I am *in!*" Felix shouted, now getting Selena's attention as she stirred back to reality and joined Arielle in front of Felix.

A smile stretched over his face with a look of complete shock that he had achieved this goal. His eyes were bloodshot from late nights staring at the screen, chugging caffeine to keep going. Arielle had warned him to take a break a week earlier, on Christmas night, but he hadn't.

He had worked straight through, insisting he had already celebrated 2013 Christmas in his Original Time, back when he was seventeen years old.

Now he could rest, satisfied with the work he had accomplished.

"I can see everything," he said, eyes refusing to break away from the laptop screen. "Internal chat messages, emails, HR reports on different departments."

"We're called *POPS*," Selena corrected him, her words falling on deaf ears.

"Look," Felix said, raising his hand, showing them how much it was trembling.

"*Felix,*" Arielle said in a disappointed motherly tone. "You need to go to sleep. I can't have you killing yourself on this mission."

He shook his head. "I'm not shaking because I'm exhausted—which I am. I'm shaking because I'm nervous . . . excited. I don't know. But we're in. We can find any communication that has taken place within WonderHome. Look."

He spun his laptop around to show the email inbox for Michelle Garrison.

"Holy shit!" Selena said. "Felix, you've just changed this mission. Do you know if you're going to stay in this, or is there a chance you somehow get kicked out?"

"There is always a chance of getting kicked out. But it's not likely. WonderHome keeps a running log of all activity happening on their VPN. Every single computer that logs into the VPN, all of their activity gets tracked. So yes, technically someone with the company *could* look over these logs and see I'm a non-employee with access."

"Well, that doesn't sound too promising," Arielle said, crossing her arms. "This will be fairly short-lived, then."

Felix raised a finger, spinning the computer back around to face him. "Not so fast. I'm logged in with full access, which means I can view this log and what happens within it. It appears to get checked every two weeks. This is fairly common because there are hundreds of thousands of line items on this log. Keep in mind, it spans the entire company, and not just the Seattle office. WonderHome has remote workers all over the country who sign in to this VPN at strange hours of the day. Most likely they make sure nothing looks out of the ordinary—say a mysterious login from a foreign country, or repeated attempts to log in to the company's bank portal. Things like that. My activity, while logged in, will look no different from a sales rep checking their email on the weekend. It will get lost in the shuffle with everything else, as long as we work out of it during business hours. We can do a couple of things on weekends and after hours, but I'd advise we only do that for urgent matters."

"Should we even be looking at anything right now?" Arielle asked. "The office closed at noon, and is off tomorrow for New Year's Day."

Felix looked at her, balled a fist, and pursed his lips so tightly they turned white. "No, you're right. We probably shouldn't. Dammit! We probably should wait until Thursday now."

Arielle reached out and grabbed Felix by his trembling arms. "Felix, breathe," she demanded. "We've been here two months without this access. I think we can wait two more days."

Felix's face soured. He despised this feeling. "I know, but it's right *here.*" He jammed his finger into the laptop's screen, his voice coming out above a defeated whimper.

"Does the duration we're on a particular screen account for anything?" Selena asked.

Felix stared blankly at his laptop, Arielle releasing her grip from his arms.

"Felix?" Arielle asked.

"It shows up on the log," he said. "But I doubt that's something they even look for."

"Good," Selena said. "So instead of calling this feat a waste, we can at least examine Michelle's inbox. See what we can find out from there."

Felix grinned. His mind was wandering. He felt like he had just run a marathon, only to be told at the finish line that he actually had two more miles to go. Emotions rarely got the best of him, but he suddenly felt the urge to run through a brick wall.

He slammed the laptop shut, causing both Arielle and Selena to jolt back.

"Felix, really?" Arielle said, crossing her arms.

He stood up, hands elevated, all ten fingers spread wide apart. "No. You're right—I need to take a step back. I've been swimming in this mess long enough. I accomplished what we needed, but now we have to wait two days. Looking at those email subject lines will only drive us crazy and crank up the temptation. It's New Year's Eve. Let's celebrate with the rest of the world, and tomorrow we can find something else to do." He pointed a firm finger at the laptop. "Because if I flip that open one more time before Thursday, I cannot control what I do. So what do you say?"

Arielle checked her watch. "It's almost six o'clock. Why don't we go see a movie? Then we can grab a late dinner somewhere and decide what we want to do for the rest of the night."

"Deal," Felix snapped, his reply cutting off Selena, who had parted her lips.

"Okay then," Arielle said. "Let's head out. I believe one of the *Hunger Games* movies is showing right now."

Within five minutes, they had gathered what they needed, Felix looking over his shoulder on the way out, the laptop remaining on the couch.

Chapter 34

January 2, 2014

On the second day of the new year, Felix woke up at six o'clock in the morning to dig through everything he could find within WonderHome's system. Arielle and Selena had returned to the office, and hurried home at four o'clock that afternoon to see what all Felix had found.

Arielle had sent him a couple of text messages throughout the day hoping to learn something new. But he never responded.

When they strolled through the front door at 4:22, they found Felix still dressed in his pajamas, eyes sunken while he sat at the dining room table with his laptop open, papers scattered to cover nearly every inch of the table.

His work entranced him, eyes scanning up and down, before grabbing his pen to scrawl notes on a piece of paper. He repeated this action three times, paying no attention to Arielle and Selena, who had shuffled into the dining room.

"Felix?" Arielle called out.

He dropped his pen and jumped out of his seat. "Christ! Is it already four o'clock?!" He swiveled around to find the clock and smacked his forehead. "Oh, my God. I haven't eaten today. I haven't even brushed my teeth."

"You're nasty," Selena said, Felix blowing off her words and her friendly giggle.

"Felix, this isn't healthy," Arielle said. "We can't ask you to keep working if you're not taking care of yourself."

Felix shook his head, his hair a raggedy mess. "I know what you're saying, but I promise this wasn't intentional. I just . . . lost track of time."

"For *ten* hours?! Felix, c'mon. This is truly unacceptable."

"I know, and I won't do it again. And do you know what I have found after looking through hundreds—no, thousands—of emails today?! Go head, take a guess!"

He looked at them with crazed eyes and a somewhat terrifying smile.

"Not a single fucking thing!" he cried, slamming a fist on the table, sending a couple sheets of paper flying off the edge. He tossed his hands in the air. "I've read emails between Michelle and every executive in the company. Between her and the software development teams responsible for launching the real estate portion of the website. The legal department outlining the best way to launch this program free of lawsuits. Executives from the other national brokerages, some threatening her with those same lawsuits. All I could find was that Michelle Garrison doesn't give a damn what anyone has to say about her launching this new real estate team."

"So Michelle isn't responsible for the money laundering?" Arielle asked.

Felix shrugged. "Hell if I know. Let's talk about our guy, Adam Marshall. This dude gets hired and his first email is a list of responsibilities from Michelle. They're all over the place. Helping with the social media team, checking in with customer service on recurring issues. So many items, but nothing I could find regarding the real estate team. This is suspicious because his own wife admitted to Arielle at the holiday party that Adam was working a ton on the real estate matter. So why isn't there a single trace of it?"

"Felix, relax. We will figure this out together."

He laughed. Not at Arielle, but at the thought of there being an explanation to the mystery.

"I'm not sure what else we can do to figure it out. I looked through the inboxes of everyone on the executive team. All I could find was that this whole real estate thing was the CFO's idea, but even he had little involvement in getting it launched, aside from approving budgets for hiring and development."

"Okay," Arielle said, speaking forcefully to take control of the conversation. "Let's take a step back and consider all of this. We're just too early. And that's fine. This tells us they didn't launch the real estate program with the intent of money laundering. It started out as a legitimate stream of income. If we can't find anything connecting Michelle or Adam, or any of the executives, to the laundering scheme, then it has to mean it hasn't happened yet."

Felix nodded. "Okay. So I'll monitor things every day until we see something. But something is drastically off if Adam said he's working with the real estate team and nothing is showing up. How do you explain that?"

"Keep in mind it wasn't Adam who said that. It was his wife. We'll never understand how she's interpreting what Adam is telling her each night when he comes home. For all we know, Emily Marshall understands WonderHome is a real estate company her husband works for. We can't put too much weight on her words."

Felix crossed his arms, unsatisfied with such an explanation.

"Okay," he said. "So let's assume nothing has happened yet—I still don't buy it. What do we do next?"

"Selena and I will crank up our efforts at the office. Mainly to see what people are gossiping about. Perhaps we can start a rumor about Adam. Something that will look bad on him, and force Michelle to have a conversation with him. As of now, this might be our best play until new information comes through."

Selena smiled. "That's a good idea. And being in the POPS department, I'll get the inside scoop on how it all plays out."

"Perfect. We can plan to get that in motion tomorrow. What a better time to start a rumor than on a Friday. People will go out to happy hour after work and definitely let the gossip fly. Let them bask in it over the weekend, so when they come back on Monday, they'll have convinced themselves the rumor is true."

"What's our angle?" Selena asked. "Sexual harassment? Racism?"

Arielle shook her head. "I don't want to do anything like sexual harassment that could get the actual authorities involved. Too messy. Do you still have access to that first application Felix submitted under Adam's name?"

"We should."

"That's our play. We'll start a rumor that he sent in a fake resume. Make his entire presence at the company feel like a big lie. If we can get this rumor started tomorrow, maybe Felix can start planting the seed in Michelle's mind on their date on Saturday."

"That's already this Saturday?!" Felix gasped. He ran his fingers through his hair, making it stand up in messy spikes like he had just woken up. "I really have been so far out of the loop. I can't believe I have to go on another date with her."

"You do," Arielle said. "And it's going to be productive. If we can't find anything through the WonderHome system, then maybe we need to shift our focus to these executives' personal email accounts and phone lines."

Felix scoffed. "Oh, so now you just want me to do it all over again. For how many people? Forget the last two months I've spent trying to get into this damn system, right?"

Arielle pointed at Felix, anger rising to her surface. "That's not what I'm saying. I'm not even suggesting we do it, just throwing it out there as another option. Of course, we're going to exhaust everything we can before that point, which includes capitalizing on your next date. That said, I'm ordering you to not do any work tomorrow or Saturday morning. I need you to wash yourself up and get ready to play your role as her executive love interest. Because if we sent you out like this right now, she'll be sending you right back."

"What?! I don't think—"

"It's an *order*," Arielle snapped. "Not up for debate. Thank you."

The air left the room in a hurry. Even Selena's jaw hung open.

Felix balled a fist as he stared down Arielle, and she thought he might actually take a swing at her.

But he didn't.

"Look, Felix," she said. "Don't take this personally. You've done fantastic work, but I think you're overcompensating for all the downtime you had when we first got here. Look at you. You're still in your pajamas. I know you enjoy that your work is mostly from home, but this is a first for you. You look like someone who hasn't slept in a month. And *you* admitted to not even eating today. Are you hearing these words? Are they processing in your mind, or are you still stuck in the WonderHome system? Does any of this sound healthy or reasonable to you?"

His fist uncurled, but his burning glare remained fixed on Arielle. She could tell he was biting the inside of his mouth.

"She's right," Selena said, Felix swinging his head around to look at her. "We're just looking out for you. We all know you can get so deep and lost in your work. This time is bad, and you need to be pulled out. When's the last time you took a shower?"

Selena put her hands on her hips as she cocked an eyebrow to Felix. He licked his lips before shaking his head.

"I honestly don't know. I . . .I feel so dead inside."

Arielle noticed his bottom lip quivering and rushed to his side, throwing an embrace around him. He broke into intense tears, their moisture seeping through Arielle's shirt as Felix buried his face into her shoulder. Selena joined them, running a hand up and down Felix's back.

"Felix," Selena said. "Our work is important, but you don't have to take it to this extreme. It's okay to take a break and go for a walk. Breathe some fresh air. It will be better for your work in the long run. You *need* to take care of yourself, or else you become this...zombie."

Felix pulled away from Arielle, wiping his tears away as he stood to face his friends. "I don't know how to be any different," he said through a hoarse throat, prompting him to clear it. "I've always been this way. Since elementary school. If I'm working on something, and it requires any sort of problem-solving, I can't step away until I've solved it."

Selena grabbed Felix by the shoulders, and Arielle took a step back, knowing Selena had a more personal relationship with Felix than she did. Selena knew how to get through to him. "Dude, this is a seven-month mission. Don't you remember us talking about all the free time we'd get because the mission is so long? You can take weekends off. You can work normal hours and enjoy your evenings. We still have over five months until Adam gets arrested. You're not going to solve this mission overnight or on your own. Set a schedule and stick to it. Pace this out."

Felix nodded. "I'm too hard on myself. Part of me still believes we can finish this mission sooner than planned if we can just crack the code. But it won't be that simple."

"If it was," Arielle said. "We'd have no jobs."

Felix laughed. "Okay. Thank you both."

"I mean it, Felix," Arielle said. "Take tomorrow off, and the entire weekend—beside your date with Michelle. Go do something fun to clear your mind. And jump back in Monday morning refreshed. I bet you'll look at that WonderHome system with a whole new perspective."

Felix nodded. "Okay. I'll do that. Now, what exactly do I need to prepare for this date with Michelle?"

Chapter 35

January 4, 2014

After a day off, where Felix spent the morning walking around Pike Place Market and the afternoon at Mount Rainier National Park, Felix not only felt like a new person, but empowered to take control of his role.

What Selena had said was true. They had five months left until the authorities would barge into the WonderHome offices and take Adam Marshall away. Five months meant it wasn't time to panic, but to focus and use time efficiently.

The opportunity in front of Felix was uniquely his. He had access to Michelle Garrison's work inbox and was currently driving to his next date with her. If he could nail down the intricacies of a faux romance and truly get Michelle interested in him, there was no telling how he could leverage all the information he would gain.

The first date had gone well enough, considering he had been a nervous wreck. Now, on the second date, he could finally appreciate this as part of the mission and something he was being entrusted to handle for the sake of the team. Gaining Michelle's trust was simply another puzzle he needed to figure out. Her desire for a second date proved she had some sort of interest in him.

Felix pulled up to a sports bar called My Oh My in the Pioneer Square neighborhood. With their first date at an obnoxiously formal restaurant, Michelle asked Felix what he would like to do on their second date. He suggested they grab a quick dinner downtown before going on one of the underground city tours offered all around town. He expected Michelle to push back and was pleasantly surprised when she agreed with much enthusiasm.

"I've never done one of those tours but have always wanted to!" she said over their brief phone call to make arrangements.

Felix had suggested the date idea not just to avoid the lights and glamour of the filthy rich. Getting Michelle out of that scene would loosen up her personality. She would get to be a regular person on a normal date. Maybe they'd even get ice cream at the end of the night.

He parked and entered the bar, finding it crowded with people watching the Saturday slate of NFL playoff games. The local Seahawks were in the playoffs as a big favorite to win the Super Bowl (they would), but they were on a bye week, leaving everyone to watch who they would match up with the following weekend.

Much to Felix's delight, he found Michelle seated at a booth for two along the outer perimeter, away from the drunken, howling fans. He pushed his way through the crowd, admiring the decorations on the walls celebrating the Seahawks, Sounders, and Mariners.

"Well, this is fun!" Michelle said with a big smile, standing up to hug Felix before he sat down. She pulled him in a little tighter than he expected.

"I know it's not a fancy place," Felix said. "But what do you think?"

Michelle looked around. A table of five men doing shots. A couple trying to find the back of each other's throats with their tongues. Waitresses somehow navigating through it all with wide trays of drinks that never spilled.

"I love it," Michelle said. "I never come to places like this."

"Why not?" Felix asked, his focus kicked into the absolute highest gear. If conversation veered into a random void, he'd guide it back to something relevant, even if just getting to know Michelle better as a person. Felix had learned from his last mission that the better you understood your subject, the better you could anticipate their next actions. And that ability only came from knowing someone as deeply as possible.

Michelle drummed her fingers on the table. "Not to sound like a total snob, but when you reach a certain level of wealth, your circle of friends changes. It's nothing malicious or intentional. I guess lifestyles and interests change. I don't exactly have friends these days who would invite me out for beer and a burger at a sports bar, even though I totally enjoy it."

"You like sports?" Felix salivated at the opportunity of having something they could actually bond over. No acting needed.

"I grew up in a small town where Friday night football games were as important as going to church on Sunday. I've never gotten into other sports, but I love me some football. I'm so excited for the Seahawks right now. I really think they can win it all."

"I have a hunch they will," Felix said, offering a sly grin. "They'll cruise to victory. Do you ever get to go to the games?"

"I go to a few each season. I'm good friends with Jody . . . the owner's sister."

Of course you are, Felix thought, actually doing cartwheels inside. The woman sitting across from him knew Bill Gates, so naturally she knew his co-founder of Microsoft, Paul Allen, and his sister. *Five minutes in, and not one mention of work.*

"That's really cool," Felix said. "So how has work been for you?"

He hoped the question didn't come out as dismissive of what they had been talking about.

"Oh," she said. "It's been good. Always exciting to have a new year ahead."

Felix nodded. "I know what you mean. How was the holiday party? Last time we went out, I think you said it was the following night."

Michelle smiled, reminiscing. "It was spectacular. My team really went all-out. It was more of a production than a party. I'd say everyone left with a big smile on their face. How was the Starbucks party? I assume they had one."

Felix froze. If Starbucks had a holiday party, he had no idea where it was, or what day it had fallen on. And it was entirely possible Michelle knew these details, considering she was connected to everyone in Seattle.

"It was good, from what I can remember," Felix said with a laugh.

"Ahhh, one of those nights? Can't blame you. You're young, though—you can handle it."

Michelle bit her bottom lip, and Felix could sense the lust radiating from across the table. He had never been so grateful for a mob of people to holler like they did when a running back for the New Orleans Saints broke free for a sixty-yard touchdown run. The distraction made it impossible to hear anything else, forcing their conversation into a brief hiatus.

"Lots of Saints fans here tonight," Michelle said once the noise returned to a more bearable level.

"I'll say."

A server stopped by their table to take their order. Michelle ordered a beer and wings, impressing Felix, who ordered the same thing.

"I heard something interesting last night about an employee at your company," Felix said.

"Oh, gossip? This should be good. What was it?"

Michelle seemed genuinely unconcerned, as if she heard this type of statement at least twice a week.

"Well, the word is someone named Adam—I forget his last name—applied with a fake resume and still landed a job. An important job, by the sounds of it. The details weren't too clear."

Michelle sat frozen, her eyes reading Felix, trying to figure if this was a joke. "How did you hear about this?"

Felix's stomach flipped in a violent cartwheel. He struck a nerve and had no clue how it would all play out. She could storm out of the bar right now, and he would forever beat himself up for ruining the mission. Self-doubt immediately crept back into his mind for the first time on this date. Had he gotten too greedy?

"I, uh, I was at a happy hour last night. Lots of execs from all around Seattle. I don't even remember who I heard it from, but people were talking about it."

"Fuck," Michelle muttered under her breath, shaking her head. "Not good. How the hell do people already know about this? Do people have no lives in this city?"

Felix sensed rage from across the table, but didn't feel it directed toward him. "So it's true?" he asked in a soft voice that could barely be heard.

Their server returned and placed two steins of beer on the table, along with a basket of French fries. Michelle immediately stuffed four into her mouth and washed them down with an exaggerated swig of the beer.

"I don't even know the details yet. They literally alerted me of this yesterday, but honestly, it's not as big of a deal as everyone might think."

"How do you figure?"

Felix leaned forward in his seat, elbows planted on the table, the beer the furthest thing from his mind.

"The employee in question is my assistant, Adam. He started about a month ago, and has been exemplary in his work."

"How does something like this even happen?" Felix asked, needing to test the waters and make sure nothing was being tied back to Arielle or Selena.

Michelle shrugged. "Word of mouth. We could try to trace it back to the source, but with over 500 employees in the building, that would be nothing but a pointless witch hunt. I have my recruiting team looking into the matter, and they should have something for me on Monday."

"Have you asked Adam about it?"

"No. I had sent him home a couple of hours early yesterday. We're still a little slow to start the new year, so I always try to make life easier for my assistants when I can. That way, I can grind them to dust when it gets busy again." She let out a laugh and took another long drink from her stein. Felix finally did the same.

"You know, I think you should take this a little more seriously. Regardless of what you find, people might think they can fake their way into WonderHome, especially if they hear this happened, *and* the employee remains with the company. In a time where so many people would love to work for a company like yours, you need to show you take this allegation serious. Or else you'll be bombarded with fake applications."

"Is that what people are saying they'll do?" Michelle asked in a near gasp.

"No, no, no. Nothing like that was said. I just know how people in my generation act, so I'm imaging how it can all play out if you do nothing. Worst-case scenario, of course."

"I can talk to Adam, but would he admit this so freely?"

Felix shrugged. "I don't know the guy. You'll have to be the one who reads him. Maybe wait until you see him in person."

"I have a hard time believing it. Adam is an incredibly focused worker and a good family man."

"Good people can do bad things when they're desperate. How well did you know him before hiring him?"

"One of my close friends had suggested I interview him. They said they knew Adam, his family, and vouched for him. I have no reason to think my friend would be in on some sort of scheme. Then again, he had a guaranteed interview because of the mutual connection. He had no reason to lie because I was going to interview him regardless of what his resume said. He used to manage a grocery store—not exactly the qualifications we look for when hiring an administrative assistant. What do you think? Have you ever heard of something like this happening?"

Felix drew a deep breath and looked around to feign deep thought. Inside, he was dancing. Boogeying. Michelle had complete trust in Felix for even entertaining this conversation.

"I think you need to take a step back and look at the big picture. As of now, this is just a rumor. So someone started it, completely made up, intending to harm Adam's career. Does he have any haters at the office? Anyone who can gain something by him losing his job? Or on the flip side, it is true, and Adam bragged about it to someone, setting in motion the rumors himself. Because if it's true, who else would know about it besides Adam?"

Michelle leaned back and rubbed her fingers frustratingly on her temples. "I don't know what to think. I don't want to deal with either of those scenarios. Damn it all."

Felix reached across the table and caressed Michelle's arm. "Look, maybe it's not a big deal like you think, but you need to do *something*. Brushing it under the rug is the absolute wrong choice."

The move startled Michelle in a good way. Her eyes fell to Felix's hand, then moved back to him. She leaned back and grabbed his hand.

"Thank you," she said. "I'll have to deal with this on Monday. I need to know how widespread this rumor is. Do I need to address the entire company, or is it much smaller than that? This is not how I was planning to start the new year."

"If you give it proper attention, this whole matter can be behind you before next weekend, and you can get back to your regularly scheduled plans."

The server returned, this time with two baskets of chicken wings. Michelle's mood had gone through a whirlwind in the last ten minutes. Felix almost felt bad about it, but this was business, after all. And business was good today.

Then it got even better.

"Say," Michelle said. "Would you like to join me at the Seahawks playoff game next weekend?"

Chapter 36

January 8, 2014

On Wednesday, Arielle and Selena arrived home after work, Selena steaming with fury. Felix was in the kitchen, tending to a boiling pot of chicken noodle soup he had prepared for dinner.

Selena tossed her purse and car keys on the counter and immediately poured herself a glass of wine.

"What's wrong?" Felix asked, looking at Arielle for guidance, only to receive a tight-lipped grin.

"Your girlfriend is letting him off the hook," Selena said, taking a sip from the wineglass as she leaned back against the counter, staring at the ceiling in disbelief. "You know, it would be one thing for her to actually acknowledge what happened and address it. Share her thoughts on the matter. But *no*, she wants to leave us all out in the dark."

"Selena," Felix said. "I have no idea what you're talking about. Would you mind explaining?"

"We've had this investigation open since the first thing Monday morning. It was supposed to be perfect, because I was directly involved, especially since I was the one who 'accidentally' deleted the application from Adam that is now in question. This was supposed to help our mission. I spent all of Monday and yesterday digging up the details, and writing a report to make it look like Adam definitely submitted a fake application. I spoke with everyone involved in his hiring. My team lead even asked me questions and helped me write this report—I'm so pissed! We *had* him right where we wanted."

Selena took another sip of wine and paced frenzied circles around the kitchen, looking like a college professor so deep in her lecture that she wouldn't hear anyone's question.

"Yesterday afternoon, we sent the report with our findings to my manager. She read it, agreed that Adam had applied with a fake resume, and sent it further up the chain to our VP. Within thirty minutes myself, my team lead, and my manager were called into the VP's office. She thanked us for our work and basically double-checked everything we mentioned in the report. 'These are serious allegations,' she told us. 'Adam will probably lose his job. Michelle isn't going to like it, but that's where we are after reading this.' Do you have any idea how excited I was? I wanted to break open the window in her office and shout it to all of Seattle. We had done it. Somehow, some way, we framed Adam Marshall for this silly offense and he was going to be fired. Mission complete. Let's go home."

"I take it that's not what happened," Felix said, earning the most intimidating glare from Selena.

"I take it you haven't checked Michelle's sent messages this afternoon," Selena replied, mocking Felix's voice.

"I haven't since about three o'clock. That's when I started on this soup."

Selena pointed to Felix's laptop, still sitting on the kitchen table. "Why don't you turn that on and pull open the email she sent to the four of us who put this report together?"

Felix turned the dial down on the stove before crossing the kitchen and taking a seat behind his laptop. He flipped it open and punched in his password, then logged in through the back-channel VPN he spent months figuring out.

"Okay, I got it," Felix said.

"Read it out loud," Selena said, crossing her arms as she finally stopped walking in circles. She returned to the counter where she had left the bottle of wine and poured a second glass.

"From Michelle Garrison to Susie Foster, Amara Edwards, Janina Victoria, and Selena Nicole. This one, right?"

"Mmhmm."

"Hello team," Felix said, eyes glued to the screen as he read the email. "Thank you so much for your hard work in preparing this report. Me and the executive team have reviewed the details and have decided, at this time, to disregard the incident as a misunderstanding. Mr. Marshall will remain employed with WonderHome. Thank you."

Selena shuddered. Felix thought her head might fly off the hinges of her neck.

"The past," Arielle said. "Always protecting itself. This one is impressive. I wonder what was said that allowed this to happen."

"Let's see if we can find anything," Felix said, clicking out of the email and searching through the rest of Michelle's inbox.

"I'm just in so much shock," Selena said. "This was a slam dunk for us. I don't understand."

"How did your bosses take it?" Felix asked.

"I don't know about Susie, but I'm pretty sure Amara threw a stapler at the wall. She was in her office with the door closed when this email came into our inboxes, and we all heard a loud bang. All we could see was her standing over her desk, huffing and puffing. She's always so gentle, despite my intimidating first impression of her. I've never seen her so pissed off; I could only assume it was because of that email."

"Well, we can likely eliminate her as a suspect. Why would she get involved with the other execs after something like this?"

"Not necessarily," Arielle said. "If anything, I'd say this makes her a bigger suspect. We're trusting the laundering scheme is coming from somewhere in the executive team. What if Amara comes up with the idea of framing Adam to get her own personal revenge for this? I don't think it's likely, but we should see how things play out in the coming weeks."

"I don't get it," Felix said, rubbing his forehead. "There are no emails between Michelle and anyone else regarding this matter. Not even an initial one that brought it to her attention. Do people in the company not email her? Do they just stop in her office to share information like this?"

"Did you check Adam's email?" Arielle asked. "He might field everything for her before deciding what she actually needs to deal with."

"I did, and still nothing. Obviously, they wouldn't include him in anything about this. I checked all the executives' inboxes and none mentioned this. Michelle claims to have met with the executive team, but did she really?"

"We need to bug her office," Arielle said. "I wanted to avoid it because of the risk, but we have no choice. How can we go about it? There are security cameras in the hallway outside of her office pointing right at her door. It records anyone who goes in and out."

"Do you know how closely those are watched?" Felix asked. "What if you tried after hours?"

"I'm honestly not sure. It's my understanding that both WonderHome and the building security have access to the feed. Do you know, Selena?"

She nodded. "They're watched and reviewed pretty regularly."

"Does Michelle ever have groups meet in her office?" Felix asked, running down a mental checklist of possibilities to get into the coveted office.

"As far as I know, only with the executive team," Selena said. "I can't imagine a scenario that would get me or Arielle into her office on official business. Even if we had a concern for the CEO, we'd get told to run it through Amara."

"Same for me," Arielle said. "We don't even know what the inside of her office looks like, either. Say we got in somehow, we'd have to figure out where to plant the bug, and how to do it without getting seen by anyone else in the room. All on the spot."

"For an office," Felix said. "Under the desk is always best. It's the one area that gets completely neglected, even by the cleaners—they don't dust the underside of a desk."

"What about tapping her phone line?" Selena asked.

Felix shook his head. "Way too risky. Especially if the feds will investigate her in a few months. They'll find the wiretap, and who knows what kind of mess that would cause."

The room fell silent as they all grew discouraged at the prospect ahead of them. After a minute, Felix cleared his throat and said, "I have an idea that just may work, but it all depends how my date with her this weekend goes."

Chapter 37

January 11, 2014

A chilly wind slashed across Felix's cheeks as he stepped out of the car. Arielle had just dropped him off outside of CenturyLink Field, home to the Seattle Seahawks and their playoff game against the New Orleans Saints that would begin in less than an hour.

The energy outside the stadium hummed unlike anything Felix had experienced at a sporting event. Swarms of fans wearing navy blue and neon green crowded the sidewalks and streets as they made their way into the game. People poured out of the several neighboring bars, marching toward the stadium.

Felix needed to fit in, especially if he was going to be in a private suite for friends of the owner. It was the one shopping trip he had wanted to make, going out to buy a Russell Wilson jersey and a Seahawks beanie hat to match. He looked and *felt* like he belonged as he pushed through the crowd toward the exclusive VIP entrance that had a line of only two other fans getting wanded by security.

Michelle had left his ticket at will call on Friday, and he picked it up that same day to avoid the long lines before the game. The mission aside, Felix couldn't believe he was actually going to experience a playoff game from the comfort of a luxury suite. Sure, he already knew the outcome of the game, but the energy was about to boil over inside the stadium that had become known as the loudest and most difficult to play in for visiting teams.

Felix checked in at security, a chipper guard patting him down before running the metal-detecting wand across his body. After being cleared, Felix stepped into a world he had never seen before. Even with all the money and connections he had through the Road Runners, he had never watched a game from a suite. Front row was his preferred location, but he was already seeing how the closest seats lacked the amenities of a suite ticket.

Instead of walking on the typical dusty concrete floor most outdoor stadiums had, he strolled along a carpet decorated with the Seahawks logo in a dizzying pattern. The entryway turned into a hallway with a concession stand, merchandise shop, and private elevators.

Felix took the elevator up to the suite level, where he found himself on a concourse that seemed much too quiet for a playoff game. It was a fairly even mix of fans dressed in Seahawks attire and others in suits and dresses. The suite concourse welcomed luxury. A massive sculpture of a flock of twelve hawks flying hung from the ceiling. There were fondue and carving stations, a handful of bars serving top-shelf liquor, a dessert tower, and an array of concession stands serving everything from sushi to hot dogs and the typical stadium grub.

These people know how to take in a game, Felix thought, suddenly wondering what he had been missing out on his whole life. *I wonder if I can buy a suite at Coors Field or Ball Arena when I get back.*

Overwhelmed, Felix checked his ticket for his suite number and made his way through the concourse, scanning the ticket outside the door of suite number four to unlock it. He pushed open the door to a suite full of at least thirty people, surveying the room for Michelle.

He found her at the suite's own private carving station; the chef preparing top sirloin. Through the window, Felix saw they were right around midfield, and was delighted that the view seemed closer to the field than he had always imagined.

"Why, hello there," Felix said, sliding next to Michelle.

"Oh, my goodness!" Michelle cried, throwing her hands in the air and wrapping them around Felix's shoulders. "I'm so glad you made it. You got in no problem?"

She released him and took a step back, Felix relieved to see her dressed in a Seahawks hoodie and jeans to match his casual outfit.

"I wouldn't miss this for the world. This has already been an incredible experience, and the game hasn't even started."

"First time in a suite?" Michelle asked.

"Yes, actually. I didn't even realize it was my first time until I stepped into the private entrance. I'm hooked!"

"Well, that's good. Let me introduce you to my friend."

Michelle grabbed Felix by the wrist and pulled him through the crowded suite, where huddles formed with the different cliques present.

They reached a standing table near the window overlooking the field where both teams were finishing their warm-ups. A woman wearing a Seahawks jersey with the name "Allen" on the back was enjoying a plate of lobster when Michelle reached out to touch her shoulder.

She turned around, brushing back her short reddish blond hair.

"Jody," Michelle said. "This is my good friend Felix. Felix, this is Jody."

Felix's eyes bulged as he reached out a shaky hand. "It's such an honor to meet you, Ms. Allen. I'm a big fan of you and your brother's work."

Jody smiled and shook his hand. "Why thank you, sir. I'd like to say Paul will make it to our suite today, but he's dealing with some business on the other side of the field. Besides, he likes to wander down to the sidelines a couple times during the game. I'm glad you're here. Make yourself at home and let Benny know if you need anything."

"I still need to show him around and introduce him to Benny," Michelle said, running a hand up and down Felix's back. He was too awestruck with everything to even realize it.

"Of course. Hopefully, we'll have some champagne to celebrate a win at the end of the game."

"We'll win tonight," Felix said. "We actually won't lose again for the rest of this season."

"Now that's what I like to hear," Jody said. "I like this guy, Michelle. You bring him back next week if we win. I'm sorry, *when* we win."

Felix looked over and saw Michelle blushing, snapping him back to the reality that he was on a date with the CEO of WonderHome to learn who was responsible for the money laundering that sent Adam Marshall to prison.

"*When* we win, of course," Michelle replied.

"You two have a fun time. I gotta check on a couple of things, but I'll be popping in and out during the game." Jody grabbed her plate and vanished through the crowd on a mission.

"She's not Bill Gates," Michelle said to Felix. "But what did you think of Jody Allen? It's not every day you get to meet the owner of a sports franchise."

"She's a lot more down-to-earth than I would have thought."

Michelle nodded. "She's always been that way. The money never changed her. She believes in her work and the causes their foundation supports."

"That's admirable. I hope to be a billionaire one day. It's sort of a life goal of mine."

"Well, if that's your goal, you're in the right room. Obviously, not everyone here is a billionaire, but there are several worth nine figures. Strike up conversations, pick their minds. It's honestly the only way to get anywhere near that sort of status."

Michelle's response caught Felix off guard. Normally when he shared this dream—often to others his age—people would laugh it aside, not taking it seriously. But Michelle didn't so much as flinch, and even encouraged him. Presumably, everyone packed into this suite wanted to become a billionaire one day, and that was simply what everyone was talking about, from what Felix could hear from the surrounding conversations.

Minutes before a playoff game was about to start and not a single discussion of how the Seahawks would beat the Saints. Stocks, investment accounts, business ventures, risks, failures, success stories. Rich people talked about money almost exclusively, and Felix was taking notes.

He also felt bad for them. For Felix, becoming a billionaire wasn't a matter to elevate his status in society. It wasn't even to afford himself a better life—he could earn unlimited funds through the Road Runners. He wanted the challenge of earning such an astronomical amount of money through his own work and ideas. And when he reached it, all that money would go right back into the community to lift others to the next level in their lives.

"Well, I appreciate you bringing me today," Felix said. "I'm honored."

"You're a good guy, Felix. I can tell that much already, and I see nothing but bright things in your future."

"Thank you. Can I get you anything else before the game starts?"

"No, I'm good for now."

The mood had lightened, and Felix was ready to attack. "Say, I've been wondering since we saw each other last. Whatever happened to that employee at your company?"

Michelle rolled her eyes. "A false alarm. There was definitely cause for concern, but it looks like there was another applicant who had the same name as my assistant. They applied a few days before my assistant did, which caused all of this suspicion. It was a brief hiccup, but everything is back to normal now. And thank goodness, because Adam has been an absolute lifesaver. I invited him to join us here today, but he wasn't able to make it. He'll be free next weekend, if there's a game."

"Well, I look forward to meeting him."

Felix was content to let the conversation drift wherever it needed for the rest of the evening, for a new opportunity had come into play. There *would* be a game next weekend, this he already knew, and he'd get his chance to question Adam Marshall.

Chapter 38

January 19, 2014

The next week flew by for all three Angels. Arielle and Selena had put in another routine week at the WonderHome offices, where Arielle continued to fake her way through her job. She considered leaving the job in the coming weeks to dedicate more time with Felix in trying to resolve their mission from behind the scenes. Her colleagues rarely carried on meaningful conversations, let alone shared gossip from around the office. She was finding her time at the office a headache and a waste of time. Felix was still figuring out the logistics of keeping their access to the WonderHome system without Arielle's VPN connection.

Selena had received an Employee of the Month award for her efforts in December, for not only ramping up so quickly after her training, but hitting the ground running. The perks of the award came with a wooden plaque, an extra day of paid time off, and a fifty-dollar gift card to spend on Amazon.

Sometimes Selena seemed to veer off into her own world, and they wondered if she forgot she was working on a mission and not actually an employee for WonderHome.

None of that mattered on the following Sunday evening, when the Seahawks were to square off against the San Francisco 49ers for a chance to advance to Super Bowl XLVIII.

Felix was indeed invited back. Michelle had been out of town all week for a conference in Texas, so Felix had no opportunity to execute his plan to get into her office and plant a bug. He'd have to navigate one more successful date to keep those hopes alive.

By the time he arrived at the stadium, dressed in the same attire as the prior week, he strolled through the VIP entrance with an extra hop in his step. His confidence soared after last weekend, and knowing he'd have the chance to meet Adam Marshall today had carried him through the week.

By the end of the first quarter, when Adam had yet to appear, Felix asked Michelle where he was.

"Adam isn't going to make it," she explained. "I guess his in-laws are in town and he couldn't make it work."

"But it's the NFC championship," Felix said, as a genuinely concerned citizen of sports fandom.

Michelle shrugged. "I suppose that's one reason to not get married."

She cackled at this, and Felix joined.

He had rarely given thought to marriage, considering he rarely even went on dates. But if missing a hot ticket item like the NFC championship was at risk, then maybe marriage would forever remain off the table. Sweat dripped down his back just thinking about such an atrocity.

So they sat through the game, carrying on the usual small talk with Michelle, high-fiving at the opportune moments. Despair hung in the stadium at the start of the fourth quarter when the Seahawks were trailing by four and looking out of sorts. After a long touchdown pass to take their first lead of the game, the building erupted with the energy it was known for, staying that way while the team closed out their rival and punched their ticket to face the Denver Broncos in the Super Bowl two weeks later.

Champagne bottles popped in the suite, some for drinking, some for spraying around to celebrate. Felix was glad to have remained in the outdoor seating on the other side of the glass when this happened, but appreciated the sentiment just the same.

Michelle tapped him on the shoulder while they watched the team gather on the field to receive their NFC championship trophy. "Would you like to come over to my place and have a drink?" she asked, the question instantly removing Felix from the excitement on the field and spinning his stomach into the tightest knots he could remember having ever felt.

He gulped, leery of how Michelle envisioned the night would go.

I can't bail right now, he thought. *I haven't even bugged her office yet. If I don't go, she could get upset. She's not afraid to jump around to different men, and I can't get left out of the picture.*

"Sure," Felix said, trying to sound remotely interested.

A grin spread across Michelle's face. "Let's go."

They spent a couple minutes telling people goodbye as they made their way out of the suite. Everyone had been too drunk or too distracted by the celebration to pay them any attention.

"Do you need a ride, or did you drive here?" Michelle asked when they reached the street level.

"I drove."

"Great. You can follow me. Do you know how to get to Medina?"

"Yes."

They walked one block to the parking garage that had a VIP section on the main level, an added perk to having a suite ticket. Felix walked Michelle to her car.

"Race you there," she said, winking at him as she closed the door.

His stomach dropped more. *This old lady wants to sleep with me.*

Felix tried to erase the image from his mind. He had never tried to get out of sex before, and wasn't even sure where to begin. Headache? Stomachache? He could take a bunch of shots of alcohol when they arrived and give himself whiskey dick. He even considered being honest with Michelle by explaining he wasn't ready to get physical.

Michelle, however, was a wild card. It had been four dates, and he couldn't get a solid read on the things that bothered her, or the things that brought her pleasure.

You are the pleasure she wants, Felix thought, gagging at the thought. *You and your young, tight body.*

"Fuck," Felix cried out as he found his car and got behind the wheel.

He backed out and saw Michelle waiting ahead at the garage exit. Since everyone was still inside the stadium celebrating, traffic was at a minimum. Part of him had hoped it would take too long to leave the premises, and he could make up an excuse that he had to go home and get ready for work in the morning.

But it was only 7:30, and the city of Seattle was rocking with their Super Bowl ambitions.

Because there was no traffic, it only took them twenty minutes to arrive at Michelle's home.

It wasn't the castle they had all expected, but it was still a stunning two-story home with a perfectly manicured front lawn. Michelle pulled into the driveway and parked in the garage. Felix stopped behind and stepped out of the car with hundreds of different things he could say to throw off the scent of attraction.

"Do you mind if I use your restroom?" he asked as he entered the garage, Michelle promptly closing the door behind him. "I'm not sure those nachos are sitting too well with me."

"My goodness, are you okay?" she asked.

"I think so. Just need a minute."

"Absolutely. Let's head in."

She hurried out of her car, a silver Mercedes sedan with a license plate of *WONDER*.

When she opened the side door, they entered a dark foyer until she flicked on a light to reveal a laundry room complete with a coat rack and a small bench, where she slipped out of her shoes and tucked them into a basket.

"If you don't mind, please take off your shoes here," she said, pulling out a second basket from under the bench.

Felix obliged.

The foyer opened to a hallway connecting the living room to a family room, a spiral staircase in the middle that led upstairs.

"I'm sorry, Michelle, but where is that bathroom?" Felix asked, trying to make his words sound urgent. He hoped Selena would approve of his acting skills.

"Yes, second door on your right." She gestured down the hallway, where the door stood ajar across from the staircase.

Felix let himself in and raised the toilet seat with an audible *clank!* for dramatic effect.

Okay, how the hell do I get out of here? Felix asked himself, standing over the sink and studying himself in the mirror. He took off his Seahawks beanie to find his hair a frazzled mess. He debated cleaning it up, but left it to look as unappealing as possible. *How long can I stay in here until she comes knocking?*

Felix didn't know the rules of etiquette that most of society played by, and wondered if this was even a thing. Surely, common courtesy called for a host to check on their guest if they were in the bathroom for over five minutes. Ten, maybe?

His face flushed a light shade of red, so he turned on the sink to splash some water on cheeks.

"Dammit," he muttered under his breath. Felix always kept a backpack with tools he might need, and he'd love to bug Michelle's house in as many places as possible. But the backpack was on the passenger seat of his car.

Just don't ruin the night. She likes you, and you need to leverage that until you can at least bug her office at WonderHome.

Felix grew nauseous and wondered if he hung over the toilet for a minute, if he could force his body to vomit. Then he wouldn't have to pretend to be sick to leave.

He shook his head and froze at the sound of footsteps approaching from the hallway outside.

"Felix?" Michelle called out. "Everything okay?"

It had been five minutes, and Felix knew he had overstayed his welcome in the bathroom.

"Yes," he shouted back. "I'll be right out."

"Would you like a drink?"

"Yes, please. Whiskey or scotch."

"Okay. I'll meet you in the kitchen."

Felix had no idea where the kitchen was, nor did he care. He figured he had one last minute before needing to step out.

He flushed the toilet and blasted the sink. "Okay," he said to himself. "One drink and we're out of here." His reflection nodded back in understanding.

Felix killed the flowing water and drew a deep breath before spinning around to open the door.

The hallway was abandoned, but the lights were on everywhere in the house. Music carried from down the hallway, some sort of smooth jazz, so he followed it towards what he presumed was the kitchen.

"Jesus Christ," he whispered to himself as he stepped in. Sure, the kitchen was state-of-the-art and would have normally earned all of his attention, but what had really caught him off guard was Michelle.

She stood along one counter, pouring two glasses of whiskey, dressed in lingerie. Navy blue panties and bra, and a neon green see-through robe that stopped at her upper thighs, opened at her chest to reveal her cleavage while a bow tied the rest of it snugly around her waist.

Michelle hummed along to the music, grinning while she screwed the top back onto the bottle of whiskey.

"Did someone ask for a drink?" she asked, grabbing the glasses and gliding across the floor toward Felix.

His heart drummed madly in his head, adrenaline slipping into his veins as sheer panic settled in. He had mentally prepared for this moment—granted, not so soon.

Michelle stopped in front of him and extended a glass, which he grabbed and promptly took a sip. As much as he had dreaded this, he couldn't resist looking her up and down. Her body was tight and chiseled, but what Felix was now finding the most attractive was her confidence that seemed to seep through every crack in the house.

"What do you think?" Michelle asked, swaying her hips side to side to ensure Felix saw every curve of her body. "It's Seahawks colors. Don't you want to keep celebrating?"

Discipline was a universal trait across all members of the Angel Runners. When altering the past, temptation was practically guaranteed on any mission, whether emotional, mental, or, in this case, physical.

Michelle reached out with her free hand and ran a finger down the center of Felix's chest, not stopping until she reached his waistband. Heat pulsed in his crotch, and he knew it was time to make a move.

He threw his head back and gulped the remaining whiskey. "I'm sorry, Michelle," he said, keeping his voice soft and his eyes on her face for a reaction. "I'm not feeling too well right now."

"Oh?" Michelle took a step back and placed her glass on the counter. "Is there something wrong with me?"

"Whoa, no, not at all. My God, it's my *stomach*, not you. You're . . . incredible."

A tender smile touched her lips at this compliment.

"I really think something from the game is not settling well with me," Felix continued, running his hand in a circle over his stomach. "I thought the shot of whiskey might help, but I'm not feeling any better yet."

Felix wondered how many other men his age had found themselves in this same predicament in Michelle's house. They probably raced to take their clothes off, of course, not find an emergency exit out.

"Do you want to lie down?" Michelle offered, now hugging herself to keep her lacy robe closed over her body.

"I think I should get home, actually. Would hate for me to get worse and have to drive home any later. I think I can make it right now, and will probably dive straight into bed."

"Oh," Michelle said to herself, disappointment tangible in the air. "Okay. If that's what you need to do. I hope you feel better soon."

Felix's heart hadn't stopped pounding away, apparently looking for its own exit. He needed to ensure this wasn't the last time he'd see Michelle, because he understood a debacle like this could very well cancel his next invitation for a date.

He took a big step forward, reaching out to grab Michelle by her hips and pulling her in toward him. Their faces hovered inches apart for five seconds before Felix closed his eyes and pressed his lips against hers.

There was no resistance from Michelle, who promptly gave in, throwing her arms around Felix, where her nails scratched seductively along his back.

Felix pulled away right when he sensed Michelle about to open her mouth to challenge him to a game of tongue Twister.

"Don't take tonight to heart," Felix said. "I *really* want to see you again."

Michelle tasted like wine, and the flavor was stuck on his lips. She had three glasses during the game that were still making their way out of her pores, apparently.

She bit her bottom lip and nodded. "Me too. Now go home and get better, so we can try this again."

For good measure, he kissed her on the forehead. "I'll call you this week and we'll plan something."

Felix wasted no time leaving, relief flooding over him when he sat down behind the wheel of his car.

Crisis averted.

Chapter 39

January 22, 2014

Arielle and Selena couldn't help but bring up the story of Felix escaping Michelle's sexual advances every day since it happened. Arielle couldn't believe how quickly it had all escalated, and told Felix he could bail on this mission whenever he pleased. Selena simply liked to poke fun.

"Not until I've planted the bug in her office," he said. "Which will happen this week if all goes according to plan."

It was Wednesday, and Felix was beyond ready to execute his plan that he had kept to himself so far.

"Look at you, Felix," Selena said earlier that morning at the breakfast table. "Acting like Arielle with your mission secrets. You're going to pull this off, aren't you?"

He only smiled. "I've learned from the best. That's all."

Felix had joined them on their drive to the office, spending the morning hours wandering around downtown, stopping for a coffee around nine, and spending the rest of the freezing morning walking underground at Pike Place Market. When 11:30 rolled around, he sent a text message to Michelle.

Good morning! I'm off work today, but have some business downtown. Can I bring you lunch at your office?

It only took thirty seconds for a response. *Good morning, handsome. Yes! Floor 34. Excited to see you <3*

Felix shook his head. Was Michelle truly falling for him, or was the past trying to force the issue so he couldn't interfere with its plans for the Marshall family? It didn't matter to Felix either way. He needed to plant the bug this afternoon and get the hell out of whatever relationship was forming with the WonderHome CEO.

"Okay, I'm getting in the building," he said, finding a deli to stop at for two sandwiches. Once he had the sandwiches in hand, he patted his pockets to make sure the two bugs he had brought along were still secure. With that confirmation, he made his way out of the underground portion of the market, back up to street level, where the WonderHome office waited only two blocks away.

The sidewalks were filled with those who liked to take their lunch on the earlier side. Felix never understood how anyone could eat lunch before noon.

He strolled into the lobby of the Wilson Investments Center, confidence creeping back into his mind. *This* was the part of the job he thrived in. Sneaking around and planting bugs. There was no one better, and nothing else gave him the rush of getting away with it.

Felix entered the elevator and rode it up to the thirty-fourth floor, the doors parting to reveal a hallway that stretched far into the distance. It only ran in one direction, so he followed it, passing a bathroom and several conference rooms before he saw the first sign of life.

"Can I help you?" a woman with short, spiky hair asked. Felix immediately recognized her as Mila Bachman, the chief marketing officer.

"Yes, actually. I'm meeting with Michelle, but this is my first time here. Which way is her office?"

Mila looked him up and down and crossed her arms. "Fresh meat, huh?"

Felix stared back, not sure how to respond. Not even sure what the comment was supposed to mean.

Mila broke into howling laughter, stepping forward to clap Felix on the back. "I'm just messing with you. The big boss is at the end of the hall, corner office so she can hog all the space and have two views of the city.

Good luck in there."

Mila didn't wait for Felix to respond and walked off, disappearing down the elevator he had just arrived in, still cackling to herself as the doors closed.

The floor seemed deserted, only a couple of other people appearing in the hallway as he made his way to the furthest end. A small group of employees huddled around a computer monitor in a miniature bullpen area.

The end of the hallway opened up, a desk sitting outside of Michelle's office.

There you are, Felix thought, seeing Adam Marshall for the first time in the flesh.

He was busy typing away on his computer when Felix approached, stopping when he saw him.

"Hello," Adam greeted him. "Are you Felix?"

"Yes. How did you know?"

"Michelle told me you were coming by for lunch. Feel free to go on in."

Adam gestured to the open door and returned to typing on his computer.

Their encounter was clearly not a big deal to Adam, nor should it have been. But Felix had so many questions he wanted to ask, not sure how, realizing he wasn't getting that opportunity today.

One thing at a time. Get this planted and so much more is going to open up.

"Thank you," Felix said, receiving no further acknowledgment from Adam.

He let himself through the door, finding Michelle in a similar position, typing from her desk.

"Felix!" she cried, jumping out of her seat and rounding her desk, which was oddly centered in the room, at least twenty feet away from the windows. She hugged him, and he hugged back. "This is such a pleasant surprise. Do you want to go eat on one of our balconies?"

"No. In here is fine. It's cold outside, anyway."

"Well, they have those outdoor heaters, but that's fine. We can eat in here."

Felix had only ever been in offices for high-ranking Road Runners, and Michelle's compared rather closely. She had her own refrigerator, a microwave, stovetop, sink, and a couch. Being the corner office, she had the dual view that overlooked both the bay and downtown Seattle. If anything, the view made her office even better than the Road Runner ones, since theirs were always underground without so much as a window.

Michelle shuffled to the door and closed it.

"I met Adam just now," Felix said. "A man of few words."

"Oh, don't mind him. He's had a ton of work this week. We sold a lot of homes over the weekend, and he's processing all of those contracts."

"I didn't realize he worked on the real estate side of things. I thought he handled more of your daily tasks."

"He does that, too. But the real estate program is off to a much better start than we expected, and there's been a backlog in contracts to process. He's just helping until we can get more people hired on that team. Besides, the entire program is an initiative from our CFO, so it's not exactly busywork."

"How important," Felix said, mentally tucking all of this information away for later.

"Look in the fridge and grab yourself a drink. I'll have a Sprite, please."

Michelle returned to her desk and cleared it free of papers, wheeling two seats around the corner of the desk so they could sit side by side.

Felix rummaged through the fridge, looking for a reason to get Michelle out of the room. He saw cans of Coke, Sprite, Diet Coke, Fanta, bottled water, and lemonade.

"Do you not have Pepsi?" Felix asked. "I prefer it."

Michelle gave him a look as if wondering if Felix was being serious or not. Could he really not find something to drink out of all the options?

"We have Pepsi in our kitchen. I'll get you one."

"Thank you so much, Michelle." Felix hadn't expected it to be so easy. Until it wasn't.

Michelle only moved to the center of her desk and laid her finger on her work phone's intercom button. "Adam, are you there?" she asked.

His voice crackled in response.

"Can you do me a favor and grab a Pepsi from the kitchen?"

"On it," he replied.

Well, shit, Felix thought, his confidence now wavering. How could he get Michelle out of her own office if she didn't *need* to leave it for anything?

He hurried back to the desk and unwrapped his sandwich, flipping up the top piece of bread. "Dammit! I asked for ranch and mustard, and they didn't put it on. Do you have any?"

Michelle was about to unwrap her sandwich and paused. "I think I only have ketchup in the fridge. We should have mustard and ranch in the main kitchen."

"The one Adam just left to? Of course."

"It's just down the hall if you want to go look."

"Could you?" Felix asked, fighting to make sure his voice didn't sound too desperate. "If you can go grab those for me, I'll finish setting up our little picnic here."

Michelle studied him for a couple of seconds before agreeing. "Okay. Anything else we might need?"

"Just the condiments and I'll be set."

"Okay, I'll be right back."

Michelle stood from her desk and started for the door, Felix's heart pounding away in angst. There was still a chance Adam would return and Michelle would send him right back. When she opened the door and stepped out, Felix stuffed his hand into his pocket and pulled out a microphone disguised as a functioning pen. He jumped out of his seat to round the desk and dropped the pen into a cup of a dozen others sitting on the far edge.

Felix had brought a few options for bugging the office and wanted to use one more besides the pen that only had a 50-hour battery life.

The supreme bugging device was burning a hole in his pocket, so he whipped out the USB flash drive that doubled as a recording device. The advantage of the flash drive was that it plugged directly into a computer to keep a constant charge. No concerns over the battery life. An added plus was that Felix already had access to Michelle's computer, so he'd be able to log in from home and access the recordings without an issue.

Footsteps echoed from down the hall, so Felix dropped to the floor, found the computer underneath, and stuck the flash drive into a port on the back side, out of sight from Michelle, who would never suspect a thing.

The footsteps grew louder, high heels clacking on their way to the office.

Felix lunged out from the desk and returned to his seat, where he hurried to unroll Michelle's sandwich and tossed some napkins around just as she entered the office with a can of Pepsi and bottles of mustard and ranch.

"Are you okay?" she asked. "Your face is super flushed."

Felix's heart rate and breathing had ramped up, and he fought to control at least his breathing, giving a slow nod. "Yeah, I'm okay. Just hungry, I suppose."

Michelle frowned at him while she returned to her seat. "Okay, silly. Let's eat."

And they did. Felix enjoyed his lunch, eager to get home to listen to Michelle's private conversations, and overjoyed he'd finally get to end his fake relationship with her.

Chapter 40

February 8, 2014

Two and a half weeks passed since Felix had planted the bug in Michelle's office, and they hadn't gained a single bit of valuable information. The bugging had worked as it should, and this finally gave Felix something to do throughout the day while Arielle and Selena continued working at WonderHome.

Felix had grown more suspicious since planting the bugs. If the real estate program truly was thriving as Michelle had mentioned, then why was there never a conversation about it? Or why in the hell did Adam Marshall not have a single email regarding the matter? He was supposedly taking on much of the work. Did it just magically fall on his desk? Did the company not keep any electronic records of the real estate transactions? That might make sense if they had planned out the money laundering from the start, but that had never appeared to be the case.

He even spent two days combing through the emails of everyone on the real estate team. It mostly consisted of back-and-forth messages with clients to schedule appointments, review contracts, and answer basic questions. But where were the contracts going to be completed and signed on behalf of WonderHome?

It was like the entire process fell off the grid as soon as it was time to sign.

Felix couldn't find a trace anywhere in the WonderHome system.

The frustration was growing heavy on Felix. He felt like he kept running into one dead end after another. There was literally nothing further he could do than directly asking Michelle if she was laundering money through the company's real estate program.

But that conversation would never come, for it was time for Felix to end the relationship. He had confirmed all was running smoothly with his bugging efforts over the past couple of weeks, and felt confident about never having to step foot inside Michelle's office again. His relationship with her had served the mission's purpose, and he didn't need to waste any more of his free time dodging her sexual advances.

They actually hadn't seen each other since their lunch date in her office. He lied about having plans already that following weekend, and the weekend after that Michelle had gone to the Super Bowl with Jody to watch the Seahawks dismantle the Broncos and bring the first Lombardi trophy back to the Pacific Northwest.

She returned from that trip and had a busy week at work, asking about Felix's plans for the upcoming Saturday, February 8. He said he'd let her know that day if he'd be available that evening.

Snow fell outside while the three Angels gathered in the living room, Selena most eager to hear the phone call Felix was about to make.

"You know," she said. "It's much better to do this today and not drag it out closer to Valentine's Day. That would be so fucked-up."

"The whole thing is fucked-up," Felix said. "I know this is going to hit her hard. I had to listen to some of her conversations with her therapist because they do some sessions over the phone, and this lady actually brings my name up. She's genuinely into me."

Selena laughed. "It's because you're playing hard to get. That woman has gone through life getting whatever she pleases, and you're probably the first man to be so difficult to get in the sack."

"You're sick."

"It's true. Just saying."

Arielle nodded. "Definitely true."

They all burst out laughing.

"Now, before I do this," Felix said. "Have we thought about the repercussions? This relationship didn't exist in the original timeline, which means we have no idea what the breakup might do."

"I've thought it through," Arielle said. "I can't speak to what it will mean for Michelle, but I can't imagine it having much of an impact on our mission. The sooner the better, so we don't get too close to the day of the arrest."

"And neither of you have heard anything around the office?" Felix asked.

"No," Arielle said. "No one is mentioning anything. I've tried to launch a new initiative with our accounting department in hopes of spending more time with them and getting to really dig into our bank accounts, but it's going nowhere fast. I've told you for a while now how I'm considering stepping away from this job, and I think that day is coming soon. My time is being wasted. Selena is thriving and gaining trust from people all around the company, so I think we'll be okay with having her there while I focus on other aspects of the mission."

"Are you asking for our permission?" Selena asked. "Because that's kind of what it sounds like. You've been thinking this for weeks and haven't done anything about it. That's not like you at all."

"No, I'm not asking for your permission, but I'd love your input. What do you think?"

"If we're not gaining anything by you being at the office every day, then you should absolutely leave the job and figure out what to do here with Felix. Surely he can't cover the entire company himself. There could easily be something slipping through the cracks."

Felix nodded. "We can make it work. As long as that flash drive stays plugged into Michelle's computer, I can get into the system no problem. If you can, maybe sneak a computer out of the office before you leave. I know IT always has some lying around that aren't accounted for. Take one of those, so we can have a backup in case Michelle gets a new computer or discovers the flash drive. I'd need about a week to get it configured to match your computer's setup, but after that, you'll be home free."

"Okay," Arielle said. "I'll grab a computer on Monday and we can get this in motion. I'll be out of this job by the end of the month."

"How long does it take the feds to investigate the laundering?" Selena asked. "Won't they be starting that soon if Adam gets arrested in May?"

"It can take a few months for them to sift through records and trace it all to the responsible party," Felix said. "Forensic accountants get tasked with this sort of work, but a good laundering scheme can make their job incredibly difficult."

"Are they allowed to do this without the company's knowledge?"

"Yes. It's sort of a loophole when it comes to electronic data. If the feds need access to electronic data, they can go through the company's service providers to obtain it. All they need to do is present a case for their investigation to a judge to sign a warrant for such a request between the feds and WonderHome's internet and phone provider. That way they can investigate in the background while WonderHome has no idea what's going on. I'd imagine, if they haven't already, they'll be starting their investigation within the next month. We're getting a little off track, though. Can I make this phone call I've been dreading for weeks?"

"Why are you so nervous?" Selena asked. "It's not like you're in love with the woman."

"I'm just worried about what will happen. I want to get it over with and see."

"Go for it," Arielle said, prompting Felix to pull out his cell phone.

His fingers trembled as he clicked on Michelle's name and the phone started dialing.

"Why hello there, handsome," Michelle greeted in a cheerful voice. "I thought I'd never get to see you again."

Felix's stomach plunged. This would not be easy.

"Hey, Michelle. How are you doing? How was the week?"

"It was a busy, stressful week. But I'm doing better now that I can hear your voice."

Jesus Christ, Felix thought. *Is the past really going to make this so difficult?*

"Well, I'm glad to hear that. Do you have a minute?"

"Sure. Is everything okay?" The cheer left Michelle instantly, zapped with a sudden concern.

"Yes, I'm okay. I just need to talk to you about something?"

"Oooookay? What's going on?"

"It's about us. I don't think—"

"Are you breaking up with me?" Michelle snapped. "Are you kidding me right now?!"

Her voice elevated, and Felix felt the instantaneous rage radiating through the phone.

"Look," he said. "I've enjoyed the time we've spent together, but I just don't feel this is working out. We hardly get to see other. We're both so busy."

"Is this because I didn't take you to the Super Bowl? They only offered me one ticket—you know that."

"No, it's not the Super—"

"Am I just some ticket whore for you? You got a taste of the high life at the Seahawks games, and now that the season's over, you just toss me aside."

"Michelle, you're not letting me talk. I promise it has nothing to do with the Super Bowl. I can't speak for you, but I don't feel like I can dedicate the time to our relationship that it deserves."

Arielle and Selena both nodded, impressed with Felix's cool demeanor as he navigated through what was certainly unknown territory. He had to look away from them and paced in the other direction.

"This is *bullshit*, Felix," Michelle said, through what sounded like gritted teeth. "After all I've done for you. And you don't even have the balls to *fuck* me! You're such a chickenshit!"

"Michelle, that's enough."

"You fucking slimeball! I could have slept with a different guy every night while I was in New York, but I didn't! Because I thought we had something. You have some nerve. I'll give you that, you rotten piece of—"

Felix hung up the call, wheezing as the tension lingered.

He turned back around to face Arielle and Selena, who had settled on the couch, and watched him closely.

"So . . ." Selena said. "It's done?"

"She completely exploded," Felix said. "You'd have thought we were dating for years. I don't understand. Do people really fall this strongly for someone after such little time?"

"It happens more than you think," Selena said, standing from the couch to approach Felix. "Everyone is searching for love in some capacity, and when they get hopeful that they may have found it, the reality can catch them completely off guard. You can call yourself a heartbreaker now."

Felix chuckled. "I don't think that's something I'll be bragging about. That was the worst thing I've ever done. Thank God she doesn't know where I live, or I might be worried."

"So it's going to be a dark mood at the office on Monday," Selena said, laughing at herself. "I wonder how long until she gets back to her normal self."

"I don't know," Arielle said. "It can take some time to recover from the unmatched charm of Mr. Felix Francisco."

They all roared with amusement.

"I'm just glad it's finally over," Felix said. "That was *not* fun. I never want to be put in that kind of situation again, if you're taking requests, Arielle. In fact, I'll be fine if you don't even mention anything in the mission report about me doing that. The last thing I need is requests coming in for me to do it again."

"You did so good, though," Arielle said, Selena nodding in agreement. "Even if you don't realize it, what you did has made a major impact on this mission. We're officially set up for the home stretch."

Chapter 41

February 10, 2014

On Monday, Arielle had grown eager enough to finally step away from the job at WonderHome. Her department, though critical for helping Felix gain access to the company's system, lacked opportunity in all other ways. Her colleagues couldn't care less about the happenings outside of their individual projects.

The team was comprised of mostly middle-aged men. They'd gawk at Arielle occasionally, but were otherwise harmless. Before she could turn in her notice to leave, Arielle spent an hour hovering outside of the IT department's workspace, a counter with garage doors that opened up to the rest of the office on the thirty-second floor.

She took one of the open desks in the nearby bullpen, keeping an eye for whenever the rep inside the IT station would step away. Once he did, she stood up and rushed to the aisle, where she saw him disappear down the hallway and into the restroom.

Took long enough. Dude only drank a quarter gallon of water an hour ago.

The coast was clear, the IT station surrounded by only a handful of quiet employees from the accounting team.

Arielle slipped into the IT station, already knowing the table along the back held stacks of laptops that were undergoing repair or being prepared to ship out to remote workers across the country.

Felix had known what he was talking about, as most of the computers on the back table were unassigned in limbo. A junkyard of sorts, with some in perfect shape and others on their final, technical limb.

Arielle snagged one that looked fairly new—she could tell because the charging cord plugged into was still wrapped in plastic, and there wasn't so much as a scuff on the laptop's surface.

She had brought her company backpack and slipped the computer and charger inside, vanishing from the IT station without a peep.

When she returned to her desk, Arielle jumped back into her side project of combing through different email inboxes from employees on the real estate team. She kept running into brick walls like Felix had, and expected as much, since she still had limited access compared to Felix at home. Within the confines of the WonderHome office, Arielle was still an entry-level software engineer and could get nowhere near bank account information or the private inboxes for upper-level management.

Shortly after her lunch break, which she spent hunkered over her computer, desperate to find something and continuing to come up short, when she received a text message from Felix:

Meeting in Michelle's office. 2pm w the execs. She sounds pissed.

Arielle checked her watch to find the time as 1:52 and responded: *Any chance you can share the feed with me? Slow day here.*

She waited for a response, knowing her team was losing hope on this mission. It was hitting Felix the hardest. He had put so much effort into setting matters up for success, yet answers continued to elude them. Arielle didn't waver, though. The money laundering was happening, or going to happen, and every day that passed was one closer to them finally learning the truth. Sometimes, no amount of effort or planning could yield the desired results. Sometimes you just had to wait and let the truth come out on its own.

Felix replied with a link for some sort of screen share to view and listen to his computer screen. Arielle opened it, gratified to find it worked. She saw his screen, showing the inbox of Michelle Garrison, along with another open window she presumed was the audio software connected to the bugged flash drive sitting in Michelle's computer.

He sent a follow up text: *No audio yet. It's voice-activated. We'll hear everything.*

Arielle sent back a thumbs up emoji, grabbed her laptop, and shuffled down the hall until finding a small conference room with only two seats and a desk. They didn't frost the windows to obstruct the view like the bigger conference rooms—these smaller ones were meant for quiet workspaces instead of actual meetings. With her laptop open in front of her to give the appearance of her working, she slid her cell phone on the desk next to it and plugged in a pair of headphones.

It occurred to Arielle that this was the first instance of a meeting in Michelle's office since Felix had bugged it. He had listened to plenty of phone conversations and small talk with Adam, none of which ever discussed the real estate department.

A gnawing suspicion grew in her gut. This meeting was the one to turn the corner on this mission. Why call for a sudden meeting with the executives with virtually no notice?

At 1:58, a hollow knocking sound came from the headphones, along with a static white noise as the flash drive kicked on.

"Come in!" Michelle's voice called out. "Landon, how are you doing?"

Arielle listened as the CFO and CEO caught up after the weekend. Michelle mentioned nothing about being dumped by Felix.

Over the next three minutes, Mila the CMO, and Raj the president trickled into Michelle's office, followed lastly by Adam Marshall.

"Are we expecting anyone else from the team?" Raj asked at 2:03.

"No," Michelle said. "I just wanted to meet with you four. We have an issue, and I'm not sure what we're supposed to do." Her tone shifted into one of intensity. "Landon, what the *fuck* is going on with this real estate project of yours?"

"I beg your pardon," Landon said, entirely surprised.

"We are *bleeding* money for this initiative of yours," Michelle said. "You told us it would only take a few months to get it up and running and bringing in serious money. Now, it didn't look too bad to end the year, but we have another seven weeks until we have to share our first quarter reports to the board, and as of right now, this real estate department has lost over half a million dollars. Are you trying to get us all fired?"

Michelle's tone was furious, accusatory. Arielle wished she could see inside that office.

"I know it looks bad, but lots of things are in motion. This can very well turn into a half a million dollar profit by the end of the next seven weeks."

"Is that true, Mila?" Michelle asked. "Because from what I've seen, there have been virtually no marketing efforts pushed behind this initiative. How are people supposed to buy and sell their houses through WonderHome if they don't know it's even possible?"

"I'm not here to point fingers," Mila said. "But Landon, you haven't submitted any requests to us. We have no idea what kind of language or material we should push publicly. And since we're the first in our industry to do something like this, we're not just going to make something up. I've worked with legal to understand the things we *can't* say, but I need something from your team to actually push out into the world."

"The new section is live on the website," Raj said. "It just released over the weekend. We had a team working all weekend to make sure it ran smoothly, so we really should start seeing some traction."

"That's too organic," Michelle fired back. "Sure, we get millions of visitors to the site every week, but how many go straight to the map or search bar to look for homes? No one is going to notice the new tab on the menu unless we tell them about it. My apologies for sounding like I'm attacking you, Landon. This is a team effort, but since this was your initiative, I expect you to take more control over it. I shouldn't be the one calling this meeting to demand answers—you should have done this yourself."

"I understand," Landon said. "And so you know where I'm coming from, I'm just not worried. I truly believe by the end of March, you'll be looking back at this meeting and will say how silly it was. The money will pour in soon enough. Mila, can we at least get an email and a social media campaign sent to our existing users about this new feature?"

"Done," Mila said. "I can have something out tomorrow."

"Why do I hear about all these contracts Adam has been working on and the bottom line doesn't reflect it?" Michelle asked.

"We've run into some issues," Landon explained. "Nearly every lender has been hesitant to work with us, but I'm working on that issue, too. It's taken some manual work on my part. I'm on the phone all day with different banks trying to explain our program."

"Are you shitting me?!" Michelle cried. "We launched this without having that part of the equation in place?! The actual financial logistics. Absolutely sloppy work."

"Michelle," Landon said. "I'm telling you, it's all under control."

"It'd better be. Because if we report this kind of loss at the end of the quarter, they're going to make us gut it, or worse. I've seen entire teams get fired for reporting losses much smaller than this. Maybe they'll give us the benefit of the doubt, but I don't want to find out. You may not be worried, but honestly, I'm freaking the fuck out. Turn it around, immediately."

"Yes, ma'am," Landon said, cool and confident.

"If you need my help on anything, just let me know. Thank you all for stopping in."

Chapter 42

Arielle rushed home with Selena after work, explaining what had happened.

They found Felix at the dining room table, buried in his laptop.

"Can you believe that meeting?" Arielle asked, pulling out a seat and sitting across from him. Selena joined them at the table, pouring a glass of water.

"Yes, that was really intense," Felix said. "I almost feel bad for Landon, but doesn't it kind of seem like he might be the one responsible? Michelle all but threatened their jobs if he can't get this turned around."

"My thoughts exactly, but how does laundering money help his cause? Isn't the purpose of laundering to *hide* illegal money?"

Felix nodded. "It is, but this is a golden opportunity to kill two birds with one stone. If we assume he's involved in some shady dealings, he can then dump that money into the real estate side of WonderHome by having moles purchase real estate. That gets money onto the books *and* it also masks the dirty money."

"You don't seem entirely convinced it's him," Arielle said. Felix was usually confident once he grabbed hold of an idea, yet that aura wasn't present.

"Don't get me wrong, I feel great after today. No matter how you look at it, this was a breakthrough for us. All signs point to Landon, but we can say with confidence the scheme is tied to anyone who was in Michelle's office for that meeting. I actually don't think Michelle is involved, based on the way she was speaking. She sounded like a pissed-off CEO demanding answers for a suffering portion of their business. Nothing more."

"I heard she was in quite the mood today," Selena said. "Word around the office this morning was to steer clear of Michelle. Someone saw her at the coffee machine. It was broken, and Michelle just started punching it over and over. Busted two of the side panels. Must have had a rough weekend."

Selena laughed at herself and rolled her eyes when no one else did.

"Not now, Selena," Arielle said. "We're on to something here. Felix, I know you started digging into Landon's stuff after that meeting. What did you find?"

"He placed multiple phone calls after that meeting—seven, to be exact. All were to masked phone numbers, so definitely suspicious. No internal calls, as you might think—all were outside of the company."

"Did you find it weird that Adam didn't speak during the meeting?"

"I did at first. It became obvious during that meeting that Adam is *not* the brains behind this scheme, or else he would have had a lot more to say. Michelle acknowledged his workload, but that was it. He's definitely a puppet in all of this, and I don't think he has a clue. We need to find out who is pulling the strings, and our search should obviously start with Landon. He has the most to lose, the pressure is on him, and he's the CFO overlooking all the funds for the company. What we need to find out first is where the illegal money is coming from."

"I can tail him," Arielle said. "In fact, I'd *love* to do that. Gives me something else to do besides rotting in the office. I'm gonna submit my notice tomorrow."

"Tomorrow? Did you even get the—"

"Right here," Arielle said, reaching into her backpack and pulling out the stolen laptop.

"Okay then. I can start setting it up tonight, and you can leave your job in peace."

"Thank you." Arielle sensed a fresh wave of optimism, even if it was just between her and Felix for the time being.

"So you're just gonna leave me to go to work by myself every day?"

Selena asked.

"I'll still be there if I'm following Landon around. I'll just be spending most of my day outside the building waiting for him."

"I've got his address here," Felix said. "Looks like he lives in the Broadmoor neighborhood in northeastern Seattle, right by the bridge that crosses over to Medina. That's over fifteen minutes from here. Rich neighborhood. Not mansions, but large houses and yards. Lots of cars parked on the streets, so you should be able to do your usual stakeouts."

Those words had never sounded so sweet for Arielle. "It's crunch time," she said. "If the laundering hasn't started by now—which it doesn't sound like it—it's going to soon."

Chapter 43

February 11, 2014

The following morning, Arielle stopped by her manager's desk and asked him to speak in private. She told him something had come up in her life that wouldn't allow her to continue working at WonderHome. She needed to return home, and while she could wait out the next two weeks, it would be ideal, if possible, for her to step away today.

Her manager, Adrian Decker, folded his hands on the conference room table. "Is everything okay?" he asked. "If you don't mind me asking."

"Just a family matter," Arielle said. "Trust me when I tell you this was not a simple decision at all. I guess sometimes you just need to roll with the punches in life."

Arielle could dance around this matter until her feet fell off. She had mastered the craft of bullshitting and knew precisely how to use words to create sympathy from others. Here she was, making up a story about nothing, offering no details, yet Adrian leaned back with a concerned face.

"I think we'll be okay if you need to leave today," Adrian said, defeated. "Do you have plans for work wherever you're going?"

"Not yet. I just need to move and get settled before I worry about that."

"Understood. Well, if you need a recommendation from me, just let me know. I'd be more than happy to help however I can."

"Thank you so much." Arielle hadn't realized until this moment just how beneficial having Adrian as her manager had been. Sure, he provided nothing of substance for their mission, which is why she had long considered him useless in the grand scheme. But things could have played out drastically different if she had a different manager. Adrian never micromanaged. He could have easily questioned why Arielle needed a setup at home so soon, or browsed her online activity throughout the day and grilled her about how she spent her downtime. As long as her work got done on time, he stayed out of her way, and that alone brought its own value to the mission. "Thank you for everything. I'm gonna miss this place."

"The pleasure is all mine, Ms. Lucila," Adrian said, standing up and extending his hand. "And if life ever brings you back to Seattle, call me and you'll have a job in no time."

"I appreciate that. Thank you, again. So, do I just go pack up my desk now and leave? I've never done something like this before."

"Yep. I'll take care of everything with POPS. Take care of yourself, and good luck."

Arielle nodded before stepping out of the conference room and returning to her desk that would take only five minutes to pack into a small box.

* * *

When Arielle reached her car before nine o'clock, the whole day ahead of her, she sat behind the wheel in silence to plan her next move. Landon was in the office that she no longer had access to, but that didn't concern her. He was definitely tied up in the laundering, but it was unlikely that he conducted such illegal activity from within the building.

She had only made a handful of friends during her time at the FBI academy, and now was a time she wished she had paid more attention to those relationships. A quick phone call could answer a lot of questions and help point her in the right direction, but she hadn't spoken with any of those colleagues since she left several years ago. She didn't even know which of them still worked with the agency.

Arielle sent a text message to Felix and Selena, letting them know she had quit her job with WonderHome. Felix called her immediately.

"What's up?" Arielle answered.

"I've been diving into Landon's world. Still nothing concrete in his email inbox, but I found his calendar. He keeps everything fairly broad, but I have no idea if that's intentional or just his personality."

"How do you mean?"

"Like his work meetings are just marked as 'meeting' or 'meeting with accounting team', things like that. But I'm noticing a weekly meeting he has scheduled for every Thursday, after hours, titled 'Down by the bay.'"

"Down by the bay? Do you know if he has kids?"

"One sec. Let me check my notes." Arielle waited for a minute while Felix fell silent, the only audible sound his frantic clicking as he rummaged through digital data. "He does not. Why?"

"'Down by the Bay' is a popular kids' song. I thought maybe the calendar event had something to do with a child. What time is the event scheduled for?"

"From six to eight. Every single Thursday."

"Is he married? Girlfriend?"

"Not married. Not sure about a girlfriend. His Facebook profile lists him as single."

"Well damn. It could mean anything. It could be a weekly dinner date, not necessarily romantic, either. Could be a session at a gym. Doctor, therapy."

"It doesn't help that we're in Seattle. There are five bays all within a quick driving distance."

"Exactly. It could even be a weekly fishing session, for all we know."

"I think we need to follow him and see what it's all about. And by we, I mean *you.*"

Arielle laughed. "I'll plan for it this Thursday."

"Good. I wouldn't have called you about it if I didn't think it was suspicious. Nothing else on his calendar is labeled, except for that one recurring meeting."

"Thank you. I think you're right. Psychologically speaking, he may mark it different because it has an elevated importance in his mind. He wants it to stick out when he looks at the calendar. Has he made any noise today?"

"No. He's apparently in meetings until lunchtime, so you might not see him slip out of the building until then."

"Good to know. Back to my long days of staking out the bad guy. Beats sitting in front of a computer all day, I suppose. No offense."

"Whatever floats your boat, Number One."

Arielle giggled. "Hey now, I thought we were past that kind of name-calling."

"We are. Just thought I'd remind you that you're the best. I think sometimes you forget it."

"Well, thank you, Felix."

"No problem. I gotta bounce. Gonna spend my day in front of the computer." Arielle could hear the sarcasm in his voice. "Just promise me you'll be careful out there. We're getting closer, and I have a feeling you might get mixed up with some bad people."

Chapter 44

February 13, 2014

Arielle had followed Landon home Tuesday after work. He stopped by a sandwich shop to grab dinner, which he took back to his vast house and didn't step foot outside for the rest of the evening.

On Wednesday, his regiment had included a stop at a gym for an hour, before grabbing food to-go from a local Italian restaurant just outside of his neighborhood. He stayed in the rest of the evening.

Arielle expected nothing less. It was the middle of the work week, after all. On Thursday, however, they were all expecting something of significance. Felix had dubbed it "Bay Day" and believed whatever the mysterious event on Landon's calendar was would lead to answers for the mission.

The three Angels had gathered on Wednesday night to discuss their ideas on the mission. Arielle liked to do this once a week, but had lost a regular cadence while they all fell into the grind of day-to-day jobs. Besides, nothing was changing during that time.

Confidence reached its peak in the belief that Adam Marshall had no direct involvement in the money laundering. This allowed them to shift their focus on saving Adam from the downfall awaiting him in just three months. They were even ready to cross Michelle Garrison off the list of suspects, but Felix fought against it.

"I don't think she's part of it, either," he had said. "But we need to understand the full picture. She is the CEO, after all, and she *could* be tied in at some capacity we don't understand yet."

They concluded Landon was most likely operating with help from someone else within the company. It could have been anyone on the executive board, or possibly a lower-level employee he could have bribed to help him cover his dirty tracks.

Arielle had found a parking spot in the garage around lunchtime, and took the place directly across the aisle from Landon's blue Corvette. She had backed in to make it easier to follow him on his way out.

Landon had left the office at five o'clock sharp on Tuesday and Wednesday.

He didn't reach his car until 5:35 on Thursday, and Arielle had grown plenty anxious by the time she saw him appear. He wore his usual suit and tie, a heavy briefcase in hand he tossed onto the passenger seat before pulling out of his spot and leaving the garage.

Arielle followed the Corvette, a tight grip around the steering wheel turning her knuckles white. They paused at the gate as Landon swiped his badge to get out. Selena had left her badge with Arielle after swiping herself out earlier to go home, so Arielle used it in the same fashion to get onto the road promptly behind Landon.

The heavy downtown traffic made it nearly impossible for Arielle to lose sight of Landon as they were stop-and-go for the first few minutes rolling down First Avenue. Once they broke free into a clearing, Landon floored his Corvette to blast down westbound Elliott Avenue, eventually merging with Fifteenth Avenue that took them north.

They drove this way for ten minutes, hitting minimal red lights and making great time. When Landon exited at the Port of Seattle, Arielle's stomach fluttered.

"*Down by the bay* definitely meant something near the water," she said to her empty car. They drove through a neighborhood of businesses entirely dedicated to marine life. Boat repair and care. Terminals. Fishing Gear. Seafood restaurants.

They put the Port of Seattle behind them when Landon turned onto Twenty-First Avenue, a road that split civilization on the left, and the bay and piers on the right.

Landon slowed down to drive at a reasonable speed, thanks to the road being filled with cars parked along the sides, pedestrians filling the sidewalks. They reached the end of the road, and Arielle turned off her headlights. She had maintained a safe distance of about fifty yards since they had exited the highway, and it was becoming clear they were about to enter an area in the middle of nowhere.

Landon turned onto a side road labeled as "NW Dock" and honored the posted speed limit of eight miles per hour. The road stretched about a quarter mile, and Arielle found the mixture of boats peculiar as they made their way down the dock. They passed private yachts, fishing boats, and cargo boats. There was even one rather large cargo ship undergoing construction. Parked vehicles filled both sides of the roads. Landon reached the end of the dock and parked under a massive sign that read: *NO PARKING. FIRE LANE.*

A blue fishing boat was anchored around the tether at the end of the pier. A handful of people standing at the boat's entrance waved to Landon when he stepped out of his car.

Arielle found a tight parking spot along the side of the road, and sandwiched herself between a muddy pickup truck and a worn-down Crown Vic. She was roughly one hundred feet away from Landon's car and had a clear view of his illegal parking space.

Two white vans without windows were parked on either side of Landon's Corvette.

Arielle pulled out her binoculars for a closer view.

The people on the fishing boat looked to be all men, though it was difficult to tell since they were all bundled up from head to toe, thanks to the whipping wind that swirled the winter's most recent cold front.

The men stepped off the boat, each shuffling toward Landon, where they stopped and huddled in front of the Corvette. Landon sat on the hood of his car, reached into his suit jacket's interior pocket, and pulled out a packet of cigarettes.

After offering one to each of the men gathered around, he popped one into his mouth and lit it, taking a deep drag before blowing long clouds of smoke into the brisk air.

The men were all dressed in dark colors, and each wore a pair of gloves. One was carrying on the bulk of whatever conversation he and Landon were having, the CFO occasionally nodding and responding.

After three minutes of this back-and-forth, Landon stood up from his car and followed the men onto the boat. Arielle had paid little attention to the contents on the boat, but now saw the stacks of wooden crates lined around the deck's perimeter. The crates were each about five feet long, three feet tall, and two feet deep, all stacked in neat columns of three.

The group on the boat gathered around a crate while one man fiddled with the padlock hanging from it. They shared a round of laughter once the padlock was removed and tossed aside. He lifted the crate's lid and reached in, pulling out a gun nearly as big as his arm.

"Holy shit," Arielle whispered to herself.

Another man reached into the crate and pulled out a second gun, Arielle now able to tell they were both AR-15 rifles. Landon pushed through the huddle, stood on his tiptoes to see deep inside the crate, and reached in.

When he pulled out a bag full of white powder, all of the dots started connecting.

"Son of a bitch," Arielle said. "Cocaine and guns."

She pulled out her cell phone and started snapping pictures, most of them coming out grainy from having to zoom in too much, but still clear enough to tell what was happening.

Landon patted the bag of cocaine like a proud father might pat his child on the head. He tossed it back into the crate. The two men with guns followed by returning the weapons, and watched as the first man put the padlock back on.

Landon shook hands with all five men before one of them ran into the cockpit and returned with a black duffel bag. He dropped it on the floor at Landon's feet, who promptly bent down to unzip it and examine the contents.

Arielle couldn't see. The boat's exterior walls cut off her view of everyone just below their waists, but it was obvious Landon was most likely counting money.

"That money is going to appear in a WonderHome bank account soon, isn't it?" she asked, shaking her head.

She had seen enough, and turned on her engine to get the hell out of there before anyone could spot her.

Chapter 45

"It's Landon," Arielle said, having just burst into the house, where Felix and Selena were watching *This is 40* in the living room.

Felix powered off the TV, vaulting off the couch. "What happened?!"

"His calendar event is a meeting, all right. He drove all the way to the docks at Salmon Bay for a drug and weapons deal."

"Jackpot," Felix said. "There's the source of the dirty money. So Landon is facilitating these deals and collecting enormous sums of money to launder through the real estate program. We did it, guys. This knowledge makes the mission pretty straightforward from here."

Arielle shook her head. "This is just important information. We still have to figure out what to do with it."

"Well, sure," Selena said, finally standing to join the conversation. "But do you honestly think we're not going to? All we've needed to know is who was behind this, and now we have our guy. The next step is just figuring how to tie the crime to Landon instead of Adam."

"Exactly," Arielle said. "This is where it gets dangerous. We don't know anything about those men on the boat tonight. I had no way of identifying them. We don't know what we're going up against."

"Why get involved with those guys?" Selena asked. "We shouldn't need to. For all we care, Landon can keep on having his weekly meetings and bring in the money. We just need to figure out the part of the equation that takes Adam Marshall out of the picture and leaves Landon as the lone target."

"I'm aware of all that, but we don't know how it's going to play out.

We should still be prepared to deal with these drugs and weapons dealers because we don't know how the rest of this mission will play out. We're still going to follow Landon every time he steps out of the office, and that could mean getting close to these people he's dealing with. And I agree with Selena. We shouldn't interfere with Landon's illegal activities. Our job was to prevent the murder-suicide of the Marshall family, and that begins with painting Adam as innocent."

"How do we know Adam *isn't* involved?" Felix asked. "Sure, we know Landon is the one pulling the strings and not Michelle. But Adam's supposedly working on real estate matters on behalf of WonderHome, and we can't find anything that actually shows this as true. Something still isn't adding up."

"That's all a good point, and I'm sure it's just a matter of sorting out the moving parts," Arielle said. "I've actually been toying with the idea of us trying to sell this house to WonderHome, just to see what happens from our end. The laundering has to take place when WonderHome buys property from someone selling their home. I don't see another opportunity where such a thing can happen. But that opens up another question. If Landon is laundering his own money through the company, there is still a disconnect somewhere. He can't just show up to the bank and deposit duffel bags of cash into the company's account, can he?"

Felix nodded. "He actually can if he's an authorized user on the company checking account. And as the CFO, I'd imagine he definitely is. Even so, that wouldn't work. Companies this large have accounting teams dedicated entirely to making sure every cent is accounted for. If money comes in, they must notate a reason. Same when money goes out. They balance the books at least once a month, from what I've been able to find digging through the accounting team's work. And if there is even a single discrepancy, the accountants reach out to all parties involved on a particular transaction, demanding answers. This is literally how companies remain compliant and avoid money laundering."

"But he's the CFO," Arielle said. "Literally in charge of the entire accounting department and all money activity for the company. It wouldn't be a stretch for him to have fudged these cash deposits as something related to the business—especially with it being cash. All he'd really need is one or two people to be in on the scheme to pull this off."

"Or an entire team," Selena said. "Felix, have you reviewed the members of the real estate team?"

"Of course," Felix said. "Their activity looks completely normal. They negotiate contracts with home buyers and sellers. It's all pretty standard."

"I think Arielle may be on to something. We need to investigate the process, and what better way than to do it by selling our house?"

"Well, I don't think we can sell this house," Felix said. "It belongs to the Road Runners, and we can't just decide to do that for the sake of a mission. What I *can* do is check in with *our* real estate team and see if there is a property in the area they're willing to sell. If so, I can handle that transaction with WonderHome, and we can follow the paper trail from there. I'm not sold that WonderHome buying properties from sellers is when the laundering takes place. That's money going out. Laundering has to be when the money comes *in*."

"So, when WonderHome sells the property they've purchased," Arielle said. "That would mean the people buying the homes are part of the scheme. That doesn't seem possible. Aren't they selling hundreds of homes each day across the country?"

"I don't think it's as many as you think," Felix said. "It might grow to that now that Landon is getting desperate to save his job and his entire scheme. But their team doesn't have enough members to pull off that many transactions. I'll look through their recent contracts again, but nothing stood out in terms of suspicious deals. Maybe that's all about to start now after that heated meeting with Michelle."

"Do you know how many people are on that team, Selena?" Arielle asked.

Selena looked upward, thinking. "I can double-check when I'm in the office, but I would guess around forty."

"And I assume these realtors get paid on some sort of commission, yeah?"

"Definitely."

"Felix," Arielle said, turning to face him. "Would you be able to get into payroll's system and see what each individual realtor is making on commissions?"

"Yeah, I can do that," Felix replied. "Where are you going with this? I see your wheels turning."

Arielle's wheels were always turning. "I think we need to have a talk with one of these realtors. Perhaps one who will talk to us about what really is going on. Selena, you have access in your department to see these realtors' personal information, right? Like their marriage status, children, things like that?"

"Absolutely," Selena said. "That's all standard information I can get easily."

"Tomorrow is Friday. I don't want to take this into the weekend. If we can get profiles completed for each realtor, we can narrow it down to who we want to approach."

"How do you plan on confronting whoever we choose?" Felix asked, brow furrowed in curiosity. "You worked there—someone might recognize you."

"I doubt it. We were on completely different floors. I don't recall seeing anyone from the real estate team after finishing training. So we can avoid anyone from my training class, and we should be fine. I'm not Ms. Popular over there." Arielle nodded at Selena, who responded with a satisfied laugh. "Depending who we select will determine my approach. I'd love for it to be a civil conversation—I don't even mind paying off one of these realtors to get the info we need. I also don't mind shaking one of them down. We need our answers."

"Well, well," Felix said, crossing arms and shooting a smile across the room. "Look who's back to being herself now that she's out of the office. It only took one night of following Landon when he actually did something, and you're firing on all cylinders. I wouldn't be surprised if we're going home next weekend at this rate."

Arielle grinned. "I've been here this whole time—just hasn't been much of an opportunity to do anything. Now that we have some action, it's time to get shit done. So, what do you both say? Let's get those profiles ready tonight. Tomorrow is going to change everything."

"I'll say," Selena said. "Felix, why don't you give me one of those spy pens?"

Chapter 46

February 14, 2014

On Friday morning, Arielle was ready for the day by seven o'clock, but not because she *needed* to. Felix was right. She was back on the ball since leaving her job behind at WonderHome.

She hadn't even realized how dead she had felt during that time, stuck inside the office like a fish in a glass bowl, unable to explore the town and dive deep to investigate suspects in this ever-changing mission.

Felix and Selena worked hard into the night, providing Arielle with a list of forty-three realtors employed by WonderHome, along with their commission averages, performance reviews, and familial situations.

Arielle had received the list shortly after 10 P.M. and reviewed it thoroughly until one o'clock in the morning, when she called it a night and selected who she would approach the following day: Owen Adams.

Owen had been working at WonderHome for six months, one of the original ten realtors hired at the launch of the company's new real estate program. Despite the experience in the role, Owen was currently on a performance improvement plan, also known as a PIP, because of lackluster results in the field. He averaged one closing per month, while many of his colleagues from the same class averaged one per week.

Owen's placement on a PIP meant he had ninety days to improve or risk losing his job. According to the metrics Felix could find, satisfactory performance meant at least two closings per month. It had been fifteen days, and he still had no closings in February.

What stuck out the most about Owen, besides his potential to lose his job, was he had married just over a year ago and had a two-month-old infant at home. Arielle needed someone vulnerable to approach about the shady dealings taking place at WonderHome, and who better than a fresh realtor—WonderHome had helped him get his license upon his hiring—who couldn't afford to lose his only stream of income.

He was twenty-six, eager to prove himself, and failing miserably.

Arielle had sent him an email through WonderHome's portal, asking to view a house the following morning. She stressed she was only available between eight and ten and wanted to see the property as soon as possible.

She didn't know if such a simple request would work to lure Owen, but it was his job, after all. When her phone rang at 7:30 from an unknown number in the Seattle area code, she knew it was him.

"Hello?"

"Yes, hi," Owen said. "Is this Arielle? My name is Owen—I'm calling in response to a request you sent last night to view a property."

He spoke fast, as if he had been used to getting hung up on while delivering his spiel.

"Yes, Owen, good morning. Thank you for calling. Are you able to show the property today?"

"I sure can, and I can meet you there at eight, if that works."

"Can we make it eight-fifteen? I'm running just a few minutes behind."

"Absolutely." Owen's voice elevated to a higher pitch filled with glee and hope. She wondered if he treated every showing like this, only to have something go astray before a closing could happen and dampen his dreams.

"Perfect, I'll see you there."

Arielle hung up and left the house, stopping first at the bank where she had to wait until they opened at exactly eight o'clock. She had heard the desperation in Owen's voice, and figured two thousand dollars would be enough for him to share everything he knew. She didn't want to rattle the man, who sounded like he might jump away from his own shadow. It was no wonder he wasn't cutting it in real estate. Successful realtors had confidence. They could walk into a home and tell you everything right and wrong with the place with a quick fifteen-minute tour. They knew what they could squeeze out of the seller during negotiations and how to lower all the bullshit costs and fees that typically fell upon the buyer. Just hearing Owen over the phone, she figured he probably struggled to even get the front door unlocked.

At eight, Arielle was first in line at the bank, withdrew the cash, and was on her way. She had found a property listed on WonderHome's website just outside of her neighborhood, a short five-minute drive away.

She arrived at the property and found the one-level home a disaster. Shingles were missing from the roof. The main window had a wide crack webbing out from the center. The screen door hung crookedly off the hinges. And the lawn was nothing but a scatter of dirt and weeds, trash littered about.

Parked in the driveway was a Toyota Prius, so Arielle pulled up and parked behind it, ensuring Owen couldn't leave until Arielle was ready.

Owen got out of the Prius, and Arielle immediately recognized him. She had seen him around the office, if only in passing. He was tall with a messy mop of black hair, his face droopy. If Arielle hadn't known any different she would have figured he was the IT guy for some startup tech company operating out of the CEO's basement.

"Arielle?" he asked, sticking out a hand.

"Yes, you must be Owen."

The stench of coffee oozed from his breath. Dark bags clung to his bottom eyelids. He was clearly the parent of a newborn, dodging sleep at every opportunity.

"You're aware this is a home for flipping, correct?" Owen asked. "Just always like to make sure of that before we go in. It needs a *ton* of work."

"Yes, I figured as much," Arielle said, following Owen to the front door where a lockbox hung from the doorknob.

"Good. It's honestly the best way to get a killer price, assuming you know how to do a lot of the repairs on your own."

He fumbled with the combination lock on the box, cussing under his breath as he had to do it three times before the little door popped open to reveal the key.

I knew it, Arielle thought, fighting off a laugh. *This poor guy has no future in real estate. He needs to take the money I'm about to offer and run.*

Owen unlocked and pushed the door to find it stuck. After another failed attempt, he lowered his shoulder into the door with enough force to get the damned thing open.

A musty smell flooded their senses immediately as they stepped into the house.

Carpet covered the floor as far as they could see, frayed along the edges. The walls had holes and splatters of random paint colors.

"The kitchen has carpet?" Owen asked, more to himself, his face drawn in complete bafflement. "Who in the world would do such a thing?"

He let out a nervous laugh, probably assuming he was already losing his next opportunity at a sale.

"Well, there's no need to worry," Arielle said. "I'm not buying this house."

"Oh?" he replied, not sounding entirely surprised. "But we just got here."

"I know. But I was never buying this house. I needed to get you in private to speak with you, if you don't mind."

Owen's eyes focused on Arielle, and she could see his mind trying to figure out what the hell was going on.

"I'm sorry," she said. "I shouldn't have led with that. Owen, I'm a private investigator looking into the dealings of the new real estate team at WonderHome. Would you mind if I ask you a few questions? I understand you've been there for six months now, working in this same role, correct?"

Owen gulped, his fingers fidgeting .

"You have nothing to worry about," Arielle said. "This isn't about you directly. You're not in any sort of trouble. I can't just barge into your office and demand to speak with someone, so investigators like myself have to get creative. Hence, why I've asked you here this morning."

"Okay," Owen said, unsure of himself. "I don't know if I can be of much help."

Arielle sensed the anxiety emanating from Owen, could almost smell it over the rotten stench of water damage that had never been treated. Somewhere inside these walls were pipes and framing devoured by mold.

"I can sweeten the pot for you," Arielle said, reaching into her coat pocket and pulling out the wad of cash. "I know you're not doing too well selling houses. Here is two thousand dollars to help you get by if you'll just answer some questions for me as honestly as you can."

Owen's eyes bulged, and she figured she could have gotten the same reaction with half the amount.

"Okay," Owen said. "What do you want to know?"

"Thank you. And seriously, relax. This has nothing to do with you."

Owen nodded, and she watched the tension leave from his hands as they stood awkwardly facing each other in this abandoned home.

"You've been on this team since it first launched, right?" Arielle asked.

"Yes. My training class was first."

"And the CFO, Landon Greene, created this entire team. Is that correct?"

"Yes."

"Did he have any involvement during your training?"

"Yes. He basically trained all of us himself."

"Interesting. Did you not find it odd that the CFO would take, what, two to three weeks out of his schedule to do training? Doesn't WonderHome have a team of dedicated trainers?"

"Well, sure, it was weird. But WonderHome isn't your typical company. They do things differently, so I didn't think anything of it. It was all his idea, and he had mentioned how no one on the training team had ever done real estate before, so there was no point in having them try to teach it."

"And who does the training now? I can't imagine Mr. Greene is still taking time out of his busy schedule to train new realtors."

"Our team takes the training directly after the new hires finish their orientation part of training. We have two managers who take the bulk of training, but sometimes us realtors get called on to help."

"And how often does your team hear from the CFO? Whether that's in-person meetings, or even an email to the team."

Owen scrunched his face, his lips crookedly pursed while he thought. "I'd say about once a week. He still sends out a lot of emails about our team's performance since we're still pretty new. He's always done that. I guess he likes to be transparent with our performance."

"And how has that performance been? What did he say in his most recent email?"

"He said our team is struggling to stay afloat, and that we need to close more deals, or else. He told us to keep doing the work, and we'll find the qualified buyers in no time. Stressed to not get desperate."

"And do you feel desperate?"

"I do, yes. This is my first job in the professional world and I don't want to lose it already. I feel like I'm just getting the hang of it."

"I see. And what can you tell me about the actual closing process? How involved are you, as the realtor?"

"We help all the way until the actual closing. We do the showings, communicate with lenders on behalf of the buyers..."

"So you work with only buyers?"

"Personally, yes. But our team has other realtors who specialize in working with sellers, and they try to negotiate deals for them to sell their home directly to WonderHome."

"Aren't realtors typically present on the day of a closing? It's a big moment for everyone involved."

Owen shrugged. "I told you, this is my first professional job, so I don't know what the norm is. I just know with WonderHome, they take care of the contract and transaction, so I can move on to the next showing and hopefully find the next deal we can close on."

"And that's how it's always been, this part of the process?"

"Yes."

"Do you know who at the company handles the contracts? Someone *has* to put their signature on the form."

Owen shrugged. "No idea. When I come to an agreement with a buyer, I draft up the basic details and send it to my manager. He takes it from there, and I have no clue what happens."

"Do you ever deal with Adam Marshall?"

Owen stared at Arielle as if his mind were absent from this conversation.

"I don't know who that is. I think I've heard the name Eric mentioned around the closing part, but I don't even know an Eric at the office, so don't hold me to that."

The mention of Eric caught Arielle off guard. She wasn't familiar with the name either, which gave her hope that they were on to something new.

"You're doing great, and I thank you for that. I just have a few more questions and we can both be on our way. Let's pretend the person's name is indeed Eric. Once Eric signs the contracts, you get paid your commission, right?"

"Yes, five percent of the final closing amount. Gets paid out on the following paycheck."

"And you've never had an issue? They've always paid you on time?"

"No issues."

"And do all of your potential clients reach out to you how I did, or are there other ways?"

"There are lots of ways: an online form like you did, inbound phone call, and sometimes we get a list of home buyers sent to us. That's where I've had most of my luck."

"I see. Where does that list come from?"

"We get it from our manager. They assign everyone a list of clients to follow up with and see if they're still interested in buying properties. I think WonderHome uses some of their internal information, since they can see who is browsing the site, because most of these calls the people sound surprised to hear from us. But now and then, it's like we make the perfect connection and the buyer is ready at that moment to get a deal done."

"Interesting," Arielle said, more to herself. "And how often do you get this list?"

"About once a week. We were told yesterday we'll start getting more of these types of clients, and they're hoping to make them more qualified. But I haven't seen anything yet."

"I see. I think that's all of my questions. Are you okay if I reach out to you down the road if I think of anything else?"

"I guess," Owen said, eyeing the money that Arielle held in her hand during the entire questioning. She had no plans of ever speaking to this man again, and handed over the money.

Owen examined it like it couldn't possibly be real. Once he realized it was, he stuffed the wad of cash into his pocket. "Thank you. This actually helps me more than you know."

"No, thank you, Owen. You've been a tremendous help and made this process much easier than it usually is. If I can leave you with one piece of advice before we part ways. Leave your job at WonderHome. Just trust me on that. Start looking now, and get out as soon as you can."

She turned and left him dumbfounded in the house. When she reached her car, he still hadn't appeared outside. Poor guy was probably suffering an anxiety attack after everything that had just happened, but Arielle had to leave.

She understood what was happening, and how to bring the entire scheme down.

Chapter 47

February 17, 2014

Selena had taken one of Felix's microphone pens to work on Friday and planted it in Landon's pen cup with no detection. Only Michelle kept her door closed on the executive floor. Selena found a conference room along the hallway with a direct view of Landon's office. Once she saw him step away and enter the bathroom, she glided right in and planted the pen. The executive floor was known for being a ghost town, and it was even more abandoned so early on a Friday morning.

No one saw her, and she vanished without a trace.

Felix began listening immediately, and Friday ended with nothing of substance. Landon had even called it a day after the lunch hour and was gone for the weekend.

Arielle had followed him home, but he simply ventured into his house and hadn't come back out when Arielle decided she had wasted enough time and left at five o'clock.

Over the weekend, with not much else to do, Arielle demanded they unplug and take a step back to prepare for a chaotic week ahead.

"We're going to get aggressive starting next week," she had told them. "We have a basic understanding of what's going on and where the obvious opportunities are for the money laundering to occur. Let's apply some pressure on everyone involved and see if we can't cause a panic."

They agreed to spend their Sunday at the EMP Museum and its dozens of exhibits covering American pop culture throughout the years.

By the time they arrived home later that night, after a fun dinner out downtown, Arielle knew her idea for a laid-back weekend had worked. Felix and Selena were not only ready for Monday, but excited at the prospects of the new week.

On Monday morning, the breakfast table hummed with an anxious anticipation.

"All right, the weekend is over," Felix said. "You said you wouldn't talk about the mission until Monday, so let's hear it. What do you have up your sleeve for this week?"

Arielle took a bite of her Fruit Loops before answering. "I don't want to get our hopes up, but I think we can end this mission this week. If not, next week at the latest."

"Say what?!" Selena cried, jumping out of her seat.

Arielle raised her hand to silence the energetic Selena. "My ideas take time to marinate. I may have not discussed the mission, but trust me, it's all I thought about this weekend. The way I see things, Landon is playing two different roles at the same time. He's the CFO for WonderHome, and also the one behind these drug and weapons deals—who exactly he is in *that* whole scheme, I don't know. I also don't care. We're here to get Adam Marshall off the hook. If they want us to investigate Landon and his dealings separately, they can assign another mission for that."

"So, what are we doing?" Selena asked, urgency clinging to every word.

"There are a lot of moving parts, but I think we can cover all of them. Landon is desperate right now. His job is on the line, and if he loses it, he can kiss his laundering operation goodbye. Felix got us some snapshots of the company's bank accounts. They've spent a ton of money buying properties across the country. Properties that are not selling at the prices they're looking for. I don't think Landon has ever worked directly in real estate, because he didn't entirely think the program through. Their whole angle was to buy properties needing lots of work, to then resell at a higher cost. Now, I don't know if this was intentional, or if this somehow fell through massive cracks, but WonderHome has no way of improving these homes they're buying. It would have made sense for them to hire contractors directly to their payroll and deploy them to each home needing repairs. But that never happened, and it makes zero sense why not. Because of this, I believe it has always been Landon's intent to use the entire program for his laundering purposes."

"So, this has all been going on for months?" Felix asked.

"Not necessarily the laundering, but the plans for it. The real estate program was the framework to make it all possible. With it now fully in operation, Landon can start funneling the funds back into the company."

"I still don't understand how this gets Landon paid," Selena said.

"Felix, shed some light on that part, please," Arielle said.

"Yes," he replied. "I found the original email conversations from before the real estate program even launched. The CFO is to receive fifty percent of all profits from the real estate program, paid out monthly as a commission."

"Fifty percent?!" Selena gasped. "That's outrageous and makes no sense. He's losing a lot of money by doing that."

Arielle nodded. "He is, but this is all being set up for the long term. If this runs smoothly, Landon can have a constant supply of bonus money coming his way, completely legal in the eyes of the government, all without ever having his name tied to anything illegal. On paper, the company makes money from this program, which keeps them happy with his employment, meanwhile he's pulling in half of whatever he's making off these drug deals without a worry in the world. It's actually kind of genius because it can literally last until he retires. And at thirty-six years old, that's a lot of money to be made. It makes sense why he didn't seem worried at all during that meeting with Michelle, and it's because he's pulling all the strings. I've done some more reading on major laundering schemes over the years, and I'm fairly confident his next move is to pay off people to buy these worthless properties. We're ahead of him."

"How do you figure?" Selena asked.

"Because whatever money he's made from his illegal dealings hasn't made its way into WonderHome yet. Now, it's clear Landon is not some evil genius, or he would have covered more bases. I think the higher-earning realtors are in on the scheme, but Landon hasn't entrusted everyone on the team. Too many people involved opens up the possibilities of getting caught. Someone always gets too greedy and blackmails the ringleader. It's a tale as old as time. Now, Landon needs to turn things around quickly, and there is a simple way he can do that. He can bribe people to buy these properties for a certain amount of money. He can do this a couple of ways. Option one is by paying someone a flat rate to do it. He can offer, let's say, ten thousand dollars to call into WonderHome with an interest to buy one of their properties. He can have them claim they want to buy the property with cash, which eliminates the need for a lender and all of that paperwork. Since WonderHome owns the deed on the property, all they need to do is take the paperwork and sign it over to the pretend buyer's name. The buyer leaves with their ten thousand, and WonderHome can file the paperwork as a successful closing, all while depositing the cash from the alleged purchase. Boom, the drug money is now legally on the books for WonderHome.

"Option two would include Landon preying on those less fortunate. He can seek out the poor and make them the same offer, only instead of a cash payment, they can live in the house rent-free. He can literally offer this to the homeless and they'll agree to it. They won't *need* the running water or electricity, since they can't pay those bills, but it's a roof over their head. A lot of these properties are already in pretty run-down neighborhoods, so it's not like some trust fund family will have a homeless person moving in next door. *That* would cause many problems for Landon. But the way it's all set up now—intentionally, I'm sure—no one will bat an eye."

"So if he's thinking of the future, option one is probably the most likely route," Felix said. "Less opportunity for things to go awry."

"I agree," Selena said.

"As do I," Arielle added. "Now, where do we come in to this? I want to scare some of these hired home buyers. We will follow one of the top-earning realtors from WonderHome, and if we see them showing a run-down home to someone, we'll know that's exactly what's at play. There are only five real estate agents at WonderHome who are bringing in big money. Everyone else is struggling, like my friend Owen. The five have to be working directly with Landon while the rest get left out to dry, trying to sell homes that no one actually wants to buy. I think the new classes that keep coming in for the real estate team are intentionally big. It's all a numbers game. New hires come in, and Landon sorts through them to find even just one person who can join his small team on the scheme. They have to be trustworthy, in Landon's eyes, and if so, they all get to make tons of money together, sworn to carry this secret to their graves."

"Do you think he threatens them?" Selena asked. "I can always ask for a transfer to the real estate team."

"I'm sure he threatens them with reality. If any of them get caught, they're going to prison for a long time. It's simple. And if someone else gets caught, you keep your mouth shut. Now, after my meeting with Owen, I'm quite confident we can continue to play the role of a private investigator. I want to approach these fake home buyers and threaten them. I'm not interested in taking their money or anything like that, I just want them scared. If we scare enough, one of them will crack and reach back out to their WonderHome agent who crafted the deal. That agent will tell Landon what happened. And once Landon gets word that his real estate program is being watched, well, we sit back and watch the fireworks."

Felix laughed. "You wouldn't sit back. That's not the Arielle Lucila way. Once you smell that blood, we all know you're going to pounce like a lion on a wounded zebra."

Arielle smiled. "That's probably true. I want to go home, and I know you both do too. That's why I've already called in for you today, Selena, and for the rest of the week, in fact."

"What?! How did you—? When did you—?"

"I called this morning and said you had an unexpected family emergency and won't be in for the rest of the week. The attendance line is just an answering machine. It wasn't too hard to sound like you." Felix burst into laughter. Arielle turned to him with a devilish grin. "And what's so funny over there, Mr. Francisco? I called out for Selena so you wouldn't have to join us today in acting like private investigators. Unless you'd like to, of course."

Felix's laughing and his grin halted immediately. "No. Thank you for doing that."

"Exactly. Selena, I have the names of the agents we're going to follow. These high-performers are collectively closing three deals a day, but I suspect that will start ramping up even more now that Landon has to show some big numbers coming into the company. Felix can access their schedules, so we'll know exactly where they're going. We won't be together this week so we can cover more ground, but our job is simple. Look for the transaction that makes no sense, then approach the pretend buyer once they're out of sight from the realtor. Tell them we're investigating real estate fraud and have some questions. Make up the questions, it doesn't matter, because by the time you've already said all that, they're going to be shitting their pants. Leave them in peace afterwards and tell Felix once you've done it. Felix, you'll need to keep a close eye on Landon's inbox and potential conversations in his office after these encounters."

"How do you figure this takes a week?" Felix said. "We have no idea if or when any of these people will reach out to their WonderHome agent."

"Exactly, that's why I said a two-week cushion," Arielle said. "Some-one *will* talk. I'm confident about that. It's human nature to panic if you think you might go to prison, especially for something you just did, like we'll be doing with these fake buyers. It's even more natural to seek blame and point fingers, which is what will happen when they reach out to their agent. Then the dominoes fall, and we swoop in to complete the mission."

"This is honestly a brilliant plan," Selena said. "But what if it takes some time before someone calls back in? Then what?"

"Well," Arielle replied. "We can wait patiently. I have no issue with that. But we know where Landon will be every Thursday night. I don't mind sending him a little warning shot while he's there. Hell, I might do it either way. That warning shot can do a lot more damage if he already thinks he's being watched. Then he'll really unravel. Because if I've learned one thing about these types of criminals, and further confirmed through his lackluster planning of the real estate program, is that they never have plans for getting caught."

Felix nodded and stood up, prompting Arielle to do the same. "I'm ready to get to work. But I have one question. How does all this get tied back to Adam Marshall?"

Arielle walked her empty cereal bowl to the sink and turned around, crossing her arms. "I haven't been able to confirm this yet, but I'm pretty sure Adam is the one signing these real estate contracts on behalf of WonderHome. It's why we haven't been able to find anything—it's all physical paper contracts with his name in ink."

"But how does that responsibility fall to him?"

Arielle laughed. "Do you really not see it? Because that's what they hired him to do."

Chapter 48

Arielle and Selena each took a car and went their separate ways after the motivational breakfast. Felix hung back to monitor the surveillance activity set up in both Michelle's and Landon's offices.

Selena had yet to feel this level of optimism while on this mission, content to enjoy the ride as a popular new employee at WonderHome. Even that honeymoon was fizzling, the energy fading quickly as she got deeper into a routine at work, every day feeling like the same thing after another. She supposed that was natural, and a reason many in her generation hopped around from job to job.

Knowing she had a week off from going to the office (and potentially never returning), driving across town energized her in a way she hadn't realized she needed. She had no idea what awaited over the course of the day, no clue when she might return home, and no idea who she might meet today. Plus, she got to act in a different role when approaching these realtors.

According to their schedules for showings, Arielle and Selena would each confront two different realtors during the day.

Felix had shared the details with them about how WonderHome managed these transactions, and where they would be best suited to intercept the fake buyers.

The transactions were unorthodox for real estate purchases, where the alleged buyer would meet the realtor at the property. They would enter and do a final walkthrough, and sign the paperwork there on the spot. Even for a cash transaction, this process seemed strange, but

WonderHome touted same-day closings for cash buyers as a perk of their program.

How this wasn't seen as a red flag by whichever authorities monitored money laundering was beyond Selena. Or perhaps that was exactly what led to them being caught in the original timeline of events where everything was tied to Adam Marshall.

Selena's first target of the morning was Cody Hayes, the top-ranked realtor on the real estate for WonderHome. According to their records, Cody was closing at least three transactions per week for the last two months, most of which were run-down homes that sold for well above their value.

Arielle had insisted Selena take Cody, claiming she had earned the right.

That familiar sense of destiny worked its way through Selena's body as she entered the neighborhood. Vehicles with deflated tires, scratched paint jobs, and cracked windows lined the curbs. Nearly every business had bars over their windows, graffiti sprayed on the side of the buildings. Stray dogs roamed the streets, and not a single property kept a maintained front lawn. Most had more cars parked right on the patches of grass and weeds outside the front door.

The houses were in even worse shape, and Selena figured none of them could sell for more than one hundred thousand in 2014, if that.

I'm in the right place, Selena thought. *It's going down right here to start the day.*

The meeting between Cody and the buyer was scheduled for ten o'clock, and Selena arrived at 9:45, parking across the street and two houses down where she could have a clear view of the property in question. For a neighborhood that lacked any sort of colorful cheer, the bright green and yellow WonderHome "For Sale" sign stuck out like an orange in a batch of apples.

Selena parked and killed the engine, checking her surroundings. She had turned off the main road and found herself on a long block of ranch-style homes, trees providing plenty of overhead coverage.

She parked in front of a house that appeared abandoned, one of the few without cars stuffed into the driveway and lawn. Most of the homes on the block had their dumpsters rolled out to the curb for trash pickup. It was the middle of the morning when the kids would be at school and most people at work.

Selena watched as a shiny black car turned onto the block from the main road, rolling steadily down the street and stopping in front of the house for sale.

"There you are," Selena said, leaning forward for a better look, but unable to see anything through the blacked-out tinted windows. The car, an Audi of some sorts, was clearly out of place.

The door swung open and out stepped Cody Hayes, a tall and skinny kid with black hair slicked to the side. He wore a long gray peacoat and black gloves, and strutted to the house's front door with plenty of swagger and confidence.

"You slimy motherfucker," Selena said, shaking her head, wishing she could hop out and key this cocky dude's car.

While she had known plenty of rich and narcissistic people, she suspected none of them earned their money in such a fake way. Most had taken gambles in the stock market or risky business ventures that ended up paying out. And most donated money to charitable causes, even if only for a tax write-off.

How low could a person go for a quick buck? Selena was now finding out, and hoped all the realtors who took part in this scheme would go down in flames with Landon once it all collapsed around him.

Cody disappeared into the house without so much as a look over his shoulder. That told Selena that he had become comfortable in such settings, especially considering he hadn't even locked his Audi despite it being out on the curb.

"There is definitely a closing about to happen."

She only had to wait five more minutes until the next car appeared on the block, parking in the driveway.

A heavyset bald man stepped out of the Ford Focus and scratched his gray goatee before stretching. He was much bigger than Selena and could pose issues should he get physical when she encountered him. But there was no way he was fast on his feet, something she would play to her advantage if matters escalated to that point.

"Where do you even find people to do something like this?" she asked the empty car. Was there a network of regular folks looking for easy money to help money launderers?

None of that mattered, and when the bald man let himself into the house without knocking, she had one hundred percent confidence this was all part of the scheme.

The urge to disrupt the transaction from even happening swelled within Selena, but she knew better than to step into a situation where she'd be outnumbered. They still didn't understand exactly what *type* of people they were dealing with.

Fifteen minutes passed when Selena grew antsy, wondering what was taking so long. But it was only another five minutes after that when both men emerged from the house, a shit-eating grin smacked across Cody's face.

They made their way to the WonderHome sign standing tall near the sidewalk. Cody grabbed both sides and wiggled it out of the earth, tossing it into the next-door neighbor's dumpster.

The men laughed and shook hands, the fake buyer patting his pocket where an obvious wad of cash had been stuffed, appearing like a bulge of rocks in his pants.

Cody hopped into his car first and sped away with a quick wave out the window to his most recent buyer.

The man trudged down the driveway, moving gingerly as he strolled around his vehicle.

"I can take this guy," Selena said, slipping on a pair of sunglasses, stepping out of her car, and dashing across the street.

The man hadn't seen her yet. As she approached him, she shouted, "Hey! Excuse me!"

The man was getting ready to open his car door and had his back to Selena when he heard this. He stopped and spun around, a dumbstruck look on his face.

"Can I help you?" he asked, his voice deep and slow.

"You sure can. Start by telling me what happened in there."

The man's hand gradually inched toward his bulging pocket, and he covered it with his massive palm. "I don't know what you're talking about."

"Of course you do," she said. "This house has been up for sale. You went inside and came out, and now that sign is gone. Did you just buy this house?"

The man looked around the neighborhood, and Selena had no way of knowing if he was scared or planning to try something. Either way, she was prepared.

"Do you live on the block or something?" he asked. "You one of those nosy neighbors?"

Selena grinned and crossed her arms, glaring at the man from behind her sunglasses. She knew wearing them would intimidate him. The oldest trick in the book was to interrogate someone and not allow them to see your eyes.

"I'm not your neighbor," Selena said smoothly, growing confident the man wouldn't try to hurt her. "I'm a private investigator looking into WonderHome. Did you just buy this home from one of their real estate agents?"

The man gulped, looked up, looked down, all the while his fingers clenched the bulge in his pocket. "I, uh. Yes, I did. I bought this home."

"Really? Do you have any paperwork proving this?"

The man parted his lips and started looking in every direction *except* at Selena. "I, uh. No, I don't. My realtor just left here. He's going to finish the contract so I can sign it."

"Right," Selena said, taking one more step closer to the large man. "So, when do you close?"

Beads of sweat formed around the man's forehead, despite the morning being a cool forty degrees. "Next week," he said, continuing to avoid eye contact.

"I see. Are you aware that I know you're lying? I can see right through you. Standing here sweating like a Catholic in church. If you're going to be involved in such criminal activity, you should at least learn how to lie and remain calm under pressure, because people like you are the ones who always end up in jail."

"I didn't do nothing, lady," the man said.

Selena smiled. "Let's take a step back. What's your name?"

The man hesitated, not replying for twenty seconds.

"Well?" Selena asked.

"Ed," he said. "Ed Zimmerman."

"If you say so. Ed, let me start over and say that you're not in any sort of trouble. I'm not here to investigate *you*. I don't care about that cash in your pocket. You will walk away from this conversation with your money. If someone else wants to come after you later, then that's their business. I want to know what WonderHome is doing. How much did they pay you just now?"

Ed was squeezing his pocket so tightly his knuckles were a sheet of white. "Ten thousand dollars."

"Ten thousand?! Christ, I'm in the wrong line of work. And for what? All you had to do was sign a deed for the house, yeah?"

Ed nodded slowly.

"Again, I'm not coming after you, but I'm just curious. Are you aware that you're assisting WonderHome in a money laundering scheme?"

Ed nodded again, not speaking, still not making eye contact. Selena figured his throat had probably tensed completely shut.

"Are you aware of the punishment for aiding in such a crime?"

Ed shook his head.

"It's twenty years, Ed. Twenty years in prison. *And* you have to pay back all the illegal money you received, *plus* some. If I were you, I'd think twice about doing such a thing again. You'll get caught eventually—I can promise you that. You signed your name on a legally binding form, after all. If WonderHome ever gets caught, the feds will investigate every single piece of property they've ever sold. It's only a matter of time before they find your name on that deed, which you don't even have in your possession. You signed it and let the bad guys take it with them. You, sir, are truly a fool."

"I'm sorry," Ed pleaded. "I have kids. I lost my job. My wife is sick and can't work. This money is all I have to keep us in our home for the rest of the year."

Selena tossed up her hands. "I'm not taking your money. It's yours. You've taken the risk and earned it. Just be ready for when the feds come knocking—they won't be as kind as me. Now get the hell out of here before I change my mind."

Ed nodded one last time before hurrying into his car, flying out of the driveway and zipping down the block.

Selena stood there, alone in the silent, eerie neighborhood, smiling. She had definitely gotten through to him, but was it enough to help their cause?

Chapter 49

February 18, 2014

Monday had passed with Arielle and Selena successfully approaching all of their targets. Three of the four encounters played out similar to Selena's with Ed Zimmerman. One man dashed away in a mad sprint that Arielle had no intent of chasing down. Her only goal was to scare these people, and clearly that had happened, judging by his record-breaking speed.

All of their work had turned up zero results by the end of the workday on Monday. No emails, calls, or direct meetings with Landon occurred around the topic. It was deflating, but Arielle assured them they just had their hopes too high. She gave a two-week cushion for a reason, though admittedly agreed she believed something would happen much sooner.

Tuesday morning, Arielle and Selena were back out in Seattle, following WonderHome's best realtors, and shaking down the fake buyers. Arielle commented how absurd it was that they weren't even trying to disguise what they were doing. They made no efforts to sprinkle in actual home buyers interested in legitimate properties.

"That's what the rest of the real estate team is for," Felix had said as he wished them a good day out the door.

And it was true. He had taken a deeper dive into the financials of the real estate team. Outside of the top performers, everyone else struggled and had much lower deals, on average.

Felix spent his Tuesday morning how he preferred; a hearty breakfast followed by a light jog around the neighborhood, then back home where he planted himself in front of his computer to get started for a fun day of work.

He still listened to Michelle's conversations, convinced she was involved in the scheme to a lesser degree. Surely a CFO couldn't pull all this off without the CEO knowing. She could have even caught wind of what was at play and turned a blind eye, giving that public shaming of Landon for appearances.

The morning passed with no drama. Landon had meetings from nine to eleven, then an open block where he returned to his office for an hour until lunch time. Michelle's schedule was similar, although her meetings took place in her office, leaving Felix to listen to a heated discussion around hiring more sales agents to further expand their market reach across the nation.

It wasn't until ten minutes after one o'clock when a knock banged on Landon's door and another voice immediately started speaking. "Hey, boss," a man said. "You have a minute?"

"Charles," Landon replied. "Come on in. Close the door and have a seat."

Felix looked over his list of WonderHome realtors and identified the man as Charles Hawkins, the team's second-highest performing agent.

After a few seconds, Landon spoke first. "How is everything going out in the field? Looks like you've got more closings lined up."

"Yes, I can't complain," Charles replied, then lowered his voice. "I just got an interesting phone call I think you need to know about."

"Does it pertain to Eric?" Landon asked, followed by a silence Felix assumed was filled with Charles nodding his head. "I see. What was the call about?"

Charles continued just above a whisper, but Felix's pen microphone was plenty strong enough to pick up the discussion. "My buyer from my first closing this morning just called me. He sounded terrified. He said some lady in sunglasses walked up to him after we left the property, claimed to be a private investigator, and was asking all kinds of questions about the transaction."

"And what did the buyer say?"

"He said he made up some answers as best he could. The lady asked if he had received any money for signing the contract. Luckily he had it in his backpack and he told her he didn't know what she was talking about. But why would she ask such a specific question? Landon, is someone on to us?"

"Well, it certainly sounds like it," Landon said, not sounding too distraught. "That's a lot of details. I wonder if someone tipped off the feds. Who do you think it could be?"

"What do you mean? Like someone from our team? No one's crazy enough to do that—way too risky."

"Unless they were approached first. The feds could have figured it out some other way and started snooping around. If they got hold of one of our agents, they could offer immunity for the truth about what's going on. But let's slow down. I don't want to jump to conclusions."

"With all due respect, sir, I think jumping to conclusions is exactly what we need to do. This wasn't some chance encounter. Whoever this lady was, she knew exactly where to go, who to follow, and what to say. We're being watched."

"How did your buyer say this meeting ended?"

"He said the woman questioned him, and he gave made-up answers until she finally decided she heard enough and left."

"No threats?"

"Not that he mentioned. But I could hear the fear in his voice. He sounded on the verge of tears."

"Just shaken up, I'm sure. Easy money is never actually easy. Did anyone ever tell you that, Charles? Easy money still requires a lot of hard work. Some might classify what we're doing as easy money, but I don't see you sitting on the couch picking your nose all day. God no, you're out there busting your ass every single day, even if it's all rigged. You still gotta show up and put in the work."

"Yes, but none of that means a thing if we're in prison."

Landon laughed. "Prison. Slow your roll, young man. Nobody is going to prison, remember? This is all set up in a particular way, with certain checks and balances, to make sure no one on our team is ever held responsible. Is your name on the contract your buyer signed today?"

"No."

"Exactly. If shit were to hit the fan, we'll get questioned, sure, but nothing is falling to us. We're just a team of real estate agents out doing our jobs. Eric is the one pulling all these other strings for his own agenda. Don't forget that. Tell your buyer to not worry and to keep his mouth shut. Maybe we need to lie low for a bit, but we can't really afford to. Our entire department is on the chopping block unless we show more money coming in. For now, business as usual. Okay?"

"Yes, sir," Charles said. "Do you want me to bring this up to you if it happens again, or are we really going to keep pretending everything is fine?"

"Excuse you. Everything *is* fine. I have everything under control. Speak to me like that again and you'll find yourself unemployed. I don't appreciate the accusing tone you've had since you walked in here. Get back out there and do your job."

"Yes, sir, my apologies," Charles said, and left the office.

Once in silence, Felix listened as Landon let out a frustrated, "Fuck!" followed by frantic typing on the keyboard.

Everything was becoming clear, except for this Eric character. There wasn't a single Eric listed anywhere in the WonderHome database. It had to be a code name for someone, or perhaps something.

Once Landon's typing stopped, Felix watched closely for any outgoing email messages. After a few seconds, it popped up, and Felix's heart sank. Landon had just sent an email to Michelle, calling for an urgent off-site meeting in ten minutes.

Felix picked up his phone and called Arielle.

Chapter 50

Arielle was finishing a burrito bowl for lunch when Felix called in a panic, urging her to get back to the office as soon as possible.

Fortunately, she had been in the general vicinity after approaching the last fake buyer and demanding details they didn't have.

She didn't think she could make it in ten minutes, but would try. Selena was even further from the office, so it would all depend on traffic. Her GPS said she was exactly twelve minutes from the office, so she hopped in the car and sped off. If Landon and Michelle were to *meet* in ten minutes before heading out of the office, that would give Arielle just enough cushion time to make it to follow them.

The mission gods must have been looking over her because traffic was light, and she caught very few red lights and she raced across town, tight grip on the steering wheel while she pinched her tongue between her lips, weaving around cars going much too slow.

It had been 1:22 when Felix called, and she pulled up to the front entrance of the Wilson Investments Center at 1:33, screeching to a stop in the loading zone that only allowed fifteen minutes for parking.

"Shit!" Arielle cried, seeing Landon and Michelle step out from the building. She looked around, saw no metered parking available, and opted to leave her car in the loading zone.

Arielle jumped out and hurried around to the sidewalk, where plenty of people crowded the walkway. She set her eyes on Landon and Michelle, who strolled along at a leisurely pace, one block west, until they entered the Starbucks on the corner.

All three Angels had visited this Starbucks back when they first arrived in Seattle. It was famous for being the first and original location for the chain that would eventually rule the planet. Selena had wanted to see it, and insisted they stand in the ever-growing long line.

But in the middle of a workday afternoon, there was no line out the door like there was in the morning, so Arielle took cautious steps as she entered, delighted to see a decent amount of people sitting at the tables inside.

Landon and Michelle didn't even bother waiting in line for a drink. They headed straight back to the corner nearest the bathrooms, where they huddled together at a two-seater table. Landon planted his elbows on the table, both hands balled into fists that covered his mouth. He was speaking, and it was impossible to read his lips. His eyes were also scanning the Starbucks, as if expecting to see someone.

Michelle matched his positioning, the two looking like a baseball coach and pitcher convening on the mound, hiding their mouths so the cameras couldn't pick up what was being said.

Both of them kept scanning the room, causing Arielle to turn her back from them as she pretended to stand in line. It was too risky to get any closer, at least without something to conceal her face. An open table was three spaces over from them, and she might be able to sit there while keeping her back to them.

Arielle cocked her head downward and started walking toward the table, looking ashamed of herself. Just before she arrived, a couple pulled out of the seats and sat down, leaving Arielle stranded in the middle of the room, standing awkwardly among the patrons enjoying their afternoon treats.

She spun around and headed back toward the line, keeping her back to Landon and Michelle. Arielle grew paranoid about getting caught—that was too risky of a decision to get that close. If only she had one of Felix's recording pens, she could drop it next to their table without them even noticing.

But she only had herself, and remembered one of the key lessons she had learned during her rise as the top-ranked Angel: Never force a matter under any circumstance.

The line inched closer to the counter, bringing Arielle gradually closer toward the direction of her two targets. Standing in line was simply a way to blend in—she needed to get closer to actually hear their conversation.

Arielle stepped out of line a second time, this time pulling out her cell phone and holding it down by her waist. She shuffled into the narrow walkway that led to the bathroom and strolled confidently past the table where she could overhear Michelle saying, "You need to fix this."

Those five words tantalized Arielle as she slipped into the restroom, leaning on the door. She could spare thirty seconds before stepping back out and not appearing suspicious. And the way they were both looking around the café, she couldn't take a chance of them having already noticed her walk by.

Once the thirty seconds passed, Arielle stepped back out of the bathroom, the short hallway giving her just enough room to see Michelle sitting at the table, facing Landon. She pulled out her cell phone again and pretended to be texting as she walked by.

This second trip was a waste, with neither Michelle nor Landon speaking as Arielle wandered by their table.

Once Arielle was three steps past the table, Michelle's voice called out to her. "Hey!"

Arielle felt every muscle in her body tighten.

You forced the issue, and now you pay.

Arielle continued forward, calm and confident, not looking over her shoulder.

"Hey, you!" Michelle called out again, this time loud enough to earn the attention of others in the room.

Arielle was about fifteen feet away from the exit when she looked over her shoulder, still not stopping. Her eyes locked with Michelle's, who had stood up to face her.

"Stop!" Michelle snarled, but Arielle had already turned back around and bolted out of the Starbucks, breaking into a full sprint away from Pike

Place Market and down the block toward the Wilson Investment Center, where she had left her car parked.

It had only been ten minutes, so she was still within the time restrictions for the loading zone. She didn't look back until she reached her car, gasping for air after the unplanned cardio workout. She saw nothing but crowded sidewalks. No Michelle. No Landon.

Stupid, she told herself, disgusted with her performance. *High-risk, no reward. That's all that was.*

Arielle didn't chalk up too many losses on missions, but this blunder would weigh on her mind for the rest of the day.

Chapter 51

The three Angels gathered at the dinner table Tuesday night, mentally battered, sitting in silence.

Arielle had just shared the story of being spotted by Michelle at the Starbucks.

"Better than spotting me," Felix said with a laugh that failed to lighten the mood.

"We're getting close," Selena said. "I had a situation arise today, as well. I'm pretty sure it's the past resisting *because* we're so close."

"What now?" Arielle asked.

"I got a call today from work."

"But you're off for the week."

"Exactly. It was my VP, Amara. . . she had some questions about why I was in Landon's office the other day when he had stepped out."

"What?!" Arielle cried.

"Shit," Felix said.

"Someone saw you?" Arielle asked. "I thought you said there wasn't anyone around."

"There wasn't," Selena said. "She said the surveillance cameras caught me. Apparently, Landon submitted a request to the security team to review footage of the outside of his office and to report anything out of the ordinary. Sure enough, there I am, seconds after he steps out."

"But they couldn't see *inside* his office, right?"

"Correct. All they saw was me go in. They didn't even mention anything about the pen, so I think we're in the clear."

"What did you tell Amara?" Felix asked.

"Told her I was looking for Landon to review some payroll questions. I have no idea if she bought it—I don't think so. She said I'm to meet with her, Landon, and a security rep when I get back on Monday. We need to finish this mission this week—we can't keep going at this rate. I'm pretty sure they're going to fire me if my story makes no sense."

"That's probably true," Felix said. "But you're absolutely right. We *are* close. We rattled Landon. That's why he called an immediate off-site meeting with Michelle. Unfortunately, we don't know what they said, but it's obvious—again—that Michelle at least knows about the laundering scheme. It doesn't seem she's actively taking part in it, but her knowledge will be enough to put her away. I suppose the biggest question now is, where do we go from here? We have Landon against the ropes."

"He thinks he's being watched," Arielle said. "The call to review the security footage. The way he was looking around Starbucks. That's the only reason I'm not outside his house tonight. He's probably sitting at his window waiting to see anything that looks remotely close to someone following him."

"But we have a slight advantage," Felix said. "He thinks the feds are watching him, not us. And why would he think any differently? It's not like he knows there's a team of time travelers coming to bring him down."

"Exactly," Arielle agreed. "We can do whatever we need to stop this entire scheme from getting pinned on Adam. Speaking of, does anyone know how he's doing?"

The other two shrugged. No one had kept an eye on Adam over the past couple of weeks. As far as Arielle was concerned, Adam didn't need to be stopped. He was just going about his job and minding his business.

How Michelle could stand by and watch him get taken to prison proved everything about her character. Adam did nothing to deserve such a brutally harsh life. He had a family and dreams for a bright future. Still, Felix questioned how they pinned everything on him without a trace going back to Landon.

"He was fine, last I heard," Selena said. "I never got to see him at the office, but the POPS team hears everything. Everyone wanted to talk about the secret boyfriend who dumped Michelle after she got back from the Super Bowl. It made the gossip start about Adam and if Michelle would try to make a move on him, as she had done with past assistants. Honestly, it's all gibberish. People talking out of their asses. Still, we need to do the right thing. Not just to save Adam and his family, but to make sure these evil people get what they deserve. Michelle and Landon are literally using people like pawns in a sick game of chess. I'm sorry, but I have no sympathy for people like that. They really don't need to exist in our world."

"I completely agree," Arielle said. "Which is why we're going to ramp up the pressure. I think we've done enough to send the entire executive team into a frenzy. Think we can get away with placing some threatening calls?"

Felix nodded. "We have some ways to do that without being caught, yes."

"Good. I think we can end this Thursday night. Landon is going to be so paranoid by the time he meets with his drug mules. Who knows, he might even bail if he's scared enough. But I don't want it to get to that level. Not yet. We need evidence tying everything back to Landon. I'm going to take pictures of him at his next drug meeting. Tomorrow, I want pictures of the realtors and fake buyers making their make-believe transactions. And instead of approaching the buyers, let's approach the realtors in the same way. Once Landon gets wind of that, he'll have no choice but to call off the entire operation."

"Do you think that's safe?" Selena asked.

"Of course. Landon is the criminal—that's who we should avoid for our safety. These realtors are nothing more than realtors. They won't take a shot at us or anything like that. Some might get mouthy, but I'm not too concerned."

Selena nodded to herself, taking a sip from her nightly glass of wine. "We're gonna make these assholes sing our praises to Landon. And I can't wait."

Chapter 52

February 19, 2014

The following morning, Arielle and Selena followed their same routine. Arielle was to confront two of the real estate agents in the morning before heading back home, where she would call Landon's office. Selena would remain out during the afternoon to intimidate more realtors.

Arielle's goal, by the end of the day, was to have the walls closing around Landon. He probably still believed they would tie every trace of criminal activity to Adam. But the phone call to Landon would throw a wrench into that belief. He wouldn't get away with it, and she'd make sure he knew that.

Before any of that could happen, Arielle had business to tend to. She sat outside another beat up property. This one had missing pieces from the roof and didn't look like anyone had lived in it for at least ten years. It was an abandoned property that stood alone across the street from a business strip offering tires and auto repair work.

Cars zipped by on the main road, and this would work to Arielle's advantage. The realtor she was about to approach, Rodney Perry, had been in Arielle's training class. The two had never spoken, and she was counting on a simple pair of sunglasses to keep her unrecognizable when she strolled up to him.

She had watched Rodney and his fake client go into the battered house ten minutes earlier. Once she saw them step out, Arielle immediately hopped out of her car. She didn't care if both the realtor and buyer were present. If she could scare both at once, then it would be that much sweeter.

She had her pistol tucked into the rear of her waistband, just in case, and walked up to the house with her arms crossed.

"Excuse me," Rodney said. "Can I help you?"

"Yes," Arielle said. "I'd like to see the property."

Rodney frowned. "I'm sorry, ma'am, but we just closed on the property."

The buyer shuffled away to his car, hopping in and taking off in a hurry.

"Do you always pay your clients to buy a house?" Arielle asked. "I'd love to get in on that sort of deal."

"I don't know what you're talking about."

"Did you not just bring ten thousand dollars for that man to sign his name on the deed for this house?"

"Nope," Rodney replied, smug. He clutched a briefcase at this side.

"Kind of strange to close on a property *at* the property, isn't it? I've never heard of such a thing."

"Cash transactions can happen anywhere."

Rodney was a lot sharper than Arielle was expecting. Aside from the overly tight grip on the briefcase, he showed no signs of worry.

"I see. And you have the cash in the briefcase?" Arielle nodded to it.

"I don't need to speak to you, ma'am. I'm sorry, but this property is no longer available."

"Then you should probably take down the 'for sale' sign, don't you think?"

"I'll do that as soon as you leave. This is private property. If you don't leave, I can call the police."

"Oh, that would be fun. Let's get the cops over here. Maybe they can take a peek inside your briefcase and all the cash I'm sure you just got. I saw this house listed on WonderHome for $250,000. Most estimates show it's valued at $80,000. That doesn't make sense. And now that I'm standing here, I suppose even the eighty is too high. How much will it cost to fix that roof?"

"Look. I sold that man this property. He wants to turn it into a restaurant. My job is to sell properties, not worry about what happens to them after the deal is done."

"I didn't see your buyer with any paperwork. Shouldn't he have had a copy of the deed? Especially with a cash purchase. No need for all the other paperwork those pesky lenders ask for. He gave you cash, so you should have given him the deed and the keys."

"I don't know what you're talking about."

Arielle sensed a growing frustration from Rodney. This was not the way he had planned his morning on going.

"Well, a deed is a piece of paper showing who owns—"

"I know what a deed is," Rodney snarled through gritted teeth.

"Oh, well then, why do you keep saying you don't know what I'm talking about?"

"Look, lady, just leave. There's nothing here for you. Okay?"

"I'm not here to make any trouble for you. Just answer some questions and we can both be on our way. First question, are you aware of the money laundering taking place by WonderHome with these fake transactions you're processing?"

"Bullshit," Rodney said, continuing to his car.

"You'll go down as an accomplice when this all comes crashing and burning. And it will. I can promise you that."

"Have a good day."

Rodney got in his car and slammed the door. Arielle didn't think he actually wanted her to have a good day.

"Tell Landon hello for me!" she shouted from outside the car, an older Honda Civic.

Rodney threw up his middle finger before blazing out of the driveway, swerving onto the main road and narrowly missing contact with an oncoming vehicle.

Arielle pulled out her cell phone and called Felix. "Hey, stay tuned. This guy left extremely heated. I'd be surprised if he's not already on the phone with Landon. His name is Rodney Perry."

"Got it. You're still going to the second realtor on your schedule now?"

"Yes. I'll see you after that for my call to Landon. Probably another hour."

"I'll be ready."

* * *

Arielle arrived back at their house just before noon. Her second encounter was with Cody Hayes, the top-ranked performer on the real estate. Cody had already spoken with Landon about someone being on to them.

He mentioned how he was "expecting" Arielle and had nothing to offer. He professed his rights as a free American, and without a warrant signed by a judge, she had no grounds to keep questioning him. Cody insisted he had committed no crime.

Arielle hounded him with another half-dozen questions, but he simply ignored her like a celebrity pushing through a crowd of paparazzi and reports.

The meeting did nothing to advance their cause, but gave Arielle all the assurance she needed to know they were making substantial strides.

"Your buddy Rodney called Landon like you said," Felix explained to Arielle as she joined him at the dining room table. "I could only hear Landon's half of the conversation, but it was obvious the discussion was about you. We're getting to them. He told Rodney to take the rest of the week off while he brainstorms ideas to get the feds off his back."

Arielle laughed. Landon really had no clue what was going on, and that couldn't have played any better to their advantage. "Let him brainstorm all he wants. Tomorrow night, I'm kicking the wheels all the way off. Are we ready to make this call?"

"Let's do it."

Felix handed Arielle a headset, and she slipped it on while he configured the computer to make the outbound call. "This software records the call and masks the number. When the feds eventually pull all the records, they'll see we placed this call with an untraceable number. And by that time in the investigation, they'll just assume it was another one of Landon's illegal dealings. Why else would he receive a call from an untraceable number?"

"Genius," Arielle said, earning a grin from Felix.

"Okay, dialing now," Felix said, clicking in rapid succession on his screen.

The phone rang in Arielle's ear, and she waited patiently while it rang for fifteen seconds. She almost gave up when the familiar voice of the CFO spoke. "Landon Greene."

"Hello, Mr. Greene," Arielle said in her most professional voice. "This is Lucia Ariano, and I'm an agent with the Federal Bureau of Investigation. May I have a few minutes of your time?"

"Hello, Ms. Ariano," Landon replied, calm. "I have a few minutes right now."

"Thank you. My team is investigating a money laundering suspicion at WonderHome, and I'd like to ask you a few questions. First off, you are the company's chief financial officer. Is that correct?"

"Yes."

"Great, and are you familiar with the company's real estate program? It's my understanding it was just launched within the last few months."

"Yes, we have a team dedicated to that."

"And may I ask who is in charge of that team?"

"I'm not entirely sure. It's not a department I work with."

"But you just said you're the CFO. Don't you work with all departments?"

"Well, sure. I overlook all funds for the company. I know how well every department is performing financially."

"Yet, you don't know who you would reach out to if you needed to speak with someone on the real estate team. Hard to believe, Mr. Greene."

"Look, Ms. Ariano, I don't know what this is about. And it sounds like it has nothing to do with me. And if you're with the FBI, shouldn't you be speaking to the company's legal department? I'm not sure what I'm even allowed to say on this phone call right now. You know, confidentiality and all that."

"I can respect that," Arielle said. "And I've attempted to contact the WonderHome legal team. No one has ever responded, so now we're going through your company directory for people who might be of interest. Naturally, since you're the CFO, you're at the top of our list. Now, I'm not accusing you. If anything, this phone call can help clear your name and help us narrow our search for whoever might be responsible."

"Okay? I'm not involved in anything illegal, so I'm not sure what you can even clear me of. You should speak with our legal team. I'm happy to go down there and find someone right now."

"That won't be necessary, Mr. Greene. I'll try them again after we speak. Since I have you on the line, I was hoping you could answer some questions about the real estate team, mainly about some properties that have been reported as sold through WonderHome."

Silence.

"Mr. Greene, are you there?"

"He hung up," Felix said. "He's probably running out of the office right now because I hear nothing on his office feed."

"This is a big deal. If he's really convinced he's being watched by the FBI right now, there's no saying what he might do. He could run. And if he does, then what are we supposed to do?"

"I wouldn't panic. That only opens another opportunity for us. He'll be away from WonderHome. Him running might be the best option. We can have Selena plant the evidence after hours, and we can get out of here."

"We'll have to see how it plays out. If he still goes to his meeting at the docks tomorrow, I think we can bring this all down."

Chapter 53

February 20, 2014

Thursday morning arrived after a long night of the three Angels debating their next move. Arielle had driven to Landon's house half an hour after he had hung up on her. She sat there for six hours before leaving.

He never showed up.

Arielle had driven through Michelle's neighborhood, just to see if Landon was maybe hiding there. But the house was also abandoned.

Selena frightened one more realtor on Wednesday afternoon, and with that, Arielle ordered they remain home on Thursday.

Selena argued against it, believing they should continue to follow the realtors until they broke down and stopped showing up at their fake closings. Felix urged Arielle to make additional calls to the WonderHome office. Why not dig deeper and call other members of the executive team or random employees? Combine some rumors with Landon presumably not showing up to the office, and it just might guarantee the employees at WonderHome would jump to their own conclusions about their CFO's guilt.

Arielle listened to their proposals and offered reasons for her rejection. First, Landon was right where Arielle wanted him. As long as he showed up at the meeting at the docks, then he hadn't abandoned all hopes for his scheme. They could live with him not showing his face at the office. Arielle expected as much. Wherever Landon was hiding, he was surely plotting his next steps. She had seen enough greedy criminals to know he wouldn't pull the plug on the operation. If anything, he was fielding different ideas for how to launder the money without using WonderHome.

They didn't need to approach any more realtors. Calling other employees could backfire. They still didn't have a full understanding of who was all involved. Contacting anyone else could risk others to cover up on behalf of Landon. Because if he went down, they were all going with him.

Selena and Felix understood Arielle's perspective on the matter, and braced for an eventful Thursday ahead.

Arielle made plans for the evening when Landon was to meet with his drug runners at the dock. They had no way of confirming if Landon had actually called out for the day. Felix listened to the bug in Landon's office and didn't hear a single peep all morning. Emails came into Landon's inbox and remained unread. Selena floated the idea of stopping by the office, but Arielle shot that down as unnecessarily risky. With Landon about to be in the spotlight for highly illegal activity, and Selena already on the radar for having snuck into his office, conclusions could be drawn, and they did not need any more targets on Selena's back.

Felix would remain at home while Arielle and Selena ventured out to the docks.

"Do you really think the gun is necessary?" Felix asked as he watched Arielle pack her backpack with the camera, pistol, and throwing knives.

"I'm not planning on even getting close enough where I'd need to use it. But I'd rather have it than not. Keep in mind, we'll be outnumbered, but we'll keep a safe distance when trying to take the pictures. That's my primary goal for the night. If we can get clear shots of Landon involved with drugs and weapons dealers, the rest of the mission will be smooth sailing."

Felix laughed. "Smooth sailing. Right. We've heard that one before."

"This can end tonight. Tomorrow at the latest, depending if we can get these pictures printed."

"And what's the plan with the pictures? Drop them off at the police station? Pin them to Michelle's office door?"

Arielle smiled. "No. We'd deliver them to Adam Marshall, of course.

Is there any sweeter justice—granted, he has no idea what's awaiting him—then to let him be the one to have those photos when the feds come in to arrest him?"

"That seems just as risky," Selena said. "We don't have evidence that he *isn't* involved, aside from unknowingly signing these contracts on behalf of the company."

"You're right," Arielle said. "And that's why we're going to have one last conversation with him, if we can. We can go to his house and explain what we've been investigating. He has to understand what he's been signing all this time. Maybe he's playing dumb and is getting part of Landon's money under the table, but unlikely. He never spoke up in that meeting in Michelle's office, and I would think for someone putting his name on every transaction, he might have more to say. I think it's a menial task he does. Probably doesn't even read the contracts anymore and just signs away to keep Michelle off his back."

"Do you not fear the risk of telling all this information to Adam?" Felix asked. "What if he really is working behind the scenes, knowingly, and just staying out of the limelight. If so, delivering him this info could do even more harm. If we can't risk calling others on the executive team, I don't see why we're treating Adam any differently."

"We have to tell *someone,* and it should be someone who still has a connection. Handing it off to someone completely random—say my old manager—is even higher risk. They may not take it seriously and nothing ever comes from it, or they blow things out of proportion before it's time. In that case, it's most likely to end up right back with Michelle or someone else on her team."

"We can plant some of these documents somewhere in the office," Selena said. "Even my desk. If I go after hours and leave it in my desk drawer, it will get found soon enough. Once I don't show up on Monday, it would probably be a few days until they realize I'm not coming back and clean out the desk."

"That's actually not a bad idea," Arielle said. "I still want Adam to have all this information. He's ultimately going to be accused of orchestrating this whole thing, so he needs to be equipped with the truth. During the trial, all he had was his word against his own signature on all the documents. And that's how we know he wasn't playing dumb about all this. He couldn't defend himself because he had no idea who was pulling what strings behind the scenes."

"We might as well hit everywhere we can with the proof once we have it," Felix said. "We can deliver it to Adam, the WonderHome offices, even the local police station. Hell, we can even send it to a news station. Having that many bases covered can only help our cause. Are we planning on leaving as soon as we deliver the evidence, or waiting around to see what happens?"

"Let's see how everything plays out first. I don't want to make any assumptions this close to the finish line. We still have work to do this evening. I expect fireworks—Landon has his back against the wall with nowhere to go. Felix, do you have one of those body cameras I can wear tonight?"

"I should be able to get one before you leave."

Arielle checked her watch. "I'm heading out with Selena in six hours. Get me that camera. I want every single movement recorded tonight. I'm not taking any chances."

Chapter 54

Arielle and Selena arrived at the docks an hour before Landon's scheduled time. They didn't know what to expect—Landon hadn't shown his face at WonderHome since the call with Arielle.

It was entirely possible he wouldn't even show up at the docks tonight, considering the size of the target he perceived to be on his back.

They parked three hundred feet away. Arielle killed the engine and lowered the windows an inch, allowing the cool breeze to seep into the car. Seagulls cried out from the bay, gliding above the water in their search for dinner. Bells gonged on the buoys, swaying with each subtle gust of wind.

"Which one is it?" Selena asked.

Arielle pointed straight ahead to the end of the dock. "Last time, there were four or five guys who showed up on the boat. Landon was the only one who came to meet them. If it's that small of a group again, what do you think about firing some warning shots their direction?"

Selena scrunched her face, glaring at Arielle. "Don't take this the wrong way—I think that's the dumbest thing you've ever said. Fire a warning shot? What is that supposed to do? Aren't you supposed to kill the bad guy?"

Arielle smiled. Hearing Selena voice a strong opposition strengthened the trust she had in her teammate, her sister in this mad world of time travel.

"I only kill people who cause physical harm to others. Murderers don't have a place in this world."

"What do you consider yourself?"

Arielle paused. She could recall every single person she had ever killed. Even in her line of work, the sensation of removing a life from existence never grew numb. Each kill was a reminder of her own mortality, the fragility of life. Each time the guilt of playing executioner would twist her thoughts. A universal trait across all the villainous men and women she had encountered was their self-manipulation to justify their horrid actions. Was she not doing the same thing?

Was there really such a thing as good conquering evil, or was assassinating the wicked of the world simply good wrapped in evil?

"I consider myself an Angel," she finally said. "I don't like it, but I'm one of the few who can shoulder the burden of taking multiple lives. Not only am I numb to death, but I got to witness firsthand how powerfully cruel humanity can be. I guess that makes me the perfect candidate for a job like this, now that I think about it."

"Which is why you're *not* going to fire a warning shot. Doing that won't change anything of substance. You can either kill this guy or not, but don't settle for middle ground."

"It's not middle ground. There *is* a difference. What Landon has fallen into is being driven by greed. Maybe he'll never satisfy his hunger for more, but he deserves a chance at reform. A murderer does not."

"So it's settled. No warning shot—no shot at all. He can live for another day. Because if you fire that gun, these goons will look all over until they find us."

Arielle had once picked off an entire drug cartel one-by-one without any help. A handful of drug runners hardly posed a threat. "Good point," she said. "Looks like someone is coming."

She caught a glimpse of a car turning onto the road in her rear-view mirror, and lowered her seat back to stay below the windows, prompting Selena to follow suit.

"Is it him?" Selena asked in a whisper.

"Couldn't tell. Could be, since we only have half an hour until the planned meeting time."

They remained low for a minute, waiting as the vehicle took its time cruising by, the engine a gentle hum, gravel crunching beneath the tires as it passed.

Once in the clear, Arielle and Selena nodded at each other before raising their seats to the upright position. They saw the rear of the vehicle, a black Lincoln Continental with windows tinted too dark to see inside. The license plate was a regular tag from Washington state.

"That's not Landon's car," Arielle said, brows narrowed as her eyes followed the SUV rolling down the dock.

"It looks kind of familiar," Selena said. "But I'm not sure from where."

The vehicle had nothing unique to identify it. They could probably stop by the airport and find another dozen that looked just like it.

The Lincoln stopped at the dock they were watching and parked in the same spot Landon had last week. Plumes of smoke puffed out of the exhaust pipe as it remained parked, no one stepping out.

"What's going on?" Selena asked, looking through her binoculars.

Arielle did the same. "I don't know. We've already altered things enough that we can't predict what's going to happen next."

She put the binoculars down and reached under her seat, pulling out a handgun and flicking off the safety.

"Whoa, what the hell?!" Selena cried out, shifting closer toward her door. "I thought you're not going to shoot anyone."

"I don't plan on it. But it's good to be prepared for anything."

They waited another five minutes before a second vehicle appeared on the road, and did their same routine as it passed by. This time it was Landon in his Corvette, and he pulled up right next to the SUV.

Arielle and Selena both returned to their binoculars, watching the two vehicles, still no one stepping outside.

"They probably think they're being watched—well, at least Landon thinks that. Explains why they're hesitant to get out of their cars."

"Do you think they have someone checking the area?"

"If he's that concerned about it, I wouldn't be surprised. But I haven't seen anyone besides the few sailors closing up their boats for the day."

The same blue boat from the prior week finally appeared, carefully drifting up to its anchor point.

"That's the one," Arielle said. "Crates of drugs and guns, and who knows what else. Looks like the same size crew, too."

They watched as a half-dozen men gathered at the center of the boat, waiting for it to dock.

"Shit!" Arielle shouted. "Get down!"

She yanked the lever and snapped her seat all the way back in an abrupt motion. Selena only paused for a second before realizing she needed to do the same.

"Someone's coming from behind," Arielle said. "Walking."

"Shouldn't we get out and fight?"

"We don't even know who it is. Could be an innocent bystander."

"Let's hope."

They braced themselves in the car, the only sounds those from the bay still carrying through the cracked-open windows. They lay flat on their backs for a clear view of the world outside. A long shadow cast over the car, swaying with each step its owner took.

Maybe we should have just gotten out of the car, Arielle thought. *They still wouldn't see us from the dock.*

Something in Arielle's gut, which she was listening to more, told her the person approaching their vehicle was no coincidence. As the shadow grew larger and closer, her stomach tightened to the point she thought she might vomit. She had the gun in her grip, but had never felt in such a defenseless position.

The pace of the walking shadow moved consistently. Confidently. The footsteps became audible, clopping along the road.

Please just keep walking by, Arielle prayed.

The footsteps stopped, and a pistol rapped against the driver-side window.

Chapter 55

"Put the gun down and get out of the fucking car!" the man shouted.

Arielle wasted no time releasing the gun from her grip. The man outside could blast right through the window, and she needed to buy time to find a way out of this situation.

"Both of you OUT!" the man yelled, tapping the gun on the window again, this time with more force. "And don't try anything cute."

"Just keep your hands visible," Arielle whispered to Selena, elevating both hands as she crunched her stomach to sit up straight from the reclined seat.

"Good girls," the man said, keeping the gun pointed at Arielle as he reached down to open the door. "Get out slow and put your hands behind your head—we're going for a walk."

Arielle and Selena both rose from the car, fingers intertwined behind their heads. Selena circled around the front and stood next to Arielle, where the man moved the gun back and forth between them. Arielle saw an opening to kick the gun out of his hand, but didn't want to take such a risk so soon. She hadn't seen where this guy came from, and didn't know who else might be hiding in the distance.

She assumed the man knew Landon. Who else would have any interest in watching them once they arrived?

They were still far enough where even if Landon saw Arielle take this man down, there wouldn't be much he could do aside from blasting some incredibly long-distance shots. They could be back in the car and out of the docks in a matter of seconds. She had left the keys in the ignition—a detail the man didn't notice.

They continued forward, and both vehicles at the dock now swung their doors open. Landon stepped out of his car, and another man stepped out of the Lincoln. They were too far to make out who it was, but Landon and the other man met in front of the Lincoln, shook hands, and proceeded onto the boat.

They didn't even look back this way.

Could Landon really have been that cocky, to trust one of his thugs to handle whoever was following him? He assumed the FBI was tailing him, so why would he run such a risk as holding a federal agent hostage?

Arielle looked around, scanning the top of the shipping containers. That's where *she* would hide in this scenario, and it appeared the man had no backup. She needed to distract the man. She needed Selena to understand this, but had no way of getting her attention as they continued walking at a gradual pace down the boardwalk. They were side by side, elbows almost touching, while they kept their hands behind their heads.

Over the next couple of steps, Arielle exaggerated her sway from side to side until she nudged Selena's elbow with her own. Selena took it in stride, continuing at the same pace as they continued toward the dock.

Selena didn't draw attention to the intentional contact, but Arielle could feel her staring at her from the side, begging to know what to do next. She could only imagine Selena's simmering fear, having never been in a situation like this. Fortunately for them both, Arielle remained calm and under control. One of the many lessons drilled into all Angels responsible for carrying out the dirty work was to always find a way out. No matter the situation, setting, or how many people were involved, there was *always* a way out.

She had no way of communicating what she wanted Selena to do. Reading each other's thoughts was a skill that would only come after years of working together. This being only their third mission together, Arielle would have to create the distraction and hope Selena understood what to do next.

Arielle slowed her pace, gauging how far behind the man was. She guessed about four feet. What she couldn't tell was where his gun was precisely located. He could have kept it lower by his hip to not appear so obvious. Or maybe he didn't care who saw what was happening and kept it elevated, level with his shoulders as he aimed directly at Arielle's back. That left Arielle with a two-foot window where she could spin and kick, but she didn't like those odds. Her foot could swing and miss everything. Then he would certainly fire the gun and draw the attention from the drug dealers on the boat.

She needed to guarantee the gun's placement and knew going to the ground was her best option. She slowed more and sensed the man—or rather the gun—now two feet behind her back.

Now.

With her next stride, Arielle drifted her right foot toward the center of her path, much like a model might walk down the runway, and planted it firmly on the ground, forcing all of her body's weight onto it. Her left foot continued forward, where she let the tip of her shoe clip the back of her planted foot, sending her sprawling forward. Her hands flew away from her head as she braced for the landing.

On her way down, she caught a glimpse of Selena's bulging eyes, and saw just enough understanding in them to know this half-baked plan just might work.

"Hey!" the man growled, lowering his pistol to Arielle on the ground, having caught herself in a position resembling a difficult push-up.

Arielle looked over her shoulder and saw a clear shot to kick back and knock the gun out of the man's hand, but she was too slow.

Selena hammered down a fist on the man's wrist, causing his hand to lose all sensation and drop the gun, where it clattered along the concrete. Arielle jumped to her feet just as this happened, the man letting out a howl of pain, so she reared back and punched him square in the teeth to silence him.

The punch knocked him off his feet, sprawling him where he landed square on his back, blood immediately spouting from his nose. Selena leaped for his gun, swiftly turning it on him.

"Don't make another sound," she said, crushing the gun into his cheek. "Or I promise you it will be the last."

The man moaned, rocking his head from side to side, not opening his eyes.

"Easy, Selena," Arielle said in a near murmur.

She had turned around to find the dock. They had only walked about one hundred feet, leaving another two hundred to the boat. Had it been a silent evening, the commotion might have carried toward the drug dealers, but the wind continued to whip and blew the sound of the man's painful whine into the void.

They were still far enough to not appear as anything concrete to the men on the boat.

"We need to get him out of the road," Arielle said. "Help me."

She crouched to grab the man under one shoulder, and Selena joined her as they lugged him twenty feet and lay him against one of the shipping containers. He continued to mumble incoherently, so Arielle kicked him on the side of his head, leaving him completely silent.

"Jesus Christ!" Selena gasped. "You gotta warn me when you're going to do something like that."

"Sorry. We can't take any chances. I'm quite certain this guy is a decoy sent from the past."

"How do you know that?"

"Think about it. If he had any relation to the events taking place on that boat, don't you think they'd be watching what happened to us? Or even helping once they saw trouble?"

"The past can't just create a new person to come impede with our mission. That doesn't fit the reality we know."

"I'm not saying the past *created* this guy. Keep in mind, we have already altered things in this timeline. The ripple is always wider than we can understand. We have no idea why this man was taking a stroll down the docks today, or why he had a gun and wanted to seek us out. But something over the past five months has led him exactly to this point. Clearly, he thought we were someone worth hunting. But none of that matters right now. He's out of the way and we can only hope that was the last big hurdle the past can throw our way."

"So, what are we doing now? Going back to the car?"

"Do you have your cell phone?"

Selena smiled and reached into her pocket to pull it out, waving it in front of Arielle. "Always."

"Good, we're going to need it for pictures. We've already come this far. I want to get closer to the boat. Let's go."

Chapter 56

There were enough obstacles between them and the boat to hide behind, so they hurried from one parked car to another, to a row of oil barrels, and eventually to a stack of empty wooden pallets, placing them a mere seventy-five feet away from the boat full of criminals.

"How well does your camera zoom?" Arielle asked as they crouched behind the pallets.

"Decent enough for a 2014 model," Selena replied. "Let me see what I can get."

Selena pulled out her phone and zoomed in toward the group of men chattering on the boat. Arielle watched as Selena's face pinched into a confused look.

"What is it?" Arielle asked.

"I think that's Raj."

"Raj? The vice president of WonderHome?!"

Selena nodded cautiously, as if she was still trying to convince herself of what she saw. "Here. I took a picture."

She handed over the phone, and Arielle snapped it out of her hands, studying the pixelated photo. She looked up and squinted toward the boat. "Holy shit, I think you're right. I *knew* there had to be more involvement from the executive team. No way in hell Landon was pulling all this off on his own."

"And Adam Marshall is nowhere to be seen. He has to be completely innocent."

"We need to get closer." Arielle took a step forward, just as Selena grabbed her by the arm.

"Are you crazy? There's nothing left between us and the boat. We're sitting ducks if we go any closer."

"Nonsense," Arielle said. She had done far riskier things. "We're going to use their cars to shield us. If it was only one car, then no, we wouldn't be doing this. But there are two, and they're parked in a V-formation. It's literally a wall if we stay low enough. Trust me, missions rarely throw you a bone like this."

Selena shook her head. "I don't think I can do it."

"Don't kid yourself. You saw what you did back there, right? I had no idea if my plan of tripping myself was going to work, but you took care of business. You have nothing more to doubt about yourself. You are *good* at this work. I'd even say *great*, if you had a little more faith in yourself. It's getting darker by the second. The wind is loud. This is our chance. C'mon."

Now Arielle grabbed Selena by the arm and pulled them both out from the pallets, crouched like stealthy burglars ready to escape.

"We don't do all those lunges for nothing," Arielle said, gaining speed as they crossed the road where it curved to the right, leaving them vulnerable out in the open.

The two vehicles provided just enough coverage. They reached the Lincoln in a matter of seconds, Arielle stopping at the rear bumper.

They were now less than twenty feet away from the gathering on the boat, and could clearly hear the voice of a shouting man.

"Raj?" Selena whispered.

Arielle nodded. They couldn't see anything, but it was obviously the vice president's voice, elevated to a pitch they had never heard before, his slight accent growing thicker with his mounting rage.

"You have got to be shitting me, Landon," Raj bellowed. "Two million dollars of product on this boat, and you want to send it back? Do you know how ridiculous that sounds?"

"I'm trying to protect us," Landon shouted right back. "You put me in this role so you could keep your hands clean. *I'm* the one with the real estate team. Everyone knows it's my team and my idea. If only they could know the truth, you weasel."

"Well, I'd say you're doing a real shitty job," Raj fired back. "If nothing is supposed to be tied back to me, then tell me why I am on this fucking boat right now. I was never supposed to meet any of these people. Now they all know who I am and what I look like. You feel some heat and now you want to bring everyone down with you. You're a coward. A pussy!"

"Be that way, Raj. Go crawl back to your office where you can hide and be safe. I'll take care of things like I have been, this *entire time*."

Raj laughed. "Landon's a funny guy, don't you guys think? Take care of things, you say? Like sending away two million dollars. I don't think you should be involved any more in this project. But I can't take you off, because clearly you're a coward and will bring the entire company down. You weak little man. I told Michelle to not hire someone so young for this job."

"Was that before or after you were sucking her tits? We all know it's true!"

Raj erupted with laughter. "Oh, Landon, you truly are one lost puppy. You're letting your dark thoughts win. You're no longer equipped to do this job, so consider yourself removed from the project. We will shift the real estate team to someone else and make all this go away for you."

"The feds called me on my office phone!" Landon screamed, as if he had mentioned this three dozen times already today. "What are you not understanding about that, you ignorant little fuck?!"

"You really don't trust the plan we set up, do you?" Raj asked, letting out a laugh. "It's fool-proof. Everything goes back to Michelle's assistant. *Everything.* Why do you think we went through so much trouble building a secret server to operate all the real estate transactions? And the fake accounts we made for him. Every single transaction for your team is on that hidden server, and every single one is tied to him. We may get questioned if the feds find out, but once they take a closer look, they'll find Adam Marshall was the brilliant mastermind behind the entire thing, and no one will doubt it. He can swear against it all he wants, but the proof is all on that server. *Thousands* of emails in his name, all related to these real estate purchases. It's his word against his own, and I think they'll believe the written proof over his denial."

"You'd better hope so, because they're getting closer."

Raj laughed again. "Let them look. If they really thought something was going on, they'd be here right now busting up the party. But once again, you're blowing things out of proportion. Typical Landon. All emotion and no substance. It's people like you who cause the downfall of a great thing like what we have going. There were always going to be questions surrounding our business practices. Whether from the feds or our competitors, it doesn't matter. Maybe our competition asked the feds to look at what we're doing. At least we don't have to worry about them speaking to you anymore."

"HEY! WHOA!" Landon screamed, fear slipping into his voice.

This caused Arielle and Selena to stare at each other. Arielle rose just enough to see Raj with a gun aimed at Landon.

She hurried back down. "Take a picture. Now!"

Selena circled around Arielle, hand extended with the phone in her grip.

"I'm sorry, Landon," Raj continued. "But you are currently the most dangerous factor in this entire operation. We still have a chance if you're out of the equation."

"You can't just kill me!" Landon cried, terror and desperation thick in his voice. "If I go—"

The gun fired, a crisp, cracking sound that echoed all around the docks. Seagulls screamed as they flew away in a hurry.

Arielle and Selena instinctively crouched lower to the ground, nearly sitting.

"You all work for me now," Raj said to the men on the boat. "Nothing needs to change in your weekly routine. I'll meet you here at the same time every Thursday. You will not speak of this. Now, help me toss his body into the water. Do we have anything that can weigh him down?"

Arielle and Selena exchanged a glance. Arielle had to force down a gulp to clear her throat before speaking. "We need to get the hell out of here."

Chapter 57

They only waited ten more seconds before Arielle peered around the Lincoln to see the men gathering around Landon's dead body. As much as it tempted her to get even closer for pictures, she knew they had enough to protect Adam.

Dusk had taken hold, turning the sky a bluish-purple tinge.

"Now," Arielle whispered, breaking into a sprint away from their hiding spot, Selena quick to follow.

Their footsteps made plenty of noise, but they had to take the risk. Hiding out any longer would only increase their chances of being caught. The wind had actually picked up in speed, and they could only hope it blew the sound of them running *away* from the boat.

Racing at full speed, they reached the car in thirty seconds, both panting for breath as they sat inside. Arielle hadn't looked back once, and was delighted to find no one following them.

"Oh my God," Selena panted. "What the fuck was *that?!*"

Arielle turned the key and sped out of the parking spot, flipping the car around as smoke spewed from the rear tires. That would surely have gotten the men's attention, but it was too late for them to do anything about it. Arielle blazed down the road.

"Raj was behind it the whole time. Michelle too. I don't think she had much of a role aside from ensuring certain people remained employed at WonderHome."

Selena flipped through the photo gallery on her phone. "I got it all. Pictures of Raj and Landon shouting, their crooks standing around the background. One is even holding a rifle. It might not prove what was on the boat, but it's a picture of the last time Landon was alive. Raj has the gun pointed right at his face, so it shouldn't be too hard for them to piece this all together."

"Excellent work. Text those pictures to Felix so we have them backed up, and he can start sorting them out."

"Where are we going now?"

"Home. We got through the hard part, but we still need to package this all up to deliver something substantial. I'd like to get it done tonight so we can get out of here. Every moment we hang around here now becomes a little more dangerous. As of right now, nothing has changed in Adam Marshall's life, but that's all going to change once they rule Landon as missing. We don't know Raj's next move, either. Will he tell Michelle what happened, or is he taking this to his grave? Either path alters the rest of the future for everyone involved. Tell Felix to print five sets of these pictures."

* * *

Twenty minutes later, they arrived home, jumping out of the car and dashing into the house. Felix was at his post in the dining room, laptop flipped open as a wire ran from his phone to the computer, and another from the computer to a printer.

The printed pictures lay in five stacks on the edge of the table, the top photo on each stack showing Landon getting out of his car when he had arrived at the docks.

Felix sprung out of his seat. "Are you two okay?"

They each gave him a quick hug. They were far from okay.

"We're alive and well," Arielle said. "We need to get these pictures out to the proper channels tonight. I want a set of photos dropped off at the *Seattle Times*, one directly to Adam Marshall, one to the police department, and one to the WonderHome offices. Let's leave it in the desk of Amara Edwards. I'm certain she has no involvement in any of this."

"That's only four copies," Felix said.

"The fifth one's for us. We're not going back without evidence."

"Are we just dropping off the pictures with no context?" Felix asked. "We can't assume anyone will know what to do with them."

"Can you print out a note to include with each? Say 'WonderHome money laundering. Raj Kalan killed Landon Greene. Body in Lake Union. Adam Marshall innocent.'"

Felix nodded and returned to his computer to type.

"It was never our job to piece this together for the authorities, just to clear Adam's name. I think we've done enough to do that."

"Are we going to split this up?" Selena asked.

"I was actually thinking we pack up and all head out together. Everything is close by. The office, newspaper, and a police precinct are all within a two-mile radius of each other. Adam's home is maybe another six miles away from the office. We should stop at his place last."

"You want to go there so late?" Felix asked. "It's already 7:30. It'll be close to nine o'clock, maybe even later, if Selena takes forever to pack all her shit."

Selena crossed her arms. "Hilarious. I may pack heavy, but I can do it all in thirty minutes. Can we say the same for you and all of your tech gear, nerd?"

Felix chuckled. The mood had definitely lightened now that a return home was on the table.

"Let's settle down," Arielle interrupted. "Go pack your things. We still have a lot of work to do."

Selena lowered her hands to place them on her hips, jutting out her head toward Arielle. "You're already packed, aren't you? This was your plan since you woke up this morning, wasn't it?"

Arielle grinned. "I packed last night."

"And you didn't tell us to do the same?" Felix asked.

"Sorry. I didn't want to impede your work today if you knew we might go home. That's how people get rushed and do a poor job. Besides, none of it was guaranteed. Still isn't, but I'd rather be ready to leave right after we drop this stuff at Adam's house because who knows what will happen once he gets it." Arielle checked her watch. "Your thirty minutes starts now. Let's get to it."

Chapter 58

They met by the front door twenty-five minutes later, all with wide, nervous smiles.

"It's not over yet," Arielle reminded them. "I know it feels like it, but we still have to be on our toes. We've altered this timeline beyond recognition."

"Good for the timeline," Selena said. "All I see is *my* bed in *my* house. And it's glamorous."

"Soon enough. This couldn't be a worse time to let our guards down. Shall we?"

They followed Arielle to the car, loading their luggage into the trunk. Felix took shotgun, while Selena settled into the back seat. Arielle started the car and pulled onto the road.

"Where to first?" Selena asked.

"The *Times*," Arielle said. "Then WonderHome, police, and Adam last."

"Have you thought about how you're going to give this to the police?" Felix asked. "You can't just walk in and hand it over."

"I'll tape it to the door, or maybe slip it underneath. We'll see what looks easier once we get there. We need to move quickly everywhere we go, especially once we reach the police station. They won't be able to tie anything back to us. But we can't hang around to see what happens."

"Not like we ever do," Selena mumbled.

"For good reason. Sticking around afterwards has never led to anything good. That's why we have a Futures team to scout things after the fact. The longer we're around, the greater the chances of getting tangled in whatever mess we leave behind. Think about it, by tomorrow morning the WonderHome offices are going to be teeming with police and detectives. As an employee there—and one who was recently seen sneaking into Landon's office—do you really think it's wise to stay? You'll be a suspect, even more once they find out you called out for the entire week Landon goes missing. We may have the proof with the pictures, but your name will come up plenty of times. It's easiest to vanish without a trace. It stirs up the suspicion, sure, but it leaves the authorities with nothing to pursue."

"I see," Selena said as they pulled up to the office for the *Seattle Times*. "And what do you plan on doing here?"

"Easy," Arielle said. "The building is open. They still run their printing press upstairs. I'm not going that far, but I'll be able to get this envelope into the hands of someone. Now, if you'll excuse me."

Arielle grabbed the first envelope from Felix, who held the stack in his lap. She parked along the sidewalk and stopped the engine, stepping out without another word. The downtown skyscrapers blocked most of the wind gusts that had been plaguing the area, making for a rather pleasant night. The block around the newspaper was deserted, save for a handful of cars parked across the street.

The building entrance had glass double doors, and Arielle saw a security desk right inside, an older man sitting behind it as he flipped through a recent edition of *Sports Illustrated* highlighting the Seahawks' Super Bowl victory.

She tried the doors to find them locked, the rumbling sound getting the guard's attention. He looked up, and Arielle smiled and waved.

He tossed aside the magazine and took his time getting out of his seat, Arielle imagining all of his old joints cracking and popping as she interrupted his nightly routine. He shuffled to the door and returned a grin as he pushed it open enough to stick his face through.

"Are you lost, young lady?" he asked, his voice gentle.

"No, sir." She held up the envelope. "I'm a private investigator with an incredible story that needs to be shared. I was hoping you could pass this envelope along to the proper person."

The guard studied the envelope with curious blue eyes. "This isn't really the way this works. You can mail it in, or you can email the editor about your story. Unfortunately, the world is a mad place, and we have protocol for a reason. Lots of sick people out there like to send mail into newspapers laced with poison."

"And I completely respect that. But I can assure you I'm no criminal. In fact, I've caught the criminal. It's all in here."

The guard looked at the envelope again, and Arielle could tell a part of him wanted to take it. He was trying to convince himself.

"Look," Arielle said. "It's not sealed."

They had only tucked the flap into the envelope to keep its contents secure, so Arielle flipped it out and stuck her hand into it. She did this for ten uncomfortable seconds while the guard looked from her to the envelope and back.

"My story is true," Arielle said. "I hope you can take my word for it. A bad thing has happened tonight, and I need to make sure the story gets to the right hands. I'm leaving town tonight—my job here is done. I'm sure the mail room has a procedure to check for poisons. You can even take it straight there. Just make sure it gets addressed to go to the correct person, which I'm assuming is the editor."

"I hope I don't get in any trouble," the guard said, reaching through the door, but not opening it any more. "Hand it over."

Arielle hadn't realized the tension building in her shoulders until the relief flooded over her. "Thank you so much, sir. You're helping make the world a better place tonight."

"Uh-huh, I'm sure."

"It's just some photos with a note about the situation. Front page news story."

"I've heard that one plenty of times. But I'll do this favor just this once."

Arielle clapped her hands together. "Thank you, again, you won't regret it."

The guard chuckled. "Honey, at my age, regret is simply a word. Have a good night. I'll get this sent upstairs for you. Good luck."

He offered one definite smile before closing the door and trudging back to his post. Arielle didn't need to wait around to see what he did with the envelope. He was likely going to open to have a look for himself. That would be all he needed to see before knowing it most definitely had to go upstairs.

Arielle returned to the car, and continued to their next stop at Wonder-Home.

Chapter 59

The parking garage was practically deserted. Even the workers who prided themselves on staying late had gone by 8:30.

"This one's all you, Selena," Arielle said as she parked by the elevators.

"Excuse me," Selena replied. "How is that smart? What if security sees I'm in the building and comes to find me?"

"Building security won't do anything. WonderHome has questions for you, not the building. They're going to know you're in the building, regardless, since you need to swipe your badge to enter. If me or Felix were to enter with your badge, that would only draw more suspicion."

Selena sighed. "Fine."

"This should take five minutes, most of it riding the elevator. Just put the folder on Amara's desk and come right back. Nothing to it."

"Okay."

Selena grabbed the envelope from Felix. "Good luck," he said, as she opened the door and stepped out.

She drew a deep breath, taking in the musty smell from the garage, before heading for the elevators. Each footstep echoed multiple times, making it sound like someone else was walking nearby. But there was no one.

Selena pushed the button to call the elevator and waited as it hummed. The chime rang out emphatically, and she realized her elevated senses. The slightest tremor shook the envelope in her hands as she stepped into the elevator, throat swelling with tension as she watched the doors close, cutting off her view of Arielle and Felix.

Alone in the elevator as it climbed thirty floors, Selena paced in circles. She wasn't sure if it was stress being back inside the office, or a true gut feeling that something was off.

We didn't even confirm who's in the building. We're just assuming everyone is gone by now. Michelle could be here. Even Amara.

Selena talked herself out of it. Possible, but unlikely. She had never known Amara to stay so late.

"Home by dinnertime with the family," she always said, and encouraged the rest of her team to live by the same rule.

But Michelle didn't have a family. WonderHome was her spouse, so she *might* be around.

The elevator stopped, and the doors parted to the executive level. Selena had been on the floor plenty of times, but never had she seen it so dark. The lights were all off, minus a couple above the backsplash in the kitchen area. The refrigerators purred as the only sound.

Selena looked around to see all the doors closed, figuring there was a new mandate to do just that after the footage had leaked of Selena slipping into Landon's office.

Landon.

His door would remain closed for how long? Likely until tomorrow, once word spread about what had happened.

Selena felt the cameras watching her, capturing her face clear as day as she wandered through the office after hours.

I'm definitely going to be a suspect, she thought, realizing how questionable her actions looked on the surface. Hopefully, the proof in the envelope would clear her name, but people would still speculate on Selena's involvement. Her presence in the office mere hours after Landon's death didn't exactly paint her as innocent.

She passed Landon's office, not so much as looking at it, but feeling the haunting presence that always made her head spin when she thought about death and her own mortality.

She passed Mila's office before arriving at Amara's, reaching out her shaky hand to the door handle.

Damn. Locked.

She wiggled the handle a couple more times to confirm, pissed she didn't think of asking Felix for his lock pick.

Selena squatted, finding a gap of about a quarter inch beneath the door, plenty of space to slide the envelope through.

"It'll have to do," she said, dropping the envelope flat on the floor and sliding it under.

Selena had been so focused on her task that she never heard the elevator chime down the long hallway. Never saw the figure approaching her from behind. All she felt was the cold metal of a gun pressed against the flesh on the back of her neck.

"What do you think you're doing?" Raj asked from behind.

Even in a squatted position, Selena's knees locked. She thought she might have been having a heart attack because she couldn't feel it beating in her chest.

"Please don't shoot me," she said. "It's not what you think."

"I think it's exactly what I think, Selena Nicole. If that's even your real name. Turn around and don't make any sudden movements."

Selena did as instructed, pivoting around on her knees, raising her hands for the second time this evening.

"Stand up, dammit," Raj snarled.

Selena rose, her legs wobbly. Surely they would give out any second.

"Please," she said, scanning the area for anything she could use as a weapon. But she had no options. She was pinned against the wall, twenty inches between the gun and her face.

Staring into the tiny black hole brought a flood of emotions.

I'm going to die, she thought. Raj had clearly gone off the deep end with blood already on his hands. He had proven he would do anything to keep his scheme alive, but could he go as far as killing someone on camera? Did he have connections to make the tapes disappear? Crazier things had happened with corrupt, greedy men.

"Who are you?" Raj asked.

Selena focused on her breathing, hearing, but not listening to Raj's words. He wanted to talk, and that meant she had time to buy.

"Answer me, dammit!"

Raj reared back and whipped Selena across the face with the gun. Pain erupted in her cheek as a tingling numbness spread across her entire face. She didn't know blood was oozing from her nose until it seeped into her mouth and she tasted the metallic flavor.

"I'm Selena Nicole. Like you said."

Raj cracked his lips into a menacing smile, madness raging behind his eyes. "I looked into your file. No one on your resume has ever heard of you. It's all fake. Tell me who you really are and what you're doing here."

Selena's mind felt like a game of whack-a-mole, one idea popping up after another, unable to nail one down she liked. What could she say that would decrease the chances of Raj pulling the trigger?

"I'm undercover," she finally said. "Undercover with the FBI."

"I knew it," he replied, satisfaction in his voice.

"You can't shoot me. We're on camera."

Raj threw his head back and laughed. Selena stared, wondering how Arielle could ever muster enough courage to throw out a punch toward a gun. Not that Selena currently had the physical strength to attempt such a thing.

"I'm not afraid of the cameras. I can erase the footage before anyone ever knows what happens to you."

"My team will know," she said. "Do you really think I came here by myself?"

Selena saw a sliver of doubt creep into Raj's eyes and knew she had bought even more time for herself.

"Bullshit," he said. "Probably another lie like everything else you've told since you've been here. You're snooping around the money launder-ing. Why else would you have gone into Landon's office?"

"Of course, that's what I'm here for. My team has been watching you guys for the past six months. I'll admit, we had no idea *you* were involved. We were entirely focused on Landon."

"That's because Landon was the brains behind it, so you were correct there."

Fucking liar, Selena thought, then said. "Okay then. If that's really true, maybe we can work out a deal. Immunity for all the information you know, including Landon's whereabouts. We haven't been able to find him since Monday."

Raj stared deep into Selena's eyes, the gun never wavering. He was giving it deep thought.

Selena saw a small motion out of the corner of her eye, accompanied by a whizzing sound, followed by a *thump!* on the wall further down the hallway.

They both looked over to see a sharp object sticking out of the surface like a dart.

"What the—" Raj began, his words cut off.

Selena looked back at him and saw a throwing knife lodged in the side of his neck, blood shooting from the wound.

Raj dropped the gun and flailed for the knife, falling to his knees as his hands scrambled helplessly. Selena watched as all strength fled his body in a matter of seconds. His shirt turned black from all the blood it had already soaked up. He tried speaking, but his words came out in bloody gurgles. His eyes bulged from their sockets, the life slipping out of them.

Selena jumped aside as Raj fell forward, his body smacking the ground with a heavy thud, blood pooling all around his head and seeping into the carpet.

She looked to her left, toward the elevators, and saw both Arielle and Felix panting for breath.

Chapter 60

"Let's go!" Arielle yelled.

Felix lunged toward the elevator and pushed the button.

Thirty seconds ago, Selena thought she was going to die in the middle of the WonderHome office. Now, she looked down at the company's vice president, who had choked to death on his own blood.

Selena turned and sprinted, her legs still weak. She tumbled, even tripped, but held herself along the wall as she whirled toward the elevator lobby. Her face throbbed with excruciating pain, the cheekbone likely fractured. The blood from her nose slowed, but hadn't stopped.

Despite the suffering, she made it to the elevators where Felix was already inside, arm extended to keep the doors open. Arielle wrapped an arm around Selena's waist and helped her into the elevator.

"What happened?" Arielle asked, propping Selena up against the wall. "Your face is smeared with blood. I don't even know where to start."

Selena pointed to her cheek where the gun had struck her. "Pistol whip," she said.

"Jesus Christ," Arielle said, still panting. "You're so lucky. An inch higher and you'd probably have lost your eye. An inch lower and half of your teeth would've been knocked out."

Selena nodded. "Lucky. Yes, that's it." She tried to smile, but winced at the pain burning from her nose to her jawbone.

"Seriously, Selena," Felix said, also panting like a thirsty dog. "This could have gone so much worse."

Selena noticed Arielle had another throwing knife in her hand, a gun tucked into her utility belt.

"How did you know?" Selena asked through closed teeth like a ventriloquist, not wanting to cause herself any more pain.

"We saw him in the parking garage," Arielle said. "He pulled in like a maniac and we knew something was wrong. We knew his office was on the same floor as Amara's and that he'd probably find you."

"How did you get in without a keycard?"

Felix reached into his pocket and pulled out his lock pick. "No keycard needed, but we had to run up thirty-four flights of stairs. That's why we still can't catch our breath."

Selena wanted to question this further, but saved her strength. How the hell could they have run up that many flights of steps? And Arielle still delivered the deadly blow to Raj's neck, even if it took her two tries.

Selena wanted to smile, but knew better than to try. "How do I look?" she asked.

"You look like you just last lasted twelve rounds with Mike Tyson," Arielle said.

"But you should see the other guy," Felix added, laughing at himself.

Despite the throbbing injury and the tension from just surviving a close call with death, Selena broke into tears of gratitude.

"Selena, what's wrong?" Felix asked, the humor in his voice replaced with sudden concern.

She shook her head. "I can't believe I'm alive. You saved my life. Both of you. How can I ever pay you back?"

The elevator stopped, and the doors parted to the garage. Somehow, it had already felt like a lifetime ago when Selena was last here.

"Your legs feeling better?" Arielle asked. "You want to try walking?"

Selena nodded, some resemblance of normalcy returning to her legs during the elevator ride. The adrenaline was fading and her body felt like itself, aside from the piercing pain on the left side of her face.

They got into the car, Arielle moving with urgency. Building security might have not had an initial interest, but if they caught a look at what had just unfolded on the executive floor, a pursuit would surely follow.

Arielle turned on the car and flew out of the garage, driving at a calmer speed once they reached the road and blended in with the rest of society.

"You don't owe us a thing," Arielle said, speaking to Selena in the rear-view mirror at a red light. "Everyone in this car would do the same thing for each other. We sensed danger from the moment we saw Raj show up and knew we had to literally run up those stairs for your life. It's why we put in the work to keep our bodies in tip-top shape. If we had been two steps slower, who knows what might have happened."

"Arielle's right," Felix said. "It was like we both knew exactly what we needed to do. I'm not sure we even said anything to each other. We just got out of the car and figured out how to get to you."

"It's all instincts. We've all gone through the same basic training where they teach survival techniques—you're not allowed to go on missions without it. You retain more than you know. Once you've done so many missions, that sort of thing comes second nature."

"Well, thank you," Selena said. "The margs are on me when we get back."

"Wait," Felix said. "Are we still going to the police station right now?"

"Of course," Arielle replied, nonchalant. "Why wouldn't we?"

"Because you just murdered someone on a live camera feed. The police could already be looking for you, for all we know."

"I'm not worried about it. We'll swing by and see how it looks. If it's a quiet night, I'll slip the envelope under the door and we'll be on our way. We're only two minutes away."

They rode in silence, pulling up to the police station, a two-story building surrounded by towering skyscrapers.

Arielle parked along the curb. The entrance had two sets of glass double doors. A couple of officers walked out of the building, sharing a laugh as they strolled to a patrol car parked across the street.

"See," Arielle said. "Quiet night. Two people have been killed and they don't even know it yet. I think it's your turn, Felix."

Felix laughed. "I don't think so."

"I did the newspaper, Selena just did WonderHome, and now it's your turn. We're all going to approach Adam together. Just open that first door, toss the envelope on the ground, and come right back. Nothing to it, and we're all right here."

Felix shook his head and stepped out of the car without another word.

They watched as he looked around, then hurried to the door. No one had appeared once he reached the door and pulled it open. He threw the envelope down and pivoted around to run back to the car, jumping into his seat.

"Easy," he said. "Now get me out of here."

Arielle put the car into drive. "We have one last stop."

* * *

They arrived at Adam Marshall's house fifteen minutes later, relieved to be further from the WonderHome office that would soon swarm with police activity.

Selena's face remained in a tolerable pain, but she could speak a little better without wincing on each word.

"Okay," Arielle said. "Game plan. We're a group of private investigators with important information. We don't know how he's going to react, so we'll need to roll with it. At the very least, we need to make sure he's aware of the envelope and that we're leaving it with him for his own protection. The past has removed both people who should take the fall for this, leaving a line of evidence that will point back to Adam. As soon as we deliver the envelope, we don't owe Adam another second. We come back to the car. I'll drive around the block so we're out of his sight, and we'll take our Juice to return home. Does that all sound good?"

"Sounds perfect to me," Selena said.

"Let's do this," Felix said.

"Okay. I don't expect any fireworks from Adam, but let's still be on our toes, just in case. We're not home yet. Let's go."

Arielle stepped out first, the other two following her up the path to the Marshalls' front door. A light on the upstairs level was on, but Arielle could see another through the narrow window next to the door. It was past nine o'clock, so Arielle knocked instead of ringing the doorbell to not wake the kids.

Arielle took a step back and crossed her arms in front of her waist. Felix and Selena remained a step back, the envelope clutched tightly in Felix's grip.

"Any snooping neighbors?" Selena asked, scanning the area.

It was much too dark to see if anyone was out for a late night walk. The block had a few lampposts stymied by the tall trees.

"I think we're okay," Felix said.

Arielle knocked harder.

"Do we just leave it if he doesn't answer?" Felix asked.

"He'll answer."

On cue, they saw the movement of a shadow appear through the window, growing as it approached the door. When it reached the door, the shadow stopped.

Arielle forced a fake smile, knowing whoever was on the other side was looking through the peephole.

A snap came from the door as the deadbolt was unlocked, and it swung open to reveal Adam Marshall dressed in his pajamas, reading glasses perched on his nose, a John Grisham novel in his grip while a finger held his page location.

His eyes jumped across all three Angels standing on his doorstep, then behind them to study their car.

"Can I help you?" he asked, keeping his free hand on the door.

"Yes, good evening, Mr. Marshall. Do you have a moment to speak with us?" Arielle said.

Adam kept looking back and forth between the three of them, pondering the late-night visit. "May I ask what this is regarding?"

"Your freedom," Arielle said sternly. "Your future is at risk. We just need two minutes of your time, and we don't even need to come inside.

Everything you'll need is in my colleague's envelope."

Arielle turned around and Felix handed her the envelope.

"Let me grab a jacket," Adam said, closing the door and re-opening it ten seconds later. He stepped out, looking over his shoulder before closing the door behind him. "Okay, what is this about, exactly?"

"I'm afraid you made a mistake taking a job with Michelle Garrison," Arielle said.

"Michelle?" His voice elevated. He wrapped his arms around himself to keep warm, but unease spread across his face. "What does she have to do with this?"

"As far as Michelle is concerned, we're still not entirely sure. Wonder-Home has been laundering money from drugs and weapons sales through its real estate program. Landon Greene and Raj Kalan overlooked the operation. Both men are now dead."

"What?!" Adam cried. "Dead?! I just saw Raj this afternoon."

"I'm afraid so," Arielle said. "All the real estate transactions are run through you, correct?"

Adam looked past Arielle into the distance, running through his memories. "Yes. Michelle assigned me as a special assistant to the real estate team. My only duty is to sign the purchase agreements on behalf of the company." Adam leaned back against his door. "Oh my God, am I going to jail?"

"No. That's why we're here. You'll definitely be questioned and, like I mentioned, you are meant to look guilty. In this envelope are pictures of Raj and Landon on a boat full of drugs, weapons, and their dealers. Raj shot Landon and dumped his body in the water. The location is noted in there, as well."

"I'm sorry," Adam said. "Who are you? This all sounds made up. I need to make some phone calls."

"I'd advise against that. We're a team of private investigators. We were looking into the laundering scheme and have uncovered a lot about it, including how it's all tied back to you. There are other names involved, sure, but it sounds like Raj and Landon were running a fake email account in your name on a hidden server. We couldn't access the hidden server, but we can only assume it is full of all the information meant to paint you as guilty."

Adam laughed. "You know this is crazy, right? I can't just accept this and move on with my life."

"No one here is laughing, Adam. If you brush this all aside, you're going to prison for a long time. We've already delivered this information to the *Seattle Times*, Seattle PD, and even left a copy in Amara Edwards' desk. We did that in case you really don't believe us, you'll at least have a fighting chance."

"I can't just *believe* you. This is the most absurd thing I've ever heard."

"It's all true," Felix said, stepping forward. "We do this for a living. We see absurd all the time. You're an innocent man, and we saw the opportunity to help you. That's all this is."

Adam stood up tall and nodded to Selena. "And what happened to her?"

Clearly, Selena's face had been morphed out of recognition if Adam didn't recognize her from the office.

"This is Selena Nicole," Arielle said. "From your POPS team. We planted her at the company to help with our investigation."

"Selena?" he asked, jutting his head forward for a closer look. "Can't be. She's . . . wow, it really is you?"

"Hi, Adam," Selena said. "Listen to what we're telling you. It's the best thing you can do."

"We need to go now," Arielle said. "Our work here is done. The rest is in your hands. Let's go."

She turned and started walking.

"Wait!" Adam said. "The envelope?"

Arielle grinned to herself before turning back around. "Apologies." She handed it over.

"How can I get in touch with you?"

"You can't. We're off the grid for a reason. Don't even mention us to anyone, or we'll know, and we can make you pay. If anyone asks, just say this envelope was left on your doorstep. There will be footage of us, and they'll probably print some pictures to ask if you've ever seen us before. You will tell them you have not. Are we clear?"

Adam nodded, eyes wide. "Yes, ma'am."

"Good luck with everything, Mr. Marshall."

Arielle turned back around and started for the car, Felix and Selena hurrying to her side as they returned to their seats. She fired up the engine and drove off, Adam remaining on his doorstep, watching them disappear into the night.

"Do you think he believes us?" Felix asked.

"Once he looks in the envelope, he will," Arielle said. "He just needs to see the faces of Raj and Landon, and then he'll start picking apart every contract he's signed. He'll be fine." Arielle turned to the next block over and parked the car in front of a house with all of its lights off. "Does everyone have their Juice ready?"

"Oh, it's ready," Selena said.

"Got mine," added Felix.

"We still have a long journey back to Denver, but let's just get back to our present time first. Before we do, I want to say how proud I am of this team. This mission took a ton of resilience, and you both showed it. We're going home really banged up. But we're still going home—that's all that matters."

"I can drink to that," Selena said. "Cheers."

They raised their flasks of Juice to the center of the car before taking a swig to return to the present.

Chapter 61

Present Day

The trio's transition to the present passed seamlessly. Thanks to Arielle having access to her own private jet, they didn't need to wait around for a particular flight to leave. They did, however, stop by the Seattle Road Runners' offices for Selena to get checked out. Each office across the continent had a resident doctor, along with a closet of medical equipment.

After an hour at the office, the doctor cleared Selena for their return travel home. X-rays showed no structural damage to Selena's facial bones, but her cheek would remain swollen and bruised for at least a couple of weeks. The doctor gave Selena painkillers and prescribed her a heavy regiment of ice and pressure to the injured area to help bring down the swelling.

They headed to the hangar where Arielle had already arranged their flight home. It was midnight by the time they boarded the jet, leading to the rare instance of all three Angels sleeping during the three-hour flight back to Denver.

They landed at four in the morning, local time, and were back at the Denver headquarters by 4:45, both the city and office nearly vacant.

"Is this a bad omen?" Felix asked once they entered the basement.

"What do you mean?" Arielle asked.

"Well, the last two missions ended with us having a margarita at D'Corazon. They're not exactly open right now. How are we supposed to cap off another victory?"

They had all regained some energy thanks to the extended nap, the drive to the office rather chatty considering the hour.

"*You* want a margarita right now?" Selena asked.

Felix shrugged. "I believe in tradition. And I suppose if we let it die after only two times, then it isn't actually a tradition, and just something we did on those first missions."

Arielle definitely didn't want a margarita, but she understood Felix's point. Having the margarita wasn't about the drink itself, it was the endcap to a mission. The final stamp of approval. Until the next one.

"Well," Arielle said. "We can alter it. As much as I'd love for it to be D'Corazon each time, that's just not feasible. There will be other instances we come back at weird hours and they're closed. There might even be times we stay overnight in whatever city we're in—I'm strongly giving that some thought after tonight. But we can still have a margarita, no matter where we are."

"Are you suggesting we have one here?" Selena asked coyly.

"We should have everything we need in the kitchen, so why not? We can't just go our separate ways tonight without having our celebratory drink."

"What the hell is going on?" Selena asked. "Felix and Arielle are the ones pushing for a drink at five in the morning. Am I hearing this correctly, or was the doctor wrong about me not having a concussion?"

Felix laughed, the sound echoing around the office. The three Road Runners who were still awake and working in the bullpen all turned to look at them.

"Trust me," Arielle said. "I don't want a drink, but Felix is right: doing it for the third time will cement it as our tradition. It's our thing. If thinking about that marg pushes us to the finish line on these missions, then so be it. I'm not here to interfere with whatever motivates us."

Selena half-smiled, unable to give a complete grin. "Okay then, let's go find the blender and tequila."

They started across the office, Felix stopping when they approached three men working in the bullpen.

"Hey guys," he greeted them. They were all focused on their computers and spun around to face the three superstar Angels. "This might be an odd request, but are any of you able to do us a favor and find some news articles from the *Seattle Times* in the year 2014? We're looking specifically for the week after February twentieth for a story regarding a company called WonderHome. We know the Futures Report won't be available until tomorrow, but just want to know what happened."

"That's not a problem at all, Mr. Francisco," one of the men said, swiveling back around to face his computer. "Give me five minutes and I'll get something printed out for you."

"Thank you so much, and please, just call me Felix. My dad is Mr. Francisco, and that makes me sound old."

Selena laughed, shaking her head. "You're the one who acts older than your dad."

"Don't sass me," Felix said, pointing a stiff finger at Selena.

"Thank you again," Felix said to the Road Runner. "I look forward to it. We'll be over in the kitchen area."

Arielle led the way and rummaged through the cupboards, piecing together the blender, margarita mix, and tequila, while Felix gathered the ice and orange juice. He also grabbed an ice pack for Selena, who instantly pressed it against her purple cheek.

"I still can't believe my eyes," Selena said. "Arielle Lucila playing bartender and making margaritas. In the middle of the night. Are you sure you know what you're doing?"

Arielle flipped off Selena and continued mixing everything in the blender, her tongue clenched between her teeth as she concentrated on getting the perfect measurements. "Hope no one's sleeping right now," she said before flipping on the switch to start the blender.

Once it fell silent, leaving a smooth and frothy mixture in the blender, Arielle poured the drink into three cups. "I'm afraid they don't have margarita glasses here, but I promise it tastes just as good."

She passed out the glasses, and they all lifted them to the center of their informal circle.

"To another mission in the books," Arielle said. "And to all of us returning home. May we never take that for granted."

They touched glasses and took their first drinks.

"Holy shit, Arielle!" Selena cried. "This is incredible. How do you know how to make these so good?!"

"Well, I am Mexican," Arielle laughed. "Seriously, though, who do you think played bartender at my family parties growing up? Once I was twelve, my dad taught me how to make drinks and never looked back. It was funny because I couldn't drink anything I made, so I had to experiment based on how people reacted. I just kept tweaking things until I got reactions like the one you just had."

"It really is good," Felix said. "So smooth."

The man from the bullpen made his way toward the kitchen with a sheet of paper in hand. "Excuse me," he said. "I'm sorry to interrupt, but I have what you asked for, Felix."

"Thank you, kind sir," Felix replied, taking the paper. "We really appreciate you doing that."

Felix shook the man's hand and waited for him to return to his desk, walking with his head high and chest puffed out.

"I know you don't read the Futures Reports," Felix said to Arielle. "But this isn't one. Are you okay with me reading it out loud?"

Arielle crossed her arms and considered this. "That's a fair point. I suppose it's fine because I'm not sure how much the Futures Report will even discuss WonderHome, since the mission was about Adam Marshall. Let's hear it."

"Okay, here it is from the *Seattle Times*, dated February 22, 2014. Police have reported several suspicious tips regarding the murder of Raj Kalan, the vice president of the online real estate marketplace, WonderHome. They have a person of interest, and believe the murder to be related to the disappearance of the company's chief financial officer, Landon Greene, who hasn't appeared in the office since the start of the week. The tips officials have received suggest Mr. Greene was also murdered, and that both men were involved in a corporate money laundering scheme together.

"This separate matter is being handed over to the FBI for further investigation. Police are trying to determine the validity of these anonymous tips. Michelle Garrison, the CEO of WonderHome, has not responded to our requests for a comment, nor has the company's legal team. This is an ongoing story. Please check back for updates, and if you have any pertinent information, please contact Seattle PD."

Arielle smiled, nodding to herself. "We did it. No mention of Adam Marshall, even though I'm sure he's being grilled by the detectives."

"You thought the murders would hurt his case, but I think they're actually helping him," Selena said. "They'll be able to clear him of the murders, and that's only going to allow him the chance to explain his side of the story."

"It's a success," Arielle said. "And that's all that matters. Adam will get to live his life with his family and never have to go through all that pain and suffering."

"Cheers to that," Felix said, raising his glass once more. "I know we're all looking forward to a long rest and recovery after this one, but let's soak it in. We made the world a better place, and *that's* all that matters."

They clinked their glasses one more time and sipped margaritas until the sun came up.

READ THE FUTURES REPORT!

Just because Arielle Lucila doesn't want to look at the Futures Report to find out what happened after the mission, doesn't mean you can't!

Enjoy an exclusive look at the official Futures Report that is prepared for the Commander's office following each mission.

All you need to do is join my e-mail Reader Club!

Angel Assassin (Mason Gregory Report) - https://dl.bookfunnel.com/874f27yoy3

Secrets in the Vault (Bank Massacre Report) - https://dl.bookfunnel.com/mncpe0ispw

Dirty Money (WonderHome Report) - https://dl.bookfunnel.com/7e0mheonzi

Author's Note

Thank you for reading Dirty Money. To date, this is the longest book I've written. I planned it that way, too. I wanted to try things differently with this book by diving deeper into the three main characters of Arielle, Felix, and Selena. I also wanted to experiment with writing scenes from the perspective of the troubled Adam Marshall, hoping to bring some humanity to the subject in question, so that it wasn't just another notch in the belt for the team of Angels.

In the next book, I'm looking to add more scenes from the perspective of the potential suspects involved.

This is all part of what I consider the next logical step in my growth as an author. Past books have always revolved around three characters or fewer. I want to expand the universe I have created, and the only way to do that is by bringing in new characters. Who are the Road Runners that make all the arrangements behind the scenes, and deliver them in a simple file for the Angels to begin their mission? I look forward to finding out with you and seeing who else we can bring into the mix.

More on that later.

Dirty Money was inspired by my time in corporate America. No, I've never worked for a company that played along with a money laundering scheme, but a lot of the vibes in the office, the executives, and other employees in this fictional company of WonderHome are all drawn from real-life experience. I imagine you can relate to working under money-hungry executives who will do anything to improve the bottom line, even at the expense of the regular folks.

It was my great pleasure to bring these fictional executives down, along with the company. Too often in our society, we see the filthy rich maneuver out of justice. I couldn't dare let this story end that way.

I hope you enjoyed how it all played out, and that you are growing closer to all three of the Angels as they continue to grow together as a team and learn about each other.

Thank you to everyone who helped with the production of this book. Special thanks to my editor Stephanie Cohen-Perez, my narrator Cynthia Farrell, and to all my fans in the Gonzalez Gang. You've kept me going for nineteen books now, and I look forward to the many more!

Lastly, thank you to my wife Natasha for continuing to support me on this journey. None of this would be here without you.

Andre Gonzalez

August 17, 2022 - February 15, 2023

Enjoy this book?

You can make a difference!

Reviews are the most helpful tools in getting new readers for any books. I don't have the financial backing of a New York publishing house and can't afford to blast my book on billboards or bus stops.

(Not yet!)

That said, your honest review can go a long way in helping me reach new readers. If you've enjoyed this book, I'd be forever grateful if you could spend a couple minutes leaving it a review (it can be as short as you like) on the Amazon page. You can jump right to the page below:

https://www.amazon.com/ebook/dp/B0BRW8BQTR

Thank you so much!

Also by Andre Gonzalez

Arielle Lucila Series:

Dirty Money (#3)

Secrets in the Vault (#2)

Angel Assassin (#1)

Wealth of Time Series:

Time of Fate (#6)

Zero Hour (#5)

Keeper of Time (#4)

Bad Faith (#3)

Warm Souls (#2)

Wealth of Time (#1)

Road Runners (Short Story)

Revolution (Short Story)

Amelia Doss Series:

Salvation (#3)

Nightfall (#2)

Resurrection (#1)

Insanity Series:

The Insanity Series (Books 1-3)

Replicate (#3)

The Burden (#2)

Insanity (#1)

Erased (Prequel Short Story)

The Exalls Attacks:

Followed Away (#3)

Followed East (#2)

Followed Home (#1)

A Poisoned Mind (Short Story)

Standalone books:

Snowball: A Christmas Horror Story

About the Author

Born in Denver, CO, Andre Gonzalez has always had a fascination with horror and the supernatural starting at a young age. He spent many nights wide-eyed and awake, his mind racing with the many images of terror he witnessed in books and movies. Ideas of his own morphed out of movies like *Halloween* and books such as *Pet Sematary* by Stephen King. These thoughts eventually made their way to paper, as he always wrote dark stories for school assignments or just for fun. Followed Home is his debut novel based on a terrifying dream he had many years ago at the age of 12. His reading and writing of horror stories evolved into a pursuit of a career as an author, where Andre hopes to keep others awake at night with his frightening tales. The world we live in today is filled with horror stories, and he looks forward to capturing the raw emotion of these events, twisting them into new tales, and preserving a legacy in between the crisp bindings of novels.

Andre graduated from Metropolitan State University of Denver with a degree in business in 2011. During his free time, he enjoys baseball, poker, golf, and traveling the world with his family. He believes that seeing the world is the only true way to stretch the imagination by experiencing new cultures and meeting new people.

Andre still lives in Denver with his wife, Natasha, and their three kids.